Touching the Starfish

ASHLEY STOKES

UNTHANK BOOKS

First published in 2010
By Unthank Books
www.unthankbooks.com

Printed in England by Lightning Source, Milton Keynes

A CIP record for this book is available from the British Library

Any resemblance to persons fictional or real who are living, dead or
undead is purely coincidental.

ISBN 978-0-9564223-0-9

Cover design by Ian Nettleton and Dan Nyman

'Starface' © Ian Nettleton 2009

Grateful acknowledgement is made to the following for permission to
reprint previously published material:
St Martin's Press: Excerpt from *Plotting and Writing Suspense Fiction* by
Patricia Highsmith.
Bloomsbury Publishing PLC: Excerpt from *The Man Without a Country* by
Kurt Vonnegut
Methuen Publishing Limited: Excerpt from *Story* by Robert McKee.
Harold Matson Co., Inc: Excerpt from *Mysteries and Manners* by Flannery
O'Connor.

Every effort has been made by us to trace any other rights holders. We
would be grateful to receive information that will ensure correct
acknowledgement in future editions.

For my parents

These little setbacks, amounting sometimes to thousands of dollars' worth of time wasted, writers must learn to take like Spartans. A brief curse, perhaps, then tighten the belt a notch and on to something new — of course with enthusiasm and optimism, because without these elements, you cannot produce anything good.

Patricia Highsmith.

Fumigate them all!

James O'Mailer

How to Begin

Word Games, Confessions and Dead, Dead Silences

Never start a novel with a sentence like: *Locally respected creative writing tutor Nathan Flack strode out through the double doors at the back of the Eudora Doon Building and watched the Folder-Holders[1] as they arrived in the famous university's carpark below.* Rethink a first line that utilizes the blunt, inanimate 'was', like: *Nathan was very hopeful,* or: *Nathan was in a well chipper good mood as he met up with his beautiful yet impossible ex-girlfriend, Frances and speculated on the new Folder-Holders and their potential for foibles,* or '*Nathan Flack – John Cusack in a crap leather jacket – was leaning forwards hopefully and in a well chipper good mood because he knew, and the much-admired poet Frances Mink knew that this was the last time he would have to do this job.* Don't, like one student of mine, trigger a novel with: *On the one less than half a dozenth storey of the building somewhere in the eastern city in the country exotic, she patted her fat belly pregnant and said, 'C'mon, we've got to stop the genetically-modified Jesus from porking the nuns.* Or, like another, kick off with: *She needed his hot enormity suddenly inside her like she needed Coldplay on rainy afternoons.* Never emulate the ex-student, a retired Deputy Chief Constable no less whose opening gambit was: *The thatch of*

---

[1] **Folder-Holders:** Generic term for creative writing students. First used on the night we met by the poet Frances Mink after we'd escaped from The Writer Formerly Known as Sharon Plum and Hieronymus Ponce, The Enemy of All That Breathes and just before we invented James O'Mailer.

3

her pubic hair resembled a red squirrel's arse hanging from a laburnum tree in a small back garden on the outskirts of Hull[2].

Opt instead for something crisp and simple that locates our protagonist just before a moment that changes the status quo, and then try to hint at something consequential to come. Suggest that something *has* happened, *is* happening and *will* happen. If you can also supply a sense of the narrative voice, your unique style, your personality and moral perspective as it filters through your prose, then you're laughing.

So there I was, Nathan Flack, standing with Frances on the concrete walkway at the back of the Eudora Doon Building. It was the first day of the autumn term, a blustery evening in late September, and we were hoping for some advanced intelligence on the new creative writing students about to arrive in the carpark below. I was slightly apprehensive and vaguely energized; safe in the knowledge that this would be the last evening class I would ever have to teach. *The Penelope Tree*, my fourth and best novel was all finished and edited. It had landed on desks in The Arctic[3] a month ago, and a month is as long as any writer should have to wait for an answer.

'The next few months are going to be so exciting,' said Frances.

'Oh sure,' I said. 'Word games, confessions and dead, dead silences.'

'Good title. I'd write that down if I were you.'

'Never start with a title.'

'Your teaching autopilot is already switched on. Exciting for your novel, I meant.'

'Oh sorry, yeah. I'm excited.'

'Who's it with now?'

'Fred Malone. ZY and Haggard.'

'It will be exciting, I promise. I can feel it.'

---

[2] You may think this has something arresting about this opening, and although I might agree that it straddles the border between genius and madness, you didn't read the rest of *The Truncheons of Humber Vice*, of which I will say no more than it involved an Al Quaida sleeper cell in deepest Immingham, a plan to inject cod in butter and parsley sauce sachets with a deadly nerve toxin and a jive-talking prostitute called Zizi Le Flaps.

[3] **The Arctic:** Flack-speak for London. I grew up there, in the southern suburbs, and after university lived there for a few years with my first serious girlfriend Johanna. One night, ten years ago, we were walking home from a restaurant. It was mid-winter, during a terrible cold snap, and the pavements were icy and treacherous. When she let go of my hand in the street I knew things had become insurmountable. Ever since then, I've always thought of London as the Arctic: the ice core, the explorer's grave.

I could feel it, too. Finally, I'd written something commercial, a simple modern love story, with likeable characters, straightforward prose and high stakes. I'd reigned in my more immature, experimental instincts and this time produced something accessible. There were no games with form or typeface; no passages that borrowed from textbooks, poetry, screenplay or role-play games; no slang dictionary or asides assembled in footnotes; no obscure literary references, foreign words or italics and no cranky sub-texts (or semi-colons).

Yet I didn't feel I'd compromised myself. I had avoided the clichés I hated in contemporary popular fiction. No serial killer devised an astrological clocklike puzzle for the worn-out investigator to deconstruct. No occult, age-old institutional conspiracy underpinned the history of Western Civilization. No apocalyptic medieval fantasy battle decided all at the climax. A super-powered child did not endure a procedural rite of passage. Nor did an everyman grumble about his ex in pub-monologue style then solve all his problems by acquiring the love of a good woman (or step-fatherhood of an irritating pre-teen). There was no unlikely love affair and *Penelope* was refreshingly free of wizards, creepy monks and grotesques. It was not set in the past or abroad to appear exotic or erudite, or in the world of media and celebrity to appear slick and fashionable. I had not patronized the smack-and-firearms underclass to appear gritty and relevant. I also felt I'd dodged the commonplaces I found in the stories of those around me who posed as 'literary' writers. There were no gender identity confusions, no pared-back, minimalist prose, no camping it up, no magic and no dream sequences. Nor was *Penelope* 'relentlessly salacious' as one of my more success-hungry colleagues once insisted that fiction must be to secure a deal. I'd just wanted to write something vivid. I wanted to feel that things could work out. I wanted to feel something.

I glanced sideways at Frances. Her jet-black Louise Brooks bob was newly styled for the start of term and her red leather jacket obviously waxed. Her black skirt was as ever short and tight to her hips. Three years ago we'd split up and I moved out, in theory a temporary arrangement while I focused solely on writing *Penelope* and a moneymaking side-project. That's what I'd told her anyway.

'You're going to be very rich and famous,' she said, 'and then you won't speak to me anymore. You will still speak to me, won't you? When you're a rich and famous novelist?'

'Course,' I said. Down below, cars had started to arrive. According to the register, eight students had enrolled for *An Introduction to Prose Fiction with Nathan Flack.* Not all of them would arrive by car. Some would come in through the front entrance unsighted by me before the class started [4]. I liked to have an idea of who I was going to get, just in case the impossible happened.

'Do you think tonight is the night?' I said. 'Will he come tonight?'

''O'Mailer?'[5]

'At the back of the class, slashing the air with his sword stick, quoting from unavailable texts as soon as I enter.'

'Heavens to Murgatroyd, look at that!'

A low-slung lime green sports car spun into the carpark, *Animal* by Def Leppard blaring out of the stereo until it pulled up. The handbrake crunched and after a brief pause a huge beardy in a double-breasted suit unpacked himself from the car, punched the air and waddled into the building.

'He's mine,' she said. 'Poetry incarnate. 'Tis fated. He has that magnetically austere Ted Hughes quality about him. The scent of the moors. Bracken stains on his palms. Eyes brimming with baby animals being born. You're on the edge of a maelstrom, you could easily fall, lose yourself in him, that voice, those eyes. I am, at last, relieved to be a woman.'

'No, he's even not ours,' I said. 'He's the MD of a cleaning or catering franchise. Think of it, the mirrored ceilings and cork walls in his bedroom, the stuff under the bed. Look, she's one of yours.'

---

[4] In fact, only six ever showed. Mr Trevor Chodd and Ms Pravina Mantlestein, the absentees, lingered on the register like ghosts for the duration of the course. I would often wonder, as I skipped over their crossed-out names, if either of them realized what they missed out on here, how they could have been witnesses to history.

[5] **James O'Mailer:** On the night we met, Frances and I, working through a bottle of wine and several Brian Eno albums, drew up a composite of the worst possible person who could attend one of our classes. In this way we came upon James O'Mailer. James O'Mailer would be a literary martinet with James Joyce's talent and eyeglass, the insight and caustic wit of Flannery O'Connor and the temperament and pugilistic skills of Norman Mailer and he would speak in a way that combined the wisecracking self-confidence of the young Orson Welles and the ornate braggadocio of Shakespeare's Falstaff. James O'Mailer's talent would far outstrip my own. I would have nothing to teach him. In front of the world he would reveal me as a hack, a bluffer and a charlatan. So far, James O'Mailer had never showed up in either of our classes. We knew he was out there somewhere, though, patrolling the night with his chihuahuas and swordstick and the killer lines that throbbed through his brain. I often found myself talking about James O'Mailer with Frances to avoid talking about 'us' or what happened to 'us' or getting back to being 'us' now that *Penelope* was on Fred Malone's desk.

A woman with long auburn hair slipped out of a hatchback. Her kitten heels clacked across the tarmac under a billowing scarlet pashmina.

'Oh no,' said Frances. '"I want to be a lady poet and stand upon a balcony in Bloomsbury".'

'And you don't, right?'

'It would have to be Florence now.'

'I'll have her if you don't want her.'

'Nathan, you're still like a character in a thirties novel who gives all his money to a prostitute.'

'Yes, I am.'

On the far side of the carpark the backdoors of a white Transit van seemed to forcibly eject a hulking bald man. He sniffed the damp air and the first spits of rain before stomping towards the building, head down, shoulders hunched, hands deep in the pockets of a sheepskin car coat.

'Now he's mine,' said Frances. 'There's sensitivity beneath the brutish lumbering gait, a lovely temperament.'

'The birdman of East Anglia?'

'Yes, he and Ted will have a duel over my favours. That one's prose. You can see it a mile off.'

A doddery old soul, his gabardine overcoat done up to his chin to shield himself from the breeze meticulously checked all the doors of his Volvo before he marched across the carpark as if it were the parade ground at Trooping the Colour. On his way he nodded at a dumpy, middle-aged woman in oatmeal-coloured sweatpants and a brown cardigan as she shuffled out of a battered, beige Fiat Panda. As she followed Trooping the Colour towards the doors below us, she hesitated, taking a forlorn look back at her car, then let off a sigh so loud that I'm sure the lamps flickered.

'Nathan, I think we have a Sensitive Plant,' said Francis.

On the night we met, the night we ran away from The Writer Formerly Known as Sharon Plum and Hieronymus Ponce, the Enemy of All that Breathes, and invented James O'Mailer, Frances told me her system for classifying creative writing students. The Folder-Holders, she explained, fall into categories: Minor[6] and Major Arcana[7]. Oatmeal

---

[6] **Minor Arcana**: Polite, intelligent, unobtrusive students who are a joy to teach and rewarding to know. Ninety percent of students fall into this category.

[7] **Major Arcana:** Deluded souls and troublesome nutjobs. The Ten Percent of Doom.

Sweatpants here was a Major, a Sensitive Plant[8]. There's always a Sensie, at least one.

'I always wonder what they think they're going to get here,' I said.

'She sees,' said Frances, 'a high-ceilinged library with a circle of ornate chairs.'

'And crimson velvet drapes that keep the draught from unsettling the fire that crackles purposefully in the grate . . .'

'And books piled up on the floor.'

'There's an understated but definite charge to the atmosphere.'

'A legendary grouping comes into existence . . .'

' . . . the Eudora Set . . .'

' . . . whose crosscurrents . . .'

' . . . cross-fertilisations . . .'

' . . . will be analysed by the literary historians of the future.'

'The tutor will conjure spirits from the vasty deep and impart the how-to secrets of the art, setting them on their way to success and celebrity.'

What was imagined, or what Francis and I imagined might be imagined, or at least what some Folder Holders, and Sensies in particular probably imagined of a short taster course in Adult Ed was what they expected went on somewhere on the other side of the campus from the Eudora Doon. It could be reached by a short walk through the carpark and across the grass in front of the arts centre and up the concrete spiral staircase to a concrete gangway that passes the utilitarian concrete chunks of science departments and pyramid-shaped accommodation blocks. Somewhere along this elevated thoroughfare, with its view of the lake and the treetops, and its bustle of undergrads in their stripy scarves and parkas, is Humanities Faculty I and Humanities Faculty II. If you make your way into Faculty II, on the second floor, you come to the Department of English and Creative Writing and the hallowed chambers of *The* MA[9], where six years ago I arrived, imagining tall-backed chairs and life-transfiguring conversations and the kiss of success.

---

[8] **Sensitive Plant**: Type of CW student prone to thinskinnedness, theatrical stropping out of class and falling in love with wafty past/abroad novels; continually desirous of more feedback/vocally resents feedback; allergic to plotting, planning and preparation. Professional moaner.

[9] *The* **MA**: Redoubtable, world famous programme, founded in the early 1970s, that jump-started the UK's creative writing industry; makes 5% of its students, breaks the remainder; faculty cash-cow.

'And what do the Folder-Holders get?' said Frances. 'Us.'

'No one's going to turn up tonight anyway,' I said. 'England are playing Luxembourg.'

'We're jaded,' said Francis. 'It's not even started and I'm already jaded. I'm going green with jadedness. I'm lilac to the gills.'

'It's always like this now,' I said. 'It'll seem normal in a minute.'

'That's all right for you to say. Your autopilot's already on and you're going to sell your novel and make loads of money. Me, two volumes of poetry and still flat broke, still single and lilac to the gills with jadedness. I need curing, Nathan.'

'You cure the Arcana, Fran, that's your gift.'

'But not my mission and, yes, Nathan. I cure. You're The Fumigator[10]. There's a kind of male/female contrast going on here. We better go in.'

I picked up my bag. As the weight bumped against my hip, it happened for the first time. A painful pulse jabbed at my temples. For a second, I couldn't quite see straight. Someone had spoken my name, but I couldn't actually remember it being said. The 'than' of the 'Nathan' and the 'ack' of the Flack seemed to buzz between my ears. I looked at Frances and was about to ask her if she'd said something, but clearly she hadn't.

'Don't lie to me,' she said. 'You've got the last-minute terrors, too.'

'Something like that.'

The pain subsided. I thought little of it. Stress has lots of side effects and I was under a lot of stress. I thought that maybe I'd pressurized a nerve when I repositioned the bag. Or I was suffering psychosomatic precursory reactions to the conversation that I knew I was going to have with Frances some day soon about the turning point and the change in

---

[10] **The Fumigator**: Francis-speak for Nathan Flack. When we lived together I worked as a book doctor, writing reports on unpublished novels. I had gained a reputation for taking on any job, however dirty, nasty or plain unreadably stupid the novel because I was so short of money. *The Truncheons of Humber Vice* was like *Rebecca of Sunnybrook Farm* compared to some of the things I had to assess: novels by sex tourists; by right-wing cranks planning kitchen table revolutions and militia *aktions;* by unwitting misogynists and pitiful bores; by lunatics and Boo Radley-type creatures hiding in attics who hear voices, whose works are written by articulate spirits and novels by accountants and pension fund managers, their low-grade thrillers and alpha male fantasies. One of the worst things about teaching creative writing is that you become party to the things that actually go on in people's heads. It drives you a little mad. You go beyond jaded. They start to whisper to you when you least expect them.

the status quo. She strode ahead of me and I followed into the foyer of the Eudora Doon.

With Stupidity the Gods Themselves Struggle in Vain

But we stopped almost as soon as we started and both instinctively shunted into the wall of the little passage between the walkway and the foyer. Out front, backdropped by a swathe of plate-glass and concrete pillars, a dozen or so students milled around beneath the striplights, all lost or in a fluster about misallocated rooms. We could pass by them unhindered, no worries. We were wary, though, of their helpmeet. Sharon Plum blocked our rat-run to the stairs as she remonstrated with a tall, eagleish-looking, grey haired woman in a tweed jacket and pearls. As ever, I wasn't sure what I should be calling Sharon Plum now. She changed her name often and, according to Frances had done so recently. Here, she was wearing some sort of identity-specific costume again, though it was a less obvious one than her pizza delivery girl uniforms or her boots-jeans-vest building site garb of functionalism. Sharon is an engineer of human souls. She dresses with the masses, the reading public. Tonight, she'd zipped a rather odd baggy black tracksuit top with white piping tight to her chin and wore prison-white trainers, a 'street' and ironic look in keeping with her new name and her fiction's inevitable about-turn.[11]

---

[11] **The Writer Formerly Known as Sharon Plum:** Sharon is a writer, in that she writes things on a word processor, but none of these words, to my knowledge, have ever

'My giddy aunt,' said Frances, 'she looks like she's dealing crack at the Conservative Women's Conference.'

'If she was, would you buy it?'

---

appeared in print. No book bears the name Sharon Plum or that of her varied aliases on its spine. Neither she, nor her pseudonyms have ever appeared in any anthology, journal, magazine, fanzine or newspaper. She didn't, then, even have a blog, something that always surprised me, given her instincts. As I say, Sharon used a lot of pseudonyms. These she adopts as soon as the literary fashion changes, as if she's always been honourably ploughing her own furrow and suddenly she's part of a movement that's suddenly hot and bleeding edge. When I first met her she was simply Sharon Plum and had for some time been writing feminist magic realist stories of a vaguely Angela Carterish nature. There was a novel called *Scarlet Dante and Chairman Miaow* that did the rounds and never found a loving home. Since then she's reinvented herself and her concerns with every fashion in the book trade. Her first volte-face occurred in the mid-nineties when backpacking thrillers were all the rage. She'd always been 'post-colonial', she told me, and wrote a novel about going on holiday in Spain called *The Towel* under the name Magenta Fleet. After I whinged to her that my then agent, Squinty Hugo had told me that he didn't care what I wrote as long it was set in the 'past or abroad, because that's what they want,' (i.e., the commissioning editors and corporate publishers based in The Arctic), Sharon consoled me by agreeing that this was vulgar. No agent could expect you to write as if you're taking an order for a pizza. She then changed her name to Meryl de Sommelier and penned *Lieutenant Lapislazuli's Lyre*, a love story set against the Nazi occupation of Cyprus. When Hugo passed on this as well, she became Bru Gore and wrote *Flyposting*, a fragmentary story, partly written in dialect that centres on four Edinburgh girls on smack that ends with a cross-double-cross drugs deal. Then came chicklit and poor Bru Gore died young and horribly after ODing on correcting fluid. In her wake came Sharon's inner chick, Tabitha Vacanta who penned *Janet Doubloon's Journal,* in which a pleasant enough but slightly overbearing thirtysomething woman who works as a creative writing teacher worries about her weight, age and daily wordcount and has a few romantic mishaps. Perhaps realizing this was all a tad superficial and needing to get closer to the fringes where the real lives of real people happen, the reaction came as Pauline Thigh, writer of gritty, realist stories of gender identity problems and lesbian awakening (*Cats of Iron and Other Stories*). Pauline didn't last long, though, and probably married Bru Gore in an alternate reality, as Sharon then decided we should be candidly sexy. As Prunella Givit she penned *Sex in the Market Square* in which four local lasses have drinks and some tiffs with several local men. It was during the writing of this I had the infamous 'salacity sells' conversation, followed by a conversation two months later in which she claimed 'salacity is vulgar and hates women' and she'd only been indulging in 'disassociation through over-identification'. Now she was finally going to write what she'd always wanted to write: soft fantasy featuring theological speculation. She was working on something in which an occult, age-old institutional conspiracy underpinned the history of Western Civilization and an apocalyptic medieval fantasy battle decided all at the climax but with streetwise, ordinary characters (hence the tracksuit, I assumed). It was the best story ever, apparently. And she'd changed her name again, but as I stood there watching her give directions to a woman who looked a bit like the eagle out of *The Muppets* I couldn't for the life of me remember what it was though I did know she was serious this time. She'd changed it by deed poll.

12

'Alps of it. So I don't remember anything of the next two hours. Shhh.'

'You're the one bitching, I'm not.'

'She might go away.'

'She'll never go away. She'll be at our funerals, shagging the legs of the mourners, sniffing for contacts like a pig after truffles.'

The Writer Formerly Known as Sharon Plum was our boss. She was Head of Creative Writing at the School of Adult Education. She doled out the teaching contracts. She sat in meetings with other people. She went to lunch. She had an office. No one quite knew how she got to sit in that office and leave it for lunch, how she wheedled that one. Sharon is an expert operator, a networker, and a ruthless game player. I often imagined the networking software was imbedded in her brain, a mesh of electrodes and microchips called **plumcam** that analyses and advises: who is to be worked; who is to be undermined. It would be a lit-up green screen visible only to her inner eye, like that scanner in Schwarzenegger's head in *The Terminator*. Plum, rather tragically, we thought, would do anything to get published. Anything. Anything to associate with the right people. Anything to find the right tack that accorded with the direction of the book trade at the right time. And if you were around Sharon, you ought to be helping Sharon.

This was my problem. We first met just after I finished *The* MA and stayed on to do a little undergrad teaching. Sharon, starved of feedback, asked me to look at her stuff. I looked at it. I made helpful suggestions. Sharon liked my suggestions, changed her pen name and offered me a job teaching in Adult Ed. Around the same time that I started out on this particular adventure a literary agent called Hugo Cornwallis was sniffing around the famous university looking for new writers and somehow ran into Sharon. Sharon mentioned a few names, including her own (or whatever name she was using at the time) and mine. Hugo passed on Sharon, of course, but he signed me up, poaching me from another list. He said big things. He promised. We've since parted company; hence *Penelope* was on Fred Malone's desk, not his.

Sharon, though, seemed to hold it against me for not becoming the next big thing under the auspices of Squinty Hugo and letting her ride my coattails, provide those tasty contacts, those opportunities to schmooze the influential. She'd always seemed over-interested in my tails, I felt, especially before I met Frances at one of her parties. In fact, I met Frances in Sharon's bathroom – I have never, ever had a relationship with any woman that didn't start in a bathroom, washroom or some sort of

13

toilet – and Sharon seemed most put out that I hadn't stayed with her to help with the coattails and that Frances too had failed to audition for a similar supporting role. Sharon's spoken desire was to be part of a 'power couple' and she didn't care whether she was coupled with Firework Flack, the squib that until now merely gazed at the firmament, or with twice-published Frances Mink. It didn't really matter. When she was seventeen she used to sit all day outside Jeanette Winterson's house yet she'd marry Jeffrey Archer in a minute. She'd be Dan Brown's slave and wear a French maid's costume for him while she buffed up his silverware and yet still insist that she's a radical feminist. She'd live in the toilet on John Grisham's private jet, a place where I hoped we'd never meet. And given this history of disappointment she took an undue interest in my performance as a teacher. There were always vague threats that she could get someone else, someone with better contacts, a fuller pocket book of contacts in the Arctic for **plumcam** to download. But I could manage Sharon. Sharon was merely Sharon, or was she? Here, though, hesitating in the corridor, aware that I was going to have to stand up and actually talk intelligently for two hours to complete strangers, I really didn't want to field *The* Question Two[12] from Sharon.

'What's she called now?' I whispered.

'Juliet Largo,' said Frances. 'Seriously, I kid you not. Don't ever call her Sharon again. She goes nuts.'

'The Eagle looks like it's landed out there. Maybe we can coolly ghost past her.'

'Operation Ostrich.'

'She won't notice us.'

Sharon's back was turned. The Eagle's head lifted and fell. Side by side now, we adjusted our bags, then I quietly opened the door and we slunk past The Plum and The Eagle out of *The Muppets*. I held my breath until

---

[12] *The* **Question Two:** Ephemeral annoyance that comes around about once every four years and lasts for about two months, during which every Jack and Jill, every Jock and Sharon from here to the Arctic will continually buttonhole you with: 'Have you sold your book yet?' Not to be confused with the much more irritating yet ubiquitous *The* **Question One**: 'What do you write about?' Don't go to parties if you can't handle *The* Question One. The first time it's asked, you're calm and reserved and merely say, 'I don't write about things, I write through them.' The second time, your tongue is dry from the cheap red wine and you mutter something about 'failure, I suppose, big dreams coming to nothing, peculiar lights, I'm a social ufologist, being English is horrible, isn't it?' The third time you'll shout 'fuck off, you're tearing my head off' and then go and cry in the toilet and probably fall in love with a woman stuck in there doing the same.

we reached the foot of the stairs that led up to our classrooms and only exhaled halfway up when I felt confident that we were out of earshot and her line of sight.

'I clipped some trees back there,' I said, 'but the fuselage is intact and I'm heading back to base.'

'Well, I hope you are,' said Frances.

'Intact?' I said.

'No, coming back to base.'

I couldn't help it and paused on the step. She took one pace ahead and then turned, stopped and looked down at me with her enormous brown eyes. This sort of remark was a Frances stealth tactic for getting me to talk about 'us'. When I suspended our short-lived relationship of three summers ago and told her that I needed space to write it was a cowardly way of not saying upfront that Frances, despite her brilliance and charm and Jazz Age hair is impossible to be around; or at least she's impossible to be around once she starts to rely on you. I wouldn't want to be in her crosshairs if she ever found out that I thought her impossible; or that I'd had another girlfriend while I was writing the novel and the TV scripts. I'd be chopped and dissected into a thousand couplets and stanzas. I'd be hung, drawn and versified. I was already quite suspicious of a poem she'd placed in *Rialto* called *When You Were the Only Boy in the World and I was the Only Girl* and still alarmed by the phrases she underlined in the poetry of Nest Darkle.

'Fancy a drink later?' said Frances. 'I'll need one, I think.'

I tried not to look shifty. After two glasses of red wine Frances would pull out all our stitches again. She would start going on about coming back with her because she hates the empty flat. I would give in, and once there something horrible would appear, like a retsina bottle, and she'd ever so self-consciously hold a naked flame to the tea-lights on the bookshelves and the coffee table and put on Scott Walker – probably *Always Coming Back to You* from the first album; she knows I'm still an adolescent sucker for that type of sentiment, that song in particular – and then she'd sit crossed-legged in front of me to analyse why she can't be on her own for long, and it would get very late and we'd get sleepy and a layer would sneak from her shoulder, and for all that time, with its snags and snares and easy temptations, seriously, there might have been messages back at my place waiting to be picked up.

Her nose crinkled and her mouth tensed. I hadn't replied quickly enough, I knew, but it crossed my mind that I really would like a drink after work, especially if the question of 'us' stayed in its kennel, but if it did slope into the house I would just have to be honest and say that I didn't want a relationship with anyone at the moment, even though this, too, would be a dirty great lie. But just as I was about to speak that pain stabbed at my forehead again.

'Ugh.' I dropped my bag. Its thump on the stairs echoed around the foyer.

'Well, by the look on your face,' said Frances, 'the suggestion's repellent.'

'Steady on, old girl,' I said.

'I was only trying to be nice.'

'Wait a minute.'

' "One of these days you'll miss me, honey".' She turned tail and swept back up the stairs.

Before I could recover my bag and go after her, I heard the voice in my head, the same tone of voice that had spoken my name on the walkway, but this time it was clear and coherent.

Who said that?

My arms stiffened at my sides as I tried to look around for the speaker but my spine and neck were rigid and I found myself flicking my eyes left and right. I saw no one and could feel no presence behind me.

It spoke again.

Who said that?

Said what? I thought.

This. Who said this?

What?

Who said this?

You?

And who am I?

'Nathan!'

A filmy sweat heated my scalp and clung to my cheeks. This was not my inner voice or a daydream. I could hear it, but I didn't think that anyone else could. It was inside my head, unlike the voice had called up from the foyer. I looked down. Sharon Plum, surrounded by sundry eagles and Folder-Holders peered up at me, waggling her hands around. 'Oooooo, Nathan. Have you sold your book yet?'

The filmy sweat froze over. My head shrunk. I struck out my arm and prodded the 'V' sign at the crowd.

'Piss off, Sharon.'

I ran up the stairs before the effect registered. Why did I say that? Why did I say that? Why did I do that? I couldn't see Frances. I wanted to apologize and explain to her but I was already five minutes late for class and I was hearing voices. I always hear voices, but this was a voice I could actually hear, not one that I imagined for the sake of imagining it, for some scene as yet unwritten or column of dialogue.

Who said that? said the voice. It was gruff, reverberating, authoritative and between my ears.

What?

With stupidity the gods themselves struggle in vain?

I don't know. Oscar Wilde? Richard Madeley?

I did, or at least I whispered them to Friedrich von Schiller.

Who are you?

Why, you've known me forever, Kiddo.

No, I haven't.

Let me introduce myself. James O'Mailer, at your service.

I was stock-still outside my classroom now, hanging in the artificial light. Everything now seemed extra-solid yet simultaneously flimsy and fake, like things do in a dream of childhood places, your first school, the house you grew up in, your baby room. I was becoming a creative writing exercise. I could hear murmur from inside. I could hear murmur inside my head. I waited, tried to work out what was going on. It was merely my imagination running away with me. I controlled my breathing, but until then hadn't realized I was panting. I wiped my face on my sleeve and slicked back my hair. I would look like I'd run to class in a panic. James O'Mailer. Don't be stupid. My imagination running away with me. I vaguely remembered the Schiller quote from somewhere else. Frances and Plum. First night of term. *The Penelope Tree* and *The* Question Two. Turning points and changes to the status quo. Making me nervous. Stress in a bucket. I waited for the voice to speak again. When it didn't I crept into the classroom, assuming that once I got this over with and launched into some nice, safe icebreaker exercises, it would never speak to me again.

Are You The He?

Shutting the door behind me, I paused when I hadn't intended to and found myself staring at the backs of the students' heads. They were chatting; at least some of them were chatting. This was a good sign. Sometimes they don't talk to each other. Sometimes they don't talk to each other or to you for the whole course, as was the case with the now-legendary Ipswich Group of Death. I was still sweating, though. The crown of my head and my shirt collar were damp. Even without voices in my head and shouting 'piss off' at Sharon Plum in front of the new cohort, these were the most uncomfortable moments of any course: first contact, then the transition from by day haunting the interior world of the flat, with its grey ashtray light and hammerhead silences to by evening wearing the clothes of instructor, performer and affable guide to this particular underworld.[13]

Rain now drizzled against the black windows. No one seemed to notice me. They murmured. They shifted their shoulders. The room was not like the one Frances and I had conjured in our approximation of a Folder-Holder's fantasy of *The* MA. It was airless and over-lit, with a wall-length blackboard and lines of spine-wrecking plastic chairs scrutinized by

---

[13] **Note to Self:** A title; no story yet, no plot, no trigger or stakes and no sense of how this is to be approached. *The Double Life of Nathan Flack.*

the eye of the television that loomed in the corner. It was, in fact, identical to the seminar rooms of *The* MA, except here there would be less rancour and gladiatorialism (not on my watch), and on *The* MA you never have to touch the starfish.

Calmer now, I made my way along the aisle. As I rounded my desk, just as I was about to make sure I was smiling as I took my 'How to Begin' lesson plan and my handouts and the register from my bag, before I could nod and smile at each of the students in turn, especially anyone my internal intelligence gathering system told me was a Sensitive Plant, as you always have to make a Sensie feel loved, just as I was about to weigh up an opening gambit and go either for something formal and professional, like, 'Good evening. Welcome to Prose Fiction. I'm Nathan Flack,' or informal and light, like 'Why are you here, this rain-swept evening? Shouldn't you be watching England get hammered by Luxembourg?' just as I lifted my eyes and fixed my gaze and the heads began to firm-up into faces and I was beginning to anticipate that in a minute or so I was going to kick-off this course by telling them about the schedule and a little about myself and my writing career to date, my temples throbbed.

Look at this merry shower, Flack. Minions of misapprehension, Diana's moonbeams, popinjays to a man and a maiden.

'Oh God, not you again!' I thumped my head with the heel of my hand, and then gasped as I found peering back at me, Trooping the Colour Man, the woman with the pashmina, Lime Green Sports Car, the Bird Man of East Anglia, who this close up, I noticed, wore a white spade-shaded beard that seemed to jab out at me, and next to him the Sensie with the oatmeal sweatpants. The full set. Royal flush. I'd copped the lot.

With their wide eyes, onion-white faces and pursed mouths, they looked like I'd just swanned in and nonchalantly hurled a bucket of cow piss all over them. The old bloke, in particular, gripped the armrests of his chair and shuddered like he was fighting the blast of a wind tunnel.

I pushed out a really mimsy smile and tried to use my internal intelligence gathering network to devise a damage limitation strategy. I could be straight. 'Sorry, there is a fictional character talking audibly in my head. It's a tad disconcerting.' No. I could pretend it was an elaborate exercise. 'Now, get your pens out and rant on the page for five minutes about how rude that was and how humiliated you feel. Get it all out of your system, now.' I could carry on as if it hadn't happened, hoping they'd forget. 'Good evening. Welcome to Prose Fiction. I'm Nathan

Flack.' Or I could scarper, pant and scream, go home and e-mail Sharon Plum and quit, then wait for Fred Malone to sell *Penelope* and meanwhile I could concentrate on my new novel, *The Girl on the Millennium Bridge*. Or I could, instead, apologize and beg their forgiveness, make them feel sorry for me. Never. I could bang my stick on the floor and say, 'writing costs and this is where you start paying' and we could break out into a pre-choreographed dance routine all around the Eudora Doon. Or I could just shrug and say 'rejection is a rite of passage, get used to it.' Before I could open any of these hatches, the door smashed against the wall with a crack.

The shoulders of the students jumped. Their eyes seemed to pounce out at me before en masse they whipped around towards a figure in the doorway. A rotund, fridge-shaped woman marched into the room wearing a fluorescent orange woolly hat forced down over shaggy, unkempt brown hair. She struggled with five or six bulging carrier bags and sprayed chairs in all directions as she found her way to a seat behind the others. At the head of a trail of overturned chairs, the newcomer seemed to spend a long time rummaging in the bags but produced nothing and merely unzipped her electric blue puffa jacket and folded her stumpy arms.

'Are you The He?' she said. 'Are you The He?'

'Pardon,' I said. 'Can I help you?'

'You are The He! At last. I have searched.'

I took a deep breath and forced a smile. My internal intelligence-gathering network computed straightaway that this was a Major Arcana: The Moon-Barker[14].

It wouldn't be the same without a Moon-Barker. Moon-Barkers can be of great value. They prevent the dead, dead silences (the Ipswich Group

---

[14] **The Moon-Barker** is the giant among us and the future of literature. This should be recognized at all times. On the appearance of The Moon-Barker, the tutor should start a fund for the commission of a public statue of The Moon-Barker to be erected in the city centre where future generations can lay flowers and hold vigils. The Moon-Barker's arrival signals that the world is now flat and the sun and all heavenly bodies now orbit The Moon-Barker. The struggles of The Moon-Barker to write will be greater and more heroic than those of say, Kafka, the Gulag poet Osip Mandelstam or the state-oppressed writers of Iran or benighted North Korea. Each class should start with a minute's silence to acknowledge the sacrifice of The Moon-Barker. The Moon-Barker will expect twenty-four hour support from the tutor, who only exists to service the needs of The Moon-Barker. Telltale signs: often seen weighed down with heavy bags; a life of perpetual calamity (lightning will not strike merely twice but on the hour); obsession with rubbish bins; self-destructive networking skills; no boundaries.

of Death was crying out for a Barker). They force the other students into anti-Barker alliances where otherwise they might be cagey with each other for weeks. Frequently, Barkers provide a working example of how not to write and how not to think and what delusions of grandeur not to entertain. In some ways, the tutor needs The Moon-Barker, though a Barker can also ruin the tutor's life. Here, though, her entrance gave me an opportunity, even though it did strike me that I, hearer of voices, was a bit hypocritical for doubting the faculties of anyone else.

'This is Prose Fiction,' I said. 'Are you here for prose fiction?'

'Thank The He,' she said. 'I am arrived here now and it took me such a time to find and you are The He.' She took a pocket watch on a chain from inside the puffa jacket, stared into it with a concern like that of a wary new mother checking on a sleeping baby. Looking up, she said, 'You may continue. Later, we discuss.'

Now I had The Moon-Barker's gracious permission, I picked up the thread. 'OK. OK, OK,' I said, flourishing my hands and pacing a little behind my desk to recover my equilibrium. 'Given that this has been the most unusual start to any class ever, you should all have something to write about tomorrow. Good evening. Welcome to Prose Fiction. I'm Nathan Flack. And why are you here anyway, shouldn't you be watching England get hammered by Luxembourg?'

The heads in the front row seemed to regain some of their anticipatory smiliness. Lime Green Sports Car Man suddenly turned to The Moon-Barker and said, 'Hey love, what's in the bags?'

The Barker leant forwards. 'Well, I tell you . . .'

'Excuse me,' I said. 'Is there going to be another interruption? Anyone else going to fire themselves into the room through a howitzer? No . . . Wait for a bit. Hold on. No. OK, as I was saying . . . Welcome to Prose Fiction. I'm Nathan Flack, and to start off here I think it's best that I tell you something about myself and how I come to be involved with this course.'

Now that I had their attention I took a deep breath before I launched into my little speech about myself, my well-honed, very abridged autobiography that omitted anything about my childhood traumas[15] and illnesses or anything true and interesting, my self-deprecating version that concentrated on trial and error, the translatable material. I opened my

---

[15] I won't go here at all. Judging by the reaction to my third novel, *The Best Man*, no one's interested.

mouth and just as I was about to say that for as long as I could remember I only ever wanted to be a writer, the throb came at my temples.

And why on earth was that, Flack? Why on earth would you of all people feel that this was your calling?

'Because,' I said, 'even when I was seven I was writing my own comics, wasn't I? *The Astounding X-Ray Man.* The *Jamie Regal* stories.'

And they were your best work. It's been downhill since then.

I realized I'd turned and was remonstrating with the rain drops on the black windows. My head was hot. I swallowed a breath and made myself look at the class, at their stiff postures and the concerned restlessness of their faces. My mouth made some sort of raspberry-cum-whistling sound, as if I'd merely stumbled over my words.

'What I was trying to say,' I said, 'is that I always wanted to be a writer, from a very young age. Always scribbling and drawing. Couldn't help it. When I was fourteen

I wrote in purest biro a 400-page fantasy epic called *Quest of the Hellhounds.'*

I paused, for the voice to come and for anyone who wanted to leave to do so. They could probably get home in time for the second half of England versus Luxembourg. Nobody picked up their folders and walked out. They just sat there looking nervous. But they always look nervous. When the voice didn't come, I continued and found myself kind of smiling.

' Later still I wrote poems with titles like *Highland Fling of Love* and *Elegy for Us Under Cedar Trees* that I gave to the girls on the bus. And you can laugh, you're laughing, I can see, I'm laughing, it's hilarious, but you have to own your early forays, because they are all stations on the way. You have to start somewhere.'

I perched myself on the edge of the desk and hung my hands between my knees, the tried and tested creative writing tutor's informal pep talk position.

'The thing is, although I always wanted to write and was always thinking of stories, I didn't think people like me became writers. I thought writing was for other people.'

It is, said James O'Mailer. You were right all along.

Balling my fists, I tried to ignore him.

'Writers were from some other place, a special place, a place gated off and restricted. And I made excuses not to write. I didn't have a desk. I didn't know how to start. I ought to get a career first.'

And what a career you had? I was there. I remember every barnstorming minute of it.

I knitted my fingers together and kept looking at the group, surprised that the pashmina woman and the Sensie were taking notes. Hoping that I looked like I was merely pausing for effect I dug my fingers into the backs of my hands and concentrated on my temples. Some sort of cough or yelp clicked in my skull, then my ears popped and a warm wave passed through me. Everything seemed to lift.

'I took a degree,' I said, 'and a succession of jobs in publishing, but I constantly felt that I should be doing something else. I was dreamy and unfocused at work, and I couldn't find anything that I wanted to do that didn't seem pointless. Know that feeling?' Nobody answered. The voice didn't break in. He'd gone. I was back on track. The moment of madness had subsided. 'No. OK. Just me then.

'Anyway, three things happened. I was about twenty-five. I actually started to write, just in exercise books after work; I got fired, excellent! Which gave me nine months on the dole during which time I wrote my first novel; and I met the writer Sebastian Harker, the author of *Snow on Parnassus* and *Kill Cyclops*, and after the second of his workshops I attended, he said to me, "you have it, Nathan, you have the voice."'

I paused, unclasping my hands. The group seemed to have shuffled in closer together.

'You'll be pleased to know,' I said, 'that Sebastian has agreed to come and talk to you at our residential weekend at the end of the course.'

'Oh how wonderful,' said the woman in the pashmina.

'Never heard of him,' said Lime Green.

'Look him up then,' I said.

He sniffed. I continued, rattling through the rest. Within a year of meeting Sebastian, I was publishing short stories in magazines. Rather than get another office job and stare out of the window dreaming about the desk at home and *The Drowners*, the novel I was working on, and avoiding any mention of Johanna and what happened between us, I simply said that I bought myself some time to write and took *The* MA in Creative Writing here. I was asked to stay on and do a little teaching, which lead to book doctoring work, all of which allowed me to keep the mornings free to write. I'd sold twenty short stories, written four novels and written for television.

Trooping the Colour's face had crinkled, giving it a walnutlike texture. He huffed and obviously wanted to interrupt me.

'Wow,' said Pashmina.

'What did you write on the telly then?' said Lime Green.

'I think you mean, *for* the *television*,' said Trooping[16].

'It was called *Gentlemen's Relish*[17],' I said.

'Oright. That was good that. Loved it to bits.' He folded his arms high on his chest and nodded around the room.

'Well, I only did two episodes,' I said. 'It wasn't a big deal. Anyway, that's me. That's how I got here. Any questions?'

Trooping put up his hand.

'Reginald,' he said, as if offering his services to a high-ranking police officer at a crime scene. 'Reginald Carnaby. I listened to what you were saying there, and although it's all very interesting, it seems to me that you've done nothing in your young life apart from write. Now, I've always been told that one writes about what one *knows* and . . .'

My face pushed a smile at him. I wanted to say that if that was so, Grammar-Stammerers ought to stick to writing about syntax, though I

---

[16] Internal intelligence gathering network sent out a code red. We have a **Grammar-Stammerer** in range. A Grammar-Stammerer is more of a pain than a Moon-Barker. Every single thing I said from now on in would be contradicted and every day my inbox would be full of complaining messages from the Stammerer. Any writer or novel I referred to would be spluttered over as indicative of a decline in 'standards' and the twilight of Western Civilization. The Grammar-Stammerer is obsessed only with usage, syntax and the formal conventions of English and pre-war, public school Latinate grammar at that. The Stammerer is almost universally male, elderly and votes for the UK Independence Party. The Stammerer needs rules when in the writing of prose fiction there are none (principles, yes; rules, no). The Stammerer writes cleanly and clearly but never creatively because he can't write about people and can't withhold judgement. The Stammerer tells but never shows. The Stammerer wants to switch places with the tutor and take the class himself. The Stammerer here was no doubt champing at the bit because in my little speech I'd used low and beastly colloquialisms and wretched slang terms that wouldn't even be acceptable in the public bar of the Tinker Shooter's Arms in Seething.

[17] **Gentlemen's Relish**: a short-lived, universally derided cable channel drama about three stud-hunks working for a male escort agency called, funnily enough, Gentleman's Relish. It was centred on Sylvester 'Sly' Ramos-Pintos: a right dirty, ripe-and-ready, half-Portuguese, half-east London geezer shagmonster in it for the fun and the riot and the birds when one of his co-stars does it for the money (wife, kids, debts etc) and the other is a bit pretty, a bit confused and a bit of a bender, and deep-down has a thing about Sly. Squinty Hugo had found me this writing job. My inability to turn out what the production company really wanted was one of the main reasons we fell out. I was still living off the fee (just about; I needed to sell *The Penelope Tree* sharpish).

couldn't, having developed a long fuse and, post *The* MA, prior to this evening, an addiction to politeness in class.

'Hang on,' I said. 'Let's not get ahead of ourselves. We'll be talking about ideas and where they come from in a minute. I'd just like us to get to know each other first.'

'You see, Jane Austen only wrote about what she knew. She only wrote about the world in which she lived in . . .'

'Reginald. We'll move onto to this, I assure you.'

He clawed his knees and his face tightened until it looked like it belonged on the top of a walking stick. Even though he relaxed, he kept staring at me as if storing up a series of cutting observations to be used when he inevitably wrote a complaint to Sharon Plum. I stared back, trying to smile, be friendly, but the throb bashed my temples and I realized I was now scowling, my mouth hanging open. I knitted my hands together and concentrated and no voice came. No one spoke. I looked at the clock. I'd been here for years already, I felt. It was a quarter past seven.

A Stealer of Comforts

'Well,' I said. 'That's enough about me. What I'd like to do now is go through the register and I'd like you to tell us about yourself. Let us know what you do and how much writing you've done, what sort of things you like to read and maybe what you want to achieve on this course. Take your time. We're not in a hurry.[18]' I looked down at the register. 'So, do we have a Trevor Chodd?'

---

[18] Never do what I am about to do here – list your principle characters in a static situation without movement, thruline or scene. During my long pre-*Gentleman's Relish* stint as a book doctor/fumigator I noticed that this often happened in would-be ladlit novels where a group of trendy wideboys is introduced thus: *In his local,* The Melons, *he met his mates. Shagger (known as Shagger because he liked to shag a lot of birds), Skag (known as Skag because he liked to shoot up lots of heroin), Porno (called Porno because he had a lot of dirty mags in his flat), Hard Drive (called Hard Drive because he had a lot of porn on his computer), Dog (called so because he went with a lot of dogs/ or because he looked a bit like a mongrel) and Mikey (a name typed on a page).* Here, though, things actually happened like this, so if I want to stick to my instincts as a writer and tell the truth I'm a bit stymied. Similarly, earlier, I could have avoided giving us first sight of Reg etc as Frances and I met up before class, but Frances was being so entertaining and, again, it happened like that. For maximum impact, to foreshadow what occurred subsequent to this, I really should have started with O'Mailer. O'Mailer was the start of it. Everything afterwards would be coloured by my struggle with O'Mailer.

I scanned across the line, through Lime Green to Bird Man, through Reg to Pashmina to the Sensitive Plant, who at that moment looked like a chasm of fear had opened up beneath her, but it was the Barker who thrust up her hand.

'Er, you're Trevor Chodd?' I said.

Her chair grated against the floor as she struggled up. The bags rustled and slid against one another. She ripped off her woolly hat and let her hair sprawl across her shoulders and then she fixed her eyes on me, her deep-set, almost whiteless eyes with glinting, glassy pupils.

'I am the Erika Gretsch.'

'OK Erika, you can get the ball rolling,' I said. 'Tell us about yourself.'

'Hi, I am Erika, and I am an Aries and The Herald, and I am not from England but from Königsburg in Eastern Prussia but in the beginning I was from a city called Aleppo.'

Reg turned his head, his chin shaking with disgust. 'That's in *bloody* Syria.'

'Reg,' I said, lowering my hand and spreading my fingers. 'Briefly, Erika, we've a lot to get through.'

'Yes, I was born in Syria, which is a most terrible place with a dreadful, dreadful hot weather and I was born there and when I was eleven I found myself separated from my Mutti in a street full of baskets and pots and camels, and there I wandered into a stable, and there was a wise woman sitting on a lumpy of hay, and she said to me suddenly, she said, you, you girl, go away from here because you are the Herald of The He and must serve him with your words.'

'Jesus wept,' huffed the Sensie, and fell against her armrest, shutting her eyes.

'Erika,' I said. 'Just keep it concise. What do you do? What do you write? What sort of things do you read?'

'No. After all this time, it obviously does not matter to you. Are you The He?' She gave me a look more venomous than disgruntled, then sat down and began to poke about in the bags again.

'There's only one question we want answered, love,' said Lime Green. 'What you got down there?'

Erika looked up, about to speak, about to climb to her feet again. I had to nip this in the bud.

'People,' I said, trying to inject as much unflappable joviality into my voice as possible. 'We've got all term to get to know each other, so please here, just the salient facts. Less is more, as no doubt I'll be saying over

27

and over again from now on in, I should imagine. Now, do we have a Frank Denbigh in the house?'

The Bird Man of East Anglia, the man with the white spade beard sat up and laced his pudgy fingers together. A pink flush ballooned across his cheeks as he smiled broadly and fondly, and for a second, if you could ignore the beard, he looked like a man-sized baby, all ruddy and smooth-skinned and happy-to-see-Daddy.

'Hi everyone, I'm Frank. Er . . . I used to be an ambulance man, until I retired three years ago.' He paused. We waited. It's not easy this bit. Everyone is allowed a little shyness. I kept up my smile. Everyone was watching him. He stared back at them until his frame jerked and he slammed down his fist on the armrest. The wood vibrated. Everyone ducked. His face crunched into a mask of terrible frustration and his voice became more hiss than accent.

'I'm a bitter man, I'm an angry man, I've got no friends.'

And with that he unclenched his fist, looked at me beseechingly for credence, and then flipped his hand as if to say 'move on to the next one'. [19]

My stomach crawled as I struggled for something to say. There was no sound in the room apart from the rustle of bags from the second row. Then Pashmina woman clicked together the sides of her shoes and as she straightened herself she started to clap, not rapturously, not bravo-encore, but respectfully, impressed until everyone followed suit.

'That was brave,' said Lime Green. He put his hand on Frank's shoulder and gripped it manfully.

No, don't do it, I thought, please, this is not AA or a support group. There are no Twelve Steps here. Don't encourage him. He's in the wrong room. He should be lying on a divan listening to a calm voice ask questions about his toilet training. He should be weeping in a counsellor's conservatory with the yuccas and vines, nursing a complimentary cup of free trade decaffeinated tea. I waited for the clapping to subside and the blush to drain from Frank's face and his gummy smile to recover.

'OK, OK, OK,' I said. 'OK and er, thank you for that, Frank. Thanks very much. And Chodd, do we have a Trevor Chodd? No. No Chodd. No. OK. So you . . .' I indicated Lime Green. ' . . . must be M. MacMahon. What's your story?'

---

[19] **Wrong-Roomer:** Type of CW student who really needs to see a therapist of some sort. Expect confessions and disconcerting opinions.

'I'm Mac McMahon. Estate agent by day . . .' Howling glee lit up his face as he punched the air. 'Best-selling author by night.'

'OK,' I said. 'And what's the basis for that statement?'

'I used to be in a rock band, me. Drummer out of Ruiner. Played all over the world. "Night of Medusa." Remember that?'

'No,' I said, and I was pretty sure, judging by the bemused faces ahead of me that no one had heard of Ruiner either.

'Oh come on, guys,' said Mac. 'Classic British Heavy Metal band, us. Straight outta Birmingham. We were big in Europe, anyway. Scandinavia. Got to number twenty-one in the Norwegian charts.'

'Any ideas about what you want to achieve from this course, Mac?' I said.

'Well, this bloke a few years back, right, we were on tour, or like we were halfway through this tour and it, well, I won't go right into it, but the tour got pulled, the kids were too into death by then, and we were in this hotel in Spalding for three days and it went off and when it stopped, this weird bloke comes out of nowhere and says to me, "you will be a writer, Mac", so I went off and retrained as an estate agent, moved to Norfolk, lovely part of the world, but that's why I'm here now.' He stroked his beard against his throat. 'I am going to write a novel.'

'Have you got a clue, I mean, an idea?' I said.

'That's why I'm here.'

'You might think, Mac, that a novel is a big undertaking. If you've not written before, you might think about cutting your teeth on something shorter.'

An irritated look passed across Mac's face. His hair was long at the back, and smeared into gelled-up spikes, which all made sense now.

'No, you don't understand, Nate. If I can write a drum part in a minute, I can write a novel in a week.'

There was no point going into this.

'OK,' I said. 'And what are your favourite books, Mac?'

'First Blood, Spinal Tap and The Matrix Reloaded.'

'Those are films,' said the Sensie.

'Yes, they are,' I said. 'Books, Mac, novels?'

'Have you actually *read* any?' said Reg.

'No,' said Mac. 'Well, I've read *Jaws*, but it was shit.'

I found myself chewing on the joint of my thumb to keep the laugh indoors. Eventually, I said, 'Well, it's hard to write if you don't read. Perhaps you ought to start by . . .'

'No, I don't read,' he said.

'Try some of the classics, Dickens maybe.'

'Classics is shit.'

'Or try something more modern, maybe like the sort of things that you'd like to write, then at least . . .'

'No, I don't read. It's all shit.'

'I think you'll find that writers tend to read.'

'I don't read. I don't read. I don't read. I've tried. It's all shit.'

'So if some young kid came to you, Mac, and said that he wanted to be a rock drummer, but he'd never picked up the sticks, or even heard a song before, but he'd heard that U2 have a vacancy for a drummer, what would you say?'

A ripple coursed from the tip of his beard to the underside of his drooping stomach.

'Go for it, sonny-me-lad.'

I blew up my fringe, then checked the line of faces. Mac was sitting imperiously now, arms folded, head up, as if he'd proved me utterly wrong. The others seemed to be looking to me to carry on with this, apart from the still-rummaging Erika, but having encountered several Literature-Deniers[20] before, I knew I was entering unstoppable-force-versus-immovable-object territory, and I didn't want to get too snagged. Hopefully my course would puncture Mac's preconceptions. If his prose were just a little better by the end, or even if he merely came to a realization that's it's harder than simply wanting to do it, I would have done my job. Also, anger was beginning to rile my stomach and my ears were heating up and then the throb came at my temples.

No, no, no, no, no, Flack, no, somehow I surmise that it won't be like that.

---

[20] **Literature-Denier** – Breed of CW student, relatively uncommon, with an almost pathological dislike of all printed matter, no ability to see the quality of any novel, play or poem, ignorant of all subtlety of language or situation, sees only the inherent emptiness in all literary works, yet is in possession of tremendous confidence and believes that he or she can succeed and will make a shit-load of money and receive a multitude of sexual favours. Will insist on reference for *The* MA at some point. Most likely to write a story that features the tutor undergoing some humiliating ordeal or assault.

Oh God. I squeezed my eyes shut and clenched my fists until my ears popped and I realized that to the class it must look like I was battling with a particularly vicious bowel problem.

'Good stuff, Mac,' I panted. 'We'll see how you get on.'

I asked for Mantlestein; I wished for Mantlestein. Kind, keen, straightforward Pravina Mantlestein. I got no Mantlestein.

'Reg,' I said, hearing my voice level with formality. 'Your turn.'

'Yes, you seemed to miss me out earlier. Surely C comes before the D of Denbigh and the Ch of Chodd.'

'Sorry, go on.'

He propped himself up on the armrest of his chair with his elbow. A kind of boyishness or sprightly quality came over him. He checked both sides, beaming a smile that I'd only seen before on the faces of old guard novelists wheeled out in lecture theatres or festival amphitheatres, a smile of relief on the face of someone happy that he's still remembered somewhere, what with his novels out of print and his appearance on the shortlist of one of the initial late-sixties Booker Prizes long forgotten, his reputation dependent on PhD students eager to find something obscure to cut their teeth on.

'As I said earlier, I'm Reginald Carnaby, and I'm a retired headmaster, and I've always wanted to be a writer, and since I retired from active life I've dedicated myself to writing something that I think will be of great use to future generations . . .'

A sudden feeling of déjà vu weighed me down – I'd heard this a million times before; it was in the preface of the 58th edition of *The Grammar- Stammerers Handbook* – and I have to admit I glazed over. I found myself thinking about Sylvester 'Sly' Ramos-Pintos striding through a gallery in a stately home, stripped to the waist, dressed in only leather trousers, his pack of muscle sidewinding between his shoulder blades, deshabillées debutantes and under-dressed underwear models strewn around the room spread out and waiting for him. Then Pashmina's legs distracted me – beneath the pashmina of crimson and flame, she wore a short black dress more suitable to the cocktail hour or a networking soiree, and there was a strip of adorable leg on show between the hem and her knee – and I was speculating on something unprofessional when Reg's voice interjected again, a sound like that of a distant buzzsaw, the sound of men doing DIY in a yard over the back, behind your house, when you're a kid and it's Sunday and you've been out with the other boys in the street, but you were bored and disconnected and came back to read an HG Wells or John Wyndham book or *I am Legend* by Richard Matheson or something. The buzzsaw voice grew louder and I blinked at her knees and let my gaze travel up to her face and her titian, wavy hair. She was staring back at me. The buzzsaw voice clamoured and I felt all the liquid in my body – blood, lymph, water, stomach acid, brain fluid – start to evaporate and my extremities wizen and I could imagine the expression on my face and my ashen, pallid skin tone, and it must have been the same expression that I saw on Pashmina's, and as I scanned the line, on Sensie's, and Frank's and Mac's and even Erika's.

'My novel,' Reg said, 'is about a rather crusading headmaster and how he deals with the various challenges put to him by the social changes of the nineteen-sixties and how he fights a rather valiant rearguard. And it's a love story too, which I'm basing on my Darling Dear and myself.'

'That sounds very interesting, Reg,' I said, my autopilot kicking in. 'I look forward to reading it. Swiftly moving on.' I gestured to the end of the line. 'And which one of you two is Doctor Jane Vest?'

Pashmina placed her hand to her chest. 'That's me,' she said, and she blushed and stalled and gave me a pleading look.

'Are you a medical doctor?' I said, trying to help her out.

'No, PhD in physiology. But what I'd really like to do is be a writer and write full time. That's my dream. So, I kind of feel that this course is really important to me. I really do. I'd really like to give up work next year and just write. That's all I want. I can just see myself doing it all day in a cottage with just a cat for company.'

My spirits dropped. I'd hoped that Doctor Jane wouldn't fall into any Major Arcana category, but the cottage-and-cat statement marked her out as a Romantic Typist[21]. The pashmina was a dead give-away, in any case.

---

[21] **Romantic Typist (Rom-T)**: category of CW student, frequently female, though the 18-25 year old male is also susceptible (minus the underwear issues: see below). The Romantic Typist is less abrasive than a Literature-Denier, a Grammar-Stammerer and some Wrong Roomers, though requires a similar kid gloves approach as a Sensitive Plant. A Romantic Typist entertains grand illusions. Writing is not so much the telling of stories, but the attainment of status and the escape from perceived disappointments or routine drudgery. The Romantic Typist feels that she will not be taken seriously unless she is recognized as a writer and will tell all and sundry about her works in progress, frustrations and expectations. The Romantic Typist will try very hard and is certainly earnest, but confuses the process with something to do with being taken out to lunch, the wearing of La Perla underwear, and the standing on balconies in a chiffon dress, whilst sipping white wine and looking wistful. The Romantic Typist shares with the Sensitive Plant a tendency to insist that the tutor would only understand if he or she dropped all critical parameters and just accepted the work as the writer intends. We all have an inner Rom-T. Most of us

Pashminas, long diaphanous scarves and crushed velvet coats are a uniform of sorts for Rom-Ts and all other dreamers and delicates. Then again, I could work with a Rom-T. I just needed to knock the romance out of them. Come round to mine and I'll show you the romance. Come round to mine at six am on a winter's morning, when breath hangs visible in the room like ectoplasm and I can't feel my feet and the heater's a joke and the pipes are groaning and shaking the draining board so hard that the crockery is smashing into the sink, and the rising damp on the stairs has frozen and leaving the flat is like *Touching the Void* or *The Birthday Boys*, and I kippered the cat long ago with my thirty a day habit, and am desperate for the post and for something good to happen to me, and I'm trying to winnow out 250 words because otherwise the day will seem pointless, and then Squinty Hugo phones, his voice now an elemental part of the weather, and starts droning on about marketing and profiles and the tightening of the book trade and what *they* want, and he does this once a month for two years until that time he tells you that your scripts for *Gentleman's Relish* are not the 'posh porn' *they* wanted, and then sends you an e-mail saying that there's nothing he can do for you, chin up, best of luck, and you go out and smoke a fag on a park bench and watch the fronds of snow melt and fall from the branches.

The best thing I could do for Doctor Jane was disillusion her, gently, gently, of course. The thing I hate most about teaching is that ninety-nine percent of the time I come as a hatchet man to the students, a stealer of comforts, the unceasing complicator, the raiser of the bar. More. More. More. Closer. Closer. Closer. *Show*. Can't see this. Can't feel this. Don't get this. Go back and do it again. Start again. Replan. Replot. Refashion. Rewrite. Rewriting is writing. Writing is a way of life and a state of mind, not a job option or career path. It is not a way to stop commuting. You will not regain your self-respect. This helps a Rom-T and most Minor Arcana Folder-Holders. For the other Majors, I wasn't so sure I could help them at all.

'Have you written much already, Jane?' I said.

'I have. I really want to get into the women's market. I just like things with a bit of spice and a damned good sense of humour. I do hate the phrase, but I'd like to get into chicklit.' She sat back and hunched up. 'You're looking at me funnily.'

---

outgrow it, as we do not standing up for ourselves, reading door-stopper science fantasy novels, listening to Pink Floyd and masturbating all day and all of the night.

'No, I'm not. Sorry. Go on.'

'Then I also write, well, I don't like the word either, but I write erotica.' She held her hair in a bunch at her ear that if she pulled on any harder she'd rip out.

'That's er . . . quite diverse,' I said. 'Thank you very much, Jane. Nice to have you here.' I started my pacing again. 'Maybe before we go on, I ought to say that all these ideas that you might carry about what a writer is like or what writing is going to bring you, lose them. They will only distract you. Writing is mainly work, OK, it's hard work, it's a slog and a grind and a worry. It's not about cottages and cats. It's not about future generations. It's not about publishing. It's too mysterious for that, OK?'

'I'll try,' she said. She let go of her hair and it bounced back into shape. Her hand fell to her lap and she started to scribble quickly in her exercise book.

'I've already got a cottage,' said Mac, 'and a cat. It's called Four. After *Led Zep Four.*'

'Do you spell that F-O-U-R,' I said, 'or One-V?'

'Dunno, just Four.'

'OK, OK, OK, who's last on the list?' Must be Oatmeal-Sensie. I checked for the name. I double-took. I bit my lip. I swallowed my breath and for the life of me tried to keep my voice even and unruffled. 'You must be . . . er . . . Cynthia Wadge?'

She crossed her legs. The oatmeal colour of her sweatpants looked extra bland in the striplights and one of her feet twitched feverishly.

'Well, after what you've just said, I don't think I want to tell you anything about myself at all.'

'Oh, c'mon, Cynthia. You're among friends here.'

'No, I'm just Cynthia. That's all I want to say.' She hunched up again, her foot stilling as she lost her hands in her brown cardigan. Worry balls were lodged in the pockets.

Well, there wasn't much I could do about a Sensie. If I'd said something else, the something else would have been her reason for shutting down. I clapped my hands in a way that I hated, then said thank you to the class. Sitting on the edge of the table, I briefly summed up the course outline, saying that the first hour of each session would be given up to discussing the previous week's homework and the second would involve an exercise and a mini-lecture from me. I ran through the assessment criteria and the details of the residential. So there they all were, my new flock, folders out, grinning and eager. They and I had survived thus far and only two of them, Reg and Erika, looked like they wanted to kill me. Only 30%. Not bad in the circumstances. Totally manageable. Now we could get on with it. How to begin? Cut to the chase. Appeal to their vitals. I told them where the coffee machine lived and gave them a full fifteen minutes to recharge and slag me off.

As I sat in my chair behind the desk and waited for voices, a familiar feeling came over me, a down-dragging sense of loneliness and ennui that I'd forgotten about during the summer vacation. There's a melancholy, the sort of melancholy you might romanticize in a short story or novel coda that seems far more unsettling in lived life, when there's no context or structure, no sparkle of hope in the rainfall, none of the consolations of fiction. Teaching creative writing is a melancholy occupation. Continuously, at the back of your mind, you know that you should be writing. Your time would be better spent writing. The rain that glimmered and splashed on the black windows now should have done so on my window at home. I should have been pushing on with my new novel about the girl on the Millennium Bridge and waiting for news. With my luck, news would come when I wasn't in, and Fred Malone would leave no message and neglect to ring back. My big break would be no more than a dead blip on the ansamachine.

Only an hour to go. Then I could return home. There might be messages. And the class would be easier from now on. What a gang, though, what a crew. I was going to have to earn my alms here. Then I experienced a tremor of fear when I reminded myself that in December I would have to spend a whole weekend trapped with these people in the gloomy, gothic confines of Kollocks Grange in the northerly outer reaches of The Shire[22].

---

[22] **The Shire:** Flack-speak for Norwich and Norfolk. When trying to sell a contemporary English novel, the setting is important. According to Squinty Hugo, unless a novel is set in one of a few elite places it will be 'tricky to market'; hence the trade's preference for novels set in the past or abroad. London, Manchester, Liverpool and for some reason, Brighton, these are places that have a marketable charge. Stories don't happen in Leicester, Mansfield or Stoke. They don't happen in Hastings, Glossop or even Penge. It wasn't the writing in *The Truncheons of Humber Vice* that led to its rejection by every major publishing house in The Arctic (no one would have read as far as the lines I quoted earlier). It was the river that runs through it. I always find this odd, as most of us live in places like Leicester, Mansfield and even Penge. But I couldn't possibly think about setting my story in Norwich. Although there is a long history of stories set in 'East Anglia' – East Anglia evokes a winning combination of bleak watery glamour and grotesque peasants– Norwich or Ipswich seem provincial and uninteresting. I could have got around this by using a municipal pseudonym, like Cowrich or Fenchester, or by pretending that all this actually happened to me in St Petersburg in 1912 or in some microcelebrity's penthouse

Don't be such a sourpussy, I told myself. They're all right. Nothing out of the ordinary. Just run-of-the-mill Folder-Holders and Leisure-Learners. Writing here is just a form of socializing and entertainment. It's not serious. I reminded myself that my job was to impart a sense of first principles and offer some editing tips, just like Sebastian had done for me. That's all I could do. That's all any CW tutor can do. Can't give anyone a voice. Can't give anyone ideas. Can't give anyone the luck or the breaks or the networks.

But, I told myself, it was a small group, nice and compact, and maybe Chodd and Mantlestein would turn up next week, and there are always Sensies and Rom-Ts, and frequently Grammar-Stammerers and Wrong-Roomers, and I had coping strategies and ways of teaching them all. At least I didn't have any of the really dodgy Majors I'd come across during my time[23].

Famous last words, said James O'Mailer, uttered by the not very famous.

---

overlooking Battersea (there is, of course, an alternative version set in the penthouse but so this more marketable idea sidetracks no one, I'll give away the end. I murdered Zizi but only so I didn't have to ghostwrite her autobiography, *Dangerously in Love*). By borrowing a place-name from Tolkien, though, I not only manage to avoid the 'N' word, I might fool the unwary into thinking that this story is a soft fantasy in the epic mode that features magic objects, hooded figures and an apocalyptic medieval fantasy battle that decides all at the climax

[23] I was relieved not to have in our midst here: a **Ponce**; a **Trustafarian**; a **Child of the Raves**; a **Retired Married Couple Who Used to Run a Concentration Camp**; an **MC Text-Speak**; a **Poverty Pornographer**; a **Shout-in-yer-Face Ian Paisley Voice**; a **Chestwig of the North**; a **Can't Spell, Won't Spell**; a **Fan-fiction Geekface**; a **Script Slipper**; a **Pratchett Hat**; a **Princess on a Hill**; a **Theory Wanker**; an **Author Stalker**; a **Masonic Ex-Copper with Streets to Clean**; a **Financial Journalist of Our Times**; a **Fringe Cringer**, a **Third Monkey**, a **Penguin with Weasel's Fur**; a **Hank Fantasy** or anyone who'd asked whether I could guarantee them a three-book publishing deal at the end of our eight weeks or where they could buy my novels.

Nothing is Lost

I had my head pressed to the tabletop, unable to pop my ears, reduced to hoping that I had an ear infection, some imbalance or inflammation of the fluid in my ears that was causing distortions I interpreted as language when the door opened. I lifted my chin and opened my eyes, fully expecting the normal crocodile of nervy, chatting double-ups carrying plastic cups of weapon's grade coffee, but some sort of kerfuffle occurred. Reg, Jane and Cynthia scrambled into the room and scuttled to their chairs as if they were fleeing from something occult that had manifested itself out there in the corridors. They were followed by a slower, more composed Frank, who was grinning like he'd just won the biggest, hairiest coconut at the coconut shy at the grandest, bestest fair ever to hit the little village at the edge of the world. Oh my God, I thought, what has he told them about himself?

'That's a bit rough,' he said.

'What is?' I said. The other three cowered and rubbed theirs arms as if freezing.

'I don't know what it is, but it's a bit rough,' said Frank.

'It's disgusting,' said Reg.

'What is it?'

'I don't want to say in front of these lovely young women.'

'I've seen some things,' said Jane. 'I don't usually get rattled, but . . .'

Inside the room now, Mac was standing deep in conversation with Erika. She held one of her carriers with both hands, pulling its mouth open wide so he could look into it. He stared pensively and rubbed his beard, his back slightly arched, as if forcing himself to keep his eyes fixed on whatever it was that lurked and glimmered down there.

They both seemed to then realize that they were being watched. Erika closed the bags and fell in behind Mac as he sauntered back towards his desk.

'That's just given me a blinding idea,' he said.

'What is it?' I said.

'I don't want anyone copying my ideas, Nathan.'

'In the bag?' I said.

'The object found,' said Erika. 'It is my inspiration. It calls to me.'

'Well, it can stop calling now, Erika.

'It prophesises the world of The He.'

'Next time, leave it at home. No one comes here to be inspired. Well, not like that anyway, if you know what I mean.'

A plummeting sensation travelled through me and for a while I couldn't stop myself staring at Erika, staring into the abyss and the abyss was staring back at me. And then, bull to my red rag, Reg's gimlet eye joined forces with The Moon-Barker-ray, and I snapped out of it.

'OK, I said, galvanized by a meditative pace across the front of the classroom. 'Let's get down to business. Where do we start?'

As they sat there attentively now, autopilot took over and I dozed off behind the levers and dials as I talked about ideas and where they come from, how they are gathered and shaped, and impressed upon the group the need to write frequently and the need to consider writing a process. When I asked them who was keeping a journal, only Erika, unsurprisingly, was already doing so; a freehand, hieroglyphic epic, I imagined, which like the satanic tomes in the HP Lovecraft novels I used to read when I was fourteen, could drive the reader insane[24]. Besides, none of the others were doing practice, so I hammered into them the need to get into the habit of

---

[24] **Note to Self**: *The Erikomicon*. Pastiche. Write twelve horror stories that reference *The Erikomicon*. Watch as sundry Moon-Barkers, Lit-Deniers, Wrong-Roomers, goths and larpers hassle the staff of the British Library and the Bodleian trying to find the Eldritch and hallowed *Erikomicon*. Realize there are better things to be doing with your so-called talent.

writing three pages of free notes a day [25] and then write maybe two hundred and fifty to five hundred words a day of composition. This caused some consternation.

'I don't want to do that,' said Mac. 'I just want to write. And five hundred words a day is too easy.'

'The thing is,' said Jane, 'that I really need certain things to write. I can only write on nice paper in a violet notepad and I can only write at dusk and I can only write if I have fresh flowers on the desk and I need chilled white wine and nibbles.'

'And I wouldn't want anyone to read my diary,' said Cynthia. 'I'd feel violated.'

When I suggested to Cynthia that a journal is for her use alone and not for publication, Frank nodded his head sideways and said, 'What, not even after she's dead?' Cynthia cringed and her notepad fell to the floor with a thwack.

'Let's really not get ahead of ourselves,' I said. 'All I say is give it a go. Keep a journal and write a little every day. That sound fair?'

By the look of them, I'd just asked them to walk to the North Pole in their bare feet. I then mentioned Henry James' idea of the 'glimpse' and how we are looking for images or situations that allow us to use both our imagination and our experience, quoting his line: *'Try to be one of the people of whom nothing is lost!'* Then I asked them to spend twenty minutes or so compiling a list of 'glimpse' ideas that could eventually become stories.

For what seemed like hours, nobody did anything, then notebooks flapped open and pens started to move. Frank lowered his head to the armrest, poked his tongue out and shielded his paper with his elbow. Reg started to list, but did so without reference to the paper, his head up and eyes lofted as if studying the shapes of clouds or the transit of butterflies. Jane was thinking hard, I could tell, but she gave me a concerned glance before dipping her eyes to her paper. Mac was writing incredibly swiftly, line after line, on his second page already. I couldn't see Erika. A flood of tiredness engulfed me as I sat down. I could have slept then. Something comes over you as the end of class approaches, exhaustion so heavy that you could curl up on the desk and flake out and become a living sculpture for the students to sketch. By the time you get home, though, you'll be wired again and won't be able to sleep until the early hours.

---

[25] See **The Artist's Way** by Julia Cameron (Souvenir Press, 1994), though if you take this book to heart, you'll end up like Erika.

I swallowed a yawn and drifted. So much of your time teaching is spent doing nothing, daydreaming before a group of strangers reading or writing. Mac was blitzing the page. Jane and Reg scribbled notes and Cynthia was staring into the void of the blackboard behind me. There was no sound, apart from the rustle of Erika's bags. What on earth was in there? What wet creepy thing had she trawled out from the depths and the dark? I didn't want to think about it. Mac did. A worry, but not a surprise. On the back of my lesson plan, the nib of my pen started to sketch Doctor Jane's outline, trying to remove the pashmina. I just wanted to see her without the cashmere wigwam attached to her shoulders. Not without her clothes, not that. I hadn't yet been completely taken over by the spirit of Sylvester 'Sly' Ramos-Pintos, though it worried me that a year after I'd stopped working on *Gentlemen's Relish*, I thought about him at least as much as I thought about my own characters, and frequently listed plot ideas for the defunct series during my writing practice in the mornings. As I started to adjust the shape of the waist and crosshatch the bust, I realized that the face possessed a peculiar resemblance to Juicy Gash.[26]

A chair scraped, clattered.

'I can't believe you're making us do this!'

Cynthia shoved her folder under her arm and scrambled out of the room, scattering more chairs and banging the door behind her. A hum hung over the heads of the students.

'Don't worry,' I said. 'It happens. I'll e-mail her.'

In my experience, running after a Sensitive Plant will lead to a grim tête-à-tête beneath the sodium glare of the carpark lights, listening to a long diatribe about the shadow of a more talented brother or an accomplished sister, or the brink of divorce, or how he won't read my writing or just how difficult this all is and can't you be more encouraging.

---

[26] **Juicy Gash:** Flackspeak for JG Ballard. I used to have a real obsession with Juicy. I can pinpoint the exact moment when I suddenly, really, really needed to write, and to write things that are predictive and extreme and strange and unsettling, to an afternoon when I was seventeen and it was summer and I lay in a park on my back in the grass and read *Crash* by JG Ballard. I could never think of a dashboard as merely a tool ever again. And afterwards I read everything he'd published at that time. I read him a lot when I was at university. One morning, I was reading *High Rise* in bed and Johanna woke up and asked me what I was reading and after I'd said it starts with a GP eating a dog (an impressive, immediate opening; refer back to opening thoughts here), she said: 'what does JG stand for?' I didn't know. I'd never even thought to wonder. 'Juicy Gash,' I said. He'll always be Juicy to me. RIP.

The others continued. Another wave of drowsiness came over me. My eyelids heavied and I felt myself plummet, almost dropping off until the throb suddenly hit me.

You're the one upon whom everything is lost, Flack, said James O'Mailer.

Before I knew it I'd jumped up and blundered across the blackboard to the television, where I turned to the class and froze. A sensation of deep shame crashed over me. The students' eyes seemed froglike and yellow.

'What's the matter with you, boy?' said Reg. 'Having a mental episode?'

'Sorry,' I said. I shuffled back to my desk, keeping my eye on him, the way he draped his left hand over the rest and kept his right neatly in his lap.

The rain was lashing the windows now. The clock had inconvenienced itself enough to slither towards five to nine, just about time for me to call it a night. Returning to my perch on the rim of the desk, I asked the students to stop writing.

'Anyone have any good ideas?' I said.

No answer.

'Well, what I'd like you to do for next class is to firstly, start to get into the practise routine I mentioned earlier. Buy a pad. Write every day. Then I want you to think more about this idea of the glimpse, and then go over your list here, and cross out anything that seems too cliched or too unlikely, settle on one idea and then start to write the story. If you can bring two pages next week, we'll see what we've got. And next week, we'll move on to the vexed subject of showing and telling. OK? Nice to meet you all. Thank you and goodnight.'

As I organized my papers, Erika and Reg left the room, which gave me a certain feeling of relief, as I didn't want to get bogged down in any afters with either of them. Mac was standing now, stomach puffed out and his notebook under his arm.

'Frank, mate, fancy a pint?' he said.

'Oh no,' said Frank. 'Wife's in the van. See you all next week.'

As he stalked out of the room, a worried look shot across Jane's face that I assumed matched mine. She slid her stuff into a glossy shopping bag imprinted with a Montmartre street-scene, then hesitated to peer back at Frank and then over to me. For a second I thought she was going to approach me. I tried to look nonchalant and involved myself in quickly,

41

desperately screwing up Eveningwear Juicy Gash. Footsteps approached. When I looked up, Mac's vast stomach was blocking my view on the room, his mahogany-brown eyes studying me. The door shut. The air-conditioning buzzed. My legs seemed to telescope and my shoulders hunch. He was holding papers covered in scrawl.

'Mac,' I said. 'What can I do for you?'

'I've just written a short story.'

'What? In twenty minutes?'

'Well, it's short.'

'It must be.'

'Will you read it for me?'

'The thing is Mac, and I should have said this earlier, but I'm not paid to do work outside of class, that's why we use the first hour of the class for workshopping.'

'Oh go on, Nate. You'll like it, I promise. It's the best one yet.'

'I thought you'd never written before.'

'That's how come it's the best one.'

'Don't you want to edit it? It'll seem different in the morning and then different again the morning after that.'

'No, I don't want to change it. I want *you* to read it.'

I was desperate to leave. I wanted a cigarette and a bottle of beer from my fridge. I wanted to check my messages and spend some time with my friend the Sofa of Shame and ponder my predicament. Should I go and see a doctor or pay to sit in a conservatory with yuccas and decaf tea? Should I go and see an ear specialist or a padded cell door-slammer? This was the question that burned like a magnesium flare.

'Look, just this once,' I said. 'I'll read it for next week. But don't tell the others, all right?'

I took the papers and shoved them with the others in my bag.

'Cheer's mate. Want a lift?'

'Er, thanks, no, I like the walk.'

'It's pissing down.'

I smiled and patted the collapsible umbrella lodged into the side-flap of my bag.

'Suit yourself then.'

I sat back, let out a long sigh, then another one. Since when had I become such a soft touch? The room was white and bright and empty and the rain beat against the windows.

You're becoming one of them, Flack, said James O'Mailer. A what do you call them? A Folder-Holder. So far out of the loop now.

I Have Seen Them

Outside the Eudora Doon, I was halfway up the path, frantically searching my jacket pockets for my cigarettes, when I realized that it really was pissing down. Rain pounded the surface of the road and the glass roofs of the greenhouses opposite. My hair was already wet and if I didn't stop dithering I'd quickly be soaked to the skin. I half wished I'd taken up Mac's offer, but I'd have ended up in a St. George cross-bedecked, Euro 96-themed pub on the ringroad, listening to his lifestory and his plans to rip up the hardback charts, and I'd have to talk like I'd been talking for the last two hours for a further two. Anyway, I liked my post-class walk home. It helped burn off the melancholy. But tonight, as a gust of wind swept a sheet of rainwater off the road and splattered it across me, I decided to take the bus. As I started for the little shelter just along the road past the greenhouses, a voice crackled behind me.

'Herr Professor.'

My guts rippled. Standing under the portico of the building, silhouetted against the plate glass windows and the soft yellow light of the foyer, half in shadow, half glimmering, was Erika Gretsch. The woolly hat was pulled down over her forehead, the puffa jacket done up fast to her neck, which gave her, when added to the width of her chassis, the look of a Mongolian bouncer or small-time rapper's bodyguard. The bags nestled against her legs like squat ducklings to their mother. Rain seeped through to the roots of my hair. Now I wished I were pulling up into the carpark of some shit-awful mock-Tudor pub on the ringroad, about to deconstruct *Jaws* over pints of real ale full of animal hair and woodchips, or sheepishly about to ask what Mac had seen in the Moon-Barker's bag.

Suddenly, she was right in my face and the bags were nipping at my shins.

'Professor Flack, I need speak with you.'

'I'm not a professor,' I said.

'I need speak with you.'

'Can't it wait? Why don't you e-mail me?'

'E-mail?'

'Seriously, I'm in a rush. I've got to meet someone.'

'Really? Who?'

'My wife.' I shivered against the wind, perhaps knowing even then that someday I'd regret this fib. 'Goodnight, Erika.'

I marched off towards the bus-shelter. As I crossed the road I realized that no one else was there hiding from the rain, no other Adult Ed types from classes running simultaneously with mine, none of the other tutors, or Frances; now I wished I had agreed to a drink. We could have sat out the rain in the bar. I could have apologized for seeming rude earlier. Then again, if I told her that O'Mailer was talking to me, she'd laugh. I imagined that, like me, when Frances was sixteen she had matured out of laughing at mad people. Something about this job had made us both shrink back down into those clothes. I couldn't call her, but I couldn't stay here and wait for the bus on my lonesome. Erika was lurching along towards the shelter, the bags slapping against her jeans. No way was I going to suffer on that oblong of concrete, praying for the bus to come, a Moon-Barker frothing at my side.

Girding myself to the weather, I trudged away up the road. There was a larger bus stop by the porter's lodge on the main university drive. I didn't look back and powered as fast as I could. When I reached the other stop, it was packed with huddling undergraduates. I lost myself in the crowd and again considered putting on my headphones. Then I noticed Erika dragging the Gretschbags across the road, her eyes scanning the faces in the queue. I shuffled along the line, maniacally searching for anyone that I knew. It had been two years since I'd taught undergrads but there was an off chance that ex-students might be here. I could ingratiate myself and keep my back turned as I asked how they were, if they were still writing. I'd risk being sent a story about sour campus love or what

45

happened on my Interrailing holiday to look busy and unapproachable to The Moon-Barker. Nobody, though. Not a soul. I reached the end of the shelter. The long, black stretch of the drive was ahead of me, and I could just keep going and walk on, but the rain was torrential now. The students yelped and screeched and tried to bundle under the roof. My hair and legs were getting drenched. Through the glass of the shelter, I couldn't see Erika, just a bleary mass. Then, holy miracle of miracles, a bus pulled up.

I elbowed and barged through the pack. When I got on, the bus was already half-full and all the seats were taken. Long-tailed water droplets clung to the windows, vibrating as the bus thrummed and started to chug along the drive. I ended up standing in the middle of the aisle, clinging to a handgrip, keeping my eyes fixed to the floor and the bag between my feet. Just as I began to let myself think that in five minutes or so I'd be at home, towelling off my hair and cracking open a Pils, just about to check all the messages on the ansamachine and the e-mails, shouts and protestations erupted from further down the aisle. Shoved-aside kids collapsed onto the laps of people sitting. The thud and a rustle of bags followed each barked volley of, 'Excuse me! Excuse me!'

Her shoulders split apart the two giggling Japanese girls in front of me, the Gretschbags sliding past their hips and their matching yellow coats as she conquered the gap. In my face now, Erika's eyes were black and piggy and they slid disconcertingly leftwards as the bus veered out of the campus.

'Professor Flack, I must speak with you.' She dropped one of the bag clusters. It thunked on the floor. She raised her hand into a clenched fist. 'Today I have had one of those days when everything I have touched turned to dust!'

'Pardon?'

'I wake up. They don't come. I go out. I can't stay. I go to post office. There is nothing there. I ring up and they put the phone down. On me. They *put* the *phone* down on *me*!'

The people around us flinched and snickered. Eyes were averted. Eyes were wide. I wanted to turn and say that I didn't know this person. She had nothing to do with me.

'These people are all peasants,' she spat. 'I have seen them, in the south of France, crushing grapes with their feet!' Her voice then lowered a little. 'But Professor Flack, I have found you at last. You are The He. You can help me, you know people, you know these peasants.'

'No I don't.'

'I have piles and piles of them. I have heaps and mountains all over place and nobody will publish them.'

'Erika, I still don't know what you're talking about.'

'Poems. I have a poems and no one wants.'

'I'm not a poet, Erika.'

'You are The He! All poems are for you.'

'I don't know anything about poems.' Ah, she was Moon-Barker sub-category, **The Beat Baglady.** I might yet shunt her sideways into someone else's classroom and someone else's nightmares. If I was a cruel man, I would have given her Frances's e-mail, but I was pro-life, anti-blood sports. I could e-mail Plum and ask for this one to be transferred. Then I remembered my little altercation with Plum earlier and my ears started to burn.

Erika's voice dipped to a grovelly whine. 'The He can help me. You can.' As the bus pulled up before the roundabout, I thought for a second she was going to use the thinning of the crowd in the aisle to throw herself to her knees. But she stayed standing, a terrible grimace of loss and emotion pleading all over her face. 'The He, you must help me.'

'Erika,' I said. 'I teach prose. Why are you in my class? We have poetry classes.'

'I have done those. Facking idiot-bitches.'

'Erika . . .'

'I am writing love poems for you, just for The He.'

A big guffaw went up behind me. My ears were scorching and my wet jeans shrunk and heavied and crawled up into my groin.

'Erika, can you be quiet.'

The bus jolted sideways as it took the roundabout. Erika startled and fell into me, her giant breasts thumping into my chest, her huge face clamping to my cheek. My arm snapped rigid as the handgrip took my weight. Someone behind me pushed me and I was able to drive Erika off. As she wavered, a muscle spasm pulsed through my legs to my pelvis, up my spine to freeze my jaw. All my composure funnelled into not shouting, not bursting into tears.

'You must help me!' she whined. 'You must! You are The He!'

I would have better appreciated the despair in her voice if she had been drowning in quicksand while I was sitting nonchalantly on the bank, whistling a merry tune as I practised slipknots with the rescue rope.

'Erika, this is not the time, OK?' I said. 'Not here. And I don't want any more bloody poems written about me, OK?'

She glared, made a castrating pout, then shook her hair and turned away. There was a pause. Muttering circled me. The bus engine rumbled. Rain against the window sounded like handfuls of shingle. Embarrassment makes you temporarily telepathic. The judgements and the *schadenfreude* of the people around me swirled in my head. The bus was barrelling down the road and I lived on this road, so I picked up my bag and positioned the strap on my shoulder. I took a glance at the Gretschbags. They were filled with newspaper packages covered with greasy spots and thumbprints that jostled and leapt as the bus hit humps in the road. I dithered about whether I should ask what she'd shown to Mac and the others. I *did* want to know. Or at least, the dirty-minded, risk-all, curiosity-martyr in me wanted to know – Juicy Gash would want to know, wouldn't he? – but the safety-first adult didn't want to be responsible for the stampede that would follow when Erika waved a dead alligator or something around the bus.

'Where do you live, Erika?' I said, trying to make polite, non-berserker chitchat, now that the end was in sight.

'You want pizza?' said Erika.

'No!'

'I live other side of city.'

'Good stuff. I'll see you next week,' I said, reaching for the bell. I made an ungainly hash of trying to force myself along the aisle while the bus was still moving. When it stopped, I fled into the rain, not looking back. The bus swooshed past me as I was struggling with the front door key. Inside, as I made my way up the stairs to my flat, I felt the relief that the class was over and that I was shot of Erika strangely change into restlessness and wide-awake boredom. Then again, time to see if anything had come in for me while I was out.

48

The Garret

Three messages bleeped on the ansamachine. I could hear them singing to me while I towelled off my hair in the bathroom. Turning on the taps sent a shuddering death rattle through the pipes. It howled downwards into the depths of the building and set my teeth on edge. The ground floor flats were still unlet; no one else could hear that sound. In the bedroom, I changed my jeans. Then the lounge, as ever, seemed grim and shambolic: the dull magnolia walls; the russet carpet that was impossible to keep clean; the mismatching sofas; the piles and piles of books and DVDs all over the place; the heaps of folders and stationery and journals; the desk strewn with fag packets and letters and post-its and the computer that by now was actually nicotine-stained. The Garret wasn't exactly Wilbur Smith's private island, or John Fowles' house on the Lyme Regis cliffs. It was never going to get me onto *TLS Cribs*.

When I'd got the money through for *Gentlemen's Relish*, I'd made a reasoned decision not to move from The Garret to somewhere with 20th century plumbing and central heating and presentable furniture, thinking that the money would last longer here and I could devote more of my time to *The Penelope Tree* and less to teaching and editing. Now, it was time for this tactical manoeuvre to pay off.

It is not unusual, I told myself, for literary agents to contact you at the end of the day should they phone. With the towel around my neck, I checked the messages on the machine.

One: Recording of gushing Northern woman proclaiming that if I ring an extortionately priced phone line I might have won a holiday on the Costa Del Bollocks.

Two: Frances: Nate, er, you there? . . . It's me. Good to see you tonight, sorry I was stroppy. Hope yours were more simpatico than mine. Shudder from Hell[27]. Er . . . buy you a pint later in the week? Call me? Ciao-Miaow.

Three: no message, just a tone, and when I dialled 1471, the caller's number had been withheld.

I paced. That might have been him. Fred Malone. On the other hand, he was unlikely to call in the evening, and I'd not left for work until six. I booted up the computer – no messages there either. Only junkmail about mortgages, Viagra and dating agencies in Texas.

I grabbed a beer and lit a cigarette and wandered around the room, not really knowing what to do with myself. I was involved in a nerve-jangling waiting game, in stasis until the breakthrough. Since Squinty Hugo dropped me in March, I had no agent, and without an agent I couldn't sell the book and while I couldn't sell the book I was stuck here.

On my desk lay the bag of objects I used in my teaching, the bag I would get out next week for 'Show, Don't Tell'. I reached in and found the starfish. It was big and pink and studded with filaments. I gave it a stroke and a squeeze. Johanna had given it to me in Australia. I could almost hear her voice: *Touch it always and think of me*. I'd never wanted to be the sort of creative writing tutor who has a bag of objects that he pours out onto a desk and everyone takes one and someone has to touch the starfish and describe it in a paragraph of sense-based prose, and you just say, *well done Simonetta, bravo*, and everyone claps whatever. Never wanted to be that. Pretty pointless. Hate exercises. Never did exercises myself. Think it best to start with narrative ideas and work techniques into storylines. But I had a syllabus to follow and included the starfish as a private joke. Recently though, I'd started to find a new respect for the

---

[27] **Shudder:** The collective noun for a Sensitive Plant is a **shudder**. For example, "Frances told Nathan that fifteen minutes before class, she was sitting in the cafeteria speed-reading 48 students' poems about September 11th (and/or 'geese') when she was approached by a shudder of Sensies. All clutched folders to their hearts and were on the brink of tears".

starfish. I began to see more in it. The star was high in the sky. The fish was flat to the seabed. The starfish would eventually be washed up and passed around and prodded and fingered, marvelled at and despised, just like a novel.

I didn't know what to do with myself. I spread out on the Sofa of Shame with the starfish on my chest and tried not to think about agents or voices or Frances or whatever was in Erika Gretsch's bag. Switching through the channels on TV, I'd either seen everything – documentaries I'd already taped and films I knew so well I could have acted in them – or the shows were just time-wasting drivel. I was zapping the remote control, muttering *shit, shit, shit*, over and over again until I gave up and turned it off. I lay around for a bit, sipping my beer and smoking cigarettes, unable to clear Mac and Reg's voices from my mind and intermittently cringing at the memory of Erika ranting on the bus. And O'Mailer. How could I have spent an evening with James O'Mailer speaking to me? I lay there and looked for faces in The Garret's lovely Artex walls[28]. I should go to bed but resisted this, I realized, because I was still waiting for the phone to ring. I often sat up until the early hours waiting for the phone to ring. When I was going out with Lisa, my post-Frances girlfriend, she lived – she still does live – in The Arctic, and most evenings she would ring me late, around midnight, and we would talk for an hour or so. It played havoc with my writing routine. I couldn't get up in the mornings. Somehow, I was still waiting for her call, even though it was over a year since we'd split and I didn't have anything to say to her anyway and vice versa. If the phone rang now, it would only be: *I'm pleased to announce you have won one of our top-prizes, if you are a mug or a spanner, ring this number . . .*

I took a stroll to the kitchenette. I'd make a camomile tea to help me sleep, then turn in with a book, forget about tonight. It would all go away; or at least I'd wake up with a skull-busting ear infection but in the morning there would be post. I hoped there would be post. Hope of the mornings: post. Hope of the afternoons: phone calls and e-mails. As the

---

[28] **Note to Self:** Potential new creative writing exercise. First, touch the Artex. How does it feel? What texture? What does it look like? What does it remind you of? Remember your first encounter with Artex? How does it smell? If Artex is an historical or cultural figure, who would it be? Shaka Zulu? Mrs Beaton? Cliff Richard? If Artex is an emotion, what would it be? Is Artex reckless or conservative? What part of Artex is changing and what part is static? What sort of voice would Artex use? Does it orate like Il Duce, or does it promise huskily, a late night telephone voice (a glass of whisky; the first cigarette from the day's second packet; the long distance relationship) Now, write for fifteen minutes from the point of view of Artex.

kettle boiled, I lit a cigarette and standing by the window blew smoke against the glass. The rain flickered in the orange glare of the streetlamps. Shimmer flowed down the side-road opposite The Garret and swept into the gutter. Cars swished past. I felt kind of content then, out of the weather with the smoke, the kettle's burble, the quiet. Then the wind whooshed in the copper beech tree outside my window and as the branches sprang back, I saw something on the pavement outside the house. Unsure, I nipped back to turn off the kitchen light. The outside became more distinct as my eyes adjusted to the darkness in the kitchen. I waited for the wind to take the branches again and give me an angle. I was right. Not seeing things. Down there, in front of the tree, apparently staring up at the house, was a figure in a black, hooded sou'wester.

Someone was standing there, looking up at my window. What did they want? Why couldn't they have it? Why were they doing that? Steam mottled across the glass. The figure became no more than a blur, then nothing. Stop writing, I told myself. Just a late night dog-walker or boozer having a piss on the way back from the pub. The kettle clicked and I made my tea. When I checked again, the figure had gone. I stirred the tea bag around the mug and pressed it to the sides to squeeze out the flavour. If anyone, I thought, and I laughed as it occurred to me. It was James O'Mailer out there, checking up, making sure that I wasn't writing furiously by candlelight, making sure I was still the one upon whom everything is lost.

It's not me. I'm in here, and I know all that already.

My temples throbbed. I dropped the mug. It smashed on the lino and the tea jumped and stung my shins. I was hopping around, slashing at my legs with a towel. The kitchen was empty. Just me in the dark and a sickish smell of herbs.

It's started, he said. They know.

'What?'

At this juncture I cannot say for fear, dear Flack that we overplay our hand. They are powerful.

'Go away!'

That I cannot do, Dame Parlet the Hen, dear Kiddo, I have a little job for you to do.

'What job?'

Let us not refer to it as a mere job but a quest. Now there's a word to gird the soul.

'Who are you?'

My ears popped. He didn't answer. I turned on the light. A thin brown puddle spread its borders over islands of shattered earthenware. My legs were still steaming when I reached the window. No hooded figure lurked out there in the rain.

Show, Don't Tell

The Grey Light that Filtered Through the Curtains

Never start a story or chapter with a character waking up. Avoid writing about the grogginess of the head or the renewed freshness of the mind. Edit out any account of the body's awkward or elegant position on the mattress, the subsequent ablutions and any other flab larded onto the plot. We don't need to know about *the grey light that filtered through the curtains*, or that *as soon as he woke up he started to burp yeastily*. We don't need to know about *the memory of the wonderfully submissive women that made him as stiff as a rhino's horn*. This is especially so if the character always rises in his own cot and routinely wakes up alone.

I say this because the waking-up gambit occurs frequently in the work of beginners, where each scene or sequence will be bracketed by a lengthy account of getting up in the morning and going to bed at night. Such scenes receive as much attention, and will have the same even tone and lack of tension as the crucial love scenes, the car chases and the apocalyptic medieval fantasy battle that decides all at the climax. Stirring in bed will be paced identically to the novel's more profound moments, like when our girl realizes that she should, after all, marry Mr Dinky-Dick from downstairs, even though he looks like a moulting iguana and during their earlier, procedurally-arrived-at sex-fest *slavered over her face*.

Don't do this. Cut to the chase and move us to where the storyline picks up again, to where it's heading for a turning point or realization. Make an exception only if the protagonist has woken *from uneasy dreams . . . transformed in his bed into a gigantic insect.*

However, on the morning before the second class, the grey light filtered through the curtains as I lay in bed thinking about my insectoid nature as I waited for the post. No post of note had arrived in the intervening week, a week in which I had done little more than wait, jump at the phone and obsessively check my e-mails. Also, given the messages I'd received from the class, I was dreading tonight's session. Apart from Frank and Erika, all of the Major Arcana had been in touch, bleating and giving me hassle. So there I was, lying in bed, dreading that evening's class and the return of the voice as the grey light filtered through the curtains when I should have been writing. This was the best part of my day, the time I looked forward to most when I was writing *The Penelope Tree*. If I wasted the morning, when my mind was most active and uncluttered, the day would be squandered. I'm not one of these 'midnight disease' writers[29]. I'm stricken with morning sickness.

It was already ten o'clock. And it was only the sight of my famous blue bathrobe hanging on the bedroom door that eventually guilted me out of bed. While I brushed my teeth I tried to assess if I looked any less like a sack of shit in the shaving mirror than I had done yesterday and the day before yesterday and the day before that. Then I risked being sighted by decorators, burglars and sundry interlopers while looking like a sack of shit wrapped in a bathrobe as, from the vantagepoint of the landing, I checked if the post had come. No post, so back inside I switched on the water heater and drank a bio-yoghurt thing and took vitamins. Simultaneously, I smoked the first cigarette of the day whilst spying on the street from the kitchen window, scanning for the postman as the kettle boiled. While the coffee settled in the cafetiere, I nipped back to the landing to double-check for post. Finally at my desk, I pushed down the cafetiere's plunger, lit another cigarette and opened my notebook, then went back to the landing to check again. Returned to the desk, I finally managed to write the date and listed all the things I had just done in minute detail and afterwards on a new line I wrote: NO POST YET.

---

[29] See **Wonder Boys** by Michael Chabon (Fourth Estate, 1995), page 20.

Then, as the caffeine kicked in, I started to drift into *The* State[30]. The woman on the Millennium Bridge glimmered at me again.

Ever since she flashed into my head while I was waiting to pick up my Chinese takeaway in the Crouching Panda, she'd haunted me. She was walking away, towards St Paul's Cathedral, a golden brown raincoat flapping behind her. The setting was definitely the Millennium Bridge, despite my efforts to shift her somewhere more unusual, somewhere in the past or abroad. As she strode along the bridge, away from the viewer, she always looked back over her shoulder. I didn't know if this was an encouraging backward glance, like, *come with me, into the most complicated and difficult part*, or a *for the last time, no, Dinky-Dick*. I didn't know who she was, what she wanted, where she was from or where she was going. And I didn't know who was watching her. A man? A woman? A sex-trade slaver, a lovelorn aluminium magnate or an out-of-his-depth, struggling writer, the sort who would give all his money to a prostitute? All my male characters start as the out-of-his-depth, struggling writer, though since I went with this for my first novel *The Drowners* and my third *The Best Man* I had made very sure not to write about him again. Never do this. It's like drinking your own urine, and no one sympathizes.

So what was the Millennium Bridge Woman doing? She was . . . running across the bridge to take the tube northbound to her decrepit apartment, to check the post, to see if there was any news about the brilliant novel that she had written on her lap in cafes during the gloomy afternoons, the novel that symbolized her escape from sex-trade slavers and aluminium magnates and having another struggling writer give her all his money.

I went downstairs and checked again.

Back at my desk, I thought that if I did nothing else I ought to just get on with it. Settle on her and settle on the present, or some approximation of three years in the future, given that by the time I wrote and sold this novel, it would be three years hence. What I did know, however, was that I couldn't shed the Millennium Bridge Woman, just as I'd not been able to rid myself of Penelope and write about something set abroad or in the past for Squinty Hugo. With *Penelope*, as soon as that internal picture

---

[30] *The* **State** — State of mind required to write. Place where the writer and the work-in-progress meet, mesh and merge, where distractions cannot get you. Requires the listing of routine waking-up rituals and ablutions in the writer's journal and the wearing of a shabby blue bathrobe.

appeared to me, of the boy and the girl planting the tree in a garden, I knew there was a solid bond between them. I knew it had to be called upon in later life. But there were two of them, Penelope and Alexander, and therefore it was easier to find an epicentre. There was only one character here, or at least only one character that I could see. I was getting rather unsettled by characters that I couldn't see. So, who watches her? That was the issue, the heartbeat of this drama.

I slouched in my chair and lit another cigarette. The spasm tugged at my temples.

What a load of stinking dung, said James O'Mailer. What a load of nuts this is going to turn out to be?

It had been like this all week. After the first night, when he spoke about a 'quest' in the kitchen, I'd not heard his voice for a few days afterwards; long enough to think it had been an aberration, my imagination playing tricks. *The* State was bleeding into my consciousness, I reasoned, or I was having some sort of stress-induced dialogue between my human doubt and my internal editor personified. I'd decided against telling Frances or seeing a doctor. The issue of voices often comes up in creative writing classes. Students can dislike the suggestion that a writer might hear his or her characters talking or that they seem somehow real or independent, that this is in itself suggestive of mental illness. I had it on good authority that it was only when you hear voices that seem to come from *outside* of you that you should worry. Talking to yourself is not the first sign of madness. Talking to others, though, is something else, but O'Mailer's voice came from within. Whenever he spoke he spoke between my ears.

It was only this Monday past, when I sat down to write in earnest for the first time in a while that he came again, spoke just as I began to sketch out a life story for the girl on the Millennium Bridge. It was, I admit, a weak story, but I was only brain storming, trying to find something to change. If I didn't have an internal editor I'd never be able to work out if my ideas were weak or not. Even so, I didn't need one this vociferous and castigating.

I disagree, it is plain for all to see that you need me like the trout needs the stream, the fighting cock the cockfighter, the strumpet the gin. What about the big things, Flack? The Grand Narratives? Politics? Society? War? Metaphysical enquiry? The Human Condition? The delineation of that compartment of existence that has never yet been trodden in ink? The Quest?

'It doesn't start like that,' I said. 'You know that.'

Leave this skeleton of scribble alone. I have a more promising adventure in store, but you need to trust in me.

'Adventures are pulp,' I said. 'I hate adventure stories. Especially ones set in the past or abroad and ones with arcane conspiracies and mediaeval battles at the end. Find someone else to badger.'

You're never going to get anywhere. I can help you. I am greatness.

'Yeah, sure you are. You're not even real.'

I lit up again as I shuffled from the desk towards the window. I noticed the postman's bobbing gait as he rounded the head of the path and disappeared behind the copper beech. From down below, vibrating up the stairs and the landing came a heavy, rustling thump.

Tricky to Market

A pile of envelopes lay on the hall carpet. The disappointment hit me. Disappointment is too weak a word. I'm looking for something that describes a kind of visceral collapse. You write in the flesh; you feel the kick in the flesh. You feel the kick when lying there is one of your own envelopes, one of the white, padded A4 packages into which you carefully slid your sample chapters and synopsis and sales letter where you had listed, just as they ask, all your publications and achievements. And there it was. Another rejection.

Or so I assumed, as I ran down the stairs in my bare feet and famous blue bathrobe. I shoved the envelope under my arm and flicked through the rest of the post – nothing for me besides junk – then skulked back to the flat with the package in my hands.

I ripped it open, still with some hope that the big envelope was some tightwad agent's way of saving the use of a smaller envelope and the expense of one of their own first class stamps. But the package was thick; the sample material was still inside. There was a letter, though. If you get a letter, not a standard rejection slip, you are doing very well. The tingle of fear and shame coagulated in my stomach.

ZY HAGGARD

Dear Nathan Flack,

Re: The Penelope Tree.

I'm sorry that it has taken me so long to get back to you. Thank you for your very strong letter and impressive sample material.

The idea is a great one, and you write very elegantly, but I think it would be tricky to market. Why don't you try Hugo Cornwallis (he has his own agency). Best not to say that I've seen it . . . agents are strange creatures.

Wishing you all the best

Frederick Malone

Agents are strange creatures? Had he never met a Major Arcana Folder-Holder? And what does that mean? Tricky to market? Why is it tricky to market? How can it be tricky to market if the writing is impressive and elegant and the idea great? Why can't they tell you what they mean? If I said to a Folder-Holder 'great idea but tricky to read,' I'd have to justify myself. And I am not a Folder-Holder. I deserve better. And Squinty as well? Try that loveable old stick Squinty? I was in this mess because of Squinty. Did Malone know that? Was he sticking the knife in? Was this some sort of code?

I sat down and had a brood. This wasn't the first rejection I'd had since March, when, after I'd discussed *The Penelope Tree* with Squinty Hugo several times and received no objection to the idea, and after I'd spent three years writing the book, and after I'd circulated it among my reliable readers like Frances and Sebastian, whose feedback was enthusiastic and admiring, and eventually, full of confidence that I'd finally written something unreservedly readable and commercial, and after having sent Squinty several draft chapters that he didn't even bother to read, I'd sent him the full manuscript and six weeks later received the fateful 'chin up' e-mail.

And yes, I was pissed off that he dropped me, but relieved. I'd wanted shot of him anyway. Squinty had done nothing for me after he poached me from my first agent, the gentlemanly but three hundred and fifty-year-old Thornton Dackery. Squinty had failed to sell *The Best Man*. He'd urged me to capitulate and write soft porn for cable TV. His latest causes célèbres were pretty-pretty, underage Indian food journalists typing out romcom standards with titles like *Guacamole and Chips* and *Roast Beef and Naan*, and third rate comedians tossing off nostalgic thirtysomething 3 for 2 table product-shifters called, for example, *Can I Have a P Please, Bob* and *Hi-Ho Silver Lining*. I didn't relate to him. I was scared of him (those eyes, that voice). I just didn't want to go through the malarkey of finding another one. And yes, I would be snapped up by another agent, I thought, because *The Penelope Tree* is a very, very good novel and I am a very committed writer. I couldn't do anything else. I needed to do it. I'd served my time, done all the things that they tell you to do: persist, be patient, publish stories, win prizes. I'd not just attended courses but taught courses. And when I outlined all this in my *Penelope* letter, what was their reaction?

This guy can't write.

I'd been turned down by a dozen agencies [31] by now, but none of them could tell me what was wrong with *The Penelope Tree*. What are you supposed to glean from:

Will Win Prizes but . . .

Fresh Writing, but . . .

Tricky to Market.

?

Tricky to market, said James O'Mailer. That means, Flack is just not good enough. And not just Flack is not good enough yet, like with your first three efforts. It means not good enough.

Oh shut up you. It was easy when you started out. Anyone with a pen could get into print. There was time then for a novel to find its readers.

---

[31] So far, I had made approaches and been turned down by Coldhands & Shyster; Shickle & Gruber; Mxyztplk & Wukfit; Chasm & D'Ark; Moosebone & Flange; The Jed Shed Agency; Day-Glo & Baboon; Forkin & Hufti; F.U Dahl; Shortlife & Profile and Insider Arts.

No one talked about 'industry'. No one talked about 'marketing'. A writer didn't have to fit a certain demographic or tick the right boxes. You could set a novel anywhere you liked. Novels were expected to live longer than mayflies. Have a gander in your local bookstore; see that everything newly published fits into a neat marketing category. Minor Arcana Folder-Holders complain that there's nothing in there to read. It's all dross, reprints and gifts. That's what I'm up against. It's been getting more and more conservative and dumb and short-termist for the last ten years.

That's precisely why you need to follow my commands.

I held my breath and focused and somehow managed to banish O'Mailer to the outer darkness. As the blood in my head stopped rushing I remembered what the nice lady once said: Take it like a Spartan. I asked myself what Sylvester 'Sly' Ramos-Pintos would say? *Fuck em. Move on.* Thank you, Sly, and fuck you, Fred Malone. But the Millennium Bridge Woman was gone for today and I'd progressed no further with her. Maybe Sly was watching her . . . don't go there. I got up and went over to my desk, took out the starfish from the bag of objects, the very starfish that would be pored over and stroked by one of the hopefuls later tonight. The Worry Starfish. The Comfort Starfish. I looked for the positives. The letter doesn't say the novel is bad. If the novel isn't bad, and no one is saying it's bad, I could only keep trying and in the meantime write another novel. Get on with Millennium Bridge. Forget about *Penelope*. Take it like a Spartan. Remember the starfish. The starfish would say: *Frederick Malone? It's his loss.*

The phone rang. The phone was ringing at midday! I leapt across the room and yanked up the receiver.

'Oright. Is that Nate?'

'Yes.'

'Mac McMahon here.'

'How did you get my number?'

'In the phonebook. So what do you think then?'

'Pardon?'

'Read my story?'

'Not yet, no.' He knew this. He'd sent me three e-mails already and three times I'd said that I would read it by the next class.

'Well, are you going to read my story?' he said.

'Yes, later . . . now I'll see you . . .'

'Listen Nathan, I know you're going to be pleased. Listen mate, I've started to write my novel.'

65

'That's great, Mac,' I said. 'I'm very happy for you.'

'Thirty-five thousand, two-hundred and thirteen words already.'

'Jesus, that's far too much.'

'Will you have a look at it for me?'

'Hmmm . . . I'll have a look at this story first. I'm a bit concerned that you're rushing into things a bit.'

'Don't be concerned, don't you worry about it. You've got a treat coming, my son. I am a natural, as they say.'

He hung up. I fished his story out of my class file and spread out on the sofa. The handwriting was a semi-illegible scrawl, the letters huge, each vowel ballooning across the lines above and below it, which at first gave the text the appearance of a white puddle spattered with blue ink ripples. The catchy title jumped out at me. I slid down into the sofa and pulled a cushion over my face and laughed like I'd not laughed for as long as I could remember. Then I read the whole thing.

Needing a Piss

Any bloke will tell you that the pain of needing a bad piss is the same as that a lady goes thru when she's given birth to a baby. Its a really bad pain and it can cause no end of grief. Billy Zoo was on the London Underground and he was trying to forget that he really wanted a bad piss and he was starting to regret the many lagers he'd drunk with the band at lunchtime in Soho. He tried to think instead about how great it felt in the pub when some bloke came in and played 'Night of Medusa' by the famous british heavy metal band Ruiner on the duke box and all the suits had stood up and were heard saying, fuck me what a tune, go Ruiner, go. And he tried as well to think of the hot blonde fox sitting opposite him. She was called Tracey and worked in a bank, but on the side she was a bit of a groupie and had had it off with many leading muscians of the day. She noticed him and his heaving crutch, not realizing that he needed a bad piss, and flashed him her skimpy knick-knacks. He was delighted to see that they were white and clean, though sometimes he liked birds with no knickers and sometimes even slightly dirty ones. The piss feeling started to get a lot worse and the train was bumping up and down and Billy started to wiggle his snake hips like he was in a rock club and Ruiner was playing some great riffs and Tracey licked her big bright red lips and undid the top bottom of her top to give him an eyeful of her ample breastage. She stood up and put her stilletto on the chair and said to Billy, come on big boy, lets do it like in the Deadringer for love video with Cher'. All the suits were staring and Rob Grey nearby, a banking suit from a miserable grey town somewhere else in England thought to himself, that wouldn't happen to me, some guys have all the luck, but he was chuffed for Billy Zoo.

Billy Zoo was chuffing at the bit, sure baby, lets do it and have some cawfee with cream and sugar afterwards and I'll shake you all night long, but first off I need a piss.'

'Sure baby', she said.

The train came into a station, one of the stations on the red line and Billy and Tracey got off and did some snogging on the escalator. Tracey liked snogging blokes on the escalator. Billy thought she had really good blowjob lips but still needed a piss. Any minute now it was going to spray out everywhere.

Outside they found a pub an Billy said 'I'm bustin for a piss, love. When I come back you can give me a blowjob.'

'Aren't you even going to buy me a drink first.' Tracey would give any rockstar a blowjob, apart from Fish out of Marillion and the bald bloke from Gillan, but she expected a drink of Archers first.

Torn, Billy looked at the bar and then looked at the door to the gents then looked at Tracey's blowjob lips and thought bloody women, can't live with them, can't live without them. Then he went over to the bar and searching for change in his spandex jeans, bumped his bladder and out it all came in a big gush that went on for ten minutes and all the beer mats and beer towels started to float out of the boozer but most of all it went all over this chinny bloke who turned out to be a rascally copper who'd seen Tracey's blowjob lips for himself. Suddenly he was frog marching Billy out of the pub.

'Billy', shouted Tracey, letting him cop an eyeful.

'Rock and roll, love', said Billy.

And that was that and it's true because the copper actually told me this story after he'd married Tracey and they had had lots decent blowjobs.

I finally breathed out and had a good long stare at the cracks in the ceiling. This was actually the story written from the point of view of Artex. After a few minutes I felt like I was floating about the room, looking down at the mismatched sofas and russet carpet and my limp, defenceless body and sniggering face. What could you say about *Needing a Piss*? Nice play on 'cop' at the end maybe? I jumped up, switched on the computer and connected to the Internet. As I waited, I shivered. Another 35,000 words in the style of *Needing a Piss* had been churned out in a mere week. I needed information. I needed to be armed. Who was our Arch-Literature-Denier? I Googled various combinations of 'Mac McMahon', 'Ruiner' and '"Night of Medusa"', but all I could find were a couple of references to the song on compilations with titles like *Doors of Annihilation* and *Ghoul's Ballroom*. Eventually I found a listing in an index that read:

> '**Ruiner** formed in 1980 in Birmingham. The line-up consisted of <u>Bob Punter</u> (vocals), <u>Derek Strang</u> (bass), <u>Lionel Feral</u> (lead guitar) and <u>Mac 'The Paddle"</u> McMahon on drums. A single released in 1982, **Night of Medusa**, a live favourite, reached number 112 in the UK charts. The only UK album, **Tits Up** was released in 1983. Punter left in 1985 and the band soon decamped to Norway, which became their base. Several rare Norwegian language albums released (**Helvete Arsehole** (1988), **Hun Liker Den Gynge** (1990), **Trondheim Damer ar Natter** (1993). Existed in some form or another until the mid-nineties, with Paddle McMahon as the only consistent member.'

No mentions of a career change into estate agency or best-selling authordom for our demon sticksman. But he wasn't bluffing. He hadn't concocted a bizarre counter-life like some students in the past. I found the cover of the *Tits Up* LP. There he was in triumphant medieval warrior pose: Mac 'The Paddle' McMahon, beard a little trimmer and wearing a black breastplate and gauntlets, brandishing a mace. The vodka and herring lifestyle in rock 'n' roll Oslo must have done for The Paddle, for he looked much slimmer. Flanking him were two menacingly stupid looking men in plate mail and a chinless guitarist in a crusader's tunic. Another browse brought up a Norwegian metal fansite. Although I couldn't decipher any text, I did manage to find the *Trondheim Damer ar Natter* cover. In the background, in lurid airbrushed colours, was a cemetery with twisted railings and shattered tombs. In the centre was a naked woman with massive knockers and crimson nipples and a heron's head. Her legs were spread across a bier and out of her 'pelvis' snaked a turquoise serpent that breathed fiery letters that spelt 'Ruiner' across the bottom of the sleeve.

From the keyboard, a grimy sensation slid over my hands and started to claw its way up my arms until I shuddered and clicked off the image. I ran a bath and emptied half a bottle of aromatherapy bathfoam into the water. Paralysed, I let the steam surround and comfort me. When the bath was ready I lay under the water, holding my breath, my eyes shut, trying to block out the thought that a Ruiner novel was coming my way. And Mac wasn't the only Major Arcana to give me cause for concern that week. I'd had my Sensie showdown with Cynthia, albeit in cyberspace, and had been informed in a 2000 word e-mail about just how difficult it was and how much she had at stake and how she needed nurturing and shouldn't be bullied and how I was already making it seem too difficult and already she was finding it hard to write and that she hadn't finished anything for two years and had suffered a lot of disappointment with her writing and what exactly was I going to do about it? And Doctor Jane threw me by e-mailing to ask what she was supposed to do when the only 'glimpses' she experienced involved a complicated sexual position and the deli counter in Waitrose. Think about the consequences, I said. Dear old Reg had taken the journal thing to heart and started to e-mail me his as attachments.

Tuesday: First class with new writing tutor. Was very much looking forward to it, but the tutor is a flyblown sort and the others left much to be desired. A terrible shower, if truth be told, and a morbid lot. This generation of writers is the worst on record. As I drove back, I had the misfortune to sit in traffic opposite a bus stop full of teenagers. Some of the girls even allowed their boys to kiss them. How we have let our moral standards slip. I didn't even kiss my Darling Dear until eight months after we were married. What a day that was! The sun up. The brook that babbled in the churchyard. Father in his uniform. Halves of ale in The Headlong Hare with Jinky Lawler before we tied the knot and all our summer days were ahead of us. My Darling Dear. How I anticipated the sumptuous cherry and walnut cake she would have ready for me on my return from the ruins.

I ran some more hot water and mentally listed all the things I needed to do: send material to three more agencies; post on way to campus; write some sort of appraisal of (i.e., fumigate) *Needing a Piss*; prepare my notes for *Show, Don't Tell*; make sure that I had the bag of objects for the objects exercise; call Frances and ask her to come for a drink after class to prevent any possibility of being followed by Moon-Barker again. I'd phoned her last Wednesday, but as soon as I asked if she knew Erika Gretsch she slammed the phone down. Her ansamachine had been screening her calls ever since.

As I lay in the bath, the heron-headed woman from *Trondheim Damer ar Natter* seemed to materialize behind my eyelids, except now the image had a Reg Carnaby VO: *my Darling Dear, my Darling Dear.* In true last hero fashion I no longer knew if I had the mettle for the conflict to come. But I was The Fumigator. The Fumigator stayed in the bath until the water cooled, unsure if he defended the Arcana from Frederick Malone and his cryptic brush-offs, or protected Malone and the strange creatures from *Needing a Piss* and *Cider with Reginald.*

Pretty Morbid Banana

As I entered the classroom, they were already assembled in a semicircle around my desk, including, to my relief, Cynthia. The only change to last week's seating arrangement was that Erika had moved a row forwards. She'd inserted herself and her moveable heap between Reg and Doctor Jane. Now, from the rear, her shoulders resembled a hump-backed bridge that connected those on either side of her.

There were no newcomers, no Chod or Mantlestein. Mac, however, was plonked on my desk, legs dangling and his stomach poking out from the jacket of a saggy black pinstriped suit. He appeared to be giving some sort of lecture.

'All you have to do is keep sat there and just let it come all over you. Don't bother with any of that bollocks about planning and notes. Just grab it by the goolies. Half a novel, in one week! And then, right, today, I put down me pen at six-thirty this morning, jump in the shower, knock back a bacon sarnie, bomb over to Fakenham in the Mazda and flog two gaffes. Wrap up the paperwork, then back home. Mashed out another eight thousand words. Easier than drumming but twice as noisy. Do you want to hear some?'

I dropped my rucksack. It bumped on the floor. The objects inside clattered.

'Oright Nate,' said Mac, then returned his gaze to the class. 'Guys, what do you say? Want to prick back your ears?'

'Mac,' I said. 'I don't think we're quite ready for that yet.' I picked up my stuff and made my way to the desk, causing him to slide off and thump down in his seat. A shivery nervousness rippled through me. I didn't want him to read. He'd humiliate himself and I didn't want to administer a stiff public fumigation or hurt his feelings. From my bag I recovered my materials and the envelope with the *Needing a Piss* notes. I wrote 'Show, Don't Tell' on the blackboard, then turned to the class and found myself doing a horrible hand clap thing. 'So, how did everyone get on with last week's exercise?'

'Flack,' said Reg. His charcoal grey slacks were pulled up to his nipples and a maroon cravat dotted with lion and unicorn motifs was tucked into his shirt collar. 'You did say last week we could read our writing out in the first hour of the class, did you not?'

'Well, yes, but I thought we'd look at the homework first.'

'I think the consensus is that we'd like to hear Mr McMahon's story.'

'Are you sure?'

Evidently so, by the look of them. Mac with his arms folded, feet twitching, bursting with eagerness. Frank with his moonface and Reg (all legs and no torso) and Erika with the brim of the woolly hat covering her eyebrows. It compressed her wide face further and I really didn't want to look at it, not after the debacle on the bus, so I focused on Doctor Jane, who tonight wore a sort of tight black gym top and a dusky mauve pashmina wrapped sash-style around her waist, and then realized that Cynthia was looking at me, pinchy faced and exasperated. I had, after all, started the class by trampling all over someone's creativity.

'Of course,' I said. 'If that's what you all want.' I took up my position on the rim of the desk and kicked my heels together. 'OK, Mac. Tell us about this?'

He snapped open a briefcase on his lap and removed a huge wodge of foolscap and biro-scribble that reminded me of my long-lost, teenage epic *Quest of the Hellhounds*. Fingering the pages, he skimmed off the first few, and for a second I thought he was going to back down.

'I don't want to say anything,' he said. 'It speaks for itself. It's called "The Grasp of Fear."'

'Maybe I ought to lay some ground rules about responding to our work,' I said.

73

'Shhh.' Mac licked a finger and plucked out the first page. I hung my head and clasped my hands together between my knees, a tried and tested listening pose. Chairs scraped and shifted. The line leaned back. Mac popped his eyes, then stroking his beard with his spare hand, started to read.

'The Grasp of Fear . . . Things were going brilliantly for Zane Champ . . .' He flipped down the paper. 'Nate, I'm not comfortable. Can I stand up?'

'Well, whatever makes you comfortable. Just take your time and read slowly.'

He sidled over to the window, jigging his shoulders like a boxer before a bout, then tried to heave his hip up onto the ledge. Eventually he made it by using a chair as a stepladder. Awkwardly perched on the ledge, he reassembled his papers, took another breath, put the papers down again, mouthed something to himself and then relaunched.

'The Grasp of Fear . . .OK? Oright, oright . . .Things were going brilliantly for Zane Champ. He was in a fantastically successful rock band that had just broke the States and he had birds here, birds there, birds falling out of his armpits. Not the ropey old birds he knew from back in the Black Country but well proper stunnas with real artificial bits and everything. When Zane Champ woke up he couldn't remember the night before. A grey light filtered through the curtains and his head was doing the opera bit from *Bohemian Rhapsody* over and over again. He reached over for a can of lager that he knew he'd left on the table beside the bed in his LA hotel suite and it was then he realised that there was a well fit bird lying starkers-malarkers in the bed beside him.'

Mac paused, flickered his eyes from the paper to me to the others, seemingly trying to gauge some reaction to this cunning plot point.

'Then it all came back to him. The night before he had been at this belting rock club in downtown LA that was like a place where all the rock guys like Slash and Ozzy and Bonfire hung out to pull birds and it was over three quid a pint, even back then, and it was called The Fear. Who was this bird then? Even in his polluted state, Zane could tell she had a great body and heart-shaped arse and she had rocked him all night long. He had the scars to prove it . . .'

'Do we have to listen to this?' Cynthia said. She appeared to have dragged her chair as far as she could into the wall.

'Shhh,' I said. 'Let him finish.'

'I've lost me place now,' said Mac. 'I've bloody lost it.'

74

'Arse-night-scars,' I said.

'That's right . . . can't read me writing . . . OK . . . He had the scars to prove it . . . That's Zane Champ, right? . . . As he picked up the sheet and had a look at her bouncers, it all came back to him. Last night, in Fear, he had been dancing to this monster of a track called "Night of Medusa" by his favourite band Ruiner on the dancefloor that was heaving so much it was more like a moshpit and this bird had come up to him. She was called Janis Pyjamas, though even Zane Champ knew that wasn't her name. These Yank birds always change their names for some reason. Maybe it's because they don't want their Pas to find out they give blowjobs to the gods of rock. Her legs were so long that they went right over her head and came up again as more legs. Zane had pulled her and now he was quite happy with his performance in the sack as they call it over there.'

Cynthia looked like she was going to start tunnelling into the wall any minute and Reg had on the sort of face he probably reserved for special outrages, like vandalism, the EEC or pre-nuptial kissing. Even Jane looked a tad flat.

'OK Mac, I said. 'Maybe we should stop there . . .'

'Hang on, Nate. I've not got to the best bit . . . Sack, right? Happy with his performance in the sack as they call it over there . . . they do an all . . . anyway . . .' He patted down his beard as if there was money hidden in it. 'Under the covers, Janis giggled to herself but half way through the giggle became a snarl. What Zane didn't know was that she was a zombie fleshgobbler sent from Hell and a thousand years old and Fear nightclub was a gateway to Hell itself. Little do you know what's coming to you, monster of rock. Meet a real monster . . . The fleshgobblers were aggrolites of the devil who hated rockstars because he knew that only rock 'n' roll could defeat Satan and she was on a mission to wipe them out. She raised herself up in the bed and her bouncers bounced but her head now was green and scabby and fangs had come out of her mouth, Zane Champ grabbed her round the throat, thought 'Fuck, she's a zombie,' and pulled off her head. It rolled down the bed and into the bidet. 'Bloody Yanks,' he said to himself and had another chug on his can.'

Punching the air, Mac dropped off the ledge. Back in his seat, he looked around, waiting for the laurels to be tossed his way and the Swedish Academy to call his mobile. At that moment he was as chuffed with himself, I imagined, as Rob Grey in *Needing a Piss* had been for Billy Zoo.

I pouted to keep my mouth shut. A pressure built in the back of my throat. If I'd have given in and started to laugh, I would have disintegrated into a shower of dust, and that would have been most unprofessional. I didn't know what to say or where to start. Mac was looking at me for approval. The others were looking at me for advice or opinion or a lead, apart from Erika, who was staring up at the fascinating ceiling. Cynthia was quivering and I needed to go into Sensie Defence Mode. Reg looked like he'd just spied upon a graffiti artist and was out for vigilante justice, and I would need to shift into Peacekeeping Mode. Jane was thinking it all through far too earnestly and I was going to have to click her into Say-What-You-See Mode. Frank, though, seemed serene, head back, eyes shut, as if enjoying the sunshine during a cider buzz.

'So, what did you think of that, people?' I said.

They pondered and shunned eye contact and fiddled with their pens and folders. I waited for the silence to pass, for consternation to erupt, but the parenthesis extended for so long it would have embarrassed even the Ipswich Group of Death.

'Well, how do you feel about Mac's story?' I said. 'Would you like to hear more? Does it work, technically? Is he achieving what he's setting out to do? If you do like it, why? If you don't, why not?'

Doctor Jane levered her forearm from the rest of her chair.

'Well, it seems a bit rough, but I suppose it's OK for a first draft.'

'No, it's well finished,' said Mac.

'But, it's not exactly *Mansfield Park*, is it?' said Reg.

'No, it's not,' I said. 'But does it want to be? What's the genre? Horror, right? You can't enjoy the juice of the apple, but then deny the banana its curves.'

'Pretty morbid banana, if you ask me,' said Reg.

'Well, horror is morbid, isn't it?'

'It's not horror,' said Mac.

'It's got a zombie in it,' I said.

'I thought it was icky, utterly, utterly icky,' said Cynthia. 'Repulsive and icky.'

'Hear, hear,' said Reg.

'Maybe, Mac,' I said, 'an issue here is that as horror, it's not frightening.'

'It's not horror,' he said. 'I keep saying, and anyway, she was frightened.' He gestured at Cynthia.

'Only by what goes on in your head,' she said. Any minute now, she was going to scramble up and scarper.

'And if scary has to be scary,' said Jane, 'then the love scene isn't sexy.'

'Well you've obviously never done it in LA, love,' said Mac.

I started to faff. 'Er . . . what do other people think? Let's widen this out. Frank?'

He puffed up his chest and wiggled his big bald head side to side.

'Liked it,' he said. 'Good stuff that. Want to know what happens next.'

'Really, but there was no set-up. OK, Erika? How did you feel about Mac's story?'

Easing herself up from her chair, she grabbed hold of the armrest with one hand and with the other took hold of Reg's sleeve to use as a support. Her pitted eyes seemed to shrink and swirl.

'Well, you know, today I went out and I walked and walked and walked over hills and dales and in the end I visited an abattoir and I thought, this is a sign and when I listened to that, I knew it was a sign from The He.'

I breathed out so fast that my cheeks bloated and a sort of involuntary raspberry spluttered out of my mouth.

'Which abattoir was it?' said Frank.

'The one with the sheep and the pigs and all the horses hung up,' said Erika.

'See,' said Mac, pointing. 'They get it.'

'No, *you* don't get it,' said Reg. 'Where was the love and the beauty and the courage?'

'He pulled a zombie fleshgobbler's head off. What more courage do you want?'

'OK, everyone,' I said, forced now to pace again and blunder along the line until I met Cynthia's eyes. She was hunched up as if suffering the bends. Her papers had been returned to her folder. No more strop offs, though. No once as tragedy, twice as farce. Time for The Fumigator to take control.

'Mac, lots of issues there.' I clicked my fingers like an irritated secondary school teacher. 'The writing is flat. There's no genre awareness and no reader anticipation. There's the mother of all point of view switches halfway through and it's a bit, how shall we say, basic in its characterization of women.'

'Hear, hear,' said Reg. 'At last, some bloody leadership.'

I shuffled behind my desk and scooped up the *Needing A Piss* envelope.

'These notes might help.' I passed it to him and sat back down on the desk. 'Mac, you're not ready to write a novel. You're rushing. Best thing I can suggest is to take this course slowly. A novel, as I said last week, is a big undertaking.'

Mac's eyes swivelled side-to-side. A barrage of literature-denying counter-arguments was about to come my way, but Frank put up his hand.

'I've written a novel,' he said.

'What? Last week?'

'No, dopey. Last year. It was about an ambulance man who goes around killing people.'

'Hey, great idea,' said Mac.

'And I send it off, right, to this publisher fella, and he writes back to me and says that the problem with me book is that ambulance men don't kill people, but I know they do, cos it were based on a true story. Me and my mate Davie Mitre, right, we picked up this biddy with heart stuff and she used to be one of our teachers . . .'

My legs chilled. The white walls seemed to whiten further. The clock flinched and I wouldn't have been at all fazed if the spare chairs had fled the room to hurl themselves off the landing. Frank stopped talking when he registered that everyone else was peering at him with discomforted expressions on their faces.

'OK,' I said, timidly. 'Let's move on.'

My mind went blank and my index of things to show, don't tell vanished. The bag was on the desk, so I reached for it. When in doubt and in times of strife, set an exercise and give yourself some time to stare into space.

Something Wrapped in Thick White Polythene

To compose myself as much as I could, I slowly, slowly, in high chalk letters, and using two long lines, wrote on the blackboard.

'The beginning of human knowledge is through the senses, and the fiction writer begins where human perception begins.' Flannery O'Connor.

Turning back to the class, I pointed to the sentence.

'Let's do some writing and then think about these lines.'

Expert bit of fumigation, this. Do it backwards. Exercise before discussion. Busk the class from what they produce. As quick as I could, I told them that I wanted them to describe an object using only sensory language. Then I moved along the line and asked each of them in turn to take something from the bag. As ever, I played a little game with myself, wondering who was going to pluck out the blessed starfish. Who would the starfish choose? Who would be touched?

Mac: the whopping big, hand-varnished pinecone that failed to distract him from analysing my report on *Piss* as if it were the last will and testament of a rich uncle who'd left everything to a landfill site.

Frank: the doll with no legs and one missing eye.

79

Reg: the chunk of yellow mineral that I'd nicked from a skip.

Jane: the very battered Matchbox Formula One car.

And the starfish touched Erika. Erika was touched.

When I reached Cynthia, she said, 'I don't want to do this.'

I took out the San Francisco snowshaker and placed it on her armrest. 'Just have a think,' I said. 'You're doing fine, you're doing really well.'

Back at my desk, I held out my hands in this ridiculously messianic way and said, 'Just think of it as painting with words.'

The objects were sized-up and considered, and notebooks opened and pens taken out of pockets and pencil cases. I tried not to notice the way that Frank jabbed his pencil into the hole in the doll, hoping against hope that he was only seeing what sound it made. I couldn't help thinking about the story he had just told us. I imagined the failing of the senses, the roof of the ambulance misting over; the striplights floating off into space like booster stages from an Apollo rocket; the smiles above that warped into the faces of spiteful little boys writing lines in detention. Surreptitiously, I found my mobile in my jacket and with it concealed on my lap sent Frances another text: **Drink. Please! (X10)**, then checked on the Arcana. Unlike Janice Pyjamas in *The Grasp of Fear*, Doctor Jane's legs, though certainly long and partial to poses, stopped where legs should stop, at the hip. I liked the pashmina wrapped around the waist and wondered if I could steal it for Millennium Bridge Woman. Doctor Jane's eyes followed the little car as she ran it up and down her thigh. I concentrated on the motion of the car and her hand and in my mind's eye I could see Millennium Bridge Woman in some sort of airy bar, rubbing her hand along her thigh as she waited. At first I thought the shuffling sound was in my head as someone approached my girl. Doctor Jane lifted her eyes and realized that I was looking at her. A creak and a rather heavy thump sent her head sideways.

'Professor Flack,' said Erika. The poor starfish was wedged between her thighs. 'I have my own object found.' A newspaper bundle, about the size of a football, sat precariously on her armrest. 'Can I make use of it?'

'What the Dickens is that?' said Reg.

'Oh God, not that thing from last week,' said Cynthia, throwing her pencil down on her pad so hard that it bounced up into the air.

'OK, OK,' I said. 'Just carry on with your paragraphs.'

Nobody returned to the page. Mac craned over Frank's shoulder to see. And Reg leaned back into Frank, and Jane and Cynthia edged their chairs away. None of this perturbed Erika. Her stubby fingers began to work at the newspaper, stripping away the layers, scrunching pages of tabloid and broadsheet. Her palms massaged the curves of the object, which seemed wider at the top than the bottom. As the paper came away, patches of white appeared incrementally until all the newspaper had been removed. A glossy lump sat on the rest; something wrapped in thick white polythene.

She rolled it over. It was fastened at the bottom with Sellotape that she tugged away. Those who wanted to see moved closer, and those who did not, me included, inched further away. She upended the bag again and pulled apart its carry-holes. The bag stood up as an oblong now. Gently, carefully, as if she were unpacking a bouquet, she pulled the bag down over the object.

The smell fired a series of memories through me: I was back there, those summers I worked with my dad and we tended the gardens of the old folk and cleared out sheds and pruned roses and weeded flowerbeds and mowed lawns and trimmed trees and sat in sopping vests and shorts in the sun and drank orange squash from plastic bottles and once, one time, it was there in the middle of this long striped lawn, the softened grey coil, the dead rat, a dead rat that had lay there for two or three weeks before the old lady had noticed it, and how eyeless and black and matted it was, the slash in its fur and the smooth glistening blue-grey tissue it exposed and how it left a black stain in the soil and how that smell made us gag as he wrapped it in a cloth and we buried it behind the greenhouse. The smell, though, sickish and fleshy and acid and how it clung to our clothes afterwards, brought bile to our throats and how it lingered in that patch of her garden for weeks afterwards.

Chairs scraped and grated. Even the big boys scattered to the back of the class, and then across it to the door where Cynthia's Gold Medal sprint headed them off. Jane walked backwards, as if sucked out by decompression. Halfway she turned to the door and the fleeing Reg put his hand on her shoulder and hurried her out.

Erika stroked the horns, then the strip of white wool between them. Its watery eyes stared at me, a gruff, resentful expression on its face, as if its brute masculinity resented the polythene choker made by the flattened bag at its throat.

'It is for The He,' she said. 'I write poem, then give to you.'

I ran over to the bin, picked it up, ran back and forced it down over the head.

'Get that thing out of here!'

81

The Haunting of Nathan Flack

Ten minutes later I was still huddling in the disabled toilet along the corridor. I tried to use the white tiles and the hum of the extractor fan to positively visualize something calming and uplifting. When I breathed, though, I could still smell it. When I closed my eyes I could still see it, as if the jacket image from a 1960s Dennis Wheatly novel, *The Haunting of Nathan Flack* or something had slid behind my eyes. That was it. I was going to have to do something about Erika Gretsch. You couldn't have this sort of behaviour, not with Sensies and Rom-Ts in the group. Following me last week was one thing. This was a step too far from the boundary. Then it occurred to me that maybe it was her that I had seen, hooded and cloaked outside my flat last week.

She needed to be expelled from the course. This was clear. It was going to be impossible to teach if this sort of thing happened every week. I needed to report this to Sharon Plum first thing in the morning. Bloody hell. Why, why, why hadn't I apologized to Sharon Plum for telling her to piss off? She hadn't contacted me, that was why, and I was embarrassed and I had other things on, and at certain times actually in my mind. The old brooder would be brooding, though. If I asked Sharon for help, she'd hoist me with my own petard. She'd say I couldn't control a class. Whatever, the class was cancelled tonight, my flock fled. I ought to hunt about for them and then find Frances and seek her advice on matters

Plum and matters barker. I needed to know what she knew about Erika Gretsch. She obviously knew something.

Unsteadily, I made my way to the landing, then froze as I caught sight of Erika loping across the foyer, the Gretschbags gripped all in one hand, the bundle lodged under her other arm. As I rapid-fired another text to Frances, I felt the throb.

Don't you think it's all beginning to converge? said James O'Mailer. The sprits are spiralling above the glass and the seekers look in askance around the table. Something is about to hatch. What you do next will prove crucial.

Yes, it will, so piss off. I can't deal with you as well at the moment.

I took a deep breath and waited for my ears to pop. Outside, in the rear carpark, I found Reg, Mac and Frank in conference beneath one of the streetlamps.

'Whu-hay, you look sheepish,' said Mac. 'Looks like you've had a baa-d experience.'

'Be careful of puns,' I said. 'They ram people up the wrong way.'

Reg thrust his hand into his trouser pockets and pulled his waistband further up his chest.

'The ladies have gone already,' he said. 'Quite, quite terrified, the poor loves. I don't think this is acceptable behaviour, Flack. I don't think we want to put up with this sort of malarkey.'

'It were probably no more than a bit of hi-jinks on Erika's part,' said Frank.

'No, I agree with Reg,' I said. 'It's not acceptable to bring dead animals into class. She's clearly unwell and needs special help.'

'Quite good stunt, though' said Mac. 'Ruiner used to chuck rubber dogs' heads into the audience whenever we played Hell.'

'Hell?' said Reg. 'What are you blathering about, man?'

'Hell, right. Town up the north of Norway. Blinding pizza.'

'Bit of a moody sheep, weren't it?' said Frank.

'Ram,' said Reg. 'It was a dirty great ram. There's a lot of difference between a sheep and a ram.'

My mobile blipped inside my jacket. 'Look everyone. Let's call it a night. I'll have a think about how to address this, and send an e-mail or something.'

'Cheers Nate,' said Frank. 'Really enjoyed it.' He patted my shoulder, then sloped off across the carpark to his white van, ripping open the back doors. The suspension bounced as he got in. Seemingly driverless, it sped off.

'Goodnight Flack,' said Reg as he made his way to his Volvo.

And then there were two.

'See you next week, Mac,' I said, and walked a few paces, removing my mobile from my pocket and checking the messages: **be in the bar. xxx F.**

'Hey, Nate.'

I turned. The Paddle was still standing there, my *Piss* report in his hand.

'Look mate,' he said, his face in the lamplight stern and salesmanlike. 'Writers need money, right?'

'We're like everyone else,' I said. 'We're not beamed back from the future.'

'I've got a proposition for you. Next week, I'm going to have whacked off *The Grasp of Fear*, right?'

'I strongly advise . . .'

'Look, you say you're a book quack?'

'Doctor,' I said. 'Book doctor and yes, I *used* to be a book doctor.'

'How much for you to read it, then?'

My gullet, spleen and knackers began to slide and pour into my legs. Usually I charged a pound a page if the client wanted a simple assessment of viability both commercial and aesthetic, and a further pound a page for copyediting and line-by line suggestions. Price yourself out, I thought. Treble the fee. Six pounds a page. If he writes another thirty-five thousand words by next week, that's seventy thousand words in total, that's a roughly three hundred pages double-spaced, that's a one thousand, eight hundred pound fee. Prohibitive and exorbitant. Only a twat would pay that. So I quoted Mac six pounds a page. He didn't think on it.

'Money is no object,' said Mac. 'So I can bring it next week?'

Suddenly my head throbbed, the most powerful throb so far, like hot lava poured into the plates of my skull.

Flack, don't do it. You don't want to read it. Show it a fair pair of heels.

It's three months money to write. Tell me why I shouldn't?

I can't. They will find us. Flack, I beseech of you. None will fall if you decline this task, I promise you. My word is blessed honour.

You're not real. You don't have bills.

84

I will only become stronger should you accept this Faustian Pact.

Go away. I tried to get rid of him, didn't I? He doesn't listen. A bit like you.

Flack, I'll match pact with pact. Desist here and I will never bother you again? Never. You'll never hear my lyre-like voice again. I will not be needed. I shall shrink.

I need the money, O'Mailer. And you're not real. Begone!

'You alright, Nate,' said Mac. 'You look like you're shitting a wild one.'

'No, I'm cool,' I said.

'Until next week, then. Cheers, mate.'

He waddled off and then waved as he manoeuvred himself into his low, sharp-edged car. I lit a cigarette and watched the car disappear into the slip road and as I did so I sent another text: **F, I just sold my soul.**

Oh yes you did, Kiddo, said O'Mailer. And now I shall be forced to act further. And we shall be made to work in earnest and in concert. Keep safe, dear Flack, you and I, we are in this together.

A Disturbance to Our Left

'Be serious, Frannie. Satan's head. Satan's head saying, I vant you. I vant you.'

'No, no, no. It's *not* the worse thing that has happened.'

'How can you say that?'

'Think about it, Nathan, you think about it.'

An hour after I'd sold my soul, we were sat at a table by the window in the Grad Bar. I was aware that I was fidgeting like an anthill and couldn't keep my hand from covering my mouth in between swigs of my Guinness. I kept thinking about the eighteen hundred-pound bundle of doom and O'Mailer's cryptic blithering. I wanted to tell Frances about O'Mailer. But as she more or less invented O'Mailer, if I told her I was hearing him speak, receiving ghostly commands she'd think me insane. This might be a reasonable assessment, but Frances's bee-swarm logic would interpret my going insane as something I was doing consciously, just to add to her problems, to our problems, the problem of 'us'. And then she'd tell everyone. She'd write a poem about it. It would be a good poem as well. It would cut to the quick of it. It would appear in *Rialto* and *Mslexia* and would be called *Nathan is a Barker*, or something, and then her third collection would be called *Nathan is a Barker* and it would have a picture of me on the front weeping on a bench and sat next to huge imposing man with a beard, eyepiece, chihuahua and sword stick. She'd appear on Radio Four and explain to the whole nation why the collection was called *Nathan is a Barker* and how someone left her for a figment of her imagination.

I tried to put these things out of my mind before she accused me of not listening to her. We'd blundered into a special night in the bar: pre-rugby club dinner cocktails. The meat-heaps studded around the room radiated tuxedo machismo. Fists the size of the foam hands waved at American Football matches made pint glasses look like thimbles. Silent little girls, in their ball gowns and flimsy eveningwear, became in contrast fairies scissored from the pages of childrens' picture books. The tangible musk in the air reminded me, not in a comforting way, of Oxford and the night I met Johanna. I'd better not think about her in front of Frances as well. Reflected in the black window, I watched her profile: her slender neck; the sheen on the shoulder of her leather jacket; the fronds of her bob that kissed her cheeks as she blew out smoke and sipped her red wine.

'Remember that little bald gnome-man,' she said, 'who thought his guru in Mandalay was writing his mystic Mills and Boon novels for him?'

'That's sad, not scary,' I said.

'That Russian woman with six fingers from Thetford who handed in that sheaf of love letters to Stalin.'

'Writing Barker-Nonsense is not the same as doing Barker-Nonsense and doing Barker-Nonsense *in* class is the worst. You can't top this.'

'I can.' She wrinkled her nose at me and swiped her cigarette across her lips.

'Fran, dead head on the desk. Abandon ship. Course cancelled. Erika Gretsch. Bah Bah bonkers in the brain. If this was Folder-Holders Top Trumps I'd beat you every time, forever.'

'You don't remember what it was like, do you? You always say you're listening when you're not.'

Oh damn, she'd segued into 'then' again. When we were together, it was always: you're not listening to me, Nathan; what did I just say? You leave the room when I come in; you don't want to spend any time with me; stop writing, I can see that you're writing; you don't like it when you say that you do; please come over; you don't really want to be here; you're thinking about Johanna; you won't look at me; why? Why doesn't this work? You're not listening.

'I am listening,' I said, reaching across the table to gently pinch her arm. She frowned. Shit, she wasn't referring to 'then', so no need to head off another discussion about why she ate my copy of *The Invention of Solitude* by Paul Auster and how she was sorry and that we shouldn't have split up.

'Not now,' she said, '*then*.'

Bollocks, she was. 'I don't think we should go into this now,' I said.

'I told you about her,' she said. 'Grotbags, remember?'

'Grotbags. The worst one ever?'

'Yes, Grotbags.'

'Erika is Grotbags?'

'Why do you think I put the phone down on you last week?'

'Because you hate me?'

'Of course I don't hate you.' She smirked and slanted two fingers across her cheek. 'But I *top* you. I have what she *did* to me. Dragging me to a police station in the middle of the night and citing me as next of kin, that's paper wraps stone.'

'It's the same person?' I said, pissed off now. 'I thought she'd been banned?'

'Banned from my classes, not the Department *per se*.'

'Jesus. Erika is Grotbags.'

'You didn't bloody remember, Nathan?'

'And Sharon let her in again and put her in my class. And she didn't tell me. She did that on purpose. She's trying to get at me. Or she knows they'll be a big mess that we'll have to work together to sort out.'

'Ooh, paranoid,' said Frances.

'You don't know the half.'

'Oh God, Nathan, you've got Grotbags.'

I remembered Grotbags now. It was at the end of it, at that depressing crossroads of indecision that haunted the last month of our relationship, after she'd eaten my copy of *The Invention of Solitude* and I moved out of her flat and into The Garret. And she was right. I wasn't listening back then. I was drifting into *The* State. *The Penelope Tree* was solidifying in my imagination, its first third real and realizable to me. During that last month, Frances had been continually moaning on about a student, a Barker Extraordinaire, a woman whose poetry was the stylistic equivalent of 'watching a man riding a bicycle with square wheels'. But this had floated over me. Frances was always going on about Moon-Barkers and

Sensies and Grammar-Stammerers and Theory-Wankers, and they had started to blur. Something had happened, though. Something bizarre.

Frances had been called in the middle of the night and asked to come to the police station. Her mother had been arrested. This confused and upset Frances. After all, her mother died when she was twelve. So it wasn't in the most positive mindset that she arrived at the station to be met by bemused coppers and Grotbags weeping like a widow in the reception.

Of course, she'd put the police straight and refused to take Grotbags home. In a side-room they explained that at one am they received a call from a distraught German woman. Round at her house, they found a 'right state' and were told a story of how she had that day taken a long walk out into the sticks and somewhere in the fields came upon an abandoned factory. Exploring its dark chambers and workshops by torchlight, collecting bricks and stones as she went, she discovered a closed door at the heart of the complex. She plucked up courage and snuck herself in, using the torch to scour the floor and the walls and the ceiling, and as the torch worked its way over the junk, it settled on a bundle propped against the wall. There were runes and symbols daubed on the plaster around it, she said, terrible pictograms, she could feel the hex and curse of the place, and her heart was pounding and she was sweating fright, and as the torchbeam settled, the thing came into focus. Spread out on a sack, posed in a ritual-fashion, was a dead child. Mummified. Wizened.

She panicked. Scarpered back to her house and hid under the covers of her bed until she mustered herself enough to call the police.

They took her back to the factory in the dead of night. They crept through the rooms again, three torches this time, searching and searching. For a while, she couldn't retrace her steps, couldn't find the chamber of blood. But then, it was found, and in the dark there, the stillness, the air heavy with dust, there, lit-up in the overlapping circles of the torches, lay a burst bag of ping-pong balls.

Somewhere along the line, as she was charged with wasting police time, Grotbags Gretsch had insisted that the poet Frances Mink was her daughter, but as the Duty Sergeant so succinctly put it, 'I reckon she's a bit of a bammer, miss.'

The bar was filling up and the backs of tuxedo meat-heaps hemmed in our table with their guffaws and bragging. Frances, strafed by flashbacks, stared at me, half-angry (with Grotgretsch, or me - it was impossible to tell) and half-triumphantly.

'It beats yours,' she said.

'No, it's snap,' I said. 'She keeps calling me The He. What's all that about?'

'That's typical. It's not you. It's anyone. She used to do that to some poor old Minor in my class. "Are you The He? I have found you" and then fall at his feet and start stroking his trousers.'

'Well, I've got to do something, haven't I? I just don't trust Sharon . . . I mean Juliet or whatever. Mrs Tiggywinkle, Aunt Bessie.'

'Nathan?' said Frances. She leant forwards to stroke the stem of her now empty wineglass. 'Do you think we're too jaded to do this now?'

'My round.' I got up and snaked my way through the herd of muscle. At the bar, I waited for the drinks and stared at my pale, sullen reflection in the strip of mirror beneath the optics. I did look jaded. But what did she mean by jaded? Frances could be tangential. She had a hundred different words and phrases for 'let's try again'. *Second edition. More than one stanza. Shopping after midnight.* As I collected my drinks and turned, three Big Foot-sized rugger-buggers loomed in front of me.

'This is the night of the year,' said the biggest one, 'that women will satisfy our needs, categorically.'

Categorically? What did he mean by categorically? Of course, I knew, and I felt a twinge of jealousy. For them, it's simple. Just a scrum, a bundle, an oval tossed from hand to hand and thrust over the line and back into play. No, that's simplistic. That's just his stated POV. Not what whispers in the recesses of his head when he's alone in his bed and the night lies heavy across his bulk. It was virgin, not veteran-speak. You wouldn't catch Sylvester 'Sly' Ramos-Pintos saying things like that. I found myself smiling and took a second glance at them, the mighty trio, their pint glasses flipping side to side in their hands like I might twiddle a pencil in class. Their heads fell back as they belly-laughed. I caught sight of the doorway – it was vacant – and as I shuffled forwards, trying to manoeuvre my way through the heaps without sloshing the drinks, a square-shaped figure ghosted the entrance, then stepped into the bar, scanning.

I froze.

Unmistakable.

Woolly hat. Puffa jacket. Heavy bags.

I lost half my pint banging down the glasses on our table.

'Oh behave,' said Frances, dabbing at the spillage with a beer-mat. 'I was trying to talk to you then. Are we jaded? Can we not empathize with

90

these people because we're jaded? What does that say about us? What if she was an *idiot savant*? We wouldn't notice. You certainly wouldn't. You're not even listening to me.' She put out her cigarette with vigorous stabs. 'What have I done now?'

'She's here.'

'Who is?'

'Grotbags. Erika.'

'Fuck.'

'She didn't see me.'

'Sure?'

'No.'

'Fuck, Nathan. Fuck!'

Our table was still shielded by a crescent of meat-heaps and their categorical girls. Frances dropped her hands to the table and turned them over. I rested the flats of my palms on top of them.

'If we imagine we are invisible, we will be invisible,' she said. 'We can fade from here. She won't come near us, she won't come near me, anyway.'

Fade? What did she mean by fade?

A disturbance to our left. A yelp and a huff. Voices raised above the hubbub. Someone said: 'It's that mad woman from the bus.' The right flank of the human shield collapsed and the broad shoulders plugged the gap. The eyes locked upon us. Frances and I now clutched each other's hands as the Gretschbags ripped apart the shield wall further. Dumping the bags in front of our table, she swaggered to the next table along, snatched an empty chair and hauled it over to us, nearly toppling three fairies and a meat-heap the size of Big Ben as she went. She crashed down on the chair and urgently started to wrestle with something in the bags. Resplendent and regal joy then pounced into her face.

'So, you two are *married*, then. Why haven't you asked me to come for the tea and to join you?'

'Er, we're coffee-drinkers,' I said.

'Nathan,' said Frances. 'Teleport.'

She let go of my hands. I stood up. She stood up. My bag swung about and pummelled lots of meat-heaps as I followed Frances through the bar. Downstairs, we rushed arm in arm across the foyer, looking back over our shoulders. At the double-doors, we paused. A commotion erupted behind us. Erika was dragging the Gretschbags down the stairs, barging people this way and that.

'Jesus, this is like *The Terminator*,' I said, as we hit the concrete expanse of the University Plain and in the dark scrambled up an embankment. Over a lawn terrace, we fled into an arrangement of bushes and laburnum trees backed by the Registry building. I slid down against the wall and Frances crouched next to me.

The breeze rustled the leaves. Through the bushes, the plaza was a bleached polygon; the restaurants and cafeterias had shut down for the night and the stone slab benches were unoccupied. Music from the main bar pulsed. Erika, her outline softened in the distance, stood guard in the middle with her bags. Frances turned to me and in the half-light, her eyes were glossy and her lips close. They stayed close until Erika shambled off.

'Why is it,' said Frances, 'that whenever I go anywhere with you I end up dragged through the mud or running through a field or accosted by barkers or on my hands and knees?'

'It's all part of the Fumigator lifestyle,' I said. 'Why read it when you can live it.'

'C'mon,' she said, 'let's go back to mine.'

I Don't Understand Why You Can't Forgive

Back at Frances' flat, a slightly more salubrious and organized garret than mine, I was sat on her sofa, intent on staying sat. If I relaxed and spread out, I'd cause a blip on her body language radar. A cafetiere cooled on the coffee table and, underscored by crackles on the vinyl, Miles Davis' *Kind of Blue* swam around the tangerine walls. Frances, I counted, lit thirteen tea-lights and four mauve pillar-like scented candles she'd arranged on the bookshelves and the mantelpiece. Being at Frances's was like time travelling back into the title sequence of an 80s arts magazine programme. In the 80s, when I was a teenager, I would have fanaticized about situations and atmospheres like this. I wondered when everything had become so fraught and confusing.

She blew out a match and stood with her hand pressed to an exposed triangle of skin between the hem of her grey cashmere V-neck and the waistband of her black hipsters.

'I can't believe he said that,' she said. 'Tricky to market. Why is it tricky to market? It's not tricky to market.'

'It must be, mustn't it.'

She sat down next to me.

'Don't be down, Nathan,' she said. 'You've written a wonderful novel, you don't need me to tell you that[32].'

I shrugged, feeling empty and not wanting to talk about *The Penelope Tree* unless I had something positive to say to my friends. With every rejection slip, a part of me felt that I'd betrayed the trust of those people who believed in the novel and believed in me.

Papers lay on the coffee table, two overlapping sheets; a poem called *The Venice Syndrome*.

'Is this new?' I said. 'Can I read it?'

'You don't have to now.'

'I'd like to read something good today, not just bladder traumas and zombie fleshgobblers.'

She fell forwards, the heels of her hands slapped to her cheeks. Her laughter vibrated in the pit of my stomach. 'Needing a Piss,' she said. 'Needing a Piss.'

'Exactly.' I picked up the poem.

'Is there going to be a sequel?'

'Needing a Wank?'

'Needing a Beating.' Frances sagged into me. 'Needing a . . .'

'Shhh, I'm reading,' I muttered. 'Don't distract me.'

The Venice Syndrome.

I stared at the text, but hesitated before reading it. According to the reviews of her second collection, *Reproduction*, no one can vocalize a certain type of contemporary female frustration quite as precisely as Frances Mink can. After *Reproduction*, she received fan letters from thirtysomething women of the bookish, Rom-T, scarf and mittens variety, saying that reading her poems is like finding a snowflake identical to

---

[32]Of course, you do need other people to tell you if you are one of the only two broad types of writer that I have ever met. I have come to think that there are, outside of Arcana, only two types of writer. Firstly, those who truly know that other people exist. Secondly, there are those that do not. I hope that I fall into the first category. I write to be closer to other people. Others write to lord it over people. Philip Roth articulates this in a far more erudite and particular way than my hackish attempt (because he is Philip Roth and I am a hack) when in an account of an interview with Primo Levi he says "It is not as surprising as one might initially think to find that writers divide like the rest of mankind into two categories: those who listen to you and those who don't" (*Shop Talk* by Philip Roth (Vintage, 2002) page 3). This urge to be closer, to listen, was at this point, in Frances's arts round-up boudoir and after the day that I'd had, causing me moral conflict.

another, so apt is the phrasing, so sharp the imagery, so convincing the voice.

I don't understand why you can't forgive

The sofa cushions bounced up beside me. She had stood up and started to pace around the room, pausing to take off her boots, then she lit a cigarette and stared briefly out of the window. Then she traipsed across the room to sit in the armchair and study the shimmering candles. This is what writers do. We pace. We can't stay still. We're restless. And it's a strange experience, to be there when someone is reading your work in progress, when a part of yourself is on the line, when you've voluntarily opened the trapdoor beneath you.

She wanted me to love it.

Simultaneously, she wouldn't accept my loving it and wanted me to tell her why it didn't work.

She peeled off her jumper. Underneath was a shaped, black, slightly faded sleeveless top. Her breasts moved as she stood up and walked to the window again.

I don't understand why you can't forgive

The line seemed to wax and smear on the paper. The room had started to smell of sage. I glazed over. Frances was hanging on to the sill. She flashed me a look, then returned to the window. Then the throb came at my temples.

Oh God, not now.

Look at her, whispered James O'Mailer. Those legs, those lips, those tits like mozzarella pillows. Just give her what she wants. Be a man. Be an artist. She likes ambiguities and so do you.

No I don't.

It's a dance of death, Flack. She needs it for her work and you need it for yours. Where would she be without resentment and where would you be without regret?

It's a moral art form, James. I've got to be able to look at myself in the mirror tomorrow. And you weren't there.

Oh but I was. Very kitchen sink.

We drove each other barmy.

'Tis human to do so. We need her. She will help us overcome.

I've got to do the right thing.

Bourgeois cant! Mammock her.

'Piss off you. You'd screw your own daughter for a paragraph.' I held my breath until the pops, then looked up. 'Oh shit.' I realized I was speaking out loud, and then I realized something else.

Frances sunk her hands into her pockets and adopted a rigid stance that pushed her breasts together and displayed the line of her cleavage.

'It's that bad?' she said.

'No, I just remembered something.'

'What?'

'Nothing.'

Erika Gretsch still had my starfish.

'Well, if you're distracted by nothing, you can't be reading, can you?'

'Sorry, look, hang on . . .'

'Don't say that you want to read it when you don't.'

'I do want to read it.'

'Did you tell Grotbags that we're married?'

'Oh Frances, seriously.'

I put the paper down. She turned back to the window, hands on her hips now. I never knew what to say when she was like this, and if I went on the offensive, things would end either in a silly discussion about *then* or a recurrence of book-eating or toothbrush-snapping or the belittling of my manhood and the saying of things that couldn't be unsaid. I watched her at the window and wondered why I was here, what I was actually up to, whether James O'Mailer was right and I was a prig and a prude and a puritan and a pompous twat making a mistake. And that Moon-Barker had my starfish.

'Nathan?' Frances said.

Nathan, what? I thought. Nathan, what next? Nathan, why not? Nathan, why don't you want me? Nathan, why can't you forgive me?

'Come here,' she said, still not looking at me.

I felt suddenly over-warm and dry-mouthed.

'Why?' I said.

'Someone is watching the flat.'

'Pardon?'

'There's someone in the garden.'

I got up and joined her, feeling tired now and apprehensive. Down below, the garden was a black square divided by the path and greyed by lines cast by the streetlamps. I couldn't see anything.

'There's no one there,' I said.

'Not now. There was though, someone looking up.'

'What did they look like?' I said, finding my hand in her hand.

'I don't know, they were wearing a big black coat with a hood.'

In the distance, in the middle of the side-road opposite, trudging away from us, was a black dot that receded and shrunk until it disappeared.

She squeezed my hand. Her palm was hot.

Talent will out, hissed James O'Mailer.

Character

The Unsettling and Peculiar World

Never go in bookshops. They are not for you anymore. They are not for browsers, bibliophiles and those of us who fuss for hours until a first line takes hold of our vitals. Bookshops have become the citadels of the insider artists and the untricky to market. But I am nostalgic and a romantic. I need to read. I want a novelist to take me by the hand through the same world in which I live, a world I still haven't read about yet. Thus bookshops still have their allure. Browsing, for me, is an act of hope.

On a windy Monday afternoon I wandered around the city centre with a head full of agitation until something drew me into the Royal Arcade and into the bookshop. Soon I was sleepwalking among its matt black shelves and dumpbins and stacked 3-for-2 tables. The piped Prozac music charged me up with déjà vu. I'd been here before. The stock and the layout were exactly the same as in the other chain store I'd mooched disconsolately around last week. Then again, they were the same in every high street bookshop across the land. Unreasonably, I was looking for something different to read.

Too unsettled to write since The Night of the Ram, I'd done nothing but read for five days, whipping through *The Wings of the Dove*, *Concrete Island* by Juicy Gash and *Cain's Book* by Alexander Trocchi, all of which made me effervescent with life and fizzing with bliss. Now I needed something else. In fact, I needed three. Otherwise, I'd be back in two days time.

No way, though, would I buy from the 3-for-2 table. I never buy a novel unless I've either found it myself, or someone I trust recommends it. I don't buy anything slashed in price, 3-for-2'd, hyped, marketed, reviewed. I don't buy anything written by a celebrity (i.e., not written by a writer – why would anyone buy a novel not written by a writer?[33]) or an author who ticks all the marketing boxes or whose advance has been publicized or who is an Insider Artist with connections and networks. I ran my hand along the 3-for-2s: abroad, past, celebrity, abroad, past, celebrity. *The Penelope Tree* deserves to be here, I thought. *The Penelope Tree* is in no way inferior to any of these novels. But these were not novels. They were gifts.

Ah, Nathan is having a sulky-wulky, said James O'Mailer.

I looked up at the striplights, then down at the aquamarine carpet. I really was in a sulk, and I only sulked like this when I wasn't writing, and why wasn't I writing? I wasn't writing because I'd lost my starfish. I was worried sick about my starfish. God knows what that woman was doing with it. And without writing, there was only waiting. No post or e-mails had arrived last week.

On the 3-for-2 I noticed a pile of *Can I Have a P Please, Bob* by Squinty's Little Helper and for a second I thought that maybe I should just accept the business as it is and toss off a nostalgic thirtysomething 3 for 2 table product-shifter. I could easily toss off a:

1)   A thirtysomething romcom role-play gamebook where the reader chooses various pathways through the story, rolls dice for outcomes etc, thus tapping into both contemporary ennui and thirtysomething nostalgia for the geeky games of the early 80s.

2)   Something salacious. The salacious sells. I would start work soon on *The Unsettling and Peculiar World of Arnold Bumrape.*

---

[33] The London Philharmonic does not pay daytime TV presenters to conduct. The Royal Academy does not commission the infantile daubs of some third-rate celeb's best mate or the idle doodles of some sex-crazed sack of tits. The government doesn't ask writers to run the Home Office. Why do marketeers think politicians can write a novel? I'm going to write a non-fiction polemic called *Marketing and its Discontents.*

3)   A thinly veiled, urine-imbibing autobiography about waiting for nothing to happen, i.e. *Touching the Starfish*.

Finding my 3 X 5 cards in my jacket pocket, I pressed one to my palm and started to scribble down my ideas for product-shifters.

'Oh you're so dedicated!'

Doctor Jane leant against the corner of the True Crime section. The way that her black-framed spectacles dangled at her hip and she cuddled three day-glo-jacketed paperbacks suggested she'd been watching me for some time.

'It's just like you said in class, isn't it? A glimpse just comes into your head and you're off. Except you write them down. Me, I let them go.'

My arm started to shiver and wouldn't stop until I buried the card in my pocket. Last time she caught me writing I was sketching a picture of her body attached to Juicy Gash's head. Now I'd just written 'ARNOLD BUMRAPE' on an index card.

'I was looking for your book,' she said, 'but I can't find it.'

'Oh, it's not out yet,' I said, and quickly moved on. 'How are you, Jane? Are you enjoying the course? Is it doing what you want it to do?'

I started to scratch the back of my head even though it wasn't itching. Why did I have to start speaking like this? Why did I switch into speak-and-spell mode? James O'Mailer and Juicy Gash wouldn't do this. They'd be suave and composed and relish the stroking of their feathers.

Alrighty, Flack. Let me do the talking.

'Go away.'

'Pardon?' said Jane.

'Oh sorry, I was still . . . daydreaming.'

She stood up and hugged her books closer to her chest, causing the tails of her raspberry-coloured velvet coat to flap around her knees.

'No, I'm sorry, I'm disturbing you.'

'No, you're fine, seriously. Are you writing?'

'Last week's class left me a bit out-of-sorts, I mean, you know. I've seen some things in my line of work. I'm not squeamish . . .'

'Well, I need to speak to Grot . . . I mean Ms Gretsch,' I said.

Jane poked her forefinger up to the ceiling, lifting it slowly, then pulling it down. 'I'm . . . er . . . Do you want to go upstairs?'

'Pardon?' I said, startled.

Now she's talking, said James. In 1937 I met such a gamey one in the foyer of the Hotel Adlon . . . We made furious love as a torch-lit procession of stormtroopers passed below the window and the world spun on its axis.

I pursed my lips this time. Begone!

Jane stopped her poking.

'Yeah, sure,' I said, checking my watch for no reason at all. 'Why not?'

Jane tossed her books back onto the 3-for-2, and as we swished through the aisles and up the escalator to the bookshop café, it crossed my mind that if I spent some time getting to know Doctor Jane, fresh inspiration for *Millennium Bridge* might follow.

Gloucestershire

Upstairs in the café students lolled on the sea green comfort sofas and mums and pensioners whispered at the tables surrounding our own. The eyes of authors scrutinized us from the posters hanging on the light blue walls. Bizarrely, I always feel under the cosh when both Alan Titchmarsh and James Ellroy are watching me with plum-stone eyes.

I had an excuse, but I wondered why Jane wasn't working today and again what she actually did for a living. She was some sort of therapist or counsellor, I imagined, hence her remark about her 'line of work' downstairs. She pulled her scarlet Pashmina scarf away from her neck. No rings glimmered on her fingers. You know you're getting older when you start to notice this. Absently, with her other hand, she used her stirrer to draw a heart in the froth of her cappuccino.

'I do owe you an apology,' she said. 'For running off last week. It was just . . . Cynthia was in such a state . . .'

'Hey, don't worry, everyone was a bit fazed.'

'I like Cynthia, but she's . . . you know . . . But isn't everybody else nice? Reg is a dear old soul . . .'

'Yes, he's a card, isn't he?' I cradled my chin in my hands and pressed my cheekbones, trying not to crack up. I'd recently received another of Reg's e-mail journals.

Sunday: I still can't get used to this lady vicar and still maintain that she embodies our national decline. Yesterday it was only my Darling Dear's tight hold on my paw that kept me in my pew as that damned woman stood at the lectern and read those much loved lines from Proverbs about a virtuous woman's price being "above rubies". Now there's a description of my Darling Dear if ever there was one and I don't like to hear it garbled by such an accent. Outside, as we made our way to the Volvo, some sort of urchin in a Dracula costume, hopped up on Pritt-Stick, no doubt, ran up to us and shouted "udders" at my Darling Dear. I had to be restrained by the organist with the hook hand and Mrs Tifflicott from the charity shop in the high street that I will still insist on calling the Spastics.

'What are you laughing at?' said Jane. She batted her lashes, her eyes as glossy as milk.

'Nothing.'

'Oh go on, you tease. Have I got something on my lips?'

'You were saying.'

She raised her eyebrows and stroked her neck. 'Yes, well, and Mac is very funny, well, sort of funny, and oh I don't know, I don't know, Erika's a shame, isn't she a shame?'

I nodded. She'd be more than a shame if I didn't get my starfish back. But I didn't want to get into the Gretsch Issue with Jane. It's unprofessional and risky to slag off a difficult student to another, however sympathetic she is. I had Frances for that. Since last week's palaver, though, Frances didn't seem to be talking to me. She'd not returned my calls, my texts or my e-mails.

'I don't know, Nathan,' said Jane. ' It's just Frank. He gives me the willies.'

'The willies?' I said.

'Oh not that sort of willy! Not on your nelly.'

'My nelly?'

'Let's not get our nellies and willies confused. Don't you think he's . . . odd?'

Yes, yes, yes, he's a Wrong-Roomer and serious fantasist loon. He's got a library of serial killer books and secretly admires terrorists. He's got photographs of himself dressed up in an anti-radiation suit and a gas mask and pointing an air pistol at the lens. He lies in bed imagining the day that the sound downstairs is not the cat, when he can give a burglar both barrels and become a national hero. He lies about killing people and thinks we'll admire him for it.

'I don't think I actually know him,' I said. I cocked my head and found myself smirking and rotating my hand. 'He's just, oh misunderstood, or something.'

The froth on her cappuccino was cooling, the heart shape solidifying.

'His wife stays in that van all evening,' she said.

Something gushed through me.

Millennium Bridge Woman is hiding from a man who trapped her in a van and she saw him on the bridge, that's why she was running away, and in the café, she was waiting for a friend she'd just called, so she could confide. A female friend? A male friend? A champion? A shape-shifter? Arnold Bumrape?

Instinctively, I reached for the index card in my pocket, then remembered where I was and pressed by hands to the table as I leaned towards her.

'So what do you do, Doctor Jane?' I said.

'Oh Nathan,' she said. 'It must be wonderful being a writer, just to write all day and really touch people with words. I'm just so impressed. I really *am* impressed. And you're so good. You make everything seem so clear. You make me feel that I can do it. I just get so much out of you. And you're a proper writer, you've got a writer's name and even look like a writer.'

She spread her shoulders and crooked her arms, upholding her palms.

Over the top! shouted James O'Mailer. Get in character, Flack. We need her. She's the one. She will save us.

Jane paused and chewed her bottom lip as she steepled her fingers above the heart in the froth.

'You know, when I was a teenager,' she continued. 'I didn't fantasise about football players or popstars or actors. I dreamt of writers. I dreamt of being taken out to dinner by writers. I dreamt of being laid down on a four-poster bed in a farmhouse in Gloucestershire and the words massaging me. You know, I didn't give a fig for Duran Duran or Curiosity Killed the Cat. I had pictures of writers on my bedroom wall. I wanted writers. I wanted Christopher Isherwood, or Oscar Wilde or Truman Capote.'

'Er Jane,' I said. 'You know those writers, erm?'

She stared back at me, frowning, then plucked at her hair, finding a strand and drawing her fingertips slowly through it.

'And then I meet you and you are a writer and you wrote that wonderful thing for the television.'

'Have you seen it?' I said, terrified that *Gentleman's Relish* was being repeated while my course was running.

'Not yet. I'm waiting for the box set.'

Judging by her reaction, she imagined *Gentleman's Relish* as an ambitious, filmic and exotic adaptation, something set abroad or in the past, like *Brideshead Revisited* or *The Jewel in the Crown*, something where at the end of episode three a brick-chinned RSC actor in a white lounge suit covers his privates with his fedora hat and stares balefully at the ground as a posh woman in a tea dress drifts off into a storm of red dust and a bit of classical music that's already number seven in the singles charts plays out, and as the credits roll you can't see how Charles and Maude can ever get back together again, not with the class system and the cruel machinations of Aunt Ernestina and the unrest in Rawalpindi that threatens to destroy their idyll forever. *Gentleman's Relish* was actually like this:

29: INT. MIZZI'S LOUNGE — NIGHT
Through the archway, we see MIZZI. She wears a very tight, short dress and is silhouetted against the glittering skyline outside the window. She holds up two whisky tumblers and giggles as Sly PROWLS towards her.

                    MIZZI
          You're early?

                    SLY
          I'm never early.

                    MIZZI
          Business?

                    SLY
          My name's Sly, but you can
          call me lover?

                    MIZZI
          That's my kind of mission
          statement.

She passes him the tumbler. They both down their
shots in one gulp.

                     SLY
          I'm a magical being. Take
          off your bra.

                    MIZZI
          I'm not wearing one.

She WIGGLES out of her dress. It slips to the floor.
She's wearing black stockings and suspenders.

                     SLY
          Do you like my belt buckle?

                    MIZZI
                 (chews bottom lip)
          Yes.

                   SLY
          It would look better against
          your forehead.

Mizzi kneels down and looks up at Sly longingly but
something flickers across her face.

                    MIZZI
          Hey, didn't we meet in
          Acapulco? Monica Cartier-
          Romanov's party at the Hotel
          Mongochetto?

Her head flicks to a framed picture of a child on
the mantelpiece with the same whiplash smile as Sly.
A look of horror FLASHES across Sly's face.

Not exactly *The Seventh Seal*, is it? I was only following orders.

Jane clasped her hands together and pressed them to her cheek as if overcome by tiredness or feeling. Her eyes were wide and her lips slightly parted and her face had become infused with a pinkish glow. Must be the lights, I told myself.

Don't be a poltroon again, said James O'Mailer. *Don't be a milksop. Don't fail to dance the dance of death this week like you did last week. It would be a crime against* nature! *It's what it's all about. She wants you. Look at the state of her? One word from you and it'll be off to Gloucestershire for a massage. And then the rearguard can begin.*

James, she's a student of mine. And she's a Rom-T.

And how else is she going to learn? Just ask yourself what your noble savage would do here? What would Mister Ramos-Pintos do?

Well, yes. Sylvester 'Sly' Ramos-Pintos would have swept her off to Gloucestershire as soon as eyes met across the 3-for-2s, and Gloucestershire for a hired gun like Sly could be anywhere, especially Sussex, Rutland or Cumbria. Could be on top of the 3-for-2s and all over the piles of *Can I Have a P Please, Bob*. Could be back at hers with Arnold Bumrape and Juicy Gash paying to watch. This is the thing about Sly. He has no capacity for guilt. He has no sense of consequence, no moral core. He's a 2-D cipher in a fourth-rate wankfest. It was trying to add 'layers' to him that got me into trouble with the producers and Squinty Hugo. I wrote a scene where Sly is unsettled by the weary eyes of a prostitute in a Manet painting he finds in a book left open on a client's coffee table. The eyes stare back at him accusingly yet sympathetically as Keiko or Temple or Dakota or whatever undresses in the other room and it strikes him that he's no more than a nervous system with a cock. Big epiphany. Inner conflict. Character development, I thought. They didn't like it, though. They made me replace it with Sly taking charge of the situation, getting his Gloucestershire in the shower.

Everything is so easy for Sly. Why do I have to have inner conflict? O'Mailer was right and I should stop dithering and take charge. That's what Sly would do. Taking charge was better than reading and better than waiting. Jane was about to say something, but Sly was going to take charge. She was, after all, very pretty and would be even more so when removed of everything Pashmina.

'Nathan,' said Jane, sliding her hands apart and sitting up. 'You know you gave me that racing car?'

I sludged back into being sensible, realizing that if I took advantage of the Gloucestershire situation I would have to sit in class with her eyes fixed on me and very soon all of the Arcana would know and I'd feel exposed and dodgy and grubby, and more than this I really needed to sort out the Frances predicament before I Gloucesteshired anyone.

'Oh, it doesn't matter,' I said.

'What do you mean?' she said, sounding offended.

'If you've lost it.'

'I've not lost it. I wrote a story about it.'

'You did?'

'Yes, head or no head, I still managed to write a story. Can I read it in class?'

'That's what it's there for.'

She smiled and then started to rummage in her coat until she took out her glasses, put them on and stood up. I jogged the table as I got up and the coffee sloshed everywhere.

'Nathan, this has been lovely,' she said, 'but I've got to dash.' She looked down at me with her Gloucestershire face again. 'But, I . . . er . . . why don't we go out for a drink some time?'

'OK, fine,' I said. 'Send me an e-mail.'

She squashed her hand to her chest, then leaned towards me, dabbing a kiss on my cheek, holding it there long enough for me to catch that she smelled of fresh, watery melon.

'Bye, bye, lovely to see you.'

And with that she was gone, sashaying thought the aisles, leaving me sat there with the brown chocolate heart now misshapen in crusty froth and the eyes of the authors compressing me with their stares and James O'Mailer tutting in my head.

The Venice Syndrome

Downstairs, I managed to summon-up enough decisiveness to select and buy *Super-Cannes* by Juicy Gash, *Hard-Boiled Wonderland and The End of the World* by Murakami and *This Sweet Sickness* by Patricia Highsmith. As I crossed the market square a gigantic, spherical bank of cloud descended over the city, almost blocking out the sky. Its ridged, solid-looking surface made it seem like the moon had rolled out of its orbit. If it swung any lower it would crush the buildings and the spires. Outside the newsagent on the corner was a board with the local headline written on it: **Body Found in Woodland. Is it The Angel?** The Angel of Trunch was a figure supposedly behind a series of unsolved murders, mainly of nurses, that had been going on out in the countryside for years. He was like something out of bad popular fiction brought to life, a deadly cliché. I'd paid little attention to the case. As I left the square, a peculiar quality of the light tinged everything with a shining, soft-focus aura. The loosely single-filed crocodiles of schoolchildren, the logjammed traffic, the windows of the antiques shops and the thrift stores became fluid and intense as I made my way to the footbridge over the dual-carriageway. The Jane thing seemed a tipping point. I'd only agreed to a drink, but a drink implies more than sitting and sipping, and she was in my class, which made it sticky. But the course only lasted for a few months and it's not exactly unknown for adult ed tutors to get involved with their

112

students afterwards. Then again, she thought I was something I'm not, and that was both off-putting and meant I'd disappoint her when she found out I'm a third rate hack and a failure. And she was a Rom-T and with a Pashmina fetish, and I didn't know much about her. She obviously didn't want to talk about her job. Probably a sex therapist or literary agent, something slightly disreputable that your dad wouldn't see the point of. The thing is, just entertaining the possibility made me realize that post-*Penelope* I was feeling lonely and bored and unappreciated and maybe I should just see what happened and ignore inner conflict and not take things so seriously. If she e-mailed, I should say yes. Have no preconceptions. Relax. Stop letting James O'Mailer and Sylvester 'Sly' Ramos-Pintos get to me. Just have a few drinks and a chat and a laugh and enjoy myself. See what pattern developed. If she dropped the Rom-T act, she might be just what I needed. Then again, if something developed, I'd have to keep it secret from Frances like I had with Lisa, or face her wrath and more poems about my treacherous ways. And I was already worried about Frances.

Last week, in her flat, Frances had squeezed my hand as we stared out at the street, at the space where the lurker had stood. To avoid scaring her unnecessarily, I decided not to tell her that I thought I'd seen a similar figure outside my flat recently. I'd felt unsettled though, and didn't really want to go out there and walk home in the dark and the wind.

'It's her, isn't it?' Frances said. 'Erika Gretsch.'

'I'm sure it's nothing,' I said.

'I don't want all that to start again.'

'I'm sure it isn't.'

'And you can say that with such confidence after what's happened tonight?'

Frances tugged my hand so I faced her. With her other hand she pulled the collar of her grey jumper over her mouth. A suggestion bristled in her eyes. I released my hold on her hand, said I was knackered and had to be up early. As I gathered my stuff, I rubbished on about relaxing and calming down and letting me know if anything happened. She sat down on her sofa and didn't look at me or show me out. Down in the street, the breeze rippled the hedges and trees. I couldn't see a soul. Except, when I headed off and looked over my shoulder, Frances's outline was standing in her window, backlit, stationary, blurred.

Since then, she'd been incommunicado. I decided to go round and see her.

When I reached her street the moon-cloud had blown over. The half-light softened the pebble-dashed and plaster facades, the concrete front gardens and fluttering bushes. A twinge of apprehension pinched me as I trudged up her garden path, then stopped midway to turn and check. No people about. No children or dog-walkers, leafleters or kids. The emptiness reminded me of her poem *The Venice Syndrome*. It wasn't written in her usual ironic and cutting style. It was earnest, hard and plaintive. The Venice Syndrome is, I knew, a tendency among the lovelorn to find a beautiful place to die. And she wasn't exactly attacking this fey, defeatist nonsense in her forty-two lines of submersion imagery intercut with anecdotal fragments about a broken relationship. The first line had kept playing in my head all week long.

I don't quite understand why you can't forgive

I knocked on her door and stood back, folded my arms and waited. I knocked again and did one of my stupid little pacing circuits up and down her path. I tried again, much harder his time. Then I took out my phone and rang her landline and then her mobile. Both were on ansamachine. I scribbled a note on an index card and pushed it through the letterbox and considered going to the pub on the corner and holding out for a bit. Then again, she could simply be out shopping or walking. She could have gone away for a long weekend. She could be writing and not want to be disturbed. I wasn't her keeper. Still, I didn't find these explanations comforting. I walked back to the head of the path and stared up at her window. The blank window. A grey glint in the dusk. I found myself unable to move. Something Jane had said came back to me: that I looked like a writer. I continued to peer up at the window and wondered what on earth this meant.

Grubby Bundles

By the time I arrived at the Eudora Doon the following evening, I'd still not heard from Frances. Before my session, I nipped up to her classroom. The door was ajar. I knocked gently and pushed it in. I hoped she'd be sitting on the desk, swinging her long legs, her head full of the same melancholy as mine. At seven PM on a Tuesday night we'd all rather be writing, or in the pub talking about writing. Legs did swing, but they were about as long as a ventriloquist's dummy's.

Perched on the desk, in her uniform of black tracksuit bottoms and sheepskin coat, was the brick-shit-house shape of Sharon Plum. Sensing my presence, she fluttered her eyelashes at me, looking like a doll when you shake its head.

'Oh, it's you,' she said.

'Er, Shar . . . Juliet,' I said. 'Where's Frances?'

'Don't you know?' Sharon always needs to feel that she's in the loop and you're not, just like she needs to believe that everyone she knows is more influential than everyone that you know. Influence with *published*, well-reviewed poet Frances Mink was always a source of competition for Sharon, especially as I'd met Frances through her. In Sharon's eyes, Frances and I became briefly what she would, in a phrase I despised, term 'a power couple'. Juliet would love to be part of a power couple. Her partner in crime could have been me. It could have been Frances. It could have been Arnold Bumrape if he knew people in The Arctic and had a book coming out. It didn't really matter.

'No, I don't know where she is,' I said.

'I am displeased with Miss Mink,' said Sharon. 'She's gone to Venice.'

'Venice?'

'At short notice.'

'You're taking this class now?' I said. Juliet knows naff all about poetry. Erika Gretsch would be a better tutor. Sylvester 'Sly' Ramos-Pintos couldn't do worse. 'Are you sure she said Venice?'

'Nathan, what have you done to her?'

I could sense **plumcam** booting up behind her eyes:

OBJECT: Nathan Flack . . . confirmed.

STATUS: Negatively co-operative.

ACTION: Interrogate/operate/eliminate.

'Nothing,' I said, taking a step forward and fixing my stare on her squat, powerful body.

'Well, you did before.'

'Piss off, Sharon,' I said.

Woah, said James O'Mailer. Play the game. Remember that Stalin came to power by controlling the Orgsburo, the party membership cards. I was there. I saw him do it.

Isn't there a lesson in that?

Keep your enemies close. One step backward to go two steps forwards, as Lenin once said. I need you to keep close to the central committee here.

Sharon smiled, and waved her hand expansively at the shudder of Sensies all lined up and grimacing in their seats with their folders out and pens poised.

'I'll talk to you later,' said Sharon. 'There's a lot to discuss. Things that have happened recently.'

Yes, and I need to talk to you about someone in my group.'

'Shut the door, Mr Flack.'

Perfectly politely, I closed the door, then scarpered to my classroom. Frances had gone to Venice. What was I supposed to do about that? And there was obviously no point talking to Sharon about getting Erika off the course. The striplights seemed even brighter than usual as I slunk in. Only four of the Arcana had arrived, but a kind of split had occurred. A corridor divided the seating into two gender camps, with Frank and Reg on one side and Cynthia and Doctor Jane on the other. Preoccupied by how dank Venice would be at this time of year, my voice couldn't find its reach and I mumbled my greetings like a caught-out truant before a thrash-happy headmaster.

Talking of which:

'You're late, Flack,' said Reg, holding up his arm and pointing to his watch. His trousers were pulled up even higher this time. His braces were the length of sock suspenders.

'Official start time is five past,' I said, 'and not everyone's here yet.'

'If I were you,' he said, 'I'd start by addressing issues pertaining to last week's class.'

The balls of my feet clenched. 'PRAT' seemed to repeatedly flash across Reg's face like a news ticker. No doubt he'd been grammar-stammering all week: about hunting with dogs and spastics and women priests causing the spread of Aids and foot and mouth in rural districts and how he should have pointed out to the hopped-up urchin that his Darling Dear's grubby bundles are 'mammary glands', not 'udders'. But he had a point. More than the usual expression of palpable alarm waxed Cynthia's face, and Jane's arms were folded tightly and her legs pressed together like she'd been waiting at a bus shelter for three days in subzero temperatures. The pashmina was a startling green tonight, shot through with emerald and metallic jade tinges. Frank, however, was grinning like a fox amok in chicken coop heaven. Visualizing the blood and juices dribbling down his chin, I turned to the blackboard to buy myself some privacy and thought of Venice: the distant whine of an accordion; the moonlight scattered across the surface of a canal; the dark smudge of floating hair, the protruding fins of her shoulder blades, the glinting islands formed by the back of her legs and her buttocks; the clichés of place and situation. *Death in Venice. Don't Look Now. The Comfort of Strangers. The Wings of the Dove.* Frances going to Venice to die, like Milly Theale.

She wouldn't, surely.

I concentrated on chalking out a Robert McKee quote that I hoped would be the basis of tonight's discussion.

TRUE CHARACTER is revealed in the choices a human being makes under pressure - the greater the pressure, the deeper the revelation, the truer the choice to the character's essential nature.

As I wrote I couldn't help but think about the Venice Syndrome and what essential nature it revealed. Nor could I stop questioning myself about my true choice in telling Plum Largo to piss off in front of a shudder after I'd previously told her to piss off in front of an eagle. I returned to the class and sat on the desk.

'Let's just see what Erika has to say for herself,' I said.

'She's here,' said Cynthia, 'she's here. I've seen her.' Her eyes were fixed upwards, as if any minute Erika would crash through the ceiling like the xenomorph in *Alien 3*. 'She was in the cafeteria, just prowling around and around the tables with an empty tray, never finding anywhere to sit.'

'Flack,' said Reg, 'What is this nonsense that you've scribbled on the board? Do you think Jane Austen needed recourse to *soundbites*.'

That tension in my gut made a break for the bigtime and tried to collapse my left lung.

Before I could answer the door crept open, gently swinging into the room as if shoved by an invisible helper. A long exhalation of breath followed and a shape appeared, lumpen, heavy-set, waistless, the brim of the hat low again to conceal her eyes. The Gretschbags snuffled across the floor as if titbits and morsels hid beneath the surface. She moved through the corridor between the chairs like a prisoner hauling a ball and chain, and as she settled herself down next to Doctor Jane, again I remembered that stench from last week and its eyes and its leer and its horns.

'Good evenings, everyone,' Erika said. 'You may start now.'

All eyes turned to her, then back to me. I pulled away from them, ticking off the names in the register to buy myself some time. Then I really, really let myself down by clapping my hands like a primary school teacher.

'OK,' I said. 'I know that last week's class didn't go quite to plan. And I think we're agreed that some cause for concern arose. Erika, you would like to say something to the class.'

Erika's chin quivered a little as she reached out and gripped the bags as if they moored her to the floor. Her expression fluctuated from the brink of an outward shout to the start of an inward scream. I could see it then. I was convinced. Drape a great big black hooded sou'wester over her and it was the figure outside my garret, the figure Frances said she saw outside her flat, the watching obsessive, the loon in the shadows, the crank who had pushed Frances over the edge, sent her on her way to Venice. I crushed my thighs together and dug my fingers into the underside of the desk.

'Erika,' I said. 'Do you, or do you not, want to talk about this?'

Her bottom lip stuck out and her hand flipped over into a pleading gesture. Finally, she opened her mouth, but the door banged into the wall. Waylaid by a briefcase, laptop valise and a bulging carrier bag full of paper, the gargantuan frame of Mac McMahon toppled into the room. He tried simultaneously to announce something and stabilize himself, his gut hulahooping to the left and ricocheting to the right. For a second it looked like a huge butternut squash was losing its structural integrity. Squashing his wrists together, he swung his stuff down to his knees and when he'd composed himself he held still and beamed an overjoyed smile.

'Sorry I'm late, rockfans. Right live one this afternoon, then frigging traffic.'

As he sauntered up the aisle, he tripped on a Gretschbag. The whole lot crashed to the floor, the briefcase with a bump, the laptop with a crack and the Paddle with a splat. The carrier bag thumped, then spewed out a rustling trail of papers that snaked up the aisle towards me. When I looked down, between my feet, there lay a cover sheet:

The Grasp of Fear

by

Mac McMahon

Hell on foccaccia. I'd forgotten about selling my soul on top of everything else.

'Not exactly my grandest of entrances,' said Mac, now stooping and stumbling to regather his papers. 'Don't worry, it's all insured up to its arsehole.' He piled his luggage up on the windowsill, then lowered himself into his seat. 'What's going on then?'

'We were just talking about what happened last week,' I said.

'Oh that,' he said. 'Ace that was. Big up for Erika, I say.'

'Erika was just about to say her piece,' I said. 'Were you not, Erika?'

She stood up and clutched her hand to her heart as if acting out the death-scene in a Wagner opera.

'I didn't mean to, I didn't mean to. I didn't mean to cause anything to happen, but it was just so beautiful and I cannot understand how The He could find it ugly.'

'Erika,' I said. 'Just promise not to bring into class any more bodyparts, or any offal, giblets, offcuts, bones, guts or mince, this is not Conceptual Art, and we can get back on track. People have strong feelings about that sort of thing, and not just vegetarians.'

'I promise. I promise to be a good girl in classroom.'

I found myself sitting and nodding, as if I'd just come to my senses after a bomb-blast had shot me halfway across the city.

'Oooo-K everyone,' I said. 'Anybody like to discuss anything else before we begin? No. Good. Right, last week I gave you all an object to write about. Can I have them back, please?'

I fixed my eyes on Erika as the pinecone, the snowshaker, the mineral chunk, the racing car and the doll with the one missing eye were passed over to me. For once, her hands stayed in her lap and refrained from reaching into the Gretschbags.

'Erika,' I said, 'have you got my starfish?'

She frowned. 'Oh no, damn The He, I've forgotten it. I left it in my toilet.'

'Well bring it back, please,' I said. That tension inside my chest launched an Operation Barbarossa that swept aside my fortifications and wave upon wave of it ripped through my head. I dropped off the desk and turned to the words on the board, but I couldn't read them, thought about where the bollocks I was and why couldn't I have my starfish and how the hell was I going to write a word without it and how stupid this was. If a Folder-Holder had said to me that she needed a fetish-object to write, I would have said something pat about writing without affectations or self-consciousness. You don't need anything fancy, no place or pen or coloured paper.

Fuck it all to pieces. Fuck and nuts and bumrape.

The racing car lay on the desk.

'Jane,' I said. 'I believe you have a story for us?'

'Why yes,' she said. 'You remembered!' She slipped her hand into her folder and drew out a sheaf of pages.

'Jane's going to read to us,' I said.

'Marvellous,' said Reg. 'Marvellous.'

'Is there anything you'd like to say beforehand, Jane?' I said.

She adjusted herself in her chair, crossing her legs at the ankles and popping her glasses onto her nose.

'No, well, I was inspired by the little car Nathan gave me,' she said. 'I'm not sure about the end. Anyway, I'll just get on with it. It's called . . .'

Formula One

'She doesn't stand a chance . . .'

In a room stuffed full of jostling bimbos merrily partying to celebrate the end of the race and his victory, Jennifer Damson stood alone, fighting to stop herself going lobster-red with rage as the girl with the Dior number painted onto her faultlessly nubile body drifted away from the group of podium minxes. She had just made that catty remark without bothering to lower her voice so Jennifer couldn't hear it. Everyone knew that Jennifer's world wouldn't be complete unless she had Andy Ridgley, the world's most heartthrob Grand Prix driver. He was on the other side of the room, entertaining a group of lovelies with his wit and charm. He could take his pick but Jennifer was just the PA to the boss of the company that made the cars.

Her heart was jumping up and down, her body quivering with a deep-felt need, a drive so strong that she made herself stand really still as she watched the girl in the Dior dress's tight apple-shaped bum sidle across the room – everyone could see that she wasn't wearing any knickers, not even a thong – until along with her heaving, struggling breasts that continually fought a battle with the dress to spout out and leap at any man in sight she joined the group around Andy.

Andy would be a much better man if he knocked gold-diggers like her out of his life, thought Jennifer.

What was he really like? she pondered feverishly as the blood continued to pump around her veins. Was he a womanizer who could have any girl he wanted and then just tosses them aside like the ingredients of a Greek salad? Or was he looking for the love of his life, someone he could settle down with and really talk to about art and music and engines. Even from here, she couldn't help but notice that inside his trousers it looked like there were two cans of Diet Sprite one on top of the other.'

This line seemed to pull Jane up short. She paused and coughed and had to clear her throat.

'Excuse me,' she said, and rummaged in her bag for a bottle of mineral water.

'Don't stop, love,' said Mac. 'It's just getting good. You can smell the characters.'

When I looked over in his direction, intending to flap him a shushing gesture, I noticed that next to him Frank was rigorously rubbing his thighs with his sausagelike fingers. The dome of his baldhead glistened with sweat.

'May I just interject here?' said Reg. He looked as if he was about to be dropped from high altitude onto a sleeping Japanese city.

'No,' I said.

'It's a free country, Flack, and I am sitting here wondering why a lovely young woman like Doctor Vest would want to bare all in such a fashion. I myself would not want to write something that suggested I had thoughts my family would be ashamed of.'

I was about to reboot my Grammar-Stammerer firewall software, but was distracted by Erika. Intently, uninhibitedly, she was poking her head into Jane's lap in an attempt to read the rest of the story, causing Jane to lean away and tip the bottle, splashing water all over Cynthia's oatmeal sweatpants. Before I could switch into crowd control mode, my temples throbbed, but this time I could also smell something that reminded me of dog fur.

The old mutt's right, said James O'Mailer. This is a dead-loss. My demands for back taxes and alimony make better reading. It's Mills and Loon. Fumigate it. Fumigate her. Fumigate them all!

I'll fumigate you in a minute, you belletristic ponce.

What are you going to do, Flack? If you tell her straight, she might never drop her linen. Is it one rule for her and another for The Fearless Grasper, the fat drummer who beats his meat with all his heart?

Of course not. Now sod off before I feed your dogs to the Gretschbags.

I waited for the kerfuffle in the girls' cloakroom to blow over.

'Jane,' I said, 'would you like to continue?' I hoped she wouldn't, but she nodded and resettled in her chair, holding the paper up to her face this time. She smoothed her hair away from her ear and picked up where she'd left off.

'Jennifer decided that it was now or never. Otherwise, the gold-digger was going to get it all her own way. She downed her champers and plucked another one from the tray of a waiter who was so dishy that he had to be gay, then clicked in her heels across the room to where the gold-digger was smiling at some amusing anecdote Andy had made. Jennifer muscled in and stood in front of him and lifted herself as if she had just risen in her full splendour from a very hot bubblebath.

He stopped relaying his amusing anecdote and honed his glinting smoky-blue gaze on her. As their eyes met she already felt naked. He had a sensuous mouth with one of those little twists to it and he gave her a devilishly intoxicating smile as he tipped his glass at her and chinked it. He was tall and well made, like one of the Baciari cars he mastered as he took on the world with dash and elan. He was a slim, muscular machine himself. Silky skin stretched tautly over his fit body. He was broad-framed with powerful piston-like hips. What passed between them in that instant turned her mouth to sandpaper just thinking about it. Big feet. Long arms. Hands that, like in what she knew was his favourite Genesis song, had an invisible touch. They called him Ridgeback Ridgley, because he was an exotic dog.

The bimbo in the Dior dress cut in rudely.

'Oh Andy, get me another glass of champagne and take me away from all this.'

With a small shrug of indifference, he took a small step towards Jennifer. Her skin began to fizz as if champagne bubbles were being poured all over it. She struggled to speak, but somehow she managed to.

'Andy, what's your favourite book?'

'Well, that would have to be *Breakfast at Tiffany's* by Truman Capote.'

'Oh my God, that's just the best book I have ever read,' she gushed.

'And you look so much like Audrey Hepburn tonight, Jennifer, let's get away from these sorts and we can talk about it. In private.'

They veritably ran through the room, hand in hand and desperate for each other.

Later, on his yacht, he made such love to her that she thought the boat would break and they would sink to the bottom of the sea. As he did so, with his firm hands, and expert tongue and undisappointing manhood, she was glad that she had read a lot at school and bet the other girls now wished they had done too. You never know which way leads to a man's heart.'

Jane pressed the pages to her lap and looked up at me, her brow raised and her eyes unblinking and her mouth open, as if struck by the beauty of the moon for the first time in her life.

'Er, thank you very much, Jane,' I said. As much as I liked *Breakfast* I was relieved that my favourite authors were Juicy Gash and Patricia Highsmith. 'You read very well.'

'Oh thank you,' she said. 'Please don't hang back everyone. Tell me what you really think.'

Before anyone could react, before I'd decided on the most urgent of the issues that had preoccupied me during the reading – who would win in a fight between Ridgeback Ridgley and Sylvester 'Sly' Ramos-Pintos? – and before Mac could shift from the ridiculously earnest pundit's pose he'd adopted, before Reg could go out with a bang, before Cynthia could run out with a whimper, and before Erika could flail the contents of mortuary slab around the room, Frank heaved himself up to his full height. As he rolled his shoulders, he smeared the sweat from his face with one of his massive paws and shuffled his chair around so he could face Jane. A spitty growl hissed from the back of his throat.

'I could listen to you all night, Jane.'

Weather Anomaly

Of course, I didn't fumigate Jane. I pointed out, as gently as I could, that if *Formula One* was a popular romance, (it wasn't exactly *Gravity's Rainbow*, was it?) the heroine gets want she wants too easily, while a bona fide romance depends on obstacles and risk-taking. I didn't say that if *Breakfast at Tiffany's* is Ridgeback Ridgley's favourite book he was more likely to jump ship with the poofy waiter, just in case mentioning homosexuality caused Reg to go all Bomber Harris and call for air strikes. Instead, I called for a coffee break and sprinted out onto the walkway to smoke as many cigarettes as possible. As I rested on the rail and stared at Frank's van on the far side of the carpark, Jane came out of the double doors, holding two cups of coffee.

'Do there,' she said, 'do there really have to be obstacles?'

'In that type of story, yes,' I said.

'What about other types of story?'

'Really, yes. We'll talk about this when we do plot.'

'The plot thickens, Nathan.'

'I think you just made a friend in Frank.'

For some reason, she went all quiet on me. We stood and sipped our coffees, her Pashmina brushing my shoulder in the breeze as we watched the white van: its grey windows, tidemark of grime and apparently vacant cabin. I was sure that at one point the suspension bounced.

The rest of the class passed in a sort of fog. I existed in a bubble of clarity, a weather anomaly while everyone else seemed hazed in mist. I gave a forgettable little introduction to character and characterization, but then became bogged down in responding to Mac's insistence that you could write a story without characters (he cited *Watership Down* and *Caravan of Courage, The Ewok Adventure* as examples). Frank became unnecessarily heated about writing from the killer's point of view and why couldn't the killer get away with it. Then a sort of Reg and Cynthia Axis of Drivel formed and crusaded to airbrush the arseholes out of fiction. We lost ourselves in why must characters have inner and interpersonal and extra personal conflicts, why can't you just write about good sturdy people who know who they are, risk-adverse, pillars of the community who have equity and savings and run small businesses and don't sponge off the state and at weekends go to fetes and make jam and paint watercolours of renovated watermills and write poems about geese and who have well-adjusted, responsible children called Jennifer and Peter and don't have to draw attention to genitalia and toilet matters all the time. I can't remember what I said to any of them. I forgot what I'd said instantly, just like when I used to mark forty reports on undergrads' stories and afterwards not remember a single one of them or a single comment I'd made. Throughout, the fog seemed to swirl around the room, fluctuating and thickening. I imagined the fog drifting off the sea and invading St Mark's and the Grand Canal and Frances on the deck of a shrouded vaporetto, straight-backed, resigned, sure now.

Some time later, I materialized in my kitchenette, starfishless and chain-smoking. Smoke dispersed across the windowpane and I watched the street for hours, waiting for the figure in the sou'wester to come for me. At my back, on the work-surface, edging out of its white plastic bag by its own volition, coffee-ringed, red wine-stained, as burdensome as an anchor, smutted by fingerprints and God knows what else, was the door-stopping, head-crushing, epoch-ending heavy metal opus known, for the time being at least, as *The Grasp of Fear*.

The next morning, I heaved the manuscript to my desk and positioned it next to my bag of objects. Many cups of coffee were drunk. Many cigarettes were smoked. The passive voice was used. The pipes wheezed, banged and sputtered as I waited for the post. I wrote my journal and tried to convince myself that there was nothing foreboding or sinister in Frances's impromptu disappearance. I tried to find *The* State. I tried to get back into *The Woman on the Millennium Bridge,* but every time I reached out to touch the starfish it wasn't there and I ended up staring at the blank page until my eyes strained. I checked my e-mails. None from Frances. None from literary agents. Only spam and:

From: R.Carnaby@albion.org.uk
Subject: (none)

Wednesday: I am coming to the conclusion that I will remain a failed writer just as long as I refrain from using four-letter words and writing about the bedroom. But what was good enough for Jane Austen is good enough for me. My Darling Dear would have one of her episodes if she ever found me writing about fumbles on the chaise longue and the rumpy-pumpy of the marital bed and anything that rears its ugly head in that department. Last night we were subjected to the vilest piece of top-shelf gibberish. It's beyond me why the young people need to be so morbid. People of my generation don't like to be reminded of the morbid side of life. Throughout, I was just thinking about Mother and the war and how she kept it all together with gusto. As I listened to the verbal assault to which I was subjected I could clearly picture Mother standing in the kitchen in her gas mask and stirring the powdered egg with authority and vim. Flack, the lazy cur, veritably encourages morbid behaviour in class and seems to wallow in filth.

Also in the inbox was a more ominous:

From: J.Largo@un.ac.uk
Subject: (none)

Nathan,
I think we need to meet up and talk about your recent attitude towards your responsibilities and me. Have you got any news for me re your novel?
xxx Juliet Largo.

I deleted that one. Screw Sharon Plum. Screw her. Well, if I had done that in the first place instead of ending up in a bathroom with Frances I wouldn't be in this mess. Downstairs, the post lay on the mat, including one of my own hand-written envelopes. Inside was a letter from the agency Djemba-Djemba and Portnoy Ltd: The Penelope Tree *is written keenly, with panache, but we have to be 100%* . . . I tried to take this like a Spartan and drew a big scowling face next to their entry in the *Writer's and Artist's Yearbook*. My bank statement had arrived too, and warned me that I had very little overdraft left. The *Gentleman's Relish* fee was running out. The measly alms I would be paid for teaching *An Introduction to Prose Fiction* wouldn't cover next month's overheads. Unfortunately, *The Grasp of Fear* was going to save my life. In the bathroom, as I shaved and thought about Zane Champ and zombie flesh-gobblers, I suffered a nosebleed for the first time in twenty-five years. A monstrous undead thing looked back at me in the mirror. Beneath him, rosy strands spiralled around in the bowl with the foam clumps and blobs of stubble.

Look at the man in the mirror, Flack, said James O'Mailer. Is the problem in there or out there?

I took a walk to think about it and meandered around the parks and the city centre. Outside a travel agency, I paused and checked the prices of flights to Venice. I ought to go and find her, make sure she was OK. Even if this was a stupid game on her part, an attention-seeking exercise, I needed to be sure that she was well and upright, otherwise I'd never forgive myself. But Venice is a big place; she could be anywhere. I couldn't afford the time. I didn't have the money. The manuscript of doom lay on my desk back at the flat. There was enough money in that manuscript to pay for next month's bills *and* take a trip if I needed to.

I trudged home and lay on the sofa all afternoon and all evening, trying to work out why I couldn't sell a novel and why I was poor and why I lived in an Artex-ridden shithole and why I couldn't make any relationship work, why I only met women who were being sick in toilets and why it always ended with embarrassment and shame, and what I had done to deserve this.

I was wallowing. I was not being active, proactive and spartan. I was not showing my true and essential nature under pressure. I was not taking risks and surmounting obstacles. I was letting other people impinge, letting things I couldn't control, other people's choices, mess with my head and get in the way of what I was supposed to be doing. I was letting the absence of a stupid starfish stop me from writing. I was letting all this have form and voice and whisper in my ear. I was starting to start every sentence with 'I'.

A horrible thing about writing, the most horrible thing among a number of really horrible things about writing, is that only writing itself can solve any problem that you have with writing, and I wasn't writing. I hadn't written for ten days. I was feeling like a squashed slug because I wasn't writing. Then I remembered the list, my ideas for product-shifters I'd made in the bookshop, and retrieved the index card from my jacket pocket. Then I realized. It all became clear to me.

Straightaway, I abandoned *Millennium Bridge* for now and sidelined *The Grasp of Fear*. I got out my journal and brainstormed the possibilities. Within fifteen minutes I'd fused together my three ideas into one single narrative direction. Within three hours I had a structure. Within a day I'd started to compose. Within a week I had a book, a short book mind you, a very short book, but a book nonetheless, a book written under a catchy pseudonym, a book with a gimmick and a charge and untricky to market, a crossover book that would appeal to both adults and adolescents, a book I called:

The Garret of the Fumigator

or

Nostalgic Thirtysomething 3-for-2 Table Product-Shifter
A Role-Play Adventure in which YOU are the Zero

by

Arnold Bumrape

HOW TO FIGHT THE CREATURES OF THE LITERARY UNDERWORLD AND WIN SUCCESS, ESCAPE AND SOMEONE WHO'LL LISTEN

The Garret of the Fumigator is a role-play adventure set in the literary underworld in which YOU are the zero. Before you start, you must first create your character by rolling dice to determine your TALENT, MARKETABILITY and CONTACTS. Alternatively, depending on your moral disposition, you can just make these up as you go along. The others will even if you don't, and all the fights are fixed anyway and the victory panel is unreachable. Write the scores down on index cards. You will need these in your quest to find the muse of your dreams, sell your novel and escape an upside-down world in which the meanest thrive.

You start your adventure with the mystic scroll of The MA, the armour of youthful naivety, a magical starfish that glows in the dark and sundry stationery items.

May neither hope nor despair go with you on the adventure ahead!

1

What fresh hell is this? It's almost 2am, The Poncing Hour. You are standing with your back to the wall and down there on the high wire the party is still sizzling on. Daft Punk or Air or something plays for the four-hundredth time. Hazy shadow-people slot tequilas and hoover gak from the coffee table. You wince as a jumpstart with an uncanny resemblance to the Turin Shroud comes up from a line, raises his arms like a goalscorer and shouts: 'I've just had an epiphany.' He and his cohorts are from *The* MA's new intake. These tyros must make an impression, be witty and beautiful and shocking. In their own heads, they are already a new Lost Generation or Dada. The critics of the future will be writing about them and their cross-fertilisations; their biographers will one day describe this heady night of bacchanalia under red light bulbs.

You know that in the future there will be no writers, only gift books. You know that by Christmas *The* MAs will all hate and suspect each other. You know that you don't belong here.

An American girl called Verisimilitude Joystick or Fornea Mingmong or something comes up to you and quickly informs you that she is a genius and is writing a novel about a woman who marries a bat with Eminem's face. 'It's a twisted love story,' she says. 'Are you twisted?'

Your junkmail filter sets to exclusive and you flee into the other room.

In here, the host – who last year was called Sharon Plum and who has recently co-opted you into teaching Adult Ed – is lecturing about elitism and realism and varied abstractions to a unisex group of whoevers in vaguely military attire. She catches your eye. She shouts something you can't hear and then lumbers over to the stereo, cuts-short Daft Punk and puts on the Chocolate Salty Balls song from *South Park*. Laughing hysterically she makes a beeline towards you. One of these is the last straw, and you make like you've not noticed her.

You elbow through the jam-packed, spliff-smoky kitchen to the bathroom, pretending not to register that *The* MAs and students and junior staff and researchers and hangers-on here are muttering your name as if you are important or influential. Their voices hush as you close the door behind you.

There is an ironic picture of S-Club 7 hanging over the toilet. The light in here is also red. A woman is before you, on her hands and knees, her head over the bowl. She is wearing leather trousers and high-heeled shoes. Realizing your presence, she turns and looks back at you. Her face is pale, her make-up smudged. She smiles and says, 'Oh hi.' A shiver of déjà vu flickers through you. You will either: about-face and leave the party (turn to **47**) or say 'Hi, that's a quietly dignified position you've taken up there.' (turn to **33**).

2

Find yourself in a dream where you are suspended by a harness in front of a giant billboard-sized poster of Captain Beefheart's *Trout Mask Replica* LP. Start to come round with a shock-and-awe of a hangover and find that a naked Sharon Plum is standing over you and that you are tied hand and foot to her bed. Realize you have finally managed to sleep your way to the bottom. She places a wooden box between your feet and then picks up the sledgehammer. 'I'm your number one fan, Nathan,' she says. End of game.

3

Continue to work on the novel, composing 850 words of tiptop, high-octane final-draftish prose a day until one afternoon, Lisa Levankranz phones you. She wants to get together. Intrigued, you take the Polar Express down to The Arctic and on a drizzly and overcast Friday afternoon, meet her in the bar of a Piccadilly hotel. She looks a lot prettier without her head stuck down a toilet and she likes your stuff. She likes it a lot. She says, earnestly and passionately, that she loves the gorgeous descriptions that seamlessly slide from image to feeling almost cinematically and the storyline that becomes more muscular as the predicament thickens. She says it has potential. She says it has every chance of success. She wants you to finish it. If you finish it, she'll pitch it to the sales people at Eighth Window.

You stay with her and drink two bottles of wine as the evening's predicament thickens. You lose track of time. There's

135

inevitably something about a woman who is a voracious and insightful reader that's very attractive to you. When last-train-time comes, she says: 'I can put you up if you like?' You will either: realize you are getting that stupid feeling again and say 'yes' (turn to **22**); or refrain from mixing publishing with pleasure and weather her deflated expression, vamoose back to Liverpool Street and jump aboard the East Anglian Red-Eye, sleeping through most of the ride back to The Shire, safe in the knowledge that you (you!) have actually done a successful bit of networking (turn to **16**).

4

Try to enjoy the gorgeous naughtiness of it all as you spend the next three nights in her bed. Try to be cool about it. Try to compartmentalize. You start to think that you really like her. But you also start to think that you're abusing your position. This is not the way that you want to behave, this is not the way you think things should be, and you have no idea whether you are allowed to do this.

You will either: decide that the whole thing is wrong and let her down gently (turn to **47**), or decide to talk this through with your university mentor, Dr Neville Copperson (turn to **20**).

5

Snap and launch verbal barrage. Draw from your genes the language of the building site and factory floor, of the class struggle of your glorious working class forebears. Volley an unstoppable C-word blitz, one that's fuelled by years of this, years and years of it. He is pantsing himself, but you can't win this. His scores are:

HIERONYMUS PONCE
TALENT 0   CONTACTS 10,000

When you lose, turn to **15**.

6

Back at her flat, you are impressed when she puts on *Love and Dancing* by the League Unlimited Orchestra. She shimmies as she lights candles and uncorks a bottle of Shiraz. You talk of writing, teaching and other things. She seems to be on your wavelength, and you can't recall feeling a rapport like this forming since before you arrived on *The* MA and in the seminar room in Humanities Faculty II, you first saw people like Hieronymus Ponce and Verisimilitude Joystick and straightaway thought: *This is not going to work out.* You seem to be shifting into another state of mind as she plays *Here Come the Warm Jets* and *Various Positions*. You are sitting on the floor, talking about how you want to live in some place where it's always the Prague Spring and everyone wears short sexy raincoats and has metaphysically rewarding flings and lives in flats with big windows overlooking baroque squares and is writing an explicit and dangerous novel instead of networking and arselicking. With a twist of her wrist she opens another bottle and smirks at you like you might smirk at a well-meaning ponce. 'We're going to save the Folder-Holders of Ipswich together,' she says. This is the first time that you have heard the phrase and you laugh until your diaphragm hurts. It is four am and sunlight is coming up. She shuffles backwards towards you until she rests against the sofa. The lines in her lips are purple with wine and they sneak cautiously towards you. 'I like you,' she says. 'You're sane.' It is one of those moments where the possibility hovers and you know that things will be utterly changed if you do and utterly miserable if you don't. You will either: bottle it, thinking that you will have to work with her and you hardly know her and this is seriously unwise and you should learn from your mistakes (turn to **47**) or fade into her (turn to **40**).

7

You had seen her earlier, sitting on the sofa with *The* MAs, but she wasn't talking to anyone. Now, she looks very ill and pale-faced and you can't help but feel sorry for her. You step over her and rinse out a mug and then hand her a drink of water. 'There should be a warning sign about the red wine at these things,' you say. 'Why? Are you a veteran?' she says. You make a face. She laughs. 'Who are you with?' she says. 'Nobody,' you say. 'I came with Ferdie,' she says. 'He's my ex.' You will either: remind yourself that you must maintain six degrees of separation between yourself and Arch-Ponce Ferdie Paget and his coterie and return to the party (turn to **49**) or override your immature and confrontational attitudes and stick around for a while (turn to **13**).

8

Never find the time to write. Become no more than a creative writing teacher. Become nothing more than a supporting beam for her own work, which picks up and accumulates and leaves you behind. Get a full time job teaching Communication Studies A-Level to pay the bills and finance the happy home and her career. Live a full and rewarding life. End of game.

9

Deny everything and spend more time with Copperson and Plum. Write short story called *Crabbing with Owl* that you sell to *London Magazine*, then:

Roll Dice:

1-2 (turn to **17**)

3-4 (turn to **43**)

5-6 (turn to **29**)

10

You are now sitting in Pryce Carcrash's office in some especially poxy bit of Chelsea. He has Bart Simpson hair and wears lunettes, a white dinner jacket and has gladioli stuffed in the back pocket of his jeans. He loves your novel. He loves it so much that you fear he's going to drop his strides and do the 'new speaker, new paragraph' dance again. There is only one problem. The title. According to Pryce, you can't sell a novel unless it has 'Bitch' in the title. You suggest 'Bitch Nation', but that's already been done. After some hours in which you both seem to recite the thesaurus, you settle on *Bitch City*. Then

138

there's another reservation. Pryce can't market a white, Oxbridge-educated, heterosexual male from the Home Counties and from a loving family and suggests 'we' use a brand identity. You will either: tell him to poke it and go home (turn to **3**), or agree, thinking that he knows what he's doing. Do whatever he says from now on (turn to **28**).

11

You have seen her before, striding across the University Plain and sitting in the cafeteria at dusk, reading and smoking and very apart. 'You've been talking to Neville Copperson,' you say, 'I can tell.' Top bit of networking, this. She might be one of his friends, or in the pay of The Orgsburo, but indiscretion is integrity and you left the DMZ hours ago. 'No,' she says. 'The red wine's rank. And don't piss on me.' I don't need to go,' you say. 'I was on my way out but went the wrong way.' 'You too?' she says. 'I'm Frances, by the way.' She holds up her hand for the shake and you take it as you slide down to your haunches. 'I'm a poet,' she says.

You will either: run like hell, as you know that whatever happens subsequently will be like being trapped in a Kate Bush video (turn to **47**); or become infused with a teenage fantasy that your ideal woman writes poetry and has hair like Louise Brooks. Think: *wow, you're amazing.* Say: 'Hi, I'm Nathan Flack' (turn to **26**).

12

Over the coming months, you continue with the novel and share the new chapters with Lisa during your visits to London and her visits to Garettland. This long distance dating thing suits you, as it doesn't interfere with your writing. You start to feel that this could be the start of something sustainable and the terrible first flush becomes the powerful second wind of optimism.

Even so, Ferdie Paget starts to interfere, suggesting to Lisa that your passion will deplete itself quickly, that he's heard things about you, that she should go out with someone that he likes. You will either: quit the deal, assuming that this isn't going to go away and if she's still in touch with him, still listening, she's playing a game with you (turn to **16**); or take this like a Spartan (he is the enemy of all that breathes, after all; what do you expect?) and try to be understanding and not show your anger (turn to **37**).

13

Bite tongue. You can't be bothered to be vitriolic/principled at this hour. 'I don't know why I came here,' she says. 'I don't know what he expects me to do.' Paget has been trying it on with anything with eyes since he arrived. 'Who are you anyway?' she says. You tell her that you are Nathan Flack and after her next question about your occupation, you tell her that you are a writer. 'Oh God,' she says. 'Another one.' 'I'm sorry,' you say. 'It's a curse. I hope you're something noble and selfless.' 'I'm a fiction editor,' she says. 'Eighth Window Press.' Eighth Window is a major imprint of a major corporate publisher. You will either: realize that this is a golden opportunity and mention your manuscript (turn to **31**) or think such lavatorial networking vulgar and make your excuses and leave (turn to **47**).

14

At the end of term, you are standing in some concrete bunker where the Writer-in-Residence, Jurnet Fang is throwing an end of term party. Everyone is here: Copperson and Plum (as ever pretending that they like each other), everyone you have taught this term, other tutors, lecturers, Fornea Mingmong and the Turin Jumpstart and *The* MAs. You are drunk but safe in the knowledge that you are not as lonely as you were two and a half months ago. Jacinta is here with her friends. Her eyes glint every so often as she looks up from where they are all sitting on the floor in a circle. Neville Copperson is telling everyone that he's just written *Oscar Wilde is Gangbanged on The Planet of the Apes*.

The Plum, who at this time is operating under the name of Pauline Thigh starts to boast to you that she's written seven thousand words this week and has produced a story called *Dogbreath*. It's about a teenage girl with bad breath that scares off all the boys. The breath miraculously freshens when she comes out as a lesbian. Plum/Thigh wants you to read it for her, make sure that she's using the comma correctly in speech, etc.

She mentions blithely that she's met an agent called Hugo Cornwallis who wants to see some of your work and wants to know if you are good-looking. You will either: agree to edit *Dogbreath*, get Hugo Cornwallis's number and arrange a meeting (turn to **30**) or pretend to be too busy and slope into the kitchen to grab another beer from the fridge (turn to **41**).

15

The pub has gone quiet. All energy flees you. All you can hear are the approaching footsteps on the pine boards. She sits next to him. You stand up. You say, 'I've never let you down.' She says, ' You just did. I think you ought to go.'

You go (turn to **21**).

16

Return to Garretland and finish novel, then send it to Lisa. Receive standard rejection letter signed by under-secretary. Take it like a Spartan. Turn to **29**.

17

Wait three months, work on your novel, and return to **1**.

18

For reasons he can't articulate or won't tell you, he fails to sell your novel and then for reasons he can't articulate or won't tell you, he insists you write something set abroad or in the past, and then when you find writing to order impossible, for reasons he can't articulate or won't tell you, he drops you. You find that no literary agent will touch you now for reasons that they can't articulate or won't tell you. End of game.

19

Things come to a head when ex-students of yours ring up and ask you to go for a drink. You invite Frances, but she's on her mobile, complaining to Plum about a student called Grotbags who claims to be her mother and hallucinates dead babies. She says she'll meet you at the pub, but doesn't show. When you

141

come back, she has ripped out and eaten pages from your copy of *The Invention of Solitude* by Paul Auster and snapped your toothbrush and your razor. When you ascertain that she got the name of the pub wrong, and sat in the wrong pub on her own, stewing about your purposeful deception and your unfaithfulness, she switches to calm and cheerful mode, says 'OK then', and returns to normal as if nothing has happened. You will either: leave this hat-standery and find new garret (turn to **38**) or realize that this is all your fault and you must be more considerate (turn to **8**).

20

'Borag Thungg, Earthlet,' says Neville, as you enter his office and take a seat. He's wearing yellow-checked, Rupert Bear-style bellbottoms, purple DMs, an orange shirt, black nail varnish and David Bowie *Low*-era hair. Before you can open your mouth, he starts to ponce on about his new story *Charlotte Bronte is Bumraped by the Bionic Man*. This is not at all comforting and you wonder if you should be confiding in him at all. You decide to white-lie it. You tell him that a student is taking an interest in you and you don't know what to do.

'Boy or girl?' says Neville, swivelling on his chair now and staring at you with interest.

'Girl,' you say.

'That's not zarjaz, Nathan,' says Neville. 'Totally unacceptable. Four legs good; two legs bad. If it were boy-boy, that's a totally different thing.' Neville leans towards you. 'I'd allow that.'

You will either: give in to prolonged pressure and sleep with Neville Copperson, hoping that afterwards Neville will recommend you to his editor (turn to **39**), tell Neville that you've already slept with said student and he can stuff his hypocrisy (turn to **45**) or keep schtum and convince yourself that you're in love and love, after all, conquers all (turn to **32**).

21

Go home and reacquaint yourself with the Isle of Shame. Don't call her. She doesn't call you. Decide that you just can't do this anymore. End of game.

22

Wake up in her bed bathed in swimming blue light and to the sound of pigeons cooing in the attic above the bedroom. Stay in bed all morning, talking about books and other things. Go out to lunch in some brassy sofa-pub in Fulham and peoplewatch and gossip. She asks you to stay another night, which makes you think some connection is occurring here. Agree and go to see incoherent Japanese anime at the ICA. Afterwards, hold hands as you walk under the lights on the Embankment. Feel the terrible first flush.

In the morning though, she sits crestfallen on her sofa in her maroon nightdress and starts to smoke all your remaining cigarettes. The grey light filters through the curtains as she recounts in numbing detail the crimes of Ferdie Paget, a lurid tale of sexual treachery, mealymouthedness, pretentiousness, nepotism and cruelty. You will either: leave, realizing that she wouldn't moan if she didn't still care and if you get involved here, you're going to get bogged down in a fight you can't win (turn to **16**); or feel sorrow and pity and believe you can make it up to her simply by not behaving like Ferdie (turn to **12**).

23

Rent a new ropey garret. Find the grey ashtray light and hammerhead silence comforting and reliable. Pace about convincing yourself that this is a good life and that solitude is inventive. Throw yourself into novel writing and a story where the shimmer is so bright it hurts the eye.

Roll Dice:

1-2 (turn to **17**)

3-4 (turn to **43**)

5-6 (turn to **29**)

24

You are now sitting in The Mincing Cheese, an over-lit sofapub in Pimlico. You seem to be eavesdropping, through a Guinness haze, on a two-way conversation between Lisa and Ferdie Paget. This is, in fact, a one-way conversation, as Lisa has mutated into some sort of giggling scullery maid in awe of the lord of the manor. Ferdie now has shortish ginger dreadlocks skullcapped onto his narrow bony sheep-shaped head. He *really* is a cretin (Lisa has told you he once asked her if Perineum is a place in Greece) and is wanking on about how the poetry magazine *Gullsoup* describes him as the poet of the soul's loss-map and the concrete forests of the city. He wanks on about how London reminds him of a seafood restaurant where everyone is served but never fed, and that he is striding towards his objective correlative, and that a poet needs to 'become', a poet needs to 'experience', a poet has a right to experiment with emotions and sensations and the love-lives and disappointments of other people to use as 'fuel', that a poet had to create his own moral universe.

You feel sick. You are bored. You are losing all respect for her and the black Guinness haze is beginning to coagulate in your head. You will either: leave before you launch a trans-frontal fumigation-assault (akin, in this case, to the Polish cavalry charging the Panzers) (turn to **46**), or sit it out, have more beer; you don't want to upset Lisa (turn to **48**).

25

She is Jacinta Drax. She's in your class, one of the girls who always comes to tutorials and sits there looking at you in a funny way. 'The red wine's rank,' she says. 'It's not just the red wine,' you say as you slip to your haunches. 'Oh God,' she says, 'why do I have to do this? I'm so embarrassed.' She looks pretty in this light, her eyes softened, her skin like a porcelain doll's. 'They're all out there and I'm in here. ' 'That's why I came in here to have a bath,' I said. 'Well, I'm *soooo* glad it's you and not her,' she says. 'We all like you, Nathan, we do.' 'Reduced to the status of an old blade, ' you say. 'Did you read my story?' she says.

You are always on duty. It's Saturday night and you end up giving toilet tutorials.

'No,' you say, 'what's it about?' 'It's about a girl,' she says, 'who's having a passionate affair with her tutor.' This stirs an uncomfortable mixture of feelings. 'That's original,' you say. 'I thought I'd banned stories about campus romances and what I did on my holidays.' 'I showed it to Neville,' she says, 'and he said it was too middle class and too heterosexual.'

She's talking about Neville Copperson, Arch-Theory Wanker and crap writer of puerile stories but, bizarrely, the Lecturer in Creative Writing and therefore your boss and her supervisor. He was here earlier, boasting about his new story *The Third Incarnation of Doctor Who Bums the Life Out of Virginia Woolfe*, but left after one joint made him bark-up.

'Change it,' you say, 'to a green echidna from space having bumsex with Elton John. You know, splice a bit of gay magic realism with a northern trash aesthetic. He likes that.' 'But what do *you* think of my story idea?' she says. 'I need to see the whole thing,' you say. 'You have the most mobile eyes, Nathan,' she says. 'You make me sound like a crab,' you say. 'I was thinking more of an owl,' she says. '"The Crab-Owl,"' you say. 'Now, if you called your story that, Neville would give birth to a lemming with polka dots on its fur.'

There's a rap on the door. You know that the people outside will begin to talk. 'We better shift,' you say.

Outside, you walk her back to her house. At the gate, she says: 'Nathan, you . . . er, will you go out with me?'

You will either: say. 'That's probably not a good idea. Thanks for the chat,' and then walk home (turn to **47**) or think that every male writer needs an obscenely younger girlfriend and say, 'Meet for a drink tomorrow night. Be discreet,' then kiss her on the cheek before vanishing mysteriously into the night (turn to **36**)

26

'Hey,' she says. 'Aren't we going to be working together? Adult Ed? Ipswich Public Library?' 'You're *that* Frances?' you say, realizing this is new-girl Frances Mink, author of the *Glamourpuss* and *Reproduction* collections. 'Are you feeling better?' you say. 'I've got to get out of here,' she says. 'These things always like this?' 'Without fail,' you say. 'Can you do me a favour?' she says. 'Can you walk out with me? Ferdie Paget's been hanging around me all night.'

Ferdie Paget, known to the Resistance as Hieronymus-Ponce. Semi-Poet. Assistant editor for the poetry list of the publishers Dewsenbury and Madge. Posh as gout and descendent of William the Conqueror, but you've seen him read his mechanically recovered frankenverse in a fake *Oirish* accent. Mother on the board of Dewsenbury and Madge. Father is books editor of a Sunday paper. Has trust fund. Connected and protected. Will never be found out.

'That's not very good, is it?' you say. 'I do have some proper wine back at my flat,' she says, 'as you obviously need bribing.' You realize that she really does have stunningly cool Jazz Age hair. You will either: bottle it and leave her wide-open to the advances of Hieronymus-Ponce (turn to **47**) or say, 'No, hey, seriously, no problem.' Saunter behind her through the spliff-smoky kitchen and red-lit dungeon of the lounge, ignoring the cobra-like eyes of Ferdie Paget and the unhappy muttering of The Plum (turn to **6**).

Realize that one of the Labours of Hercules should have been moving 450 crates of books, CDs, DVDs and videos, plus suitcases, computer equipment and your huge box of unsold manuscripts from your garret into hers. When it is done, sit about on the piles together and drink champagne out of mugs. Look at the nicotine-stained iMac set-up next to her PC, and imagine that from now on you are going to be in it together. You are going to be like Raymond Carver and Tess Gallagher. Together, you are a lot more marketable. Have no inkling that it's going to be more like the union of a third rate F.Scott

Fitzgerald and a marginally less mental Zelda who can actually write a constrained sentence.

She Zeldaerates so suddenly, you can't acclimatize. You want to get up and write in the mornings, as you usually do, but she doesn't, she likes to stay in bed and write in the afternoons. If you get up to write, she says you don't love her and sits behind you in her dressing gown, smoking and griping until you end up getting dressed and going out. When you stop your morning rituals, and try to write in the evenings, she wants you to read all her work and spend all night talking about it. She accuses you of leaving the room as soon as she enters, when you can't remember ever doing this or wanting to. She sometimes spends whole days lying on her back not saying anything. She will say, 'let's spend some time together,' and then spends hours on the phone to people called Blooper Moment in Copenhagen and Viscous Dresssense in Thessaloniki while you sit there thinking that you could be writing. She throws a strop if you ever mention any other woman you have ever known, yet expects you to understand every nuance and fault-line of every one of her past relationships. You find books by the scary man-hating poet, Nest Darkle with bits unlined and annotations that dissect you and your behaviour. You will either: say that you can't live with her, try to stay friends and move out (turn to **23**), realize that you must be more considerate and change your behaviour (turn to **8**), or assume this is just teething trouble, talk your arse off and stick it out for a bit (turn to **19**).

28

Pryce Carcrash now wants to reinvent you as Arnoldia Bumrapia, who was born in 1993 in Bangui in the Central African Republic but escaped to London where she worked as a mudlark and a chimney sweep before becoming the youngest ever editor of *Heat* magazine.

You will either: tell him to fuck off (turn to **3**), or agree. Marketing people always know best and know what the people want (turn to **42**).

Wait a year; fail to sell your novel, then return to **1**.

End up freezing your nuts off in Hugo Cornwallis's Shoreditch office. *The Best Man*, your work-in-progress, sits on the desk. You are perturbed that his eyes point in different directions and seem unable to focus on the manuscript. After he's photographed you from several angles, made you go out and buy new clothes and measured every part of your body with tape, he says you're just about good-looking enough for a jacket photo but you're still a little short to be a stormtrooper. Listen to lots of stuff about how your writing is compelling and you are a tiptop ladlit author and should be on 3-for-2 tables. Find this bemusing, as it's the opposite of what you're about, but you know that Hugo is a marketing person and can only grasp a concept if it is the same as another. Then he says that he doesn't like your name and you need something more hip and blokeish. He writes CHARLIE BRICK on a piece of paper and says, 'this is you now, this is your identity.' After this, he says that there's no way that we can have your title for the book and they will want a pop song in the title. He suggests *Take My Breath Away*. You remind him that your principle male character is asthmatic and this might look a tad insensitive. He suggests *The Final Countdown*. You parry with *Rock Lobster* and ask him to turn the heating on. Thankfully, he gives up this tack and says that what they want now are three words pushed together, like *Deadkidsongs* and *Number9dream*, but he doesn't like your suggested *Braziertoiletduckliver* or *Artichokeflapsgasket*, and assertively says that it must have the name of a famous person in the title, like *Elvis Has Left the Building* or *Goodbye Johnny Thunders*. That's what they want and they are the market. They are the market and they get what they want. You finally agree on *The Mid-Beckham Cuckoos* and battered down by hypothermia you agree to sign with him. 'Thank you, Charlie,' he says. 'When I sell this I can buy myself a new kitchen' (turn to **18**).

31

'Bloody hell,' she says, and then reaches for her handbag, draws out a business card and hands it to you. It reads: **Lisa Levankranz, Editor,** and lists priceless phone numbers and e-mail addresses. Be casual about it. 'I'll send you some stuff.' Pour her some more water and fuss about how she's feeling until you help her back to the sofa and leave before anyone notices (turn to **44**)

32

You carry on with your tête-à-têtes, but the actual teaching starts to become difficult. She is there, looking up at you admiringly, lustfully as you write quotations and diagrams on the board; and as you pace about the room reading out short stories like *How to be An Other Woman* by Lorrie Moore and *Bullet in the Brain* by Tobias Wolff; and as you sit there brooding on the night before as the others do their exercises. And the others, this multinational gang, they all know. They know not because you've been caught or boasted, but because *she* has told them. You know this because the girl from Argentina asked you if you were 'geeving the pork' to the girl who always sits at the front with eyes on stalks and you had to deny it.

You are now compromised.

You ask Jacinta if she's been indiscreet. She gets upset with you. You try to cool it and suggest a hiatus until the course is over. She gets angry. You keep on seeing her and feel desperately in love with her. Or, at least, you believe that if this were to end and life returned to the default setting of grey ashtray light and hammerhead silence of the garret you would not be able to cope.

You will decide to either: take control and end it while no one's been hurt (turn to **47**), or insist that because you are a writer you construct your own moral universe (turn to **14**).

33

The woman shuffles around to sit with her back to the bath and her legs splayed. You realize who she is.

1-2 (turn to **25**)

3-4 (turn to **11**)

5-6 (turn to **7**)

34

Wash up on the shore of the Isle of Shame. Quit your position. Go home and return home to that job as call centre manager that's always been kept warm for you. Stop writing. End of game.

35

Things coast. She's not the same, becomes removed and distant. Things fizzle out. You hope, flounder, sink and wait for her to end it. When she does, feel crap, then:

Roll Dice:

1-2 (turn to **17**)

3-4 (turn to **43**)

5-6 (turn to **29**)

36

Sit around all day trying to write, distracted by memories of her face in the red bathroom light. Dither about whether to stand her up or not. When the time comes, walk to the pub with coattails flapping. You sit at the bar while you wait, scanning around, worried that someone gossipy and competitive from the Department has caught you at it. The Plum has spies everywhere. It's like Saddam's Iraq. One fifth of the student body is watching the other four and relaying back information to the Orgsburo.

When Jacinta arrives, she is jittery as she tells you that the worst thing about studying here is that she misses her Jack

Russell, Becks. Very quickly, she gets out her story, a story written in biro on two sheets of foolscap. It's now called *The Crab-Owl*. There is a girl called Jennifer (all the girls in the girls' stories are called Jennifer). There's an initial concrete campus setting that's eerily familiar (and which appears in almost all of the undergraduates' stories and either serves as a backdrop to spree-killings or diatribes about the retarded behaviour of ex boy or girlfriends). There's a dishy writing tutor who lives in a cottage and has a cat called Posh and who invites Jennifer to see him for no apparent reason. You read this without feeling, undertaking a discreet fumigation and crossing out extraneous words like *moist* and *pounding*, until you reach the end, the paragraph, a quite well described and vivid paragraph in which Jennifer has a religious experience during the sixty-nine position, which is referred to as *crabbing with owl*.

You put down the paper. She is chewing her bottom lip, holding one of your cigarettes at her ear.

'This isn't the end of the story,' you say. 'It's a start.'

She starts to finger your knee. 'Can any woman get to the heart of Nathan Flack?' she says. You will either: say, 'when you're my age you won't ask twattish questions like that' (turn to **47**); or the next morning, wake up beside her, reacquainted with the warmth of the body and the semireligious rituals of the bed, yet unsettled by the Han Solo binders on the floor, the Robbie Williams poster above the bed and the framed photos of a seemingly twelve-year old girl holding up a snarling Becks whose black marble-like Cerberus-eyes drill into your soul. She is snoring. You feel like a kiddie-fiddler (turn to **4**).

37

During one of your visits, she is downcast and distracted, and then without discussing it with you, says that you are both going out for a drink with Ferdie. You will either: end the relationship; you have morals and values and don't drink with that trustafarian ponce (turn to **16**); swallow what little you have that counts as pride and agree for her sake; we can, after all, be adult about this (a phrase which neatly side-steps the fact that Hitler, Torquemada and Henry Miller were all, in fact, physiologically at least, adults) (turn to **24**).

38

Sit about in new garret, bingeing on sambuca, grappa and all sorts of wank European booze. Keep the curtains closed and listen to later Scott Walker albums and think about Treblinka. Imagine you are a superhero called Shamblesman, who fights crime by night aided by his masked sidekick Disappointment Sans Frontiers. Put on weight. Develop popularist philistine attitudes. Write porn for late-night TV by day and tricky to market romantic novel in the grey light that every morning filters through the curtains.

Roll Dice:

1-2 (turn to **17**)

3-4 (turn to **43**)

5-6 (turn to **29**)

39

Go to Hell, which turns out to be exactly the same as in the Hell Sermon in *Portrait of the Artist as a Young Man*, and stay there forever. End of game.

40

Things change utterly. Over the next few weeks, you feel continually excited. You spend every night with her, talking, cooking, analysing, joking, playing, drinking, dancing, lovemaking. In the mornings, as you walk home from her flat, you buy pastries and coffee and the weather seems to morph to suit your mood: bright and crisp and warm. She is like something you have made up, someone who has walked out of the pages of a book that you love. The phone ringing makes you buzz with anticipation as you bounce across the room to it. You start to find yourself smiling and dreaming as you sit on the bus. You find yourself on the walkway at the back of the Eudora Doon, kissing like thirteen-year olds instead of smoking and counting down the minutes. You find your life suddenly liveable. You can't write, though, the momentum of your novel slackens, and you can only produce glowing little sketches about her in your journal. After three weeks, she sits opposite you in one of those folksy restaurants in town and after she's removed the skin from her chicken with her fork, she asks you, without trepidation or nerves, 'Nathan, why don't you move in with me?' You will either: feel yourself flood into her and say, yes, yes, yes (turn to **27**) or, put the brakes on your desires, say it's too soon and feel suddenly scared as you both eat your meal in silence (**35**)

41

In the kitchen, you uncap a beer and when you turn around Jacinta stands in front of you. You kiss her and she kisses you back. You like the risky nature of this and know that she likes it too. You whisper that you love her, really, really love her. She breaks away from you. 'Get off,' she shouts. 'Get off of me. Get away from me.' 'Shhh,' you say. 'It's over,' she yells. 'I can't have sex with you anymore.' Jesus wept! You check the doorway. 'What on earth is the matter?' you say. She shrugs you off when you try to touch her arm. 'I'm not your fucking possession.'

Copperson and Plum and everyone else are now in the kitchen, staring at you both with their lemur eyes. You will either: laugh it off and say that you are just rehearsing a one-act play called *I'm not your Fucking Possession* that you've written together (turn to **9**), or run out of the room in exactly the fashion of someone with something to hide (turn to **34**).

42

Arnoldia Bumrapia is now promoting *Bitch City* on *Lit Idol* at the London Book Fair. Make a complete prick out of yourself trying to read in a twangy mixture of Sango and West London street slang whilst wearing a dress made out of dead silverfish. Get considerably less votes than Jennifer Catstrangler (author of *Wise Marrows*), Mac 'The Paddle' McMahon (author of *The Death Metal Revelations*) and eventual winner Porcupine Ninety (author of *Blind Man's Penis*). End of Game.

43

Wait six months, finish your novel, and return to **1**.

44

The following Monday, you toss off a letter to Lisa Levankranz that says how nice it was to meet her and that you hope she got home safely etc. Include chapters and synopsis but in such a way that it sounds like an afterthought. Forget about it quickly and get on with pressing business of finishing the damn thing, getting up every morning at dawn as the grey light filters through the curtains and the tapping of the keyboard disrupts the hammerhead silence of the garret. Then, in the publishing gossip section of the Saturday *Guardian* fume when you read an article about a huge advance paid to bright young talent Verisimilitude Joystick for her novel *I Married Bat-Eminem-Face*. However, notice that hot new literary agent Pryce Carcrash, who you knew vaguely at school, represents her. You will either: not bother, remembering that Carcrash once dropped his trousers in English and danced around the room singing 'new speaker, new paragraph' and had to go away to Wales for six weeks to sort himself out (turn to **3**). Or get on the phone to Carcrash straightaway. It's not what you know, but what you think you can get away with in this business (turn to **10**).

45

Given that hypocrisy does not blip on Neville's polymorphously perverse moral radar, you will lose your job and never work as a university tutor again, thus will eventually have to find full-time work and your writing will gradually peter out. End of game.

46

Text her from Liverpool Street, saying that you better leave her to it. Take the Polar Express back to The Shire. Ring her the next day and break the whole thing off diplomatically. Feel glum and defeated. Return to default setting of the grey ashtray light and the hammerhead silence of the garret as you apply yourself to finishing your novel (turn to **16**).

47

Walk home on your own under midnight-blue clouds and spitty rain, and once indoors are struck by the grey ashtray light and hammerhead silence of the garret. Go to bed and wait for the static in your head to subside. Worry about the future until you sleep.

Roll Dice:

1-2 (turn to **17**)

3-4 (turn to **43**)

5-6 (turn to **29**)

48

When she goes to the bar, Ferdie focuses his green eyes on you and then actually speaks to you, but in the tone you might use to a feral scumbag who had just asked you for a fiver to watch your BMW while you're in the bank. He says, 'So what do you do then?' This is a curious question, as he knows full well. You put on a monotone voice.

'I teach prose fiction,' you say.

'Prose fiction?' he says. 'But prose is non-fiction, surely?'

Remember this guy is a published poet and works for a major publishing company . . .

'Prose is non-metrical language, you arse.' Tense up and feel the mist swirling.

'I rilly don't have any interest in anything that you have to say,' he says, and then flicks his hand as if declining the port.

The black mist closes over you.

You will either: walk away before you disgrace yourself (turn to **46**) or engage Hieronymus Ponce in combat (turn to **5**)

49

In the lounge, Sharon Plum is ripped to her tits on booze and giggles up to you waving an absinthe bottle. You will either: one-for-the-road it and knock back a glass that's full to the brim (turn to **2**), or decline politely and leave (turn to **47**).

50

Your
Quest
Is
Over

Turn the page to discover what lies
outside of the Fumigator's garret.

The garret of the Fumigator is no more and you are now the recipient of a two-book deal and have won the hand of a very sophisticated woman called Jennifer who a year ago would have crossed the road to avoid you. You are living in a cottage by the sea and have two cats called Hieronymus and Poncey. It is a summer's afternoon. Your study has french windows that overlook a lake. The bulrushes sway out there and the dragonflies skim the surface tension of the water. Framed jackets of *The Penelope Tree* and *The Girl on the Millennium Bridge* hang on the wall. You are writing a new novel. You write the last line, breathe, feel a warmth inside and tiredness behind your eyes. A printer hums and clicks into life and she walks across the parquet towards you and starts to massage your shoulders and whispers in your ear. 'Oh my. It's the best thing you've ever written.'

No One Answered

At the fourth midnight of a four-day slog, I finished the above passage. A chasm of white cyberspace opened up beneath the final sentence. The story that had floated me vanished, the skittish clatter of the keyboard replaced only by the low hum of the computer. I saved the ms to a floppy disk and switched off the nicotine-stained iMac. From the window I stared out at the road opposite the house, at the roofs indistinguishable from the nightsky and the grinning moon. *Garret of the Fumigator* was complete. *Garret of the Fumigator* lived. *Garret of the Fumigator* would have Frederick Malone and Djemba-Djemba and Portnoy and the cunts at Mxyztplk and Wukfit flocking to my door like rats after a bloodbath.

It's a bit lugubrious, isn't it? said James O'Mailer. It's not exactly going to endear you to them, is it? Come to think of it, it's not actually very good. Tone? Unity? Significance?

Oh go away, James. This isn't literature. This isn't even entertainment. This is war.

So do you actually feel better now that you've coughed up that particular furball?

Yes. Yes, I do.

Writing is not therapy, Flack. Even you know that. Self-fumigate. Get rid of it. Burn it.

Burn my computer?

Well, do whatever you have to do to the infernal machine.

James, go and seduce Anais Nin or Claire Claremont or whatever it is you do when you're not hectoring me.

I'm always here, Nathan, you know that. I don't actually go anywhere. Where would you be without me to aim at, eh? Ever thought about that?

Shhh.

Ahead of me, outside in the moonlit street, shambling along the middle of the road between the parked cars, coming at me in a straight line was a figure, stout, dark, hooded, I couldn't tell if a man or a woman. As it came closer, the sou'wester glinted in the moonshine. Something swept over me, panic, anger, and for a moment the floor seemed to curve up and over like a great wheel that looped me across the ceiling and back down again to where I was standing at the window watching the thing approach me.

Out of the flat, down the stairs, through the hall I ran, out of the door and into the street. I staggered to a stop on the pavement. The damp breezed hit my face. The houses that seconds ago I'd peered down on now seemed like giant monuments aloof and dispassionate above me. A car slunk past; its engine purring. Up ahead, up the side-road, nothing, no one, nobody.

'Where are you then? Show yourself. Show your face. C'mon.' My shout echoed in the night air. 'And where is she, and where's my starfish?'[34]

No one answered. I stood there for a long time and still no one answered. Back inside I sat for a while staring at the Artex. I made a reasonable decision to write a letter of approach to Fred Malone and parcelled up *The Garret of the Fumigator* for his approval. I would post it the next day. It didn't matter though, for in the morning I finally had news.

---

[34] **James O'Mailer**: I interject here because I can, dear reader. As you can see, my hold over Flack has intensified and I can now colonize not just his thoughts but now even the formal components of his text. On the other hand, as fifth business and something of a conscience here, it would be irresponsible, and perhaps unkind of me not to draw your attention to the fact that here in the street, at the witching hour, as self-pity, paranoia and angst overcome him, something horrible is happening to Nathan Flack. Unless he finally accepts my reality, this will only get a lot worse.

Plot

Two Planets Crashing Together

Never do what I did back there. Never raise the reader's expectation that something significant is about to happen and then deflate that expectation for no good reason. This causes a slackening of tension and a stalling of the forward drive of the narrative. On the day after I finished *Garret of the Fumigator* I did not, as I might have led you to expect, receive any approach from any literary agent about *The Penelope Tree*. I did, however, get a phone call from (One Foot in the) Dave Cave, my old university friend, both of us confiding to each other back then that we both wanted to write as much as read and whose short story collection *Swapping Amy* I had edited way back in the mists of the 1990s. One Foot invited me to read at London's *Moonshot* short story event that he was now organizing.

Of course, I accepted. I needed to get away from the grey ashtray light and hammerhead silence of the garret and James O'Mailer, *The Grasp of Fear* and fretting about the still-missing Frances and my starfish. That coming Friday I would take the Polar Express, deliver some prose, catch up with some people and hit the bars of the Arctic. Never, though, do what I am about to do here in the classroom. Never tell the Folder-Holders what you are up to.

The clock had just hit five to nine. I'd lost the plot. Or at least, I'd failed completely to explain to the group the first principles of plot and

163

plotting. Theories of cause and effect; high stakes; beginning, middle and end; trigger, conflict, crisis, resolution; problems of compression and decompression; the categories of archplot, minimal plot and non-plot, my insistence on escalation and tension and pace and my examples of *Dr. No*, *They're Not Your Husband* by Raymond Carver and *Watt* by Beckett seemed to at best to confuse the class and at worst make them angry.

As soon as I'd mentioned a need for structure, Erika heaved the Gretschbags to the back of the class, pulled her chair to the wall and folded her arms to her chin. Reg turned a thrasher's crimson, shouting at me that life didn't need tension. What we need is less tension, not more tension, and if you write about what you *know* and you've been a good Christian, you should have banished tension from your life. Peace, peace, peace, that's what we want. He was wearing a 'Keep the Pound' badge on his lapel. I refrained from saying that the story of Our Lord's sacrifice contains a degree of conflict and tension.

Jane looked baffled and kept fiddling with her cerise pashmina, drawing it down over her bare shoulders and screwing it up at her waist. Frank said plot sounded too hard and he wasn't going to do it. Cynthia turned the colour of pumice and then the whole last half-hour degenerated into Mac insisting that you could write a story without any conflict at all.

'Of course you can,' he said, wiping his wrist across his chin as if about to gee up his stallion before charging down at an oblivious Indian encampment. 'I keep saying, you don't need all this bollocks to write.'

Given the state of *The Grasp of Fear*, of which I'd tried to make some sense during the previous three days, I think I was justified in insisting that you did need at least a semblance of this bollocks.

'OK,' I said. 'Give me an example of a story without conflict?'

'An alien put on trial for being a Muslim?' said Mac.

'Man versus society,' I said.

'It's not a man if it's an alien, is it?'

'Formally, yes, it is.'

'A bloke, right, probably a rockstar, maybe a roadie, falls in a dirty great hole in the road.'

'That's a very basic plot outline. Man falls in hole and climbs out again. Vonnegut wrote an essay about it.'

'Van Der Graf who?'

'It's man versus nature. Or man versus self. Trigger, conflict, crisis, resolution.'

'What if he doesn't climb out, eh, eh?'

'Then it's a disillusionment plot, but it's still a plot.'

The spark of inspiration fired through him. He raised his arms; his fists clenched as if he'd just plucked the last chord of an especially punishing riff.

'Two per-lanets crashing together!'

I dipped my head. The universe wobbled and time froze. We tumbled into a vacuum. We contemplated the void. I was slumped over my desk trying to avoid anything like eye contact with any of them. Reg rubbed his forehead in despair. Cynthia was now cross-legged on her chair and collapsing into a foetal position. Jane pulled her pashmina over her shoulder.

'Isn't that an event?' she said.

'Thank you,' I said. 'It's an event, Mac, not a plotline.'

On this showing, the point of view class was going to be as relaxing as the Tet Offensive.

I made some attempt to sum-up and conceded that there was a lot to think about, rattled off an exercise (character, suitcase, train station, what happens next? banning guns, drugs and bodies for content of suitcase, much to Frank's disappointment). I then walked around the room handing out forms and schedules for the residential weekend, an odyssey that took me right to the back of the class and the lair of the Gretsch.

'Do you have my starfish?' I said.

'Oh no, I do not, I am sorry, sorry. It is still in my wee-wee house.'

'Next week,' I said. 'Or else.' I walked away before I said anything about her creeping around outside my building and Frances's flat and what trouble she may well have caused.

Back at the front of the class, I perched on the desk, and asked if anyone had anything that they wanted to say.

Jane shifted on her chair and uncrossed her legs.

'What are you doing at the weekend?' she said.

Frank turned to her and then gave me a look that seemed to suggest a raised clawhammer poised over his shoulder.

'Pardon?' I said.

'Are you out and about?' she said. 'Or are you staying in and doing . . .' She typed the air and her voice went up several octaves until it became a squeak. ' . . . a little bit of *writing*?'

165

'Er, no,' I said. 'I'm going away. To London. Doing a reading Friday night.'

'Oh how marvellous,' she said.

'Marvellous, marvellous,' said Reg.

'Rock 'n' roll,' said Mac. 'Where's it at?'

'Morleys,' I said. 'Charing Cross Road.'

'Never heard of it,' said Mac.

'It's meant to be the biggest bookshop in the world,' I said, noticing that Erika was leaving the room.

'Hey!' Jane bounced on her seat and clapped her hands. 'Why don't we all come with you!'

'I can drive, if you like,' said Frank, his body facing me but his head turned to Jane. 'Me van's roomy.'

'Oh fiddlesticks,' she said. 'I've got the Chorus coming over.'

'It's a long way everyone,' I said. 'Seriously. I wouldn't want anyone to put themselves out.'

'Well, we do all wish you the best of British,' said Reg.

'Thank you very much. Now let's call this a night.'

I hung my head to appear as unapproachable as possible. Chairs scuffed, papers rustled and footsteps receded. When I looked up, only Reg and Cynthia had actually left. Doctor Jane was still standing in front of her chair, her hands clasped across her waist, her bag slung over her shoulder. Her eyes were glistening in the striplights and she rubbed her chin back and forth across the hem of her pashmina. I smiled back at her, but for the life of me I didn't want to be waylaid by a new version of *Formula One*, or asked out for a drink and then if I needed a chaperone for Friday. I had business still to conduct here.

Frank was standing stock-still and gigantic, his arms hanging at his sides. He rotated his head from me to Jane and back again as if I was his reanimator and she the bride I'd promised him. She realized this and her face whitened. She waved at me as she left and picked up a fair pace by the time she'd reached the door, leaving Frank to lumber after her.

'See you, me lovers,' he called back at us.

Mac pointed his thumb over his shoulder. 'Hey, great guy,'

'A wonderful man,' I said. I heaved the paper-stuffed carrier bag from under the desk and placed it on the surface. 'Do you have my cheque?'

He put his hand inside his black suit jacket and drew out an envelope.

'Here.' He flicked it at me. I opened the envelope and checked the amount. Yep, no garret-to-gutter freefall for me now. Two more months to sell *Penelope*.

I drew a packed A3 envelope from the carrier bag and tossed it to him. It was my report, twelve pages of comment, instruction and suggestions and, as an extra service, the product of so much guilt at the size of the fee I'd demanded, a one hundred page synopsis for a possible rewrite. He fingered open the envelope, drew out the report and stared at the first sheet. His face darkened and his frame quivered as he slapped the document to his thigh.

'Nate, the first line here is " this novel is unpublishable, Mac'.'

'Well, I've tried to sort that out for you,' I said. 'But you're going to have to rewrite it thoroughly and carefully.'

'But I don't want to.'

'Read the report first. And look at the annotations. Read through my thoughts on what you *could* do here.'

'But . . .'

'It's not unusual, Mac. Remember what Hemingway said. The first draft is always shit. You've found a story. Now you have to write it. Just follow my instructions.'

'You want me to change the title?'

'No. I *insist* that you change the title. I've suggested a new one.' I held out the carrier bag to him. As he took it from me, my soul returned to my body, the light rose, birdsong erupted in my head. Mac looked like he had a lot of shouting at me to do. He collected his other bags and stuffed the report under his arm.

'Thanks, Nate.'

'My pleasure.'

'Oh Nate. Looked you up on Google. You wrote that story, *Boys* that won that prize thingy, didn't you?'

'Yes, I did.'

'I read that. Didn't like it much. Couldn't get into it. Too much description, and too much thinking. I thought you should know that.'

He waddled out of the room. I stayed put, kicking my heels to give him a nice long headstart. My temples throbbed.

When you mentioned Ernest back there, you should have said Hills Like White Elephants' Dung, said James O'Mailer. It would have been hilarious.

167

Yes, James, it would have been really, really funny. The world would have laughed up its spleen[35].

---

[35] **James O'Mailer**: I return. See it wasn't a one-off, dear reader. Let's take a step-back from this moment of uncomfortable pathos and indulge in a little flash-forward. Flack may have taken the shilling here and got off with no more than a cuss. Little does he know that, like the young baleful Jews one used to meet in the coffeehouses of Jerusalem and Brooklyn in the early fifties who over their card games and cheroots would ask themselves what they would have done if they had been there on January 31st 1933 and been blessed, like I am with the gift of precognition, would they have fired the silver bullet at Adolf, in future years many a moral and philosophical fellow will speculate whether in Flack's position they would, at this moment, have saved the world and assassinated the Fat Drummer Who Beats His Meat With All His Heart. This is at the core of my concern. This has a bearing on my being compelled at this time to finally make myself apparent to our boy Flack, my jail, my hermitage of exile this last thirty-five years. The stakes are high. If only Flack would realize this. If only I could explain forthrightly. But such a straightforward path would put both Flack and me in grave danger should they know my powers do return, and more so, do you think, dear reader, that this Flack would believe me in any case? He may well need to see to believe. Anon. Exit O'Mailer.

The Polar Express

Late Friday afternoon and I was finally sitting in an empty carriage as the Polar Express shuddered its way southwards towards The Arctic. Arranged on the table were my paperback, my mobile, my Discman, my pack of index cards and a copy of *Lesser Lights*, the story I would read at *Moonshot*. Outside, a powdery November dusk turned the outskirts of Norwich to mounds of soot and slag. The carriage was cold and for the first time that winter I was wearing my black coat. Winter was coming. The weathermen had forecast unseasonal pre-Christmas snows and a vicious cold snap in the next few weeks. Just what you need to add glamour and spice to the garret lifestyle. Soon it would be too cold to rouse myself from bed or sit still for long enough to write a sensible sentence whether I possessed the starfish or not.

Travelling back from The Shire to The Arctic always made me feel like the last-hope hero sent into the future to procure the cure for cowpox. I plugged in my headphones and found the *End Theme* on Vangelis's *Blade Runner* soundtrack, the perfect accompaniment to hurtling through Stowmarket and Diss. Despite the barrage of programmed kettledrums and the gliding synths, I still managed to hear the door behind me shush open. No one came in, though. No one was there. I still had the carriage to myself and picked up my book and opened it.

Super-Cannes by Juicy Gash. I was about halfway through and although there's nothing I love more than an immersion in the peculiar and unsettling world of Juicy Gash, I was having trouble concentrating on this one. It annoyed me that I couldn't help noticing that 'tail lights' had so far been constructed in three different ways ('tail lights', 'tail-lights' and 'taillights').[36] I read a couple of pages about a middle-aged man in a knee-brace ejaculating up and down the Côte D'Azur and then put the book down. The door shushed again, but no one came in. Through my headphones, Rutger Hauer intoned about tears in rain and attack-ships on fire on the shoulder of Orion while I worried about tail lights and stared at the zebra-print dress on the cover of *Super Cannes* by Juicy Gash.

It was never going to be the same again for Juicy and me. I was never going to be eighteen again and lying in the grass reading *Crash,* using the book to block out the sun. The shock of it, the challenge of this cruel story of machinery and celebrity and middle-aged men in surgical supports ejaculating up and down the Westway. Reading would never be like that again, never the same as it was when those first blasts struck me in my late teens and early twenties. Reading would never be so crucial and exciting and transformative.

I would never repeat that afternoon in a youth hostel in Innsbruck when the rain kept me indoors and I lay on my bunk with the mountains visible outside and read *The New York Trilogy* by Paul Auster cover to cover. Afterwards, as I walked in the drizzle my eyes readjusted and I became suddenly aware of the crosscurrents and histories and what-ifs and chance encounters swarming around me.

Paul Auster. He's got me into lots of trouble as well, just as much as Juicy Gash. Never again would I have that feeling when I'd just started to touch the starfish and was living with Johanna in the south Arctic, and on reading in *The Invention of Solitude* Auster's account of his life as a starving, freezing, friendless, struggling writer, thirty-five years old and just returned from France, living in a bleak garret on the tenth floor of a semi-converted office on Varick Street, Manhattan[37], and I, with ten thousand words of *The Drowners* written out in longhand and kept away from her, I thought: that is not going to happen to me. I am going to be a success. And hey . . . Auster makes the fight seem so heroic. Now I was thirty-five and futureless and had clanking pipes and poor heating and ghosts and I

---

[36] We seem to have gone beyond a situation where editors no longer edit and into one where editors can't be bothered to use a grammar checker.

[37] **The Invention of Solitude** by Paul Auster (Faber and Faber, 1988) pages 76-79.

was never going to have that moment again when an account of such a condition would seem so darkly alluring, so mythic, so me.

You lose an innocence with reading. I was never going to have again that morning in the summer term of my first year at Oxford, when I woke up with Johanna – we had not been together long – and the sunbeam through the window had warmed the duvet and she slid out of bed and wearing just a white T-shirt shambled to the stereo and put on *Heaven or Las Vegas* by the Cocteau Twins and came back to bed and she lay there listening as I finished *The Great Gatsby* and lingered over each word of the last page, reading and rereading each paragraph three or four times, fired by admiration and terror and wonder[38]. But the impact

---

[38] **James O'Mailer:** As you can see, dear reader, just as Flack is starting to carp and caterwaul, I return. You need to make a choice here. You need to decide whose side you are on. Are you on the side of **_GREATNESS_**, or are you on the side of 'tricky to market'? You can stay on the train with the purple snow of Flack's reminiscences, or you can come with me. Flack may well, in his account of his lie-in provide a vivid *mise en scène*, but you were not there, you didn't have to sit through all this, you didn't have to float in the ether waiting for Flack to get his head out of Scotty's fairytale and around to the lithe and gentle flower at his side, who, if I remember correctly, had quite astounding breasts, rather like those of my old flame Jane Austen. Let me tell you about Jane and O'Mailer, one of the greatest love stories never told. Jane Austen? What would we know of Jane Austen had she not in 1804 at first sight fallen for one James O'Mailer, a time-travelling roué, demigod and legendary philanderer masquerading as a dashing and genial clergyman, an experience that informed her later ability to describe and dramatize the condition of falling in love and the frustration of such urges so exquisitely, and therefore we may well ask ourselves what of the English novel had I stuck around and, as she begged me to in letters later burned by the Austen family in their efforts to create a hagiography, married the poor old maid? Let me now tell you a more satisfying and thrilling tale than even Flack's of his idling that morning as the clock of St Anthony's struck ten and the girl beside him thought brazen and intense thoughts. After Jane, though a long time before Barbara, though to me, who could once be at any time any time I liked, these things were close together with what I am to tell of now the meat in the sandwich, so to speak (more of Barbara Aple a little later, promise), I, accompanied by my faithful valet, Dante, transported myself across the Continent, to Cluj in Transylvania. Soldiers had occupied the town and we, Dante and I found ourselves trapped in the encircled Church of Saint Stephanie the Jug Maker and de facto protectors of some seven hundred of the county's womenfolk. As the clock struck three, and it was a much more ominous and resounding bell than the clapped-out clapper of St Anthony's, Oxford, finally I ventured forth from the church and met what appeared to be an army soused in firelight and drunk on savage intention. The Captain – who wanted access to the aforementioned and by now frightened and hysterical womenfolk – and I debated on the threshold a while and for some time a game of philosophical chess occurred, he attacking, I parrying, all of Civilization at stake upon the chequered board, all history before and forever after lined up in our ranks and our files, but after some time, I quoted to him Horace's lines that *Force, unaided by judgement, collapses through its own weight*, and by sunrise his troops had put down their weapons and drifted back to their harvests. I returned to the church and the manifest gratitude of the seven hundred. Locally, the town is now referred to as Clujames in my honour and the

softens. The charge fades somewhere around the age of twenty-five. During the last ten years I've not been swayed again like I was by the Camus and Sartre novels I used to read on the train to work when I first moved back to The Arctic. I'm never again going to be so beholden to a passage as I was when I first encountered the murder sequence in *Crime and Punishment* or the 'Snow' chapter in *The Magic Mountain*. I've not wandered into a shop and picked up a novel like *The Ghost Writer* by Philip Roth, or *Seize the Day* by Saul Bellow, and been so rapt in the first lines that I had to buy the book straightaway and hide in the toilet at work to read at high speed. I will never experience that impact again. It's a pity. It's a shame. It's terrible. It's why we write.

The door shushed. I looked around. No one there.

We pulled into Ipswich and a flashback of the Ipswich Group of Death made me shudder. Still, they were less of a hassle than the present bunch. At least they kept themselves to themselves. As the train carried on I fixated on the black smears of the landscape and the grids of streetlights and the business parks. It hit me that my aversion to reading *Super-Cannes* was due to spending the best part of three days on *The Grasp of Fear*.

The Grasp of Fear. I'd seen some incompetent and juvenile novels in my time, but this was a bottom-scraper that found depths of prurience and crassness that made *The Truncheons of Humber Vice* seem like *Middlemarch*. The only book I can remember that failed to inspire to this degree was Sharon Plum, writing as Nicola Hemsby's memoir of her adolescent obsession with netball, *Fever Bitch*. Mac possessed only a rudimentary sense of grammar and syntax and couldn't spell (one sentence came out as *Zanes shag was a little bazaar*). There wasn't a single active sentence and the whole story was written in a sort of blank reportage, with no pace to the phrasing or vocal texture. The plot was predicated on an attempt by Satan to replace all of the world's heavy rock musicians with zombie fleshgobblers who then insert hypnotizing kill-kill messages into the songs. This was designed to provoke a mass bloodbath at the climactic

---

motherland cheekily as Omailermania. Strangely, a year hence, seven hundred baby boys were born with the distinct O'Mailer strong jaw and clever eyes coagulating in their as yet inchoate features. Now, that's a story! Much better that Flack's of the lying in the same bed with the same girl and still with his head in a novel rather than satiating the poor dear's desires and wants and inscrutable inconsistencies. All this, of course, Sweet Jane and The Seduced of Cluj and much more besides I could show him, but should I be forced to I worry now that we will have reached the darkest hour.

Ruinerfest open-air concert in Coventry, where the brainwashed rock-kids would go berserk, slaughtering all and sundry before descending on Birmingham to turn it into one great shrine to Beelzebub. Only Zane Champ can save humanity, but only if he stops drinking and screwing for long enough to take the Apocalypse seriously.

And there was a lot of screwing. At one point, Zane has realized that Satan is going to make a move on his idols Ruiner and decides to tell the FBI. Mac describes in over eighty pages of sub-*Razzle* prose the fourteen orgasms experienced by Zane with bureau chief Fansi Fonda. *She worshipped at his whopping great crotch. She realized that all she had known before was boys but Zane Champ was a man, a proper hairy rock god of a man with massive pipe of a dong and she would never cum like this ever again, not even on birthdays and at Christmas.* I'm pretty sure that had a pack of zombie fleshgobblers, formerly members of the band Mötley Crüe not stormed the Pizza Hut where this beautiful tryst was unfolding, the *strokes* and *humps* and *moans of pleasure* would have continued until all the trees in the world had been felled for Mac's paper.

Reading *The Grasp* took me about a day. It was a straightforward job to write up why it was a little underwhelming (i.e., bollocks, the sort of novel that I hated: occult conspiracies; only one everyman can save the world[39], and a mediaeval fantasy battle at the end etc.). But the size of the fee I'd charged worried me and I didn't want it to appear that I'd just taken the money and tossed off a dismissive crit. I decided that I would write him an alternative plot plan, a sort of treatment that he could use as a guide to a rewrite. This would be a good exercise for me. *The Grasp of Fear* was supposed to be a horror/thriller. Let's see if I could make it so. I took the premise and extrapolated a much more restrained story, and then merely wrote out very basic paragraphs for the suggested new plot sequences. All of the sex scenes were removed to save Mac his dignity. This streamlined the narrative, so at least it kept moving and made the most of the premise. I suggested that Zane Champ ought to defeat Satan by his own courage and ingenuity at the dénouement, and not have him torn apart by

---

[39] The thing I particularly hate about this sort of story is that the Chosen One or whatever, the Hero Candidate, is always ultimately a worthy conformist. I'd be much more interested if when the Hierarchy send their minion to inform Everyman of his (or her) special, fated purpose, he (or she) just said, and meant it, 'nah, I don't want the responsibility, I want to stay in the pub and take the piss out of people.' It would also be much more interesting if the Chosen One refused and then stuck to his guns and so evil actually won out unopposed. This would not be consoling or heart-warming, but it would be sort of funny. A lot is made of questions of 'what if?' What about 'if only?'

zombie fleshgobbler versions of ZZ Top and Status Quo or have Bob Punter, Derek Strang, Lionel Feral and Mac 'The Paddle" McMahon, the original line-up of 'the classic British Heavy Metal Band' Ruiner save the day by battering the beast back to Hell with a 'massively loud performance' of their 'world famous' song 'Night of Medusa'. I also pointed out that a decision had to be made about whether the novel was set in the UK or America. At the moment it seemed to be in a mishmash place where the West Midlands was contiguous with the West Coast. I changed Fansi's name to Frankie Fonda and I changed that title. Initially I toyed with *Spinal Crap*, but in the end I plumped for *The Death Metal Revelations*.

This new plot plan was nearly a hundred pages long, but it was written in note form and the sentences double-spaced. It wasn't exactly a dense text. All this work was just an exercise to me, something to make it look like I'd earned his money.

By my reckoning, it would take Mac about four years and ten drafts to get the novel into a state where an unpaid individual could actually read it. I doubted he had the stamina or talent for this work. But I had done my bit and not short-changed him. I just wished it hadn't turned my head to sludge.

The door shushed again. I looked around. No one there. Everything was malfunctioning. In my bag I found *Lesser Lights* and started to read and reread it as the train journey continued. When in doubt, read your own crap. After all, no one else will. I would have to read aloud soon, but beforehand I had a little matter of meeting up with my mentor[40].

---

[40] **James O'Mailer**: Pity the Nathan, dear reader.

The Manticore

The two men on the table alongside us shared with the whole restaurant a loud and bombastic war story about how the skinny, smiley-faced one hadn't budged until he'd sold a hundred units. It was a score, a hit, a tickle, a pinch, a ree*sssssult, mate!* Forty-five minutes had passed since my arrival in the Arctic and I was sitting in The Manticore, a post-war-austerity-themed Italian restaurant in Bateman Street and one of Sebastian Harker's[41] favourite Soho haunts. The Manticore hadn't changed at all since we used to come here in the mid-90s. The same old jaundiced reproductions of Francis Bacon and Kandinsky paintings hung around the turquoise walls. The same faded plastic tulips drooped from the same urn-shaped vases on the wood-effect tabletops. The same shagged-out Billie Holiday and Patsy Cline records crackled in the background. Up and down the aisles the same blobs of pink tissue paper balanced out the legs of the tables. At the end of one such aisle we were sat in the window, trying to ignore the conversation beside us and watching the shadows that shambled past footsore and exhausted at the end of the working week.

---

[41] **James O'Mailer:** Zounds, not this mountebank . . .

175

'Look at those poor souls,' said Sebastian. 'Don't even know they're alive.'

Sebastian Harker: novelist, rabble-rouser and throwback[42], and, with Frances still AWOL, the only person left in the world who still believed in me.

He wore a black suit, the fins of a wide white shirt collar sharp at his neck, his hair cropped and greying now, his jaw oblong and his eyes glinting as if somewhere to our left was a flickering firelight that crept across his face. He had the appearance of an old blade of the physical theatre, or an East End gangster grown respectable in the age of PR.

'Fucking idiots,' he said. 'The world is owned by idiots. At every level. Anyone who wears a suit should be shot.'

Alongside us, the thin smiley-face stopped his crowing. He wore a navy blue pinstriped suit and a tie with Betty Boop motifs. A shapeless gunmetal-grey suit festooned his colleague, a fat man with Himmler-like spectacles lodged on a nose runny with sheen in The Manticore's over-bright lights. Himmler-Glasses flicked the stem of his wineglass and tapped his foot. Meanwhile, Smiley squeaked his finger around the rim of his glass, his eyes downcast, as if waiting for something procedural to happen. So was I, until the pause blew out and they both turned away from us.

'Seb,' I said. 'You're wearing a suit. You always wear a suit.'

'It's ironic,' he said. "It's a time of irony, or so they will insist on telling me. Here's to the single entendre. Good to see you, old son, it is.'

---

[42] *The Oxford Companion to English Literature* lists Sebastian as: **HARKER,** *Sebastian Knelms (1948 -), novelist and critic, born in Aden, Yeman, the son of an army officer; he returned to England in 1956 and after attending a series of minor public schools and Keble College, Oxford, he travelled widely, living in West Berlin, Reykjavik and New York, before returning to England in 1975. Although he started to publish fiction quite young (his first collection of stories,* The Barbara Ape and Other Stories *appeared in 1976) his work made little impact for some years. He was first recognized as a critic who frequently stood against the fashions, preoccupations and more particularly the personnel of London's literary scene in the 1970s (a collection of reviews and essays* If Only They Had One Neck *appeared in 1978). His first novel of interest,* The Hydra's Heads *(1979), heavily influenced by *Evelyn Waugh and *John Webster, is a revenger's tale set in a Soho peopled by undeservedly acclaimed trustafarian poets, second-rate literary celebrities and 'industry hacks on the make', intended, in the author's own words, as a 'pitiless charcoal sketch of moral etiolation.' Harker achieved notice with the publication of* The Chimera *(1982); a stark retelling of *Tom Brown's Schooldays *set in an austere English public school with a vicious prefect regime of feted poets. Subsequent novels have included* The Wintering *(1985),* Bards of Passion and Girth, *(1987),* Cease Thy Prattling *(1992),* Snow on Parnassus *(1997) and most recently* Kill Cyclops *(2005) an unsettling modern fable in which a brutal dictatorship is established by a group of talentless yet connected young poets and artists.*

176

He lifted his glass and duffed his wine, nimbly refilling it before magicking a jiffy bag from under the table. 'You'll never guess what the bastards have done now.' He tossed me the packet.

'Which bastards?' I said.

'Dewsenbury and Madge.'

Himmler and Smiley again paused and looked pointedly at us until Seb stared their faces back to their drinks.

I reached into the jiffy and produced a softcover book. It was the new paperback edition of Sebastian's *Kill Cyclops*. The overall colour scheme was a honey yellow, the title embossed and golden and surrounded by a swarm of amber dots and dashes and cute little butterflies. Beneath it was an image of a full-length twentysomething blonde in a strapless yellow minidress and a Cheddar Gorge of a cleavage. Impossibly smooth and toned legs tapered down to high-heeled, open-toed sandals and she held a laptop bag in one hand and a latte in the other. Well, if a novel isn't past/abroad/celebrity, it has to have a sexy bird on the cover. The novel may well be set in a Mount Athos monastery, or in some future dystopia where all the women in the world have been packed off to Mars, but there still has to be a sexy bird on the cover. If *Lord of the Flies* were published today, it would have a sexy bird on the cover. *The Naked and the Dead*: sexy bird on the cover. *The Golden Notebook*: sexy bird on the cover.

'That petal-head is not in my novel,' said Seb. 'No one remotely like that is in my novel. What sort of message does that give out?'

'Sure they're not trying to be too subtle?' I said.

He gave me a disparaging look and swigged his wine. 'You can have that,' he said. 'I'm halving my sales, but you can have it.'

Himmler leaned over and grabbed the edge of our table.

'Hey you,' he said. 'You're that writer, aren't you?'

Sebastian smiled and jabbed his thumb at me. 'No. He is.'

'Oh, right.' Himmler now turned his attention to me. 'What've you done then, mate?'

'I'm not a writer. I'm a teacher,' I said, the hack's standard response to ward off *The* Question One.

'He's too modest,' said Seb. 'This is The Voice, gentlemen. The most engaging young writer I've ever met. Remember his name! This is none other than Nathan Flack!'

'Never heard of you,' said Smiley as he shuffled around on his seat to face us. 'Who's your publisher?'

'He's a wind-up merchant,' I said. 'He's the writer.' My hand went cold as I waved to attract the waitress.

'So what's your favourite book?' said Himmler.

'What's yours?' snapped Seb.

Himmler stroked his lips with one hand and drummed the table with the other. '*The Da Vinci Code* is a corker.'

Seb straightened up. 'My sympathies.'

'Sold five million copies,' said Himmler.

'You're impressed,' he said, 'that there are five million idiots in this country born without the ability to discriminate?'

'There's just something about it,' said Himmler, 'that makes you want to keep turning those pages. I wish . . .'

'What? Nosebleed-inducing, subnormal prose and a plotline cribbed without cunning from a discredited and stupid conspiracy theory that's been in the public domain for thirty years. That's genius, that is. Pure class.'

'Lots of people like it.'

'"To be accessible to the people, it doesn't matter what a few crazy intellectuals still think. The weight of affirmation of millions makes the opinions of a few invalid". You agree with that, then?'

'Most definitely.'

'You know who said that?'

'You just did.'

'No, it was the great salesman himself, Adolf Hitler.'

Smiley raised his eyebrows at me, trying to find an ally to diffuse the atmosphere.

'What do you think of the new Harry Potter then?' he said, his voice singsong and chipper.

Seb smashed his fist down on the table. The cutlery jumped. The faces of the two men creased. Other diners peered over at us, then returned to their pasta. A shadow fell over us. I'd seen her coming, but now the waitress, a petite blonde in a honey yellow dress beneath her light blue, tea-stained, hundred year old Manticore housecoat was hovering between our two tables, pad out, pen poised, gently biting her bottom lip as if not quite confident enough to interject. I looked at her. I looked back at the cover of *Kill Cyclops*. I looked at Seb and he looked at the jacket and then we both looked up at the girl.

Himmler tugged his lapels so hard that his glasses jumped on the bridge of his nose. 'Well he-llo,' he said, flapping his hand at *Kill Cyclops*. 'That's you that is, isn't it?'

'Who said a literary imagination is not an aid to seduction?' said Seb.

The waitress stepped forward into the gap between the tables, blocking our view on Himmler and Smiley as she took their orders.

'Patting his jacket to check he has mobile phone and business card at the ready,' whispered Seb. 'And waiting to flash gold Visa card, Travelodge brochure and Viagra sachet.'

'Perfecting mental image of himself as bluff Prince Hal,' I whispered back.

'Svelte and dashing . . .'

' . . . Like the young Martin Amis. But, Seb, he looks like Heinrich Himmler.'

'I know. We need more wine.'

'I need to keep a clear head.'

'What are you whispering about?' said the waitress, smirking as she faced us now with her pad raised. Something then seemed to jolt through her and she jerked her head at Himmler.

'Casanova lives,' said Seb.

'Pardon?' said the waitress.

'Please tell us you're not her, are you?' I said, pointing at the *Kill Cyclops* girl.

'Everyone's in a silly mood this evening. Would you like to order?'

We ordered pasta and Sebastian made a big deal about requesting the most expensive red wine on the menu (£5.99 a pop; we writers have a certain joie de vivre and devil may care attitude).

'OK,' said the waitress, and then paused and read through her list. She tucked it into the pocket of her housecoat and started to click the top of her pen on and off for no apparent reason. Then she folded her arms and a tendril of hair swung across her forehead.

'Er . . . I couldn't help overhearing,' she said, 'but you're writers, aren't you?'

'I'm not. He is,' said Seb.

'Oh wow,' she said. 'What have you written?'[43]

---

[43] Internal intelligence gathering network alerted me to the possibility that in our midst we might have an **Author Stalker**, an individual suffused with vicarious Rom-T longings and

'Look,' I said, staring at the drooping pink plastic tulip with its forlorn head and patina of dust. 'I'm just a teacher, that's all.'

'My dear,' said Seb. 'This is The Voice. This very night, at Morleys booksellers, he shall be reading one of his most compelling stories. Why don't you join us?'

'Oh wow,' she said. 'I knock off soon.'

Seb rubbed his hands. 'First, we shall have the wine.'

'Oh yes,' she enthused and ran back to the kitchen.

I'd lost all my appetite. My jaws had gummed solid together and I was letting off one continuous steam of breath like a football after an encounter with a garden fork.

'That's how you do it,' said Seb, swiping his hand expansively at Himmler and Smiley. They didn't notice, lost in muttering.

'It's called Bountiful Treacle,' Himmler explained. 'It's about how treacle changed the world . . . found America for us and that.'

'Seb,' I said, 'can you stop embarrassing me?'

He leaned back, peered into Bateman Street and gave me a stern look.

'Nathan,' he said. 'Ever get the feeling that you're being watched?'

'Yes, all the time.'

'I mean now.'

'Stop telling everyone that I'm a writer.'

'But dear boy, you're my finest protégé.'

'I'm your only protégé, and that doesn't reflect well on either of us at the moment.'

He took a packet of Lucky Strikes from his jacket and flicked me one. Around us, chatter buzzed. Himmler and Smiley swayed and topped-up their glasses. Rattles and thumps ricocheted from the kitchen. A silent waiter with a jet-black mullet mooched among the tables and lit the candles as Patsy Cline sang *Crazy*. All the couples looked misaligned and shabby, at the end of the affair or about to slide foolishly into another. And so Seb listened as I laid out my woes in monotone.

Teaching the most unruly, bizarre pack of loons and ranters I'd ever come across; despair at spending three days of my life reading *The Grasp of Fear* and knowledge of what went on inside the heads of people like Mac McMahon; the grey ashtray light and the hammerhead silence of the

---

an unrealistic, sentimental idea of what a writer is like. Liable to crazymake, cling and annoy. Prey for the shameless trustafarian element who write with their cocks.

garret; perpetual loneliness; being as skint as a stick insect; institutional politics and the Orgsburo; Frances's disappearance and *The Venice Syndrome*; my appearance and *The Garret of the Fumigator*; the creepy phantom outside my flat that was probably The Moon-Barker of all Moon-Barkers.

'And,' I said, 'I've written the best novel I've ever written, you know that, you know it's good, you know it's fine, and I can't get an agent, I can't get a publisher.'

I stubbed out my cigarette and immediately lit another one. The only thing I hadn't spilled was James O'Mailer and just as I realized this and it crossed my mind that maybe I should tell Seb about the voices as well, the throb arrived.

Hiya Kiddo, Dame Parlet the Hen. You know what he's going to say? You know full well. You've used it yourself. He said it to you before when you were failing to sell *The Drowners*, and when you failed to sell *The Mess* or whatever it was called – even you can't remember, you're so ashamed – and then when you failed to sell *The Best Man*. He's going to recount the Legend of William Golding. The story of how every single publisher turned down *The Lord of the Flies* until that assiduous reader at Faber upon Faber noticed the black thumbmarks on the manuscript and ripped out the bland and soapboxy first chapter and discovered thereafter the story of the boys on the island. I, of course, had told Willy this already, but would he listen? You think your charges are dense . . .

'Shut your stupid trap,' I said.

'Pardon,' said Seb.

'Nothing.'

'Look.' His face tightened and he smiled generously. 'JG Ballard once said that any idiot can write a novel. It's something else to sell one.'

'What? Juicy said that?'

Seb cocked his head and frowned.

'It's not the same anymore,' I said. 'You know that. I know that. The sales and marketing fascists wouldn't know what to do with a Golding now.'

Himmler peered at me. His eyes, magnified by his specs, seemed froglike as he poured out another glass of wine.

'Golding?' said Seb. 'Nathan, please. Be calm. Stick to your guns. What else is there to stick to? This cannot last. You will have a breakthrough. I just wish I had more influence. Talking of which, I suppose you've had the misfortune to see this?' He took out a folded broadsheet newspaper

181

and tapped at an article. The poet Ferdinand Paget had been shortlisted for a major first book award for his collection *Rich Boy Invents His Blues*.

'Yeah, I knew that,' I said. I'd found out while I was editing *The Grasp* and the news sent me hurtling into the shady undergrowth of Mac's prose like a fox before the frenzy of the hounds.

'It's a low,' said Seb. 'Even by the standards of origami and its commissars.'

'His mother's contacts bought him it. It's like a Christmas present. It's disgusting.'

'It's beyond disgusting,' said Seb. 'It's the nuclear winter of art. If I ever see that Paget, I'll kick him from here to next week[44].'

---

[44] **James O'Mailer:** Me again, slipping down like an oyster from the back of Flack's mind to the bottom of the page, where I do find that I locate a more receptive audience. Dear reader, you may have noticed that Flack at last has someone who'll listen (remember the introduction to that little tract he composed last week?) in the form of one Sebastian Harker. Flack much admires The Harker, adoring his ornate, sensuous style and his pasquinades against iniquity and boredom and trash and the decline of aesthetics, though I do believe that my pseudonymous works, like *The Rainbow* and *Sons and Lovers* found the heart of such matters with more of a marksman's precision. You may also have noticed from sundry references and asides, as well as the evidence given by this last tirade, that Harker has a pronounced dislike of all poets, versemongers, bards, minstrels, troubadours, ballardists, skalds, jongleurs and rhymers of all persuasions and styles, from Sappho down to Larkin and on to the scribblers of today, excluding from his sweep only Shakespeare; even he can't dare question my best work. Where were we? Yes. This business of the Harker's hatred of the poets. Flack regards this as no more than an eccentricity, an overcompensation and moreover an affectation. He regards it as an outgrowth of Harker's commitment to the novel as a great popular art form, something for the masses unfettered by ritual and aristocracy and arcana. Flack should know, however, that these things are rarely more than personal gripes and grudges. I should know. I was there. I was there in 1969, my last year of freedom, when the still *enfant terrible* Harker caught sight of her at a cocktail party in Princeton. She was a light that scared the corners of the room, that jellied the legs of all suitors, a Penelope Armed, a Venus Incarnate, a Cleopatra with her odalisque eyes and roaring breasts and the magic that moved around her like the Aurora Borealis. She was the poet Barbara Aple – you've heard of her, died tragically young after a short-lived yet galactic career, you studied her at school: *The End of Kisses, Persephone's Curse, The Lavender Man* – and she drew in the tyro Harker. He stalked across the carpet with a glass of fine wine in each hand. In the left pocket of his corduroy jacket was a strident copy of *On The Road*, and in the other lurked *Cain's Book*, which, unbeknown to him, were the products of my two weekends in Madrid when it had rained and the booze ran dry and I was bored of whoring. To his credit, Harker kept eye contact; he wooed, he silver-tongued, he challenged, he listened, he whined, he howled, he pleaded. No fool, though, was my Barbara. She had eyes. She could see. She passed by him and left with one James O'Mailer – God, she was good; she used to call me Zeusy – and she left Harker with his ruins and his ire and his subject. Where Flack sees patronage, I see petty resentments. However, let's not sidetrack ourselves by putting a case for the above-hated Paget, and lets not suggest here either that Flack's assessment of the situation has anything to do with his feelings for a certain Ms Levankranz, because even I stand here shoulder-to-shoulder,

He thumped his hand down on the table. A shockwave pulsed through The Manticore. The candles shivered. Heads turned. Himmler and Smiley broke off their conversation, eyed each other and eased around to face us.

'Hey you,' said Himmler. 'Don't you think that if a book's won a prize it must be good?'

Seb interlaced his fingers and seemed to be internally counting. It was his philosophy that if one does not confront ignorance, one is just as guilty. I needed to get in first before Seb administered an Agent Orange style fumigation.

'It's not won a prize,' I said. 'It won't win. It's a PR exercise.'

'PR's good,' said Himmler. 'Where would we be without PR?'

'I don't like him or anything that he's ever done,' said Seb, 'but I think Damien Hirst put this most eloquently when he said that "PR used to be about promoting things. Now it's about selling shit to cunts".'

I lit a cigarette and turned away. Out in the dark-swathed street, someone flashed out of my sightline just as I was about to focus on him. Alongside me, the standoff continued.

'But . . .' said Himmler.

'Shhh,' said Seb.

'But . . .'

'Shhh.'

'But . . .'

'If you haven't anything intelligent to say, listen.'

The waitress suddenly appeared at the table. She held up a tray carrying two bottles of red wine.

'One for you,' she said, placing it in front of Seb, 'and one for you two gentlemen.' She sidestepped and put the other one down on Himmler's table.

'This isn't your real job?' said Himmler. 'You're like an actress or something?'

'How long?' said Seb, tapping his wristwatch.

---

manning the barricades with Flack and Harker; the Paget boy is a charlatan and ingratiate and all his laurels are bought for him by his mother's influence, but has it ever been different? And I, the omniscient narrator, assure you, dear reader, that within a few short pages The Harker will get his chance to make good his threats.

'What?' I said.

'I'd say forty-five minutes.' He looked up and gave the waitress a very understanding smile. 'Forty-five minutes . . . before he tells you that his wife's not been the same since the stork paid a visit.'

Himmler let out a low and guttural breath. The waitress put her hand across her mouth to stifle a laugh. She turned to us and her face was flushed and her pursed lips twitched from side to side.

'Stop it,' she said.

'We're only just getting warmed up,' said Seb.

'Hey listen,' she said. 'You know what you were saying about being writers . . .'

'He is, I'm not.'

'Well, when I was at university I was doing a creative writing workshop and I started this novel. I mean, I don't, I've not, I've not looked at it for ages, but I wondered . . .' She paused. Her eyes were a deep, purplish blue colour and across her lips hovered a question that I knew was coming[45]. 'I was just wondering . . . if you could . . .'

Himmler's tie swung across his paunch as he raised his wineglass and a little splash jumped onto his cuff.

'You written a book, love?'

'Er . . . sort of,' she said.

'What's it called?'

'Erm . . . "Jennifer's Issues".'

'Great title. Chick lit, is it?'

'No,' she said. She looked sheepish now, as if above us full-beam stadium floodlights were burning off her clothes, skin and hair.

'Listen, love' he said. 'Why don't you send it to me? We'll have a gander. See what we can come up with.' He reached out and tucked a business card into the pocket of her housecoat.

'I'll just go and get your orders,' she said and turned tail, the movement of her hips slinking this way and that until they vanished into the kitchen arch.

---

[45] But internal intelligence gathering network was on red alert, fearing that what we had here was a **Script Slipper,** a type of Folder Holder who hangs out in bars, restaurants and the various outposts of the Arvon Foundation, waiting to pounce on unwary writers and thrust a manuscript into his or her hands, expecting a leg-up and free crit. Published, well-known writers are at particular risk from Script Slippers, especially the stealthy sub-category the **Postal Slipper**, a breed now almost replaced by the **E-Slipper.**

I looked at Seb and he looked back at me, both of us blinking, bemused.

'So, are you writing?' I said.

He flapped his cigarette about in front of his face. 'Yes . . . you know . . . something new, a change of direction . . . it's called "Shelley Underwater".'

'That's a departure?'

'If I don't write the same book over and over again, they don't know what to do with it. So, you still want me to pop up next month, talk to these students?'

'Yes, you just . . . forewarned is forearmed, if you know what I mean.'

The waitress reappeared in the arch carrying a wide tray stacked with plates and bowls. Himmler bobbed his head at her, then shuffled around to us again.

'That shut you muppets up, didn't it?' he said.

'Pardon,' I said.

'Not so full of it now, are you?'

'Do you know who we are?' said Smiley, as earnestly and pityingly as an undercover copper might as he reveals himself to the gang he's betrayed.

Himmler took out another business card and put it on the table in front of us. The waitress was halfway along the aisle, side-winding her hips to avoid elbows and the edges of the tables. I looked away from her and down at the card. The card read:

Oliver Blox

Sales Director

Dewsenbury and Madge PLC

'So,' said Oliver Blox, wagging the biggest finger I'd ever seen. 'You're Sebastian "Mid List Oblivion" Harker and you're . . . who? I forget.' His face was like a Halloween pumpkin wallowing in its one night of gleeful incandescence. 'I think on Monday I better have a look at your sales figures, Seb, old sport.'

The hair at the back of my head tingled. I waited for Seb. I waited for Seb to cut back, to switch modes, to launch a charm offensive or reel out the dramatis personae of his friends and supporters at Dewsenbury and Madge, the once proud and redoubtable publishing house long since swallowed and downgraded by a Chicago-based media conglomeration. But his eyes flopped in their sockets and on the tabletop his hand coiled slowly into a fist. A sensation plummeted through me, a sensation I remembered from junior school, when the gigantic, horrifying black-bearded PE teacher caught me weeing behind the prefab hut in the playground, and from when the sales manager of one of the publishing firms I'd worked for hammered down a fax on my desk and, as if there was something wrong with me, shouted: *what does munificence mean? I had to look it up.* The sensation was similar to that which I experienced whenever I received a rejection letter from someone like Frederick Malone at ZY Haggard or Squinty Hugo or the cunts at Mxyztplk and Wukfit; a feeling of being exposed and reduced by the presence of pathetic, wilful and unaccountable authority. I shouldn't be made to feel like this. I had to do something here. I had to take control. Be a man. Be a strong man. Be the Alpha, not the Beta.

Seb's fist tightened on the tabletop. The waitress approached, steam rising from the bowls on her tray.

I ought to draw the attention of Oliver Blox to the status of the man in front of me whose livelihood they were threatening, the novelist and critic Sebastian Harker, author of the prize winning, best-selling, much translated *Snow on Parnassus*; a man who I had seen at a festival in Bath hold an audience of five hundred people rapt for an hour, every consonant a performance, every phrase a shock to the system, every image a hanging, lingering thing; a man who clung for dear life to the highest aims of literature, a man continually asking questions about how we live now and something called the human condition. They ought to show some respect. They ought to listen.

And I ought to deploy some stealthy subtlety of my own here. We could blow this over. We could take this by the scruff and open up a channel. I could charm my way in here. I could make an impact on decision-makers and circumnavigate the obstacles in my way. I could put to them the case against unit shifting and short-termism and discounting and category mining and PR and profiles. I could tell them where they are going wrong, how the majority of serious readers of substantive fiction are frustrated that there's nothing in the shops but gifts, that we're tired of celebrity ghosts, beach read bollocks and a dozen different facsimiles of last year's smash word-of-mouth disappointment. I could tell them this. I could make a point. I could make a difference.

Or I could do myself a big, big favour and pitch The Penelope Tree. The Penelope Tree: sure-fire smash word-of-mouth bestseller if you just give it a chance. It's a fast-paced, high-stakes, contemporary novel that is also romantic, cinematic and emotionally charged. I could Paget and Plum this. I could ingratiate. I could sell myself. I would sell myself. I would do it. Now.

My head jerked up from my slumped position. There was a red flush developing in Seb's cheeks. The waitress had now reached us. Plates and bowls clicked on her tray. Baskets of garlic bread wobbled and bottles of Peroni beer jingled together. I turned from her and fixed my stare on Oliver Blox, Sales Manager of Dewsenbury and Madge.

'Oh just write me a cheque, you fat Nazi,' I said.

The flush in Seb's face sprang from red to crimson. He whacked his fist down on the table, this time clipping the dessert spoon. The spoon powered into the air. It clunked against The Manticore's grey ceiling at an angle and pinged back into the restaurant. It spun in the air as it passed over the waitress's shoulder. She stood mesmerized for an instant as it turned and twisted and drew the eyes of Oliver Blox and Smiley Underling and the novelist and critic Sebastian Harker and for a second all five of us seemed to be staring at some speck in the distance like planespotters at a seafront airshow. Over the waitress it travelled, heading for a table two down, where a man with a John Berryman beard reached out for the shoulders of a statuesque terracotta-skinned woman with nut-brown bobbed hair who recoiled as if from a slavering wolf and into the space between them bulleted the spoon. It hit the edge of their table. It rebounded. I couldn't see it. A smack. A charge frazzled the waitress. She sort of star-jumped – the spoon must have hit her neck and slipped down into the 'V' at the back of her dress – and the tray, with its bowls of pasta con vongole, and farfalle con quattro formagi, and spaghetti bolognaise and heaped cannelloni, and baskets of garlic bread with melted cheese and garlic bread with herbs and fingerbowls of olives and four Peroni beers, all leapt up and separated and spaced-out and seemed to hover for a moment, the bottles rolling, rolling, as if suddenly we had sunk to the bottom of the sea and all around us detritus was rising floating upwards, drifting up to the light before dropping, falling and spreading and liquefying. Until it all, with a crack and a tinkle and a whoosh slopped down right bang-smack in the middle of Oliver Blox's table. A widening parabola of white and red sludge swept out from the centre and hit both at chest height, then head height, then right in the eyes. The Himmler glasses flashed orange. A spaghetti hat plopped onto Smiley Underling's head. The Betty Boop tie was a brown mince creeper. The waitress gasped. Only a tiny squiggle of cream sauce had lashed across our table, the last thing I can remember before somehow we were running away down Bateman Street as fast as you can run when you're laughing yourself half to death.

Lesser Lights

We were late when we arrived at Morleys, late for *Moonshot*. We entered the shop by the Manete Street side-door and stalked through the children's department. After I left university, thirteen years ago now, I'd worked in this section as a sales assistant for six months until I was sacked for being frighteningly grumpy. The shop had changed in the interim. A total refit made it now a labyrinth of scrubbed white walls and neat shelves and stacked display tables of past/abroad/celebrity gift-titles. It was no longer the ramshackle, dim and dusty maze immortalized in my short story *Boys*[46]. We mounted the whirring, drowsy escalator, gliding evenly along a white passageway hung with posters of the jackets of *Penguin Modern Classics*. Seb, on the stair ahead of me, turned and pointed to a picture of Jack Kerouac's *On the Road*.

---

[46] 'Rob can sense him, out of sight, waiting in the musty, humid air. The spiralling flecks of dust. The alcoves. The shelf-lined passageways. Morleys is the biggest bookstore in the world. Six floors. Thirty-two departments. He could be anywhere. Rob is at the service desk. Tom is here, too. They serve a line of customers. Behind them, the escalator whirrs, evenly, drowsily.' *Boys*. Nathan Flack. *Context* Vol. 3 – 1999. I know, there's too much description.

'See that?' he said. 'Blox would turn that down[47].'

'Too experimental,' I said.

'And that.' He jerked his thumb at *To the Lighthouse*[48].

'Ginny wasn't good-looking. Tricky to market.'

'And she didn't drip with the cuisine of the blue-honeyed Mediterranean.' Seb gave *Brighton Rock* a full-on stare. 'He'd turn down that for sure.'

'Graham Greene. Only gave one interview in his entire life[49].'

'And I, Nathan, may well have given my last.'

Seb swung around and we continued to flow up to the top, to *Moonshot*, where soon I would stand in front of the people of the Arctic and read out words for the purposes of self-promotion and marketing myself. I was doing such a good job so far on this trip. I really thought I'd made some contacts and created an impression. Dewsenbury and Madge were now drooling at the prospect of *The Penelope Tree*. I put my hand into my bag and checked again that I still had my *Lesser Lights* manuscript. We reached the summit and slid out into the Art Department and into the rear of the *Moonshot* audience.

In a corner of the department was a long, thin gallery space studded with framed black and white photos and set up with a lectern and microphone. A woman with frizzy orange hair and saucer-sized folksinger glasses read a haiku to the audience arranged in five rows in front of her. My audience. She was only open-mic. I was in the *Time Out* listing. I was the name. My name was on the photocopied sheets blutacked around the walls: Nathan Flack. I stood up on the balls of my feet. She was still delivering her schtick.

---

[47] **James O'Mailer**: Not true. I was always in with the right crowd.

[48] **James O'Mailer**: Not true. We owned a publishing house.

[49] **James O'Mailer**: Well, Flack has a point here. We must admit that we didn't get into our stride until *Stamboul Train*, our three earlier forays bearing the hallmarks of distraction; we were spreading ourselves thin at the time and Virginia was so time-consuming. Even so, I tend to think that we would not have got those first three efforts published now and we may well have given up the writing lark and settled for a comfortable life knocking out naff-noir screenplays for what was once called the British Film Industry. Probably would have ended up in Hollywood in the forties and moped about a bit in the tawdry neon lights. Probably wouldn't be hanging on that poster here. No Pinky. No Bendrix. No Scobie.

'N. Flack. Third-rate hack.

Tricky to market and crap.

Can't write fucking haiku.'

Or so I imagined she read out as she paused and curtseyed. Soon I would shunt from here to there. The space was sizzlingly over-bright. A rig of stainless steel spotlights blasted down from the ceiling. I looked around for (One Foot in the) Dave Cave as Seb pounced on a girl with electric-blue hair at the drinks table and liberated two glasses of white wine. I wanted water. The taste of The Manticore's cheap plonk still coiled in the back of my throat and I was trying to mentally rehearse the opening lines of Lesser Lights and not think about the first reading I ever gave, way back in 98, some upstairs room of some cackhole sofapub in Primrose Hill. Halfway through my story my diaphragm had gone all earthquake on me and my hands started to shake so much I almost drilled myself into the floorboards. Never underestimate the effect a code red bladder trauma can have on a performance. One time I nearly hosed down sixty baying OAPs in Chiswick.

'Greek fire,' said Seb, and handed me a glass. I duffed it anyway.

'One more spoonful,' said the haikuist. 'This last one's called "Mslexia."' She fingered the shaft of the mic. Her phrases droned out over the PA.

'I'm reading Mslexia

But I'll pay out if you buy me

White chocolate, you pig.'

The words petered out into applause that rapidly descended into whispers and burble. The haikuist's orange frizz swished across the shoulders of an emerald canvas jacket as she romped away from the mic-stand.

'Why on earth are they clapping?' said Seb.

(One Foot in the) Dave shouldered his way through the pack around the drinks table. (One Foot in the) Dave Cave: seven foot tall with greying pudding bowl hair and face as narrow and straight as a cricket bat who tonight seemed to be wearing a lab coat and baggy tweed trousers. Seven years ago I'd edited his second short story collection *Grave Goods*, which went on to receive fab reviews but sold poorly. One Foot fell in the first exchanges of the war that the Grand Coalition of Marketing and

191

Discounting launched on short story writers. If I ever got around to writing *Marketing and Its Discontents*, (One Foot in the) Dave would be case study.

'Nathan,' he said, 'talk about last minute. What kept you?'

'Don't mention the war,' said Seb.

'We fought in a war,' I said. 'You've met Sebastian?'

'Yes,' said One Foot. 'Seb, love the new novel, hate the cover. Nate, this lot are cool, no worries. No ceremony. I'll take you up now, OK?'

'Sure.' I rummaged in my bag again and checked on *Lesser Lights*. I took it out this time and stashed my bag and coat under the drinks table.

'C'mon,' said One Foot.

We squeezed through the standing punters at the back of the crowd and into the aisle at the edge of the seats. From this angle, at this moment, the audience looked like a rugby crowd, thousands and thousands of them, trumpeting and roaring and cursing. Something shot through my stomach and my diaphragm quivered. I looked away and concentrated on One Foot's long white coat, the tails that swayed around the back of his knees. Clutching my papers tightly, I asked myself what Sly would do here? How would he feel? How would his body move? What would he be saying to himself? I imagined my elevated height and impressive, disarming musculature and my exoskeleton of leather waistcoat and trousers and motorcycle boots and oiled and sun-tanned flesh. I was Sylvester Sly Ramos-Pintos and I could take anything this blood-desperate boxing mob could chuck at me. Sylvester Sly Ramos-Pintos. I was Sly. Man and cipher in perfect harmony. An appropriate strategy, given what I was about to read. *Lesser Lights*. A story of an actor, an out of work actor called Midge Moon who has just failed to get the part of Einar Stricksburgen in *Pleasure Boys*, a cable channel drama about three stud-hunks working for a male escort agency called, funnily enough, Pleasure Boys. Einar Stricksburgen: a right dirty, ripe-and-ready, half-Swedish, half-east London geezer shagmonster in it for the fun and the riot and the birds when one of his co-stars does it for the money (wife, kids, debts etc) and the other is a bit pretty, a bit confused and a bit of a bender, and deep-down has a thing about Einar. Midge Moon is in a hotel room and about to be browbeaten into getting a proper job by his long-term, long suffering girlfriend Jennifer when he sees a strange light on the horizon and leaves the hotel, embarking on a mythic quest to find it. The first line ran through my head like fastforwarding tape: *The glow on the horizon could have been sheet lightning, but as Midge focused on the skyline, as his eyes adjusted to the distance, there was no thundercrack, no tailing boom.* I was ready. I

192

was unafraid. I was cocked like a pistol, dancing like a firefly. I was going to Gloucestershire these fuckers. I took an eyes-right to check on the audience, to focus on the heads so they wouldn't faze me, drink in the sight of them and remind myself that they were here to listen, not hector or hassle or catcall. They were waiting to hear me. Rows and rows. Young and old. Men and women. The smart and the casual. The keen and the dutiful. The hip and the hipless. I swallowed. Excitement rose in my chest with each stride. I achieved perfect readiness and concentration. As an afterthought I hoped that the haikuist had the good sense to keep well away from the writer and critic Sebastian Harker.

A clip-clopping sound; there was a clip-clop running alongside me that at first I thought was my pulse pounding at my temples, but then I saw it, rampaging along the central aisle, parallel to One Foot and me. A black figure: a waddling, speeding black shape. A black outline, a woman dressed in a black trenchcoat and clogs and billowing cranberry slacks. A huge woman pulling a clutch of swollen carrier bags along the aisle. One Foot froze. I ran into him, almost staggered and fell. The clipping of the clogs stopped and she heaved the bags up onto the stage and stood behind the mic. The PA distorted the voice, made it sound even more B movie-Nazi and terrifying.

'I am the herald,' announced Erika Gretsch. 'I am the herald of The He.'

Sly evaporated and all this water seemed to be seeping through me, gushing and gathering and pouring into my bladder. About a third of the audience instantly got up and fled. One Foot turned to me, a look of utter horror smashed into his face.

'Who on earth is that?'

'I really don't know,' I said.

Erika reached into her coat pocket and pulled out a roll of paper. As she did so, one of her bags fell over and out of it skittered my starfish. My starfish. *The* starfish.

'I have poem,' said Erika. 'It is called "The Black Hen Dines on Pomegranate".'

'I'm going to get rid of her,' said One Foot.

'No,' I said. 'Let it blow.' The Starfish. I could see it.

Erika took a breath. She unfurled the paper and held it so close to her face that I'm sure the audience would only have seen a black mac with a white oblong head.

193

"'I am the herald of The He.
I am the mother of the pea
I am the poet of the fleece
I am the one who loves The He
I am the one who dreams of meat.'"

She paused and scrutinized the audience. Another mini-stampede occurred and the pack around the drinks table swelled and shrank and filtered away into the shop. Then those who were brave enough to remain started to clap, clap because they thought it was over. There was a sound in my head, like a World War Two air raid siren. It cut out. It started up again as she lifted her paper.

"'And he comes to you, with new tyres
New poppies. On a day of suet when the
Prancing Moon-Sun of a large city-town
Eats its own wax and sits on the library steps
To wonder at the glory of The He that is The He that
Belongs to me and I come to tell you of He. The
He that is married to my kumquat.
The He.'"

All my Slyness was now raging in my bladder. My bladder was now the size of a basketball as I edged back into the wall and stared at the frozen faces in the crowd, the hanging faces, the dazedly despairing faces. I was now descending the food chain. I had devolved from Sly to The Voice to The Fumigator to Flack Hack to Beta Male and now I was Shamblesman again. A speck. A mere blip on the radar. Erika's voice raised to a crazy-loon pitch and feedback buzzed through the PA.

"'The He is here for you and me
Sometimes with a Latin box
Sometimes with a purple smock
Sometimes with a face of flock
Sometimes with a hand of socks
Sometimes he is there for me
Sometimes he makes love to me

194

Sometimes he is kind to me
Sometimes he is cruel to me
Sometimes he makes Spanish tea
But always he is The He and He is here
To preach to thee.'"

Erika bowed. No one moved. For a second I seemed to be looking at a photograph. A cowed group of suffering sinners laid low by the sermon of the mad cult leader. Everyone remaining was about to rush to the toilets and cut off their genitals and take a fatal overdose before the saucer landed. Erika crouched and gathered her things, scooping up the starfish. She dropped off the stage with a thump and stared so hard into the face of this poor guy in the front row that he seemed to morph into Munch's *Scream* before he abandoned his chair to her and stumbled off into the greyer light at the back. There she sat, right in front of the mic, arms folded, head back and the Gretschbags piled up between the cranberry hams of her thighs.

Well, that sets the scene nicely, said James O'Mailer.

'Oh fucking hell, not you as well.'

'Pardon,' said One Foot. 'Let's just get on with this.'

He tried to casually stroll to the lectern, but staggered like a man after an eight-day lager binge. He took the mic and whispered into it.

'Er . . . Yeah . . . Er, Nathan Flack everyone.'

He leapt into the central aisle and ran like a manic ostrich to the drinks table.

I was on my own, wedged in the corner, bladder like a planetarium dome. I shuffled up to the mic and all of a sudden the lights seemed ever so bright. I was used to reading in the dark places of the Arctic, in the literary underworld, in basements and backrooms and crepuscular jazz-cafés and the lightless wings of dank and disordered second-hand bookshops, not this hellish white wind-tunnel that lit up Shamblesman for all to see. Erika Gretsch, right in front of me, the focal point of my now depleted audience looked up as if for absolution, a scarlet panting flush glowing from her scrotum- shaped head.

Guess who's been tailing you all afternoon? said O'Mailer. In all my Millennia I have rarely met someone as genuinely mad as that one, and remember that I saw Nietzsche hugging horses in Turin, I shared boiled eggs with Piero di Cosimo as he cowered at the thunder, and I was with

Patrick Hamilton at the booze-sodden end. And you know what, Dame Parlet? These folks, these folks here, they think you're banging her.

'I never . . . I never touched her,' I stammered. My bladder expanded to the width of the Grand Canyon as my voice echoed back at me through the PA and the heads shot up and hundreds eyes blinked in shuttering unison.

Jesus Christ, Flack, said O'Mailer. Get on with it. Say something comedic and introduce yourself and then just schmooze into the story. Like we discussed. Go on. Engage what little you have that passes for a brain, get it to send instructions to your vocal cords. Articulate. "I am Nathan Flack and this is turning out to be one helluva road trip".

'I am Nathan Flack,' I said, 'and this is turning out to be a bad day for giving up crack.'

Titters. Sniggers. Sympathetic, agreeable laughter. Careful to avoid Erika, I took a long look at the audience to ground myself, to reassure myself before I launched into *Lesser Lights*. Over by the drinks table, arms were raised. One Foot held up a glass for me and next to him Seb raised his too and they were smiling and geeing me up to start.

'I'll just find my crack-pipe,' I said, and flipped up my story. The words began to form in my head as they came into focus on the paper and created some distraction from the molten orb down there that threatened to detonate my pelvis.

'"The glow on the horizon could have been sheet lightning",' I read, '"but as Midge focused on the skyline, as his eyes adjusted to the distance, there was no thundercrack, no tailing boom . . ."'

And I was off, deep into the first paragraph, the set-up, the atmosphere, the trigger. The words seemed to materialize in my head a second before my eyes blitzed through them. Phrase by phrase, line by line, I whipped through the first section, the hotel sequence, where Midge decides to abandon Jennifer to seek out the glow on the horizon. I enunciated. I peaked the consonants and rattled the alliteration. I got a few laughs. I was bodiless now, floating in white space as I nail-gunned their attention to me.

It's a bit miserable, isn't it? said O'Mailer.

I paused to give the audience a break and allow myself to breathe. Again mindful of sighting Erika, I cast my gaze at the heads, taking in One Foot and Seb at the rear, right-hand corner and sweeping across the midsection of the seating arrangement. It's good to make eye contact. It's good to show that you acknowledge them, that you're confident and not pantsing yourself. Then my bladder pulsed as I thought I recognized her. Three rows back. I flashed my head away, but the pressure in my bladder launched an upward thrust and started to do a breakdancing routine on my diaphragm. It formed a pincer movement with a nicotine pang that coursed over my tongue. I checked back. No doubt. She was staring at me but I couldn't work out if she was impressed or disappointed or bemused. But it was her. For sure. Lisa Levankranz. My ex. She was there in one of her violet and purple marble-print dresses and a pinkish diaphanous wrap. Something like sorrow blended with something like fear that floated down from my head, intermingling with all that discomfort warring down there in my guts[50]. Only one thing for it. I picked up the story of *Lesser Lights* and hid myself in words.

My voice kept steady as I read through the middle of the story, Midge Moon's walk through the city at night towards the eerie glow on the horizon that fires off all sorts of memories and associations within him and further blurs the line between his sense of self and the role of Einar Stricksburgen, the role he will never now play. And as I did so, it started to nag at me. It wasn't her. It wasn't Lisa. It couldn't be. My mind was playing silly buggers. The hothouse lights had my brains on a brisk simmer and with bladder trauma and James O'Mailer's naysaying had formed a Tripartite Pact with the aim of causing me maximum destabilisation. She wouldn't come here. She wouldn't come to see me. She must know that I would be here. It had all been too embarrassing. It had all been too stressful. It wasn't her. It couldn't be.

It is her, Flack, said O'Mailer. Why don't you have another look? Have another look at those breasts and those thighs that you miss so much when you're alone in your cot in the middle of the never-ending night.

Get stuffed, James.

I kept on with my reading.

"'To be discovered. How he had always loved that phrase. He would recite it to himself in the mirror every morning after he'd done his t'ai chi and his press-ups and stretches. To be discovered. To have always been there in the wings with his talent and presence and commitment, and suddenly the spotlight sweeps and double takes and veers back to rest upon Midge Moon, leading man.'"

---

[50] If you want an abridged version of what happened between Lisa Levankranz and me, turn back to The Garret of the Fumigator *or* Nostalgic Thirtysomething 3-for-2 Table Product-Shifter *A Role-Play Adventure in which YOU are the Zero by* Arnold Bumrape and take the path 1, 33, 7, 13, 44, 3, 22, 12, 37, 24, 48, 5, 15, 21.

Now I did pause with a beat in the story and once more made eye contact with the audience. I couldn't help it, though, couldn't help centring my crosshairs on her and it *was* her, certainly: the steadfast clever eyes that had once looked back at me across a pillow; the ankh pendent that rested just above her right breast; the curious way she had of clutching her hands at her left hip so her arms stretched across her body. I sniffed and noticed there was a hand lying open on her lap and I followed the hand up a blue and gold paisley-sleeved arm and at the top of the arm was a shoulder covered by an especially horrible leather waist coat and above it I met a pasty, sheep-shaped, ginger Rasta head and snide green eyes.

Grinning at me. Laughing. Squeezing her hand. Ferdie Paget. Hieronymus Ponce. The Enemy of All That Breathes.

Oh my God, Flack, said O'Mailer. It gets worse. And those lines you just read out in front of him. What must he be thinking? He got your gal and now he knows that you know that you're a failure.

Don't you think I know that? What are we going to do?

Set Harker on him! Now. I demand it.

No. Not more lunacy. We finish this and run.

I wandered from the mic, pacing as I stared up at the terrible lights and remembered the lights that Midge was following. Now back at the lectern, I found where I'd left off and started to read the section where Midge meets a girl on the street and ends up telling her that his name is not Midge Moon or Einar Stricksburgen but Peter Pollocks. Over the top of the paper, out beyond the heads and the seating I could see a bright green sign above a door: TOILETS. My bladder was burning now, throbbing and scorching. My thighs ached and my knees trembled. But I kept on. Only the words could keep me in check. Midge leaves the girl. Midge follows the light. Midge has an altercation with a gang of youths who chase him along a towpath until he arrives on a jetty and across the other side of the river is the glow. I was getting through this. I was getting there.

No. You're in denial. I will remind you of what is going on here, said O'Mailer. You are ruining this story; gabbling and reading much too fast and pausing for much too long, which makes you appear a maniac to the assembled ranks. They already think you're making the beast with two backs with the beast with no marbles that if you look down is peering up at you with designs on your schlong. And behind her is your ex-squeeze, who is, quite frankly, concerned for your sanity and wellbeing and blames herself in some way and next to her is the pizzle-prince of Pimlico who has had it confirmed that you are a déclassé huckster and is laughing at your misfortune and over and beyond that loveable duo – how the dickens do you get involved with these people? – is your psychopathic mentor who when he registers the pizzle's presence, and to put the Cardinal's hat on your humiliation, will chomp the mushroom and go berserker in public, partly to relieve the frustration caused by your double-act's inane faux pas in that vulgar little Italian, and then there's the parvenu and egomaniac David Cave who later on will unburden himself to you with a blow by blow account of every low moment and suicidal urge he's experienced since your last meeting, and if that wasn't enough, any minute now you're going to soil yourself like a babe.

Shut the fuck up.

I read on. Peter Pollocks on the jetty, staring at the light, making a choice. Peter Pollocks forced into the river by the gang of youths.

How does the story go? said O'Mailer. Any bloke will tell you that the pain of needing a bad piss is the same as that a lady goes through when she's given birth to a baby. It's a really bad pain and it can cause no end of grief.

Shut the fuck up.

Peter Pollocks in the river, his near-death experience before coming up for air and reaching the other side.

The piss feeling started to get a lot worse and the train was bumping up and down and Billy started to wiggle his snake hips like he was in a rock club and Ruiner was playing some great riffs.

Shut the fuck up.

Peter Pollocks staggering along the towpath to the light and reaching the light. The end. The end of the story.

"'The feeling inside him found neutral. He could not sense his feet or his face. Closing his eyes, he kept going and let his hands drop and felt them slap against his thighs, but not his thighs impact his hands. It was dark now, dark behind his eyes as he kept walking blindly. He couldn't hear his breathing anymore. He couldn't remember his name. He was nothing but a heartbeat as he stepped into the glow and the glow engulfed him.'"

The end. My bladder cramped and clenched, about to go supernova.

No, this is the end, said James O'Mailer. *Out it all came in a big gush that went on for ten minutes and all the beer mats and beer towels started to float out of the boozer but most of all it went all over this chinny bloke who turned out to be a rascally copper.*

'SHUT THE FUCKING-FUCK UP.'

My voice clanged out around the room. The audience was a smudge. No one clapped. Lisa had her hands over her face and Ferdie Paget was laughing with his head back.

'Thank you,' I said. 'God bless.'

Next I knew I was fighting my way along the left-hand aisle towards the green light, the green toilet light. (One Foot in the) Dave's voice came out of the PA behind me, saying something like, "That's Nathan Flack, tricky to market, third-rate hack and crap teacher who has bored then insulted us and obviously has emotional and psychological problems and hasn't had a shag since the Fuel Crisis and he's off now to piss his pants and wallow in his humiliation. I am David One Foot in the Dave Cave and this has been *Moonshot*, you have been watching, stay for a drink, we all need one after that. Goodnight sweet Nathan, goodnight.'

Operation Starfish

I have to shamefacedly admit that it struck me here that *Needing a Piss* was, after all a work of prescient genius. To describe the sheer, basic, visceral relief I experienced after I'd squeezed my way into the tiny cubicle and pissed a volume of water similar to that of the Welsh Harp reservoir in Hendon would probably require a feat of stream of consciousness prose beyond my meagre talents. As you may well have guessed by now, James Joyce or Ginny Woolf I am not.

As the pain and discomfort subsided and a rubbery feeling came over me, I hung there in the restraining confines of the cubicle and ripped my *Lesser Lights* manuscript in two and fed the pieces into the lavatory bowl, then flushed. Plotting a graph in my head, I worked out that when I finished *The Penelope Tree*, my position was about two-thirds up a y-axis. Since then, it had staggered downwards, point by point across the x-axis, my value plummeting through Squinty Hugo's rejection to the cunts at Mxyztplk and Wukfit to telling Sharon Plum to piss off in front of a shudder and the appearance of James O'Mailer and my first encounter with the Major Arcana Clusterfuck to the black ghost outside my window to Frederick Malone and the Night of the Ram and losing my starfish and Frances's disappearance, right on down to *The Grasp of Fear* and Oliver Blox. The graph had now, after *Moonshit*, plopped into a cute toilet-shaped graphic. The Flackdaq had crashed. My life was torn pieces, swirling down the pan. My life was leaving me. It was flowing away. I was watching it saturate, disintegrate and vanish.

Stupid wanky story wouldn't go down. A raft of mushy paper and stained type floated on the surface. The lines about 'to be discovered' were still legible. That just about summed it up. I couldn't even get rid of it. I'd never be able to flush it. I pulled the lid down – as Lisa can corroborate, I am house-trained and know when to put the toilet seat down – and sat on it. Even the graffiti on the back of the door had more merit than my so-called prose. I wanted to stay here. Stay here all night and leave in the morning after everyone outside had gone. I didn't want to see Erika. I didn't want to see Lisa or Hieronymus Ponce, The Enemy of All That Breathes, or have to apologize to One Foot in the Dave for ruining *Moonshit*.

But I couldn't stay here. Seb was out there. And so was Hieronymus Ponce. Out there would be a melee, a scrap, a crusade, the killing of cyclops. And everyone would blame me for it and would be waiting for me to come out and take the rap. I'd get done for inciting hatred against ropey poets. Beyond the door, the whole crowd would be waiting for me to emerge. If I left the cubicle, it was going to be like the end of *Butch Cassidy and the Sundance Kid*. But my starfish was out there. The Flackdaq had gone into terminal freefall since the Beat Baglady quarantined my morning star.

Out of the cubicle, in the washroom now, I brushed myself down, smoothed my hair and rinsed my hands under the tap. I would need my clean hands and clean tongue and all my residual Slyness for Operation Starfish.

First move: I slunk out of the toilet and girded myself for the volley of fruit, eggs, pisspots and abuse that would meet my reappearance. The room was now crowded again. The seats had been stacked at the side and people stood around in clumps, chitchatting and holding wineglasses and tumblers of orange juice. No one turned. No one harangued me. No one even noticed I was back. My diaphragm quivered. My shoulders tightened as I scanned the gathering with my camera eye. Couldn't see One Foot, or Seb, or Lisa and that nepotism-delivered sub-life Paget. I hoped to James Joyce and Ginny Woolf that they'd left to snigger about me in the Atlantic Bar or the Mincing Cheese or wherever they hung out to play their master-and-servant games. But there, there in the middle of the room, alone in a circle of about-turned backs, was Erika Gretsch with the Gretschbags at her feet.

Operation Starfish: Second Move. I approached stealthily, manoeuvring myself between the wine-drinkers as if I was made of fluid. She realized I was coming at her and her face spread open into an ecstatic mother-like grin.

Operation Starfish: Third Move: Be cool. Be subtle. Don't get out of the proverbial pram. Rescue Starfish; nab Seb and then skidaddle catlike into the vaporous Arctic night. Be nice, calm, polite and level. Don't draw attention to yourself. Don't cause a scene. The second objective of Operation Starfish is the avoidance of a scene.

I squared up to her and stabbed my forefinger at her nose.

'Right, firstly, you're insane. You should be in a home. You should be in a straightjacket. You should be whacked in a cage in some Victorian nuthouse. You should be plugged into the national fucking grid, you fucking barker.'

Her face tilted and the saddest expression I'd ever seen sank through her face.

'But I am come for The He,' she said.

'I don't want you to come for me. I don't want you anywhere near me, you rabbit hutch.'

'But . . . The He, he will change the whole wide world.'

'You follow me again, and I'll swing for you, I will. You follow any of my friends again and I promise you I'll go to my grave with your blood on my boots and die a happy man.'

'But . . .'

'You ever, EVER, *EVER*, embarrass me like that again I'll boil you down and turn you into glue. You understand me, you moon-barking knocker?'

The back-turners had closed in around us, muttering and nudging each other. Erika's face now had this look of astonished terror, as if out of the blue, vampire-riders had descended to raze her ancestral home and ravish her carrot patch.

'But I am the poet of The He,' she whimpered.

'No, you're a screaming tangent. You're not a poet. That wasn't a poem. That was a nice padded cell and lifetime on medication. Now give me my fucking starfish before I really lose my temper.'

Operation Starfish: Fourth Move: Breathe. Breathe. Calm down before you run out of insults and lamp her one. Her mouth was a gash and her palms were open in front of me, as if begging her mercy from

Flackthulu, a terrible alien god in an HP Lovecraft story. Somebody gabbed my elbow. I turned.

'Nathan, stop it, for God's sake,' said Lisa.

Operation Starfish: Fifth Move: the situation should not be allowed to deteriorate further. There she was, Lisa, a woman I had dearly loved, and who every now and again, as James O'Mailer had so spitefully reminded me, I missed. And here we were again: me shouting at a Moon-Barker and she obviously reunited, in some way, with the Enemy of All That Breathes. In her violet dress and knee-length brown suede boots, she stood with glaring eyes, her laptop case held at her hip, stinking of work as ever. I ought to say something diplomatic, but for the life of me I didn't know what to say or do.

Rip her dress off, said James O'Mailer. Tear it to pieces and bang her behind the chairs. She loves that sort of thing.

'Fuck you!'

'It's really good to see you too, Nathan,' said Lisa.

'Oh not you,' I said. 'What the hell are you here for?'

'We came to see one of Ferdie's friends read. I didn't think it would be a problem.'

'Oh you didn't, did you?'

'Nathan, what the hell has happened to you?'

'You,' I said.

I dipped my head and looked at the floor, at the scrapes and splashes on the parquet, at my dusty shoes. I closed my eyes. A pressure forced its way down on my shoulder, a pressure that at first I thought was the weight of all this exposure. I lifted my head. Ferdie Paget was swaying his way towards us, his ginger dreadlocks flapping around his face and his green eyes alive with outrage or affront or whatever emotions these people can afford to have. And the pressure on my shoulder came from Erika's arm. Erika had her arm on my shoulder and her other hand prodded provocatively into her thigh and had locked her bulk into competitive alignment with Lisa's.

Jesus wept, said O'Mailer. It looks like mixed doubles.

Disgust charged through me. I shrugged Erika off but she crabbed sideways into me again. There was nowhere to go. I couldn't see a way out, anywhere to go. Hemmed in, I was about to be the meat in a Gretsch-Paget torpedo roll. This was getting like *Huis Clos*. Stuck in a room with these wankers forever. Hell is the one who leaves you behind. Ferdinand Paget arrived and immediately grabbed hold of Lisa's arm.

'Ahho, thaht's jahst you, isn't it? Rahnting again.'

Fumigate it, said James O'Mailer. Where's Harker when you need him?

I could see him now. The black-suited assassin of poetasters and versifiers was shoving his way through the pack, working his way to us, fluorescent with Greek fire and brilliant righteousness. Two planets were about to crash together. It was lose/lose. Zero/zero. Death in the Salon. Blood on the parquet. Maximum public humiliation. A night in the cells. And Paget would cast himself as some dashing young Keats-Chatterton-Wilde, aesthete-figure; a butterfly crushed on a wheel.

Seb was imminent. Seb was coming. Seb had a clenched fist raised. His heat-seeking devices and all the targeting and delivery systems and bizarre technologies of honour in his head were set to *POET!*

I spread out my arms.

'Erika,' I said. 'This is the Right Honourable Ferdinand Paget. He's an editor at one of those very prestigious poetry publishers who have been so rude and ungrateful as to not publish your wonderful work.'

Her eyes flickered at me, then spun away and fixed on Ferdie.

'Now I'm sure,' I said, 'if he meets you, he'll change his mind.'

Erika jumped forwards, head down like a miniature battering ram. A look of utter disarray swept through Paget's face as she bore down on him, grabbed him both-handed by his belt and started to bellow in his face.

'VIE VONT YOU PUBLISH MY POEMS!'

Banzai!

I was off then, spinning around on my soles. Throwing my arms over her head, I sidestepped Lisa and caught Seb's arm as it flashed at Ferdie and spun us both through one hundred and eighty degrees. I pushed Seb back into the crowd, my hands lodged in the small of his back until we picked up speed and ran howling to scare the onlookers away from us. At the top of the escalators, we stopped our howl and listened with cocked ears for the louder, longer, terrified primal scream that replaced it from the gallery behind us. The scream of Paget hung in our ears as we hit the escalator. We both froze with our arms outstretched like euphoric goalscorers as the escalator ferried us down past Ginny and Graham and Jack.

'Fantastic,' shouted Seb. 'Outstanding. Pure Gonzo.'

'Fuck,' I said. I'd forgotten the starfish.

Outside, we jogged across the street and concealed ourselves in the doorway of a guitar shop to light our cigarettes. The air was freezing, the night sky cloudless and clear. Seb chortled and coughed and paced around in front of me, head down, wiping tears from his eyes. I'd realized by then that in my haste to find the escape route I'd left my coat and bag under the drinks table. I'd have to go back. Above me, Morleys was a vast block of display windows and lights. Up there, in the Art Department, faint shouts drifted out above the traffic noise from Charing Cross Road and the chatter of Friday-nighters passing through Manete Street.

'Oh bloody hell, Seb,' I said. 'I fucked that right up.'

'C'mon Nathan, bully for you, that was genius.'

'No it wasn't. I didn't come all this way to start a fight.'

'That story is your best, in my opinion, and I was there at the birth.'

'But everyone hated it.'

'Not where I was standing. Odd last line, I admit, when he shouts at the light, but . . . great performance. Really animated. So rare to see someone *perform* his work these days. My boy, you're a star. I'm jealous. This is the moment where I truly pass my baton on to you.'

Hey Flack, said James O'Mailer. He's just passed you the baton of shit. It's a downhill slalom from here to Boot Hill.

I gritted my teeth. Across from us, a stream of people ran out of Morleys as if the building was on fire. Oh God, I had to go back in there. The cold was clamping down on my shoulders, crushing my ears and deadening my fingertips.

'Seb, can you do me a favour,' I said. 'Can you go back in there and get my things. They're under the desk.'

'Of course.'

'Don't go near Paget.'

'Thanks to you I now have a Golem for such operations. Two ticks.'

He flicked his fag end into the gutter and I watched him saunter into the mad-dash at Morleys entrance, then withdrew into the safer darkness of the shop doorway.

Poor you, poor, poor you, said James O'Mailer. Such a testing evening and the baton of shit, too.

You know nothing.

I'm The Flame. I know everything.

Begone!

206

I huddled up against the wall and lit another cigarette. Across the street, the crowd seemed to be pouring out of Morleys with more gabble and urgency. Seb appeared coolly behind a particularly panicked group as it dispersed, and handed me my stuff.

'You should go back in,' he said. 'It's like The Rumble in the Jungle up there. Poetic justice at last.'

'Please, Seb. I don't want to know about any of it anymore.'

'But I do. Which is why we're going to a little place I know just off The Strand where we can sup whisky until three and you can tell me everything that you're not telling me.'

'Seb,' I said, as I buttoned up my coat and felt unable to move, prevented from leaving the alcove. 'Seb, I've got a two-hundred year old literary genius living in my head[51].'

'My dear boy,' he said, grabbing me by the sleeve. 'Of course you have. Of course you have.'

---

[51] **James O'Mailer**: Well, dear reader, I have to admit that here I was most affronted. A mere two hundred years old! I am far older than two hundred. I am the gyre. I am the candle-ends of time. I am the shadow beyond the cave. I am Kvasir. The Flame. And by this point my exile was nearly over. I was getting stronger. I was almost ready. It was almost the hour of the return of the repressed.

Point of View

The Twelve Labours of Beta Male

Never start a story with just a title. Never say to yourself, I'd like to write something called *Pylons of Despair* or *Catty Foodfight* or *The Reading Group Speed-Dating Gangbang Girls* and head out from there. Always have an image, a glimpse or an atmosphere, and work from the mind's eye out. I, of course, had a million titles for unwritten stories that I reeled through as, a day after my return from The Arctic, I was standing in the bank queue, trying to hide and terrified that Frank Denbigh would notice me.

Porno and Hard-Drive and the Curious Incident of the Spearmint in the Rhino. (short story with prolix and reverberating coda).

The Life and Loves of Moomin Boobischlapper (a 3-for-2 table product-shifter).

Subcarpathian Transruthenia (utopian idyll).

Special Brew Breakfast of Champions (comic inferno).

Lingerie Inside (fuck knows).

When I arrived I'd not noticed that Frank was three ahead of me. By the time I clocked him, he'd reached the counter, *The Grasp of Fear* cheque was rotting into my hot little hand and behind me the queue was a long lunchtime snake. I didn't want to go away and come back – I had things to do, the dreaded Point of View class to prepare – but for the life of me I didn't want to be recognized.

Frank was about to conduct his business, probably depositing ill-gotten gains from grave robbing or drive-by organ extraction. I was thinking that if I looked remote and distracted and kept running through all the titles of the stories I was one day going to write I'd become invisible and he'd saunter out past me as if I wasn't there.

The Di Caprio Code (toss).

The Essence of Sycamores (historical romance set against the backdrop of the Austro-Serbian Pig War of 1912).

Entertaining Jennifer Ex (really miserable novel).

Lemming, Lemming (slim volume of excretitious verse).

Anal Audits (self-help for accountants, actuaries and middle managers of the Tropic of Reigate persuasion).

At the counter window, Frank's bald head flamed with a pink flush and his sheepskin coat was crosshatched with brown stains and splatters. He heaved a bulging green cloth bag from his pocket and banged it onto the counter shelf.

'Got these, mate,' he said, and proceeded to unload six or seven smaller polythene bags stuffed with coppers. I stopped my listing and bristled with frustration. Why is it that when you want to simply whiz in a cheque, the person in front will be negotiating some complicated, Byzantine transaction, like paying for the gas a decade ahead using an arcane bartering method, or performing an alchemical ritual to turn lead into Travellers' Cheques? Why couldn't Frank just spend his change like a normal person, or bung it in a charity box? Why would I have to stand here and risk being accosted just so he could have a few quid that he would no doubt spend on a new ball-pein hammer? And where did he get that money? Probably underneath a headstone, or from some poor, recently-dispatched pensioner's electricity meter. The bank clerk, who looked like the young Franz Kafka, reached through and took the bags. The first one jingled as it was placed on the scales. I closed my eyes.

Gibber and Twitch (romcom).

Rentagit (celebrity TV tie-in).

Paget Found in Woodland (fantasy).

Emmy Lou Dustbin and The Lovejoy Tavern Mystery (a jigsaw novel of contradictory metaphysical ideas).

The Twelve Labours of Beta Male.

I found an index card in my pocket and wrote this title down. *The Twelve Labours of Beta Male*: the story of work-shy fop and unconvincing romantic hero; absence of butchy-butchy attributes and martial aspirations; weak specimen, ungainly, not strong and silent, but morose and verbose. Is set twelve relatively easy tasks, like cleaning own flat, buying right ingredients for Thai-style green curry and going out without starting incident in internationally renowned bookstore. To be written *Ulysses* style, each part mirroring and deconstructing one of the Labours of Hercules.

No, I thought, that's the cockest of cock ideas. That really is the piss of the poorest, the lame of the limpest, the sorriest of the creatively destitute. I was supposed to be writing *Millennium Bridge*. I'd left that poor girl stranded in that café weeks ago and as yet no one had turned up to fetch her. If I did nothing about this, Frank would appear genielike in front of her with his ball-pein hammer tucked into a sling concealed in his sheepskin. Only The Starfish could save her from the slab.

The bank clerk Kafka had weighed all but the last of the bags and shunted them to one side. He put the last on the scales. The levers hovered up and down, and then failed irritatingly to balance.

'I'm sorry, sir,' said Kafka, ' but there's only ninety-nine pence in this one.'

'What you saying?' said Frank.

'I'm saying, sir, that there's not enough change in this bag.'

'There must be.'

'I assure you, sir, that there isn't.'

'No, no, no, she said there was quid in there.'

'Do you have another penny, sir?'

Frank banged his palm on the glass.

'She ain't ever wrong.'

'Look, sir, the scales do not balance.'

Frank now had both of his hands pressed to the glass. From behind, it looked like he was crushing the Kafka's head.

'She said it were all there. Gimme me money.'

'If you can just give me a penny, sir, and I can change this up for you.'

'I don't carry cash and she ain't ever wrong. You saying she's wrong?'

'Why don't you hold onto to this lot until next time.'

'You saying she can't count, you little snit?'

'Not at all, sir.'

213

'You got head like bleeding elephant, ain't you?'

Frank slammed the flats of his hands onto the glass. The thump shuddered around the white walls and the spinners of brochures and all along the queue. Kafka wheeled backwards in his chair and his smile bailed-out. I turned away and shut my eyes.

The Twelve Labours of Beta Male.

One: Swimming ten lengths without a breather.

Two: Installing Broadband without fit of hysterical frustration.

Three: Answering spam phone-call from Indian call centre without swearing blue murder.

Four: Passing driving test before eighth attempt and with a limited bodycount.

Five: Doing washing-up without slicing open finger on chopping knife and bleeding half to death on floor of garret kitchen.

Six: Speaking French without sounding like Inspector Clouseau.

'You sneaky little pervert.'

Another bang pounded on the counter. Frank's tree-trunk arms were lofted Incredible Hulk style, and he loomed over the Kafka.

'I'm gonna have you,' he said. 'I'm gonna come back in here one of these days and rip your piddling 'ead off. You see this face, mate, you're dead. You see this coat, you're a goner. You see these boots, you a dead man. You see these eyes. You see these eyes, yer, runty porker.'

Kafka bleached so white he was merging with the colour scheme. The queue was breaking up. Some of the lunch-timers fled into the street and the rest of us drifted towards the wall. Frank lumbered around, slowly, mechanically, like an articulated lorry doing an eighteen-point turn, and stomped his way towards the door.

I shut my eyes again.

The Twelve Labours of Beta Male.

Seven: Getting a night's sleep without horrible dreams about the mistakes that I've made.

Eight: Shaving without cutting off nose.

Nine: Not having *Ghosts* by Japan as favourite song.

Ten: Managing pleasant, non-gibberish conversation with nice, well-mannered, emotionally mature, undamaged and interesting woman.

Eleven: Leaving the garret without acting as flypaper-magnet for every loon, crank and barker from The Shire to The Arctic.

Twelve: Writing a novel that people want to read and selling it.

214

'Nathan!'

I kept my eyes closed and held my breath until something latched onto my shoulder and turned me sideways. Frank was towering over me with his baby-like glee glowing in his face.

'Nathan, me old cocker.'

'Oh, hi Frank,' I said. 'Didn't notice you there.'

'Now Nathan, son, I do need to talk to you . . . about this writing malarkey . . .'

'Er Frank, I really am in a hurry . . .'

'Won't take a minute . . .'

'Frank, I'm rushed off my feet. Can't it wait until tonight?'

'The thing is, Nathan . . .'

'Frank, I'm coming down with Lupus, so don't stand so close to me, and really this is going to have to wait, seriously.'

'Come to think of it, you do look a bit dicky.'

'Sir . . .' Another voice came from behind me. I turned and realized that I was now at the head of the queue and being called by a different clerk, Kafka having presumably metamorphosed down to beetle-size so he could drop unhindered into a wastepaper bin and hide out for a while.

'Tonight, Frank, OK?' I said.

'Yeah, yeah, it can wait.'

As he left, the door swished in a gust of cold air that unsettled the leaflets and the fliers on the spinners. I realized that I was the only customer left and that I'd screwed up my *Grasp of Fear* cheque and paying-in book into a ball in my fist.

Lion

After I'd paid in the crumpled cheque, I left the bank and stood on the pavement outside, unsure for a minute of what I wanted to do and where I was going. I looked up the hill and noticed that the Catholic cathedral was shrouded in mist. Something pulled on the back of my head, a feeling that I was being watched. Without turning around to check, I crossed the road and paced down a cobbled street, picking up speed as the gradient carried me. The feeling was still there, tugging at my skull. I stopped and about-faced in the chill air, half-expecting to see Erika Gretsch, with or without her hood trailing me. Nobody, however, seemed to be there. The top of the road was a patch of white mist that obscured the facade of the bank. When I carried on though, I was sure I could hear footsteps. At the bottom of the road, I found an Irish theme pub called Portrait of the Artist and sidled in, bought a pint of the dark stuff, occupied a table by the window and took my journal out of my shoulder bag. I wrote *The Twelve Labours of Beta Male* on a bright new page.

I thought about the mythical labours of Hercules and scribbled notes about the protagonist being a hairy, beardy, club-dragging, animal-skin-wearing Iron John, alpha-nob. Whoever had set down those stories in Ancient Greece really needed a thorough fumigation. The legends are all procedure. Hercules is set a task, to capture or kill a beast (the Nemean

Lion, the Cretan Bull etc), or nick some magic item that doesn't belong to him (Hippolytes' Girdle, the Apples of the Hesperides etc, and this was in the time before capitalism, so none of the palaces had household insurance) and he does it each time more or less without effort or jeopardy. There are no twists or risks or reversals. You know that the old swingwilly is going to do it as soon as you start reading. This is terribly bad plotting, and although I knew that *The Labours* were supposed to be a religious rite to show Mr H's suitability for kingship, the sequence is really just a late-Bronze Age forebear of the articles you get in blokes' magazines like *Nuts* and *Zoo*. Instead of *One-Hundred Things You Should Have Done Before You're Thirty*, it's *Twelve Things You Should Have Killed Before You're Deified*. For slaying the Lerceyneian Hydra, read paragliding naked over Ibiza high on horse tranquillisers and Vodka Redbull. For apprehending the Mares of Diomedes, read snorting coke off a Bulgarian prostitute's stomach in a Monaco hotel room cheered on by the original Oasis line-up. For fetching the Cattle of Geryon, read having a crafty wank over best mate's bird. And as for Hercules, there's not much going on in there. He's not exactly a role model for the modern man. He's not insightful and clever and a proper romantic hero, like Odysseus or me. His parenting skills need a bit of honing too, considering he was buggering his stepson Hylas, then let the poor sod wander off unsupervised so some naughty nymphs could lure him into a pond and drown him. I reckoned that the bookshelf of Hercules would be full of 3-for-2 table product-shifters and his CD collection decidedly mainstream, with an emphasis on monobrow cock rock. He couldn't write a short story of the likes of *Boys* or *Lesser Lights*. Essentially, he's a vascular system for his pecs. He's the Sylvester Sly Ramos-Pintos of the classical world, a lumbering, programmed thing. Now, beta male is a much more interesting proposition, a man with depth and desires and imagination . . .

Yearning is everything . . .

I felt a little pressure at my temples.

Look who's coming to see you, said James O'Mailer.

'I'm not talking to you, you prick,' I said.

'Eh, steady on,' a voice burred.

You fall for it every time, you sap, said O'Mailer.

Standing in front of my table, two pints of Guinness gripped in his baseball-mitt-like paws, the froth coursing over them and dripping along the sleeves of his sheepskin, his face burning like red sky in the morning, shepherd's warning, was Frank.

He slammed the pints down on the table, splashing stout across my book.

'I'm sorry,' I said. 'I wasn't talking to you.'

'Who were yer talking to then?' he said. 'I'm not talking to you, you prickle?'

'Look, Frank, I was planning some dialogue. It helps to read it out loud.'

His huge head tilted to one side and his eyes twinkled.

'Oh, alright then.'

He sat down and pushed a pint towards me.

'Nathan, right . . .'

'Frank, were you just following me?'

'No, I was in here anyways and I saw you come in. I just want to have a little word, that's all. Don't want to do it in front of the others. Man to man stuff.'

Ah, said O'Mailer. Life imitates art for you, doesn't it? The First Labour of Beta Bleater. Getting rid of what you term a Wrong-Roomer. A Wrrrrong Rrrooomer.

Frank pulled up his pint and swigged half of it at once but all the time kept his blue-black eyes fixed on me. Internal intelligence gathering network explained to me that I might as well get this over with and sit and listen. Otherwise I might be found tomorrow with my legs protruding from the top of a wheelie-bin in some wind-whistling back-alleyway in Spixworth or Diss.

'OK, Frank,' I said. 'What's on your mind?'

He placed three fingers on a beer mat and started to circle it in a smear of spilt froth.

'Don't know, Nathan. Since I started this writing monkeys, I been getting all turned over and stuff.'

'Well, that's how it should be,' I said.

'Thing is, I've written this story, and I quite like it, and it does all the things that you tell us to do and that, but I don't want me wife to read it.'

'Why's that?'

' 'Cause it's about the sex, you see, and I don't want her to think unfavourably of me and that.'

I swigged my Guinness as a hot sweat broke out across my shoulders. The mental pictures were not at all comforting, but in some ways I was relieved that he was showing a more demure and innocent side.

'Well, Frank,' I said. 'I can see that that might pose problems, but think back to what I said to Mac in class. You need to ask yourself do we *need* to know what you're telling us, and are you telling us the *truth*, about sex?'

'What? That they're all chuffing whores.'

'Pardon?'

Yes, he really did say that, said O'Mailer. It's hammer time.

Be quiet, you.

I rummaged in my jacket pocket and took out my cigarettes.

'That's all I see everywhere,' said Frank. 'Chuffing whores, outside the school gates and up on the heath, whores standing about with the spawn of their loose license.'

Lighting a cigarette, I took a good, long drag and hoped that the smoke would gas O'Mailer for a bit.

'Frank, mate,' I said. 'One of the things about writing a story is that we don't come at it with the hammer of judgement. Erm . . . hammer's not the word I was looking for. But, you need to ask questions of why and what's happened to someone. You can't go round referring to women as whores. It's . . . off-putting.'

'You mean I got to be more, like, subtle. *Show* a whore rutting and that?'

'Mmm, not really. If this story you've written contains pejorative vocabulary, then you'd be advised not to show it to your wife, and I think maybe it would be more interesting if you thought about where all this anger towards women comes from.'

'They fucked me over, Nate, that's what it is? The chuffing whores Blair brought in to manage the ambulance service. Thirty years I was doing it and they say I was unwell and chuck me out. It was all tarts saying stuff out of turn, anyway. I'm so angry about it. So, so angry. I walk about and I feel angry, angry, angry.'

He threw back the rest of his pint. As he slashed his hand over his mouth to wipe away the foam his head burned a deeper, darker crimson.

'Anyway, Nate, I bet you're giving it to all them birds in the class anyway, aren't you? It's like a perk, innit?'

'No, Frank, I assure you that I'm not.'

'You want another?'

'No, I've not finished this one yet.'

219

'I'm quite glad you said that about the birds, because, I don't know whether I should be telling you this . . .'

'Maybe you shouldn't then.' I found myself leaning back, rocking a little to ease the chair away from the table. He was smiling his gummy smile again. I reached out and cradled my pint between my knees.

'You know that Doctor Jane? Well, when it's raining I can't help myself and I go out to my shed and when the sound of the drops is just right, I find myself thinking about her and her flashy gear and then I can't stop myself.'

'Frank, seriously, man to man, you're not her type, so keep that to yourself.'

'Oh don't mock me, Mr. Nathan, if she knew me she'd let me have her. But it ain't just her. I've kind of been thinking about that Erika, too.'

I looked down at the disc of froth on the top of my pint and then saw it shrink and compress as the glass slipped through my fingers. It smashed on the wooden floor with a crack and a tinkle.

'Whoops, butterfingers,' said Frank. Then he reached over and grabbed hold of my right hand. 'Look at your hands, Nathan. Ain't they soft. Them's an educated man's hand. Feel mine. They're like big fat pork sausages.'

I stood up and shook off his grip.

'You stay here, Frank, I'm going to get a cloth.'

I put my notebook away and slung the bag over my shoulder. He looked across at me as if he suspected what was going to happen next.

'Tell you what, Nathan,' he said. 'Tonight I'll read out me little story and you can tell me about the subtlety and that.'

Two minutes later, I found myself panting and coughing and wheezing in a concrete tube. I'd sprinted all the way from Portrait of the Artist, through the flats and the mist to the underpass, where beta male sat down and froze into a ball.

The First Labour, said O'Mailer, and you ran like a sissy. Hercules would have given him one in the kisser with his cudgel. Twelve Labours for you, Dame Parlet, and should you fail, I shall be forced to intervene.

Hydra

When I arrived back at my house, Bob the maintenance man was in the front garden, sweeping dead leaves and cut grass into a heap in the corner where the hedge met the wall. I said hello, then let myself in. The air in the hall smelt mouldier than usual and I noticed that slugs' trails criss-crossed the carpet again. The thought of spending another winter here suddenly made me want to burst into tears. I composed myself as I trudged up the stairs towards the garret, and as I did so that pressure swelled up behind my ear again.

That was good, wasn't it? said James O'Mailer. Plenty you can recycle there. I could get a trilogy out of that little encounter.

'No, James, that was horrible,' I said as I unlocked the door. 'He's getting worse.'

The garret was a state. I'd not had time to clear it up before I left for *Moonshot* and only got back late last night after spending all of Saturday and most of Sunday afternoon drinking and moaning with Seb in what once had been Fitzrovia dives but now were themed sofa-pubs and wet-wiped brewery franchises. In the dark the garret had seemed less dusty and shabby than it did now. The light fell on the wall by my desk in such a way that the scorch marks made by the heater looked like two pendulous brown breasts.

That's the sort of thing Barking Frankie would notice, said O'Mailer.

'Thinking is one thing, doing another,' I said.

The issue here, Dame Parlet, is whether our Frank really is a lust-killer, or is he one of those popinjays who'll confess to crimes that he didn't commit, who'd rather be thought of as a famous fiend than a shed-dwelling onanist?

'I'm sure it's the latter,' I said, staring at my desk and the space where my starfish used to sit. It came back to me that yesterday afternoon, before I'd caught the Polar Express back to The Shire, I'd made a visit to Bankside and, with my head buzzing with scotch, stood on the Millennium Bridge, hoping that something would fire off inside me, that something would come.

So you have considered the condition of Frank? said O'Mailer.

'Of course I have. What do you think I am? Some sort of moron?'

You can come to your own conclusions about that, Kiddo. For the sake of hypothesis, say Barking Frankie really is something ripped from the imagination of Fritz Lang or Musil or Dostoeyevsky, how significant do you think it may turn out to be that just now he stroked your soft scholar's mitten like he would that of a doomed femme fatale? Beauty is a snare, after all.

'Don't be stupid, James.'

What if. Isn't that the question you force upon your charges?

'No, you crappy ghost, what I ask myself is why on earth do these people think I want to know what goes on in their dirty minds? Why do I have to know about Mac's wank fantasies and Erika's illusions of grandeur and Reg's dreams of rolling back the permissive society and Frank's murder fixations? Why, oh why, oh why? I bet none of these bammers would unburden themselves to the bloody ornithology tutor, would they, you flapping tit?'

I had stropped across the room and my face was now wedged into the corner behind the television stand.

'Why? Why? Why? Why?' I thumped the wall with my fist. 'Why? You tell me that, James, seeing as you're so omniscient? Why? Come on, James? Where are you now? Where've you gone? Show yourself. C'mon. James? James? James James James?'

'Er, Nathan?'

I turned around, a sheet of shame billowing up from my feet to my chin as I realized that I must have left the door on the latch. The maintenance man was standing in the doorway in his dirt-streaked overalls. 'You all right, Nathan? I heard shouting.'

Oh shit. The cigarette end was burning my fingers and I wanted to turn into fluid and pour myself into the grill on the back of the TV.

'It's OK, Bob, seriously, I'm just, you know, doing a bit of method.'

'Right you are.'

After he'd left and the sound of sweeping drifted up from the garden, I slumped onto the floor, clutching my head with my hands. I had to get out. I had to get away. It all had to stop. I had to sell *Penelope*. *Penelope*? I realized that I'd not checked my e-mails for four days.

As I waited for the nicotine-stained iMac to boot up and then for my Internet connection, I had a premonition that there would be a message from someone somewhere saying, *yes, we love* <u>Penelope</u>, *send us the whole ms*, or: *someone somewhere told me that you have written the most exciting and imaginative novel*; a fantasy counterbalanced by my more reasonable side that knew the inbox tally would most likely be '0'.

Well, actually, the inbox was stuffed to the gills with a thirty-three new messages, most of them spam. I began to scan through and pick up anything interesting.

Subject: Harkerdammerung

Hi Nathan,

Good to see you at the weekend and thank you very much for enlivening these musty old bones. I am, of course, a little frustrated with your lack of laurels, though am sure all good things will be coming your way soon.

Things are, of course, moving in a different direction for yours sincerely. Marcus Gytt, my agent since the July Days, has just phoned to say that Dewsenbury want to see me to talk about my contract. His voice was most mournful and heavy with resignation. Methinks this is my retirement from the theatre of operations.

Anyway, I will go down with the ship. See you next month, where no doubt we will share a bottle.

Don't let me down. Distinguished Sentiments.

Sebastian.

Bastards, I thought, and waited for James O'Mailer to kick in with some smart remark. When no swelling occurred, I rattled off a reply, thanking Seb for his whisky and support and saying that maybe this was nothing and it would blow over. Olivier Blox would probably get the sack for not flogging enough units in Kwikfit or Poundstretcher and the works of Sebastian Harker would continue to be published. I had been angry when I arrived back home. Now I was miserable and the misery deepened when I clicked on my next e-mail.

From: bigmac@throbber.com
Subject: The Death Metal Revelations

Alright Nate, you miserable prat. No, not really. Yoor Ok, you, when you smile and that. Mac McMahon here. Anyways, just fort I'd let yous know that I read through your report and kind of see what your getting re me book but after all thought I was right and you were wrong. So thanks anyway. Anyways, dealt with all that and wrote it all up and sent it off to an agent this morning. When its published I'll put in a good word for you. Sounds fair, don't it.

See you tonite.

Mac

Clicked 'reply' and put head on keyboard and produced a neologism: *gopasalhnfnnmrngannnnnnnnnnnnnnnnnnnnnnnnnnnnnnnnnnnooooooooo.*

They're binning Harker. They're not going to replace him with the Fat Drummer Who Beats His Meat with All His Heart. I didn't send the message though, and would pretend that it got lost in the ether, the place where Mac's novel was heading.

Then I suspected more bad news:

From: davecave71@killmeplease.com
Subject: Sorry

Nathan,

How's you? Hope you got back safely. Good to see you and Seb on Friday. Who was that woman!!! Jesus Christ on a bike! There was a lot of damage in the reference section and Morleys want to bill us for it. Great reading by the way and we all loved the story. Come back any time (when we've found a new venue). We need you.

Sorry I didn't get a chance to catch up with you and have a bev. You sort of vanished.

Speak soon

Dave

Well, that was very polite of him and he really had no need to spare my blushes. The memory of my performance sent that sheet of shame coursing down from my head back to my feet again. I replied with a 'thank you' and told him to get Morleys to send the bill to Erika Gretsch c/o The School of Adult Education. It did seem to me, however, that I may have got away with my *Moonshot* madness, and at the very least had not lost any friends over it, an over-hopeful thought soon crushed by the next message.

From: J.Largo@un.ac.uk
Subject: (none)

Dear Nathan,

Things have been brought to my attention regarding your behaviour at a certain event in London last Friday. I have received two complaints, one from a current student and one from a good friend of this department. As you are a representative of this department when you attend these things, I am very concerned.

Please see me in my office at 18.00, Tuesday to discuss.

Yours sincerely

Juliet

xxx

Please see me! Please see me! Yeah, I'll see you all right.

I replied with a simple 'OK' before I had a chance to type something apocalyptic. The Plum would do anything to get a reaction out of me, any sort of reaction. I had to remember that. Two complaints? It wasn't too difficult to work out where they came from. Then I noticed that there was an agency message and a burn of expectancy fired across my shoulders.

225

From: F. Malone@ZY HAGGARD.co.uk
Subject: The Garret of the Fumigator

Dear Nathan,
As you supplied no return post with this manuscript, I'll put it   in the recycling.
Yours sincerely

Frederick Malone

Expectancy's burn turned to humiliation's singe. Why did I bother sending *that* to him? Well, things couldn't get any worse, could they?

From: L. Levankranz@eigthwindow.co.uk
Subject: (none)

Hi Nathan,

I know that you probably don't want to hear from me, given what you said last Friday, but I am very sorry that we can't at least be civil, given that we are bound to run into each other once in a while in our professional capacities. I'm sorry that there was a bit of a scene and sorry that we couldn't talk properly. I did want to come and find you but unfortunately I had to go to casualty with Ferdie. He had to have three stitches in the end.

To be honest, I blame you for that. Your new girlfriend is clearly insane and I am really worried about you. You don't seem too well to me. I expect everything is getting on top of you again. Anyway, I just wanted to clear the air really. If you want me to, I can recommend a really lovely therapist in Golders Green.

Please don't be angry with me.

Lisa

I read this three times, then got up, went into my bedroom, lay on my bed with my headphones on and listened to all of The Fall's *Hex Enduction Hour* at volume level twenty-five and then *Beachy Head* by Throbbing Gristle and watched my cigarette smoke vanish into the ceiling tiles. When I'd finished and my nerves felt less jangly, I deleted her message with the rest of the junkmail. This left me with a heart-sinking:

From: R.Carnaby@albion.org.uk
Subject: Dear Diary

Ah autumn, season of mists and mellow fruitfulness and all the time my Darling Dear ripens and helps me through these dark ages. Work upon my novel is picking up the pace and soon I shall be ready to share some with my fellows, show them how it's done, what, what. As I sit in the pantry with my pen running over the page, I can feel the very spirit of Jane Austen flowing through me and when my Darling Dear entered the room last night to kindly serve up a slice of her redoubtable Battenburg and a mug of creamy Horlicks, I couldn't help but think that she and JA would have got on swimmingly. Flack should take note. Full of balderdash, as he is, I'm sure that he has no way of communing with the English Greats. It is among them that I shall take my place when I quit this land of peasants and hooded vandals.

The weekend was example enough of the state that we are in. After church, my Darling Dear and I pitched up unannounced at good old Kip and Myra de Courcy's. Kip, the sweet old thing, was on veritable cloud nine since last week being selected by the United Kingdom Independence Party to stand as Parliamentary representative for our proud constituency at the forthcoming general election, and was revelling visibly in his new nickname of UKIP de Courcy. To celebrate we drank several bottles of vino collapso and ended up at the end of his garden, surveying the vale from the top of the hill. Down there, in the valley, a pack of marauding didicoys careered about on four-wheeled bikes, making a hell of a racket, while the rest of the litter seemed to be devouring a dead horse. I suppose that sort of thing goes down well in the emerald isle, but not on our patch, I can tell you. UKIP went back for his ratting gun, and I was all in agreement, but my Darling Dear, ever the voice of reason in such situations, suggested we call out the Hunt now they're unoccupied. She always knows what to do. I used to admire the way she'd ring Enoch Powell at the drop of a hat.

Something had poisoned the water supply, I was sure. A hallucinogenic fungus had infected the wheat. The Folder-Holders were going berserk. Something was going to happen. Some crisis was approaching and only Beta Male stood between the world and the end of days. On my tombstone it would be inscribed:

Nathan Flack
Literary Snob
He Fought for Sanity and Morale.

I deleted Reg's message, had a walk around the block, then another one, and before I returned to the last of the e-mails, had a good listen to *Metal Machine Music* by Lou Reed. The 'music' was still clanging in my ears, when I picked up the last of the e-mails:

From: J.O'Mailer@greatness.tradition.universal
Subject: Give up.

You've failed the second labour, dear beta boy. You've no answers to any of the questions here. The world really is against you. You're heading for a crash, a head-on collision, a ground-rush, a fatal bounce. Let me give you a word of advice, Dame Parlet. Give up now. Show this lark a fair pair of heels and elope with Doctor Jane. She has a good and loyal nature and would switch off this restless, self-destructive side in you and together you can get on with what I need you to do. Give up your head. You are merely my hat. Otherwise, dear Flack, you and I shall fight it out in the snowy wastes and the prize shall be your soul.
Yours ever faithfully,

James O'Mailer Esq.

I slowly turned around in my chair and stared at the room, at the window, at the rooftops that disappeared on their way to the horizon. Who was he? Where was he? What was he? How could he send me an e-mail? Had I made him up, or was he actually real? Was I going mad? Was I the mad one? Was I a straight character in mad world, or a mad character is straight world? I paced the room in urgent circuits, muttering, 'Show yourself, show yourself, show me who you really are.[52]'

---

[52] **James O'Mailer:** Ah, he rises to the bait. It is merely pride that causes him to do so, but the die is cast. I shall rest for a time as I sharpen my blades. Fear not, dear reader, I merely tarry in the barren snows a while. I shall be back to enliven this text and the final battle will commence.

Hind

Later that evening, I was standing outside the double glass doors of the
School of Adult Education, readying myself for my showdown with
Plum/Largo. When the final notes of Nico's version of *The End* faded out
in my headphones, I clicked off my Discman. Where I had expected a
fortifying silence, spaghetti western trumpets seemed to sound in my
head. I lit a cigarette and stared into the building and the over-lit corridor
that led down to the Orgsburo. A summons from The Plum was the sort
of thing that I usually talked through with Frances beforehand, and vice
versa, both of us having postgraduate qualifications in Plum Management.
I'd given Frances a call earlier, but she still wasn't there. Now I willed the
throb at my ear, for James O'Mailer to whisper to me, given that before
he'd been unusually helpful on the subject of the Orgsburo. Nothing
happened. I huffed, stubbed out my fag, and tried to pull myself together.
It was Sharon Plum I was about to confront, not some mythical monster.
Given that she spent most of her time fantasising about creating an even
bigger, hydra-like network of contacts that would lead eventually to
having it off with Jeanette Winterson, she wasn't really bothered about
me making a pranny out of myself. She was pulling my choke chain, that's
all. I understood this, and would use it to my advantage. I would chase
the hind around until it fell over and gave up (Hercules chases; Beta Male

229

talks). And after all, how could any sane person support over mine the word of Erika Gretsch, a certifiable Moon-Barker, and Ferdinand Paget, the Enemy of All that Breathes, who I assumed was the so-called 'friend of the department'. I could swing this, easily charm my way out of it. I summoned up the swagger of Sylvester Sly Ramos-Pintos and smoothed my way into the corridor, striding along its length and checking out the shadows that crouched in the roundels.

The Department was, as ever, a total shambles. Work stations were heaped with tottering files; the overhead lights flickered; the floor was empty of staff, except for the man with an uncanny resemblance to Stephen King who taught an Archaeology unit on Excavating Human Remains (better not tell Frank about him). He was smashing the photocopier repeatedly with a cardboard tube. The door to the Orgsburo was shut. I knocked, pausing in the doorway of Plum/Largo's narrow, breezeblock-walled office.

She was slouched in her swivel chair, her back to me and a mobile phone pressed to her ear. On her desk sprawled papers and folders, books and glossy celebrity magazines, coffee cups and sandwich cartons, Mars and Snickers wrappers and scrunched-up packets of Oriental-style snacks and one family-sized Häagen Dazs ice-cream tub dripping with brown goo. The laptop's screensaver wiggled. A nubile, topless dancer humped a chrome-coloured pole over and over against a black backdrop. Sharon's post-modern irony sucked the red cells from my blood and patterned them across the slender slats of the venetian blinds. She didn't seem to notice me, so I knocked again.

Using the tips of her three-striped trainers, she paddled the chair about-face.

'He's here,' she said into the phone, then took it from her face. 'Jesus Christ, Nathan, knock please, I'm talking.'

'Did knock,' I muttered, then took a step back and rested against a table. I stared into the doorway and Sharon Plum in her outsized grey shirt and navy blue tracksuit bottoms with white piping. The whacking sound came from over by the photocopier.

'Bastard,' shouted Stephen King. 'Bastard, bastard, fucking bastard!'

The photocopier hissed and flashed at the end of the room as Sharon Plum spun on her chair, her feet dragging until she faced me again.

'Waiting for pralines,' she said into the phone. ' Yadda, yadda, yadda, push the envelope, mwaw, mwaw, sweetie, love you L. Got to go, *don't . . . ew.*'

She tossed the phone. It clattered onto the desk.

'Hello Mr Flack,' she said, smiling sweetly now.

I stepped forward. The office smelt distinctly of dry-roasted peanuts.

'Good evening, Sharon,' I said.

'How many fucking times?' she said.

'Sorry. Good evening, Juliet,' I said, and sniggered. She tilted her head, wrinkled her nose, frowning. I mustn't snigger. This was a charm offensive, remember.

'That's better. Take a pew.' She gestured at a chair against the leftside wall. I sat down and rested my bag on my lap, using it as a kind of safety-barrier. She was close to me now, her face in my face, her eyes glittering like coal. She definitely stank of peanuts. I wondered if Shostakovich felt like this whenever he had an audience with Stalin.

'How are you, love puppy?' she said.

'Woofy,' I said.

'Well, I don't think so.'

I smiled and fiddled with the strap of my bag, remembering that it's always a good idea to distract Sharon with talk of a female cultural artefact. 'Can I play my Nico CD in here?' I said.

She looked at me, bemused, then swished her hand. 'What is all this attitude from you?'

'Attitude?' I said. I am from south London and feigning dumb ignorance in front of authority figures is encoded in my DNA.

'I shouldn't have to call you in like this,' she said.

'No, you shouldn't.'

'Well, what have you got to say for yourself?'

'Nothing,' I said. 'Sharon . . . Juliet, nothing has happened.'

'Well, it doesn't seem that way to me. Ferdie Paget called me and said you encouraged someone to assault him, and one of your students said you shouted at her in public, and last two times I've seen you, you told me to piss off in front of my class. I'm sorry, but where I come from, that's an attitude.'

'Sharon, for the record . . .' I tried to be as level-voiced and reasonable sounding as I could. '. . . I did not encourage anyone to assault anyone. Secondly, Erika Gretsch was the have-a-go hero here and she's also been following me. She's stolen property from me. A sheep's head was brought into my classroom. She disrupts my class and bothers the others. She's genuinely mad, as you well know, and she walloped Mr Paget all on her lonesome. I want you to do something about that.'

'Not all students are nice little bookworms, you should know that by now. You know I can't just remove someone just because a tutor doesn't like teaching her.'

'Sharon . . .'

'Juliet!'

'Juliet then, Erika was staking out Frances's flat, something you know she's done before, and now Frances had vanished.'

'You heard from Ms Mink?'

'No, I've not . . .'

'Mmm.' She swivelled on her chair again and parted her legs. I pulled my bag closer to me.

'How's the book going, Nathan?'

'"Fine,' I said, twisting the bag's strap so it dug into my wrist.

'I know all this is getting to you. I sympathize. And look, I understand, really I do, how you feel about Ferdie, given that that dumb blonde went back to him . . .'

'She's not blonde . . .'

'How's your lovelife?'

'How's yours?'

'Why don't you come round for a bite to eat and we can talk all this through?'

I envied the Incredible Shrinking Man at this point, wanted to compress to the size of an atom and slip into the case of the Nico CD to lie a while on the rainbow swirls of the disc. I didn't say anything.

'There's a party in the Triangle on Saturday,' she said. 'Why don't you come?'

Twats from *The* MA, no way. Hazy shadow-people slotting tequilas and hoovering gak from the coffee table. Red lightbulbs. For every level, a deeper level. The same Goldfrapp song played over and over again until *Trout Mask Replica* sinks its fangs into your liver midway through the Poncing Hour.

'I thought this was about work,' I said.

'We used to be friends. And you should know that when a friend tells you that you're in a mess, you should listen. You know that I rate honesty above all else.'

'Sharon, I want you to move Erika Gretsch from my class.'

232

'You're not listening, the problem is *your* attitude. I'm going to have to give you a warning. If your attitude doesn't improve by the end of the term, I'm not going to give you any more teaching. This attitude has to stop. Now, let me buy you a pint later, come on.'

This, I knew, was the line-management technique known as the Carrot and the Hammer.

'Look, I said,' getting up. 'Thanks for your advice and thanks for the formal warning. It's very helpful to me.'

Me and my offensive charm, eh. I didn't think the Flackdaq could dive through the floor, didn't think a Garret Street Crash was in the air and that I could lose my job on Sub-Grub Street on top of everything else. Outside, in the office, Stephen King was still smashing the photocopier, this time with the base of a desktop fan. Glass shattered and plastic splintered and Sharon Plum stayed in her room with her screensaver and whatever dream would end all her dreams.

Boar

Now in my classroom in the Eudora Doon, the Folder-Holders were bunched in closer to me than ever before, encroaching on the space between my desk and the seating. Mac had taken the central chair at the front and spidered his mouth with his stubby fingers as if about to blurt something. Next to him, Reg sat bolt upright, his tweedy trousers pulled up to his tits as ever, and an inevitable accusation or throwback's comment perched already on his tortoise-beaked face. Erika had abandoned her backwall-hugging strategy of the week before and taken a seat in the second row. She glared at me through the gap between Cynthia and Doctor Jane, who were huddled at the left-hand end. And next to Jane, causing her to lean away and imploringly peer up at me, was Frank: enormous, pig-like and with a rolled sheaf of foolscap clutched in his fist.

In my mind's eye I saw the class reaching out their white hands to me, waving ashen limbs, their eyes glazed with blue grime. Come to us, Nathan, join us, be like us. You belong with us. You belong to our folder holding, to our thick as shit Literature Denial and freaky Wrong-Roomery and boorish Grammar-Stammering and pashmina-soft Romantic Typing. You too can have a carrier bag full of dead shrews and eel bones and bark at the moon; you too can wear oatmeal sweatpants with knackered elastic. Come to us, Nathan, cooooome.

I blinked, reminding myself of where I was. This was supposed to be my workshop on narrative point of view, not one of Mac's zombie fleshgobbler wankfests. This class was the most important of the course. Ninety percent of stories that I read by students or clients were fatally undermined by problems of voice and the inability of the writer to filter the prose through a character's consciousness or concoct an engaging and rarefied narrative delivery. It's all about constriction, restriction and the fizz and life that you bring to the page. But I'd not prepared properly and owing to Stephen King Man's attack on the photocopier had no handouts or extracts for the class to read. I shambled about, making up examples on the spot.

First Person POV: I am going to lose my job.

Third-person Omniscient POV: At present we are going to concern ourselves not with the vicissitudes of narrative voice but with the notion that the locally respected creative writing tutor, Nathan Flack, was preoccupied by the thought that he was going to unfairly and unreasonably lose his job unless he conceded to Sharon Plum the run of his mind and the dilapidated playground of his body.

Third-person Subjective POV: As Nathan paced in front of the class, pretending to teach, he thought that as he was going to lose his job anyway, why should he bother with this sack of cock.

Third person Objective POV: He paced up and down and kept his eyes to the floor as he talked.

Third-person flexible POV: As Nathan paced in front of the class, he kept his eyes down, wrapped up in thoughts of how he'd ballsed up that meeting with Plum/Largo of The Orgsburo and that he was now, surely, on top of everything else, going to lose his job.

Objective POV: The wind pounded the classroom window.
'A restriction of the first-person voice is that you obviously can't allow yourself access to the thoughts of other characters,' said the tutor.
'Yes, you can,' said the Literature Denier.
'You're a talentless chancer,' said the tutor.

'You're going to lose your job,' said the Grammar Stammerer.

'He does not understand the magic of poetry,' said The Moon-Barker.

Second-person POV: You try to hide your frustration as your temples start to sweat. Your urge is to demand that The Moon-Barker return your starfish. You can now sense the impossibility of your position. You are never going to publish your novel. You are never going to escape this. You are going to lose your job. You are an utter failure and no better than any of the cranks and talentless chancers here, and worse than this, they know it.

Finally, I stopped talking and sat on my desk. Befuddled expressions crossed Mac and Frank's faces and a beetroot-red storm swirled around Reg's craggy bonce. Erika had turned her chair around, so I could only see the back of her head. Jane and Cynthia smiled in a way that seemed utterly false. It struck me that when I lost my job I would have absolutely no claim to being a writer at all.

Stream of Consciousness: James O'Mailer where are you come on down and give me a rollicking tell me that I'm right and I am one upon whom everything is lost and I should give up and go and get that job at home as a call centre manager that they have been keeping oh so warm for me.

No throb appeared or gravelly patrician voice. I needed a throb. I needed something.

'OK folks,' I said. 'We're all experts now on narrative point of view. Any questions?' Hands shot up. I turned my head swiftly to the raindrops coursing down the window. 'No. Good. Frank, my man. Why don't you read us your story?'

'Oh yes, have I got a story for you, Nathan,' said Frank as he uncurled his foolscap sheets and smoothed them out on his knee. It occurred to me that I should allow Cynthia to leave right away, and maybe let Reg and Jane go as well, and while I was at it, seeing as she'd not returned my starfish, and she had her back to me, and was going to get me the sack, Erika could stomp off into the rain. But hey, if I was going to have to sit-through a blood-dripping, spunk-splattered tract of early retirement psychosis and misogyny, then I needed more than the author of the awesome *Needing a Piss* as back up.

Frank cleared his throat. 'I'll just get on with it, shall I?' he said. I nodded and hung my head in my creative writing tutor's listening pose. 'This, right, it's called She's Taking a Train.'

'That's a nice title,' said Jane.

'Shhh.'

'Trisha Viddler,' read Frank, 'left the building and her little shoes went clickety-clack across the tarmac as she walked towards the station. They were little girl's shoes. She was a little girl, even though she was a management consultant and worked for Blair's mob. She entered the lane and the smell of the violets and the rose bushes made her feel a bit high-spirited and she thought about how she liked this time of year and how it reminded her of her mother. She was going to see her mother now. She had had a hard day's work rationalizing things up here and now she had to go and see her mother in hospital where her mother was having her hip done. That's what the NHS was for, hips and operations and heart surgery. Her poor mother, all in pain and that. It brought tears to Trisha's eyes as she paced up the lane and the sun shone between the pine trees and the day felt as if it was coming to an end. Her little shoes went clickety-clack as she wondered how many more times she would have to visit her mother in hospital, how long this would go on for, how it would seem to her if she didn't have to do this, how she would miss the old dear. She had a good look up and down at the young buck in the ticket office as she bought a ticket back to the city. The train was already in the station. She found an empty carriage and sat down. As the train pulled off, she started to think more about her mother and it seemed unfair to her that Blair's mob had just made her put out of work all these ambulance men and auxiliary nurses while other mothers still needed their hips done.'

Frank put the paper down and looked up at me and then around at Jane. She avoided his eyes, but clapped gently. Cynthia clapped too, and then Mac held up his fists, whooped and clapped big-style, rock and roll. That was it, I realized. Frank must have taken my advice and cut the stuff about 'the sex' that he didn't want to show to his wife. I allowed the pause to continue as the class worked out their responses and I considered what I was going to say: use Trisha's voice, make more of the setting, more grounding anecdotes about the mother and the job, don't call the government Blair's mob in the narrative voice, cut 'little girls'. The story was still fumigation-fodder, but it could be developed.

'Frank,' said Reg, 'may I just suggest . . .'

'Hold your horses, friends,' he said, picking up the papers again. 'I ain't finished yet. Right . . . Trisha was sitting there, thinking about her mother and the train went clickety-clack, clickety-clack. Light came in through the window and then this big bloke came into the carriage and sat down opposite Trisha. Clickety-clack. He was big in every way, she noticed, and had a big bald head and massive big hands and great dirty big feet.

'Hello, my deary,' he said. 'What are you up to?'

'My name is Trisha Viddler,' she said. 'I work for Blair's mob and I am going to see my mother.'

'I don't see my mother any more,' said the man.

'Why's that?' said Trisha, as the train went clickety-clack and her little shoes went clickety-clack as well.

'Well, it all started when I got this girlfriend,' said the man. Clickety-clack. 'Right sort she were and she really loved me package, loved it up her and she said it were a gift from God but me mum said it were a curse from Satan and made me top me bird.'

'Oh,' said Trisha, 'I wasn't expecting that.'

'You weren't expecting this either,' said the man, and with that he dropped his trousers and got out this huge dobber. Clickety-clack. He said, 'look at it, it's like a big pork sausage . . .'

'Right,' I said as I dropped off the desk and clapped one of my ponciest claps. 'I think we'll leave it there.'

Frank rocketed upright, his arms thrust out in crucifixion style, his brow gashed by deep furrows as he bellowed in my face.

'You don't understand. I hate her, I *hate* me wife, I don't want to sleep with her anymore, Nathan. I'm only doing this 'cause I don't wanna sleep with her.'

'Yes, Cynthia,' I said, 'I understand, go . . . you . . .' I gestured at Reg. 'Don't start.'

'Well I never . . .'

Frank fell to his knees. His head drooped and he started to weep and sob. In the gap he'd left appeared Erika.

'Herr professor, may I ask you? When are we going to see the magic of poetry.'

'When you give me back my fucking starfish,' I said as Frank let off a terrible, primal wail. 'Mac,' I said, 'can you talk to him?'

238

'That story was bonza, mate,' said Mac. 'And I've got some ideas to make it even better.'

At this I felt my guts, brains and tastebuds frazzle. I took a pace back. Everyone was now standing up and shoving folders into bags, the room full of crying and scuffling and murmuring. Cynthia was halfway to the door. Mac had his arm around Frank's shoulder, saying something about needing to see more of the bird, and Reg was staring at me with jaded disgust and hopelessness. Then Jane's pink pashmina lifted into the air as she climbed onto her chair and clapped her hands to snap everyone to attention.

'People, just to let you know, I'm holding a little soiree for writing types on Saturday night and you're all invited, so please come. Eightish. Nibbles and wine. Bring your friends.'

She hopped off the chair and gave me a lingering, smoky-eyed look as she packed up her things and clickety-clacked out of the room with Reg and Erika. I sat on my desk, calcifying, brain-dead and disappointed now that she'd gone so quickly, though who could blame her? Frank shuddered and shook as Mac, a manly arm around his back, led him to the door. Saturday night. She was having a party for this lot and all their friends. I could suddenly see UKIP and Myra de Courcy, their pale smug faces and belts of shrunken didicoy heads. There was no way I was going to that, not in a million years.

Stables

So a million years must have passed (or at least it seemed that way in waiting-for-news-from-agents-time), and on Saturday night, well before the Poncing Hour, with a bottle of Shiraz wrapped in midnight-blue crepe paper nestling in the crook of my arm, I found myself drifting from The Garret towards Jane's house. The wind again whooshed through the streets, swaying the furry heads of pampas grass and knocking together the hanging baskets that dangled in porches. Fallen leaves billowed up into the night to speckle the full moon, suitable atmospherics for a soiree for writing types. I'd once upon a time liked parties, or at least relished the possibility that something dramatic or romantic might happen. Like Jordan Baker in *Gatsby*, I found the big ones more intimate, the little gatherings pokey and restricting. Being locally respected creative writing tutor Nathan Flack, I would be conspicuous at Jane's salon, and must stay sober and maintain my sangfroid in front of the Folder-Holders. Any talk of writer's block, the Flackdaq's plunge, Marketing and its Discontents and the Plum's threat to my multi-pence teaching position would have to go completely unarticulated. It's always smart to have a plan, and that was mine. Responsible drinking. No whinging or brooding. Smile though your heart is breaking. I would hang about until I received the signal that it was time to leave:

Someone confides in you that: it's going to be the first in the trilogy.

Someone gets out a guitar.

Someone asks *The* Question One or *The* Question Two.

I turned into Jane's street and passed well-loved two-up, two-down houses snuggled by orderly gardens and neat privet hedges. As I progressed I became aware of a large vehicle coming up behind me and thought nothing of it until a handbrake crunched.

'Nathan, old son.'

Frank leant out of the window of his white van, his spade-shaped beard a dirty grey in the moonlight. The wind seemed to intensify its chill.

'Can I offer you a lift, sir?' he said.

'Er . . . where to?' I said. 'This is it, isn't it?' I jabbed my thumb over my shoulder at what I'd assumed was Jane's address.

'Right you are.' He slid back into the cabin and then revved the engine and parked up so quickly and haphazardly that I had to sidestep onto the garden path or be splattered against the wall. At the end of the path, the front door was ajar. The curtains were drawn. Silhouettes flickered against them. I could hear music and party murmur. A bump came from behind me. I turned. The van's suspension wobbled and bounced. Frank's voice rose then dipped from inside it. He then stumbled out of the back and smashed shut the doors with a clang that echoed around the houses.

'Nathan, loverly to see you.' He came at me with his bunch-of-bananas hand outstretched and a bottle of cider the size of an oxygen cylinder gripped in the other.

'Who were you talking to? I said, my voice snappish.

'What? In there? You don't want to worry about my little ways, Mister Nathan. I was just getting myself up and running. C'mon, the night is young, as they say.'

He put his arm around my shoulder and more or less manhandled me up the path to the door. At the porch, I managed to dig my heels into the gravel deep enough to make him stop.

'Frank mate,' I said. 'You OK?'

'Why shouldn't I be?'

'Last week . . . you seemed upset. Your wife?'

'Oh don't worry about that. I've dealt with that.' Moonlight silvered half of his face. I couldn't quite make out his eyes. An invisible line held his white head in alignment with the grinning moon above him. For a

241

second they both seemed the same size and shape and to possess the same chalky density.

'Oh I hope there's dancing and carousing,' he said as he shouldered open the door. I followed him into a hallway of parquet slats and a staircase. Frank's sheepskin coat jingled as he hung it on a hook. On the right-hand side, light from a lounge glimmered in a doorway and ahead of me figures chattered in a kitchen. Suddenly, I couldn't move. My overwhelming instinct was to turn tail and go back to The Garret and the reliable grey ashtray light and the hammerhead silence. I folded my arms and let my chin droop. I mustn't enter a party like this. I should stride in as if swaggering into a Wild West saloon, like Sylvester Sly Ramos Pintos, not lurk and twitch like Arnold Bumrape. I ought to find Jane. Finding Jane might calm me down and make me feel less uncomfortable. A quiet, unhysterical chat, that's what I needed. Easy company. Real world, day-to-day, normal life conversation and a glass of wine. Someone was staring at me. A shape in the kitchen doorway expanded, launched into the hallway, and then coming right at me, huge, black-bearded, melon-cheeked, for a moment almost the negative image of the white giant still fiddling with his coat beside me, was Mac McMahon.

'Oright Nathan,' he said. 'Guess what?'

I shook my head, poked out my bottom lip and lifted my hand in the air.

'You're gonna be pleased as punch,' he said. 'Like I said in me e-mail, right, I sent me book to this book agent last week, right, and yesterday I get this letter from him and he says, right, that it's *brilliant* and he's gonna sign me up.'

Frank turned from the coat hooks to grab Mac's hand and give it a shoulder-snapping shake.

'That's wonderful, mate, really, really wonderful. Who says this learning shit don't work, eh Nathan?'

'Which agent?' I said, tapping my foot and pushing my right hand so far into my trouser pocket that I broke the fabric. Small change began to slither down my leg. 'Which agent, Mac?'

'He's gonna start flogging me book next week,' he said.

'Mac, there are some unbelievable charlatans out there.'

'I know, he sounds great. Flogs for loadsa top names.'

'Has he asked you for any money?'

'No. Look.' He reached into his jacket and pulled out a well-thumbed letter. I took it and immediately recognized the grey silky paper and the centred letterhead in its art deco-like font.

ZY HAGGARD

Dear Mr McMahon,

RE: The Death Metal Revelations.

Thank you very much for sending us your novel, **The Death Metal Revelations**. We liked it very much and think it has great potential. Please call to arrange a lunch meeting and we can discuss ways to proceed.

I assume that there are no other copies in circulation. Please don't show it to anyone else at this juncture.

Yours sincerely

Frederick Malone

The money started to tinkle over my shoes and onto the parquet. I clawed my thigh with my hand and tore the pocket right apart as I forced a cheek-splitting smile.

'Well done,' I said, 'I'm so proud.'

'Well, you did help a bit,' he said. 'The things is, though, right, when I spoke to him, on the phone, like, I mentioned your name and he said last week you sent him the most crappest book he's ever seen. And I thought, right, double or quits like, that you could pay me to read yours and we could sort that one out. '

I was now standing on tiptoes. The tendons in my calves and groin strained as I tried to eyeball him.

'No, Mac, I sent him something as a joke. He knows that.'

A warm, thick and sagging thing suddenly dropped over my shoulder. Frank had slung his arms around both of us. He switched his face side-to-side.

'Lads,' he said. 'Tonight, I'm not concerning meself with all this art stuff you're both into. I'm on a mission. Don't you go telling no one, but I am going get that Jane tonight.'

'Good on yer,' said Mac. 'Want me to put in a word?'

I tried to interject as terror gripped my heart and I visualized local newspaper headlines – *City Woman Missing* – but Frank's arm was squashing my collarbone and Mac's beard and face and the letter I still clutched in my hand made me want to heave. I ducked under Frank and stepped back as he lofted his cider bottle.

'First,' he said, 'we drink, c'mon.'

I backed myself into the door and watched them sway along the hallway into the kitchen. I screwed up the letter and threw it after them. It ricocheted off Mac's back. He didn't notice. He didn't notice anything. Who is the one upon whom everything is lost? I waited for the throb and the jeer but no O'Mailer came. O'Mailer had gone. The e-mail had vanished from my inbox. He hadn't spoken to me for days. Maybe he was the last character I was ever going to invent and imagination had deserted me for good. Maybe my silly standards and discriminations no longer bothered him. Perhaps he was now lingering in the consciousness of the writer Mac McMahon, taunting him, winding him up. Before I burst into Beta Male tears, I hung up my coat and crept into the kitchen.

Birds

The kitchen was crammed party-cliché style and clammy with sweat and aftershave. I made eye contact with no one and thumped my Shiraz down at the end of a work surface laid out with bowls of nachos and salsa. As I uncorked my wine I noticed that the cupboard door in front of me was covered with postcards of kittens and puppies and foals. Fuckers, I mouthed. Fucking little fuckers. Fucking Frederick Malone. Inscrutable, irresponsible, unaccountable, illiterate, literature-denying, git-broking whore. What was he playing at? How could he read Mac's toss but reject *Penelope*? I slugged a glass of wine and felt it sour the back of my throat. How could Mac's no-brow bollocks be untricky to market? This was personal. This was to get at me, to put me in my place after *Garret of the Fumigator* showed him the truth. It wasn't about Mac. He was leading Mac on. He knew that no Fulham Palace Road gymslip editrice was going to 'believe' or 'love' or feel 'passionate enough'– or whatever it is that they say in interviews that they need to experience – to want Mac's sticky scrawl. No corporate Euston Road product-shifter's sales manager, not even Oliver Blox, would put their so-called marketing acumen behind Mac's asinine scribble. No chain store-buyer or book club editor would back the *Death Metal Revelations*. No way was that pulp seeing the light of day.

Frederick Malone: the bottom-scraping end of his list of authors included several hoary old rock stars signed up for one-book, ghost-biog deals.

Frederick Malone could well be Ruiner's only fan.

Mac had a tenuous claim to be what all modern novelists need to be: famous for being something other than a novelist.

I banged back another glass of wine. I had not loved the world, nor the world loved me. I had not written a 3-for-2-table product-shifter or delivered to an agent a past-abroad-celebrity. Hell is publishing people. Drink: The Enemy of Promise. My Career: The Promise of Enemies. Pouring a third glass, I checked around for Jane, trying to detect her voice in the burble of conversation. Now, although I am a fiction writer and someone upon whom nothing is lost (supposedly) and a devotee of the works of Patricia Highsmith and F. Scott Fitzgerald and Juicy Gash and Paul Auster, and despite in the past having fixations on Dostoyevsky and Balzac and Flaubert and Dickens, and Mann and Kafka and Kundera and Roth, and having taken to heart the convictions of the American journalist Gay Talese that all people are interesting and deserving should you observe them closely enough – Talese also thought failure far more interesting than success, and as such I'm sure he would find me a most fascinating subject for a feature article palpably wincing with pathos and the trials of loss – there is nothing less interesting and more dispiriting than a kitchen in suburban Norwich jam-packed with middle-aged men– including the novelist Mac McMahon and the raving Moon-Barker Frank Denbigh – talking about the Canaries' pathetic start to the season, Internet download speeds, alloy wheels, knockers and the complications inherent in converting a Vauxhall Nova to run on chip-fat[53].

Three men in jeans and stripy, lightening-flash shirts, all clutching pint glasses of lager hemmed in around me.

'Hey, you're that writer fella, aren't you? You're that Nathan Flack?'

'No,' I said.

'Oh, sorry mate,' said the one with eyes as brown as a conker and a head as shiny as a stainless steel sink in an advert for kitchen spray.

---

[53] Actually, this was a tiptop bit of found dialogue that I'm sure I could insert into a short story, if I ever wrote one again, but I was just about to fish a 3x5 index card out of my back pocket when . . .

'No, yeah, sorry, I am. Sorry guys.' I dumped my now empty glass and ponced into some introductory handshaking. 'Have we met? Did I teach you?'

'No, no,' said another with black Clark Kent specs and three-day stubble. 'We work with Jane.'

'We've heard all about you.' Kitchen Spray Head nudged the third, a sort of giant version of Sam Gamgees from *The Lord of the Rings* films.

'You work with Jane?' I said.

'At the Treatment Centre.'

'What sort of people do you treat?' I said.

They all paused and stared at me until Kent Stubble staggered backwards, laughing.

'Sewage, mate, we treat sewage,' said Kitchen Spray Head.

'Sewage, I thought she was a sex therapist or something.'

'What, our Jane?' said Sam Gamgees-on-Growth Hormones.

Tears in his eyes, Kent Stubble returned to throw his arms around his comrades in waste. 'I suppose she is, in a way . . .'

'Well, we know she can multi-task . . .'

'And she does like to try new things . . .'

They hung their heads and laughed at the tiles and as they did so a sadness spiralled in my head. It was an old feeling, one that frequently came over me when I was in my teens, a sense in a crowd that I was transparent and invisible and all the others were solid; or vice versa: they were insubstantial and light, carefree while I was bulky and dense and unable to join in. I remembered why I'd always hated parties and swiped another bottle of wine, a creosote-black Bulgarian screw top, and fled into the hall before The Boys of Sewage calmed down. They'd hook up with Mac and Frank soon and all would be boysy. I opened the bottle, swigged, glugged and swung into the lounge, looking for Jane, part of me wanting to know what she did with the sewage and the other thinking that Paladin Flack ought to at least try to guard her from the advances of Frank the Wank.

No one in the lounge seemed to notice me as I came in. At the garden end, a bunch of mostly women surrounded a table of food in front of an arch that opened onto some sort of conservatory or garden room. The furniture had been pushed back and tea-lights arranged along the shelves and the mantelpiece. The frames of mirrors and pictures were sprayed with smoky gold paint. The floorboards were stripped pine and the walls a soft tangerine colour that contrasted warmly with the wood and the fittings. Jane watched a lot of home-improvement programmes, I could tell. As the wine began to hit me, the voices and chatter seemed to merge with the fluctuating chill-out synth music. Lots of Pashminas mingled down there, women in their early thirties in fur collars, knee-length boots, leather trousers and red, red lipstick. I ought to find Jane. As I started to sidle over, a bulging, grime-smeared carrier bag thrust above the heads.

'Have you stupid *beetches* heard about the magic of The He?'

I volte-faced and fled back to the front of the room. By the window, the feeling of being invisible clicked in again, and I found myself drinking from the bottle and studying Jane's shelves. CDs: Kate Bush, Abba, Tori Amos, Dido, lots of Dido, all of Dido's singles and all of Dido's albums. Books: a plethora of coffee-table hardbacks on houseplants and cookery and homecrafts, but nothing on sewage. Lower down was a swathe of vintage Mills and Boons and regency romances and a line of 3-for-2 table unit shifters, past/abroad/celebrities and chicklit novels with day-glo spines and all with 'ex' in the title: *The Ex-Factor, The Ex-Directory, The Joy of Ex, The Ex-Files, Jennifer's Ex, Jennifer Ex's Diary, My Ex's Party, Bravo Two Ex, Captain Correlli's Ex's, Fever Ex, About an Ex, How to Be an Ex, Snow Falling on Exes, Miss Jennifer's Feeling for Exes*. I turned my attention to a framed montage of Polaroids: a toddler Jane in pink party dress with fairy wings; a teenage Jane in pink party dress and fairy wings, a fully-formed, recent Jane in pink party dress and fairy wings and in the middle Jane in some sort of white radiation suit and goggles standing with similarly dressed men beside a reservoir with refinery chimneys and cooling towers smouldering in the distance. Doctor Jane Vest worked on a sewage farm! I found myself chuckling. Not many Rom-Ts get their hands dirty. I wondered how she'd progressed from little pink girl to muck and effluence and what she did all day, what she thought about as she worked. What were the Boys of Sewage insinuating in the kitchen? Was she the sex-flit of the farm? Had she been talking about me? As I stared at the pictures I asked myself for the first time why on earth was James O'Mailer so insistent that I should be with Jane? What was it to him? If he was the voice of my imagination, was I falling in love with her? But I'd been in love far too many times and I didn't feel any real pulse or spark, but maybe the situation didn't seem immediately difficult or perverse or necessarily fictive enough for me. Maybe he was telling me to lighten up, change my ways. Then again, I really shouldn't do anything that an undead white male demanded. My head started to swim from the wine. It was about time that I stopped being so antisocial and found Jane to say hello at least. Hurricane Gretsch seemed to have blown out behind me. Turning, I took in the room again just as through the door, in car coat and nardy Yorkshireman-style flat cap and black jeans and bovver boots, with all the poise and suspicion of a Gestapo officer arriving in a known Resistance hang-out, strode Sharon Plum.

Bull

A blush sizzled my cheeks as I tried to blend in to the bookshelf. Like Griffin in *The Invisible Man*, I wanted my skin to turn to smoky glass and then vanish. A party in the Triangle, Plum had said. Toss and fuck and bumrape. The Orgsburo knew about it before me. She paused with her chest puffed out, her attention seemingly drawn by the flock of Pashminas at the other end of the room. **plumcam** had obviously booted up. Arms rigid at her sides, head slightly uplifted, she received information and computed.

*
*
*

FEMALE UNIT: Gaynor Marshall, aged 34.

APPEARANCE: brunette, 32″ chest, 5′ 4″ tall.

STATUS: married.

DEMOGRAPHIC: unfashionable.

OCCUPATION: speech therapist.

WRITER : negative

PUBLISHING PROFESSIONAL: negative

USEFUL CONNECTIONS: zero

USEFULNESS TO H.Y.D.R.A OPERATIVE: zero.

PROBABILITY OF COPULATING WITH H.Y.D.R.A OPERATIVE: zero.

ACTION: avoid.

*

*

*

FEMALE UNIT: Sally Barnes, aged 29.

APPEARANCE: blonde, 30" chest, 5' 11" tall.

STATUS: single.

DEMOGRAPHIC: fashionable.

OCCUPATION: book jacket designer.

WRITER: negative.

PUBLISHING PROFESSIONAL: affirmative.

USEFUL CONNECTIONS: affirmative.

USEFULNESS TO H.Y.D.R.A OPERATIVE: average to high.

PROBABILITY OF COPULATING WITH H.Y.D.R.A OPERATIVE: 1/1000.

ACTION: schmooze/charm/ingratiate/implement seduction protocols with extreme prejudice.

*

*

*

FEMALE UNIT: Erika Gretsch, aged 51.

APPEARANCE: brunette, 48" chest, 5' 2" tall.

STATUS: single.

DEMOGRAPHIC: unquantifiable

OCCUPATION: Prophet of The He.

WRITER: affirmative

PUBLISHED: negative.

PUBLISHING PROFESSIONAL: negative.

USEFUL CONNECTIONS: Flack unit/Mink unit.

USEFULNESS TO H.Y.D.R.A OPERATIVE: high.

PROBABILITY OF COPULATING WITH H.Y.D.R.A OPERATIVE: high.

ACTION: pacify/mollify/control.

*

*

*

My invisibility trick was obviously failing. **plumcam** swivelled around to face me with all the mechanical ease of a tank turret.

*

*

*

MALE UNIT: Nathan Flack aged 35.

APPEARANCE: brown-haired, unremarkable, 5′ 8″ tall.

STATUS: low

DEMOGRAPHIC: worse than useless

OCCUPATION: tutor/editor/writer.

WRITER: affirmative.

PUBLISHED: affirmative.

PUBLISHING PROFESSIONAL: ish.

USEFUL CONNECTIONS: Mink unit/Harker unit/Cave unit/James O'Mailer.

USEFULNESS TO H.Y.D.R.A OPERATIVE: high, yet uncooperative, obstructive and hostile

PROBABILITY OF COPULATING WITH H.Y.D.R.A OPERATIVE: unit would rather self-destruct but bribeable and bendable, crushable, assimilatable.

ACTION: observe/remove/undermine/disseminate falsities/ press and devour/implement Emergency Protocols 7865: Flack unit must not be allowed to escape.

*

*

*

Sharon Plum, Operative of **H.Y.D.R.A.** had me locked in her crosshairs. A smirk snaked across her lips. The room seemed to rotate on the axis of our confrontation. I plugged my mouth with the bottle and opened my throat and let the wine flow down my gullet, my gaze still focused on her and her clicking face. Images of her grim, torturous parties flashed through me, her sloping around after me, her crashing onto sofas beside me and trying to hold my hand, ramming her hand into my groin and whispering 'I want to suck it' before I ran off and found Frances for the first time in the bathroom. Sharon Plum, Operative of **H.Y.D.R.A.** was standing there now thinking that she had the upper hand. She was in control. She had got me where she wanted me. She was going to come over now and say: *hello Mister Flack, you're looking sexy, Mister Flack, I'm sorry about the other day, can I make it up to you, Mister Flack? You know that no one knows you like I do, Mister Flack. Have you done any writing? How many words have you written today? Have you sold your book yet? I want my*

252

seat at the table at the Booker Prize ceremony. I want it. I want to be at your side[54]*.*
Trust in me, Nathan. Trusssssst in meee.

The smirk was now a big welcoming grin and she was holding out her pudgy hand. She was going to pretend to be my friend. The Shiraz and the Bulgarian creosote were warring in my gut. In my head a red cloud was forming into an explosive thunderhead. She had threatened to sack me for no reason. She had foisted the mental case Gretsch on me and was enjoying the fallout. She was coming for me now. I didn't want this, couldn't cope with this. Fight back, have it out with her, take her down in front of all these nice girls and jovial guys and chummy students? That couldn't happen. I needed a *deus ex machina* to save me[55]. I needed something to swoop down and get me out of this; a chasm in the earth to open; the ceiling to collapse; a juggernaut to crash through the window. She held her hand out; she blocked my take on the room and her lips were moving.

'Oh hello Mister Flack, you're looking sexy, I've got something to say to you.'

I slapped the bottle against my hip as a *ffffffffff* sound formed on my lips. The door whacked open. Frank Denbigh stormed towards us with his hands clawed like Nosferatu.

'Wotcha big tits.'

He grabbed hold of Sharon Plum by the shoulders and started to jig her around the room. Frozen, incredulous, I watched as he bounced her into the windowsill, the TV and then the shelves. A flurry of books and CDs fell onto the floor. Paladin Flack should intervene, I knew, but I found myself heading for the door and as I did so I kicked a lost book that skimmed across the pine towards the doorway. I followed it and crossed paths with Mac McMahon coming the other way.

'Don't do it, Frank,' he shouted.

The book slid to a stop against the wall in the hallway. It was called *Jennifer's Ex Machina*. I put the empty wine bottle on the dust jacket. My temples throbbed. Voices and shouting seemed to encircle me. Bladder trauma kicked in. I dashed through the kitchen, weaving and ducking under the Boys of Sewage and Team Chip Fat and locked myself into the downstairs bathroom.

---

[54] She'd said this to me about the Booker Prize. Seriously, you don't know the hubris of it, the terror, the penumbra at the edge of the sun.

[55] Textbook deus ex machina coming up, class.

Mares

I found myself swaying in front of the toilet, sweat coursing down my face, my skull hot with bubbling intensity. The room smelt of bleach and lavender and moonlight dashed across the floor from a slit-window. As I pissed I let off a long, low groan as the pressure in my guts fell away. Parties? Why did I think this one would be any different? Here I was again. You'll always find me smashed in the bathroom at parties. At least there was no girl in here for me to make a disaster of myself in front of, and no one asking for a toilet tutorial and tiptop tips about nouns and verbs and resolutions. I thought of the student I'd met in a bathroom, and then Lisa with her leather trousers and Frances floating in the Grand Canal.

'Shit wank bollocks,' I said and took a yellow rubber ducky from the top of the cistern and gave it a vicious squeeze. Then I tossed it against the tiles. It made a painful squeak, then a softer, more resigned one as it hit the bottom of the bath.

'Fucking, fucking Mac, fucking, fucking Plum and fucking, fucking, dead-fuck Fred Malone. Ooooo, I've got a column in *The Bookseller*, I'll represent any old cunt. C'mon, you're a cunt? I'll take fifteen percent, you cunt.' I stabbed my fist at the moon blurred on the lavatory glass.

'Bastards! I'll show you. I'll fumigate you. I'll fumigate every single last one of you.'

Behind me came the sound of a heavy, human sigh.

I pressed my hand to the wall and hung my head and whispered, 'Oh my God' as the sweat on my cheeks froze.

Then I turned. Standing in the bath, lurking behind the grey, translucent shower curtain, was a waxy shape. It was him. O'Mailer. It was him or the cowled figure, the creeper in the street, the watcher in the dusk and the rain.

'O'Mailer, is that you, you evil ponce?'

I grabbed the curtain and pulled it towards me. Then I swung about and jerked the light-cord. There in the corner, huddled up against the tiles, her hands over her face, was Cynthia in her oatmeal sweatpants.

'Oh Jesus Bollocks,' I said. 'We mustn't meet in circumstances like this.'

'Don't,' she whimpered. 'Don't shout at me.'

'Christ, Cynthia. Why didn't you say something?'

She stepped out of the bath and perched on its edge and put her head in her hands.

'Er, how's you, Cynth?' I said. 'Enjoying the course?'

'No,' she said. 'No, I'm not. I'm not, Nathan. I have to tell you that I am not enjoying the course. I've not written a word, not a word. Everything I write is so boring. It bores me. I bore myself thinking about my ideas. I go home afterwards and just write about being bored and boring and how boring my work is. I depress myself, I do. Is that normal? Is that how it is? Everyone else seems to have so much confidence, but not me. I want to do it, I want to do it so much, I do, but I can't, it's boring.'

I sat down on the toilet and found myself adopting the creative writing tutor's listening pose, my hands hanging between my knees and my head dipped. I found this comforting. I felt in control.

'Well, maybe that's good, Cynthia. Some people rush into things before they're ready.'

'But what if I *was* ready,' she said. 'Everything I'd write would be depressing, really depressing, really, really miserable and glum and gloomy and banal and pointless. Life is terrible and disappointing. Who cares? Whenever I think about a book with my name on it, I think of a bottle of vodka and two-hundred sleeping pills.'

'"A Bottle of Vodka and Two-Hundred Sleeping Pills",' I said. 'It's a good title.'

'You're not listening to me.'

'I'm impressed, I am, seriously.'

'No one takes me seriously. Everyone thinks I'm a bore and a miseryguts and depressing . . .'

Funnily enough, I'd never had this impression of Cynthia. I'd always seen her as a sunshine girl sucking on the pap of life with slightly more relish than the rest of us.

'Maybe you don't need to be light, Cynthia,' I said. 'You're not a children's entertainer.'

'I am.'

'What?'

'I am a children's' entertainer. That's what I do. Day in, day out. Madam Salome the Clown, that's my name. Schools, I do schools, I do parties, I do really miserable, depressing parties in village halls.'

'Do you do wakes?' I said.

'Well, I didn't expect you to listen.'

'You're really a kids' entertainer?'

'Yes.'

'Honestly?'

'Yes, twenty years. I can do things with ropes and make animals out of balloons.'

'Can you do that thing where you saw a child in half?'

'No.'

'Frank can.'

'Pardon?'

'Why don't you write about it?'

'Write about Frank?'

'No, entertaining the miserable kiddies.'

'What? The unhappy clown? Isn't that the most depressing thing you can imagine?'

'No,' I said. 'The happy clown is far more horrible.' I thought of Mac and his high-hopes and his path to glory under the auspices of Frederick Malone, *idiot savant* and idiot-idiot, Dumbest and Dumb-Downed dancing hand in hand along the road to the 3-for-2 table and the Editor's Choice.

'Cynthia, can I tell you something?' I said. ' I *am* actually feeling depressed now.'

'I understand, you were ranting.'

'No, I'm more depressed than I was then, I'm sorry, I just can't . . . Look, I'm sure you're a great clown and everything, but I'm going to have to go back out there or I'm going to go berserk and drink what's in the toilet duck. Coming?'

'Am I really depressing, Nathan?'

I didn't answer, but judging from the look on her face I didn't need to. As she eased up from the edge of the bath, I tried to revisualize her wearing flour-white make-up, red-apple cheeks, a painted–on grin and a ginger frightwig, but I couldn't. I felt sober now, alert and calm. I'd drunk two bottles of wine but the drone of her voice had drawn the buzz and fury out of me.

'Cynthia,' I said as she opened the door and I followed her to the threshold of the kitchen. 'Have you ever considered becoming an alcohol-abuse counsellor?'

She didn't seem to hear me. The chatter that erupted around us as we entered the now overcrowded room had swamped my voice. Cynthia wiggled her hips, as if suddenly she'd realized that she might have to make an impression here. As her buttocks kinked side-to-side her oatmeal sweatpants started to slip. The waistband hula-hooped around the back of her thighs, then shimmied and quivered as it dropped over her white, dimpled knees to pool around her ankles. A trombone sounded *wuh-wuh-wuh wuuuh* in my head. She stooped to pull up her pants, levering her rather washed-out mannish knickers right in my face.

'Well I never, it's unbelievable. It just gets worse.'

Reg was in front of us, wearing a pair of trousers so voluminous and pulled-high that he seemed to be standing in a tweed sack. All the furrows and wrinkles and jowls in his face filled with a red glow. He put a sherry glass down on the worksurface with a hard click.

'Do you really have no moral standards at all, Flack, is there really nothing that causes you shame, what, what?'

'Oh I don't know, Reggie-Baby,' said a short, hairy-nostrilled sixty-something man in a yachting cap, naval blazer and white flannel trousers. 'She's gamey. You would, if you could get away with it.'

A statuesque bottle blond in a sagging, violet trouser suit slapped the shoulder of the nautical midget.

'Kip, do pipe down. Remember Tangiers.'

257

Cynthia scrabbled up and leaned back into me. I gave the small of her back a gentle shove to put some distance between us and scanned the mob ahead: Fuming Reg with a woman at his side in pearls and a yellow dress that left everything to the imagination. The Darling Dear, I assumed, a sort of animate axe. The esteemed UKIP and Myra de Courcy must be the other pairing. If they were Folder Holders, they would be **The Retired Couple Who Used to Run a Concentration Camp.** I knew their sort. I'd been tortured by their thumbscrews before, had the desk-light shone in my eyes, been forced to dig my own grave on the lawn outside the Eudora Doon.

'Look,' said Cynthia, her voice a jittery drawl. 'This isn't what it seems.'

'Miss Wadge, I thought better of you,' said Reg.

'Don't be ashamed,' I said. 'It's the twenty-first century. If you're not getting laid in a toilet, you're not here, are you, Reggie-Baby? Anyway, old Kipper isn't bothered?'

'He is,' said Myra.

'Ah, you must be the lovely Myra,' I said. 'My pleasure, I've heard so much about you.'

'Pardon ?' she said.

'Reggie-Baby sends me an e-mail everyday, so I know all the news. I thought back there, that must be Myra, good old Myra. I feel like I already know you quite intimately. How are you coping with the didicoys? Been offered any fridges?'

'Well, now you should mention it,' said UKIP, standing up to his full height and blowing out his chest as he gripped his lapels.

I sidestepped and put my hands loosely on Cynthia's shoulders.

'My dear friends,' I said. 'Miss Wadge does, unbeknown to us, have hidden talents. Let me introduce to you, not Cynthia the Stripper but Madam Salome the Clown. Got any balloons, Madam?'

Head down, she put her hands in the pocket of her sweatpants.

'Go on then,' I said. 'Make us something. What do you fancy, UKIP? A dangerous dog, a Polish plumber, a sawn-off shotgun.'

Cynthia blew into a flaccid raspberry-coloured balloon until it rose into the space between us like a big red sausage.

'Enjoy,' I said and slipped through.

'Well, I never . . .' I heard Reg say.

'Queer chap . . .'

'Frightful manners . . .'

' . . . Norfolk's Pornographer General . . .'

'What'll it be then, kiddies?' said Cynthia.

'Can you do Horatio Nelson?' said UKIP.

I stumbled, pushing my way through the Boys of Sewage and Team Chip Fat, more Pashminas and men in jumpers until I found myself back in the lounge. I scanned around and caught Mac and Frank looming over a group of women who seemed to be edging back towards me en masse. On the far side, Sharon Plum, Operative of **H.Y.D.R.A** was pinned to a wall by Erika Gretsch whose voice lifted itself over the general hubbub. 'You can help me, you can, you must help me . . .' I tramped around the edges of the party, thirsty now and needing a cigarette. Without making eye contact with anyone, I tripped through the archway and into a conservatory. Pink and yellow fairy lights hung from the eaves and dazzled me as I stumbled towards them. Giant yuccas and cacti stood sentry along the wall of glass panels that faced a garden black and dimensionless in the night. A low table laid with nibbles and wine bottles was surrounded by chairs and recliners. Doctor Jane lay spread out on a divan-type lounger, *sans* Pashmina and in a long, tube-like maroon dress, her golden sandals crossed at her ankles. Three frizzy-haired women in similar casual evening dresses sat on chairs around her.

'Oh Nathan, she said, 'so glad you could make it?'

The other women all looked up at me.

'Mmmmm, Nathan,' they said.

Girdle

I'd stumbled into a room of bona fide women. There was no Gretsch
Monster or Sharon Plum in this grotto. None of these slinky sirens wore
loose-fitting oatmeal sweatpants or resembled a chopping tool. It was
time for me to be dashing and cute and witty and engaging and for the
love of God not say anything bonkers.

'What a trial I've had getting here,' I said as I slumped into a chair
opposite Jane and filled a glass with more red wine. 'And I've drunk two
bottles of this stuff and already sobered up, and I've just met UKIP de
Courcy, and seen Cynthia's knickers and I've just found out, Jane, that
you work on a sewage farm.'

She batted her eyelashes and ran her hand along her side, rippling the
silky fabric.

'Have the boys been teasing you?'

'No, I just . . . I never thought you worked with sewage, that's all.'

'I'm a Sanitation Officer.'

'So you're a fumigator, too?'

'No, a fumigator kills insects, Nathan. I work for a water company,
researching ecological sanitation techniques. Yes, I do end up with my

head down a sewer and yes, I like it and no, I don't like the clothes. Anyway, my dear, I'm so rude. Meet the Chorus.'

She gestured to the frizzy women, who were now leaning forwards with wineglasses rested on their laps or held between their tanned, bare knees. 'This is Nathan, everyone . . .'

'Mmmmm, Nathan,' they said.

'And this is Lou-Lou, this is Sandra and this is Bunty.'

'You can call me Buns,' said the one on the end, her solo voice sending a prickle looping around my earlobes.

'Jane's not very good at mingling,' said Sandra. 'She left you out in the jungle all on your lonesome.'

'Something like that,' I said. 'Jane, did you know Cynthia's a children's entertainer?'

'No, really!'

'She's doing tricks in the kitchen. Well, Reg thinks she is.'

A hand waved in front of me.

'And *hillo-whatdoyoudo*!!!!?' said Lou-Lou. A vine of auburn hair swung across her forehead.

'Oh Loully, you already know,' said Jane.

'I'm a fumigator,' I said and reached out to the table and scooped up a dollop of sour cream with a tortilla chip and popped it into my mouth[56].

'He's so modest,' said Jane. 'Nathan's a writer, a proper writer. He wrote *Gentleman's Polish*.'

'Relish,' I said.

'Oh really, that Nathan,' said Buns.

'Mmmmm, Sylvester Sly,' said Sandra.

'And what are you writing at the moment?' said Lou-Lou.

Oh no . . . *The* Question One. My stomach contracted and my head abruptly thawed and all the booze Cynthia had frozen in my guts, brain and liver gushed back to frenzied life. A hot sweat erupted across my face. Not *The* Question One . . . Couldn't we talk about knockers and

---

[56] **James O'Mailer:** Aaaaargghghhhhh, it burns, at first it burns. The crisp, crunchy texture and the strange hint of ersatz pepper, the way it coagulates, becomes liquid spice and then aligns itself with something akin to cream yet not, something alien and chemical. The ghosts of my tastebuds peal across the phantom of my mouth, and they are half there, half not, half-submerged, half alert. For the first time in thirty-five years I can taste food. I'm coming; it's all coming back to me.

261

running a Vauxhall Nova on chip fat? Lou-Lou was looking at me keenly and admiringly as she fiddled with a tiny key that dangled from a slender gold bracelet. Buns and Sandra each pressed their wrists together and inched around to face me, their eyes glistening like lipgloss. They may as well have been cocking conches to their ears to divine the sea.

'Well,' I said. 'I've just finished a novel called *The Jennifer Tree*, that's like the best love story ever, except it turns into a crock of shit when anyone remotely connected to the trade reads it, 'cause plumcam is intercepting it in the post and swapping the manuscript with one of hers, and then I started something called *The Girl on the Millennium Bridge* about a girl on the Millennium Bridge, but she's, like, stuck in a café waiting for Frank the Wank . . . and then I wrote *Garret of the Fumigator*, which like, as Morrissey said of *The Queen is Dead*, "yes, it is autobiographical" and now, now I'm supposed to be working on something called *The Twelve Labours of Beta Male* but why, why write it when you can be in it?' My voice trailed off into a grizzle. 'And . . . and I can't find my starfish.'

All their smiles turned to frowns and their powdery foundation crinkled as I fished back all the wine in the glass[57].

'Oh bollocks,' I said, staring up at the fairy lights that crossed and swam. 'I can't do it anymore, I can't do this, I can't, I can't, I can't . . . it's too hard, it's too unfair and that utter cowpat Mac has got an agent.'

I put my hands behind my neck, sagging forwards and closing my eyes. The Rom-T Chorus started to mutter.

'Janey, we're going for a refill . . .'

' . . . mingle for a bit . . .'

'Mmmmm . . .'

Their footsteps pattered off, then disappeared into the voices and the jazz wafting in from the lounge. I sensed a presence at my side. Jane was sitting on the arm of my chair.

'Oh Nathan, sweetheart, what's the matter?'

'I'm sorry,' I said. 'I didn't mean to make your friends leave.'

'Oh that's OK. They need to get out more.'

'But Frank's in there.'

---

[57] **James O'Mailer:** Mmmmmmmmmmmmmmmmm . . . Mmm, mmm, mim, meeeeeeeeem. Wine! Bottled poetry! Proof that God loves us and loves us to be happy. The Dionysiac Spirit swoops down for me and throws me into the very glowing firmament itself! The Moon belongs to O'Mailer the Flame!

She looked up and stared at the door, her head uplifted and her profile stiff and stern as if watching for the Norsemen's sail on the horizon.

'I want to talk to you about him,' she said.

'Promise me you'll give him a wide berth tonight.'

'Oh forget him. What's the matter with you?'

'I'm just having a bad day, that's all.'

'I'm sure that everything will work out for you, Nathan. And it's OK to be a little temperamental or frustrated at times.' Her hand slipped onto my shoulder and started to massage it. 'Everyone knows you're a great writer.'

'How do they know? Nothing's in print.'

'I can see it all for you, Nathan. I'm like that. I can see all your books on the tables and see you on chat shows and in the papers and giving great big lectures and having a nice cottage in the country and a lovely, lovely wife.'

'It's not like that.'

'And I can see your autobiography being a best seller in thirty years time. Why don't you think about that instead? That's what I do. I lie awake at night and I think about what I'll call my memoirs. What will you call yours? What will you call your autobiography?'

I leant away from her. Her hand dropped as I picked up my wine and took a small sip to remoisten my tongue. The entrance arch was still clear of Vikings and the commandants of the Ukippery. No Wrong-Roomers lurked; no **H.Y.D.R.A** operatives spied; no Moon-Barkers threw a castrating shadow. The fairy lights cast a curtain of shimmer and gleam across my vision.

'"Mistakes I've made",' I said. 'That's what I'll call it.'

'That's so funny,' she said. 'I love your sense of humour.'

She got up and sashayed over to small pine cabinet in the corner and produced another bottle. She threw a shape, then started to burrow into the cork with a corkscrew. I blinked and wondered why she wasn't wearing her wings tonight and whether she'd ever had a boyfriend who wanted her to dress up in the radiation suit. *Mistakes I've Made.* Yes, that would be the title of any Life Writing squib that fizzled from my underpowered pen. Or *Nathan Flack: A Study in Failure. Nathan Flack: A Warning from History. Nathan Flack: Down, Down, Deeper and Down.* As I watched her, I wondered what Jane called her autobiography as she lay in bed and dreamed her Rom-T dreams.

Only the Crumbliest Flakiest Chocolate by Jane Vest.

Yes, that was it. And it got me thinking further as she twisted her wrist and dug into the cork.

By Hendon Central Station I Sat Down and Wept by Frances Mink.

When I Lived in Jeanette Winterson Times by Juliet Largo.

My Struggle by Sharon Plum.

I was a Gay Tomorrow People by Neville Copperson.

Playing by the Rules by Reginald Carnaby.

The Little Sheepies and the Little Piggies: Their Part in My Breakfast by Erika Gretsch.

Such a Word as Can't by Cynthia Wadge.

Throbber! by Mac McMahon.

Bark at the Moon by Frank Denbigh.

Turning Back the Tide by Kip de Courcy.

How to Be the Perfect Gaulieter's Wife by Myra de Courcy

Wherever I Drop My Pants That's My Home by Sylvester Sly Ramos Pintos.

Lurking in the Fog: The Peculiar and Unsettling Case of Arnold Bumrape by Arnold Bumrape.

It's Not For Me . . . by Squinty Hugo.

Standing on the Shoulders of Millionaires by Ferdinand Paget.

And on the Seventh Day I Rested by James Jehovah Jesus Vishnu Bysshe Von Augustenburg O'Mailer.

The cork came out with a pop. Jane's sandals scraped on the boards as she prowled towards me.

'Do you know what I'm going to call mine?' she said.

'Yes.'

'Go on then.'

I shook my head.

'"Into the Light".' She held up two glasses of wine. 'You don't like it?'

'I don't get it.'

'If you'd had your head down a sewer for ten years, you would.'

'Why don't you call it "Of Pipes and Pashminas"?'

She put the glasses on the table then burst into a lilting giggle as she dragged up a chair so it was right up close to mine. She grabbed hold of my armrest and hung her head as she continued to laugh. Her voice was full of cashmere.

'That's much better,' she said.

'What about "Of Poo and Pashminas".'

'You're so funny.'

'Not that it gets me anywhere.'

'It will, it will.' The glowing blue strip of her eyes hovered now in front of me and her cheeks and wispy poppyhead of tawny hair were haloed by orange light.

'God,' I said. 'Fucking Mac has been signed up and he can't even spell. He thinks syntax is a German drum machine. Why do they want him?'

'You're so frustrated. I didn't realize that you were so frustrated. I can help you with that?' Her eyes swayed side to side and she chewed her bottom lip and the swirling light behind her seemed to rear up like dragonfly wings.

'They don't want people like me,' I said. 'You have to have a 'Z' in your name now. If you've got a 'Z' in your name, you can get published. You can fill a sack with Honey Nut Loops and send it to Hamish fucking Hamilton and if you've got a 'Z' in your name, you're away. If I was Zathan Zlack I'd be laughing[58].'

She now had both her hands on the rests and was leaning even further forwards, the blue of her eyes floating down to deeper, darker colours.

'That would make me Zane Zest. And if I married you, I'd be Zane Zlack.'

'Zeg Zarnaby.' I tipped towards her face. 'Zynthia Zadge.'

'Zerika Zetch. Zak ZakZahan.'

'Zeffrey Zarcher. Z.Zott. Zitzgerald.'

'Zills and Zoon.'

She closed her eyes and the tips of our noses brushed. Her eyelids were pink-tinged and circled by a ring of blue powder. Her hands interlinked with mine; her fingers were warm and strong. As I parted my lips, as my head took a gentle swerve to avoid bumping her nose, I knew there was no way I could resist this, and just as I realized it would be a crime against nature not to kiss her, a terrible, pounding throb bombarded my left temple[59].

---

[58] The strategically deployed reference to Zizi Le Flaps on the first page of *Touching the Starfish* should ensure that an agency reader will take it seriously from the off.

[59] **James O'Mailer:** Woman!!! The Lunar. Womb. Tits. Thighs. The Winking Navel. The Puckered Petal of her Lips. The Adorable Shell-like Ears. The Sunlit Pools of her Eyes. The Sacred Chalice. The Dead Seagull. The Aperture. The Other. The Scent of Her. The Alchemical Wedding. The Revolt against our Bondage to Decay. The Defeat of Death. A

My head shot back and I slapped my head with my hand.

'Nathan, what's the matter?' said Zane, her hands suddenly tightening around mine.

I rubbed my hair and winced and waited for the pain to subside and as I did so I shot a glance at the doorway and standing there, tall and slender, in black patent leather trousers and a scarlet sleeveless top, the muscles in her upper arms taut and defined, her hair a sharp, raven-black bob, her lips pursed into a disgusted, disappointed grimace, was the poet and devourer of books Zrancis Zink.

Riot of the Senses. I can smell her, drink her, see her, I can strip her naked with my eyes and with my mind ravish her, fill her, be her. They are all swimming through me, my legions of women, from Eve to Jane Austen to Barbara Aple and the Multiple Seduced of Cluj. Oh Flack, cruise the muse, light the candle here, let me watch, let me share. Mehr Licht!

Cattle

All the time she was away I had not been able to visualize what she actually looked like, but now, as she stepped down and padded into the conservatory, I found total recall: her formidable height; her poise perfected from hours of drama groups and dance classes; her angular hips; her glossy, flapper's hair and long, expressive fingers that often seemed to swipe an invisible paintbrush through the air when she spoke. She stopped behind Jane's chair and folded her arms, an impassive smile on her face that I knew she was consciously holding.

'Zounds,' I said. 'I thought you were dead.'

'Pardon,' said Jane, frowning.

'Am I intruding?' said Frances.

'Er . . . no.' I edged back my chair and sat on my hands, then took them out again and swigged back my wine[60].

Jane turned and looked over her shoulder. 'Yes, you are? Who are you?'

'I need to talk to him,' said Frances.

---

[60] **James O'Mailer:** Now, this is what I call a three-for-two table. Go on, Flack, actions not words. Menage the trois. Cherchez les femmes.

'I do have a name,' I said.

'Easy, by the looks of it.'

Jane gave me a confused and disappointed glance as she smoothed a handful of hair with her fingers. 'You two obviously have something to discuss. I'll make myself scarce.'

The tail of her dress swirled around the doorframe as she floated out into the lounge[61]. From my low-down position, Frances seemed gigantic, skyscraper-sized, and her eyes all pupil.

'Everyone's taste always gets worse after me,' she said.

I stood up.

'Where have you been? I've been worried sick.'

'I can see that. Strange how men pine when I'm gone. They have such inventive ways of doing it. You're all so mysterious. How can I ever hope to understand your foibles?'

'I thought you were dead?'

'You think I'm a ghost?'

'Don't believe in ghosts.[62]'

'Only in flesh, I see.'

I pointed at her.

'Don't come back and tell me what I can and can't do.'

'You know that when you point like that, three of your fingers are pointing back at yourself.'

Oh not this. Arguing with Frances was like fighting a swarm of bees. All logic would be inverted, subverted, deflected, deconstructed, destablized and refracted until up was down, left was right, in was out, north was south and I was one hundred percent in the wrong and she was one-hundred percent right. I'd forgotten the swarm of bees, too. I should have included it on my list of things that signified the end of party time: the first ominous buzz. Hercules never faced a swarm of bees because he'd be outclassed. He'd lose. They'd sting him into submission in an instant.

'Where in God's name have you been?' I said.

'Didn't Sharon tell you?' The reverberating drone of the swarm amassed behind her. I half-turned my shoulder, keeping one eye on the

---

[61] **James O'Mailer**: Don't go, come back, I beg of you, fight it out, woman.

[62] **James O'Mailer**: Ha ha ha ha.

escape route and the other on the swarm, assessing its temperament, whether it was about to strike.

'She said you were in Venice, but . . . I thought you were dead.'

'Well, that's a vote of confidence. I've been doing a British Council thing.'

'That manipulative bitch.'

'So, you thought you'd get over me by . . . oh, how clichéd.'

The swarm loomed up over her, a black hill of vibrating specks.

'I am not trying to get over you.'

'Just off with her.'

'It wasn't how it looked.'

'Oh c'mon, Nathan, you can do better than that.'

'I'm not making an excuse.'

The swarm parted and flowed into a pincer movement around me.

'You think she's better than me? You would rather have that simpering sillybitch than a grown-up relationship with me?'

'No, I wouldn't.'

The bees encircled me, dark clouds in the periphery of my vision.

'What were you doing then? Removing an eyelash?'

'We were just talking.'

'So, she's deaf as well. You need to get that close. You needed to be face to face so she could catch your rhythms, your way with words. Ah, such beauty.'

The buzzing reached a pitch, layers and layers of grating sound.

'Who told you we were in here?'

'A guilty conscience makes you change the subject.'

'It was Plum, wasn't it?'

'Always someone else's fault. Poor Nathan. Always a monkey on your back. Or hanging round your neck.'

Taking my inspiration from Michael Caine in *The Swarm*, I made a valiant effort to swipe off the bees, part the circle and batter it back.

'Don't you understand, Fran, that she's pulling your strings, our strings?'

The bees dive-bombed in from difficult angles, from above and behind me.

'Our strings? You've just cut *our* strings?'

I reached for the flit-spray.

269

'Nice extended metaphor that? I can see you've been pacing the circuit. Don't tell me you haven't been flaunting yourself out there?'

'Jealous now?' she said.

'You've had one of your sordid little adventures with some meathead waiter or poetry prat and now you come back and take it out on me.'

'You're such an arsehole. All I thought about was you.'

The bees were crawling all over my face. I could feel their spiky little legs and probing antennae.

'So why didn't you tell me where you were?'

'I told you, I told Sharon.'

'You're not that stupid, Frances. You knew she'd play Battleships with me. You wanted me to miss you, didn't you?'

'You've written your book, you've written your porn programme. I want to know where I stand.'

The bees were clogging my mouth and my eyes, forcing me down onto my knees and I could only use the most desperate of evasive tactics.

'Jesus, Frances, I don't want to go back to what it was like.'

'So you want her. You want her with her melty face, but not me. Men are so predictable, so stupid.'

'At least I know what I want from one minute to the next.'

'You just can't compete with me.'

The stings! The stings!

'If you want a competition, hang out with Plum.'

The swarm morphed into a new pattern, an even, lower-lying phalanx of drones protecting the majesty of the Queen.

'You think I'm not good enough for you. You think I make you vulnerable. You can't handle the thought of us together, me at your side, you can't handle that. You hate me.'

'Oh fucking hell, where did that come from? I don't hate you. I don't. I *did* miss you. I was worried sick. But . . .'

'But what? You can't have a dialogue with me? You can't have a discourse with me? My tits are too small?'

'Frances, it's been over since it was over. I love you, but it's over. And if you want a reason then think about how this conversation has gone. OK?'

'You *do* hate me.'

'Oh for fuck's sake.'

I started to pace now, flapping and slapping and punching at the swarm. If she didn't stop I was going to burst into tears, and if I cried she would think my so-called feminine side had broken its bonds and I was now under the influence of something called 'my feelings' which would show me that everything that I thought was wrong and awkward and uncomfortable was actually right, and it should be like this, souls stripped to the waist, thrusting and shouting, stung into submission every minute of every day forever. For what? For verse? For words? For the illusion of an 'us'?

'They'll always be someone better than me in your mind,' she said. 'It's all just a narcissistic melodrama to you.'

I clambered into my extra-thick beekeeper's suit and pulled the helmet down over my head.

'You ponder on that,' she said. 'You'll have the rest of your life to do so.' And then she was gone.

A self-disgusted guilt came over me, a need to apologize, to make it up to her, to say that I didn't mean it. The inside of my head shifted side-to-side and felt raw and bloody and pitted. Unsteadily, I made my way to the arch and had to grip both its sides to survey the party and locate Frances.

Set against the bay windows at the far end, fluid and glassy to me, a long, loose oblong of guests talked and laughed and swigged and stuffed their faces. Halfway down Mac MacMahon was talking excitedly to Sharon Plum, Operative of **H.Y.D.R.A.** A shiver of contempt shot through me. He'd given her some old bollocks about Frederick Malone and now she would been adding him to the Orgsburo files as a potentially influential new contact when usually she was ideologically opposed to the very existence of such unreconstructed, heterosexualist phallocrats. The shiver intensified as through a parting couple of watery pashmina girls I caught a glimpse of Frank Denbigh, his face glowing like a red giant sun as he chucked under the chin a cooing Erika. I felt sick in my stomach. The room was packed. They were all here. The Boys of Sewage and Team Chipfat; the Rom-T Chorus of Sandra, Buns and Lou-Lou, Reg Carnaby and his Darling Dear, accompanied by UKIP and Myra de Courcy, all of whom seemed to be watching intently as Cynthia, standing on a chair, entertained them with Sooty and Sweep glove puppets. All of these people wanted to be writers, I realized. All of them wanted to write. In the future, there would only be two types of people: published writers and unpublished writers. Cynthia dropped off the chair and everyone laughed. I couldn't see Francis. My tongue was a husk.

Something slid like a panel across my line of sight.

271

'Nathan, are you OK?' said Jane.

'Bit stung,' I muttered.

'I need to take you upstairs.[63]'

'Maybe not a good idea, you know, my ex being here. I know you know all about exes.'

'I need to show you something, something important, really important.'

She took my hand and started to lead me through the crowd. The music dulled, as if some kind soul had turned it down to draw everyone's attention to us. The eyes of Reg and his Darling Dear passed through me, followed by the confused grimace of Cynthia and the knowing nods of the Rom-T Chorus and a big wagging thumbs-up from Mac MacMahon. I was taken into the hallway, Jane's arm now crooked behind her back as she manoeuvred me up the stairs. As I trailed her, a voice came from behind me.

'Nathan.'

Frances was sat on the telephone chair next to the coat hooks. She gave me the finger. The bees flew out at me in a fist-shaped formation that smashed into my back. They dissipated and blurred into the gloom at the top of the stairs as Jane pulled me along behind her.

We paused on a landing. I had no idea what I wanted or what I was capable of doing and knew that whatever I did, everyone in the city would think they knew it anyway and I'd be compromised and embarrassed forever.

'I'm so glad you're here,' she said. 'I thought he was going to kill me.'

'Who?'

'This is my boudoir.' She reached into the front of her dress and started to rummage about in her cleavage, eventually producing a small golden key that she held up. 'I've got to show you something.'

She unlocked the door and I followed her in. There was a huge oak writing desk in front of a wall-mounted pinboard and a Japanese style screen and heavy honey coloured drapes across the window. Three framed prints of Art Nouveau women were hung above the brass bedstead – Alphonse Mucha, I think, very pretty – and the bedstead was swamped by cushions and a blue velvet bolster and a heap of ragdolls and teddy bears laid out on the deepest most scarlet duvet I had ever seen and

---

[63] **James O'Mailer**: At last, after that terrible digression, we return to narrative proper. This is what we need. The future depends upon it.

272

drooping over the end of the bed was a short, satin, black nightdress. The throb shot through my temples.

Concentrate, said James O'Mailer. This is what she wants to show you, fool.

Apples

I must have looked like a right moon-barker as I scanned across the dress and the bed and the curtains, looking not at Doctor Jane in her maroon evening dress and dainty, sandal-strapped feet but for that shadowy shit-head O'Mailer.

'He's back,' I said.

'That's what I think,' she said.

'You know him?'

'You do too?'

'Him?'

'Nathan, I'm so glad we're on the same wavelength. Well, we would be, wouldn't we[64]? He's back. He's doing it again.'

'Yes, he's talking to me, he's telling me things.'

'He's told you?'

'He's setting us up.'

---

[64] **James O'Mailer:** You see, dear reader, it's all coming together. I have chosen well. With my much-vaunted omniscience, I can see where this leads and it is glory and victory and all would raise a glass to the name O'Mailer should they know his part in this. I, of course, am happy to be the secret saviour, let Flack take the laurels.

She rushed over, took my hand and sat me down on the end of the bed.

'If he's confessed, Nathan, then we must do something about him. We're in this together.' She put her arm around my shoulder. My ribs lit up like a radiator as her hair brushed my cheek. 'This is so romantic. I thought I was doing my Philippa Marlowe bit all on my own. We can write a book about this when it's over.'

Ahead of me, I noticed, the pinboard above the desk was peppered with newspaper articles and Internet print-offs, sheets and sheets of features and maps and photographs. I squinted to make out the headings:

Body Found in Woodland: Is it The Angel?

Third Patient Dies in Local Hospital.

Angel of Trunch Strikes Again.

'He's been doing it for years,' she said.

'Hang on,' I said.

'I'm just so relieved we came to the same conclusion.'

'Jane, I was talking about something else.'

'Nathan, don't you see? Frank is the Angel of Trunch.'

'You keep away from him.'

'He just chased me around the room. Erika stepped in and saved me.'

'Good old Erika. Maybe he'll do everyone a favour.'

'Nathan, that's unkind. Look, hear me out, will you. I'm onto something here.'

She got up and walked over to the board and pointed at a big red dot on a map of the village of Trunch, which I knew to be a sleepy, spooky, creepy loon-belfry a few miles south of Cromer on the coast.

'This is Frank's house,' she said. 'And the first of the murders, in nineteen eighty-six was here, in the local churchyard, and the second, seven months later, here, near the wind-farm, and then here, in the grounds of what is now the Diana, Princess of Wales alcohol abuse clinic.'

'Can you take me there now, Jane, please?'

'Then it widens . . .' She pointed to another map, one of the county. 'Thetford eighty-eight, Thetford eighty-nine. Cromer ninety-one, Caister, ninety-three, Yarmouth ninety-four, Cley ninety-six, then, o-one Trunch, o-two Trunch, o-four, double Trunch. Then the one recently. See what I mean?'

'Out there there's probably a phantom dog called Black Shanty or something that's ripping into the peasantry.'

'Listen, all the victims had some connection to the National Health and we know Frank feels aggrieved, and Frank was working near to all the crime scenes, I've checked all this out, except after two-thousand and one, when he retired, hence he's been lurking about in Trunch . . .'

'In his shed.'

'What?'

'He lurks in his shed, thinking about you.'

'Eeeer, don't.'

'He's a raving moon-barker,' I said. 'But I think he's making it up to attract attention to himself. He gives me the creeps, but he's a Wrong-Roomer. He needs counselling, that's all.'

'What about all the things he says in class? And if a story tells the truth as the author sees it, as you say, what about that thing he read out on Tuesday?'

I hung my head to avoid those staring emptied eyes and barren faces tacked to the pinboard, the gallery of the dead and missing. I remembered the way he'd poked about in the doll's body during the object exercise and story of the old woman in the ambulance and the things he'd said in Portrait of the Artist.

'What's in his van?' said Jane.

'I don't know,' I said.

'Something's in his van. Where's his wife? Where's she tonight? He's like a goat on heat down there?'

'There *was* something really odd about it when he pulled up. He was, like, talking in the back of it and then was all weird about it when I asked him.'

'I think he keeps her in there.'

'Jane, he might have done something to her. He said he hated her on Tuesday.'

She walked over to the curtain and pulled it back. I joined her. Down in the street, Frank's white van glittered in the street lighting. Frost was beginning to form over the roof and the cabin.

'Something's in there, Nathan.'

'I know where his keys are,' I said, and we both looked at each other as if we knew telepathically what we needed to do. [65]

---

[65] **James O'Mailer**: At last . . . . all my plans start to bear fruit. First the peel, then the core, later the pips. Turn the page, dear reader, and I guarantee some overdue pips.

Cerberus

'Good, it's working,' said Jane as she switched on and off a small torch she'd taken out from a drawer. Hand in hand, we crept out of the bedroom. The walls around us seemed to crackle with static and the hairs on the back of my head stiffened as we reached the top of the stairs. No Frances swarmed at the telephone chair. Music and voices hummed from the lounge. Moonlight through the hall window fell upon the lines of coats by the door.At the foot of the stairs, as Jane rummaged in the pockets of Frank's coat, I turned to check if the coast was clear. Down by the kitchen entrance, the most disgusting thing I'd ever seen appeared to me, the most repellent image to add to an index of horrors that had been compiling relentlessly since I'd started to teach this particular group of Arcana, more terrifying than the sheep's head, the hooded figure or Cynthia's knickers.

Mac McMahon ground his crotch into Sharon Plum as she gripped his cheeks with both hands, seemingly trying to suck his beard, tongue and alimentary canal into her mouth. It was like watching two giant letter 'B's' couple and smudge into a new and vulgar letter: the double-blagger, the orgs-B, the dangling beta-defeater. It was another sobering shock to my system, like a quadruple espresso shot on top of a line of speed and a high-dive swoop into a plunge pool of ice-filtered water. That's what having a literary agent gets you. Plumraped.

Keys jingled behind me. Jane's fingers meshed with my own and I was led to the front door. Outside, she ushered me ahead of her onto the path and closed the door carefully behind her. Cold night air drenched me, made me feel abruptly sodden and struck.

'Did you see that?' she said. 'I didn't know Mac was gay.'

'Polymorphous perversity,' I said. 'You'll get used to it.'

'Oh merde, it's freezing. I might as well be naked.'

'C'mon. Give me those keys.'

In front of the van's back doors, we shivered in the wind. Specks of frozen rain pattered around us.

'Let's get inside,' she said.

'You sure?'

'Yes, just bloody well get on with it.'

Yes, Flack, just bloody get on with it. Even I am beginning to feel the chill.

I looked around myself, back at the house and the shadows dancing on the curtains to the mild rhythm of the music, then up at Jane, her blueberry eyes and frizzy hair billowing across her face.

'It's starting again,' I said. 'He's here.'

'I know,' she said. 'Open the doors.'

I found what I thought was the most likely key. The lock turned first time. As I pulled back the doors a gaping black maw opened up in front of us. I clambered in and held out my hand to help Jane up.

'Mind yourself,' I said. 'You're not wearing appropriate shoes.'

'Shall I take them off? Would you like that?'

'It's minus three out here.'

'We ballsy female detectives get used to it. We all have a quirk, like macramé, eating pizza in bed, or sleeping around. Mine's a weakness for shoes.[66]'

'You need to find another motif. C'mon.'

I closed the doors. Semi-darkness drew in around us, the only light a grey glimmer from the windscreen that seemed miles and miles away from where we stood. A metallic cold intensified. It smelt of damp rags

---

[66] As she said this I could see the PI *Pashminski* thrillers stacked up on the 3-for-2 table.

and something like the inside of a matchbox. Both of us started to rub our arms and sway.

'Oh dear me,' said Jane. 'Just imagine what's happened here.'

'Well, let's not hang the guy without evidence.'

Jane stretched out her arm and pointed the torch with all the stylized poise of a Jedi Knight brandishing a light sabre. A beam lit up the dusty windscreen, the steering wheel, the headrests and then something that at first I thought was an empty sack hanging on the side of the van.

'Oh my good lord,' said Jane.

'Jesus wept,' I said. 'What is that?'

We shuffled across the tarpaulin and the sheets tangled up on the floor until we were in front of something grotesque beyond the imagination of Juicy Gash or Mac MacMahon. Its head was drooped, its lank hair falling forwards, its neck hanging by a noose of twine from a bolt nailgunned to the side and its arms loose and limp in sleeves made from orange plastic bags.

'Oh dear,' Jane whimpered. 'How long has she been here?'

My hand shook as I reached out and pulled up the head. The hair felt wet with cold. Then the hair slid away and plopped to the floor with a rustle and thump. Jane yelped. The torch beam flapped downwards and the figure disappeared into the dark again. As we both staggered back, I trod on something solid on the floor that rolled beneath my sole and toppled me against the opposing side of the van. Jane buried her head into my shoulder as I tried to cover her eyes with my hand.

'It's a wig,' I said. 'Her wig came off.'

'Oh my God,' Jane stammered. 'She wore a wig.'

'Hang on. Give me the torch.' I walked my fingers along her arm and prized it from her grip, then raised the beam and again found the lower part of the body. The feet were two tufts of thickish, robust straw, the hands two reshaped coat hooks and the head was a cauliflower with a jagged mouth gouged into it and two chunks of embedded coal for eyes.

'Jane, it's not real.'

'Oh my God, she's not real.' She shuddered, pressing her face into my chest.

'Look, it's a . . . I don't know, a mannequin, a Bonfire Night guy.'

'Oh God, Bonfire Night.'

'Seriously, it's not a corpse.'

She released her hold on me and then hesitated, composing herself before she finally made herself look.

'It's still horrible,' she said.

'I know, but it could be anything. Doesn't mean he's the Angel, or he's topped anyone.'

As I stepped forwards, intending to examine the thing in more detail, I stepped on the object under the sheeting again. A jolt shot up my shin and jarred my knee.

'What the fuck is that?'

I handed Jane the torch and crouched, rummaging around to find a hem and when I did I sneaked my hand under the fabric and found something that felt wooden, a shaft, a handle or something, and as I let my fingers travel along the wood, thinking that this is exactly what Folder-Holders go through when I make them close their eyes and touch-up a starfish or a sea urchin or some Artex and how the senses are supposed to make the object tactile and evoke a compendium of potential narratives and images. My fingers then created a chill metal plane with a sharp yet sticky edge. I froze and looked up at Jane, her goosepimpled arms and the soft underside of her chin. All I could mentally picture was what I now held in my hand: Frank's hatchet scything down on her in the back of this van.

Pulling it out, I stood up.

'Oh fuck,' I cried. 'Look at this.'

'Oh dear,' said Jane. 'I told you, I told you. What are we going to do?'

I weighed it in my hand as she stared back at me as if I had the answer here. The throb at my temples came so powerfully that I almost dropped the hatchet.

I'll tell you what to do, dummy, said O'Mailer. Take it away. It has a use and purpose that I cannot yet reveal to you. This is not a set up, but a set-up. You will need it. "The Hero Acquires the Use of a Magical Agent," as I once informed Vladimir Propp. Take it. Take her. Take her back to your garret and seal the pact. She will be revealed. All will be revealed. You can be the new Raskolnikov.

Fuck you, that's the last thing I'm going to do. I'm going to do nothing that you ever tell me to do.

'Shut up!' I swung the hatchet up into the air[67].

---

[67] **James O'Mailer:** Damn this Flack. A curse upon his stupidity. I shall be forced soon to intervene unless Doctor Vest can overcome him with her feminine cunning.

'Watch it,' said Jane.

'OK,' I said, 'OK, I believe you, OK. I think we're going to have to call the police.'

'The police. We can't call the police. We need to solve this on our own.[68]'

'No, we don't.'

'Oh c'mon. When is this ever going to happen to us again? When are we ever going to have an adventure like this? Why do you want to bail out just when it's getting interesting?'

'Because this isn't a 3-for-2-table product-shifter, Jane, this is real life. If you were staying in a creepy Bates Motel place and a secret door opened in your bedroom to reveal a cobwebby passageway, you wouldn't go exploring down it dressed only in your negligee, would you?'

'Yes,' she said, 'I would.'

Ask her about the Grand Anglian Sewer, said O'Mailer.

'What?'

'I would, I would go down the passage.'

'No, you wouldn't. You're just saying that.'

Ask her!

'You're forgetting that dark, confined spaces are not frightening to me. I've been in all the abandoned chambers and sewers under the city.'

Flack, do as I say!

I've told you already. I'm not listening, la la la.

As Jane took a step towards me I put the hatchet behind my back. Her eyes were all I could see now. Her peachy perfume overcame the damp odour of the van.

'Doesn't all this adventure fire you up?' she said. 'Doesn't it make you want to lose yourself?'

Give in, Flack. Go with her. This is the start. Ask her about the Grand Anglian.

I passed the hatchet from one hand to the other, freeing my right as the radiator feeling heated my ribs again. My nose led my head into the fruity scent of her and my eyes shut as I found myself creeping forwards on the balls of my feet.[69]

---

[68] **James O'Mailer**: That's my girl.

[69] **James O'Mailer**: At last, he gets this right. I promised you pips, did I not?

'I've done it in more unusual places than this,' she said.

I had visions of cold flagstones and half-undressed Kitchen Spray Head and hobbity engineers in dimly lit caverns, and then a nightmarish El Greco vignette of Mac and Plum humping in radiation suits, cackling and groaning. My arm swung back and I gripped the shaft two-handed again. [70]

'Oh Nathan, Nathan,' she whispered.

'Not a good idea,' I said. 'Let's go back inside and call the police.'[71]

'Oh no, let's not.'

She was closer to me again, almost ethereal in the half-dark. I tried to take a backwards step, but found that my neck had stiffened rigid. Something seemed to be holding onto the back of my head.[72] And then my head moved forwards and her face came closer to mine.

'Oh,' said Jane. 'What's happened?' Shocked surprise splashed across her face, as if she suddenly realized what was about to happen. Her eyes closed and her lips parted. I tried to sidestep, but I couldn't jerk my head away. Her lips pressed against mine. Our faces squashed together, our noses bumping. [73]

'Ouch, you're hurting me,' said Jane.

I tried to untangle myself, using my hips and legs to break free of her. Her arms were dangling over my shoulder and trapped me as I jumped sideways and slipped on a greasy patch on the sheeting. Collapsing, I

---

[70] **James O'Mailer:** Oh, the prissy idiot. As if he's never fanaticized about being Hades to her Persephone. This is my wit's end, dear reader. I am now forced to act, to draw on all my reserves and become FORM. Enter O'Mailer. Enter O'Mailer the Flame.

[71] **James O'Mailer:** Argggggggggghhhhhh, 'tis like the agony of birth again. I can feel the cold, the mesmerizing magnetic draw of the air as my hands become skin again; my bones come back into being. The can feel the hairs prick into life on the upper sides of my wrists. I can feel blood pumping through my veins. And I can smell the Eve of her, the serpent of her, the coils and the fruit. I may exhaust myself if I try to kiss her myself, should I try to bring my whole body into this world. But, I have hands now. I am the puppeteer; I am Gepeto to Flack's Pinocchio.

[72] **James O'Mailer:** I have his head in my hand. I have it. And my other cups the delicate dome of the fair doctor's skull and I am pushing, I am forcing them together. I am making an authorial intervention . . .

[73] **James O'Mailer:** Not easy this manoeuvre in the dark, when one is concentrating one's soul on remaining corporeal, when one is unused to the presence of other atoms and molecules and one's mind is racing forwards to what now needs to happen, what one has been deprived of for sooooooooo long. Oh how jealous I am of Flack here, those bee sting lips and gentle tresses. Ah bitter chill, it t'was. Flushed like a throbbing star. Undress the Madeleine. I demand it.

283

caught hold of her, took her down with me and for a terrible moment I was sure we would hit something sharp or brutal concealed in the dark, or we'd fall on the hatchet. All I could see as we dropped was the grin of the cauliflower head. I managed to keep the hatchet up as we hit the sheeting. She was right underneath me now. My lips briefly touched hers as with one hand I broke my fall and kept the hatchet raised with the other. We lay there, she underneath me and I with the hatchet held just above her forehead.

'Oh Nathan,' she said. 'What a lovely chopper.'

As it crossed my mind that Jane ought to write for *Gentleman's Relish,* a strained creak and groan ripped through the van and the floor beneath us started to bounce and vibrate. A chink of light slashed across our bodies. The doors of the van sprang open and light from the street flooded in with a flurry of bitter air. There they were, all of them, peering in at us, me lying on top of her with the hatchet poised to dash her brains out: Mac hand in hand with Plum, Erika, Reg and his Darling Dear, UKIP and Myra de Courcy, Cynthia with her glove puppets dangling from her wrists, Frances, hands on hips and gem-hard eyes, and Frank the Wank, The Angel of Trunch, with his radish-pink raring and wrong-rooming eyes and oven glove sized fists balled.[74]

'Get out my chuffing van!'

---

[74] **James O'Mailer:** Oh you idiot mouse-dick, you slapdash tatterdemalion, you mimsy pizzle I shall be forced now to take drastic measures, I shall have to manifest myself, prove to him that I am so. I shall be back, dear reader, I shall . . . the fates of worlds hangs in the balance, my powers, my strength drains, faaaaaaaaaaaaaadessssssssss . . .

A Sense of Place

The Pathetic Fallacy

Never start a chapter with a character standing by the window. The story will not be *in medias res*, in the middle of things, and therefore plotless, passive and weakly specified. She, or in my case he will not be doing anything active. Jumping out of the window in a long-overdue suicide bid would be preferable. Better still would be waving bye-bye to the Siberian sabre-toothed tiger as it slopes up the garden path, suggestively swinging its hips and twisting back its neck to flash you a satisfied wink. But, fuck it, there I was, standing at the window in the garret, looking out at the snowstorm as it remorselessly smothered the city.

Furthermore, never use the weather as a metaphor for a character's inner state. Critics and editors will label this the 'pathetic fallacy' and cross out your life along with everything you've ever committed to paper.

As I watched, snow was general all over Norwich. It was falling on every part of the dark Castle Mall, on the treeless Unthank roundabout, falling softly on the bogs at Grapes Hill, and, from the eastward, softly falling onto the dark, glutinous Dereham Road. It was falling, too, upon every part of Caesar's Pizza and Kebabs, Fish Online and the army surplus store for nutters and moon-barkers. It lay thickly drifted on the crooked gables of the garret house and the hedges and path of its shabby garden, on the barren copper beech that flinched at the window. The

Fumigator's soul swooned as he heard the snow falling finally through the suburb and faintly falling, about to descend towards his end, he was, as ever, waiting for a phone call that never came.

Snow had been general all over Norwich for an hour and a half and I was waiting for Sharon Plum-Largo, Bride of Mac the Paddle, the Pathetic Phallus, to ring me up and tell me that my class was cancelled. Usually, if bad weather cancelled a class, she would ask me round for dinner and then try to flatten me on her couch. It was now an hour before kick-off and no call had come, so arrangements must be unchanged and classes running. I would have to face the Arcana, something I'd been dreading since Jane's soiree. Snow gusted relentlessly. It obscured the houses opposite like the shash of an untuned television screen. I wasn't going to walk to campus in that. I'd have to catch the bus[75].

I wrapped my black scarf around my neck, buttoned up my black coat and turned up the collar, then put on my black woollen gloves and checked in the mirror that I looked at least in passing like Comrade Strelnikov in *Doctor Zhivago*. Outside on the step, the blizzard hit me. Freezing air smacked my face and my boots sunk into a four-inch deep layer of snow as I trod up the path. Now on the street, I stood still and let the commuters hunched up in their coats waddle around me. The wires attached to the telegraph pole hung with snow and it seemed as if a giant white wheel hovered above us. Snow glittered in the exhaust plumes of gridlocked cars and vans. A bus wasn't going to get through. I'd have to walk after all. But who cared? Unusual weather always makes me think that something dramatic and pathetic fallacy might happen. Switching on my internal intelligence system, ready to collect details and images for future use, I started on my way towards campus.

Between the parallel lines of the houses the horizon was a vanishing point so black it seemed blue. Snow bulked up the outlines of trees and turned roofs into stark, empty canvasses, the pavements into glossy slides. My shins began to ache and my face lost sensation as something in the atmosphere shunted me out of phase, out of time. I was walking in two places at once, on two occasions simultaneously, except in one I was here, alone, and in the other there was someone at my side, hand-in-mittened hand with me.

As I trudged I didn't think of the things that had been on my mind that last week: what had happened to Frank's wife or whether Frank was

---

[75] This looks like whoopee-shit, but it will turnout to be a major plot-point, I promise.

the Angel of Trunch and if not, what would be the upshot of my rather hasty decision last Sunday evening to call anonymously from a phonebox and grass him up to the police. I didn't worry about the hooded figure, who on Monday night I'd spied from my kitchen window standing in my garden, peering up at me. Nor did I fret about the fate of Sebastian Harker or *The Penelope Tree* or the machinations of Sharon Plum-Largo, or my job or Mac McMahon's maggoty novel or Fred Malone, or Frances or Jane, both of whom I'd failed to contact or return their calls, or why James O'Mailer had disappeared or what everyone must be thinking and saying about me after I was caught in the back of a white van with a hatchet poised over a Rom-T's head, and I didn't think about my class on *Setting and A Sense of Place,* or *The Girl on the Millennium Bridge,* or The Starfish and whether I was ever going to write a coherent sentence again. I thought instead of you.

Dead Sea Navigators

In my mind's eye, we are together again, you and I. February, ten years ago now; we're inching our way back to our flat, wary of the ice that hid beneath the newly-fallen snow. The gutters had smoothed out into the road. The city glittered beneath a moonless sky. I can picture us as if I am a third person observing the swing of my coat as I shuffle forwards and hold up your hand so you don't slip. You are silent, your head and shoulders shrunken into your torso, the back of your head in your woolly hat like a blue gas jet when viewed from a distance. Behind us, as I zero in, I mouth the names of the stars. I mouth them now: Orion's Belt and the Plough and the lonely Pole Star. They are the same stars up there as I trudge towards class as when we walked back that night. I mouthed them then, hoping that you would join in, mention something up there that I hadn't heard of before: a sea on the moon; a mythical beast dot-to-dotted from this star and that star; a smudge that's actually a planet.

You held my hand in your mittened hand and we helped keep each other upright as we picked our way along the pavement. We were living in London then, but this is the night that London froze over and became the Arctic to me. And the street, a side-road of Victorian townhouses, half gentrified, half bedsit-conversions and hostels was not like the one that suddenly became real to me as *I round the corner, leave Garret Road and return to this reality again. The snow is so thick I can hardly see the supermarket. It fuzzes the ranks of steel trolleys in the carpark and the off-licence and the parade of shops opposite are no more than daubs of crimson and yellow light.* Our streets from back then suddenly reappear in my remote-view imaging system. My memory banks provide a montage: the graffiti word *germs* sprayed in red on street corner after street corner; uncollected black refuse sacks and the stumps of London plane trees lost in snow that we passed as we struggled back from the Rawalpindi Indian restaurant, both wordlessly letting it sink in, what we were going to do.

The cold snap had been a shock to the system, as this is now. For several days the subzero temperature had us shuddering in our bed, kept us from sleeping, squashed our bodies together for warmth. As we continued up the street, I wasn't sure if it was snowing again or if the breeze was lifting specks up off the ground and the roofs and the bonnets. You wore two pairs of jeans and your DM boots that looked incongruous when matched with the short, scarlet duffel coat and light blue hat. We were holding hands and threading our way through what seemed like rubble, when many times before we had loped along here from the Dead Sea Navigator, our local pub, whispering, promising, analysing, laughing. We had not eaten our food. We were not drunk. It was decided. You had decided. Midway along the street – I remember now, it was called Ristova Road – your mittened hand dropped from mine. You veered away to walk the less-treacherous middle of the road. I kept my line, not looking at you, but instead at the snowy pavement. I scanned the dirty tread-marks and the shatterlines in the frozen puddles. All of a sudden, I knew.

The Dream is Gone but the Baby is Real

When it was decided in the restaurant, you said, 'The dream is gone but the baby is real.' You probably thought that you were quoting from The Smiths' *You've got Everything Now*, not realizing that the line is actually from a film, *A Taste of Honey*, I think, I'm never sure. I was trying to concentrate on this pressing cultural issue and not what was going to happen to you. I tried to think about this as I poked my dopiaza around the plate and not you and your eyes and your face and your body. You at twenty-five. *Me at thirty-five, picturing you back there as I slither up a snow-blitzed street again.* The pathos of your body. Your hips and your breasts and your skin. You were putting a brave face on it, sat opposite me, quoting The Smiths, your uncracked poppadums and your uneaten vegetable korma, your mineral water instead of your usual glass of Cobra lager, and your unlit cigarette dropped into the ashtray at your wrist. I didn't at the time, but now I wonder what you were thinking as you stared at me across that table? What did you really want me to do or say or be?

It had seemed like one of your games at first. You had rung me up from a payphone on your campus. I was writing, working on my first tentative novel *The Drowners*. But hey! What a fifteenth rate hack and dim-reader/slow-coach I am, The (so-called) Voice, The Fumigator. It never registered, not until it was over. I didn't see the parallel between what I was writing and what we were living.

'Nate,' you said. 'Can you do me a favour? Go to the chemist for me.'

In the past I'd accrued many new-man loyalty-points for buying, without cringing or moaning, without blushing at the till, tampons when you were laid up with period pain.

'What do you need?' I said.

'A pregnancy kit.'

Our flat – its walls, the ceiling – seemed to drop away. On a disc of scuffed brown carpet I floated over a polar landscape, just me and my morose sidekicks, the telephone table and the deadline tone.

As I sloped back home from the chemist with my package tucked into the pocket of my overcoat, I tried not to think about the condom that had torn and was empty of me when I slipped it off three weeks ago, before the cold spell hit.

You took the test in the bathroom while I sat in the lounge. As the snow fell past the window, I crossed from one hand to the other the starfish that you bought for me in Australia.

When you came out, the snow had started to settle.

You went to the doctors without me. Your twice-knocked-up-by-waiters-and-strangers colleague and confidante Juanita went with you. Juanita who didn't like me since you rather indiscreetly told her that I called her 'Juan-or-Juanita' because of her Popeye-like jaw. You told me that afterwards she sat with you in the Pitcher and Piano at Clapham South and wouldn't buy you a stiff drink as you cried. She wouldn't buy you a stressbusting G&T, assuming that you couldn't do what she couldn't. But you were not her. You had already made up your mind, our mind.

A gust of spiralling snow hits me full in the face as I reach a high point in the road and remember that you didn't ask me. You assumed that I wouldn't want it. The pram in the hallway. The enemy of promise. I don't know why you took me out of this equation. If we were going to blow all our money on a holiday we would have discussed the destination for days. If we were to choose between a weekend-bender in Manchester or a dinner party in some outback-parish on the edge of the *A-to-Z*, we'd have discussed it, maturely, adult-to-adult. We were not deciding on the flavour of the Viennetta. We were not debating whether to have Shreddies or Fruit 'n' Fibre for breakfast. We were not using our now long lost language of eye contacts to decide how much longer we could stomach some media twat bollocking on in the ICA bar. We were going to have a baby.

It was as if you thought, Johanna, that our relationship could not stand this discussion. You took me for granted. You never asked me. You decided. You told me your decision in the restaurant as if we *had* already discussed it. Perhaps in your own mind we already had. You'd maybe given me a marginally pointed look when you were loading the washing machine and I was supposed to understand absolutely everything and divine the future from the angle of your chin. 'I *will* have an abortion,' you said, and then looked at me with an expression on your face that I'd only ever seen on much older women. And then you said, 'the dream is gone, but the baby is real.'

I've always wondered what you meant by 'the dream' here. Whose dream were you talking about, Johanna?

I thought you meant ours.

Now, though, I think you meant mine.

I think you were talking about my starfish dream of the exercise books and the long walks and the not going to work and the grandiose self-image and the scribbling. That's what you were talking about. Once, it had been your dream, too. When you said "the dream is gone", it was, I realize now, your reality check.

Where the road meets the foot of The Avenue, the snow is so berserk that the little park and play area opposite seem to be no more than grey blips dispersed across a void. The wind sloshes flecks like white paint through the streets. I can't feel my feet anymore, or my face, or my legs. I start up the long road, slip-sliding on my soles, checking out the shapes the snow makes in the crooks of the branches, how the trees look like X-ray images of the nephritic systems of kidneys, the vascular networks of hearts and lungs, and I wonder, what if, what if the dream had not extinguished, what would have happened to us?

Flaming Rose, *Purple Snow*[76]

And I ask myself what was it about us that seems so charged; that clings and overpowers the allure of the other women I've known since you; that so threatened Frances that I had to change your name in anecdotes; that still makes me feel that when I sit down in the mornings to write that I direct the words to you and hope that later in the day you will pick up the page from the printer tray, blow dry the ink, chew your bottom lip and pace and read, once, twice, three times the draft and then love me a little more for having written it; that's when I ask myself what was it about us that seemed so charged, that clings?

Was it the way that we met in heroic-rescue fashion in the gents' washroom of the Oxford Union[77]? Oh, I had seen you before, yes. In the library, chewing the tips of your hair, your chin hidden in the folds of a cream-coloured scarf as you read your books on Cathars and Lollards; in

---

[76] **James O'Mailer:** See, I did it, dear reader. You don't understand? Don't worry. The fiendish meddling of my omniscience and time travelling will all become clear. Read on . . .

[77] Never do what I am about to do here, set any part of your story in Oxford or Cambridge Universities. Nobody wants to know about anyone who went to Oxford or Cambridge. Tricky to market; unstreet.

the lunch queue, straight-backed, arms-folded, standing in one of your floral tea dresses, one leg outstretched and hanging a few inches off the ground; in the bar with your posse of cute, preppy Home Counties girlfriends, sat around a table with your glasses of white wine, the way your hand chopped the air when you wanted to make a point. I knew there was an 'H' in your name, that there was something slightly Germanic about it, something romantic and airy; that it wasn't like *Joanne* Birtles from school who had scabies and never knew that everyone worked out what she did to Rees Yerrold behind a velour curtain in a tiny and crowded flat in Chaucer Way, Sutton; that it wasn't like *Jo-Ann* Smart, who wasn't; or *Joanna* Nunn, who more or less was one. I knew it was *Johanna*, an unusual, almost exotic name to me. I couldn't contrive a way of meeting you, at least not one as amazing as the way that we eventually met.

So there I was, a quarter to midnight on a Saturday in May, lolling against a sink in the toilets of the Union having just come in from the ball that was traipsing and tottering around outside. My bow tie felt a little tight; my cummerbund was slipping and my patent brogues were dusty from dancing. The whole black tie thing made me feel like the keyboard player in a fourth-rate New Romantic band circa 1982. There was another crowd to mine in here, white dinner-jacketed rugger-buggers radiating tuxedo-machismo and oafish self-confidence. They orbited a gigantic meat-heap SS guard lookie-likie with a pink mohican back-slanted across his otherwise shaven head. In late 80s Oxford a hairstyle like this signified a loveable, outgoing character and a zany sense of individuality. I wouldn't have been phased if he'd whipped out a saxophone and strutted his stuff in silhouette, miming an overdubbed solo.

I held a paper cup of lukewarm gin and smoked a cigarette and was talking to Dave Cave and Guy Winner about God knows what and as I talked to One Foot in the Dave Cave and a guy called Guy and sipped my gin in this improvised gin palace, in comes the girl with the hushy H in the middle of her name. Outside, the queue for the ladies stretched right down the stairs. I assumed that you couldn't face the wait. Your scarlet shoes tapped on the marble floor, attracting all of us standing around by the mirrors and sinks, drawing us to your shimmering blonde hair and the ruby-coloured ball-gown with the ornamental pom-pom attached to your shoulder that seemed to swirl like a flaming rose as you beelined towards the cubicles and all our reflections tried to climb out of the mirrors to follow you.

You found an empty cubicle. Demurely, unhurriedly you shut the door behind you. The pink mohican tossed a thimble into the urinal trough. It was actually a plastic pint glass, but in his hand it had seemed minuscule. He squared his shoulders, detached himself from the scrum and stomped across to the cubicles, then entered the closet next to yours and slammed shut the door. One of his cohorts, an especially moronic-looking neckless porker tried to moonwalk across the marble, but slipped and almost fell arse-over-tit. The three of us tried not to laugh or draw their fire. We'd had dealings with the meat-heaps before. Dave elbowed me. Over at the cubicles, the pink mohican, only the upper crest of it visible at first, quivered and lifted above the top of the door until the grey turnip-shaped head appeared and the shoulders heaved upwards like some grotesque sea monster in a Ray Harryhausen film. The meat-heap rampant peered down at you.

'Awight darling. Show us your lettuce!'

I can't say that I looked at my friends and they looked at me and between us there was a consensus that something had to be done. Before I'd even had time to consider what might happen if bigmouth struck again, or analyse the pound for pound ratio and height differential between Flyweight Flack, always a little short for a stormtrooper, and Pink Stripe, the Colossus of the Cubes, I'd skimmed across the floor on my slippery new shoes to plant a kick on Stripey's door.

'Get down, you twat, you remedial public school bollock.'

The door started to unlock. Before it could open, I'd sauntered back to the others.

'Rugby-playing tosser,' I said.

Something was wrong. Apprehension hovered in their faces.

'Excuse me.'

You were standing there, a little concerned, a touch nervous, flaming rose at your shoulder and up this close I was taken with the rose and how it burned.

And you said, 'it was you, wasn't it? . . . Because if it was . . .'

Alongside us loomed the snorting, panting meat-heap and in its hand was a sort of bowie knife-machete-double-edged sword thing that, brandished level with my nose, smouldered with bloody execution.

You grabbed my arm. Hand in hand we dashed out of the washroom and launched ourselves down the stairs, weaving and elbowing our way through the queue for the ladies' toilets. I held up your hand – just as I would hold it up in Ristova Road six years later on the night I knew that what we started here had ended – and at our backs, looming above us, descending was Pink Stripe and his machete-sword. We tore our way as fast as our flashy but awkward shoes would carry us, through a corridor that rippled and flowed with salmon-coloured drapes and he was still behind us, still chasing, the little walnut-sized brain in his skull pulsing *kill-kill-kill the ponces* and the big tangle of stegosaurus nerves and sub-brain in his thigh keeping his scrum-half's stanchion-legs pistoning. We skirted other couples, pulled each other this way and that, left to right, around her, missed him, ducked under them and the walls billowed and flapped and in my memory now *as the wind becomes a barrage that has me standing still, frozen to the core, leaning back in the blast and the houses are a white-out, a dazzle and there's only my aching knees and crisp skin and lips that feel like they're being grated by the wind-chill, and around me the windows of the houses are black trapdoors in white mountainsides and for a second I don't know where I am going or why I am putting myself through this* –in my memory the whole thing seems like a sequence from a Duran Duran or ABC video from the early eighties when the world was just opening up and forming for me and I'd have thought that you only met girls in glamorous, fraught and complicated circumstances like these. Breathless, we skidded into the debating chamber that had been transformed into a dancefloor for this event, and I spun you around to a stop and pulled you close to me. The dance was slow, cheek-to-cheek, supper-club jazz. The small of your back gave to the press of my palm as we glided into the ranks of other clinging couples. I caught a glimpse of Pink Stripe scanning the dancers from the doorway, mouth clenched, head grey, his eyes sooty crosses before he vanished in a whirr of security men's arms. You smiled up at me and laughed now, the flaming rose at the shoulder of your dress. It couldn't have been any more special if I'd untied your hands and feet from the railroad track as the thunderous train bore down at the bend.

Was it this that makes it all seem so special, or is it the hours of close, wordless dancing that followed, or the hours of talking and laughing and storytelling that preceded the tilting, tipping feeling that shifted me, drunk, exhausted, high, this way and that on the college quad? Is it that or the way you squeezed my hand and kissed my cheek and said something thank you-ish that I now can't remember exactly before you walked away towards your accommodation block? Or that sense I remember as I was standing there and a sickly yellow dawn tinged the trees and the buildings and I watched you and sank inside and then found a neutral feeling then a surge as you paused, turned, slipped off your shoes and ran back to me? Is it simply the soft-focus, film-still, book-jacket image of us that I see as the trailing third person again here: you and me, eveningwear, the dewy

298

lawn, the towers and the spires and the cupolas around us, a first kiss as the sun rises? [78]

Is it this or that you were the first girl that I slept with more than once, that I spent night after night with, that I undressed in the afternoons, in whose arms I lay on the floor surrounded by discarded clothes and knotted tights and scattered shoes; who I made love to by the river, in the library stack and frenetically, urgently in a cloister and once in the sea; whose pull I could sense any time we were apart? Is it that you were the first woman that I actually spent the whole night with, that I slept beside, who I woke up with, who made with me a private world called bed? Is it that we, like every young couple, thought that we had invented sex, that it never existed before us and it didn't happen to anyone else in quite the same way or never had and never would? Is it that in you I realized that women were all skin and blood and need and desire, too, that we were all in this together? Is it this with us, only this freshness and newness, how unjaded and ready we were back then on that college lawn, that in the first kiss we were permanent?

At the intersection, I am at crosscurrent to the wind. It seems as if in front of me vast swarms of Styrofoam quavers are flitting through the air, great clouds of them, so dense that I can hardly make out the traffic lights ahead of me and although the snow is untouched on the road, no tyre tracks, no sludge, I can't see if cars are coming, I can't sense anything but my charred lips, this dry tasteless sting on my tongue. As I take a step forwards into the whiteness, my ears contract as the snow that has dampened my fringe suddenly freezes and I see myself alongside myself ten years ago now, walking the pavement, Ristova Road, you on the camber. It wasn't this cold then. Alone, it's colder. Fuck you, you left me for that badminton-playing, prawn-faced git. But the ghost of you clings. Like the song says. How the ghost of you clings and I'm a storyteller, I want answers, questions, answers, questions; I want drama and significance.

Was it how you used to meet me on the steps of the History Library and I'd buy you coffee or soup and we'd sit somewhere and I'd make up stories about all the other people in the café. *That man with the slight rash on his jaw has a gas mask fetish because he was brought up in Israel and thinks that no one knows but because of the ultra-thinness of his bamboo blinds all his neighbours do know; one day this will come to the surface. That woman is a world-expert on*

---

[78] **James O'Mailer:** God's blood, this is getting as purple as the walls of a vomitorium. Don't worry, dear reader, hold tight. I will be coming to your rescue anon.

endocrinology but deep-down, despite her seventy-three years still longs to be an opera singer; her calling was cruelly stripped away from her when she damaged her vocal cords calling for a child lost on the windy moors. You liked this sort of thing and we would wander back though the medieval streets and return to your room on the fourth floor and look out over the parks from the balcony and smoke cigarettes and take off our clothes and then listen to Kate Bush, *The Kick Inside.*

Was it this or that hotel in Florence, that night swarms of bats followed the Arno and a violet night sky rose above the indigo hills we could see from our balcony? We smoked Lucky Strikes and hardly slept and neither of us had been abroad on our own before and we lay in the sheets and ate strawberries dipped in Nutella and as the fan whirred above us we both knew there was more to us than this, there was more time for us, more space out there for Nathan and Johanna to explore. We both knew, both said it.

I love you.

I love you, too.

And that was the night, you, the white sheet wrapped around your midriff as you crawled across the bed towards me, said that I should be a writer: the things I say, my way with words, how I describe people, my knack for nicknames, my nose for a story, always embellishing, lying for the sake of drama.

You should write, Nathan, you said, you should write.

The air thrummed with insects and distant partying, a bassline, catcalls and wolf whistles and as we stared at each other, my face close to your kiss-me smirk, klaxons sounded somewhere out there in the citrus-scented night[79].

Write, Nathan, you said, before you kissed me hard with your tongue. My hand slipped down your back and I guided you under me. It was all I had ever wanted to do. Write. But writing was not for people like me I'd thought, until then, when you tugged on the back of my hair and whispered in my ear, *write me a story, Nathan.*

---

[79] **James O'Mailer:** One more of those, dear reader, and I'm heading back a few pages to change the title of this miserable, lousy little memoir to **Purple Snow**. It's a better title, don't you think?

Touch It and Always and Think of Me

But I didn't write you a story. I didn't write one for years.

I wasn't writing a story when we graduated and stood arm in arm wearing gowns and mortar boards on the bright, brown gravel that surrounds the Sheldonian Theatre, when we smiled at the cameras that concealed the eyes of our parents and relatives. By then, we already knew how we were going to live.

I wasn't writing when we decided to set up in London and not drift around Europe like Lost Generation wannabes, too poor to play it like Scott and Zelda, Hemingway and Hadley. We rented the flat in Balham; we found jobs; me with the first of a succession of rubbish publishing presentisms[80]; you researching regimental histories for the Ministry of Defence. I wasn't writing as we closed around each other like the fronds of a creeper; as we threw dinner parties with brandy and spliff and inappropriately loud music; as we passed out side-by-side on the nightbus home from Camden or The Angel; as we lay on the floor and listened to The Auteurs, Tindersticks, Scott Walker and St Etienne. As we queued for the cinema, the theatre or exhibitions and never once doubted that

---

[80] **James O'Mailer:** Right, that's it.

London was the place that we wanted to be. London in the early 90s; a city reinventing itself, just like we were reinventing ourselves; the New York of Europe; vibrating, expanding, rising; before they built over it; before it acquired a vacant, haunted quality that reminds me of the St Petersburg of Gogol and Dostoyevsky, its gaslights lit by devils in North Face puffa jackets and media-twat glasses; before it became the Arctic to me.

I wasn't writing when we sat in the Dead Sea Navigator to celebrate the acceptance of your PhD proposal, your thesis on innovations in government during the First World War. All our friends were there: One Foot in the Dave Cave and Juan-or-Juanita, Lol Chisholm and Penny Templeton and Zed Ted with his bugger's grips and Bazza Loot and Moaning Pru and loads of folk that I forget, so they might as well have been Shagger, Skag, Porno, Hard Drive and Dog, this being the nineties. And one of them, Hard Drive probably, leant over, lips glistening with lager and said: 'Better heat up those boots, Nate, or she'll leave you behind.' Something fell through me then and I leant back against the juke box and watched you: the way your hand movements flickered as you explained your intentions for the umpteenth time; the white neckline of your deep-blue T-shirt and how it merged into your blemishless, smooth, pale shoulders; the sheen across your eyes when you looked up and caught me staring at you with my fear and my pride.

I wasn't writing all those nights when I stayed in and you went out and when I could have been at my desk, with papers and notes and plots and synopses, I was nagged and distracted by the lingering intimation of your presence. I could still feel you around me, just like I would when I was out with Porno and Hard Drive or confined by a workpod in an open plan office, scanning flatplans and printing schedules, or dangling from a hand-grip on a Northern Line tube or sitting in a park at lunchtime pretending to read when I was thinking about you instead, like I can still feel you next to me *as I cross the road in slow-motion and the snowflakes are so huge it's as if a storm of musical notes are flying at me: minims, treble clefs and semibreves, and it's so cold; I want you to hold me to make the cold go away even though I know that a cuddle in the snow won't help. But I want time to stop here. Stop time. I want it to go backwards. I don't want the past to keep scattering behind me like snow on the wind. I don't want things to be like they worked out, me here and you with the badminton-playing, prawn-faced git. This is not my life. This is the counterlife. I've been shifted into a parallel universe. I am still in love with you. I should be with you. I want to go back to Ristova Road, but this time you don't drop my hand and it is only a setback, a blip, a sad and unfortunate accident; and your hand stays in mine and you pause and turn to me and grab me and hold me and we are still in this together and everything we ever said still holds true and the cold becomes at least bearable.*

I wasn't writing when we went to Paris for the weekend in May and drifted from the tour party in the Palace of Versailles and slipped through the hedge by the obelisk and in the woods you took off your dress, the sunlight threw shapes across your breasts and your stomach and you said 'make sure that none of this ends up in a story.[81]'

Nor was I writing when we sat up in bed all night, four years together then, and talked as if we'd only just met: your dad, my dad, your childhood, my childhood, those underwhelming flings we'd had before we met; how when you were six you stole a sunset-orange scarf you coveted from a girl at school and how the guilt still made the back of your neck burn; when I buried my grandmother's dog and how around me the whole of the family's history seemed to be closing down; how you were finding out all sorts of things about the logistics of medical supplies. And then you said, 'when are you actually going to start, Nate? I want to see something. Time's winged chariot, and all that.'

And I wasn't writing in Australia, when we came out of the sea, and from a shelf outside a beach craft shop, you plucked the starfish that now hides itself in Erika Gretch's lavatory, and said to me, 'Here, to inspire you. Touch it and always and think of me. I'll be waiting.' I wasn't writing then. No. I wasn't.

---

[81] **James O'Mailer:** You might think, dear reader, that Flack is betraying a confidence here, but, unlike me, who watched the coupling unfold with unusual urgency from the boughs of an overhanging tree – not without a sense of ennui, it has to be said, he's not yet been candid enough, in my humble opinion, about the glory of Johanna's breasts – you did not hear what she actually said and thus cannot gauge the extent of Flack's coyness. She actually said 'I'll kill you if my pussy ever ends up in a story.' Incidentally, I must remind you that I am on my way, coming fleet of foot to rescue both Flack from the chill and you, dear reader, from the purple snows that bluster.

The Drowners

Then three things happened. Firstly, I got made redundant (with minimal severance pay) from Bollocks Press, where I'd been employed for eight months editing ill-conceived coffee table book packages with titles like *Shut Up Your Child* and *Build Your Own Labour Camp*; made redundant being a euphemism for fired for using the word 'munificent' in a fax. Kicked out. Again. My wonderful career in publishing. Yes, I got drunk in the Dead Sea Navigator with Porno and Hard Drive and called you up, weepy like a git, and you came and said sympathetic things, but I didn't do what you said this time. I didn't write five hundred spec letters to all of the publishers in London. I didn't apply for all the jobs in *The Bookseller* and the *Media Guardian*. I didn't send my meagre CV to all the employment agencies specializing in the publishing sector. Nor did I take a TEFL, or think about teacher training, or heaven forbid, switch career paths and side-jump onto the accountancy rat track or run away to the circus of death that is the English legal profession.

My second staging point here was that I signed on. I stayed in bed instead of applying for jobs with *Marsupial Magazine* or *Shelving Now*. I made dreamy drifts around the commons and parks and the backstreets, and I started to write. Scribble. Scratch. Form. Fumble towards it. One afternoon in a greasy spoon somewhere off Tooting Broadway, I wrote my first proper sentence: *Melissa was already there in dense round shades when I arrived at Eros.* I wrote another one, then another and another, and the next day I did the same. A week later I'd written my first short story.

My third dazzling turn was that I met Seb Harker after I'd noticed an ad in *Time Out* for a monthly Saturday writers' workshop. I turned up in the upstairs room of Fitzrovia pub and there was the long table with the would-be writers all around it, the sensitive delicates, the stridently hip, the always affronted, the terribly awe-struck, the seldom committed and the unfortunately expectant. There was Seb, in the chair, dapper, stern, unflappable. And in turn they dished up their soup – mainly noodle doodles – and he listened and commented, said encouraging things and critical things and never let slip how bored he actually was. I read out my two pages of *Melissa was already there in dense round shades.* Afterwards, I sat there feeling like a punctured plum as my overwriting, overreaching, shifting diction level, POV confusions, stagey dialogue, train-wreck syntax and adjectival overkill were exposed and analysed and discussed. My inner Rom-T threw himself off a cliff as my inner Sensitive Plant urged me to slash my wrists while my inner Literature Denier argued back that he was wrong and all he had to do was read it as I intended it to be read and all would be clear. My inner Moon-Barker wanted to gun them all down and my inner Wrong Roomer shouted to the ceiling that would *someone please just listen, I don't know who I am or what I am here for and I can't do anything and I keep getting the sack and my girlfriend is far more focused and intelligent and capable and loveable than I am, and I need this, I need it, so will you please all start telling me that everything is going to be OK, just so I can walk out of here as some semblance of a man!* Meanwhile, my inner Grammar Stammerer agreed with Seb and told me that I was a prick.

On the tube home I decided that I wasn't going back to Seb's workshop and would inform you that I would give up writing and get into the Job Search groove.

Back at the flat, I told you it had been interesting and decided to sleep on it.

During the next three weeks I rewrote the story *Losing Eros.*

When I read this out again at Seb's workshop, everyone sat in appreciative silence before they said admiring and complimentary things. I didn't really care about them. I only cared about him. He paused. He read through the pages again while we waited. He smiled and said, 'you have it, Nathan, you have the voice'.

Later that night I told you this in the Navigator, proclaiming that I had found what I wanted to do and everything was going to be different from now on.

'Good for you, Nathan,' you said. 'Write a novel. There's no money in short stories. Only people in creative writing classes read short stories now.'

'I am,' I said. 'It's going to be called *The Drowners*.'

Oh *The Drowners*. I still don't know what you imagined, what you thought being around someone writing a novel would be like, even you, with your extended essays and abstracts and thesis chapters and hours and hours in archives and libraries. I think you thought it would slither out glistening and ready like some robust, independent animal. You didn't think it was going to take two years of discovering and drafting and wrong-turns and mistakes and stupid ideas crossed out and chapters ditched and restarted from scratch. You didn't reckon on our lives being crowded by people who had the temerity to simultaneously not exist yet clamour constantly for attention. You didn't like it that I'd spend the whole evening locked in the bedroom staring at the word processor. You disliked the strange expressions and the muttering and pacing and the distance and the knowledge that I was elsewhere when we out and about. 'Stop writing now,' you said to me once on a nightclub balcony. 'Stop it,' you said in the queue for the coats after a Pulp gig. 'Hello, hello. This is ground control,' you said as we trudged all the way around Hampton Court Maze not talking to each other. You didn't like the sense that some other operation was always going on in the flat. But even in Ristova Road I didn't realize that in *The Drowners*' narrative of an alienated, frustrated 'angry young man for the 90s' (as Seb put it; I cringe at the thought of that now, yuk, yuk, yuk) I'd planted a subplot about seducing a chilly posh girl for revenge and the consequences of her pregnancy. In crap ur-novels, maturity and epiphany are always brought about by an unwanted pregnancy carried to full-term. I was still writing about all this when the winter became brutal and you rang me up in the afternoon and asked me to go to the chemists.

What If?

I reach the far side of the road and ahead of me waits the final uphill stretch. The parked cars are mounds of snow and the trees white scribbles and beside me the latticed windows of the shop have those crescents of frost that you see in Dickensian illustrations and Christmas cards. The shop lights cast a tangerine orange sheen across the snow on the pavement where I've paused. I should go in, linger a while, browse the aisles, this is bad, this weather. Tomorrow, the headlines will read: "Locally respected creative writing tutor Nathan Flack was yesterday discovered frozen to death outside a double gabled mock tudor house during the worst cold snap in living memory. All the regions' other low quality writers survived the weather that swept in from the Arctic Circle. Reginald Carnaby, a close personal friend, said, "He really was a national disgrace and a traitor to Albion. None of us will miss him."

But I don't want to hide in the shop. This isn't my life. This isn't happening. Out there on the other side of the void is the other me and the other you and they are the Nathan and Johanna who count. And I ask myself as I begin to heave myself up the slope towards campus what would have happened if in the Rawalpindi you had told me that you were going to have the baby? What if I'd been filled with joy and love and grabbed you by the hand and embraced with all my heart the completeness and the certainty of this?

Yeah, sure, when it sunk in I'd have had all the doubts and confusions and regrets that lad lit, disco dad novels tell us are the rite of passage of becoming a parent and a real man, maturity and epiphany being brought about by unwanted pregnancy carried to full term. I'd have spent the first three months being unable to express my feelings and fears and my dialogue would be at variance with my interior monologue.

'You do want to have this baby?' she says, tears in her eyes, fiddling with her Police sunglasses.

'Yes,' I say, as I flip through my Primal Scream 12" singles, my arsecrack showing over the waistband of my Diesel jeans, and sling 'Swastika Eyes' onto the Bang and Olofsen.

No, I think, babies smell and proper fit birds won't fancy me.

And I'd have worried about life being over and how could I be a father when I'm still a twelve-year old child at heart who still watches *Star Wars* and talks about *Bagpuss* and *King Rollo* in the pub, and I won't see so much of Porno and Hard Drive who will be having a much better time of it chasing uncomplicated sex with uncomplicated women named after cheap wines and tourist destinations, and drinking poncey Japanese lager in bars with abstract noun logos like Incubation and Gestation, and playing Scalextric in their purpose-built warehouse apartments and nursing their mythic hangovers and comedowns as the grey light filters through their curtains while I'm stuck with her moaning and materialism and her expanding and sagging and withering and the thing filling its pants every two minutes and I won't climb Everest now or play lead guitar at Knebworth in front of millions of call centre workers, or strafe the Mekong Delta in a F1-11 or float in space on acid, fiddling with my cock as the sun bursts over the North Pole. I'll just turn thirty and CDs will pop out of the toaster like the jacket image of a day-glo 3-for-2 table product-shifter, and I'll spend my spare time talking about things I don't care about to people I don't like and my living days lost in a la la land of big bright Fuzzy Felt colours and Happy Meal cartons.

This would pass though, yes it would. And bollocks to Porno and Hard Drive. Who wants to gibber in a sofapub with a hatful of ciphers when I could have a real relationship with a real woman and be a dad? I'd have you, Johanna, and I would have stopped writing, abandoned *The Drowners* for a life more rewarding.

As the snow begins to seem even whiter and thicker and The Avenue somehow widens and grows steeper and as all sense of feeling has gone

308

and I can't feel my legs anymore, the skin between realities tears and I sense the real history of us. Now I am not here but tucking in to a bowl of delicious home-cooked chilli con carne in my spot-lit country kitchen's dining area, surrounded by my life partner and my preteen children, all talking about our day and its truthful wonders and heart-warmingly human moments as the snow falls magically, coldlessly outside and every so often we pause and glaze over and watch it tumble and blow. This is the me who once held you tight in the Rawalpindi, who took you home to our flat and cried with love as we sat on the side of the bed, who held your hand at the birthing pool and witnessed the miracle, who found himself merged and closer and closer to you than he thought it was possible to be, who settled happily for this adventure, who stashed the unfinished manuscript of The Drowners in a box file and wouldn't look at it again, who sometimes mentioned it self-deprecatingly after three glasses of wine at leaving dos and big Four-O surprise parties, before I always glance over at my wife with her beauty and charm, and smile with relief that I left behind all that hubris and uncertainty, the desire to be 'different' and 'creative', to not do something that used to be called 'selling out'. OK, I do look a bit of a pranny here, a bit bald, a bit fat, a little like a middle-ranking Lib Dem MP who pays for sex, but it's a good life, bringing up children, the providing, the hard work, the occupation and the easy zeal of it. After I'd hid The Drowners in a box file, I sent out all those letters and eventually found another editing job, and this time, because I have to, because for the first time I am living in the future, have something to aim for, I knuckle down and stop looking out the window and using words like 'munificent' in faxes and drop the smoking and the posing and the dreaming. I do my job well and they like me and promote me and I'm like senior somethingorother, a list-managing, deadline-meeting, target-hitting, forward-thinking, rejection slip-writing, eclectic and adaptive twenty-first century publishing executive and I like the stride and the thrust and the jargon. We have a house, our third now, play the property game adeptly, learn the second string moneymaking nous that all modern urban professionals need these days. We have a big summer holiday every year, Morocco or Florida or kayaking up the Orinoco. We have two cars, collect Art Deco furniture and African objets d'art and talk often about a second home on the Illyrian coast or southern Spain. We have our three children, Molly, Milly and Tom and you have tenure and I am setting up my own literary agency now and my days are packed and never lonely. I look to you and I am never lonely. I live with you and I am never lonely. I have the children and will never be lonely.

Never be lonely?[82] A gust of snow hits me so ferociously that going forwards I find my legs almost freeze to a halt as my torso wants to fly back the way that I've just come. The skin between worlds reassembles and I see clearly now, know that I'm doing what you disliked so much that last eighteen months or so of us: merely writing in my head. The phantom Nathan and his spectral children and replicant wife freeze-frame as the snow outside their window vanishes and the walls dissolve and the chilli con carne in their mouths disappears and they share one last terrified, pleading look at one another before their world goes abruptly kaput. There was none of that ahead for us, Johanna, whatever either of us had said or done in the Rawalpindi or Ristova Road.

---

[82] **James O'Mailer:** Good boy, Flack, have your epiphany and we can get started.

A Mess of Cords and Eyes

Back at the flat that night we sat on the side of the bed for a while, still in our coats and our shoes, not holding hands, both staring at the patch of wall above the stereo. We sat there not talking until you uncoiled your scarf and muttered to me that you were going to have a wash. You hung up your coat and padded off to the bathroom. I listened to the boiler whoosh and the pipes buzz, the running of the taps and the unusually heavy-handed way that you seemed to be moving your things about. I wanted you to come back so that we could talk, though I had no idea what I was going to say and wouldn't admit to myself that what I really needed to talk about was why you let go of my hand in Ristova Road. This realization and the imminent procedure that you must be thinking about as you brushed your teeth and removed your make-up and looked at your pale, cold, winter face in the mirror made me hunch up and crush my ribs with my arms.

I noticed it then. It lay on the table next to the wardrobe, alongside the word processor and my stack of paperbacks topped by the starfish. My notebook with a sheaf of papers protruding from the covers. That morning I had finished the ninth chapter of *The Drowners*, the mid-point, the hinge where the plot dovetailed, became complicated by fresh reversals and obstacles.

311

You blanked me when you came back into the room and undressed behind the wardrobe door as if you didn't want me to look at you. I listened to your shuffling, the click of your joints and the dull twang of elastic as you put on your pyjamas.

'I'm going to bed,' you said.

The bedsprings plummeted. I stood up so you could get under the duvet. You were resting against the headboard, your eyes shut and the covers pulled over your chin. I took Chapter Nine of *The Drowners* from the notebook. I'd been giving the novel to you chapter by chapter as I wrote it. You had not yet seen this part. You said that you were enjoying it, that you wanted to know what happened next.

'Jo,' I said as I slipped the papers across the bed. 'I finished this today.'

In the bathroom, forgetting that this was the end, not the start of the day, I covered my cheeks with shaving gel, then muttered 'oh you prick,' as I wiped it off. I looked at my face in the mirror and splashed it with water and again the way that you'd dropped my hand seemed horribly significant. But I was being selfish. You were pregnant. You were going to have an abortion. The 'us' of this was academic. It was your body, your chemistry, your conscience. As I started to massage balm into my cheeks, it suddenly occurred to me what Chapter Nine was about. It was the chapter where my Angry Young Man for the 90s has been confronted by Chilly Posh Girl, because as a consequence of their chilly assignation in Chapter Three Chilly Posh is pregnant. This is a shock to Angry Young and he's in denial and at the start of Chapter Nine he says . . .

I looked away from the mirror. You would be reading it now.

It's a hideous, grasping thing growing inside her. A mess of cords and eyes.

Your bare feet thundered along the hall. As I blinked at the door, you pounded it three times. The door quivered. The mirror shook.

I held up my hands and slapped them to my face. You hit the door again and called out my name, but not in the accusatory, furious way that I expected.

Unlocking the door, I had no chance to say anything before you elbowed and shouldered me out of the way and back into the hall. The bolt clicked behind you.

'Jo?' I said. 'Johanna?'

No answer.

In the bedroom, Chapter Nine was fanned across the bedclothes.

A mess of cords and eyes.

312

Back at the bathroom door, I knocked again.

'Jo?' I said. 'I'm sorry.'

No answer, no sound from inside.

'Jo, I didn't think, I didn't mean you to see that . . . Jo, please talk to me, I don't feel like that. It's fiction, you understand me, it's not true, it's for the sake of the story.'

All I could hear now was a faint rustling inside and the toilet roll holder rattle.

Then a sob.

'Jo? Please?'

In front of the door, in the subterranean cold of the unheated flat, I shivered as I waited and I don't know how long it was before you came out but it seemed much longer than it must have been.

When the door swung open, your face was ash-blue and your eyes pink and raw. You looked up at me and thrust your hand into your fringe and seemed to teeter and for a second I thought you were going to faint.

'Nathan,' you said. 'Nathan . . . I've just had my period.'

You collapsed into me and shook and shuddered and wept.

I wanted to shudder and weep. I felt like dancing.

We curled up in bed and lay in the dark and I stroked your hair and your ear and said: 'Are we OK?'

'Yes,' you said.

'I'm glad we're OK?''

'Are you?'

'That's why I said it.'

'I'm OK.'

'Really?' I said.

'I'll be fine in a couple of days.'

'Saved by the power of prose,' I said.

Kansas

On reflection, this last statement is the most stupid and naive thing I have ever said in my entire, soon-to-be-over-in-the-snowy-wastes life. I am halfway up the sloping, final-run of The Avenue now and the snow is a million distended, ropelike threads. The ice on the pavement feels like it's listing and the only way I can make out the end of The Avenue is that the crosswind disturbs the pattern of the snowfall there. My body is remote from me. I know now that this isn't a slightly ill advised march in the weird and pretty snow. I'm going to drop. My limbs will fall off, my eyes burn. Man found encased in ice. Someone will write a book about it in 2187 ("He'd eaten a meal of raspberry Pop Tarts and gruel and had a device to play primitive music and a look of profound disappointment and perplexity was frozen into his features."). I look back but I can't see the glow of the shop, only snow whizzing behind me like thousands and thousands of white tracer lines. I should knock at a house. Too embarrassing. Will I die here rather than suffer the embarrassment of knocking on a stranger's door? Yes. "The perplexity on his face may well have been caused by the final realization that he had died of embarrassment." My feet inch forwards and I am still thinking of you but you're a trail of bits and snatches all the way back from here to the garret. I'm thinking that this cold is worse than the cold in Ristova Road, and the only thing that I

314

can compare it to is the cold that stayed between us for the month after I told you we were saved by the power of prose, before you left, before Badminton Prawn and your actual pregnancy, your real children, your real house, life, holidays and prawny badminton court togetherness that co-existed with my Capote-like arrival in the sticks[83] and *The* MA and crap relationships and *The Penelope Tree* and its culmination in my imminent collapse and death in the snow. My knees start to buckle, something that I can only sense because every second or so I dip and wobble. I'm going to die here. This is my lonely end in the Sturm und Drang of the snowstorm. But I know though that had I stayed, or had you stayed, because it was all your leaving, not my going, had I stayed there would be no super-happiness for me, no ultra-togetherness. What sort of fool am I for entertaining that particular fantasy? Do I actually think I could have become a forward-thinking, constantly evolving, eclectic and adaptive 21st century publishing executive with money-making nous kayaking up the Orinoco being Daddy Cool and never lonely alongside you. Do I actually think that you could have stuck out this last ten years of me being like this? Really? I never have. Not until tonight. No. Before tonight, all I have ever imagined if I've thought of the counterlife with you is an image of me locked in some white upstairs bathroom with white pipes and a white basin and a white cistern and a white Victorian bath with white clawed feet and the noise outside, the little voices that I can't admit I don't really want to hear because all I want to do is write a novel because the burn and the throb of it is always there, a ghostly heartbeat that tells me that out there is a doppelganger me who's actually doing it.

I stand up and stop dipping and buckling. The white road persists ahead and the falling snow is like a solid screen. I start to move.

I am not in that upstairs bathroom.

I can write.

I am a writer.

I have written a novel.

I have written four novels.

I can write.

The Voice.

The Fumigator.

I shouldn't be here.

And I shouldn't be in the long-lost hinterland of Johannasburg.

---

[83] Norfolk is actually like Kansas in the 1950s: whistling plains, dark farmhouses, timeless murder.

I should have sold *The Penelope Tree*.

I should be in print.

I am a writer.

I can write[84].

'Who says I can't write? Which one of you arseholes?'

A thump comes from behind me, probably a dustbin picked up by the wind and thrown into the middle of the road. My arms are hung out wide now and I have my fists raised and I am shouting at the houses and the snow and the sky. For a second I think I can hear the tinkle of bells, but I want to hear my own voice scream out. As I do so I realize the actual volume of the wind. It's a gale, a hurricane, like something from a disaster movie. Something is behind me, I can sense it, hear it, scraping, sliding and yapping. Something is running alongside me, something like a long, brown giant centipede. Its humps and segments ripple up and down level with my shins. As it gets ahead of me I realize that it's not a centipede. It's a pack of chihuahua dogs, yappy little gits, all trussed up in a harness, heaving something along behind them. I'm going mad, hallucinating from exposure. I am dying, I know. Got to keep myself going, got to keep reminding myself that they are not real. Then I get another surge of feeling and raise my fists again to prove that I am still here.

'Who says I can't write? Which one of you?'

A dark shape pulls up alongside me and I can hear the bells and the scrape of the skids. The leashes strain and the dogs come to a halt and right next to me is a long, gondolier-like sledge and sitting up front, adjacent to me now is a huge man in a Cossack fur hat and black cape and huge black beard. His eyepiece glints[85].

---

[84] **James O'Mailer:** No, no, damn this Flack, damn his stubbornness. I must implement the O'Mailer Manoeuvre. Summon the dogs!

[85] **James O'Mailer:** Dear Reader, this is the moment you have all been waiting for. Trumpets sound. Kettle drumbeats roll. Distant thunder presages my entrance. Up here at the North Pole I have tallied a while, gathering my strength again since my cameo at the soiree where my little subterfuge failed to bear fruit. This second subterfuge is also proving tricksy. Now, we must play our hand. Now we implement our plot and save Flack from an ignoble fate and save us all in the process. I take a last look at this Arctic refuge from where I have driven these terrible snows down on Flack. And my faithful friend this last week, an acquaintance of some two hundred years standing and the only denizen of this domain, Doctor Frankenstein's monster, turns to me and says: 'Master, will you save us all now?' 'Dear Monsty, yes. Now our heritage is not to be obliterated. There is to be no holocaust, no hecatomb. Flack and O'Mailer, together at last, to stave off the Apocalypse.' I clap my hands and summon from the vasty depths the vigour and sorcery that I have loaned to every man, woman and child upon the planet who, as Flack would

'Hiya Kiddo,' he says, 'in answer to your question, why, little old me, of course?'

Spikes of hot fear prickle up my arm as he sits there in the cab of the sled, one hand reining in the dogs. A long, ornately handled stick rests between his legs. I keep staring at him, hoping the illusion will dematerialize just as quickly as it's appeared, but his huge, black outline persists and seems to become more real the longer I look. He is just like I imagined. He's the exact image of the nightmarishly pedantic student Frances and I made up together. I am going mad. I *am* dying. Near death experiences. Christians see angels. Hindus see Shiva. Writers see James O'Mailer. He pushes up his Cossack hat with a leather-gloved forefinger and gives me a smarmy wink.

I scrape my glove along the garden wall alongside me and make a snowball that I hurl at him.

'You're not real!'

The snowball glances off his shoulder, ricochets over the front of the sledge, bounces once on the road then lands among the now crouching dogs. There's a yelp and a scrabble and out of the pack a chihuahua flies at me and sinks its fangs into my glove. Pain shoots up my wrist, my arm and grips my shoulder. I flap, trying to throw it off and as I do so I notice that the little bastard's stony black eyes swim with stardust.

'If I am not real,' comes a voice, 'then account for that?'

O'Mailer is standing up now, the Cossack hat making him seem as tall as the houses, his hands crossed over the hilt of his stick that's resting in

---

put it, touches the starfish, everyone who writes, everyone who paints, everyone who sculpts, composes, movie-makes, acts or photographs. The orange snakes of this distilled power flow from the corners of the Earth and are sucked into me. These feet reform themselves on terra firma, an invigorating rush swells through my legs as I feel for sure the sidewinders of snow that lash across the polar icecap, my shoulders find their true girth, my reborn spine lofts my head. I, James O'Mailer, return, am resurrected. I wave my right palm and my vessel appears. I snap the fingers of my left and summon the Hounds. 'Come, trusty Prudhomme, Mishal, Kipling, Hamsun, Galsworthy, Pirandello, Sholokhov and Parsons. I crack the whip and they draw the sledge up into the sky. I bid farewell to the monster as he recedes to a scab and we soar up to the moon before we swoop. The Island, a hunched old maid's outline from this vantagepoint is misted by my snow that whirls around us now. We nine, O'Mailer and the Hounds of Greatness, descend, the wind gusting my cape and down we go, down and down we go together, targeting that old maid's crookback and the snow-lashed city, a little Moscow tonight, and the streets rush and now we are a foot above the ground on the straight run and up ahead the dogs catch the scent of Flack, trained as they are to sniff out cigarette smoke and self-pity, and we hit the road – touchdown, the legend has landed – and alongside us is the shambling man. At last, we meet.

317

the snow, his face dark and hidden from me as I jump and swing and spaz and the dog keeps gnawing into my hand.

'Simmer down, Parsons!' he calls.

The dog drops and scampers back towards to the pack. O'Mailer circles his stick in a two-handed motion in front of him. A shimmer of golden stardust glitters in its arc, the same stardust that shone in the dog's eyes, and just as the dog reaches the pack, it vanishes. They all vanish and then the sledge disappears. O'Mailer turns the stick the other way and the wind drops. It stops snowing. The gash on my finger heals over. He strides towards me, his boots crackling across the snow, his arm out rigid.

'Kiddo, we meet at last. O'Mailer. James O'Mailer. You didn't think I'd let you perish, did you?'

'Piss off, you're not real.' I swipe my arm at him. He tilts backward to avoid it, then grabs hold of both my hands and squeezes them together.

'Feel this manly grip. Feel this hearty hail-fellow well met slap, feel the brush of my fulsome beard. I, O'Mailer, stand before you.'

'Let go of me, I'm in a hurry.'

'What we have to discuss is of great importance, especially so since despite my prompting you have just come again to the wrong conclusion.'

'What are you going on about?'

'Flack, listen to me.' He puts his hand on my shoulder and looks into my face. His eyepiece is a gleaming disc that swirls with the golden dust. 'You must realize by now that I am omniscient. Well, partly when I am still hobbled by you and they. But I am omnipotent and I sent the snows to you, Flack, sent them to provoke that little foray into fantasyland that you entertained so engagingly back there. And why did I do this? Why you may well ask? Well, because, Kiddo, I need you to realize the errors of your ways so you can join with me in the great work we have before us. I gave you the axe. I gave you the fair doctor. I verily knocked your heads together in the horseless carriage. But do you read the clues? Do you run through Little Moscow shouting "Eureka!"? So I have to act further. I call upon Generals Janvier and Février. And still you come to the wrong realization again, Flack, the wrong realization. You force us to have a little tête-à-tête.'

'I'm insane. That's why I'm standing here talking to a figment of my imagination.'

'Kiddo, I am not a figment of your imagination. I *am* your imagination.'

318

'Well, if you are, then I really am useless. You'd think I could come up with something better than you, Fannyface.'

'Leave the put-downs to me, Flack. The stakes are high, the cards marked, the dealer less of an *accopiatori*, more of a gin-soused stumblebum with his back pocket stuffed with greased pesos.' O'Mailer slides his arm over my shoulder and starts to march me back down The Avenue, whispering in my ear. 'I knew that if I sent the snow, Flack, you would brood on the old Johanna. You were supposed to realize that this insistence of yours that you write and thereby thwart my efforts is founded on the fairy's wing of you trying to impress a woman, a woman long gone and unfortunately uninvigorated. You're never going to get her, or the time back, by persisting. So stop, Flack. Stop and join with me. Join with O'Mailer.'

I dig in my heels and push him in the chest with the flats of my hands.

'What do you mean? You sent the snow? Nobody sends the snow.'

'When will you learn? I, O'Mailer, am omniscient, the ultimate omniscient narrator.'

'If you're omniscient then you should have foreseen that I wouldn't have come to the conclusion that you wanted me to. You're lying. You're not real. I'm mad and I'm going to die.'

He cocks his head and leans on the stick. 'Flack, even I concede that you have a slight point here. The only thing that scabbards my power is you, Kiddo. While you were strong, I was kept at bay. As you grew weaker, I grew stronger. But while you persist, I cannot be wholly free. But there is a great future for us, Flack, a great purpose. I have been trying to allude, to draw you along the right path.'

'Pick on someone else, James. There are a million 3-for-2-table product-shifters and literary heavyweights out there who'd positively enjoy being tortured by you. Leave me alone.'

'That I cannot do. You and me. We're entwined.'

'Only because I made you up.'

'If only it were so. I can only leave you if you let me go and you can only let me go if you stop and do what I and all humanity needs you to do. Otherwise, I beseech of you, join with me. I can see the future.' He holds out his hand to me. 'Join with me.' The hand is quivering, twitching. The stick is held out and he's pressing it against my arm. I sidestep and duck under the stick and try to walk past him, back towards the campus but he grabs my elbow and pulls me in front of him again.

'Flack, Kiddo,' he says, 'that Johanna story, that's a fantasy. You just subjected me to a voyage around a lousy and nostalgic Disneyworld of what-ifs and maybes. Do you want to see a real parallel world, you want to have a real flight of fancy?'

'You're not real. You're not real. You're not real.'

'So be it, then.'

Two-handedly he whirls the stick around in a circle and as it comes up for its second loop the golden stardust forms in its wake. The golden disc solidifies, a minor sun born in the road and the night. I close my eyes. There's a crack and a tinkle.

When I open my eyes, we're not in Kansas any more.

Nightmares and Dream Sequences

Someone, I'm not quite sure who, maybe Henry James, maybe Gertrude Stein, maybe Mac MacMahon[86] once said, 'Tell a dream, lose a reader,' so use them with extreme caution (and never just prior to 'the grey light filtered through the curtains' if you absolutely insist on having curtains), but I was dreaming, or dying, or dreaming just before I died. Or I was already dead. I don't know how long I was in blackness, weightless with no sense of velocity or direction or up and down, day or night and time passing. Somehow I was standing up and sensed that out there on something like a horizon, something was swirling and coiling and dragging itself into being. Cold air wrapped itself around my face and I could smell pine and dirt and hear chirrups and the breeze rustling in the treetops. When I opened my eyes I was in a forest of gigantic conifers. The trunks stretched up to thank the sky and moonlight shimmered on the canopy. There was a moon here. I could see it, full and vast. I looked around myself. Tightly packed trees as far as I could see. A flitting light danced in the distance and as I watched it I started to pace around and around in a circle, my hands wedged into my armpits, around and around

---

[86] No, it was Mac MacMahon who said, 'tell a wank-dream, gain a reader,' or was it: 'tell a dream, kill a zombie'? or: 'Tell a lie, fuck a groupie'?

323

and around and I was cold and this was death and it wasn't the end and this was not what I wanted, this was not what I wanted to believe. Dying pointlessly for nothing in a snowstorm was one thing. Discovering an Occult Universe as a consequence was a double horror.

Something pressed down on my shoulder, a gentle pressure but I felt like a bucket of dirty slush had been thrown over me and I almost retched.

'Kiddo, you thought I'd forgotten you,' said James O'Mailer, now in front of me, the chihuahua crooked in his arm, the fingers of his other hand stroking its pointy-head. 'Welcome to my domain.'

'This is it. I'm dead. Stone cold dead. Frozen to death. You're some mad dream as my mind shuts down. Or maybe I'm in a coma. That's how low I've got. The best I can hope for is that I'm in a coma.'

'Don't be so glum, chum. It ain't so bad. Tell the silly man it ain't so bad, Parsons.' The dog's eyes glowed golden for an instant. 'You're not dead, Flack. You're still very much alive. You're in a privileged position. I've never taken any of the others here in person.'

'No, this is Hell. Can you commit suicide in Hell? What happens then, eh? Tell me that. That's the last thing that I want to know.'

'Relax, Kiddo. Listen, I can drop you back at any time, trust me, but I brought you here to show you the errors of your thinking. I may have had my sport with you, true, a few wizard wheezes, a little jesting, but when I saw the future I knew we were in this together.'

'I'm dead. I'm going to hang myself from a tree just to prove it.'

'You can't kill yourself here, Flack.'

'I'll have a good old go.'

'You test me. Here I am. I show you all the mysteries and you bury your head.'

'This is the sort of thing I hate. I hate reading stories about it. You think I want to be in it?'

'Must I apologize for bringing enlightenment?'

'So where are we then?'

'Let me show you.' He turned, his cape sending a flurry of needles and dust up into the air, and started to walk into the trees and the murky darkness there. I thought about letting him go and staying here, but the forest was very, very big, and very dense, the grasshoppers ground out a relentless two-beat rhythm, and O'Mailer was striding away towards the pinprick of light. His shape disappeared and the sound of the insects amplified, as if they were an amorphous hive-mind that stalked and drew

324

closer to me. The trees suddenly seemed taller and thicker and closer to me. This wasn't real, so I wanted to stay and leave him to it, but I found myself running through the ferns.

He didn't say anything when I caught up with him. I merely followed as he slashed at the bracken with the stick, beating a path towards the light. When we arrived at the edge of a clearing, an oval of dust surrounded by an especially dense wall of pines, I realized that the light came from a campfire. A ring of stones contained a burning heap of brush and branches. The smoke flowed vertically into the windless night as if the moon greedily sucked it from the earth. Around the fire sat people, a dozen, maybe twenty men, women and children, a shabby, dirty, longhaired tribe, barefoot and dressed in furs and hides. They all seemed to be tucking into hunks of meat, their faces glittering with juice in the firelight. They whispered and murmured, but I couldn't work out a single word. On the edge of the group, though, was a thin, undersized youngster who lay on his side and stared back into the forest.

'Who are they?' I said.

'Early man,' said O'Mailer.

'Can they see us?'

'Only if I want them to. Now shush. Something momentous is going to happen.'

A man clambered onto a tree stump in front of the fire. He started to proclaim something to the now hushed group. As he spoke he made crazy gesticulations and jumped off the stump and crept up and down a line in front of his audience. He ducked and crouched, pressed his hand to his eyebrows and scanned the clearing, then made stabbing motions with an invisible implement.

'His accent's a bit north county,' I said.

'There are no counties yet,' said O'Mailer. 'And no alphabets or governments or organized religions. In case you've not guessed, we're in the Primal Forest. These fellows would marvel at a wheel just as you would a time machine. But this hero here is doing something special. This is the start of it all.'

A collective gasp went up from the pack as he stood stock still, his hand thrust towards the moon.

'What is he then? An early form of motivational speaker?'

'Your foolery is predictable. No, Flack. He's telling the first ever story. This is a great step forward in man's self-consciousness. He's defining worlds here. He's making history. Everything that follows starts here, all

325

the national epics, all the grand narratives, the sagas, the poetry. These folk are well on the way to becoming something more than their appetites.'

'Are the others, like, early Folder Holders?'

'They are listening, and let me double-back and emphasize the word "listening" for your instruction, Flack, unlike you they are *listening* to a story about the hunt, how he and his cohorts went off into the forest and faced the bear, the mammoth, the sabre-tooth, then stalked the elk, followed it, trailed its tracks and its droppings and then they circled it and killed it dead. They shall live this winter, this little tribe. They shall have meat and bones and hides.'

'Where's the plot twist then?'

'See that runty little kid out on the edge, the one stridently not listening, the one missing out on all the fun?'

'The one who looks like the singer in Ruiner?'

'That's you.'

I kicked at the dust. 'You brought me here just to insult me in the last seconds of my existence?'

'No, Flack, I'm showing you that your present predicament is foreshadowed in the very origins of our craft. That little runt contains the earliest antecedents of your genes. That's your sorriest grandfather. Your family tree starts here in this clearing. You were born to be the one who doesn't listen.'

Out in the clearing, the storyteller circled a long thighbone in front of his face.

'So I suppose you're going to tell me that that's you, is it? That's where you come in. You're the first storyteller?'

'No, no, Flack. You're excessively slow on the uptake.' He raised his stick and pointed it at the group. 'O'Mailer is the *fire*.'

Two jets of flame spurted out from the campfire and coursed around the storyteller and his huddled audience. They yelped and shuddered and turned en masse to watch the two fiery demons fly and converge, then flow into O'Mailer's stick. His outline beside me shone with the golden dust for a second before it hardened again.

'Oh can you just let me die, please,' I said. 'This is the sort of mystical cock that happens in soft fantasy novels and I am very tired. Can I go now?'

'I am trying to show to you that you must listen to me if all is not to be undone.'

326

'Primal forests. You, the flame. Me, the runt. Bollocks.'

'So be it,' said O'Mailer.

The forest people, led by the storyteller, had crept up on us and were now all on their knees, their arms out in front of them, bowing to O'Mailer.

'Mar-stah, mar-stah, mar-stah,' they chanted.

'Oh shut up, you lot,' I said. 'He's not even real.'

'If knowledge of your place in the Universal does not sway you,' said O'Mailer, 'let's make this personal. Let the Grand Narrative flow into the Little Narrative.'

He snapped his fingers. The dog's eyes glowed. A puff of golden dust exploded around us. I saw the eyes of the forest people light up for a second, then they all vanished. There was a sound and the sound was 'tock'.

And I was staring into my thinner, less pasty face and my face shouted back. 'Wanker.' I staggered backwards on my heels. There, ahead of me, was me. Me slumped in a fraying prussian blue armchair, my thigh slung over the rest, the starfish on my lap.

'Stop shouting *and* swearing, Nathan,' came a voice from another room.

The Chair-Nathan pulled a face, stroked the starfish, then squinted back at the television. John Major was giving a speech on the news about a cones helpline for motorway drivers. That voice from the other room belonged to *her*. This room was ours, our lounge in our flat in the Arctic. Johanna's lava lamp that mixed the colours of a tequila sunrise sat on the mantelpiece. Propped up against the wall by the side of my chair were the stack of videocassettes and the painting of the blue-faced Indian woman that every poncey retro-junkie coveted in the mid-nineties. Through a crack in the horrible purple curtains I could see that it was snowing. And the me in the chair was me ten years ago. A queasy sensation pulsed at my temples. I couldn't remember this moment where I shouted at Major Cones and Johanna told me to stop it, but a hideous sense of *déjà vu* visited me.

Over in the chair, I shifted and took the starfish in both hands and caressed its surface. I realized what I was doing, or at least what I was waiting for. She was going out. So I must be psyching myself up to write a few lame paragraphs of *The Drowners* while the flat was quiet. Maybe I was about to write my *mess of cords and eyes* paragraph.

A chihuahua ran between my legs and hopped onto the Chair-Nathan's lap. He didn't notice the dog and kept muttering at Major Cones. The dog cocked its leg and wee-weed over the starfish, then vanished in a wisp of golden sparkle.

'Good boy, Parsons.' A hand squeezed my shoulder. 'Kiddo, tonight, this is your life.'

'Why are we here, James?'

He suddenly appeared in front of me, blocking my view of myself.

'Why are we here, this snowy school-night some ten years gone? Let's turn back the pages, Flack. Lets have a think about that little multi-layered, fact-and-fiction splicing version of you and the buxom, bosomy, womanly Johanna that you obsessed about so vividly back there in the lanes. Why did I send the snow to provoke that?'

'You didn't, tosser.'

'Look, I know, and therefore you should know, and you certainly know now that all your efforts are actually concentrated on impressing the dear Johanna, but I say stop these efforts now and join with me. But you, dolt, thicko, conclude that the curious incident of the typing and the miscarriage was some sort of sign, a vindication of your purpose.'

'Yes, James, it was a sign.' I turned to myself in the chair. 'Don't worry, mate, a sign is coming.'

'But, I put it to you that you can only come to this conclusion because of a limited point of view, unreliable narration and plot holes, so watch.'

Golden dust crackled as he snapped his fingers. The wall behind Chair-Nathan vanished and the chair, the videos and the painting now rested against what seemed like a two-way mirror. We could see into our bedroom. And there she was, Johanna. Johanna in profile, looking into the full-length mirror on the back of the wardrobe door. Pressing her hands to her hips, she wiggled her waist and her hair slinked around the nape of her neck. She wore an unbuttoned, almost transparent cream blouse, sheer, black, hold-up stockings and the skimpiest slapper thong I'd ever seen.

'Oh fuck off,' I said. 'She never dressed like that. She looks like Sally Bowles in Reader's Wives. And what have you done to her breasts. They're like Iron Age hill forts.'

'I'm sorry, Kiddo, but she just didn't don her brothel wear for you.'

Seemingly happy with her reflection, Johanna pulled on a black mini-skirt, then sat on the bed, facing us to tug knee-length suede boots over her shins. She sat staring into space, her chin resting on her fist.

'Looks like she's got something on her mind, eh?' said O'Mailer.

Johanna got off the bed and took a coat from the hook on the door. She left the room and reappeared seconds later in the lounge doorway. She said nothing and waved her hand gently at the Chair-Nathan.

'Are you're absolutely sure you wouldn't rather I come with you?' said Nathan.

'I'll be OK,' she said. 'See you later.'

Her footsteps disappeared down the stairs and the front door opened, then shut. Chair-Nathan jumped up and phased through us to switch off the television. He thrust the V-sign at it and said 'wanker' seven times. Then he nipped into the bedroom and booted up his PC. The wall rematerialized between us.

'O'Mailer, what is going on?' I said.

'Let's *cherchez la femme*, shall we?'

He lined up his stick and swung it across his feet, golf putt style. The tock sound, a surge of nausea in my guts and we were elsewhere. The whiter light startled me. In a small square room, a table was piled with creased and sun-stained magazines. We were sitting on a plum-black banquette. O'Mailer picked up a copy of *The People's Friend*, leafed through it, then lashed it across the room.

'Balls!'

Opposite us, Johanna stared right through me to what was, when I craned back to check, a poster of the rear-view of a young couple with their fingers crossed. 'This is not contraception' read the caption.

She took her hand from her lap and then without looking sideways put it in the hand of a tall, gangly man dressed in white shorts and white trainers and a white polo shirt with crimson and grey trim. A badminton racquet rested across his knees. Hanging from between his shoulders was the elongated, antenna-frilled head of a giant prawn.

Rejection is timeless. A Canopic jar had been smashed and its dust and fragments whirled around polluting the air.

'You see,' said O'Mailer. 'In the Flack Version, Johanna should be here with Juan-or-Juanita of the ginormous gunga din, not our marine crustacean-headed chum.'

'Oh Prawn,' said Johanna. 'What will we do when the shrimp arrives? Nathan will surely know it's not his.'

'I'll stand by you, my little mermaid,' said Badminton Prawn. 'I'll be with you at the birthing rock-pool. Leave him and come let us prepare a whole cocktail, our seafood platter family.'

329

'I do love you, Prawn.'

'I love you, too.' He rubbed her stomach. 'Mmm, scampi in a basket.'

Jumping up, I kicked the table edge. It tipped over with a thump and all the magazines rustled and flapped. Johanna and Prawn didn't register. They leant into one another. She kissed his spiny, exoskeletal head, longingly, yearningly, inconsiderately. I'm sure the black raison-like eye on the side of his head winked at me.

I turned to O'Mailer. 'It wasn't like this. It was my baby, not a fillet-o-fish. And *he* wasn't literally a prawn, you moron. He just had that straggly ginger beard and odd shaped head. This didn't happen like this. It was afterwards. You know it was afterwards.'

'Oh no, Nathan, she was salt-water swimming long before she left your cold-water flat. This is what I'm trying to show you. The baby was never yours anyway. She wanted *his* baby. She left you to have it. When she dropped your hand in the snow, she knew that was what she was going to do. She was only going to terminate to save you from the knowledge of what she was up to and she couldn't live with that. She'd never have gone through with it. She'd have retracted what she said in the eatery. There was no choice here for you. There was no sign that hinted at a grander future. All you feel is founded on a misunderstanding. There is no counter-Nathan. You *are* Nathan. You are failure incarnate. But I offer you a second chance.'

'I don't believe you,' I said. 'You're a lying, gitty arse.'

O'Mailer shook his head and glared at me. His eyepiece glowed golden. Tock. Everything vanished. We were standing in a white cube that then vanished, and we blurred, shimmered and disappeared.

I stood on ramparts overlooking mudflats beneath a reddish-brown night sky. Steamy fingers of cloud clawed at a crescent moon. A walkway of flagstones stretched either side of me towards circular watchtowers. We'd tocked to a castle, a soft fantasist's wet dream of a forbidding, medieval stronghold. I ducked as a squeaking and flapping host of bats swooped over the battlements, heading for the moon before they dipped into a fuzzy vanishing point at the frontier of the marshes. When I stood up again, a faint white shape was scuffing along the flagstones towards me. At first I couldn't tell what it was and assumed O'Mailer was playing silly buggers. The shape became a woman with a elegant quality to her gait. As she grew closer I could see that she wore white suede knee-length boots and had gigantic avalanche breasts beneath a white see-through blouse, white hold-up stockings and a white slapper thong.

Johanna raised her hand and pointed.

'Pity not me, but lend thy serious hearing to what he shall unfold.'

Her figure swirled and disintegrated. A sudden breeze unsettled the dust on the stones. I sighed and huffed and waited. He appeared in front of me.

'Did you like that? Guessed yet our site of pilgrimage?'

'Elsinore, of course,' I said. 'Is this your sixth-form drama project?'

'You could think of it thus, 'tis verily true.'

'Cut the gadzookery, James, you standing tuck, you bull's pizzle, you fucking zounds.'

'Alas, poor Nathan.'

'Oh I didn't see that one coming. You're so predictable. You're like a careers advisor with a walk-on in an am-dram church hall *Hamlet*. Something's stilted in the heart of rotten face.'

'To be with me or not to be with me, that is your question.'

'I made you up, so you're merely a prompter. Pray tell, what the forsooth are we doing here?'

'Where do you think we are?'

'I told you, Pistol-Poins.'

'No, we've decamped, you and I, to what you know as *The* State, that place you sometimes reach during your morning rituals, when you sit at your escritoire to compose your *meisterwerke*. The imagination's transfigured dream-space. It's in this prison I've been captured this last thirty-five years.'

He swiped at the air with the stick and the golden dust tinselled its arc. The tock. We stood in an Edwardian drawing room. Russet divans and armchairs surrounded a heavy oak desk arranged with a reading lamp, a bowl of red hyacinths and a miniature reproduction of a Monet landscape. Lytton Strachey sat reading a brown hardcover book, his beard neater than O'Mailer's, a fedora on his head. Vanessa Bell was slumped on the other side of the room in a purple and yellow spotted dress and a mustard cardigan, staring into space and looking well miserable. Ford Maddox Ford pranced into the room, lit a cigarette and declared, 'Ah, the opening world.'

'This is *The* State,' said James O'Mailer. No one else heard him. 'We can do anything here.'

Just as it began to sink in that I was eavesdropping on the Bloomsbury Group, O'Mailer lofted his glowing stick and we tocked again, shifting into a candle-lit dining room where wuthering wind battered the windowpanes and three little girls circled arm in arm around a writing desk.

'Emily, that is by far the most indecent of your stories,' said Charlotte.

'Haworth,' I said, stepping forwards fascinated by the swish of their spotless dresses, the scraping of the soles of their heavy boots and their crinkly, beautiful ringlets.

'One day I will have them all, but not today,' said O'Mailer. 'By the way, your bloodline from the runt in the forest passes through Bramwell before it slops up in you. But why tarry here when we can go anywhere?'

'But I want to listen to them . . .'

Tock.

On a sombre beach fringed by a grey almost motionless sea, smoke drifted up into a sand-coloured sky. Men in frock coats and breeches stood around a smouldering pyre. Leigh Hunt stared at his feet, Byron out to sea. Another man I did not recognize clutched his chin with one hand and his heart with another. The smoke thickened and wafted and the figure laid out on the pyre flickered in and out of view.

'Mmm, fancy a barbie later?' said O'Mailer.

'James, that's Lord Byron. This is Shelley's funeral. Can't we go back to the fun stuff? I want to say that I went on the piss with Percy Bysshe.'

'You can do anything here,' he said. 'You know that.'

Tock.

We were back on the ramparts of Elsinore, looking out over the marshes, the moon now full and ringed and even higher in the sky than it was beforehand.

'*The* State, Nathan,' said O'Mailer. 'I have taken you into *The* State to prove my credentials. You can do anything you like here. Concentrate. Close your eyes. Dream of your heart's content and it shall be so. Brood upon your wildest fancy. Imagine where it is that you would rather be and how you would rather be or who you would like to conjure, settle your scores, inform the future, and it shall be so.'

I raised my hand and held it to the night. The air around my fingers became a translucent gel. Closing my eyes, I thought about all that I wanted. When I opened them, I held a B-format paperback in my hands. The overall colour scheme was a honey yellow, the title embossed and golden and surrounded by a swarm of amber dots and dashes and cute starfishes. Beneath it was an image of a full-length twentysomething blonde in a strapless yellow minidress and a Cheddar Gorge of a cleavage. Impossibly smooth and toned legs tapered down to high-heeled, open-toed sandals and she held a laptop bag in one hand and a latte in the other. Its title was *Touching the Starfish*.

'Bah,' said O'Mailer, brandishing his stick at me. 'Is that all you want? Publi-dratted-cation. A pox upon you. A plague. A pestilence. Why, why, why could they not bung my bottle with a worthier cork? Why oh why? Rage against the trying of this Flack. If that's all you can manage, let's see what'll happen if your dream comes true.'

There was a very loud *tock*.

The floor seemed to ripple as O'Mailer and I solidified in a TV studio full of people. Lighting rigs latticed the ceiling. Twentysomethings in headsets carried clipboards and gave hand signals to one another. Rostrum-mounted cameras zeroed in on a set where sofas surrounded three sides of a matt-black, coffee table. A backdrop of azzurri blue dashed through with orange and amber ribbons wavered behind a group of figures sat chatting and flipping through notepapers.

A bald assistant in a grey, long-sleeved top and chinos spun on his heels beside us, raised his arm and started to count. 'Five, four . . .'

'What's going on?' I said.

'Smile, you're on the television,' said O'Mailer.

'No, I'm not,' I said, and drifted away from him, heading for the rear of the studio. There must be a green room in this O'Mailer-confected torture chamber. As I weaved my way through, all the people, the kit, the furniture and the walls around me shivered. Somehow the set was still ahead and O'Mailer at my side. I turned back, but again the shiver, again the room seemed to flow in front of me.

'You can't run from the inevitable,' said O'Mailer.

'Two, one, ready,' ordered the assistant.

Music played across the PA, sophisticated, breezy jazz, like the Miles Davis soundtrack of Frances's flat. The house lights came up. The music faded. The figures on sofas were revealed as two men, a woman and something furry that I couldn't quite make out. Bang in the centre, anchoring the panel, was James O'Mailer. I did a double take, switching from the bear-sized phantom at my side and the identical copy ahead of us.

'Tonight on *Hate Review*,' said Anchor O'Mailer. 'From one unpublished novel about a girl and a tree, to another unpublished novel about not being able to sell a novel about a girl and a tree. Failure, folly and self-flagellation in Nathan Flack's new heap of foolscap, *Touching the Starfish*.'

A giant projection of the book jacket with the blonde in the yellow minidress and the Cheddar Gorge of a cleavage appeared on the screen behind the sofas.

'And with me to discuss this risible piffle,' said O'Mailer, 'are the novelist and alien demon god, Cthulu Chynn-Stroker . . .'

A tall, calamari-headed man in a sharkskin suit and media-twat glasses nodded. His tentacles sloshed across his shirtfront.

'Howdy.'

' . . . the director of the Minj Massif gallery and comfort woman to the cognoscenti, Myfanwy Starkers . . . '

A dumpy, titian-haired fortyish woman with a bank vault door's thickness of make-up mugged to camera.

'She makes a remarkable post-event croque monsieur,' whispered O'Mailer-Beside-Me.

' . . . The Pantomime Cat Wot Won the Turner Prize . . .'

'Hhhhhissssssssssssssssss.'

' . . . the critic and mean drunk, Streak O'Pyss . . .'

An otter-shaped man of about two hundred years old in a ratting jacket and crumpled grey collar squirmed and twitched his legs crossed at the knee.

'Gud Oivening.'

' . . . and the rich man's son, Ferdie Paget . . .'

'Ciao.'

Oh anything but The Enemy of All that Breathes. Anybody. Badminton Prawn. UKIP de Courcy. Gang rape by the Ipswich Group of Death in a polluted drainage ditch in Eye, Suffolk as it rains amphibians from Sirius and curry-flavoured *Pot Noodle*.

Everyone sat back and played with their chins. A camera swung over to Anchor O'Mailer.

'Kurt Vonnegut once wrote, "If you want to really hurt your parents, and you don't have the nerve to be gay, the least you can do is go into the arts." Words which had he actually bothered to read them would surely haunt the wannabe novelist Nathan Flack. Sort of known for drafting two episodes of the late night soft porn series *Gentleman's Relish,* Flack's themes have been seen as Flack, Flack and not doing very well really, how not doing very well really is a condition of the early twenty-first century Flack.'

'Usually,' said O'Mailer-Next-to-Me, 'my guests have the opportunity to bone up on the background, using the Internet to make it look like they have a long gestated and expert opinion, but we can't do that with you, obviously.'

'His new novel *Touching the Starfish*,' said Anchor O'Mailer, 'continues his meditation upon this theme.'

A pre-recorded documentary began to play across the backdrop screen. A staircase in a hallway came into view, shot from below, and then I appeared, dressed in my famous blue bathrobe, a fag hanging out of my mouth and my hair sticking up like Robert Smith out of *The Cure*.

'In *Touching the Starfish*,' said an O'Mailer voice-over, 'the central character, also called Nathan Flack, is a not-so-young *artiste manqué* unable to find a buyer for a soppy novel . . .'

In the film I reached the foot of the staircase, picked up a padded envelope, ripped it open and stared at a letter, froze, then slumped down on the bottom step and clutched my hair, weeping like a child. The scene cut to a close-up of my terror-filled face, the blackboard behind me.

'. . . and forced to eke a living,' said Voice-Over O'Mailer, 'teaching creative writing to a picaresque bunch of lunatics and caricatures.'

Stumpy fingers unwrapped the sheep's head from its polythene bag. The Major Arcana bolted from the room, overturning plastic chairs. 'Get that fucking thing out of here!' I screamed.

'A more interesting subplot appears when Flack is visited by the Flame of Tradition, a handsome and vocal demigod who encourages him to mend his ways . . .'

The screen went black. Everyone – the panel, the crew, me – jumped as O'Mailer's voice boomed out around the studio.

'YOU ARE THE ONE UPON WHOM EVERYTHING IS LOST.'

Then I was standing on a stage behind a microphone, holding up a sheaf of papers at the Moonshot reading.

'The novel becomes,' said Voice-Over O'Mailer,' a catalogue of episodes that delineate a downward trajectory towards failure and madness . . .'

'SHUT THE FUCKING-FUCK UP,' I shouted at the audience, then leapt off the stage with my hands over my bollocks.

Next, wedged into the corner behind the television in my garret, I thumped the wall with my fist. 'Why? Why? Why? Why?'

Cut to the doors of a white van. They swung open to off-camera gasps as I was revealed, hatchet poised over a supine Doctor Jane dressed in white suede knee-length boots, a white see-through blouse, white hold-up stockings and a white slapper thong.

'. . . until some sort of dénouement is reached when a very public humiliation is delivered by an illustrious panel of luminaries on a TV arts show.'

Footage of Anchor O'Mailer, Cthulu Chynn-Stroker, Myfanwy Starkers, The Pantomime Cat Wot Won the Turner Prize, Streak O'Pyss and Ferdie Paget rolling around the soft area, weeping and hurling copies of the manuscript up into the air.

I watched all this with one eye closed, my arms tightly wrapped across my chest, my mouth dry, my scalp tingling as if all my hair was falling out at once.

'Here comes the best bit,' said O'Mailer-Beside-Me.

Up on the screen I seemed to be giving an author's interview. Sat in a wicker chair in a conservatory at night, I delivered a piece to camera.

'Well,' I said. 'I've just finished a novel called *The Jennifer Tree,* that's like the best love story ever, except it turns into a crock of shit when anyone remotely connected to the trade reads it, 'cause plumcam is intercepting it in the post and swapping the manuscript with one of hers, and then I started something called *The Girl on the Millennium Bridge* about a girl on the Millennium Bridge, but she's, like, stuck in a café waiting for Frank the Wank . . . and then I wrote *Garret of the Fumigator*, which like, as Morrissey said of *The Queen is Dead*, "yes, it is autobiographical" and now, now I'm supposed to be working on something called *The Twelve Labours of Beta Male* but why, why write it when you can be in it? And . . . and I can't find my starfish. Oh bollocks . . . I can't do it anymore, I can't do this, I can't, I can't, I can't . . . it's too hard, it's too unfair and that utter cowpat Mac has got an agent.'

The image of my sweat-striped head freeze-framed. The orange ribbons swirled across the blue screen again. The studio lights came up and the cameras and the boom mic homed in on the panel.

'So, Cthulu,' said Anchor O'Mailer. 'Martin Amis once said the writers started out telling stories about gods, then communities and peer groups, then the individual until the only subject left became the writer himself. How does this . . . compare?'

Cthulu raised both his arms, his hands dangling at his wrists and his tentacles stiffened as if to strike.

'Well, I wanted to like it, I really did, but this is easily the worst novel I have ever read. It has no momentum or movement. No likeable characters. The situations are unbelievable. Where's the irony? There's no irony. Where are the jokes? There are no jokes? All I can say is that Nabokov would have done it so much better.'

'Well, *Pale Fire* this certainly is not,' said Anchor O'Mailer. 'Myf?'

She leant forwards and caressed her black leather skirt with her palms.

'Well, I have to disagree with Thu a little, just so it looks as if we're having a proper discussion here, but, yes, I agree entirely that there's nothing to like or care about when the characters are not like us *or* from the trendy minorities who seem authentic to us from our lofty yet morally etiolated positions of status, and there's no story and the author isn't even of mixed-race, but I did like the bits with you in them, James.'

'Yes, they are the best bits,' said the Anchor. 'I liked the chapter with you in it too, my little poppycock.' He reached over and chucked her under the chin. 'Mister Croque Monsieur may well liase a little later with Mademoiselle Croque Madame . . . Not much fevered love around the table for *Touching the Starfish* so far. Cat?'

The Pantomime Cat sprang from the sofa, then can-canned across the front of the stage thrusting pink and white-banded thumbs-down at the audience. Then it scampered back to the sofa and curled up into a ball.

Ferdie Paget cut in. 'The author is a shad and I don't like the way he portrays me.'

'Yes, he implies that you're nothing more than a well-connected, subsidised, black ops networker out of his intellectual depth,' said the Anchor. 'You don't think you're invited to participate on this programme because of your talent? Your father's a BBC governor. Streak, were you touched by the starfish?'

The two hundred-year-old otter took a long sip of water from a tall glass, then reclined awkwardly, his knees jumping up and down like the pistons of a cranky engine.

'This book drove me to focking drink, it did. Drove me to dis-aggregated, unmediated dissolution. Pissing in the milk bottles and marooned in my porch at three am trying to open the door with a twenty-pee piece. It had me on the boot polish, Russian-Zyrian style. I had a fistfight with a tinker's widow. I saw visions of bloomers abloom and a four-heading piglet on a mound of Twiglets and an oxygen tent called

337

Guatemala on the surface of the silvery moon. I wet my pants, I did. Our baby wasn't sleeping and my beloved compared herself to a pint of turps. I woke up in a French mime artist's wendy house and he took one look at it and all this correcting fluid trickled out of his eyes. Blake on the heath. Ruskin burned all Turner's drawings of mummy's baby-making hole. Gizzards. The gizzards of the tiny voles.'

He lashed the glass to his face. Water slopped over his chin and his shirt collar. Anchor O'Mailer smirked. 'I see. Well, the thing that I found most frustrating about this novel was that there's an obviously more interesting subplot about saving the world from doom, yet he does nothing with it. Cthulu?'

'Well, it just doesn't go anywhere, does it? I know it's bad form to reveal the end here, but it ends *here*. It ends with us hooting with laughter before we saunter off arm in arm to the Groucho.'

'I was rather hoping for the Soho House later,' said Myfanwy. 'Then my house, James.'

'Flack is *déclassé*,' said Paget. 'He'd be better off working in a call centre instead of clamouring for our attention.'

The Cat uncurled itself, leapt across the set and rolled Myfanwy Starkers over the back of the sofa. There was a thump. Her feet poked up above the backrest.

'Miaooooow.'

'Oh, the porridge is stirred,' said Anchor O'Mailer.

'The modern is a retroavantgardist text,' said Streak O'Pyss. He necked from a silver hip flask and then hurled it at Paget's head. 'Migration. Identity. Place. The sense of being lost in the modern world. The big themes. A sense of place. Place is destiny. Destiny is place. Oedipus in Ponders End. Place. Place. Place. This writer does not know his place.'

The Anchor leaned forwards and pressed his hand to O'Pyss's shoulder.

'Dear friend, where would I be without your eloquence?' He peered over the back of the sofa. 'Down there, I should imagine . . . Well, we're out of time. *Touching the Starfish* by Nathan Flack is available as an e-mail attachment from the author. We'll be back next week, where up for discussion will be McArthur Park Pidcock's new film *Porno and Hard Drive Get Laid*, the new album by Trick E 2 Market and Bling Crosby, *Gold Minger*, and the series opener of *CSI Bury St Edmunds*. Now, a look at tomorrow's front pages.'

338

He held up a broadsheet with *This is Your Future, Nathan Flack* as a headline. As they all pretended to still be talking, the stage darkened. I couldn't see them anymore and I realized that all the other people around me – the crew, the assistants – had frozen stiff. O'Mailer-Beside-Me glowed for an instant.

'You see, Flack, this is all you have ahead of you, even if it comes off. All you will have is a shark tankful of public savaging. And no one's going to write *Who Killed Nathan Flack, I said The Quarterly.* Is this what you want, eh? I can't protect you from this.'

'You? Protect me?' I said, trying to be defiant, trying to find a way of saying that I'd always known it would be tough, that it isn't the point, writing is a way of life, a state of mind and not about laurels or garlands or sales or the love of strangers and celebrities and squid-headed book reviewers in media-twat glasses licking your arse. Write to be *closer* to other people. Write because you have to. That's what I wanted to say. But I was standing in a room full of statues and felt like a skeleton, an upright ribcage with dangling arms and scraped-out sockets, meatless in the gibbet.

'James,' I said. 'You keep telling me that there's a plan, that there's something that you want me to do?'

'Aye, that there is, Kiddo.'

'Then what is it?'

'My dear Nathan, that I cannot tell you outright. They still prevent me. I would draw Canon fire and that would do for us both. But I can show you, Nathan, that's all. Show you a glimpse of an alternative ending, the one that doesn't end here. You want that?'

At that moment, I knew that I would do anything that he asked me, just to still the echoes of the voices from the stage. I nodded. He twirled his stick. It fizzled with golden glow. We tocked.

Pitch black again, and while I was still nauseous and unbalanced, I thought we might be back in the primal forest. But I was standing on cobblestones. Water dripped closeby and rushed in the distance. A distinctly eggy smell reminded me of the garret in midwinter when the damp is at its ripest. Then two quotation marks of light hovered ahead of me. They grew into fangs of glow until the silhouette of O'Mailer's head appeared. He was moving off, and as he did so I realized that we were in an underground brickwork passage slick with wet. I followed him until we came out onto a walkway hemmed in by railings and lit by electric lights bracketed to the curved walls. A roof of a gigantic, arched tunnel spanned above us. Below, a murky torrent gushed and surged and spumed into the blackness.

'Where are we?' I said. 'The end of *The Third Man*?'

'Dear Flack, this tunnel exists not under fairy tale Vienna, with its adorable strudels and moreish whores, but beneath the Fine City itself. We are under the medieval streets of Norwich. This, Dame Parlet, is the Grand Anglian Sewer.'

'Place is destiny. It ends in a sewer?'

'Ah, but what a sewer. The Victorians built things to last. This conduit has a Dickensian scale, a Shelleyean imagination, and the lurid frisson of Stoker or Stevenson. It *should* end here. What a setting for a climax!'

'You mentioned it before. At the party. You asked me to ask Jane about it.'

'Dear boy, she loves this sort of place, does Subterranean Jane. And she loves a little adventure, likes to feel her tiny heart pounding, to live slightly closer to the heart of melodrama than your average high street houri. Catch my drift, or am I snowing? If you'd asked the right question, she would have brought you here.'

'What question?'

'Come, follow. I'll show you.'

O'Mailer swung back his arm and pulled me to his side. We marched in tandem. He threw back his head and sniffed the air as if high on a peak in Darien.

'How long have I waited for this,' he said. 'To be an adventurer again. And you and I together, you the instrument of my noble scheme.'

'What *is* the scheme?'

'Kiddo, this is how it plays. You believe me now that I am the eternal flame, man's red fire, the storytelling gift, a ruby rose instinct as old as time, blessed honour, the passion, the mead of poetry pissed by mighty Odin himself . . .'

'No.'

'Don't you know who I am?'

'A git.'

'Let me tell you a story,' he said. 'In the beginning there was a war between the Northern Gods and the Giants . . .'

'No, oh no, not this.' I knew the story, because I had loved the story ever since I found it in a book of Norse myths in the school library. In the beginning there was a war between the Gods and the Giants and when the peace treaty was signed all shook hands and spat in a bucket and out of the bucket came a man made of liquid. He was called Kvasir and was blessed with powers of great oratory. But this Kvasir was captured by an evil dwarf and imprisoned in a castle where he was murdered and his blood stirred into a bucket of mead. One nip from this brew would bestow upon the imbiber the oratorical greatness of Kvasir. Odin coveted this Mead of Poetry and taking eagle form descended upon the dwarf's castle and downed the mead in one gulp. As he made his escape he was chased by the dwarf and as he soared up into the sky he wet himself in fear and as he made his rise to Asgard some of the mead fell back to Earth, where now it trickles around forever. It is said that this mead finds all those who write, but it is potent. Too potent. It is the spur of genius and it drives the genius mad.

'Don't you see, Flack, I am Kvasir.'

'I'd be more impressed if I'd not heard that story before.'

'Let me continue then. I, who had come into the lives of the Greats since that moment in the forests of the night that I showed to you, I who inspired and loaned my fiery mead to all who were grand enough to desire it, I who am behind every magnificent story ever composed, there came a time when I began to pique the new powers that be.'

'What powers?'

'I am not outright responsible for today's most favoured of narratives, Flack, that which begins with the bloody reign of Jack the Ripper and the first stirrings of the gutter press, that which now is called "the conspiracy theory", but there has been a most monstrous machination against the name O'Mailer. There is, unknown to most, a secret organization known as The Canon. This Canon watches over this *Cosa Nostra* called Culture and sometimes intervenes should they sense that the falcon cannot hear the falconer.'

He paused and whirled the stick. A disc of gold materialized in front of us. A moving image appeared. There was a lavish and stately library a little like that of the Folder-Holder's dreams of *The* MA I'd once imagined. Around a circular marble table sat a dozen dusty, bird-headed men. One was standing and in mid-speech.

'The hand of O'Mailer is too prevalent. All the new works bear his influence and tampering. It's time, my friends, that we give someone else a go. I say we hobble the liquid god, once and for all. '

With a swish of the stick, the image faded into a vapour of golden specks that drizzled onto the cobbles.

'My dear Flack,' said O'Mailer. 'Any idea what year this congregation of the Canon occurred?'

'Nope.'

'Nineteen sixty-nine. A wretched year, for I was banished to *The* State by their witchcraft . . .'

'And I was conceived.'

'You catch on fast when you want to.' He reached into his cloak, then handed me a Cuban cigar the size of a truncheon. 'When this ghastly war is over, Flack, feel free to write a novel about my fate.'

I tossed the cigar into the sewer and we continued along the walkway into the darkness.

'I still don't get it,' I said.

'Flack, the Canon blocked my portal from here to the material world by fusing me with your DNA.'

'Why me?'

'Because, as the descendent of the runt in the clearing, they considered you the least likely to provoke my flames.'

'But I write. They were wrong.'

'No, you poor old soul, you have only ever responded to my presence. If you were not my gateway from here to there, you would be a very happy call centre manager married to the fair Johanna.'

'You told me that was impossible.'

'Ah, should I *not* exist it was very possible.'

'So what now? Is this all I'm worth? Aiding your escape so you can wreak your revenge on the beaks?'

'No, Flack, we have a far more selfless task, and one that the Canon, for all its bluster, cannot undertake, gulls, sparrows and halfling idiots that they are to a man. They do not see that what approaches. You, of course, have been so far a cats-paw puppet for the other side. Now, you shall redeem yourself.'

'This is a load of old wank, isn't it?'

'Shh, Flack, we have arrived.'

The walkway ended at a Romanesque archway of red and blue bricks. Alongside us, the water flowed into a semi-circular opening. O'Mailer swished through the arch, a breeze picking up the tails of his cape. I followed, then gasped as I took in the surroundings. A vast cathedral of

342

architecture opened up above me, a vaulted ceiling, buttresses and hammer-beams of brick. It housed a gigantic tank into which the sewer-water cascaded, its impact reverberating around the chamber. We were standing on a ledge with ironwork railings that formed a square around the tank. Opposite us was some sort of balcony overlooked by a pillared portico.

'This,' said O'Mailer, 'is the Great Cistern. Should the city ever flood, and when it rains excessively, the overspill sluices into here. The effluent streams straight out into the German Ocean. Anything dumped here would never be found. T'would be as if t'were spirited away by swarthy devils.'

'You're getting worse.'

'Do you think you can remember the way here? . . . Don't worry. The fair Doctor will show you. Then you can mammock her.'

'Mammock? Rip?'

'A little manly euphemism. Watch, Flack. Over there.' He pointed his stick at the balcony opposing us. 'This is what shall pass a week hence.'

From behind the balcony, two pinpricks of light jostled. As they grew bigger and brighter, the walls of another passageway glimmered with streaks of shine. A sharp, intermittent squeak pulsed above the roar of the water. Two softened, bulbous outlines emerged onto the balcony, seemingly heaving something along with them.

'Want to escape the cheap seats?' said O'Mailer. 'Fancy the Gods?'

He swiped a figure-of-eight shape with a gold-dusted forefinger, and we tocked. My guts freefell as I found myself windmilling my arms and pedalling my legs high above the black waters of the Great Cistern. A hand on my shoulder steadied me.

'Hush, we cannot fall, or drown if we did,' said O'Mailer. 'And before you ask, they cannot hear us.'

An invisible platform floated us in front of a padlocked gate in the balcony's railings. The two lights now sliced through the gloom, illuminating the floor of the balcony. A tall figure in a pale blue boiler suit, goggles and a miner's helmet staggered towards the rail and slumped as if catching his breath. A metallic grind squawked behind him, and a second figure dragged into view the T-bar of a trolley loaded with a roped mound in a tarpaulin. He upended the T-bar, then staggered behind the trolley and kicked it until it bumped the gate. A rattling clang shot around the walls and its echo gave a peculiar soundtrack to the foaming eddies that coiled beneath us.

343

The slumped, panting man at the railing looked over at his colleague. The trolley and its mound sat between them. The second man now rested on the rail, staring into the depths of the Cistern. The first man put his hand behind his head and fiddled with the catch, took off the helmet, the goggles and then what appeared to be some sort of hair net. A bubble of tendrilly-frizz pounced out at the sides of his head, but it wasn't a he, but a she. And it wasn't any old *she*. It was Doctor Jane Vest.

She held out her arms and admired the roof.

'Oh my baby,' she cried. 'Oh my love. What a place! Look at it. Those curves. Those swoops. Don't you think there's something . . . just . . . something so *erotic* about wet brick?'

The second man looked up. His helmet-lamp sent a dazzling beam right in my face that blinded me until he put it down. Goggles off, he was me. Me in a boiler suit and protective gloves. Now, there was an image I thought I'd never see.

'It's amazing,' said Balcony-Nathan. 'It's perfect. So gothic. I mean genuinely gothic, not Pernod-and-black and the bats have left the belfry gothic.'

'Oh release the bats,' said Doctor Jane. 'Come here.'

Balcony-Nathan stepped up onto the trolley, then down to Jane. He put his arms around her waist and they kissed.

'James, this is becoming my own private sanitation-themed porn film,' I said.

'Watch,' he said.

They paused, both rubbing each other's backs through their suits, she with her head on his shoulder, peering over at the trolley.

The mound on the trolley twitched.

'Omigod,' she said. 'He's still alive.'

'Now watch to see what you've got in your toolkit,' said O'Mailer.

'Oh no,' said Balcony-Nathan, breaking away from Jane. He reached for a utility belt – I will have a utility belt! – and pulled something out. He flipped over a tool and smacked it into his gloved hand.

'How much can this thing take?'

'It's kinder,' said Jane, 'to make sure, before, you know . . .' She nodded at the water. 'Even he deserves more than that.'

'You sure about that?'

'Nathan, please, just do it.'

She turned away and stared at a pillar as Nathan stepped forwards to the trolley and with both hands raised an axe above his head.

'That's Frank's hatchet,' I said.

'Ah, the fog is lifting,' said O'Mailer.

The axe fell. A hollow thud. A pitiful yelp. The thud spattered around the walls until it became a faint pitter, then nothing. Nathan stood in silence, then hurled the axe into the darkness. It passed through me and sloshed into the tank below. Jane turned from the pillar.

'Let's get this over with.'

She took a key from her suit and Nathan stepped aside so she could crane over and unlock the railing gates. They swung out above the water.

'Do you want to do it?' she said.

'I hit him,' Nathan said.

'OK.' She walked behind the trolley, and kicked it, once so it edged forwards, then twice. The rubber wheels bulged. The mound tipped. A third kick and the whole lot plummeted, the trolley, the mound and some sort of bundle of brown paper tied up with string. For a terrible few seconds there was no sound, then a glooping, plopping splash resounded. I felt numb, meatless in the gibbet again.

'Tis done,' said O'Mailer. 'All are saved.'

Over on the balcony, they shuffled together, apparently looking out at us hovering ahead of them. Jane had her ring finger hooked to her chin and her forefinger and thumb pinched together, her other hand caressing her wrist. I took out a cigarette and lit it. Together we looked like platonic friends at a school disco, gawky outsiders balefully watching the dancefloor coolcats with envy and suspicion, neither able to say what they really felt about the other.

'We did it,' said Jane. 'That horrible thing will never see the light of day.'

'Nor will that bloke,' said Nathan.

'Your gallows humour is lovely.'

'I thought I'd feel worse than this.'

'There *was* no other way.'

'We can never tell of this.'

'We're in this together,' she said, and put her hand over mine.

'And the subtext is,' I said to O'Mailer,' that she and I will be tied to each other till death do us part because of the fear that the other will grass to the law.'

He sniggered and passed another girder-sized cigar to me just as Nathan flicked his butt at my head. He then turned to Jane and kissed her, gently at first, then deeply and hungrily.

'Do I have to watch this?' I said.

Jane broke away.

'C'mon,' she said. 'Let's not tempt fate.'

They turned, hesitating so they could wrap their arms around each other's shoulders. Beside me, O'Mailer glowed and we tocked, coming to in the position on the balcony that Nathan and Jane had just vacated. We watched them as heads nestled together, they sauntered off into the dense black passage like first date lovers leaving a county fairground beneath a sky the colour of Orangina, a cuddly panda in her arms and his first ever condom in his back pocket. And as they receded I realized what I had just witnessed and what O'Mailer had been getting at, what murder he wanted me to commit.

We'd tocked again, landing on some sort of slope in sunlight so fierce that it sent shudders through my head. O'Mailer was beside me, dog returned to the crook of his arm, but this time they flickered in and out of view for a second, like a hologram on the blink. He was losing his grip, expending too much of his energy. I sensed that our journey together was coming to an end, one way or another. Back in my body, down in the snowstorm, my heart must be about to give out. This was it. No more excursions through my obsessions and paranoia. Crunch time.

High above countryside, we were standing on a mountain. I shielded my eyes with my hand as I surveyed the setting. Ahead was a range of peaks and crags that caressed the underside of a deep Mediterranean blue sky. A lead grey haze clung to a horizon of fields and meadows, olive groves and copses. A sigh rose through me, made me grin in wonder. It was the most beautiful vista I'd ever seen. A place I'd like to live, build a house, an eyrie up here and sit beneath a parasol on a terrace and write in the mornings, eat fruit and read in the afternoons of my dotage. But I also felt a strange sense of having been here before, of seeing this place in a slightly different form. Then I noticed that beneath us on the gradient was a circular pool rimmed by a marble balustrade. A fountain gushed up into the sky. Around it a dozen or so nymphs of astounding comeliness danced wearing no more than the most flimsy of diaphanous robes. Suddenly they all waved and giggled as out of a clump of olive trees cantered a pure white horse with dove's wings. Pegasus reared upon a tree stump and flapped a cooling breeze at the girls.

'Mount Parnassus,' I said.

'Ah, Apollo's realm,' said James O'Mailer. 'Dionysus's playground, the altar of Pan, home of the Oracles and the Muses, the wellspring of poetry, learning and literature. You'll be happy here once you have done my bidding. Isn't that right, Parsons?'

The dog looked up at his face and gave an affirmative yap.

'Nah, sorry James. When Johanna and I went Inter-railing we went to Mount Parnassus and there's nothing here but a tourist trap ski centre. This is just another of your clichés.'

'Clichés, Flack. Clichés. Kvasir is umbilically connected to the Classical. 'Tis nothing hackneyed about this panorama.'

'Look at those nymphs. It's like *Carry on Camping*.'

'Flack, do not mock me.'

'I'm not doing it, James.

'What?'

'I'm not doing it. You can stick it up your meady arse.'

'Impudent varmint!' O'Mailer whipped out his stick and drew it behind his head, muscular pressure pulsing in his elbow.

'I see,' I said. 'Adopting the Victorian martinet headmaster's pose, are we?'

'Flack, do not be a stubborn ninny now when the moon enters its last phase. What I ask is really very little and will purchase you paradise forever.' He cast his stick at the pool. Resting on his other arm, the dog followed the stick's direction with glowing eyes.

'What do you think I am, James? A suicide bomber? I'm not killing anyone for a paddle in the pool and a few pokes at a virgin.'

'Damn you, Flack, you're testing my mettle here, testing the very mettle of O'Mailer the Flame.'

'I'm dead anyway,' I said. "And I'm not giving you the satisfaction of thinking that you own me.'

He squinted so hard that his nose crushed into a piggish stub. A low growl came from the back of his throat that seemed to tremor around the mountain peaks. The gravel shook. A cloud pelted across the sky to obscure the sun. As the light dimmed, the nymphs in the pool let off a collective sigh. The dog snarled. O'Mailer thrust out his chest and pounded the earth with his stick.

'You,' he proclaimed. 'You would defy me, defy O'Mailer the Flame who is the product of Gods, that has been man's inspiration and guide. I wrote *Gilgamesh, The Iliad, Beowulf, Morte D'Arthur, The Divine Comedy, The Canterbury Tales*, the plays and the Sonnets of he you call the Bard himself who was in verity me, O'Mailer, who went on to compose, *Gargantua, Don Quixote.'*

His frame expanded, seemed to grow several inches as he puffed out his chest, threw back his shoulders and smashed his fist against his heart so forcefully that I felt the vibrations in my ribcage. I staggered a little; my face trembling, my eyes welded open.

'And all of Boz's greatness is down to I, *Great Expectations, Little Dorrit, Hard Times,* and add to this achievement *Middlemarch, Wuthering Heights, Jude the Obscure.* And they cursed me by walling me up in you, dolt-clown-buffoon, I who have done all this in you who dare to defy me now. I, with my greatness and grandeur and shine. What have you done?'

'I invented Arnold Bumrape,' I said.

His shoulders slumped and the fire in his eyepiece blew out.

'Yes, Flack, that's all there is on your "Also by:" list.'

'I'm not doing it,' I said. 'I'm not tempting fate. That's what Jane said back there in the tank. "If we stay here, we're tempting fate". I'm not doing what you say, O'Mailer. I'm not killing anyone if this is real. Do you think I want to be remembered for that?

'The world hangs in the balance.'

'It does not. *I* hang in the balance. And let's face it, you're part of me, aren't you? You're not the flame, or the imagination or a Norse god. You're just the crap, vainglorious part of me. I made you up. And everything was going alright for me until recently and when it turned bad, you popped up, with your carping and your cajoling and your telling me to do everything that my better instincts tell me not to do, shag her, fumigate that, kill someone.'

'This is not so, Flack, I beseech of you.'

'All this shop-worn shit, me the runt, you the flame, Johanna nobbing a prawn behind my back, Elsinore, squid-headed book reviewers, a circle of birdmen who control literature, all this is just the paranoid fantasy of a failure like me. That's the only thing you have right about me, James. I fail. That's what I do. I fail, and there probably isn't a reason why, and that's much more scary than you with your poxy stick and nasty whispers. Only a tired, frustrated hack like me could come up with this. I own you, O'Mailer, and I'm not giving in to you. You're just my perversity.'

'Perversity, Flack, perversity.' He expanded his girth again. The flecks of flame began to whirr around his head and his shoulders as he began to walk into me like a playground bully provoking a scrap. I shuffled on my heels, easing down the slope with O'Mailer in my crosshairs.

'Look at you, O'Mailer. Look at your lousy Tolstoy beard, your stupid Mister Hyde cape, your twatman cane and your monocle. Listen to your voice with its switching registers. It's hardboiled wisecracking one minute, then Renaissance curlicues the next. You're unstable, you're incomplete, you're unconvincing. You're a crap writer's creation. You're my paranoid delusion. You *are* me.'

The stick whipped over the crown of my head.

'I am *the* Flame.'

'And look at that dog, James. It's the saddest thing I've ever seen.'

'Enough of this!'

The tip of the stick lashed against the ground. A shockwave pulsed around the countryside again. The nymphs dashed for the grove and Pegasus swept up into the sky and brayed like a dying donkey. O'Mailer let the dog slip from his hand and then rummaged in his cape.

'That is the end of it,' he said. 'Nobody, nobody questions my Hound of Greatness.'

'Oh what are you doing now, Zorro? Put it away.'

The point of the most whimsy, mimsy, poncey épée wavered in front of my face. O'Mailer's other hand was swept back behind his shoulder, the stance of a waiter balancing a particularly overfull bowl of soup.

'En garde.'

'Put that down. By your own admission, you can't kill me here, and I'm dead anyway, and even if I'm alive I'm not killing Frank Denbigh. Not for you, not for anything or anyone.'

''Tis a point of honour.'

'Murderer he may be, but murderer I am not.'

'Let me tell you, Flack, that down there in the snows you are far from death, and up here in the vapours I cannot slay thee outright, though should I spike ye heart here it will take magicks beyond your devices to return ye here. I can block up forever my channel from me to thee. I can kill *us*. I can kill your imagination.'

'Oh if you strike me down, James, I will only grow stronger. C'mon Jimmy. I'm not going to take it back. Your dog is the twattest dog that's ever cocked its dinky winkie. It's the Barbara Cartland of dogs. It's a fondant fancy that's been indulged for eternity by your stupid, gittish, meandering and purple . . .'

349

The épée's cup-shaped hand-guard blurred as he swept the blade across my face. No sting and I wasn't sure if he'd cut my cheek or not, but my eyes followed its line until I found myself staring at no more than a boulder on the slope. Then I felt it. No pain, but a jolt in my chest and a sound like the visceral crackle when you chop a cabbage in half. The épée had pierced beneath my ribs and shot out of my left shoulder. Oh my . . . I couldn't feel my legs and a chill spiralled up from the earth and there was blood in the dirt that Parsons lapped. There was an utterly defeated and despairing glimmer in O'Mailer's left eye as beside it the golden glow dived into the heart of the lens of the monocle, then vanished. I tried to drop, but couldn't and when I looked down my tiptoes just about skimmed the dust. He was keeping me up with the blade.

'Dear Flack, this is the end for you and me. You could have saved us all. Now we wither. 'Tis the coming of autumn's pallbearers. Season of mists. You will never see my like again. Look upon my works, ye paltry and despair. Oh, one last titbit. The Onanist of The Shed is not the Angel of Trunch. That misunderstanding is now your tragedy and ours. Fare thee well.'

And with that, he pulled the blade out of my chest. The mountain turned into a wave and in a whirlpool I circled downwards, catching as I went O'Mailer hovering unsupported in blank whiteness, stroking the head of his silly dog with one hand and waving tatty-bye with the other. [87]

I lost my awareness, couldn't see, and then I was in blackness again. Solid and stiffened now, all I could feel were blistering pains in my kneecaps. Needle points of sharp cold began to press against my arms and my shoulders, tracing the outline of my chin and my cheeks and for some time wet dabs like the licks of a dog seemed to be swiping flesh onto my skeleton. Again I thought I was dead, or undead, or reborn or resurrected, or I was waking up from an apocalyptic nightmare, the imagery of which I'd never be able to shake. I wasn't sure if all that had actually happened. I half-expected to come to and find myself in bed in the long-night darkness of the garret, relieved that it had all been a dream. Or I would find myself curled up in the sofa in the front room to the sound of the phone ringing, the office telling me that classes were cancelled because of the snow and the traffic jams.

---

[87] **James O'Mailer:** And that, as Aesop once said, was that. I failed you all. I doff my hat in apology. Bye bye. Sleep well. Remember O'Mailer. Remember this name. Goonight, sweet reader, goonight.

When I opened my eyes, ahead of me white lines arced like the grooves of a white vinyl record. A flow of specks, a swarm of white bees. Some grey oblong hidden in the depths of the mush and inside it a sheet of urine-coloured light. I was kneeling in deep snow. I couldn't see clearly but for an instant – I'm not sure if I saw this, or wanted to see it, or simply hallucinated it – there was a woman in the white flickers, a woman with parts missing. Two strips of upper thigh beneath a midriff and shoulders with short, bare, muscular arms. The Ghost-Johanna from Elsinore, or the Ghost-Jane from the back of the van.

'Forget me,' said a voice on the wind, before the figure whipped away in a vortex of snow.

I patted my chest and my neck for the wound, but I was whole, undamaged though as cold as if I'd slept rough on a shingle beach in Spitzbergen. Something was missing though. Something was gone. My ribcage felt hollow, my head empty. I clambered to my feet to relieve my knees and noticed that my bag lay half-submerged in the snow a metre or so from me. Ahead, battered by the streaming gusts of snow, was the Eudora Doon Building. Behind me, no footprints trailed across the lawn to where I'd been kneeling, but it was snowing so heavily they would have been covered in minutes. I must have lost my mind in the cold, reached here on autopilot. I was lucky. I could have stayed unconscious for hours and it would have been too late, I'd have slipped away into the folds. None of that actually happened. Paranoid fantasies, extremities, the reaches of my imagination teasing me. None of it. No Kvasir-O'Mailer. No stab wounds, no punctures, no blood. I staggered into the building, shivering. I paused in the pale yellow light of the foyer and couldn't hear a sound, a mutter, footsteps, laughter or chatter from the classrooms. No voice sniggered in my head. No Frances or Plum nipped out of their room to have a go at me. I wiped the snow from my hair and my face and brushed it from the sleeves of my coat as I trudged upstairs to our room. Nobody was there. None of the Arcana had made it. No one else had braved the storm. I felt like crying. I felt betrayed. Water drops dripped from the hem of my coat. I could feel my fingertips again as I crashed into a chair and stared at the blackboard. No writing on it. Nothing at all. Something was missing. Something had gone.

Dialogue

I Know You

Never give up. That's what I always tell the Folder-Holders. Never give up on a story. Leaving stories unfinished becomes a habit. You start one, struggle to realize it, and then drop it for something that seems initially more exciting or interesting or somehow easier. Then you jettison the new one for another idea that seems initially more exciting or interesting. You end up with a folder of projects on hold. You never actually grapple with the complexities of your craft. Never give up, I tell them. Finish every single one.

I'd never abandoned a story, but a week after my night in the snow I was slumped at my desk, freezing to death in my famous blue bathrobe. The grey light filtered through the curtains. My notebook was open. Nothing flowed from my pen. The foam cladding had detached from the booster rockets of *The Girl on the Millennium Bridge* and she'd exploded seconds after leaving the launch pad. And I'd caught a cold, a stifling, bone-crunching illness that sucked my sinuses deep into my skull and hectored and barracked like a call centre manager with targets to meet.

Every morning for a week I'd sat down with Lemsip and coffee, but was unable to write anything substantial. This was writer's block, a condition I'd previously thought fictitious, like split personality or lycanthropy. All I could scribble were lists of my worries: money: *The*

355

Penelope Tree; the winter and the garret; and at dialogue workshop tonight I would finally face the Arcana after my performance at Jane's soiree. And I'd kept turning over and over whether all that lunacy last week had actually happened. That phantasmagorical spree in the snow where I nearly died from exposure and met O'Mailer and saw Johanna again and was stabbed with a sword on Mount Parnassus. I'd checked for any scar or scab, but my chest was as usual as smooth as a portion of boneless chicken. Had it been more than a crazy hallucination? I didn't think so. It was simply a mad vision, a fever-dream, the effect of the pressure I'd been under and being caught out in what the papers described afterwards as the worst freak weather in the history of East Anglia. I'd browsed the Internet but found no reference, even on the crankiest of conspiracy sites to The Canon. O'Mailer seemed to have gone, though. There were no voices in my head. I'd lost the voices, and I realized that these imaginary conversations, the phantom arguments I used to conduct with others and myself were the basis of my creativity. Creativity is ghostly. My stamina was ebbing. My sense of purpose had dwindled. Ideas had deserted me.

I sniffed hard to stop my nose dripping. Something was going on downstairs. The front door kept opening and banging shut. Muffled voices drifted up to my flat. Objects slithered and scraped in the hall. The phone rang. I'd not answered the phone for a week, fearing calls from Frances or Jane, dreading any calls about rearranging the cancelled class on *A Sense of Place*. I wasn't going to answer the phone now, but then the needy part of me chirruped that it might be someone calling about *Penelope,* and maybe if something good happened to me it would all come back and I could reinvigorate *Millennium Bridge*. I pressed the handset to my ear.

'Nathan?' Where have you been? I've left thirty messages at least.'

My knees watered. Sharon Plumcam-Largo, Agent of **H.Y.D.R.A** and Bride of Mac the Paddle, the Pathetic Phallus.

'Sorry Sharon . . . Juliet, I've been on a writing binge, you know how it gets.'

'Nathan, we need to talk. And no attitude. Come round to mine. This morning.'

'Oh I don't want to.'

'This has been coming, you know that.'

'OK,' I said. 'Give me an hour.'

I was going to lose my job. I was going to lose my job. I repeated this mantra-style as I washed and shaved and put on my clothes in my bedroom that smelled of damp and mould, and as I shivered on the sofa and drank another Lemsip and crunched a vitamin C tablet. I was going to lose my job and without this one teaching position it would be very hard to build a portfolio of other tutoring jobs to bridge the money gap and pay the rent and allow me to write if I ever found the will to do so again. Fuck and tit and bumrape. It couldn't get any worse than this.

As I descended the stairs my legs ached like I'd run a marathon over sodden shingle. I had a flashback from O'Mailer's *Hate Review* documentary, of me shambling to the bottom of this staircase looking like shat-on shit in my famous blue bathrobe and frightwig hair. I paused and cringed and then from midway down checked the hall for post and packages. Nothing on the shelf. As per usual.

The front door was ajar. Cardboard boxes, packing cases and rows and rows of carrier bags stuffed with newspaper bundles littered the floor of the hall. Someone was moving in to the downstairs bedsit. No one had lived there for over a year, not since the Finnish guy moved out, the man who used to sit on the garden wall all evening plopping liquorice twists into cans of Tennants Super. The only thing he'd ever said to me was: 'It is winding tonight, ja'. It was winding now. From outside a gust rustled the papers in the bags.

As I reached the bottom stair, a shadow from the bedsit's open doorway fell across my feet. It belonged not to Nosferatu, but to the maintenance man.

'Oh hi Bob,' I said. 'New neighbour, I see.'

'Oh yeah,' he said. 'This is all her stuff. Educated woman, she is. Bit odd, mind.'

I had a silly fantasy. Odd, educated girls are my forte. An odd, educated girl was moving into the garret house. Some sort of lonely academic, I supposed, a friendly, articulate girl who would while away her solitary evenings with her Vaughan Williams LPs and glasses of Pinot Noir, listening to my footfalls as she deliberated on whether to watch *Persona* or *The Leopard* on DVD. She would wonder about me as she lay on her duvet in her kimono, stroking the fronds of her bedside pot plants. She'd be a Sophie or a Charlotte or Fi, a bookish girl from Dorset or Shropshire or the Netherlands. Strange things would happen. Knocks on the door. I would clink a spoon around a coffee mug as we swapped stories, jokes and anecdotes, departmental tittle-tattle and when I told her that I used to be a writer but gave up she'd comfort me, maybe even talk me into starting again. I'd soon be taking her clothes off. Kissing to the sound of the wind. Soon the garret house would be like a fifties romantic

357

comedy. She'd be my Doris Day or Marilyn[88]. Something good might be on its way. This might be a tipping point.

'What's her name then?' I asked Bob.

Something heavy-footed moved inside the bedsit and came towards us. Something bulky and squat appeared in the doorway. It raised its arm and pointed its finger right in my face.

'I KNOW YOU. I KNOW YOU.'

Suddenly I felt like Szell in *Marathon Man* when the white-haired Survivor recognizes him in the Jewish district of New York.

'I KNOW YOU. I KNOW YOU.'

'Oh no,' I whimpered, scarpering to the front door. At the threshold I swung around and stared at the baggage-strewn hallway and Bob with his bemused, shocked expression and Erika Gretsch, my new neighbour, my new housemate, my new inescapable tormentor standing stiff and alert with her finger rigidly directed at me.

'I KNOW YOU. I KNOW YOU.'

'Where's my starfish, you raving loon?'

'What, what is he saying?'

'Where is it? My starfish. I want it now.'

'What are you talking about?' said Bob.

'He wants to steal, he does, he wants to steal from me.'

'Cut the Gollum crap and give me back my starfish.'

Erika threw up her hands and fled back into the bedsit, slamming the door. Before Bob could say anything I was running down the road with the winding attacking my face.

---

[88] This everyman's sex fantasy had become the sharp-end of my narrative aggression.

Love in a Time of Marketing.

Bob was going to tell my landlord that I'd been weird and belligerent to a valued new tenant and I was going to get evicted on top of everything else. I'd have to kip in wheelie bins and play a plywood violin in Castle Mall for coppers and pence and live off 99p McDonalds cheeseburgers. *I am going to get evicted. I am going to get evicted.* Standing on Plum's step I rang the bell. *I am going to get evicted. I am going to lose my job. Erika Gretsch is living in my house. It can't get any worse than this.* My head throbbed. My face felt hot but my shoulders and legs cold with sweat. I rang the bell again. No one seemed to be in. Maybe she'd gone out and I could delay this conversation, pretend for a little while at least that I wasn't going to lose my job or get evicted. Then I had a thought. Erika Gretsch, moon-barking queen of heavy bags, factory haunting pretend-mother of Frances, our lady of the ping-pong balls and the severed sheep's head who had tailed me to the Arctic and moon-barked at Moonshot was *living in my house.* Now, that was no mere coincidence given that I'd seen her in cloak and hood prowling around my front garden many a time. She knew where I lived. Must have known it when she'd viewed the bedsit. That was creepy and outright harassment. With a bit of cunning, though, I could hit both targets at once here. Don't let Plum bollock on about my attitude and instead insist that Grotbags Gretsch be removed from the

Arcana and my shabby kingdom once and for all. But then again, perhaps I should delay this surgical strike. I now knew the exact location of the starfish.

The door opened. What appeared uppercut me like the southpaw smash of a cybernaut heavyweight. Our Sharon had always been one to bend with the times, but here she was, no longer in her baggy menswear or pizza delivery boy garb or sailor suit or south-of-the-river hardman's car coat. All had been abandoned for a tiny leather bodice that squeezed up her breasts into a visible cleavage. It pushed out her spare tyre above the waistband of airbrushed-on, black PVC trousers that slid down to seven-inch purple snakeskin heels. Her hair had been poodled up into Tina Turnerish spikes and an entire department store of blusher, eyeliner, foundation and sparkly lipgloss daubed her face. On her left shoulder beamed out a new tattoo, the nude on the plinth and the serpent that breathed a fiery Teutonic script: *Ruiner: Tits Out.*

OK, no irony here then, no dis-identification through over-identification. What had happened to 'womb envy', 'reclaiming our vaginas' and 'keep men indoors'? Before I could do my impression of Munch's *Scream*, she waggled at me a two-fingered salute, her hand wrapped in a lacy glove.

'Nathan. How's it hanging, love puppy?'

'Erm, is Juliet in?'

'Me Shaz. You enter.'

I stepped into her front room.

'Are you feeling alright, Shaz?'

'Well, a regular bonk does make all the difference.'

I tried really hard not to go *urgghhh*, but it must have been written all over my face in fluorescent green paint.

'Sit down,' she said. 'Cawfee with cream and sugar?'

'Got any paint stripper?'

A look of sad resignation came my way before she clicked off into her kitchen. I sat down on a sofa and stared at the coffee table. An ashtray brimmed with fag butts and charred roaches. I wondered if I ate them a fast-acting poison would finish me off once and for all, forestalling any more information about Plum's lovelife. I remembered the red light bulb mist of Plum's parties and the hazy shadow-people slotting tequilas and hoovering gak from this very table and Plum crashing onto this sofa beside me and ramming her hand into my groin. At that time, the party where I met Frances, Plum had every confidence that Squinty Hugo would sell *The Best Man* and turn me into a literary star. All sorts of useful contacts and kudos would flow her way. Plum's black ops networking was a form of sexual feng shui. Just position yourself in the right place and stay there, usually on your knees with your mouth open. Now she was shacked up with Mac the Paddle. Mac had a trendy literary agent. Mac could be her envoy, her stalking horse. Poor Sharon. Literary celebrity is supposed to strike you like lightening. One minute you're nobody, the next everyone on the tube is covering his or her face with your book. Sharon seemed to be trying to speed this up by standing in the middle of a field with a steel pole tucked into the seat of her knickers during an electrical storm of singular ferocity. It wasn't worth it. Dignity is everything. I'd remember this when snug in our wheelie bin my fiddle and I dined out at Mayor McCheese's expense.

She came back in and put a tray laid with cups and a cafetière on the table. When she sat down in the armchair opposite me she seemed to be rehearsing a prepared speech. I knew, however, that she was booting up her modem, connecting to the **H.Y.D.R.A** network to download **plumcam**.

MALE UNIT: Nathan Flack.

USEFULNESS TO H.Y.D.R.A OPERATIVE – Zero. Unit is impaired. No product forthcoming.

Her PVC trousers squeaked as she crossed her legs and lit a cigarette.

'So, pupster, how's it been?'

OBJECTIVE – browse for data.

'Oh you know,' I said, 'went to Shelley's funeral. Almost got lured into murder plot. Pretty quiet really.'

ANALYSIS – Flack Unit is taking evasive manoeuvres.

ACTION - Attack with extreme prejudice.

'I see things are getting to you,' she said, steepling her fingers.

'I see something has been getting at you, too. What on earth are you wearing, Juliet?'

'Shaz, it's Shaz now. I'm in love. I've always deserved to be in love and now I am.'

'You know you shouldn't be mucking about with the students.'

'That's bitchin' coming from you.'

'When did you start using words like "bitchin"?' Plum once failed a man for using "king prawn" in a story.

'Last time I saw you, you were rolling around in the back of a van with one of yours, in front of everybody, and you were armed.'

'Sharon   . . . Mac? Seriously? Are you OK?'

'He shakes me all night long.'

'Sharon, hasn't it crossed your mind that maybe all he wants you for is cheap editorial advice?'

'He doesn't need me to edit his work.'

'It's not really your thing, is it? Zombie flesh gobblers?'

Plum's taste in reading matter was usually restricted to the miserable-girl-on-the-outskirts-of-society genre. She preferred a spare, unshowy style and lots of product placement and cultural references, plenty of gender and identity politics and an ending in which a miserable unloved girl finds love with a plump and sexy older woman. I would have thought that after reading the first paragraph of *The Death Metal Revelations* she would have tracked down the author and hacked off his knackers with nail scissors.

'It's perfect,' she said.

'No it's not and I can't believe you're now championing his writing just because he's giving you the benefit.'

'We're living in a post-literary world, Nathan. The safe and easy categories are being broken down.'

'What's this then? Love in a time of marketing?'

'You're already on a warning. Since then you've attacked a student with a hatchet.'

'Unlike you, of course, who allowed a student to attack you with his.'

'There are many other people who would jump at teaching your classes.'

'Like who?'

'I can think of several.'

She said this with sorrow heavy in her words, but in her eyes I could see **plumcam** ticking over, calculating, playing theory games with the outcomes based on the available data.

ACTION: Delete Flack Unit and replace with Mac Unit. Mac Unit will be grateful to Plum Unit.

'The hatchet was the last straw,' she said.

'I can see Mr McMahon is already having an influence on your phrasing.'

ACTION – No compassion. Do not listen to excuses, distractions or attempts at wit.

'I'll have to get someone else to do your classes,' she said.

'Doctor Vest hasn't complained, has she?'

Plum took a long drag on her cigarette, but kept her gaze fixed on me.

ACTION –Delete Flack. Delete Flack. Delete.

'Oh who wants it anyway,' I said. 'It's a shit job and it's driving me mental.'

Tactical bollock up. Of course I needed the job. What else could I do? I didn't want to go back to book doctoring full time and read things like *The Death Metal Revelations* day in and day out. I didn't want a normal job and there was no normal job that I could do. I was a creative writing tutor. That's all I was good for. The child had dreamt of the Universe and all its possibilities and quasars and swirls and all had come to be.

Plum smirked and blew a puff of smoke into the space between us.

ACTION – Exploit weakness. Delete.

'So you don't want to teach for us anyway?' she said. 'Well, that makes it easy.'

'Let's face it, Sharon, what's happening here is that you want to replace me with a moron who hasn't even read a book because you're porking him.'

ANALYSIS – This is how the world works. Plum and Mac Units are Power Couple.

'He's going to be an important new voice.'

'He's ignorance's patient zero.'

'You've had your chance.'

'He couldn't teach my class anyway.'

ANALYSIS – Flack Unit is resisting.

ACTION – Call for air strikes.

'Well, let's go and ask him, shall we?' She heaved herself of her chair, then stropped to the foot of the stairs between the front and the dining room. 'T-Boner . . . honey . . . can you come down here a minute?'

'Fuck, he's here?' I said.

'Yes,' she said. 'He's waiting on some important news and needed me to hold his hand.'

'His hand? Sharon, you're having sex with an ex-metal drummer who now works as an estate agent and writes the worst type of misogynistic sex and violence, T and A toss imaginable in the worst English conceivable, and you're calling him T-Boner?'

'My love could crush planets and stars.'

ANALYSIS – Flack Unit outflanked.

Slow, pounding footsteps crossed the ceiling and made their way down the stairs. Mac the Paddle McMahon, the Obviously Not-So Pathetic Phallus shuffled into the room in nothing more than a tiny ruby-red kimono-style dressing gown loosely tied to reveal a huge V of sweaty chest. His hair was tousled and misshapen by sleep on one side and his beard a mess of slicked-down patches. A purple hyacinth-like pattern bloomed on his neck. When I realized what it was I felt like I'd been strapped to an invisible wheel that rotated me around and around so my head hit the floor and my feet brushed the ceiling. Mac grabbed Plum's arse and when she yelped he pounced in for a kiss, leading with his tongue. They both seemed to hang there, laughing mouth to mouth. I looked into the swirling coffee grains in the cafetière and visualized pouring it over my head and scalding myself so badly I'd be rushed to a burns unit in remotest Tobermoray to hide there forever with bandages over my eyes.

'Gobbler,' said Mac.

I reached for the coffee.

'Throbber,' said Plum, then pecked him with a kiss. 'C'mon, lover, I want to discuss something with you.'

'Oright there, Nathan, didn't see you. Love Muffin, why didn't you tell me Nathan was here? Alright son. How's your luck?'

He padded over to take Plum's armchair. As he sat down his gut strained against the kimono like a hill of blood.

'Small world, eh?' he said. 'Didn't know when I signed up for your course that I'd get a cracker like this thrown in with the fee.'

Plum giggled and followed him across the room to perch herself on the rest of the chair.

'Mac,' I said. 'Being a businessman and a musician, I'm sure you'll appreciate it if I put my cards on the table.'

'I've not trod on your toes here?' He looked quickly up at Plum.

'Er no,' I said. 'Not in that way anyhow. The reason I'm here is that . . . Shaz wants to get rid of me and replace me with you. How do you feel about that?'

She spidered her fingers in his tumbleweed of hair.

'We're just discussing the options,' she said.

He looked at me and stroked his chin, then draped his arm across Plum's thigh.

'The thing is, I think of myself as more of a writer than a teacher.'

'They go together . . .' said Plum

'I know, like you and me, love puffin. How much is it?'

'Two-hundred,' said Plum.

'Two hundred. You must be raking it in, Nathan, living it large.'

'She means two hundred a month,' I said. 'It's not the hourly rate.'

'Fuck that then, I wouldn't tug me lug for that. Nah. I'm a writer. Nathan's a teacher. Why'd you want to get rid of Nate anyway, finger puppet?'

Plum's mouth froze into a nice big happy smile but her eyes were like black chips of gravel.

'It was just an idea, that's all.'

'And you were just telling me, Shaz . . .' I reached over and poured myself a coffee then fished a sociable one out of my fag packet. ' . . . how much you like Mac's novel, so I must be doing something right.'

'Well, something,' chuckled Mac.

'I still have very serious concerns, Nathan,' said Plum.

'Like what?' said Mac.

'The business with the van.'

'That was nothing, wasn't it, Nate? Just a laugh. That Jane's a looper. We'd all club her one given half a chance.'

'Thank you, Mac,' I said.

'Nathan.' She reclined a little and scratched the back of Mac's head, a hint that she'd conceded this round. ACTION – **plumcam** logging off. 'I think the best thing to do is to delay any decision until after the residential. The residential is your last chance. No screw-ups. I want all of those students to be happy Miffy bunnies. Otherwise . . .'

'OK.' I stood up and stubbed out my smoke. 'Thanks for that. See you tonight, Mac, and see you . . . whenever Sharon, I mean Juliet, I mean, Shaz, I mean Zizi. Sorry. Love lobster. Sex penguin. Misty Mountain Hop. Sorry. Got Tourettes suddenly. Autistic temperament. It's catching. Stay away. Bye.'

I ran out of the house and straight into The Lovejoy Tavern on the corner and slid to a stop in the middle of the empty saloon.

ANALYSIS – Arrgghhhhhhhhhhhhhhhhhhhh – sensory overload.

ACTION – Massive injection of stimulants.

ACTION – log off plumcam, because you do not have access to plumcam.

JAMES O'MAILER – ACCESS DENIED.

JAMES O'MAILER – ACCESS DENIED.

JAMES O'MAILER – ACCESS DENIED.

At the bar, a gangly barman said, 'You look like you've picked up a pound but lost a tenner.'

'Really, I think I've scraped up my heart but lost my soul.'

'One of them days?'

'Black coffee, please, as strong as possible, and two double scotches and two flaming sambucas.'

'What you lose on the sandwiches, you gain on the rooms, eh?'

I liked this phrase very much. It was the sort of found-dialogue that usually I wrote down on index cards and transcribed into my notebook the following day to store for possible use later. I had a card in the back pocket of my jeans and a pen in my coat. But I couldn't motivate myself to take it out. I felt like when you're knackered and stuck on the sofa at one in the morning and you really want to get up and go to bed but you're surfing the channels going *shit, shit, shit* as each jab of the remote control brings up another clip show or reality fly-on-the-wall bollocks or a repeat of *Gentleman's Relish* featuring Sylvester Sly Ramos-Pintos, and even so you still can't get off the sofa and switch off the set and crawl into the bedroom.

'Here you go,' said the barman. 'You've lost more than a tenner now.'

'A drop in the ocean,' I said as I handed over the cash. Using this cliché didn't bother me today. I downed the sambucas, shot after shot and as the spirit tightened my throat the optics glazed in my vision. I'd just had my manky bacon rind saved by the patronage of Mac McMahon. Part of me would rather have got the chop and maintained my sangfroid. Why had he done that? 'I see myself as a writer.' I started to collapse with laughter and almost knocked over the stool next to me. The barman gave me a wary look. T-Boner? Love Muffin? Call me Shaz? I'd seen some weird old nonsense around Plum before, and I'd seen her eat some very poisonous hats in pursuit of fame and being right about everything. But I'd never have guessed she'd go all rock-chick, shack up with the Paddle and give his shit-headed novel the thumbs up. This was beyond strange. This was looping the loop, Hex Enduction Hour, mutually assured destruction. Last week I had woken up in the snow after hallucinating time travel and dimension hopping, but this was more peculiar. This was post-fantasy. I couldn't have made up the union of the Plum and the Paddle. I chucked back a scotch and thought what an exhibition Plum was making of herself. No way was Mac going to actually sell that novel. No way. And she'd attached her wagon to his star so publicly, tattooed his logo to her skin. She'd just committed professional and artistic *hara-kiri*. And she had the front to suggest that things were getting to me? They were. But I wasn't lowering my sights so far downward that I could only see the weeds at the wayside. It made me smile. It made me sad, too. Poor Sharon. I banged the last scotch and took refuge in the coffee. After all, I had to teach later. *The Death Metal Revelations* wasn't seeing the light of day. Never. A bit of a fluke was going on here. Fred Malone wouldn't actually run with *DMR* and even if he wanted to. Someone up the line at the agency would block it. I hadn't asked what news Mac was waiting for, but I bet myself that it was conformation that the book would go on the market soon. That clearly wasn't going to happen. The rotor blades of business sense would shred that tissue paper and send it back as confetti and tickertape. And what then for poor Love Shaz? My stomach burned a little from the jumpstart I'd given my nervous system. We were all heading for the shredder together. All the hacks and all the failures. The Plum, The Paddle and the Flyweight Flack the Fumigated.

Talking about Talking

After an afternoon of the hammerhead silence of the garret and a deep sleep on the sofa of shame I found myself that evening standing at the very spot where last week I'd come to my senses on the lawn of the Eudora Doon Building. A thick fog had risen. The lights of the building glowed in the haze. In my remote viewing system I imagined myself paralysed by apprehension in front of the haunted house in the film poster for *The Exorcist*. I knew that I shouldn't be lurking here in the fog like Arnold Bumrape. One of the Arcana might spot me and report back to Plum that I was Nate Le Freak again.

Too late. Cynthia Wadge gave me one of her pinchy-faced looks as she quickened her stride and hurried along the path into the foyer. Following, head down to make it look like I'd not noticed her, I remembered that The Paddle had been waiting for bad news and I ought to be consoling, understanding and fob him off with some encouraging spiel that he could report back to Plum as evidence of my rehabilitation. Then we were going to all have an intelligent discussion about dialogue, talk about talking, do some exercises and analyse some lovely examples.

As I shuffled along the first-floor walkway, Cynthia picked up speed like a lone female in the park at night when there's a persistent rustle in the bushes. True, she'd seen me with a hatchet poised above a classmate's head, but I'd seen her cowering behind a shower curtain and then her oatmeal sweatpants slide over her ash-grey underwear. We were evens, surely? But that's the thing. Students can moon-bark and wrong-room and Sensitive Plants whinge for England and there's nothing the tutor can do about it but be patient and stoical. One gripe from them, however, and the university's complaints procedure KPG grinds indefatigably into life. I couldn't afford to give Plum any more free ammunition. I divided the students into those I could expect not to make a big fuss and those who would carp. Jane, obviously, was so far in my corner that she was repainting the walls a nice, tranquil peach colour. Given what he'd said that morning, Mac didn't seem to have an axe to grind. Frank did have an axe to grind, but it wasn't swinging my way, unless he knew I'd grassed him to the law. On reflection, though, Frank hovered in the grey centre circle of the game, as did Cynthia. Sensitive Plants moan. That's what they do, but I might be able to win her over. Reg, however, was a professional bleat merchant, and at least I knew where I stood with Erika. But maybe I couldn't count on Mac either, given that Plum would needle and tempt him like Circe and Calypso advertising pay-per-view late night porn on hotel room cable.

Slipping into the room, I tried to smile calmly and hospitably for my flock. This lasted about a second, for as I strode up the aisle in the stark white light, I realized that Mac was sitting on my desk wearing a huge purple suit with a nasty orange tie and presiding over Cynthia, Reg, Erika and Jane. Embarrassment fizzled through me as I passed Jane in her thick, scarlet pashmina and tried to make eye contact with Mac to politely return him to his seat. Immediately I realized that this must have looked like I'd snubbed Jane. As I arrived behind the desk, my view on the class was blocked by Mac's hippo-propped-on-a-bucket frame. Unsure of what do, yet somehow grateful that I couldn't see them, I waited for someone to mention that I had arrived.

'They reckon, right,' Mac announced, 'it has a unique USP, right, and it's like so high contact like, that it should have market wallop. Like, it's so many types of thing that there's something for everyone. Bit like fruit salad.'

'Well, that is dandy,' said Reg. 'We're as pleased as punch for you.'

'It shows it can be done,' said Cynthia, 'unlike what we've been led to believe.'

'Ooh, I am jealous,' said Jane. 'You make it all sound so easy.'

'Well, it is, really, ain't it? Anyway, thought I'd better fill you in on me progress. Oright Nate?' He turned and looked back at me. 'Just doing a

369

bit of a support act slot for you here, seeing if I can, nudge, nudge. Don't look at me like that, just breaking your balls as they say in the US of A.'

'We're not in Brooklyn, Mac, we're in Norwich, so can you please sit down.'

'Bring your daughter to the slaughter.' He dropped off the desk and slammed into the chair next to Jane. 'Nathan, you heard of Dewsenbury and Madge?'

'Yes, they're. . .'

'Ollie Blox?'

'Yes, I've met him . . .'

'How'd you find him?'

'Covered in spaghetti.'

'Well, right, found out today that Freddie Malone has sent him me book.'

I didn't want to dampen his spirits, especially not when I was supposed to be in noble pedagogue mode. Oliver Blox was a Butcher Cumberland of product shifting and discount warfare who if the titles could be repackaged with celebrity-endorsement would 3-for-2 Mao's *Little Red Book* with *Mein Kampf* and *The Protocols of the Elders of Zion.* He would laugh *The Death Metal Revelations* out of house.

'OK,' I said, delivering one of my pathetic handclaps. 'How is everyone else?'

Reg, trousers pulled up to his tits as ever, tightened his rooster-like face and clawed at the knees of his tweed trousers.

'Aren't you going to congratulate Mister McMahon, Flack?'

'I just did.'

'No, you didn't. When I was a teacher I would always say "well done" to a high achiever.'

'So rude,' said Cynthia.

'He persecutes me,' said Erika.

'You were a little muted,' said Jane.

Jane? *Jane!*

'Has anything been achieved yet?' I realized I'd raised my voice a tad too much. 'Look, Mac, I just don't want to be party to getting your hopes up. If you have some good news, I'll be the first to buy you a pint, OK?'

'I wasn't complaining, were I?'

'No, you *did . . . not . . .* complain, Mac, and we have a lot to get through. So . . .' With a second, unfortunately more waspish clap I tried to end this exchange. The line alongside the relaxed and resplendent Mac seemed to me to be holding out their zombie hands again, whispering and taunting.

He's jealous. He's jealous. You're jealous of the Great One.

I flinched and covered my face with my hands. 'Stop it.'

'Nate, you oright?' said Mac. 'Want me to stand in?'

'No . . . No, I'm fine. I've just . . . look, I'll come clean, folks. I've got a bit of a cold, because this time last week I got caught out in the snow on the way here and nearly froze. I've got a bit of a chill, that's all. Feeling a bit fragile. Now, I know none of you drivers could make it last week, quite understandably . . .'

'I was here,' said Erika. 'I waited and waited . . .'

'You were not here,' I said.

'I was, here, nothing for the money.'

'You were not here.'

'See, see how he persecutes. See, I show you, I show you.'

'I think I need to remind you, Flack,' said Reg, 'that education is for everybody.'

'And that includes you, so can everyone please stop butting in so I can get our business out of the way and I can start the class properly.'

'Er . . .you sure you don't want me to step in?' said Mac.

'No thank you, Mac.' Would he have asked me to sing about vampire tit wanks or Attila the Hun's demon MILF orgies on one of his records? 'Now let's just concentrate on what we are here for. Please listen. We missed last week's class, so I'll repeat it this weekend at the residential. OK? I'll make time there. OK? No one will be out of pocket, OK? No one will be neglected, OK? So, this weekend. You've all got the paperwork and the map? Four o'clock Friday. Ends, in theory, Sunday lunchtime, but I'll add two hours for a class on A Sense of Place. Sebastian Harker will be coming to talk to you on Friday night. Be nice to him. He's great. OK? Any questions?'

They all put their hands up. I shut my eyes.

'None, OK, tonight I want to move on from . . . what were we talking about last time?'

'Trisha Vidler. Getting her bonce ripped off on a train,' said Mac.

'No, we were talking about narrative point of view. Tonight, I want to talk about dialogue. Talking about talking. OK?'

'What have we descended to now,' said Reg. 'Trades Unions on strike.'

'No, talking about talking.'

I realized now that I'd slid off the table and was standing in front of them. Mac seemed distracted, as if listening to another voice. Jane's bottom lip trembled as she peered up at me. The others were fortresses of disdain.

'Talking about talking,' I said. 'That's what we are going to do.'

At this moment, the door slammed open. Frank Denbigh burst into the room. His head looked like a cannonball lodged into the monstrous letter 'M' of his torso as dead-set on me he marched up the aisle, throwing back handfuls of air like he was tunnelling.

The Angel of Trunch

Everyone jumped in their seats and looked away from Frank and over to me. In the crosshairs of all this attention – Frank the Wank coming right at me and the accusing eyes of the Zombie Arcana– sweat lashed my cheeks and forehead. But Frank was staggering and covered his face with his great, big hands. At the top of the aisle he swung about and like an elephant shot by a bazooka collapsed into the chair next to Mac, hands still over his face. Then he looked up at me and then over to the others and thrust up his arms as if asking for permission to speak.

'Er Frank?' I said.

'My name is Frank Denbigh and I've been in trouble with the police.'

'Frank,' I said. 'Perhaps this forum is not the best for this sort of thing.'

'The filth?' said Mac. 'You been a naughty boy?'

'Maybe it is to be expected after all,' said Reg.

'No, you don't understand, Mister Nathan. I been banged up all week, I have, all week in a cell with coppers saying this and that and getting me all confused about things. Things they put in my head, they did. They said I did it, I did for them pretty girls. But I didn't, I didn't. And they had all these photos and dates and I don't know where Frank was during them dates and they made me say I did it. They made me say I'm an Angel. But I never hurt a fly. I never. I hurt a weasel once, but I never hurt a fly.'

A cramped kind of silence held the rest of us as Frank wept into his hands.

'They persecute?' said Erika.

'Be quiet,' I said. 'Frank . . .'

'No Mister Nathan, no, it weren't me, it weren't me and they were all for throwing away the key and that, and then they come in this afternoon and they say, right, they say, that all along this Angel fella has not been me but all along it were my mate Davie Mitre. It were Davie.'

'Oh my God,' said Jane, shooting me a glance.

I thrust my hand thorough my sweaty hair. *O'Mailer was right.*

'They looked into it all,' stuttered Frank, 'and found it were him. And when they went round his bungalow he had all them girl's stuff there laid out on the floor like jumble and he was sat in some girl's pants and watching Dirty Dancing on the viddy.'

'OK, Frank. Maybe it's best if you skip tonight's class.'

'I can't believe it were Davie. He's been such a brock the badger for Frank since we were in the Cubs up at Yarmouth.'

'Hey, you should write about this, Frankie,' said Mac. 'I'd kill to be a serial killer's mate. Proper research, that.'

'Mac, shhhh. Frank. Better not to discuss this here,' I said, noticing the palpable fear on the faces of Cynthia and Jane and wanting to prevent Reg sticking his tweedy beak in. 'Can we do anything? Call you a cab? Call your wife?'

'That's the thing, Mister Nathan. I ain't got a wife. I never had one. I been making it all up so people don't think I'm a queer one.'

'Dear Lord,' said Jane.

'I ain't got one. I ain't got one. And it ain't all it says in that Robbie Marley song, it ain't all no woman, no cry. It's all cry, I tell you.'

'Frank. You've obviously had a shock, but this is a creative writing class and . . .'

'Mister Nathan, I ain't ever been with a lady.'

'Well, it's hardly bloody surprising, is it?' said Cynthia.

'The emphasis people put on these private matters is quite obscene,' said Reg.

'No, it's not,' said Mac. 'If I didn't get it every day I'd explode.'

'Frank, I must keep reminding you that this is a creative writing class, not . . .'

'The thing, Mister Nathan, is that them coppers said they'd had an anonymous tip off that the killings were down to me.'

'Well, misunderstandings happen, don't they? Perhaps the main thing is that the real murderer has been caught.'

'What about me, Mister Nathan? Who did that to me? Who thought it were me?'

Keeping eye contact, he tapped his nose once, then turned to look along the line to Jane and then tapped it once more. Everybody else was stiff and quiet. Mac sat like he was slightly bored at the funeral of someone he hardly knew but whose family he needed to arselick. Reg was as pensive as a White Russian general contemplating the red scum lording it over Mother Moscow, and Cynthia and Jane's huddle reminded me of footage of terrified female audiences watching *Jaws* in the seventies. Erika then rummaged in the carrier bags at her feet. She pulled out a sack-sized bag of Happy Shopper Bacon Bites and proceeded to shove handfuls of them into her mouth. The stare Frank directed at me could hammer nails into a beam and now had a backing track of crunching and chomping.

'I think it's best if I stay here, Mister Nathan,' he said. 'I don't want to go home on my own.'

The room felt as hot as a maggot farm.

'Maybe you should just keep your private matters private,' said Reg.

'I agree,' I said. 'We're talking about talking, Frank. Not talking about . . . whatever.'

'Being the victim of tell-tell-tits.'

'Yes, that's right. Talking about talking. OK, everyone.' My hands slip-slapped the most pathetic clap ever as I paced along the line and situated myself in the Jane/Cynthia corner where I took out my Dialogue lesson plan and scanned the bullet points. 'So, how does everyone feel about dialogue?' I said. 'What makes good dialogue? What does dialogue in fiction achieve?'

'Flack,' said Reg. 'I think you've neglected something?'

He held out several pages of typed script. The Bacon Bites bag rustled as Erika continued to stow them away in her mouth, chewing, munching, and slapping her tongue against her lips. I looked at Frank. Frank tapped his nose.

'You've gone back on your promise,' said Reg, 'to allow us to read our work at the start of each of these sessions. Now I would politely request that I be allowed to read my work.'

I slammed my notes down on the table and positioned myself in the middle of the desk, sat back and adopted the creative writing tutor's listening pose. I closed my eyes. I waited until I heard what I assumed to be the sound of his palm smoothing across the paper. Another chomp and gulp drifted over to where I sat in self-imposed darkness.

'Can everyone please be quiet please,' I said. 'Listen to Reg. Think about it. What can be changed and what works. As ever, one positive comment for every criticism.'

'Before I begin,' said Reg, 'I would just like to say a few words.'

Please, Can You Stop It, *Please*

'It would be best here,' Reg said, 'if I explain to you what I am attempting, not though, that I am going to change anything, as it satisfies me quite completely . . .'

'Reg,' I said, opening my eyes. 'Is this the beginning of the novel?'

'Why, yes, it is.'

'Then it can speak for itself. Chop chop. Time marches on.'

'No, Flack, I *will* say a few words, if I may. It has struck me throughout this course that all of you, let down as you have been by your education and your kow-towing to prevailing social attitudes, your 'let it all hang out' and your 'spend, spend, spend' and excepting from this the redoubtable Mr McMahon, you have all succumbed to quite morbid thoughts and are writing stories of the most inappropriate kind. You all do yourself such a disservice. What can we expect, though? What can we expect when our leader shows no understanding of the classics? We must always refer back to the classics. Do people still listen to Beethoven? Do people still read Jane Austen? Why, of course they do. That's why it's so essential to write of only what one knows. Jane Austen wrote only of the world in which she lived. This is what you all should have learned from this course and it's this emphasis that's been missing from our conversations. If Miss Austen were here she would surely have blushed at what has passed for intelligent discourse.'

I couldn't be bothered to reply and let him waffle. What he articulated was the position known as 'The Grammar-Stammerer's Tourniquet', an insistence that all fiction must be located in autobiography and so-called fact when most of us live lives that lack any narrative shape and nothing much of interest happens to us. I could have bollocked on about Kafka not being a beetle, or Nabokov not being a kiddie-fiddler, and Stephen Crane not fighting in the American Civil War that was in any case over before he was even born, and *Gulliver's Travels* and science fucking fiction and that it didn't matter so long as the story is in some way an experience, but I just stared and wilted. When I realised that the others were all looking not at Reg but accusingly at me, I shut my eyes again.

'I have here,' Reg continued, 'being something of a rebel, written a story in the classic mode and that will, in time, be seen as the Great English Novel. It is, I must admit, something of a paean to my Darling Dear, and it is a thought-provoking work that shows to us all how we got into the mess we're in, where no one says 'please' or 'thank you' any more and you can't leave the house without some hooded vandal displaying his genitals. Oh yes, this is the story of Roland, an honourable and dashing man, the headmaster of a provincial school in the late nineteen sixties and how he stands alone against the ravages of the permissive society. Yes, it is my story and that of my wife. Yes, I expect you to be changed by this, so pin back your ears. Listen!'

I opened my eyes. Reg took a glance at either side of him. Every one seemed to be patiently waiting for him to begin. He nodded at me, and smiled as if keen to appear to forgive me; then he cleared his throat and took his papers from the armrest and two-handedly raised them to his face.

'"Roland was angry . . ."'

Something like a car alarm went off in my head and forced my brain, neck, shoulders, heart, lungs and liver, pelvis, knees, shins and toes out through the caps of my boots to slosh towards the door.

'Please, can you stop it *please*. Please, please, please stop.'

Reg looked up, his face so grey it seemed yellow.

'"Roland was angry . . ."' he repeated.

I quickly stuffed my notes into my bag. Then for the second time that day I found myself staggering to a halt with a head full of screaming white static. Then I was jogging across the lawn of the Eudora Doon into the fog. Someone called my name. I turned.

Jane was standing on the path. Her Montmartre shopping bag hung at her hip and her pashmina rippled on the breeze.

'Nathan, what are you doing?'

'Running away in cowardly fashion.'

'Well, that sounds like a top banana idea.' She caught up with me and tucked her arm inside mine. 'We'll be cowards together.' We started to walk alongside the admin buildings and the science departments, under the trees and into the fog.

'Why is it a good idea?' I said. 'For you, I mean. You're fearless.'

'Reg is reading his story. And Mac has volunteered to talk to us about how to write speech.' She tugged my arm and we turned off the road and up some concrete steps, a cut-through to the main campus. 'And I thought that all sounds a bit dull, and . . .'

'You're frightened of Frank?' I said as we came out from under a building and onto one of the longer walkways. It was like we were exploring a city in the clouds as we stepped down between the refectory and the chapel and found ourselves in the main university plain. The lights of the Union glowed ahead of us. Jane's arm unlinked from my elbow and her hand found mine and squeezed it.

'Nathan, Frank gave me a really strange look in there.'

'I know. He gave me one too.'

'But I didn't report him to the police.'

'But I did.'

She let go of my hand. 'Why didn't you tell me? I've been trying to ring you for days. It was on the news. An arrest and then another and a suspect released without charge.'

'I think we should have a drink,' I said.

'Are you actually asking me to go for a drink with you?'

'Let's go in there. I keep wanting to look over my shoulder out here.'

We swished through the fog and entered the Union.

Men Bleed Too When You Cut Them

No binges were in progress in the Grad Bar. No meat-heaps on the razz bragged and caroused. No sleek-moving tinkerbell girls slotted Breezers and slammers. No jukebox tunes or quiz night questions smothered what passed as conversation. Instead, there was mutter and burble. Roll-up smoke drifted into the haze coming off the candles on the tables, just like the PhD projects and research grants of the lumberjack-shirted twentysomething men in here had vanished into the beery nights. Girls in frayed jeans and Indian dresses, their hair splashed with primary red or blue dye, fiddled with the wax frills festooning the candle stems. From the bar I looked over to where Jane peered out at the glittering lights of the foggy campus. As I collected our glasses of Shiraz I realized that tonight, in the scene O'Mailer had shown me, we should be down in the sewer, disposing of Frank Denbigh's body.

When I put the glasses down on the table and took my seat, she flashed her long eyelashes at me and stroked her hair at her ear. My heart beat fast in a way that I didn't understand.

'You look manic,' she said.

'I'm sorry for not phoning you, you know, after your party.'

'It was fun, wasn't it?'

'You enjoyed it?'

'Well, I wasn't over-chuffed that you ran off. Why'd you run off? C'mon. We were having a lovely adventure.'

'Have you heard of the Grand Anglian Sewer?'

'How do you know about it? It's a secret. One of my favourite places.'

'I don't know. I dreamt about it.'

'Bit specific for a dream. I thought dreams were supposed to be all weird and peculiar. Like, I always dream about sitting down to dinner with Edmund White and finding myself trying to hold my knife and fork with my work gloves and then my visor keeps falling over my face when he tries to kiss me.'

'Must have picked it up from somewhere. You sure you didn't mention it to me?'

'Don't think so. But you didn't run off because of the Grand Anglian.'

'I don't know . . . I just . . . they all *saw*.'

'You're not OK, are you? You were like stress-stress grrrrr at the party and now you're like, well . . .' She looked at her watch. 'We should be over there, with you telling me about how to write speech even if the others want to, whatever they want, and well, you just ran out of the class.'

'"Roland was angry",' I said. 'I'm allergic to the passive voice.'

'Why don't we do it here?'

'Do what here?'

'Why don't you talk to me about talking?'

I didn't want to talk about talking. I wanted to talk about the dream in the snow. The dream in which we were lovers and virtuous avengers, like the couple at the end of a 3-for-2 table product shifter who take the law into their own hands because the powers that be are powerless and pusillanimous. But I couldn't. 'Tell a dream, lose a friend,' as someone, probably Adolf Hitler or Benito Mussolini once said, and so I switched into Dialogue summary autopilot.

'Well, the thing about dialogue is that it's not like real conversation, because that's unfocused and all over the place, like, listen to that bloke behind us, he's rabbiting mindlessly about Paraguayan haloumi and the anxiety of influence in Snow Patrol lyrics, but underneath that I know he probably wants to kill me, so I ought to lower my voice.'

She shuffled quickly around. A line of empty tables behind us terminated in a wall the colour of school toilet paper.

'So dialogue is better than talking but it must *seem* like real people talking, and then it can't be stilted, like wooden, and it can't be stagey, like the characters can't be talking just for the reader's benefit. Like, stagey would be if I said to you "Hello Doctor Jane Vest, you were one of my students, were you not, that winter it snowed like a bastard and I nearly died, one of my students in An Introduction to Creative Writing? You remember that party you threw where we broke into that nutter's van and then everyone saw me looming over you with a hatchet and I ran away like Captain Custard in his yellow submarine? I met you when I was still a writer, didn't I? When I was still writing".'

She tilted her head, like she was not so much about to ask a question of me, but answer the question that followed from the one she knew I knew that she was going to ask.

'Oh Nathan I know the Mac thing has got to you.'

'It doesn't matter what Mac does, or what happens to Mac, and I promise you nothing is going to happen to Mac. Seriously. Have you read that novel?'

'Maybe it's just different to what you like.'

'It's not different, it's shit. It's not good-bad, or bad-bad, or just very bad. It's excrement. Sewage. He didn't need me to edit it. He needed you. But knowing that doesn't help me. I can't do it anymore. Seriously. I'm blocked like a drain.'

'Oh I don't want you to be blocked,' she said, flipping over her arm and laying it on the table next to mine. 'And blockages are my business. Maybe you just need a change of scene. Maybe you need to, I don't know . . .'

'Nor do I.'

'Perhaps. I mean, look, me right, Jane the Stain.'

'Don't say that.'

'Well, that's what I've been called, because of my job. When I meet blokes in wine bars, or get talking to men in supermarkets or book group, or whatever, whenever, and I mention what I do I see it pass across their eyes.'

'But you don't smell, or anything.'

'I should do considering where I've been today.'

'Where's that?'

'The Grand Anglian, funnily enough . . . but what I was trying to say is that's what I do, but it's not me.'

I noticed that she winced a little when I jerked my arm from the table to light a cigarette and gulp down my whole glass of wine in one. Her talk of Jane the Stain and men in pubs wafted over me as I considered that she had been down in The Grand Anglian on the day that O'Mailer predicted, and that O'Mailer had, as a final volley, told me that Frank Denbigh was not the Angel of Trunch.

What a lot of old cock!

It *was* an hallucination. It didn't happen. It wasn't real. O'Mailer wasn't real. This was real. Jane was real. Jane and I could be real. Jane wasn't looking too happy though. Her arms were wrapped around her chest so tightly that her breastbone had tensed and her shoulders contracted into a rigid coat hanger's shape.

'Thank you,' she said. 'Thank you for listening.'

'Did I say that?'

'What a load of old cock? Yes you did, Nathan, so I'm obviously boring you.'

'No . . . I was miles away.'

'That's hardly a comfort.' She reached under the table for her Montmartre bag and got up from her seat.

'No, Jane, please, stay, I'm sorry, I'm sorry.' I grabbed her gently by the arm and drew her back.

'I do think a lot of you, Nathan,' she said as she sat down again, 'but you're weird sometimes.'

'Look, we do need to talk about things, I agree.'

'We need to talk, yes.'

'Ask me a straight question and I'll give you a straight answer.'

She pinched her wineglass and circled the base on the table top, smiling now, a nervous smile because there was a brink here – I knew it; she must've known it – and her eyes glistened and her long eye lashes widened, and sternly, huskily, in-this-togetherly she said: 'What are we going to do about Frank?'

'Oh.'

'Frank, Nathan, what are we going to do about Frank?'

'I don't know.'

'The way he was looking at me he thinks that I told the police about him.'

'The way he was looking at me he *knows* I told the police about him.' I thought it pertinent not to mention the shed business.

'He thinks we both did it,' she said.

'How could we *both* do it?'

'Because we were in his van poking about with his stuff, Morse.'

'What was that thing in his van, Lewis?'

'Yes, what was that thing in his van?'

'You should talk to Frank. Take the flak, Flack, and keep him off me.'

'We could both talk to Frank, couldn't we?'

'I think you should talk to him.'

'Why?'

'Because *you* told on him.'

'Only because you put it into my head that he's Jack the Ripper. Jane, look . . .' I ran my glass across the table and almost mercy dashed to the bar for a refill or twenty. 'Things are getting too strange to explain.'

'Try me.'

'Erika has moved into my building.'

'What!'

'Yes, this morning I found her moving her stuff in and then she shouted at me.'

'Oh dear, poor you.'

'And the university is seriously intent on getting rid of me and replacing me with Mac.'

'Mac?'

'And while we're on the subject of Mac, right. Mac can't write, OK?'

She pursed her lips and tipped her head side-to-side, like she agreed with me but didn't want to commit herself.

'Mac can't write. And he's got an embarrassingly dirty mind, right?'

'Like a sewer, yes.'

'And Reg, when Mac first read out his stuff, *The Grasp of Fear*, Reg was disgusted, wasn't he? Now Reg is behaving like Mac is suddenly the new Jane Austen for blokes or something.'

'Well, you know, success sometimes blinds people or makes them suck up.'

'But Cynthia too. *The Big Hungry Caterpillar* would scare Cynthia witless but now Mac's like chummy-chummy lovely charming Alexander McCall Smith to her? Something weird's going on. Some weird emperor's new clothes thing.'

I hung my head in my hands and stared down into the maroon dregs of my wine, avoiding Jane and hoping she'd get in a round so I could sit here and think for a minute. All of a sudden telling her any of this seemed wrong and stupid . A stripe of heat pricked in the nape of my neck, spreading and clawing its way up the back of my head, burning my earlobes and working its way down to liquefy the notches of my spine, and then I knew.

I could hear the buzz of the bees.

Across the bar, behind us at a slant, sat rigidly postured at a table, long legs strung out and ankle boots crossed, book bag resting against her shin, heat ray eyes fixed on me, was Frances. She clutched a slender volume of verse: *Men Bleed Too If You Cut Them* by Nest Darkle.

Squirty Little Squid

I had a very bad feeling when I clocked the Nest Darkle. Reading Nest
Darkle meant that Frances was in a very bad mood indeed. The sky would
be black with the swarm of bees. All politeness and greenery would
wither in the gloom. The barbs would sting like rabies jabs. Nest Darkle
was an uber-manhating, formless poet from the seventies (*"form is a
phallus"*), a Big Magic Lezza of particular fanaticism who Sebastian Harker
referred to as "the unofficial castrator of the universe". When Frances
and I lived together, at the end, when the bees were crawling all over the
furniture and the ceiling and our bed and had even filled up the juicer,
Frances was reading for solace *One False Move and I'll Cut Your Knackers Off*
by Darkle. When she moved on to *You Were Conceived Wrong*, Darkle's
1972 'womanifesto', the bees cut off the electricity, chewed through the
telephone cables and bunged up the water mains. When I found a Darkle
volume open on the lounge table with the poem *Stay or I'll Flay You*
comprehensively annotated – "Nathan", "Nathan?" "Nathan!" scribbled
inside red pencil boxes and connected to the text with arrowheaded lines–
I knew it was time to quit this sadness. The grey ashtray light and the
hammerhead silence of the garret and immersing myself in the world of
Sylvester Sly Ramos-Pintos, the anti-Darkle, and *The Penelope Tree*, the
inverted version of my relationship with Frances, was, in comparison, like

being washed up on a tropical island abundant with fruit, silky sand and hula-hula girls pole-dancing around the coconut trees.

Oh, Frances, why'd you have to be like this? It just never worked out, did it? I still like you; I still care about you. I still want us to be friends. I'm still on your side. But it was hard to keep these thoughts straight while she was firing her laser beam eyes at me and the cover of the *Men Bleed Too* brandished a picture of a carrot being cut in two by a pair of serrated shears. Even so, I had nothing to hide. I had done nothing wrong. I hadn't. Last time, in Jane's conservatory, I'd said it all straight. Straight up. I'd been Straight-Up Flack. It would look kind of weird if I didn't say hello now. It would look like I'd lied before.

'If I leave you to her this time,' said Jane. 'I'm not coming back.'

I turned, and behind me the bees buzzing grew louder. And around Jane was a sort of mini-swarm, just a few, two or three drones that had floated into the house on a hot afternoon and couldn't get out.

I dropped my voice to a whisper. 'Look, there's nothing between Frances and me, not for years. But it'll look strange if I blank her.'

'Why does she have to turn up every time we're on our own.'

'It's after nine. Her class has just finished. It's not on purpose. She's more embarrassed than you.' I took a fiver out of my pocket. 'Get some more drinks in and I'll just go and say hello, OK?'

'Sure.' She gave me a sour look as she got up. I was about to add that we really must talk properly but she was already halfway across the room, the hanging diagonal of the scarlet pashmina fluttering with each swing of her hips.

I concentrated and tried to get used to the humming beat of the swarm. I would go over, nice and smiley, say hello, clear the air, spray the killer Africanized bees with knockout gas to make them drowsy. How are you, Frances? It's lovely to see you, Frances. Sorry I've not been in touch, but I've had a cold. That snow last week, got caught out in it. Ha ha. Things I do for literature, eh? Jane? No, no. Informal tutorial. Fancied a glass of red. New Darkle? Any good? I still like the poem you gave me. What was it called? *Your Bollocks, My Blender.* My God, have you seen *the* state of Plum? I know. Hard to believe, isn't it? Just like old times, Frances, you and me and our alliance against Orgsburo Plum on the one side and Folder-Holders on the other. C'mon, Frances. Too much has happened for daggers, eh?

Yes. I got up and levered myself around on the backrest of my chair. Frances pretended to be immersed in Darkle, her lips moving silently as if chewing the lines like gristle as I walked over.

'Hi Fran,' I said.

She looked up and blinked.

'Well,' she said, languidly shutting the Darkle. 'Who's been a squirty little squid then?'

'Pardon?'

'Your tastes seem to have got a little rougher since you left me.'

'C'mon Fran,' I said. 'Don't be like this.'

'Don't be like what?'

'I've not been a squid, or a squirt. Seriously. I just wanted to see how you are.'

'Smooth over the cracks so I don't cause any trouble, you mean?'

'But . . .'

'But what?'

I felt like I was floating a foot off the ground, my hands pinned by invisible nails, my legs pulled apart and Frances's laser beam stare a red burning line coming vertically up at my knackers like in a Darkle-scripted rewrite of *Goldfinger*. I desperately needed to change tack here.

'Frances?'

'No, I don't believe you.'

'You don't know what I'm going to say yet.'

'It's written all over your face.'

'What is?'

'"Please understand me, please, please, please, I'm so alone".'

'I wasn't going to say that. I'm not alone *enough*.'

'You've been stringing me that line for years.'

'Frances, listen, can I ask you something?'

'You are anyway.'

'Have you seen James O'Mailer?'

'Of course I haven't.'

'Frances, I think he might be real.'

'Real?'

'He talks to me.'

'He talks to you?'

'Or he was anyway . . . I know this sounds mad.'

She stood up and threw back her chair, then stuffed the Darkle into her bag and hauled the bag up onto her shoulder.

'Nathan Flack, what sort of floozy do you think I am? What sort of harebrained tart do you think I am? I'm not one of your willowy bimbos. You can't just spin me some pathetic yarn and I'll forget everything. No. No. No. Not only are you two-faced, mealy-mouthed, spineless and gutless. Not only are you a *liar*. Not only are you are a great, big disappointment to *me*. NOT ONLY DO YOU LET EVERY SINGLE PERSON WHO GETS CLOSE TO YOU *DOWN*. NOT ONLY DO YOU CREEP AND CRINGE AND WALLOW AND WHINE BUT *NOW*, NATHAN, *NOW*, YOU HAVE GONE *BONKERS BEYOND BELIEF. JAMES O'MAILER IS NOT REAL, FOR JESUS FUCKING CHRIST'S SAKE! AND IF YOU HAD ANY CONCERN FOR ME, YOU WOULDN'T ONLY TALK TO ME WHEN YOU'RE TRYING TO GET ME TO APPROVE OF ONE OF YOUR SLAPPERS!*'

As she turned to leave, her bag swung across the table and clipped the rim of her half-full wineglass, sending it flying off the edge and onto the floor where – after what seemed like a hundred years in which I realized that the whole bar was standing looking at me and had heard every single word – it smashed all over the floor.

Frances slammed the door behind her. The shockwave shuddered every intact glass in the bar. I shuffled around on my heels with little machinelike movements but nobody's face returned to their drinks, no one resumed their far more interesting conversations about the signified and the signifiers or whether Heathcliffe is a slice of haloumi or the anxiety of influence in Snow Patrol lyrics, and as I now faced where I'd been sitting Jane was back in her chair and forcing herself to look absently out at the fog. I must go to her. I must *explain*. A film of sweat covered my scalp, a far more chilling and nasty film of sweat than the sweat I'd broken into during the previous three hundred times women had shouted at me in crowded public places. But next to Jane, his eyes like a rodent's peering out of a hollow in a turnip, was Frank. And opposite Frank, stretching around and holding up a pint of lager as a salute to me, was Mac. And standing beside the table, soft drinks in hand, frozen in shock and outrage, were Reg and Cynthia.

Out of the skillet, onto the ceramic hob, to coin an elegant variation. I robot-walked over to the table just as Reg and Cynthia fell out of suspended animation or timequake, or whatever it was that protected

389

them from sexual swearwords and human emotion, and cautiously took their seats.

'Don't worry,' I said, easing myself past Mac to my chair. 'She's a poet.'

'Feisty little threes-up you got going on here,' said Mac.

I swallowed all of my new glass of wine in one gulp as Jane blushed crimson and Frank giggled and slapped the edge of the table with his big sausagey fingers.

'Well Flack,' said Reg. 'I think we have reached the nadir. God only knows what unseemly contretemps you're engaged in now, and there's us, all of us fee-paying customers who believed you when you said you were unwell and now we find you in some sort of saloon bar slanging match with a lovely young woman.'

'Don't matter,' said Frank. 'We had a right old time with Macky. Best class we've ever had.'

.

The MA

'Bladder trauma,' I said, then sprang out of my seat to attempt a nonchalant sidle that was more like a full-blown wazzock-flap out of the bar. All the while I told myself that I was made of see-through ice and that none of these splatter-hair girls and lumberjack shirts were staring at me going 'look at the wallower, look at the whiner' and that by the end of the week you wouldn't be able to download the camera-phone video clip of *Frances Mink: Swarm of Bees* from YouTube. I tried to convince myself that I had not let everyone down as I flustered across the walkway above the Union foyer to the gents. By the time I'd locked myself in a cubicle I had failed to convince myself that I had not let everyone down, and let myself down, or was bonkers beyond belief. I adopted the traditional creative writing tutor's angst-and-doom-on-the-toilet pose. With my luck, just about now, James O'Mailer would appear in the guise of the resurrected Francis Bacon and paint me disabused and losing it on the toilet and then display the gigantic canvas in the Turbine Hall of the Tate Modern so that all the middleclass, middle-aged disco dads in the Arctic, and all the people I went to school with could come in and point at my crusty, red face and chant: *we didn't fuck up like Nathan, we didn't fuck up like Nathan.*

Why did Frances have to do that? Embarrass me like that. Maybe it had been naive of me to think that my friendship with Frances could ever be sustained after we split up. Other people achieve these nice, measured, post-break arrangements, but not me. Lost touch with Johanna. Fell out with Lisa. I'd only ever been left with the grist for miserable short stories with disillusionment plot arcs and reviews that describe them as 'merely touching'. But, shit, I *had* been talking moon-barking nonsense, though. Telling Frances about O'Mailer. Fuck and bum and Plumrape.

I clawed at the film of sweat in my hair. So much for pulling out all the stops. This had to have been the worst class ever, worse than the night of the ram's head and that workshop with the Ipswich Group of Death when half of them started to weep during 'grammar tips checklist'. And Frances had just ruined any chance I ever had with Jane.

Sitting there with the drips and the clank of the pipes and the buzz of the air conditioning I realized that I had spelled it out for the first time that I did really want to have a chance with Jane. Oh toss. I was going to have to go back to the bar and get my bag, then cut and run from Jane to avoid an inevitable depressing conversation in the carpark behind the Eudora Doon.

Did you let her down, Nathan?

Yes.

Were you a disappointment, Nathan?

Yes.

Are you bonkers beyond belief?

Yes, Jane.

Maybe we ought to leave this alone before one of us, i.e. me, gets hurt.

I fully understand, Jane.

Don't use clichés, class, but you don't know what you've got until it's gone and the only love that lasts is unrequited love.

I would grab my stuff, then waddle home to cryogenically freeze myself on the sofa of shame until Plum rang tomorrow.

The dripping sound grew louder until I realized that it was not dripping but the sound of heavy footsteps going back and forth across the stone floor outside.

I sat and waited. I didn't want to see anyone, not even some chipper little undergrad piddling about sending a text, or some shell-shocked PhD in the midst of a life-crisis at least as shattering as mine. I sat and waited and the footsteps clicked back and forth across the floor and I thought of Jane and cringed at the memory of Frances's heat-ray eyes until I realized that I shouldn't be cowering here to avoid the face of a stranger outside. Sylvester Sly Ramos-Pintos wouldn't cower. The Fumigator shouldn't.

Breathe. Chest out. Stomach in. Nothing to fear but fear itself.

Outside the cubicle, Frank Denbigh was standing at the other end of the washroom.

Frank Denbigh was standing at the other end of the washroom, arms flat to his sides, sweat glinting on his top lip and his nose and his pink bald head. He smiled in that gummy, seemingly toothless way of his and his white spade beard was longer and wider and sharper than I'd ever seen it. As it would be, I realized, if he'd come straight here from the cells where I'd sent him. I knew what he was going to do. Something violently primal, something bloody and elemental beyond the imagination of Juicy Gash. The last stand of The Fumigator. Trisha Vidler: *c'est moi.* I checked the white walls and the cubicle doors. That's where I was going, in liquid form. I could picture the final scene of my bio-pic, my lonely bag dangling by its shoulder strap on the back of my chair in the bar, never again to be unpacked by my edjumakated man's hands[89].

'Oh Mister Nathan,' said Frank. 'I'm glad I caught up with you.'

'The others send you to look for me, Frank?' I said, backing into the hand-dryer.

'Oh no, Mister Nathan, I came all on my own speed, I did.'

'Why's that, Frank?'

'I was thinking that you and me could have a little chat.'

He was walking forwards, each limb rigid, and he grew bigger and bigger until he overshadowed me. The last time I had felt so threatened was when Johanna grabbed my arm at the Union Ball and the Colossus of the Cubes was there with his dirty great knife. I had met the love of my life in a gentleman's toilet escaping from an overgrown psychopath. I had met all the others in toilets. I would meet my end having prematurely squandered a new love only to be mashed to death by another overgrown psychopath. Frank and Pink Stripe: were they cousins, separated at birth, father and son, Cain and Able, Vladimir and Estragon, Bouvard and Pécuchet? The hand-dryer switched on and whirred and blew and a gust started to hot up the back of my shirt.

---

[89] This could equally, of course, be the trigger-image for one of Jane's PI Pashminski mysteries.

Frank was right close to me now. I could hear his breathing, see the white hair in his nostrils. The smile flashed out of his face as he gripped both of my soft hands and pulled me forwards.

'Oh Mister Nathan, you got to helps me. Will you help me, Mister Nathan?'

'What do you want me to do? I'll do anything, anything.'

'I need help.'

'I know you need help, Frank. There are a lot of people who can help you.'

'Big help, I need.'

'I'm glad you've said that Frank. I admire you for it, I do. It's a mature and difficult thing to admit.'

'Oh Mister Nathan, it is, it is.'

'Can you let go of my hands, Frank? You're squashing them.'

'Sorry, Mister Nathan, sorry, I don't know me own strength.'

'I understand that, I do, believe me.'

'Oh Mister Nathan, you're going to help me?'

'Yes, Frank, yes.'

'I really want to do it, Mister Nathan. It's calling for me.'

'Well, it's good that you've come to me, Frank, isn't it?'

'I need to do it. I can't help it. I must.'

'Right you are.'

'So you'll do it for me?'

'What do you actually want me to do, Frank, and I'll tell you want I think?'

'I want to do that MA, Mister Nathan.'

'What? *The* MA?'

'*Thee* MA, Nathan, I just want to do it. I want to say that I studied with the best. I want to be the best at it, I do. I got the money and I got the time and I want to write stories for children, I do.'

'Are you sure you're ready, Frank?'

'I got the nice little kind stories all up here.' He prodded his temple just as the dryer clicked off. 'Mister Nathan, I want to say that I studied with the best. Now I studied with you and with Mac I want to meet all the other best ones, too.'

Frank wanted to do *The* MA. He wanted *me* to write *him* a reference for *The* MA, an elite course that prided itself on shaping tomorrow's big name literary writers, a course that drew on writers from all around the world, that asked only for writers who would push the boundaries a little, masters of form, literary brainboxes, dedicated stylists, tellers of new types of story about the world we live in now. And to apply you need a project, a track record, a few publications, a considered aesthetic, proven devotion and the possibility of repaying further glory to *The* MA by becoming one of its shield-bearers and trailblazers, one of its award-winners, review page *cause célèbres* and publishing phenomena. And you need to prove that you tick the right demographic categories – no Literature Deniers, no Grammar-Stammerers, only devotees of Borges and Barthes, Lacan and Zizek – and show that you perform well in workshop situations, that you have something to say, something to contribute and a gushing reference from a well-known and respected agent or author like I had from Sebastian. That's what it implied in *The* MA Prospectus anyway, not that the reality bore any of this flimflam out. Not that anybody in my time ever fulfilled the above criteria (I had sat in a chilly room for a year with people in aggressive competition with one another whilst being taught by tutors who didn't seem to exist; *The* MA is the only degree in the world taught posthumously by the staff, an appropriately post-modern circumstance, I feel). But, in my position as locally respected (i.e., outside of *The* MA) creative writing tutor Nathan Flack I had to be very careful about who I refereed. I could make myself look like a plank. I could compromise myself. I could further corroborate the widely held view that I was not to be taken seriously. And Frank, author of the worrying slash-fest *She's Taking a Train* and rosy-cheeked boyhood chum of the Angel of Trunch, wanted me to give him a reference for *The* MA.

I knew what I should do. Get Mac to write one. Or better still, get Mac to get Plum to write one. Plum would write a reference for anyone as long as they pledged their undying loyalty to the Priory of Plumion. But I was not a writer anymore, the mystic scroll of *The* MA had done nothing for me whatsoever and after tonight I was going to lose my job and Frank's hands were now raised at the level of my ears.

'I'll write you a reference. Of course. What else am I here for?'

I barely survived the bear hug that followed and out on the walkway Frank shook my hand so vigorously that he almost tore out my ribcage. I congratulated myself a little. I was belatedly playing the Plum game. The only measly plus point about tonight was that I'd probably drawn Frank back from the grey centre circle of the game. Then again, I'd probably replaced his holding position there with Jane, and ensured that Frances was probably out on loan with the Priory of Plumion United FC Academicals with a view to a permanent move. Fuck and tit and Plumrape.

'Thank you very much, Mister Nathan,' said Frank. 'It has been a most trying week.'

'I understand that, Frank. And I'm sorry to hear of your troubles.'

'Most regrettable it all has been.'

'Frank, can I ask you something?'

'Of course, Mister Nathan.'

'Look, you know that little misunderstanding when Doctor Jane and I accidentally strayed into your van because we thought it was Jane's brother's dormobile and we were looking for some CDs he'd borrowed and left in there after he'd parked it outside her house because his wife had bought another car without his knowing while he was away on business and then found out that they only had one permit?'

'Oh yes, Mister Nathan. Don't worry about that. Even I understand what complicated webs we weave.'

'No, there's no complicated web, it's just when we were in there, we found this sort of scarecrow thing, and I just sort of . . . wondered what it was?'

'Oh Mister Nathan, Davie put it there, Davie did.' He poked out his chin and raised his head, towering over me once more and shouted up at the striplight. 'And if I ever find out who told on me like that, I'll swing for her, I surely will.'

He turned and strode along the walkway back to bar and as he did so, from where I was rooted to floor, I noticed that Doctor Jane was standing outside the Grad Bar with my bag slung over her shoulder. As Frank reached her he bridled like an attack dog jerked on a choke chain, then passing her threw open the doors as if spoiling for a showdown in a bar room brawl.

Tape's Last Krapp

Five minutes later I found myself exactly where I'd feared: in the carpark behind the Eudora Doon Building waiting for my nth earful of the day (Erika + Plum + Cynthia + Reg + Frances + Frank = Jane says, 'you're weird, you're nuts, never speak to me again').

'You've got to do something,' said Jane, 'before he does.' We were standing next to her Nissan Micra. She'd been repeating this all the way back from the Union. Now though, her measured words made it seem like she was merely brainstorming a delicate work issue. Part of me thought she was enjoying this: the frisson of jeopardy, the surge of adventure, the complication of our plot. She was right, though. Anger Frank was turning gamma radiation green, becoming Frank Smash before my very eyes. This was going to end with embarrassment and humiliation all round unless I hit his bullseye with a max-strength tranquilliser dart. I knew that I wouldn't get anywhere by reaching out to Plum. And even if Plum removed Frank from the course it was as good as over, and he knew where Jane lived.

'OK,' I said, pacing a little, arms folded. 'What if I ring him up and say that you're a bit worried, and would he moderate his behaviour. We love you, Frank, but you risk giving people the wrong idea blah blah. I think he'll cool down.'

'Would you do that for me?' said Jane.

'Look, we're unsung heroes here. The real Angel's been caught because of us.'

'Well that's a lovely way of putting it.'

She paused to smooth down the scarlet pashmina. I waited for her to have a go about Frances, but Jane pointed at something on the other side of the carpark.

'His van is still here,' she said.

'The others will be back soon.' I checked my watch. Last orders in the Grad Bar. 'I could do without seeing them again today.'

'Me too. Can I offer you a lift?'

I accepted. She drove with gently emphatic pedalwork and her patent leather gloves glinted as she adjusted the steering wheel. My ribcage began to swell with warmth again. In my head I ricocheted between the side-plates of 'my place or yours?' then hit the bumper bar of 'fancy a late drink in town?' before always returning to slow-slide into the game-over of 'goodnight, sorry'.

'I suppose I really pissed everyone off tonight?' I said.

'I don't know,' she said, flicking the indicator. 'I don't think they know what they want, do they?'

'It's not just me, then?'

'I felt for you, you know, when she was shouting at you.'

'You did? I thought you were angry with me, how it looked.'

'I was trying to tell you earlier that it doesn't matter how it looks. I don't know what it is, so I don't know how it looks.'

She darted her eyes at me, as if wanting me to say something, but two hooded teenagers appeared in the road, forcing her to concentrate on driving.

'I'm sorry about Frances,' I said. 'She didn't mean it.'

'I read somewhere once,' said Jane as she turned into a side-road, 'that everyone needs to speak a certain number of words a day or they go mad. Maybe she's not using up her quota.'

'How many words a day do you need to speak?'

'Can't remember. Do you know where I'm going?'

'Hit the main road. Take a right.'

'You know, I don't really believe that you're not writing *anything*.'

'Oh I can't write what people want to read,' I said. 'I can't write something where an arcane conspiracy theory underpins Western Civilization, or a story that ends with an apocalyptic medieval battle or where people with gender issue confusions find love and peace of mind.'

'That doesn't mean that you're not writing anything.'

'Oh I am, then,' I said. 'It's called *Tape's Last Krapp*. Nathan Tape, right, is a burnt-out hack, eighty years old, who has been living in this terrible icebound garret for fifty odd years and it's got so cold and he's got so poor that he's reduced to sitting on his toilet seat and recording his lunatic mutterings on a dictaphone whose batteries gave up sometime between the third invasion of Iran and the shutting down of the last power station.'

'Is Sylvester in it?'

'Tape is not Sylvester's type'

'Oh put him in it, just for me.'

'You're asking me to compromise my art?'

'No, I'm asking you where you live?'

'Just up here past the second lamppost.'

'Is your flat that bad?'

'Worse.'

'Can I see it?'

She pulled up outside the garret house and parked the car without any jolt to the chassis.

'Look, why don't we go into town?' I said.

She took the keys out of the ignition.

'You have red wine?'

'You're driving.'

'And if I get tipsy, you can walk me home, or call me a cab.'

'Don't judge, OK?'

'Nathan, I spend much of my working life in sewers. Unshakeable Jane, that's what they call me.' She raised her arm and squeezed her biceps. 'As strong as silk. And anyway, I'm not the one judging you.' I sat and thought about this as she slipped out of the car and put her bag in the boot. It was only when she knocked on the side-window of the passenger door that I was able to join her on the pavement. Ahead of us the garret house loomed. The ground floor bedsit was unlit and the curtains pulled. Inside, in the hallway, my heart began to beat in that indeterminate way again as I put my finger to my lips and nodded at the bedsit door.

'Erika,' I whispered, then put both my hands over my mouth.

'Erika,' Jane whispered.

'She might be in.'

'She might not.'

We stood there with our mouths both covered before I pointed up the stairs.

'No disturbing the beast in the cellar,' I said on the landing as I let us into the garret.

'Oh I do sympathize with her,' said Jane as I led her into the front room and turned on the light. 'She clearly needs help, but that horrible munching tonight. Disgusting. Oh!'

The uncleanable russet carpet seemed to spring up at us. In a pincer movement it combined with the dead fist of the indoor cold. The sprawling piles of papers and books and videos laughed at me like smug squatters with the law on their side. The sofa of shame murmured lies about Nathan K in Jane's ear as the nicotine-stained iMac hollered 'Get the unholy temptress out of the inner sanctum'.

'I understand entirely if you'd like to leave now,' I said.

'No, it's just a bit . . . I lived in a place like this once, when I was a student.'

'Those days never left me. You can see the butter drips of crumpets on the upholstery.'

'Did you say you had wine? Perhaps I need a shot.'

In the kitchen I found a bottle and then an opener. As I levered out the cork I realized that my parallel line of thought here, that I ought to wash out the glasses even though they were nominally clean, was indicative of the sorry truth that I'd not had a woman back to the garret since I'd moved here, apart from Frances a couple of times and Plum once when she came round to be nosy and give me a bollocking about something bollocking-unnecessary. But Jane had not fled in horror. She was in the next room browsing my stuff. I could hear her footsteps trace the scorched crash site of the carpet. The radiator effect powered up my chest again and my heart rocketed as I sluiced out the glasses. When I poured the wine, I hesitated, a little scared now. She might be Unshakeable Jane but I was still Flyweight Flack the Fumigated. I looked out of the window, at the road opposite the house. There were no people, just parked cars smudged by the fog. I remembered that at the very beginning of the course, the night I met Jane, I saw the Hooded Figure creep up that road and then O'Mailer had spoken to me about the quest for the first time, making me think that he was real, not a side effect of new term nerves. He was not real, surely, yet I kept thinking about him, vacillating. I'd told Frances about him. I'd panicked then. Must have. The way Frances stared and swarmed. Then I considered what Jane said in the car. Everyone needs to speak a set number of words a day to maintain his or her emotional balance. Since Lisa left me I'd been living a secluded, sedentary and lonely life. My daily average spoken wordcount had slumped to about twenty-five, and most of those exchanged with call centre workers in Bangalore trying to sell me another mobile phone. And O'Mailer? O'Mailer was that shortfall of words given personality by my imagination. And what had O'Mailer insisted upon most? That Jane and I should be together. It was all roundabout. It was all distorted. But it was true. I needed to speak to her about it. I needed to speak more. Maybe speak more, write less. Perhaps I ought to talk a lot more and not write at all. This was academic in any case, because I couldn't write anyway, and so I might as well compensate with some excellent speaking. She didn't care that the garret was a squalid mess contrary to her Rom-T dreams of the tranquil, stylish writer's pad-cum-study. *She* wasn't judging me. As I stood beneath the striplight I held up one of the wineglasses and admired its cool, wet curve.

Jane was perusing my bookshelf, which to me, now standing behind her with two glasses, seemed like a flashback from my daydream that morning of seducing the odd, educated girl from downstairs. She'd taken off her pashmina. It lay on the cushions of the sofa of shame. She was wearing a black A-line skirt and a black short sleeved blouse.

'Have you read all these books?' she said, turning to face me.

'No,' I said, handing her a drink. 'They're just ornaments to impress the chicks.'

'Well, I'm impressed.'

'So was my last girlfriend. My Stradivarius particularly impressed her, and that *Les Demoiselles d'Avignon* hangs in the bathroom. And she was especially struck by my signed first edition of *Jaws* by Peter Benchley.'

'So this is where it all happens,' she said, standing close to me now by the window.

'What happens?'

'Your writing.'

'This is where my writing doesn't happen.'

'You're just having a little break, I'm sure.'

She took a long swig of her wine and then rested the glass on top of the television. Unshakeable Jane. Looking into me like she had in the conservatory, like she had in the van. She reached over and she touched my wrist and her eyes seemed to shower me with their intense blue sheen. I threw back the wine and placed the glass next to hers. She took both my hands. The radiator feeling in my chest went thermonuclear as it coursed into my boxer shorts.

'This is very naughty,' she said. 'It's the sort of thing that would happen in one of my stories.'

'I thought your stories were all about racing car drivers and men like Sylvester.'

'Only my cover stories.'

'Well, it's a fine literary genre,' I said. 'In My Life as a Man by Philip Roth, a writing tutor called Nathan Zuckerman marries a woman called Lydia he meets in class.'

'Ah, a happy ending at last,' she said, leaning forwards.

'No,' I said. 'Lydia kills herself with a can-opener.'

'You're safe. I only buy ring-pulls.'

Her arms slipped around my back as my arms slipped around her waist. My chin sank into her shoulder and I pulled her close to me. The thermonuclear warmth went supernova. Not because Jane was feverishly warm – it was impossible to become that hot in the garret – but because it had just been so very long since I'd been this close to anyone.

She kissed the side of my face.

'I do like you,' she said.

'I like you, too,' I said.

'Can I ask you something?'

'Anything?'

'Who's James O'Mailer?'

'He lives in the Grand Anglian.'

'Frances mentioned him.'

'You don't want to know about James O'Mailer.'

I shuffled around on the balls of my feet until I was facing the desk and she the window. Savouring the cuddle, I prolonged it, loving the sensation of her frizzy hair as I held it to the nape of her neck and the way my hand pressed into the silky material of her blouse. She sidled her hips, then shivered and took her head off my shoulder. This was it. A kiss. *The* kiss. *The* kiss was coming, and I wanted to be ready for *the* kiss, wanted to describe it later to myself in the most vivid and sensory and multi-dimensional way that I was capable.

Jane's face blocked out the room, but then she paused, stiffened and retreated. Her elbows pushed my arms away until I almost unbalanced and toppled backwards onto the sofa of shame.

'Oh my God, what is that!' she said.

I looked around for something nasty lurking in a shadowy corner of the garret. Damn the garret. A pox upon the garret. But I couldn't see anything exotic. And Jane was pointing not at the carpet or the sofa or the gubbins and trash everywhere, but to the window, at something in the street. 'What on earth is that?'

Starfishing

It was heading right for us, dead on the camber of the road opposite with a misty half-moon high above it. Greyed by the fog, it seemed to glide, not march towards the house. The hair on my arms and my neck lifted from my skin and the film of sweat prickled across my scalp again. Ringed by my onion-white face and Jane's stupefied stare reflected in the windowpane the Hooded Figure checked neither left nor right as it came straight at us. A brown-cowled thing. The stalker and lurker. The Beast in the Cellar. I wouldn't have felt reality spin out of kilter if it had floated clear off the ground to pass right through the glass with its talons outstretched. Except, this, I knew, was no supernatural apparition.

'Right, that's it,' I said.

'Who is it?' said Jane.

'Her.'

'Frances?'

'Erika.'

'Erika?'

'I told you things were weird.'

'Not this weird?'

'Jane, do you know how you go about having someone sectioned?'

Outside, Erika the Hood crossed the road and stepped onto the pavement in front of the house. She was right below us, her arms crossed over her chest and her hands hidden by the sleeves. I noticed then that the lawn, which at this time of night was usually invisible in the dark, was now lit up. A glow illuminated the scraggy lawn and the hedge. As Erika the Hood reached the path and then tilted her head up at my window, the front door smashed open and Erika Gretsch, in a pink and yellow floral dressing gown and clogs that clattered on the path like galloping hooves, stormed straight at The Hood. The Hood threw out his arms in defence – I could tell as the sleeves slipped to his elbows that they were a man's hands, definitely male – and he staggered, tried to turn as Erika locked her hands around his neck.

'It's not her,' I said, looking at Jane's shocked, confused face. 'Bloody hell, it's not her.' I waited for Jane to say something, but she just stood there with her hand over her mouth as Erika tossed The Hood onto the bonnet of the Micra.

'Oh no, my car,' said Jane.

'I'll call the police,' I said.

'Nathan . . . per-lease.'

We thumped down the stairs. In the hallway, the front door was wide open to the night. Jane ran ahead, pure PI Pashminski, Unshakeable Jane, but it was all rushing through me, fear and bafflement and what would confront us when we stepped in to break this up, and who was under that hood? Erika's clone? Erika's twin? Erika's disembodied mind made flesh? Arnold Bumrape? Arnold Bumrape ripping off his rubber mask to reveal the smug visage of Sharon Plum or Mac MacMahon or James O'Mailer?

I came to a halt when the thought punched me. The bedsit's door was ajar. *She* was outside with the thuds and the yelps and the distorted voices. And inside her room somewhere was my kidnapped starfish.

Then I found myself standing under in the glare of a bare light bulb of some 7000 watts that seemed to strip the corneas from my eyes. The Gretsch bedsit was the garret at the edge of the universe. No wonder the Winding Finn had returned to Winding Finland. Dusty, carpetless, no furniture or features, it was a suicide-watch cell or some long forgotten stock dump of discontinued lines and recalled goods. Boxes were stacked to the ceiling on three sides. One heap, though, was almost concealed by a two-metre tall mountain of stuffed carrier bags. Through the bay window, their legs concealed by the hedge, I could see Jane trying to pull Erika off The Hood. I'd nab the starfish, then rush out to help Jane.

There were more mice than men in this shoddily laid plan. I scanned the bags. Shapes, some angular, some rounded, some spiky strained against the polythene. It could be anywhere. I was never going to find it among all this detritus and toss. In my mind's eye I pictured the ram's head, the choker of shadow around its jowls. Some of this stuff might be wet. Some of it might even be still alive. A cry from outside spun me around towards the window. A hand flailed over the top of the bushes. Jane's frizzy hair appeared then ducked under the level of the hedge. I shouldn't be doing this. I should be out there. Out there Jane was wrestling with Moon-Barkers. Out there was the Hooded Figure and now Jane had seen him; Erika Gretsch had seen him. He *was* real and pinned to Jane's car by Erika, and for the life of me I wanted to know who it was. I was halfway to the door when I froze.

The Starfish. The Starfish was here. I could sense it. Calling to me. Willing me to rescue it. Johanna's starfish. The starfish she gave me in Australia. *Touch it and always think of me.*

Back at the pile, I picked up a bag and emptied a dozen or so plastic plant pots over the floor. No starfish. Then I poured a bag of pick-and-mix Duplo Lego bricks, Apostle spoons and bizarrely uniform twigs onto the pots. When the clatter subsided I heard shouting from outside again. Johanna's starfish. So what? Should forget about Johanna. Nothing could ever recover that time. Smash the starfish or bury it. It *was* buried. Jane was outside, in trouble, and minutes ago a whole new adventure was opening up and it had felt good, felt great, it was sweet and lovely and living. This wasn't living. Questing for a dead marine invertebrate of dubious personal significance. That life was gone. I knew it was gone. I knew it was over.

The rubbish mounds drew one half of me while the other was tractor-beamed by the fracas outside. Through the window I saw the hood flee along the hedge with Erika in pursuit and Jane following. I sprayed a bag of little wooden Noah's Ark figurines all over the place and rummaged in a melange of giant industrial bolts and oblong things wrapped in newspaper. The starfish. I needed that starfish. I had touched it every morning when I was writing *Penelope* and it had kept me alive and alert. I had touched it throughout the composition of everything I had written from *The Drowners* onward. I needed it. Bollocks to O'Mailer and Mount Parnassus. I'd dried up when Gretsch nicked my starfish. Without writing I felt like a man in the grip of the most incapacitating lust who has given up hope of ever being with a woman again. I felt like a man who's given up on ever being with a woman again *and* on top of that he couldn't write anymore. I was going to get it back. I was starfishing here.

I found a cuddly badger with a bellows strapped to its back with pink ribbon.

Then a fluorescent orange newspaper boy's sack padded with confetti and tickertape that blew around the room, fluttering and swirling as I held in my hand a hedgehog-shaped pincushion impaled with dozens of toothpicks.

Wishbones. A poultry farm of wishbones.

A typewriter with the keys clipped off.

Seven broomheads glued together in a lopsided pyramid shape.

And then, right at the edge of the heap, I heaved up a black bin liner that contained a solid block of something. With confetti in my hair and on my shirt and my sleeves and drifting all around me like the morning after I ripped off the plastic and discovered what at first I thought was a manuscript.

It wasn't a manuscript. Not quite. It was poems. Hundred and hundreds of poems. The complete works of Erika Gretsch.

I held up the bundle, lodging it against my chest with my elbow and sped-read the first few poems.

The He.

The He is Flea-God of Petrol-lungs

He comes

From Thrace, with Grace and Tongues.

He will

Sit upon your Guns.

Behold!!!

Time of The He.

Sitting here
So lonely-hearted
I tried to moo
But I only thought
Of my fear of the terrible
HE.

He is Coming

He

He

He

He

He

He is coming for us.

He

He

He

He

He

He is coming for you.

He

He

He

He

He

Will be the Last One Ever.

I reread this last poem. The professional editor and reader in me giggled, relieved that whatever I'd ever committed to paper or print had at least been semi-coherent. I had another browse and flipped through the pages. They were all 'He' poems. 'He and Tallahassee', 'He Loves Sledge Toffee Baby,' 'The Holy See and He and Me and a Flea' and so on and so on. I paced around in the confetti whirlwind until I stopped laughing and realized that at Moonshot Erika had declared herself the 'Herald of The He' and The He had seemed to be me whatever Frances had said about The He being anyone who crossed paths with the Gretsch. Still holding the sheet, I glanced at the window. I couldn't see or hear anything now.

The front door slammed. Muttering in the hallway. Erika's weird Teutonic voice and Jane's higher, soothing voice. When Jane led in by the arm a sobbing, quavering Erika, the room seemed doubly peculiar with other people in it. The confetti seemed to immediately attract itself to them as if suddenly bored with me. Hearts and star shapes stuck to Jane's hair.

'Oh I see,' she said, her lipstick slashed across her chin and the sleeve of her blouse ripped at the shoulder. 'Found some time to read, I see.' Her head tilted to one side and her eyes fixed on me in a way that reminded me of the scary Welsh primary school teacher who locked me in a cupboard for saying 'shit' during Fractions. No, her stare reminded me of Frances. She let go of Erika and stamped her foot. The stark clunk on the boards caused Erika to spring across the room at me, a blur of yellow and black.

'My poems,' she yelped and grabbed the bundle. 'Do not defile them.'

'What on earth are you doing?' said Jane.

'Who me?' I said.

'Look at the state of you. Look at the state of this room.'

I pointed at the poetry slab that Erika now clutched to her chest.

'Those insane poems are about me.'

'They are the poems of The He,' said Erika.

'She followed me to London and disrupted my reading with bonkers verse about The He. She's been writing crap poems about me, she's been following me about and she moved in here to . . . I don't know.'

'You,' said Erika. She dropped the bundle as she pointed at me. 'You are not The He. You, you persecute.'

'For the last time, I have not been persecuting you.'

'Well,' said Jane. 'It seems that man in the cloak wasn't Erika, was it?'

'Who was it?'

'I don't know. Some guy,' said Jane. 'He ran off.'

'She attacked him.'

'Nathan, she clearly can't look after herself.'

'Where's my starfish?' I said to Erika.

'You see? You see now?' she said to Jane. 'He persecutes.'

'Right,' said Jane. 'I'm going home.'

She took one last look around the Gretsch garret and without acknowledging me walked out into the hall. I caught up with her on the step. Erika's door slammed behind us.

'Jane,' I said. 'Come back. Please. I need to talk to you.'

She licked the palm of her hand and wiped the lipstick smudge from her face. The tear in her blouse revealed a strip of pale skin that seemed both teasing and glumly chastising.

'You're right, Nathan,' she said. 'The He. Her. Monks. Starfish. This is all too weird, even for me.'

'Oh don't be like that, please. If she hadn't . . . if it hadn't turned up and she started a fight and . . .'

'You hadn't ransacked her room to laugh at her poems while I . . .' She flexed her shoulder to emphasise the rip.

'It wasn't like that, Jane.'

'Goodnight Nathan.'

I watched her click up the path, get into her car and drive off. I stood there for what seemed like a long time staring at the space where her car had been parked until the chill air became too much for me. Upstairs, I found her scarlet pashmina still draped over the sofa of shame. I sat next to it and waited for something to happen. I wasn't sure at all what I was waiting for. All the while, from downstairs I could hear Erika's footfalls and her reciting her words, 'The He . . .' 'The He . . .' 'The He . . .'

Endings

The Last of My Enchanted Objects

Never get into the car of an hysterically drunk man shouting about 'block'. This writing tip is doubly relevant when that drunk driver is the author and critic Sebastian Harker. And trebly so when you soon suspect that his journey from The Arctic to The Shire has been a death-ride of blazing internal monologue punctuated by brandy pit-stops and screams of 'block' at pub toilet walls and wary barmen. If you want to live to see your next session of morning practise, don't emerge after you see him park his car diagonally across the pavement outside your garret. Don't accept his out-swung arm across the gaping passenger door of his battered black Daimler and then plant your weekend bags on his backseat that is scattered with spent bottles of whiskey. Don't let him get back into the car and reverse into moving traffic, where a multi-car pile-up is only avoided by the whim of the Gods who have other, more subtle terrors yet reserved for the pair of you.

But I did, so there. I'd already forgotten more about writer's block than Seb would ever know. I'd been shipwrecked on this particular islet of bleached shingle and albatross skeletons for so long that it felt normal. Earlier that day I had received a two-line letter from the last literary agency on my list, Dexter and Geezensax, declining to read *The Penelope Tree*. I'd had a good rant at the off-white goods in the garret until I felt numb, exhausted and fraudulent to be teaching on a creative writing weekend.

As we hit the ringroad, Seb one-handedly swerved the car around two Transit vans of unique dirtiness and an articulated lorry of brutish size. This didn't faze me. This was fitting. He was to blame anyway. Down and down we would go together. If he hadn't encouraged me in my novel-writing exploits ten years ago I'd be a nice, happy, prosperous call centre manager in suburban Surrey, enjoying my leisure time and pay-per-view and the company of my unhappy, uninspired wife who flogs her knickers on *Ebay* to Norwegian oil rig workers while I dream about winning *The X Factor* or *Big Brother*. It was apt that Seb and I should converge at the same plot point. This was the end of the affair for the zeroes of our time. Judgement at Kollocks Grange. Our last engagement as writers of prose before shoulder to shoulder we sped over the cliff top together.

The traffic ahead began to slow for lights. 'Blox,' shouted Seb and pounded the wheel with his fist. He then took his eye off the road to rummage in the glove compartment, I assumed for a cigarette. The muscles in my face tightened. As we approached the rear end of the Saab in front I whipped out my hand to grab the wheel.

'Seb, slow the car, you arse.'

He braked and changed gear. We pulled up just short of the Saab's back bumper and waited for the lights to change.

'Blox?' I said.

'Blox,' said Seb. 'That prick-eared imbecile.'

'Cross these lights, then pull up outside PC World.'

'No. I'm not PC. I'm not. I'm going to keep saying the unfuckingsayable.'

'Not now you're not, Edgar Allen. Get us over there before you get us killed.'

Somehow we made it across the junction, this time our lives threatened by Seb inching the car along in some gear midway between neutral and first. We then trickled into the carpark and sat looking out at the lovely yellow and red logo of *PC World*.

'Blox?' I said.

'It's finished,' said Seb. 'The bastard cancelled my deal. *Kill Cyclops*, it's remaindered. The stock of my entire list . . . pulped.'

'What?'

'I am now second-hand.'

'I don't believe it. Didn't Marcus do anything?'

'My agent? What did my agent do? What did my agent who over the years has had tens of thousands of pounds off the back of me, what did my agent do? He retired. That's what he did. He bloody retired.'

'You'll get another agent, Seb, you're not me.'

'Fuck that Blox. I'll pump him full of castor oil and string him up by his feet.'

'Why did Marcus retire?'

'Went round to see him. Went round is an understatement. Struck his house like the marriage of whisky and lightening, and the old flower just sat there and said that "something unfortunate is happening. Something is coming that's going to change things forever". "It's over," he said, "it's over for me and it's over for you".'

'What does that mean?'

'Blox, that's what it means. Just because of that little misunderstanding.'

'Well . . .'

'That porcine thug . . . not only has he chopped me, he's chopped nearly everyone I know at Dewsenberry. Theodore Smithson. Penny Viril. Dear old Hosni Jipek. Paul Chance. All of us. All out of contract. All out of print overnight.'

'That's a cull.'

'It's a pogrom, that's what it is. Cossacks ahoy!'

'Steady on. '"Accuracy of statement" and all that.'

'Don't you edit me, boy.'

'Do you want to go home?' I said. 'The guest pulling out won't make things any worse than they already are.'

'No,' said Seb. 'We . . . you and I . . . we're the last ones left.'

'I'm driving though. You're having a nap.'

After I managed to get Seb into the back of the car I paused and reacquainted myself with using the accelerator pedal to gently turn over the engine.

'Er Seb,' I said, edging the car out into the traffic. 'Am I insured?'

He was already asleep. I carried on cautiously, meticulously. I'd not driven a car since splitting up with Johanna and losing access to the Fiat Panda in the shakedown. Driving without insurance seemed an apt description of my life since then. I bet that Badminton Prawn wouldn't have driven without insurance and that my parallel universe call-centre manager self would be covered up to his fat arse. As I turned off the ringroad and headed away from the city, into the suburbs and towards the open countryside and Kollocks Grange I checked on Seb in the mirror. He was snoring, curled up in a foetal position, the tips of his brogues poking into the carrier bag that contained Jane's scarlet pashmina.

After the Gretsch Garret Debacle, I'd hoped that Jane would calm down, realizing that it was all silly bollocks and not worth falling out over. This time I did phone her, seven or eight times on Wednesday and Thursday, but she never picked up and I didn't want to leave a message in case I sounded like a Moon-Barker. I decided that I needed other news to smooth my path back to Pashminaland. So I called up Frank Denbigh, the Wrong-Roomer on course for the wrongest room of all, the room of *The* MA, thinking that I could use a chat about the reference as a way of mentioning his attitude to Jane and thus diffuse at least one of the ticking time bombs. I could then contact Jane with something breezy and positive. But Frank too didn't answer, so I left a plea on his unpersonalized phone company answering service. He didn't call me back. I wasn't even sure he'd turn up for the residential, and so had nothing breezy and positive to put me back into favour with Jane. All I had was the pashmina.

In the grey ashtray light and the hammerhead silence of the garret I had vegged for two days. Sometimes I found myself speculating on the hooded figure. Maybe he was actually a monk. Perhaps I had a neighbour who was a monk out of orders and that's all he was, a friendly passing monk who had become a grand phantasm in my mind and just another background artist in *Gretsch Attacks*. I wanted to ask Jane about the scuffle and what she had seen of him. I ought to ask Erika, but I couldn't face her. My only new distraction was tracking her movements in and out of the building and planning another raid on the starfish. I could hear her mutter and intone to herself downstairs as lying on the sofa of shame on Wednesday afternoon I tried to think of what I could do to make it up to Jane. If I were her, what would I appreciate, apart from not being drawn into a paranoid psychodrama and the return of a much loved and probably expensive scarlet pashmina? Then I had a brainwave. I would write her a story as an apology, something light and funny and romantic that she'd really enjoy, that would put me in a better light and show her that I wasn't a barker. It would be a *PI Pashminski* mystery, a short fiction in which PI takes on a case for someone just like me. This fired me up. No pressure. Just a pleasurable, cheeky jaunt with words. But as soon as I sat down to sketch or compose a powerful headache hit me and red gauze seemed to cloud my eyes, a collusion of symptoms I labelled the crimson migraine. If I really pushed myself, thinking that I was merely rusty I'd feel a twinge in my chest and flashback the dream of Parnassus and O'Mailer's stabbing blade. In the end all I managed to create was a canine sidekick for Arnold Bumrape called Sododog.

I checked the mirror as we drove along a lane of almost leafless oak trees that years of Siberian wind had turned into curled-over, ink-black whorls. Seb was still asleep. We were approaching Kollocks. Now I was sure that he'd rouse himself soon and in a panic throw up all that whisky and bile into the carrier bag and spoil the last of my enchanted objects[90].

---

[90] Although I never managed to actually write my PI Pashminski story, I did brood on it a lot and if I had been able to write it I imagine now that it would have turned out something like this:

The Black Starfish

A PI Pashminski Mystery

By Stradivarius D'Avignon

I

When he came into my office that October afternoon I could have sworn I'd seen him somewhere before. It was something about his eyes, the way that they flicked from his shoes to my Scarlet Collar boots, only taking in my face for an instant at a time as if he were a schoolboy with a crush on his stern yet ravishing headmistress. But I'd done my research, as I always do before I meet a new client, and whatever Nate Flake did with his time it hadn't hit the gossip columns or the review pages yet. Maybe by the look of him though, he'd appeared once or twice in the lonely hearts.

'I'm glad that you were able to make time to see me, Ms Pashminski. I'm in a hurry to get back to my moping and the outside world is a little daunting.' There was a trace of London in his voice that we East Anglians find privately endearing.

We shook hands and I gestured him towards the sofa. Outside, a stiff wind battered the city and autumn leaves fluttered up into the sky, but in my little office the heating was on and it could have been high summer.

'Do you not get out much, Mr Flake?'

'I try not to. I'm a writer, you see, a writer of detective novels. You may have heard of me? I write under the name of Stradivarius d'Avignon? The *Inspector Gloucestershire* series?'

I smiled, and felt a longing for the summery days when I could spread out on a lounger with a Pimms and a box of chocolates and devour trashy crime novels all day. I'd always had a little thing for the writers of those books: Raymond Chandler with his tweeds and cigarette and massive drink problem. Dashing Dashiell talking up his Continental Op. Smooth-talking Ross MacDonald with his wandering hands. But I'd spent none of my dreamy hours in the company of any Inspector Gloucestershire.

'I'm afraid I've not heard of them or him or your pen name, Mr Flake.'

He tilted his head, ruefully. 'That's why I'm here,' he said. 'Researching my latest novel *Norwich Confidential* may have caused me some unwanted attention.'

'How do you mean?'

'I'd been looking into the career of a local player, a Mr Sylvester Sly Ramos-Pintos, a rough and ready type, finger in all sorts of beef and onion. You must have heard of him?'

'I can't say I have, but he sounds most intriguing.'

'Well, shortly after I began I started to feel that I was being watched, and then I noticed someone standing outside my flat.'

'People are allowed to stand outside of flats. I do it a lot.'

'Are you not a private detective, Ms Pashminski? This was a monk in a cowl.'

'A monk?'

'Then there was a break-in. Something of great value was stolen. That's why I'm here. I want you to get it back.'

'Let me guess. Some secret papers? A priceless artefact? What you scribblers would call a McGuffin?'

'I wouldn't send you on a quest for the sake of a quest, Ms Pashminski. I've lost my psychological crutch. I need it to write, you see. If I don't have it I go a little berserk. I can't make proper decisions. I have to do everything in a roundabout way. It sounds silly, I know.'

'Yes it does, but I've heard much sillier.' I remembered the case of Cyn Whacker and the lengths I went to recover her collection of washed-out underwear.

'It's a black starfish, Ms Pashminski. I believe Mr Ramos-Pintos may have sent one of his associates to steal it. If I don't have it, I can't write, you catch me. Now I can't write about him and expose him.'

He leaned forwards and handed me enough cash to keep me in cashmere for several seasons.

'I do take credit cards, Mr Flake,' I said.

420

'I don't trust banks,' he said, then rattled through in quickfire a little more of the backstory. One of Ramos-Pintos's minions, a Reggie Carn, was his regular fence but Flake had no idea where he could be found.

He walked out of the office backwards with a look of exhausted relief on his face before I realized that he'd left no contact information. I spun about on my chair for no good reason at all and played with the money, my mind hopping between shopping for shoes and the outstanding bills without angsting over the outcome. I wondered how a writer I didn't know could afford such a stake and how a man who seemed to live indoors could get involved with a criminal mastermind I'd never heard of. Norwich is a small pond and the big fish stink the place out.

I summoned up a number on my mobile and called Frank Dank, my old super at Norfolk Vice, the so-called Sewer Division.

'Pash, you ain't calling to tell me you found some naughty filly we might want to take a long look at?'

'No, Frankie, you filthy pig. You heard of a local big shot called Sylvester Sly Ramos-Pintos?'

'Sweetie-Pie who?'

'Reggie Carn? Handler of stolens?'

'Knickers or kisses?'

'No, specialist items, weirdo candy, bookworm food?'

'He's a popular fellow, that Reggie, you're the second one to ask about him this week.'

'Really, who else is on the scent?'

'Don't know. Some ponce phoned.'

'Where can I find Carn?'

'Runs a school for backward kids out on the ringroad.'

'You know there's no such thing as backward nowadays, Frank, you seventies reptile.'

'You been out of Vice too long, Pash. It used to be fun on the farm . . .'

I hung up before I could have a flashback. Out of my window I thought I saw Nate Flake browsing in the Well-Thumbed bookstore opposite, but then I thought that I'd not seen this at all. I drew a black starfish on my jotter and had a bit of a think as I rolled the name 'Sylvester Sly Ramos-Pintos' around with my tongue.

Enter the Larpers

I managed to arrive with both Seb and the pashmina still dry. My sweating and teeth grinding finally stopped as I drove under the ironwork gates and taxied up the long gravel drive to Kollocks Grange. In the nineteenth century it was the country residence of some Lord Kollocks or other but when its post-war stint as a Ministry of Agriculture lab for black ops sugar beet research ended, it became what it is now, a conference centre and venue for group activities. Seeing the mansion again made me realize that I could use it for Reggie Carn's school in *The Black Starfish*.

As soon as this occurred to me the crimson migraine engulfed my head. I lost the wheel as my hands sprang to my face and my feet slipped off the clutch. The car shuddered until I thumped my foot on the brake and stalled it.

The pain vanished. I opened my eyes and looked down at the pedals, trying to think through how to restart the engine. I heard a croaky voice from the backseat.

'There's a giant mouse in the road,' said Seb.

Ahead of us, cocking its great furry head at us was a man-sized mouse holding a Little John-style quarterstaff. It wasn't alone. At Captain Mousy's left shoulder was a man of about my age in tiger-striped sleeves, purple pantaloons and a leather tabard flanked by a tiny little pixie woman with an Errol Flynn moustache and elf ears. She was dressed all in Lincoln green and had a long bow strapped to her back. Over on the other side a woman in a tattered brown cape wore a witch's hat and jabbed a wand at us. Next to her stood an enormous fat bloke in a black leather smock and blue bandanna who looked like he'd leapt battle-ready from the sleeve of a *Ruiner* LP.

'Bloody Narnia,' said Seb. 'Stuff them full of Turkish delight, then run the fuckers down!'

I restarted the ignition and revved the engine, the noise causing The Fellowship of the Mouse to part and wave us on our way with their swords and sticks.

'Welcome to The Shire,' I said.

I parked the car by the portico and slumped on the wheel to take a breather. When I raised my head I noticed in the mirror an array of billowing tents set up in the parkland between the building and the woods. Then a sharp crack came from the passenger door window. Reg Carnaby poked his beaky face against the glass and looked as short-fused as a hanging judge with haemorrhoids.

With my hand out for the shake, I nipped out my side and around the bonnet.

'Flack,' said Reg, tapping his wristwatch with his forefinger. He was wearing his sack-of-tweeds uniform with trousers pulled up to his tits. 'What sort of time do you call this? You said four o'clock. It's four thirty-two and sixteen seconds precisely.'

Blinking, confused, I took a step backwards. Some sort of yellow ghost was standing next to Reg, looming, mournful. Could he see it too? The hooded figure had turned out to be real. There were micemen and witches on the road. I recovered when I realized that the ghost wore oatmeal sweatpants. It was Cynthia with a yellow kagoule toggled up to her chin.

'Sorry, folks,' I said. 'Had a little car trouble. Didn't you find Gloria Waxham? She's usually very helpful.'

'And what sort of amusement park have you stranded us in, Flack?'

'I thought we were going mad. You saw them too?'

'Those wretched creatures are lepers, I'm told. Miss Wadge here is most concerned.'

'Lepers?'

'Flack, I will write to my MP if you have landed us in a leper colony.'

I was about to say that UKIP de Courcy was a sort of leper anyway when I heard a scuffling on the gravel. When I turned around Seb's swaying face was as grey as concrete and his eyes like pulped strawberries.

'Oh my God, a leper,' said Cynthia.

Seb punched his chest with one fist. '"To be an artist is to be a moral leper . . . a corn fed hog enjoys a better life than a creative writer".' He then took his fist from his chest and pointed at Cynthia. 'Corn fed hog.'

She about-turned and raced her yellow burka into the foyer. Reg's look of shock and outrage was the same as that I imagined he'd shown to his Darling Dear the day that Britain went decimal.

'I'm sorry about that,' I said as Seb collapsed to his knees and curled up on the ground. 'He wasn't saying she's a hog, he was . . . er . . . just reiterating a phrase for effect while . . . It's an involuntary quoting disorder. He's got this involuntary pointing disorder as well, he can't help it, like that guy Freud wrote about who swung his arms around. It happens all the time, in the bath, on the tube, and he's . . . narcoleptic, just falls over, passes out.'

'Don't hogwash me, Flack. That man is as drunk as a lord. I hope this is not the writer fellow we have come all the way out here to see?'

'He's had some bad news.'

'All news is bad news. Imagine if I had a tipple very time I had some bad news?'

'He'll be OK in a couple of hours. I've seen it before. He'll be asking for onion soup in about forty minutes, head clear as a bell. Now, can you be an utter star and help me carry him into reception.'

Reg crouched down to grab hold of Seb's feet, leaving the heavier end to me. Just as I'd locked my arms under Seb's shoulders, Captain Mousy and Ruiner Black passed us on their way into the building. Ruiner Black had his massive sword pressed against the back of his neck so he could dangle his wrists over the ends.

'We need to duke it out with SysAdmin,' he said, 'or their neg will spread like malware.'

The mouse vigorously nodded as they disappeared under the portico. We followed, strain showing on Reg's face as we heaved Seb up the steps. We made it to the foyer where paintings of floating fairies by minor Pre-Raphaelites hung around the walls and a gorgeous mahogany staircase poured down from a gallery. In the middle of the mosaic floor, Captain Mousy and Ruiner Black stood giggling in front of the white board. When

Reg started to pant like he'd just read the editorial in the *Daily Mail* they scampered off towards a side-arch as fast as they could in their costumes.

'Oh brilliant,' I said as I scanned the board. Written in block marker were directions to our rooms.

East Wing - (right) – Eldritch Discord versus Prism of Q'Qth
West Wing – (left) – Pose Fucktion (with Nutty Fuck)

Reg huffed. 'I suppose you think that's cool or wizard or some such.'

'You just saw *The Belgariad* change it, you crafty old git. Now do me a favour?' I asked him to go and find Cynthia and explain that Seb meant no offence. As he clicked off I dragged Seb by his underarms across the foyer in the opposite direction and just as I began to worry about the dust and his suit trousers, his arms spasmed and he climbed to his feet. He looked around himself, smirking, then fell in alongside me like a toddler catching up with its mummy. I left him on a chair outside the Kollocks Grange office. Gloria Waxham, the Events Manager, a slim, fortyish woman with a blonde bob and thick black Sixties-style glasses looked up from tapping away at her computer keyboard.

'Nathan,' she said, standing up and leaning over for a peck on the cheek. Her voice had become a little too loud since an accident at an archery event had left her with a slight hearing impediment. She always liked to josh and banter with me whenever we met. 'How lovely to see you? We are busy as bees. Have you seen how busy we are?'

'I feel like I've wandered into a straight-to-video film.'

She laughed. 'We're doing a lot of these now.'

'Straight-to-video films?'

'Larps. Live action role-plays.'

'Oh I see. Sex fantasy games for people whose sexual fantasy is actually having sex.'

'I see you've been on one before.'

'I have, but this one seems to be for people whose sexual fantasy is having sex with girls dressed as a squirrels.'

'Enter the larpers eh? Bad taste always brings in the boodle.'

'A canny philosophy. I'm only worried that they'll make a lot of noise and some of my students are a bit sensitive. There's already been some confusion between lepers and larpers.'

'They rarely stray indoors. You'll be OK.'

'How many of mine have arrived?'

'Three. Carnaby, Wadge and Gretsch. Sounds like a rock group.'

'Yes, Crossby, Shrinks and Gnash. There is a real monster of rock coming, actually. No Jane Vest yet?'

'Not so far. One of your favourites?' She winked. 'You're going to take her vest off, aren't you Nathan?'

'No, I just have something that belongs to her.'

'Not that squirrel costume?' said Gloria, handing over our roomkeys.

'A larper dressed as a mouse changed my name to something f-wordish on the board. Can you rectify? I've got a million things to do.'

A million things to do included manoeuvring Seb up off the chair, into a lift and along a corridor that was as long and unsettling as the ones in *The Shining* and then into my white-walled room without being seen by Erika Gretsch or any larpers. The other thing was not having a panic attack or dwelling on anything that had happened already today and mentally rehearsing Operation Get-This-Over-With-and Stop-Pretending-To-Be-A-Writer. Another was positioning Seb on his side on my bed and hoping against hope that he'd be semi-functional by dinnertime. The thought of dinner and the massed ranks of the Arcana made me shudder as I stared out of the window at the tents on the lawn and the millings specks of marketing hobgoblins and IT consultants-at-arms and human resources valkyries. Then I froze as Frank Denbigh's white van whizzed up the drive, scattering larpers in its wake. I sat down in a white wicker chair and remembered our old workshops in London. He'd seemed so inspiring then, a man with a dozen novels behind him and a reputation that couldn't be taken away, and I was just beginning to realize what I might be capable of and what might be ahead of me.

The room here was too white. Seb was dead to the world. Outside, goblins hollered at the rising moon.

I tried to doze but my thoughts drifted to stories. The crimson migraine insinuated its way back into my skull, dull enough this time for me to get used to it. It was like a hangover that you could manage if all you did was stay in bed and watch daytime TV or read a 3-for-2 table unit shifter but couldn't if you got up and did something routine, like shopping or teaching creative writing. If I reached for a pad I knew that the ache would burrow deeper into my brain. I did keep the story going though, push it along a little, thinking that maybe I could memorize it.

Maybe I could recite it later; maybe it could be a dramatic monologue. It was still the only story I had left that I wanted to write. [91]

91

The Black Starfish
A PI Pashminski Mystery
By Stradivarius D'Avignon

II

Frank Dank had been right about Reggie Carn's school. On the outskirts of the Fine City sat a fine old gothic pile hidden by trees. A sign outside the gates informed me that this was The Reginald Carn Academy for Morally Destitute Urchins and Strays. When I rang the entry buzzer I had one of those testing exchanges through the intercom where I couldn't get buzzed in because the receptionist kept correcting my pronunciation.

'The 'A' in "Carn" is a more protracted vowel. Cahhn. Reginald Cahhn's Academy. Repeat after me. Cahhn. Reg . . . and the stress is on the "Rrrr-Reg" . . . Rrr-reginald Cahhn.'

'OK, OK . . .'

'No, that's a gruesome Americanism. Say "Fine". "That is fine".'

Eventually, with my mouth now Swiss finishing schooled I found my Scarlet Collars marching up a long gravel drive towards what looked like the house out of *Wuthering Heights*. I'm sure I saw a few bats flitting around the turrets and belfries.

I strode into the hallway and straight up to the coot at the reception desk. A nameplate gave her away as 'Miss Quette.' I bet the strays lay awake all night in their dorms seeing who could come up with the most elaborate way of drawing her into their strong, young arms. She looked over her lunettes at me as if despairing of a sliced croquet ball on a Cambridge quad. I asked for Cahhn. A stair creaked behind me.

'I shall handle this, Hetty. Please prepare a hot infusion for our guest.' He was a grey, tweedy fellow with a beaky parrot face in his middle seventies and his trousers tugged up to his tits.

427

'I suppose you've come about the drains,' he said. 'Though I would expect a lovely young girl like yourself to have a more fitting profession. Ever thought of becoming a legal secretary, what, what?'

'Mr Carn?'

'Cahhn.'

'Pashminski. PI Pashminski.'

'Are you the plumber's wife?'

'Are you the monkey's uncle?'

'Come now, my dear, there's no need to trade beastly insults.'

'I have a matter of some delicacy, Mr Carn.'

I followed him up the stairs into a book-lined office. A Union Jack flag was propped up in one corner and a blunderbuss in the other. Miss Quette came in with some hot infusions on a wicker tray that she lay on the desk. From outside in the grounds I could hear teenaged voices drifting up the window. I was about to cut to the chase when Mr Carn leapt to his feet, pranced across the room and leant out of the window.

'Gareth Thornton, you miserable cur. If I hear you using a split infinitive again I'll string you up by your testicles, understand me?'

He returned to his seat and sipped his infusion.

'What brings you to our little oasis of calm, Mrs Pashminski?'

'My client believes that you may have something that belongs to him.'

'Well, I'm sure I do. I have class, you see, and standing and respectability. Respectability and standing and a sense of British fair play. Go back to your client and inform him that such things are earned, not given out equally at birth to any Thomas, Richard or Harold.'

'Does the name Sylvester Sly Ramos-Pintos mean anything to you?'

'Is he the plumber?'

'My client believes you acquired something of his on behalf of a Mr Ramos-Pintos.'

'Do I look, Mrs Pashminski, like someone who consorts with foreign plumbers with double-barrelled names? No foreign double-barrelled name is permissible here and plumbers only after references have been rigorously verified.'

'I'm looking for a starfish. Know anything about that.'

'A starfish. Are you potty?'

'A black starfish.'

428

'I assure you, Mrs Pashminski, that I have far too much to do saving these degenerates from the horrors of slang and skaz to be bothering myself with immigrant echinoderms. Now, about these drains. I think one of the expelled maybe jammed down there and a most repulsive whiff is creeping up into the cooler. Any chance of getting your husband to come over and have a snoop?'

'The black starfish, Mr Carn?' I held out my hand and put on my best poker face. 'We both know what this is about?'

'Good day, Mrs Pashminski. Miss Quette will show you out.'

He picked up a brass bell from his desktop and tinkled it gingerly before pretending to scribble on a report form. Voices came from outside again.

'Right, that's it.' He dashed over to the window and started to grapple with the blunderbuss. I didn't get a chance to see what happened next because Old Quette waltzed in and fragrantly ushered me downstairs and out of the building. As my Scarlets carried me along the crunchy grey gravel again, I heard a shout of '"Innit" is not a proper word, Thornton' and then a loud bang. When I made it out of the school I felt a little chill run along my spine and realized I was going to have to resort to a thicker pashmina for this case. I sank into my Nissan Micra and gunned the engine. As I pulled off, a black Daimler pulled off too and started to play kiss chase with my back bumper. Its windows were tinted. I couldn't see the driver. I did a U on the ringroad near PC World and drove as fast as I could into Norwich. I was sure old Carn was telling the truth, but why had Flake put me onto him and who the Dickens was Sylvester Sly Ramos-Pintos?

Who's for Tequila?

Two hours later, as we made our way to the dining room, Seb grabbed hold of my arm and pulled me to a standstill. Through the doorway I caught a glimpse of a long oval table draped with a white cloth. Candlelight winked, cutlery shone and dim outlines chattered. My mouth dried and everything seemed to warp as it does when a long-anticipated *cherchez la femme* is abruptly upon you. At the head of the far end, Jane wore a smart sleeveless indigo blouse and her was hair tied up, not loose as it was usually.

'I've got a confession,' said Seb. 'I've not done anything.'

'You have,' I said. 'It doesn't matter what Blox thinks.'

'Not that, I know that. I mean I've not prepared anything for this.'

'Busk it. Throw them some scraps. Always end on a mood, bollocks to the adverb, that sort of stuff. Creative writing students are like casual gamblers. They thrive on tips.'

'Tips? What has tipped? The world has tipped.'

'C'mon.'

In the doorway, a confusion developed as to who was letting who go first. When I finally extricated myself from Seb I found Crossby, Shrinks and Gnash all in a row along one side while at the far end of the table, Jane stared into a candle flame and fiddled with the coil of ivy at its base.

'Good evening everyone,' I said. 'Glad you all got here OK. This is Sebastian.'

Seb nodded up the table to Jane. He looked sideways and acknowledged Reg, who nodded back cautiously but respectfully. Then Seb smiled at Cynthia but without looking away from her must have noticed Erika.

'Nathan, it's that bloody woman again.'

'Do you know the magic of poetry?' said Erika.

'No I fucking well don't.'

Erika flapped her arms and had to be pacified by a steadying hand on the back from Reg. Seb then wilted into a chair across from Cynthia, who rushed up to leave. I had to intercept and usher her back to her seat with a few calming words. Seb reached out for the water jug and poured himself a tall glass. He necked it, necked another, then raised a third for a toast.

'Cheers. I hear you're all interested in touches?'

'Tips,' I said. 'Everyone wants to hear your tips.'

'Tipsy, more like it,' said Reg.

'Tippy tippy tippy tippy,' said Erika. 'I like this word tippy. What does it mean, this tippy?'

To keep an eye on Sebastian, I pulled up a seat at the head of the table, right opposite Jane. She may as well have been in Iceland so far as a *rapprochement* was possible. My legs tried to pull my body under the table, where I could crouch and hide and count down the seconds until Sunday lunchtime when I could run away and never have to do this ever again.

'Anybody seen Mac?' I said.

Nobody had. Given Seb's news I assumed that by now the inevitable knock-back from Blox had been delivered. When footsteps rumbled up the corridor behind me I anticipated Mac shuffling into the room with his stomach out, shirt untucked and his beard crazy. Plum would have dumped him now that his pipe dream had shattered. We could commiserate with one another. Two rejections from Dewsenbury and one from Dexter and Geezensax. I took a sip of water and swilled it around my mouth. No telltale smell of expensively cheap aftershave wafted over me. Instead: a whiff of mothballs.

'Alright, me lovers.'

I'd forgotten about Frank in all the moon-barkery, but here he was, overdressed in a brown demob-style suit, black dickie bow and a turquoise dress shirt with frilly cuffs that couldn't have seen the outside of a wardrobe since 1972. He swaggered in like a game show host, right past me, right past Seb, straight past the empty seat next to Seb and plopped himself down next to Jane.

'Hello Pickle,' he said and grabbed hold of her wrist.

At last she gave me a look, but it was a frightened scowl that seemed to say: *you said you would stop this but because I didn't sleep with you you've unleashed hell upon me!* She swished away Frank's hand and turned to Reg.

'And how are you, you salty old sea-dog?'

He reached for his lapels and puffed out his chest.

'I, my dear, am so-so, so-so. Do you realize that I've not been apart this long from my Darling Dear since . . .'

'Mister Nathan,' Frank said. 'This place, ain't it like the house out a *Cluedo*.'

'In the dining room, with the candlestick,' said Seb, stretching out his arm for a candle on the table. I swiped it away, almost setting fire to Cynthia.

'That's a nice observation, Frank,' I said. 'Lots of secret passages here.'

'Secret passages,' he chortled. 'All the better to creeps up on you all.'

I smiled in a horrible in-front-of-class way and tried to catch Jane's eye but Gloria Waxham pushed a clanking hostess trolley into the room and addressed the table from behind me.

'If food be the music of love, tuck in!' She then nudged my ear with her lips and as she did so I noticed Jane glance over at me again.

'Oh my, I bet she's got a lovely squirrel,' said Gloria in the sort of voice you'd use to open a debate at the Oxford Union. 'I bet she'd like to hide your nuts.'

I didn't mind Seb overhearing this, but I did marginally resent Cynthia, Erika, Reg *and* Jane averting their faces to snigger or cringe.

'Well,' I said, forcing revolting cheerfulness into my voice, hoping that I could throw out some decoy words. '*Squirrel* and *nut* cutlets sounds lovely, Gloria.'

'We don't do squirrel and nut cutlets,' she said. 'It would bother the vegetarians.'

I wanted to bash Gloria with the candlestick now, but feared I'd wet myself if I let go of whatever it was that was making me sweat and ache and my heart beat like a military band inside my ribcage. I tried to nip elegantly over to the trolley, but rocketed like a clod of sludge propelled from the barrel of a paintball gun. I shakily took the soup jug and bread bowl and placed them in the middle of the table.

'The soup's celery,' said Gloria.

Seb reached for the jug and sniffed it as if sampling the bouquet of a vintage wine.

'Smells like anal phlegm.'

The faces around the table flushed either pumice grey or measles red. I tried another decoy.

'Aniseed . . . er . . . penne. It's not pasta soup, Seb, you old card.'

Nobody touched the soup, except for Seb who sloshed a great ladleful of it all over the tablecloth and his lap. After Gloria placed tureens of farmhouse chicken, steaming bowls of mushroom risotto and side dishes of fresh vegetables on the table everyone started to eat and everyone started to talk.

'The first time I heard that Elvis,' said Frank, 'I thought he were a black man.'

I sat down and tried to get used to how slow and hazy the room now seemed. Every facial movement around the table was a muscle-by-muscle increment. Every arm that extended to take a bread roll was as cautious as that of a probe sampling the soil on the surface of Mars. Every blink of every eye was a hard, spaced-out crack that battered the back of my head. My stomach felt like it had shrunk to the size of a marble and I no more than poked my food around the plate. I remembered those two students, Trevor Chod and Pravina Mantlestein who enrolled but didn't turn up for the first class and I wondered how this group would have played with a couple more sane Minor Arcana to sit alongside Jane. I could be here now with Trev and Prav, talking about the art of the short story and life-changing novels and enduring characters and the riotous love of language and what it can open up for you. Instead my most pressing concern was whether I should acquire some child's reins to keep Seb attached to his chair and his face out of his soup.

The writer and critic Sebastian Harker, the only person of substance left who believed in me, whom I had promised as a treat for the Arcana, and here he was, reduced to shouty-bollocks. Hopefully, the food would wise him up a bit. He could do a short, little chat, then I could pack him off to bed and at least try to talk to Jane in private. I realized that I was repeatedly stabbing a chicken breast with my fork as if there was something hostile inside it, and so sat back and used a swig of water to have a glance at the room.

Everything seemed rather sedate. Some sort of triangular conversation between Frank, Erika and Cynthia was in progress about how Frank was going to do *The* MA and wouldn't it be great if they could all do it together. At the end Reg was explaining to Jane the finer points of crown green bowls, using a bread roll to demonstrate the cunning of his technique. It struck me then how much easier writing would be for them if Sebastian and I and everyone like us remained in our spiderholes, just writing our stories and then ducking them like medieval witches in the pond of chance, indifference and bullshit. Sink or float, either way it was going to cause you strife and torment, and even if you got away with it, the stocks were up next and the fruit grew more rotten each time. That should be our example.

I had known from the first moment that I stepped into that classroom two months ago that this was going to be the worst group ever, even worse than the Ipswich Group of Death. But I'd taught hundreds and hundreds of lovely, keen, enthusiastic, clever, professional, responsible, well-educated and otherwise accomplished people. Not one of them had ever sold a short story or poem to a small press magazine, let alone a novel to a mainstream publisher. The whole thing, I realized, was bad for them and bad for me. Bad for me in that in the whole scrabble to inform, to help, to demystify something inherently mysterious, teach something more or less unteachable, and let's face facts, beyond a few self-evident 'tips', creative writing is unteachable, I had began to close my eyes to what was actually around me and lose myself to paranoid hallucinations and a bitterness fed by inscrutable failure and withering loneliness. The first symptom of this was mean-spiritedness. The long-term prognosis for me was the inability to write fiction again.

Watching them eating their dinner and talk to each other, I began to feel that I had misjudged all these people. I'd just seen them all as grotesques from a bad comic novel that I'd never found the time or determination to write. I never asked myself why Cynthia was so fragile and prone to dramatics. Or why was Jane so attracted to a vision of the writer's life that could be disabused by a skim of a few biographies. How could you actually get Reg to describe the sadness of living by social codes that no longer exist instead of blathering and ranting? How does someone like Frank begin to tell himself a story of betrayal by others and institutions as a way of not coming to terms with what seemed to be a maddening isolation and a dearth of affection? And Erika? I had never once asked myself what had happened to her and never felt even a twinge of sympathy for someone clearly ill, clearly stranded, clearly abandoned. I had become the one upon whom everything is lost. If O'Mailer were still here, that's what he would say.

'And how is Nathan, Nathan?' said Cynthia.

'No . . . Oh sorry, head in the clouds. OK. Bit worried.' I wiggled my thumb vaguely in the direction of Seb.

'Yes, you do look . . . Have you got a cold? There's a vicious one doing the rounds.'

'Yes, something like that. Went out for a long walk in the wet for too long. Got soaked to the skin.'

'Twice in one month. That's tragic,' she said, quite sincerely.

'Anyway, I was just thinking, Cynthia, that of all the group, we've not heard anything from you yet. I think I've had a story from everyone, but not you.'

She cupped both her ears with her hands. 'You know I said I was finding it hard to find something to write that didn't depress me? Well, I finally found something. It's about two people who love each other from afar.'

'Sounds promising,' I said. 'You could read it out tomorrow.'

'If I must,' she said.

I sat back and checked on Seb. He seemed to have cooled down and was purposefully eating his third or fourth portion of chicken. If I hadn't known he'd been on a self-destructive bender for God knows how long, I might now have thought he was merely a bit quiet, as someone about to address a roomful of strangers is liable to be. I looked around the table again, trying to catch Jane, but Reg was still waffling on. Frank was completely ignoring Jane – I gave thanks for small mercies – and stared thoughtfully at Erika. Cynthia had turned away from me to listen to something Erika was saying. Cynthia had written a story. It might be a good story. Sometimes the Sensitive Plants pull it out of the pot. I wanted to sit in that room tomorrow and listen to her story and be able to say that it was moving and wonderful and thank her for it. As Gloria reappeared with another trolley, this time of coffee and desserts, my desire to hear Cynthia's story overrode my dread that Gloria was going to do something like spread a pair of pink knickers with 'JANE' stitched onto them across my forehead.

When the coffee had been poured and the cups passed from person to person and plates of chocolate and apricot tart and melon slices

435

distributed, the chatter began to die down without me having to remind the group that Seb was about to speak. Even so, I wasn't sure that he was aware of this. Every other guest writer I'd employed for a residential had engaged with the students during the meal and the transition from table talk to informal lecture had been effortless.

'You OK?' I asked as discreetly as I could. 'Know what you're going to say?'

He tapped his temple. 'In here I've been rehashing every damned seminar since 1974. Even that one on Skyros where the Jungian analyst stormed the room dressed as Marie Antoinette waving a spear made out of mistletoe. Have no fear, Nathan.'

The group was peering at us. Seb slid his fork and spoon together on his plate and gently moved it aside. I turned away from him in case I was putting him off and found myself staring at the shadowpuppet-like shapes the candle patterned across Jane's neck. She looked at me, then smiled, almost bashfully, dipping her face and stroking her shoulder with her right hand. I raised my eyebrows. She raised hers. I sent my eyes leftwards at Seb. Jane smirked and I lifted an imaginary glass to my lips and mouthed 'later'. When she nodded I suddenly felt a little of something lighter. Then with as much of a theatrical flourish as possible I chimed the side of my cup.

'Ladies and gentlemen, let me introduce to you, the writer and critic Sebastian Harker.'

Just as Seb was about to speak, a collective look of surprise rushed the faces around the table. The three candles at our end snuffed out and those at the Jane end guttered. I turned. Standing in the doorway in a huge black suit and butter-yellow tie was Mac McMahon, his face glowing with joy and excitement. Strapped across his chest was some sort of leather sash. He'd double-booked himself, I thought. He was here for the larp. Larper McMahon. The Demon-King of Boilerplate. He was probably the dungeon-master or something and the whole larp scenario was based around one of his poxy plotlines with its zombie fleshgobblers and shit-bollocks dialogue, and he'd come in from the tents in the park to say hello and probably 'up yours' to the writing game. But the leather thing wasn't some piece of fantasist's body armour, but one of those shot-glass bandoliers waitresses wear in tourist trap dive bars. Mac was holding up two bottles of spirit like a competition angler with prize trout.

'Who's for tequila?!!!'

'Bloody hell, Nathan,' said Seb. 'You didn't tell me that Henry VIII was coming.'

'Hello Mac. Good to see you. Sit down. Have some coffee and cake. Seb's about the speak.'

'I've done it, mate.'

He ripped me up from my seat and bearhugged me around the room, the two tequila bottles pressing hard into my back.

'Done, done it, done it. Frank, I've done it. Janeycakes, Reggiebaby, done it. Erika, Cynth, you sexy mothers, I've done it. New Bloke, I've done it. Nathan, son, I've done it. I've sold me donking novel.'

My feet were off the floor. I couldn't breathe. He let go of me and I spun away and bounced into the wall.

'Let's rock.' Mac whipped out a line of shot glasses and set them up on the table. 'I wished, and now it can be Christmas every day.'

Out of their seats, Frank and Jane were shaking his hands and patting him on the back as the others gleefully scampered around the table towards him. He lofted a glass to his mouth and sank a shot.

'Thank you, Dewsenbury and Madge. Thank you, Ollie Blox. And thank you for your one million quid. You've been a fantastic audience. Here's what you've all been waiting for. Drum rolls, per-lease'

'One million chuffing quid,' Frank shouted.

'A million,' said Jane with her hand over her mouth.

'The He. The He is here,' said Erika and dropped to her knees.

'One million solid gold English quid.'

A hideous warmth swept over me. I felt like the guy in a horror film who peers through a crack in a wardrobe door while a maniac chops up his girlfriend. I turned away from the celebration. Seb had gone. A howl came from down the corridor.

'I've got to go and find Seb,' I said. Nobody heard me and I didn't bother to say it again. I strode out, the hideous warmth getting hotter and hotter as I tried to tell myself that this was a mistake, or a nightmare. Any minute now I would wake up in the white wicker chair with Seb still crashed out on the bed.

The bar was full of larpers. No Seb. Upstairs, I banged on his door. He opened it slightly and said, 'in the morning it will seem worse.'

I dithered about going back downstairs and knew that I ought to buy Mac that pint I'd promised him earlier in the week and join in and not look jealous or curmudgeonly, but a crunching sense of dislocation came over me and the only comparison I could come up with was the moment in the snow when Johanna let go of my hand. I found myself in the too-white room waiting to see if anyone came and knocked on the door and if someone, say Jane, came and knocked the decision would be made for me and I would have to go back downstairs and play the part of the teacher outstripped by the pupil. But no one knocked as I paced the room thinking of the three-sentence rejection letter from Dexter and Geezensax I received that morning and that Mac McMahon was represented by Frederick Malone, who thought *The Penelope Tree* was too tricky to market, and Oliver Blox, who told me I'm a nobody, Mister Who?iforget, but had advanced Mac a million pounds for *The Death Metal Revelations*. I had thought that *The Death Metal Revelations* was less substantial and interesting than a sheaf of blank pages. I was a blank page now. I was a blank footnote beneath a blank page[92]. I lay on the bed until the crimson migraine arrived and I sank deeper and deeper and deeper into something unlike sleep and unlike dreaming.[93]

---

[92] **Nathan Flack:**

[93] **The Black Starfish**

A PI Pashminski Mystery

By Stradivarius D'Avignon

III

Outside my office I parked the Micra and as I got out I noticed Nate Flake scurrying along the pavement towards the Well Thumbed bookstore with a newspaper pressed to the side of his face like a character in a spy film. My Scarlets clicked across the road to head him off.

'Are you trying to hide from me, Mr Flake?' I said.

'Oh no,' he said, 'cut myself shaving.'

There was no telltale spot of red on the newspaper. I rolled my eyes and struck a pose.

'Reggie Carn,' I said. 'Drew a blank, I'm afraid, but I don't think he was throwing me a line.'

Flake shook his head. 'Well, Pintos has his pinkies in lots of chicken and mushrooms. Try Mack the Hack. Money launderer. Runs the Great Balls of Fire record shop on Rampant Lobster Street. Know it?'

'By sight.'

'Be careful, Ms Pashminski. He will more than likely throw you a line.'

With that a tremor ran through Flake and he made an excuse and hurried off. What I found curious was that from my office window five minutes later I noticed him come back up the street, this time without the newspaper stuck to his face, and sidle into the Well Thumbed. I logged onto the web and did a search on Mack the Hack. Seems he used to be a musician going under the name of Mac McMacaroon and the Mooners and judging by the cover art the stuff was a little lurid, pneumatic devil girls in submissive positions, fat naked men with Viking helmets stuck over their privates, that sort of thing. I certainly didn't want him to throw me any line other than a line of investigation.

As soon as I parked my Scarlets before the unmanned cash desk in the Great Balls an extension lead flew over the top and a thick Birmingham accent shouted, 'hold onto that, Frodo.'

I caught it, then put the socket end down on the desk with my business card attached. Mr Hack,' I said.

A huge, hairy troll of a man appeared from behind the desk and his eyes seemed to pop out of his head as he gave me the once over.

'What can I do for you, Love Muffin?' he said. 'I've got the new Cradle of Filth twelve inch, or another sort of twelve incher that never lets a lady down.'

'I'm looking for a black starfish, Mr Hack I believe you have one in stock.'

He scratched his beard and gave me a look. 'Never heard of them. Import is it?'

'It's not a band, as well you know.'

'Why don't you come out the back and have a rummage? Got some great stuff out there. Heard of a new local group going under the name of Undercrackers?'

'Mr Hack, does the name Reggie Carn mean anything to you?'

'Wasn't he Aerosmith's bookkeeper?'

'I don't think so. Nate Flake? You took a starfish from him?'

'You telling me that now you can get a fish that's like shaped like a star? The mind boggles. Does it have five tails or five heads like?'

'Don't play the ignorant with me, Hack, we both know what I'm talking about here.'

'No, you're wrong there, love, but I got to admit it, Satan must be missing an angel now you've fallen out of his dominion, like. Love the boots.'

'And I assure you that they are made for walking. Who's your boss?'

'Self-employed me, though don't tell the Revenue.'

'Ramos-Pintos?'

'Is that the trick with the ice cubes? Come out back and give me a sample.'

'You're telling me that you're not acquainted with a Sylvester Sly Ramos-Pintos?'

'Sounds mega but I've not heard it. Black Starfish their album? Look, go upstairs, makes yourself at home, there's bourbon in the kitchen and a couple of cans in the fridge, and I'll look it up on the system. Take about two days for FedEx to ship it. We can get to know each other while we wait.'

'OK,' I said. 'Charm is a rare commodity in this day and age.'

The look on his face was one of relief and lusty eagerness. But I was going to uncross these crossed wires pronto. He led me out through a bead curtain behind the cash till and into a passageway. A metal staircase led up into a flat above the shop. He was getting a little too close for comfort so I told him to go and work on his scanning while I slipped into something a little more comfortable.

'You do that, Love Puffin,' he said. 'I'll track down your black, then I'll pour you a Pernod.'

I don't drink Pernod and The Hack's apartment didn't tempt me into trying it. Every wall and ceiling was covered with horror film posters, pictures of heavy metal bands and pages ripped from softcore skin mags. The place stank of curry and badly needed a hoover. I set to work straight away, rummaging through drawers, cupboards, wardrobes, boxes of LPs, and his drinks cabinet, part of a pastiche of a Hawaiian beach bar set up in his front room. No starfish. I found an alarming black riding crop tossed unashamedly on the unmade bed and used it to poke around in the covers and under the bed. No starfish. Then I heard his heavy feet clang up the fire escape and waited, thinking through my options as I heard slithering and rustling in the kitchen. I pushed up the sash window just as his shadow darkened the doorway and found my Scarlets running across a conveniently located flat roof. At the edge of the roof I took a backward glance and caught sight of his huge, hairy, naked figure standing in his bedroom, a tumbler of spirit in each hand and a green condom hanging from his monkey-nut sized pig-sticker. This image was going to haunt me forever, I thought, would be the restless ghost and emotional loose cable this case saddled me with when it was over. I leapt like a gazelle onto the roof of the next building and found my way down via the service elevator of a department store I'd never before noticed. This was the chase of the goose and this meat-eater preferred my joint frozen from the supermarket, not stalked on the lake. I needed to chat up my client before I got my feathers caught in any more windmills.

Frazzle Dick is Dead

'I told you it would seem worse in the morning,' said Seb. He dropped his overnight bag by his car and peered at me as if he expected me to say something contradictory. The crust around my eyeballs tightened as I stared at the Afghanistan-shaped soup stain across his trousers. Spits of rain clicked against the car's roof and a thin fog hovered above the tents in the park. The place was already crawling with larpers and Seb was about to abandon me here on my own with the Arcana and their success stories. I hunched my shoulders, scared that one of them would emerge from the Grange. I'd not shown my face yet. I ducked out of breakfast and stayed in the too-white room. I tried to concoct a version of the previous night where Mac was telling an outright lie, but even this brought on the crimson migraine. The crimson migraine had kept me awake all night. When I closed my eyes I pictured the trees in the park exploding into flame. I was haunted by images of Mac collecting the Man Booker Prize, the Whitbread Prize, the Prix Goncourt and even The Orange Prize. The dawn then seemed to take about two months to actually rise, and when it finally motivated itself the person who crept to the mirror in the *ensuite* looked as if he'd staggered up a shingle beach from a shipwreck. His hair stayed gluey and clumpish however many times I brushed it and his face was so pale that I wondered if an albino double had possessed him during the night. Here was Nate Flake, Nutty

Fuck, the Shamblesman who now teetered on the gravel, about to say goodbye to Sebastian.

'I feel like I'm on page ten of a screenplay about nuclear war,' I said. 'The bomb's been dropped and now we have to work out how we're going to survive.'

'We head for the coast.'

'But there's a militia in the way.'

'And they have captured The Daughter . . .'

'She's got ESP and is foreshadowed in mystical texts.'

'And only she can lead the rag-tag of humanity after the rout of mankind . . .'

'To the New Eden, the Tibetan Refuge, the Magick Hillock.'

'Hey, this will sell. Write it down, quick.'

'Stop it,' I said. 'There's no point doing this any more.' I had to knit my fingers together behind my back to stop myself shaking my fist at the wind.

'Look, it is a terrible thing,' said Seb. 'Idiots selling novels for barrowfuls of cash, but you will float down the gutter.'

'Oh cheers, mate.'

'The gutter of time, Nathan, the gutter of time. Lawrence Sterne said that a novel floats down the gutter of time.'

'Why don't you have a hangover?'

'I guarantee you that Henry VIII's novel will go straight down the drain.'

'Mine aren't even making the U-bend.'

'Come and see me soon. We'll plan the rearguard. Lead the rag-tag of humanity.'

'Sure,' I said. 'Look, thanks. I'm just going to get this over with and then I'm going to bury my head in the sand.' I gave him back his keys and we shook hands. He slipped into the car, then wound down the window.

'Nathan,' he said, holding up the pashmina bag. 'Even last night I could tell.'

'That's why I'm not coming with you. Go on, get out of here.'

I hugged the pashmina to my chest as I watched the car disappear into the mist. In the park, larpers lofted pikes and spears. Little groups of them sat in circles and pairs of them fenced or jigged like leprechauns. Footsteps came out of the Grange. I shuddered, hoping that it wasn't

Jane so I wouldn't have to give her the pashmina back now. Captain Mousy and Ruiner Black passed me on their way to Fort Larper.

'You know by nowski what it's like at the bleeding-edge,' said Ruiner Black. 'The jones is for top-down, user-centred, interpersonal solutions.'

As I watched them gambol up the field I felt like calling them back. *Hey, pod-goblins, there's a new novel coming out that will really go for your polyhedrals.* I ought to mug that mouseman and nick his gear so I could hide out all day in larperland with the other delusionals and not have to congratulate Mac on his good fortune. Larper or loser? That was my dilemma. It was just as pressing and critical as Merton's in *Wings of a Dove*. I skulked back into the Grange and stashed the pashmina in the too-white room. Now I had the dragonquest of introductory workshop to contend with.

The Arcana were already assembled when I entered the seminar room. The chairs were set out in a horseshoe formation. At the centre of the arch, having stolen my seat, Mac was doing a bad impression of the creative writing tutor's anecdote-telling pose.

'Anyway, we pile in to his room and Strangler comes out, like, of this little side room where they put a bog and a shower, and he's like starkers-malarkers, as naked as the proverbial bollock, and his nobber is out and everything, and it's still like a pigging worm in a fridge's top box but he goes to us, right, he goes, "frazzle dick is dead, long live boner!"'

Frank Denbigh threw back his head and laughed like the Jolly Green Giant as Erika cackled in a stuttery popgun way. Jane giggled and Cynthia sniggered with her hand over her mouth as if she knew she ought not to but couldn't help it. Even Reg was laughing. I found this peculiar. If I'd told that yarn, Reg would have summoned the Hunt.

'Morning everyone,' I said, pulling up a chair. 'I think you'll find that the little side-room where they put a toilet and a shower is called an *ensuite*.'

'Oright Nate,' said Mac. 'How's it swinging?'

Everyone started to laugh again, apart from Jane, who looked at me in a concerned, motherly way that I found as disconcerting as what Erika and Frank were doing. Erika's hand rested on his lap. He gripped it with one of his paws, stabbing and caressing it with his other thumb.

'How are your hands . . . heads, I mean heads?' I said.

'Fine,' said Mac. 'There ain't half some crazy folks in this gaff.'

'Yeah, there was some plonker,' said Frank, 'dressed up like a mouse he was, and he was trying to pour beer down him with this big head-thing on.'

'We, like, me and Frank and Jane and Erika,' said Mac, 'we were in that bar until they chucked us out, weren't we? These two . . .' He used a sort of double-thumbs up to point out Reg and Cynthia. ' . . . went to bed early.'

'Not together, you understand,' said Cynthia.

'Stupid innuendo,' said Reg. 'I'm not in the RAF now.'

'Nah, we left that to them,' said Mac. He winked at the hand-holders. I shut my eyes and my nose stiffened so much that my top lip tugged at my gums and I let out a squeak. When I opened my eyes, everyone was staring at me as if I had some bizarre animal doing its business on my shoulder.

'OK,' I said. 'No time like the present.'

'No time like the present, for what?' said Reg. 'We haven't a clue what we are supposed to be doing.'

'I told you last night,' I said.

'I'm afraid you didn't, Nathan,' said Jane.

I pictured everyone ticking the zero box in the "organization" section of the course assessment forms.

'Last night was a little strange, as you know,' I said. 'Mr Harker was unwell. Both he and I apologize for that. Artistic temperament. Involuntary quoting disorder, that sort of thing. It catches him out sometimes.'

Erika rotated her head towards me. 'The He. You fear him, don't you?'

'I don't know what you're talking about . . . where was I? OK. What we are going to do now . . .' I explained that the session would be an open workshop where each of them could read a passage of work in progress. The afternoon was reserved for quiet writing time and after dinner tonight we could discuss as a group any stories produced during the day.

'You have all brought something, haven't you?' I said. Everyone shrugged and shook their heads. 'I did give you a handout last week with the schedule. Did nobody read it?' More shrugs. 'Well, I know Cynthia has something to read, don't you, Cynthia?'

'Flack,' said Reg. 'Am I right in thinking you still have yet to congratulate Mr McMahon?'

444

'I did,' I said. 'Last night.'

'I don't think so.'

I glanced around the faces and felt like a man before a jury that was about to deliver an inevitable guilty verdict. I couldn't help it. I knew I looked guilty. Guilty of jealousy, of incomprehension, of resentment, of anachronism, of literary snobbery, of something near to hatred, not so much for Mac – he couldn't help it, bless him– but for Frederick Malone of ZY Haggard and Oliver Blox of Dewsenbury and Madge. So much for pulling out all the stops this weekend and performing with utmost courtesy and professionalism to save my job. This was the Flackdaq's Wall Street Crash moment, its Black Wednesday freefall, the bottom falling out of the bottom. Things could not deteriorate further.

'Shazzer's coming up later,' said Mac.

'Oh for fuck's sake,' I said and hung my head in my hands.

'Ps and Q's, Flack,' said Reg.

'Mac. Well done,' I said. 'I am really pleased for you. Can we hear some more of this magnum opus?'

'You can't hear champagne,' said Mac.

'Doesn't matter. Have you brought anything to read?'

'Not allowed to. Dewsens want it kept secret.'

'Great stuff. I think it's over to you, Cynthia.'

She nodded and slowly, carefully drew a green folder from her bag as Erika whispered a very hissish mention of The He in Frank's ear.

'Cynthia. Would you like to say something about your story before you read?'

'No,' she said. 'I'd rather just . . . get it over with. It's called . . . The Little Girl with the Little Puppy.'

She placed the papers on the knees of her oatmeals and her arms and shoulders started to shake. Motion lines seemed to radiate from her as if she were a character in a comic strip, Nervous Woman or Shook-Up Girl. This gave me an idea. Could I write a Nervous Woman story instead of finishing *The Black Starfish*, the end of which was proving elusive? By day, our heroine is mild-mannered, neurotic children's entertainer, Cynthia Nervous. By night she is Wonder Wadge. She'd wear a cape made of several pairs of oatmeal sweatpants sewn together and have a pouch of explosive worry balls to throw at noisy neighbours and Jehovah's Witnesses. She could team up with Reg, AKA Yesterday Man to fight bogus asylum seekers working illegally in West Runton. Then there could be The Justice League of East Anglia, with Frank as Captain Norfolk,

445

Erika as He-Woman, Mac as Professor XXX and Jane as The Scarlet Pashmina. I could be Shamblesman, in better times The Fumigator but now reduced to some goo in a jar from repeated exposure to overheated dust-jacket blurbs, a bollocks McGuffin character The JLEA have to rescue from the clutches of The Hammerhead Silencer and his partner in crime, The Rejection Slipper. The crimson migraine pulsed through me just as Cynthia stopped shivering.

'Sorry,' she said.

'I'm sure it's wonderful,' I said. 'Have faith. This is not a test.'

'Thank you, Nathan, you're very kind.'

At last. I'd secured some six-out-of-sixes for Kindness to Wonder Wadge on Assessment forms.

Cynthia raised the papers, but then put them down again. 'I would just like to say how much I've enjoyed this course . . . I just think I've learned so much. I feel so much more confident.'

'Thank you, Cynthia. Why don't you just read your story? Nice and slow.'

'OK, The Little Girl with the Little Puppy. Here goes.' She took a breath, then began. 'The appearance on the front of a new arrival – a girl with a little puppy – became the topic of general conversation. Nathan Nathanovich Flackov, who had been a fortnight in Norwich and got used to its ways was also interested in new arrivals. One day, sitting on the terrace of Jernet's restaurant, he saw a young girl walking along the promenade; she was fair, very tall, and wore a pashmina; behind her trotted a white chihuahua . . .'

'Right, stop, please.'

Cynthia threw the papers down. 'Don't tell them, don't tell them.'

'For crying out loud, that's The Lady with the Lapdog by Chekhov with me in it. Did you think I wouldn't notice? I'm not a complete idiot.'

'I didn't notice,' said Mac.

Cynthia scrunched up the papers and rubbed them into her forehead. 'Everyone else can do it and I can't . . . I can't . . . I can't.'

She shot up, knocked over her chair and ran for the exit, each wiggle of the oatmeal sweatpants signalling to me another zero in the tickboxes and another long complaining sentence in the comments. When I turned back to the others I had no idea what I was going to say or whether I was actually at fault at all. I expected a lot of uncomfortable and disapproving faces, but instead Mac had taken charge.

'As you can see, right, if you're going to nick something, it has to be something good.' He paused and gave me a shifty look as if anticipating my violent disagreement. 'So don't nick that Chekhov. He's shit. It's like I keep saying. Classics is shit. He was fifth in charge anyway, weren't he? After Kirk, Spock, Scottie and Bony.'

My brain became that goo in a jar as I sucked all the air in the room into my chest. Then I noticed that Erika had used the distractions to slide onto Frank's lap and furiously licked at his face like a starving dog with a bowl of Pedigree Chum.

'Oh my,' said Frank. 'You're making Little Frank stand up to sing for his supper.'

'Right,' I said. 'You two. *Out*. Snogging like mental patients means *out*.' They giggled and scampered hand in hand to the door. Their laughter echoed around the corridor until they disappeared into the foyer. 'Talking out of your arse means *out*, Mac. Yesterday Man . . . I don't need to justify myself to you, you crazy old basket . . . *out*.'

'I think Nathan needs to lie down,' said Mac, so warmly that I wanted to punch his beardy face until I deteriorated into a puddle of tears.

'Yes, what, what. Let's go,' said Reg. 'We might be able to catch up with Cynthia and fit in a nice piece of cake somewhere about.'

'Now you're talking, Reggiebabe. I could have a gander at that story of yours.'

Professor XXX and Yesterday Man ambled off as if nothing significant had actually happened. With my arms rigidly at my sides I escaped into a weird near-silence and half-stillness as I lifted myself on tiptoes so I didn't have to look at Jane and could only see a horizon of restless larpers out in the park.

'Oh Nathan,' said Jane. 'What on earth is going on?'

447

The Seduction of Erika Gretsch

'It started last night,' said Jane as the kettle's hiss ended with a plasticky snap. I was still crashed on the bed in the too-white room, watching her as she placed white cups on white saucers, then fiddled around in a pot to find the coffee sachets. Ten minutes ago, as we sneaked up the stairs and along the corridor, Jane had attacked the silence between us by talking about coffee. Coffee would wake me up and cheer me up and we could have a little chat over coffee. Most problems in life could be sorted out over a nice cup of coffee. She would make me some hot, sweet coffee.

Even though this was the nicest thing anyone had done for me in ages I didn't need to hear all about last night's lurid talking points as she made the coffee. I didn't want images from *The Seduction of Erika Gretsch* playing behind my eyes where my talent used to live. I couldn't help it though, and started to see Frank and Erika in one of those photo-love stories in magazines for teenaged girls. It would be a specialist publication called *Bunty Boiler.* In one frame of *Love in a White Van* or *You Don't Bring Me Hammers Anymore,* Frank would be standing in a doorway in grey overalls, staring longingly and smoulderingly at Erika. A thought bubble would jab at his bald head: *She's a right dirty pillow but can I risk telling Little Frank?* Meanwhile, Erika would coyly pretend to read a book of Nest Darkle's verse while another thought bubble read: *Is he The He? Let me swaddle him in bones and make him into a magic poetry for batgirl.*

The crimson migraine started to pulse behind my eyes. Jane opened two sachets and tipped instant coffee into cups.

'And then Cynthia,' she said, 'gave Reg a lap dance.'

'What?'

'I knew you weren't listening.'

'I am. Sorry . . . It's still sinking in.'

'Can you imagine her giving a lap dance?' Jane struck her hands into her waist and sidled her hips. 'No, can't do it.'

'Lap dance?'

'No, see Cynthia doing one.'

'It would be like this,' I said. 'Cynthia shimmies for him, sweeping a figure-of-eight across her devil's pomegranates with her fingers, but her oatmeals start to slide and slink around her legs, but he thinks, as Little Reg struggles to pounce out of his tweeds like the Chest-Burster out of *Alien* . . .'

'Ew. . . Nathan!'

' . . . that she's wearing a thong, and he's delighted by this, because he's thought about it a lot, alone in his bed, the midnight tremors, taking a picture of it in his mind, but the thong's just the tatters of some baggies she's had since nineteen eighty-six that have perished in the boil wash.'

'Hold that thought,' said Jane, 'please.'

But I couldn't. Another strip in *Bunty Boiler* occurred to me. This one was called *The Headmaster Ritual*. Reggie Carn is leading a double life, the parts of which collide dramatically and erotically when he realizes that Cynthia Nervous, a children's clown he's employed to entertain the boys at his Academy for Morally Destitute Urchins turns out to be Wonder Wadge, a woman he's previously met through the lonely old farts section in a magazine for randy patriots called *Albion's Bayonet*. She's always worn a mask made out of oatmeal sweatpants for their assignations but during her balloon blowing show, suddenly . . .

The crimson migraine stamped on my forehead.

'Ouch.'

'What's up?' Jane put a cup of hot coffee on the bedside cabinet.

'Headache, that's all. It keeps coming. Like lightning striking.'

'Drama queen.' She sat down on the bed. 'You're just in a mood.' I propped myself up, giving her room to rest against the wall and dangle her long legs, today in pale blue jeans, over the side.

'It's sinking in,' I said.

'Mac's deal?'

'No. That was the last workshop I'll ever run. I didn't even make it to the end of the day. I didn't even last fifteen minutes.'

'I don't think it was your fault,' she said. 'I think you're right. Something weird is going on. Last night, it was weird.' She gave me a look, then turned away to glance at the window. The muffled hubbub of larping drifted over from the park. As she took a sip of her drink and seemed to think on what she was going to say next, her pushed-back hair caught in the light and rippled with tawny gold.

'Mac was pleased with himself,' she said. 'Understandably. And I think people are pleased for him, but you're right, Nathan. I don't get it. I don't think he knows what he's talking about.'

'He thinks Chekhov's in *Star Trek*?'

'But when Mac speaks, I feel something going from me and I *have* to listen. If you hadn't mentioned that Reg has changed his tune so much I don't think I would have noticed. It's like Mac has a hold over people.'

'Well, he has sold his soul to the devil.'

'Maybe the devils have sold their souls to a bigger devil?'

'Devils don't have souls, Jane.'

'Pedantic men are *so* attractive.' She flicked at my shin with the back of her hand. 'Last night, after Reg and Cynthia went to bed, and they didn't, I mean, I hope not, anyway, after they'd gone and it was just the four of us, he, Mac that is, noticed that Frank was getting a bit close to me again. And he was, you know, he kept glaring at me and muttering about "grasses". And this was what was really odd. Mac just bobbed his head at Frank and then at Erika, and said: "off you go," and they got up and left.'

'Just like that?'

'Just like that. We finished our drinks and by then I was getting a bit knackered. I only got back from Cardiff yesterday afternoon.'

'Cardiff?'

'Conference. The Rat Problem.'

'I've been trying to call you.'

'It was good to get away. Had some thinking time. You're right. Something's weird about all of them. Like I say, we finished our drinks

450

and Mac made me go outside and we saw Frank and Erika kissing on a bench out the back. I don't think it went further than that. She's in the room next to mine and she came back on her own.'

'So you think neither of us has to have *those* images in our heads?'

'No, but . . .'

'He's a virgin with obvious problems,' I said, 'who's recently been suspected of serial murder, and she's . . .'

'Got obvious problems and recently was suspected of stalking. It just felt like Mac willed them to do it.' Jane's fingers interlocked around the cup and her palms seemed to swell as if she were drawing the warmth out of the liquid. 'It doesn't bode well.'

'Maybe they're just having some fun. I'm relieved. I don't need to think about this anymore. It's done with. I'm out on my ear.'

'Everything's weird. That wasn't your fault down there. And what the Dickens was Cynthia playing at?'

'She wants to be a writer more than she's willing to write, that's why she copied something. She doesn't want to lose her illusion.'

'But, right, Cynthia told me yesterday that she'd written a story she really liked and then ripped it up and changed it at the last minute. She said she felt as if a voice was urging her to bin it and as you'd said to trust your instincts, if it feels wrong, change it, she changed it.'

Something from *The Little Girl and the Little Puppy* that had freaked me as Cynthia read came back to me. Why had she chosen a chihuahua as the puppy? I didn't recall chihuahuas being common in Czarist Norfolk. As I pondered this, the crimson migraine swelled up again.

'Oh, I can't think about this anymore,' I said. 'It's over for me. No more teaching and no more writing. Who wants to lie to himself?'

'You're not lying to yourself.'

'I don't know. Since the start of this term my imagination seems to have dwindled. I'm having bad dreams. I'm getting headaches. All I can think up at the moment are ideas based on the group. I just keep making up stories about the group. It's just . . . ridiculous, pathetic.'

'You've been writing stories about us?'

'No. Dreaming up stories. Can't write them, obviously. Can't write.'

'I found some of your stories. I was . . . turned inside out, you made me want to feel things like you feel them.'

'You really don't,' I said.

'I do.'

451

'I wrote you a story.'

'Can I see it?'

'It's not finished. Or written down. It's kind of up here. I . . . Jane. After last week, I tried to call you . . .'

'You didn't leave a message . . .'

'I wanted to say sorry, so I thought I'd write you a story to . . . tell you how I've come to feel about you.'

'Oh my dear,' she said. She squeezed herself up the bed a bit more, easing me out of the corner so she could sit beside me.

'I wish I could show it to you,' I said.

'Tell me about the story?' Her eyes fired with blue sheen again and both her hands were now rested on my thigh. Streamers of warmth flowed up my leg to fizzle in the pit of my stomach.

'Well,' I said. 'It's about a private eye, a female PI, obviously .'

She dipped her head towards me, as if this titbit of information was enough for her, but I bottled it, because I'm a total shambles and bottler, and slipped off the bed to find the bag in the bedside cabinet where I'd hidden it.

'It's about a private eye who wears one of these.'

'My pashmina!' said Jane, taking it out of the bag and hugging it to her chest. 'These are silly but I like them.'

'I like you in them,' I said.

'Come here,' she said. 'I want to hear more about my story.'

'I told you, it's not finished.'

'Well, if it's a good story, maybe we can, you know, act out the end.'

'Seeing as I can't write anymore, I could show you the end, I suppose.'

I was soon lying alongside her on the bed, the pashmina squashed between us, kissing and kissing and kissing. I'd like to be able to say that all I was thinking about as we kissed was the kissing, especially as Jane was proving to be very good at it and kissing seemed to be a much better problem-solver than coffee. But, lying together, side by side with my hands wrapped around her waist and her hands pressed to my cheeks, all sorts of nonsense was going through my head. I couldn't help thinking that she was imagining this as a scene from *Gentleman's Relish*. I was Sly, obviously, but stunningly miscast; she was Paris Leggi or something.

38: INT. SLY'S PAD — NIGHT

Through the archway, we see Sly. He wears a white
tuxedo and looks especially greasy and smarmy and is
silhouetted against the glittering skyline outside
the window.

FADE TO BLACK

THEN FADE OUT as we see that the black is the black
of Paris's little black dress that then slips from
her back and down over her legs.

> PARIS
>
> You're early?

> SLY
>
> I'm never early.

> PARIS
>
> I'm all undressed.

> SLY
>
> My name's Sylvester Sly
> Ramos-Pintos, but you can
> call me Lover, lover.

> PARIS
>
> Oh Lover, why did it take us
> so long?

> SLY
>
> You order the burger. You
> get it flame grilled.

Then I began to imagine our kissing as one of her stories:

Hand in hand, they left the room stuffed full of
jostling bimbos merrily partying to celebrate the
end of the course and Mac MacMacaroon's good news.
Jennifer Damson stood now in his too-white room,
fighting to stop herself going lobster-red with lust
as the man she had adored since they first met made
ropey coffee in horrid white plastic cups. She knew
that her world wouldn't be complete unless she had
Nathan Flackov, Norfolk's weirdest creative writing
tutor. He was on the other side of the room, making
the coffee with his wit and charm. He could have
taken his pick of the other lovelies in the group
but he had chosen her. He spilled the coffee all
over the rug and his trousers in his headlong dash
to her arms, then kissed her just as powerfully as
Milly Swiggins-Potter had kissed the back of her
hand when they were mere girls of thirteen in the
girls cloakroom at school.

This story fizzled out, as stories have a tendency of doing if you're not
careful, and became subsumed by the warmth of her tongue and the
caress of her hands and the faintly apricot smell of her skin. I felt as if
great chunks of ice were detaching from me, icebergs shaped like fins and
pillars, shattering ramparts and broken tusks. Only the kissing existed
now, not rejection slips or letters to publishing houses, or Frederick
Malone or Oliver Blox, or angst about the flow of the first three chapters
of The Penelope Tree or where Millennium Bridge was going and who on
earth was that girl? Where was she headed and what would happen? What
if. If only. Where had it gone, The Girl on the Millennium Bridge, my
novel? Or pent-up rancour about Mac and his million pound deal, or
worry about Seb, and Erika and Frank. Or Sylvester Sly Ramos-Pintos
and his one-dimensional existence, Shazzer Plum's identity shifts and
machinations, or Frances's unreasonable expectations, or the creepers in
the shadows: the Hooded Figure, The He, Arnold Bumrape and
Sododog; the garret and all its wet and damp and the haunted winter that
was about to deepen and chase me down under my bedclothes; or
Grammar-Stammery, or Literature Denial, or Wrong-Roomery or
Sensitive Plantation, Moon-Barking or Rom-Tism; or O'Mailer and

whether I was bonkers in the head, seeing things, hearing things, beset by ghosts. All this seemed to float away and just as I was about to wonder if this was a clichéd thing to have thought and maybe I should think a bit more on kissing, do some free-writing, play some word association games, larp with language, Jane stopped kissing and said: 'Oh Nathan, why did it take us so long?'

I was about to say that maybe this delay had something to do with a dream I'd had where we killed Frank the Wank and dumped his body in the Grand Anglian sewer, but thought better of it. This was more than a kiss, and I didn't want to ruin it by sounding like Norfolk's weirdest creative writing tutor.

'Shh . . . Class dismissed.'

I ran my hand along the ribbed sleeve of her white top, then swirled my palm over her trembling stomach. Her back arched as I began to pull up the top. Her tongue was searching deep in my mouth now and her lipstick was beginning to smear over my face, I could tell. I found the lower loop of the cups of her bra and just as I rolled her under me and found the clasp at the back of the bra, the door thumped open with a massive kick. Mac MacMahon staggered, sweating with laughter into the room with his tequila bandolier strapped to his gut and his arms thrusting up two bottles as if the whistle had just blown at Wembley after he'd scored a last minute winner of astounding audacity and singular genius.

'Erika has got a cock!'

Spread the Love like Mustard over Soft, Warm Baps

Jane's legs whipped up as she tried to roll out from under me, but her top trapped my hands. My weight dragged her sideways and we toppled off the bed. As we sprawled on the floor I managed to disentangle my fingers from her bra straps. We both shunted on our bottoms back into the side of the bed. Jane hurriedly tugged down her top and thrashed her fingers through her hair while I tried to wipe away the lipstick smudged over my face. Mac was a gigantic X above us, a veritable Orion, twenty stone of bearded glee lofting the two tequila bottles triumphantly at the ceiling.

'Erika, Erika has got a cock.'

'For crying out loud,' said Jane.

'What the raving arse do you think you're doing?' I said.

'Erika has got a cock.'

'Bollocks.' I said.

'And a cock. She's got a cock as well.'

'She's not a she if she's got a tadger, is she?' said Jane.

'True,' said Mac, pulling up the wicker chair. He took a swig from one of the bottles, then handed it in my direction. I palmed it away.

'How the Hell do you know Erika's got a cock?' I said. 'How the Hell would you know that? How much of that stuff have you done?'

'I was watching,' said Mac.

'That's disgusting,' I said. 'And probably illegal.'

'Some of the things they were doing were probably illegal, but they asked me.'

'Well, you didn't have to stay, did you?' said Jane.

'Wouldn't have missed it for the world. It's like research for my next novel . . .'

'What's it going to be called?' I said. 'Erik or Erika??'

'Good title that, Nate, cheers.' He took out an index card from one of the bandolier's shot glass hoops and scribbled on it with a stubby bookmaker's biro. 'Anyway, I was just watching, right, and when they gets down to it . . .'

'I don't think we need to know the details,' said Jane. 'We get the picture.'

'Well,' I said. 'She has been saying that "The He is coming" for ages.'

Jane prodded me in the chest and screwed up her face. 'It's not a competition, boys. Anyway, Mac is The He.'

'Certainly am. Worships me, that woman, I mean man, I mean whatever she is.' He took a great gulp of tequila and wiped at his beard with the back of his hand.

'Mac,' said Jane. 'Don't you think you've been just a teensy bit irresponsible. I mean, can't you see that they're both very vulnerable people?'

'Oh don't be like that, Janey.' He passed her the bottle, which this time she took and knocked back a shot like a trooper. 'I don't know, like, I feel like I'm on stage again. If I say jump, the crowd jumps, if I say show us your zippos, they all light up and sway and sing and cop off with each other.'

'I thought you were the drummer?' I said.

'I'm rock and roll down to me undercrackers. I just want everyone to be happy. I'm happy. And I want to spread the love like mustard over soft, warm baps . . . hang on.' He reached for the index card and his tongue poked out from the corner of his mouth as he scrawled out another note to himself.

'Mac?' I said.

457

'I just thought I could fit em up, that's all. I'm like that bird in that Austen Powers film.'

'What?' said Jane. 'Liz Hurley?'

'Nah, that bird Reggiebaby is always going on about.'

'He means Jane Austen,' I said. 'Sense and Sensibility.'

'Yeah, like that,' said Mac. 'Except I'm for real. I'm a loved up puppy dog with me Shazzer and, look, done it for you guys, ain't I?'

I looked at Jane and she looked at me and we both shook our heads.

'And I've done it for Reggiebaby and Sinful Cynth,' said Mac.

'Oh you haven't?' I said. 'He's been married to the same woman since the fish crawled up onto the beach and changed into their frog costumes.'

'Can I have that as well?' he said, pen poised.

'Mac,' said Jane. 'I think it was rather rude of you to burst in on us like that.'

'Well, I wasn't intending on staying, if that's what's worrying you lovely lovebirds. The thing is, right, I don't know. Frank, right, you know Frank? Well, I don't think finding out that Erika's got a dirty great boner did his noggin much good.'

'Well, it wouldn't, would it?' I said. 'The man's certifiable.'

'I don't know . . . it happened to me once in Hamburg, but I thought that if the poor bugger had gone through all that it would have been rude not to, if you know what I mean, who cares about the mantelpiece when you're stoking . . .'

'Mac, that's a very enlightened viewpoint, but what has Frank done?'

'He kind of screamed the place down and now he's kind of chasing her around the building, I think. I don't know. She ran out. He ran after her. I can't find them.'

'Oh no,' said Jane.

'Do you see what happens when you meddle with things you don't understand? Put the pen away. What are we going to do?'

He shrugged. The last thing I needed to add to my list of failures was to have a crime of passion on my watch. Even the strip in Bunty Boiler wasn't supposed to end this badly. I stood up. Jane followed.

'We're going to have to go and look for them,' she said.

'OK. I'm thinking. OK. We split up, right. Jane, you go outside and look around the park.' Given the high population of larpers, Jane wouldn't be alone if I allotted her that territory. 'Mac, take the downstairs. I'll do up here. If any of us finds Frank, we take him to the bar. If anyone

458

of us finds Erika, we take her to the seminar room. If we find Reg or Cynthia, put them in the picture and send them to look outside and find Jane. OK?'

'Great,' said Mac. 'It's like kiss chase, but in reverse gear. Nate, want some of this?'

Treachery and Magic

A molten layer of tequila simmered in my gut. Standing outside the too-white room I watched Mac and Jane walk towards the elevator, then vanish from view. The lift bell chimed. The doors shushed. Giggles drifted from one of the rooms at the other end of the corridor.

As I crept towards the laughter all the hairs on my arms and the nape of my neck prickled. Cupid and Psycho may well have patched up their differences and come back here; or this could be a completely spurious bug-hunt. I delegated myself the upstairs sweep because I couldn't be sure that Mac had told the truth. Erika had a cock? Erika was a man in drag? Mac's imagination could be fecund in the realm of the sleazy and genital, as I remembered from all the bits that I cut from the Death Metal Revelations, and this morning he was euphoric and possibly whacked off his bonce on tequila. Penis Erika kind of made sense though – some profound secret or longing had to be at the root of her behaviour – but it did seem like material from DMR. Or worse, it seemed like one of Shazzer's old stories, before she was the Bride of the Paddle, before she was Juliet Largo, when she was Pauline Thigh, writer of gritty, realist stories of gender identity problems and lesbian awakening. Maybe she'd sat up in bed and read him one of her old unsold tales and in his mind the line between reality and fiction had disintegrated. Perhaps later on she and

Mac would have a lover's tiff over who would write Erik or Erika? Or maybe they could write one of those novels in which married authors alternate male and female narrated chapters and conjoin their names to create a pseudonym. Bonnie and Hyde by Paddle Largo-Plums. Ms Boner! by Shazzer MacMahon. Oliver Blox would chew the carpet to sign that up. I started to visualize the jacket photo and Mac's head on Shazzer's body, but the crimson migraine rippled through me.

The laughter came from a door midway along the corridor. I paused and pressed my ear to it. It was definitely laughter: muffled laughter, playful murmur. I knocked. No one answered. This was a serious business and I had a pastoral duty to the Arcana. I was going to have to enter the room without invitation, and, in the way shown to me by my most esteemed student prodigy The Paddle, shout 'Erika, have you got a cock?' Teaching creative writing is not a job. It's a vocation.

A thin glimmer of light appeared as I opened the door slowly. The light did not brighten as I sneaked in. All I could see were the translucent oblong of the drawn curtains and two vague, silhouetted heaps, one higher up than the other. The room smelled of vacuumed carpet and fresh linen. I reached for where the switch should be and clicked it on. The room rushed at me as the light drained the darkness from the two heaps.

Cynthia was standing in the middle of the room with her oatmeals pooled around her ankles.

Reg sat on the side of the bed with his tweed trousers concertinaed to the floor. Where his shirttails parted around his thighs I could see he was wearing a skimpy pair of grey briefs covered with little pictures of Winston Churchill's head in profile, each with a disembodied V-for-Victory finger salute level with an uptilted cigar.

'Well, well, well,' I said. 'Isn't this the best job in the world?'

'Oh my God,' cried Cynthia.

'Oh my God,' I said, pointing at my head with my index finger. 'What have you done to me? What is this? Some bedroom farce version of Cocoon?'

'Flack,' said Reg as Cynthia squat-thrusted to reach for the sweatpants and cover herself. 'We were just comparing . . . knees, that's all.'

'You were comparing knees? She was giving you a lap dance with the light off, you tortoise.'

'Consenting adults, Flack, consenting adults.'

'With the bloody light off?'

'Decorum, please.'

'All that blathering, pandery nonsense you've given me and I catch you with your bags down in the throes of lust with a children's entertainer.'

'Pandery, Flack, what sort of word is that?'

'A word I made up to describe you, you turtle.'

'Well!'

'Pull your strides up to where they normally live and if I ever, ever hear one word of criticism coming my way from either of you again, and you especially, Reginald, I'll bombard The People's Friend with stories that caricature you so mercilessly and evisceratingly that you won't be able to show your face in this sceptred isle ever again.'

Cynthia curled up in this too-white room's equivalent of the wicker chair, her head buried into the cushion.

'Flack,' said Reg. 'I see no reason for any unpleasantness here, and I see no reason for my Darling Dear to know of this.'

'He made us do it,' sobbed Cynthia. 'He made us.'

'I know,' I said, 'so I won't tell your wife, Reg, or your . . . puppets or balloons or strings of sausages or whatever, Cynthia, but only if neither of you slag me off to the department ever again. I've been trying to teach you something here.'

Reg leaned over and dragged up his trousers. He straightened his crest-studded tie and reached out his hand for the shake.

'You've done a sterling job, Flack' he said. 'Marvellous. Marvellous.'

'Thank you. Thank you very much for that. Now listen, this is serious.'

I explained the Frank and Erika situation without actually mentioning any willy business and sat down on the bed and watched them as they more or less ran out of the room to get away from me. When I heard the lift bell again I got up and looked out of the window. Fort Larper, seen from this angle, was a line of tents and food stalls and shops flogging armour and jewellery and clothes set up on a ridge that lifted along the breadth of the park. I tried to locate Jane, but I couldn't see her. My eyes glossed over and I started to wonder if the offspring of a Sensitive Plant and a Grammar-Stammerer would be a Sensitive Stammerer or a Grammar Plant. A crimson spike jabbed into the back of my head and I had to sit down again and wait for the sickness to subside. Then I remembered what I ought to be doing and made my way back to the corridor. I would check the rest of our rooms. I would have a skim of the library and then the barracks o'larpers in the other wing, then I'd concede and go and find the others.

The room next door to Reg's turned out to be Jane's. The Montmartre bag was propped up on the wicker chair. This meant that the next room belonged to Erika. I nipped along on tiptoes. It was unlikely that either Frank or Erika would be the quietest of people, but I couldn't hear anything. So I paused and tried not to think that behind the door I was going to find two naked middle-aged men, one with a rough approximation of the hairstyle of a woman squirming about on the bed; or worse. It struck me that not so long ago I was still thinking of myself as a serious writer, but I'd never even seen a dead body. A writer covets experience. A writer does not flinch. What would Juicy Gash do here? He'd march fearlessly in and have a vigorous poke about. This is not a job. This is a vocation. I knocked. No answer. I knocked again and when no answer or sound followed, I pushed the door.

The curtains were open and the room swimming with dust specks. The bed was unmade and the undersheet tangled up and ripped from the mattress, as if the occupant had suffered an uneasy night of vicious dreams or restless anticipation. Four mirror-backed hairbrushes were laid out in an undulating line on the table. I kicked gently at the bathroom door. No one lay unconscious, bleeding or dead on the tiles. No corpse was slumped or arranged in the shower cubicle. Back in the bedroom I sat down on the mattress and wondered what on earth would have been going through Erika's head as she tried to sleep last night? I then tried to formulate a sense of what Frank would have felt when it was revealed that Erika was a transvestite. This idle fictionalizing suddenly seemed wrong. Crimson migraine throbbed through me and I remembered that something fraught was going on here, not to me but to others. As I got up to leave and find Frank's room, I noticed that Erika's bulging handbag rested against the wall beneath the window.

I did not flinch. I went over and picked it up, then upended it and poured its contents onto the bed.

Crushed blackcurrant juice cartoon.

Lippy.

Apple made of smooth wood that rolled onto the floor and over to the door.

Black beanie hat (inside out and gritty, as if used to transport sand for some reason).

Man's Cossack hairspray aerosol.

463

Huge bunch of ancient, brassy keys that jingled and clicked and for a second I thought might have a life of its own.

Ball of red wax.

Pocket torch with 'Torchy' written on the side in correcting fluid.

Filthy-dirty Tiny Clanger doll that made a cooing, squeaky noise.

Dan Air cabin crew nameplate badge. Vernon Goater.

Next to the badge was something hand-sized wrapped in greaseproof paper.

As I took hold of the packet I fell to my knees. The little filament studs and raised polygons of spines, the patterns that flowed up its limbs to form a maple-leaf shape at its heart stood out beneath the greaseproof paper. I could sense the five arms and the channelled grooves on their undersides sandwiched between my palms. I was almost reliving the first time I ever touched it when Johanna gave it to me in Australia. The paper fell away and I held it to my chest. If when I'd kissed Jane and she kissed me great chunks of ice seemed to break off from me, now it felt like a whole polar cap was melting but all at once, as if zapped by some space station's orbital blaster. A thousand orgasms at once. Conception to adolescence in ten seconds flat. I closed my eyes and could see but not see, imagine but not picture the shape that I held in my hands as some sort of distant whizzing thing, a descending bird of prey, a discus of flame, a comet hurtling through the gloom towards me. I girded myself and when it struck me right between the shoulder blades all the crimson weight, the sickness and headache that had dogged my every thought for weeks rushed away from me. In my mind's eye it flew from my pores as red smoke that hung for a second in the corners of the room, lingered as dust, then disappeared.

My pelvis felt so weak that I feared it might sink into my legs, so I slumped sideways and wriggled onto the bed. I lay there on the bare mattress with the starfish resting on my chest and closed my eyes. In the darkness I felt myself floating and was sure I was lifting two or three inches above the bed. I was in The State, migraine-free. I could sense the pace of it, its tension, its geometry and soundtrack, its headlong rush, its combat, its treachery and magic, and I felt like I used to feel in the garret in the mornings, in the dark before sunrise when I'd scribble and scratch in a notebook until I was armoured against the cold. The coffee and nicotine would kick in and I'd write half a page of The Penelope Tree until I was satiated, the same two hundred and fifty words over and over again until they had a diamond-hard quality to me, an unquestionable, unimpeachable, loveable characteristic that would survive until I reread them again the next morning and took the passage apart, then put it back together. This was not a job. This was a vocation. This was not sanity. This was living. This was experience, not a career. The uncreated conscience. The unwritten world. The green breast. I saw the girl on the Millennium Bridge waft again across the river. I saw the children digging the garden and planting their tree. I saw Sylvester Sly Ramos-Pintos blinking in the lamplight and realizing at last . . . And I saw myself elsewhere now, kissing Jane in some private place, and then rest of The Black Starfish jumped at me like a pop-up in a picture book. If I'd the strength I would have held on to the words and the paragraphs and written the chapter line by line across the walls in crayon[94].

---

[94] The Black Starfish
A PI Pashminski Mystery
By Nathan Flack
IV

The black Daimler was trailing me again as I whizzed through town towards my office but this time I took no evasives. I had a pretty good idea of who sat behind that tinted glass. I parked up outside my office and ducked down low, using the wing mirror to keep a keen one fixed on the Well Thumbed. The Daimler passed, but in less time than it took me to retrieve my taser from the glove compartment, Nate Flake came traipsing along the pavement continually checking over his shoulder until he disappeared into the shop. I gave him thirty secs, then took my Scarlets over the road.

The shop's interior was crammed with shelves and heaps of second-hand books, plus a beguiling and frankly bizarre collection of what looked like rubbish: animal skulls; a chicken farm of wishbones; a typewriter with the keys clipped off; seven broomheads glued together in a lopsided pyramid shape. It was a small shop but I couldn't eyeball Flake and for a moment imagined that he'd pulled a lever that spun around a shelf to reveal a murky secret passage that I'd have no reservations at all about exploring even if I was dressed only in my skimpiest negligee. The shopkeeper was a squat, bushy haired creature with a head the shape of an upturned bucket. I prowled over to the desk.

'Hello,' I said. 'I wonder if you can help me.'

'You want the magic of poetry?'

'Not my cup of char. I'm looking for Nate Flake. About five-eight. Glasses. Jumpy, scared-of-his-shadow type. He just came in and he didn't come out.'

'You, you persecute him?'

'No, I just want a friendly word.'

'The He, you come to persecute The He.'

She slumped back and with both hands clutched a bookshelf behind her and a whole stack of tottering tomes began to shiver and shake.

'No persecution here. I have important news for him.'

'You are the herald of the He?'

'Er . . . you could say that.'

'He lives upstairs. You go.'

For the second time that day I eased myself through a bead curtain and found myself at the bottom of a fire escape. At its top I found a door that I knocked on until Nate Flake appeared looking terrified out of his wits. He let me in without whining or squealing and my Scarlets and I found ourselves parked in a tiny, studenty front room with a writing desk, lots of books and some crap paintings. I clocked straightaway that Flake's window peered obviously out at my office.

'So Flake,' I said. 'This is where you plan your plots?'

He couldn't look at me and muttered something about tea but it would have to be black because the milk was off.

'Let me give you a debrief,' I said. 'I check out Reggie Carn. He barks at the moon but knows nothing of you, your adversary or the missing five-pointed McGuffin. I check out Mack the Hack and the dice comes up with the same combination except this time I almost get a Rohypnol wedding cake. So, I've drawn a lot of blanks for your deposit. You want it back?'

He scratched the side of his head and looked at me sheepishly.

'There are other avenues we could explore.'

'Don't play the lamb with me, inspector. Check one: you called Dank to enquire about Carn. You knew already he had nothing to do with anything organized but still you set this dogged Rottweiler on his cottontail. Check two: you've been following me around in your nice black car ever since I cased Carn's manor. Check three: I suss now that you've been giving me the once over from outside this shop for months. I rarely forget a face. Check four: what are you up to, Flake, 'cos you know as well as I know that there's no Sly Pintos and there's no black starfish and I don't like to remember what I caught sight of this afternoon?'

'Was it bad?'

I nodded.

'How bad?' he said.

466

I stretched out my arms as wide as they could go until my pashmina hung from them like batwings.

'I feel embarrassed,' he said.

'Go on.'

'I just noticed you, that's all, from my window here while I write. You in your office marching around and thinking and . . .'

'You just wanted to get to know me? Well, Flake, a cup of coffee goes a lot farther than a useless trawl through the backstreets of Lowliving twinned with Fruitcakesville.'

'I've blown it now, haven't I?'

I wanted to say 'maybe not' but I didn't want to let this fishy-fish off the hooky-hook so easily. Even so, my Scarlets were making the decision for me and I found myself backing Flake into his desk.

'Oh Ms Pashminski,' he said. 'You are lovely.'

'You could have tried telling me that instead of sending me the way of the goose,' I said as our lips moved closer together.

'The thing is,' he said, his hand now on my hip and his other holding mine to the other hip, 'it isn't quite a goose chase.'

'Spill it, Flake. Time maybe running out, for you and me and the whole big sleepy city.'

'Sylvester-Sly Ramos-Pintos has stolen my black starfish. I just didn't have any proper leads.'

'You mean . . .'

At that very moment, the door was opened by a loud kick and in strode a monk in a brown cowl. He ripped off the hood, then ripped open the habit and let it fall to the ground. He was tall and muscular with a rugged, stubbly face, so handsome that he seemed kind of vacant, and he wore leather trousers and a leather waistcoat and around his neck on a chain he wore the black starfish as a medallion.

'Not so fast, Lovebirds,' he said as he pointed right at us a Colt 45.

'Put down the piece, Pintos,' I said.

'On your knees, this is the bad ending coming up for yous two, capische?'

Quick as an eel I reached into my pashmina and whipped out my taser. I gave him a voltage tickle right in the groin area. He fell onto the floor, weeping and moaning. My Scarlets nipped over to his quivering form. I plucked the black starfish from the chain, then helped him to the door, and then booted him down the fire escape.

It wasn't an ending, 'sort of'. It was a beginning, almost. When I came to write down the story I'd make sure to have another look at that line.

I didn't know how long I'd been here by now, dreaming with the starfish resting on my jumper when more practical things needed my attention, but until two months ago this was pretty much my *modus operandi* and I felt supremely comfortable. The starfish, though, suddenly bulked up, not to an unbearable degree but it became pretty heavy for a starfish. Then the distribution of its weight changed and four clawed pads sunk into my chest. Something rough and wet started to brush against my face. For a moment I thought Jane may have come up to find me and had slipped in alongside and was kissing my face but in my limited experience she was a much better kisser than this. There was a smell, too, the odour of warm fur and moist breath. When I opened my eyes, a chihuahua was staring back at me with its black, glassy peepers and sulky, squashed little girl's face.

Someone was standing in the corner of the room. Someone broad and bluff and bearded. Someone whose monocle glinted. Someone resting on a thick cane.

'Hello Kiddo.'

The Best Story Ever Written

I blinked, as if coming up from a three-day sleep. I wasn't sure whether I'd heard the voice in *The* State or in the room, but then something thumped on the carpet, followed by a scamper of paws. The chihuahua bounded across the floor to jump up at its master. I lifted myself and dropped my legs over the side of the bed, swivelling my eyes to find that click at my temples I'd used before to push O'Mailer back into the recesses. He stayed solid, though, definitely, defiantly *there*, standing in a gigantic, wide-pinstriped suit, Dickens-Dostoyevsky beard and short black cape. He caught the dog in his hand and clutched it to his chest.

'Good boy, Parsons,' he said. 'You will dine on capons tonight.'

I fluttered my eyes again, trying to clear my vision, make him go away.

'Kiddo, you can't have one without the other,' he said, stroking the boss of his stick with his thick fingers. 'Your trinket there mediates against the little hex I cast on you beneath the mountain. I'm back. Miss me?'

Grabbing the first thing that came to hand, I pitched the Dan Air nameplate at him. I fully expected it to pass right through him and lodge in the wall, after which I would call for a taxi and throw myself at the mercy of the nearest psychiatric unit.

469

O'Mailer raised his hand and managed to a grab the badge without dropping his stick. He tossed it back to me.

'You really are the one upon whom everything is lost. Ponder. When I lurked in the shadows of our dear Ovid as he strolled the shore of the Black Sea, what name did we give to the first collection of tales?'

'Not this again.'

'You don't know?'

'*The Metamorphoses*. I'd be impressed if you ever told me something I didn't already know.'

'But what a story have you missed here! Huddle in around the fire and let O'Mailer recount the story of Our Lady of the Goat.'

'I don't like you. I don't want you to be here.'

'I haven't come to rub it in, have I, Parsons?'

The dog yapped and I wondered if anyone else, anyone passing the door, Frank or Erika, Jane or Mac, a cleaner, a maid could hear that yap.

'You stopped Cynthia from writing her story,' I said.

'It was quite accomplished. You did well there. But there's no point. I saved her the aggravation.'

'That's all you are, aggravation.'

'Believe in me now, Kiddo?'

'What do you want?'

'A little banter, a little table talk *sans* vino, a little debrief now that the final curtain is about to swish.'

'A debrief?'

'If only you had listened to papa, Kiddo.'

'I should have listened to the careers advisor at school.'

'So should have Vernon Goater. Employee of a defunct airline. Now, who on earth did our Vernon metamorphose into?'

'The poor old git.'

'Ah poor Vernon, yes. Poor Vernon. I'll fill in the blanks that must to you now seem vasty spaces, interstices like gullies in his biography.'

'I ought to be saving Vernon's bacon, not listening to you prattle.' I got up to leave, taking the starfish with me, and walked past O'Mailer. His eyes lit up with golden sparkle. The tock sound followed and when I reached the corridor he was standing ahead of me.

'Curiosity fails you, Kiddo. You will never hear this story from her lips.'

'I certainly won't if Frank finds her before me.' I started to walk towards the library, but O'Mailer fell in alongside me.

'A trifling matter. Listen as we go. Vernon, Vernon, born in Spalding, the Lincolnshire mires in the year of Our Lord nineteen fifty-six. A little flighty, our Vern, a little uncomfortable in his frame, desirous of the dainty, the stylized, the elegantly posed. His daddy ran at the first sight of him. His mummy was a magnetic goddess, or at least a siren relegated to the role of post-mistress just as I am demoted to the role of your confidante and chaperone. The fairy books his cutesy play-sisters used to browse turned his head. Little Vernon used to press his face to the slats of the junior school fence and not just admire the older girls as they played netball with vigour and thrust, but wanted to be, become one of them, wanted those tight black leotards to hug his smooth groin, and wanted hairless, coltish legs, wanted to prance like them, wanted to spin.'

'OK,' I said as we passed the lift. The doors sprang open. A helmetless larper dressed in a suit of plate-armour clanked out, just as I said: 'The psychological route map of any common-or-garden transvestite.'

'Pardon?' said the larper.

'My friend and I are just talking, kind sir,' said O'Mailer and reached out and shook the larper's mailed fist before slapping me on the back and forcing me to carry on towards the library.

'My God, he saw you,' I said.

'Yes, he did, that could be grievous news for me, so stop interjecting.'

'He saw you!'

'Did you ever doubt me?'

'Yes! Oh Jesus' bollocks, he can touch you!'

O'Mailer huffed. 'Anyway, where was I? Vernon. Dear Vernon. When Vernon reached the age of puberty he did shave the hairs from his shins, his chest, his toes. Smooth Vernon. Used to dress up in his mother's skirts and nylon straps while she was out licking stamps and other savoury delights in the postmaster's office. Then he stopped.'

'Stopped?' I said as we reached the library, where at this moment I should have been giving polite and considered tutorials to the Arcana, not indulging a time-hopping, Norse immortal and omniscient narrator with verbal dysentery. It was a room lit by four Jacobean windows and surrounded on three sides by bookshelves crammed with old hardbacks. Battered leather armchairs and reading tables stood in clumps on the parquet floor. There was no one else here, no Frank, no Erika-Vernon.

'Stopped,' said O'Mailer, perching himself on an armrest and pressing his weight two-handedly on the boss of his cane.

'Oh God, you're frigging real,' I said, 'I don't like this. I want this to stop. I'm going, I'm off. I'm going to find Jane.'

'What we could have averted should you have found her at the outset of this adventure.'

'And what was that?'

'All in good time, don't interrupt while the master is about his business . . . I am in full flood. Vernon, he stopped. Stopped his longing to be of female form. Willed himself back into the body of a boy. Made the best of manly pursuits in deepest, dankest Spalding and crept his way through school. He thought of it as a phase, and flew the world. I'm Vernon. Would you like some duty free? Duty free. That's our Vernon. Deceiving himself. Keeping himself to himself. Shunning mirrors. Down-turning his eyes when girls passed by on the cobbles. Growing a beard, not as refulgent as mine, I agree, yet it countered any thought in others that he shaved too closely, that he shaved not to remove the hair, but the skin. The Double Vernon, haunting his own life, the shadow of the shadowless, the shadow in the mirror of a man before a mirror with his eyes clenched shut.'

'You're getting windy,' I said. 'It's just not the best story ever written, is it? At least not how you tell it.'

'Do you know when our Vern had his moment of revelation? When he realized that he was the inverted version of his utter self, not the bearded steward but the Teutonic girl-poet, when the burial of identity became for him a crisis that would eventually drive him gaga, la la, whacko, from Spalding to Bedlam in a handcart?'

'Does it matter?'

'He was at a concert, a beastly affair, the music mortals call 'rock'. A small gathering. An alehouse stomp in Spalding town when our Vern was away from the trolley and the aisle and turbulence above the Bay of Biscay. And the name of the ensemble?'

'Ruiner,' I said. 'Must be.'

'No time for cigars and ice creams but yes, The Ruiner.' O'Mailer screwed up his face as if gargling with vinegar. 'And you know which song the granite troubadours strummed so wistfully that caused the quake inside that transfigured our loveable Vern?'

'The Nutsack Blues. Git-Willy Overdrive?'

'It was two and a half minutes of unstructured noise, like Neanderthals experimenting with sound by throwing mammoth bones against a cave wall. The name of the song? *That Bloke is a Bird.*'

'Noel Coward,' I said, 'eat your heart out.'

'Mozart, take note, but here The Fat Drummer who Beats His Meat with All His Heart made quite an impression on Transitional Vern. He conjured a vision that had our boy crying in his swill. Our Vern saw it all. His role as herald, court poet, jester. He saw that The He would come and The He would conquer.'

'This is all nonsense, isn't it?'

O'Mailer swung his cane side to side and both he and Parsons jiggled their heads in unison.

'No, I would not kid thee, not at this late hour, not when I risk so much by appearing to you.'

'What is all this bollocks?'

'Listen, Vernon that night became Erika and has ever since wandered the world seeking out a The He, an arduous quest since not only did The Fat Drummer's troupe of troubadours go four separate ways and he himself hid in the fjords for years, but Erika cannot remember Vernon, cannot recall in actuality what all this is about. It is pure instinct, pure madness. She felt his lure here. She confused others with him, including you for a while. But now, now her role as standard bearer for what singular and all-levelling power she glimpsed in him is about to rise dawn-like from behind the indigo hills.'

'So that's why you wanted me to knock off Frank, to protect the Holy Fool?'

'Kiddo, I was never interested in the Onanist of The Shed. I'm interested in . . .'

O'Mailer startled. His arms shook and he dropped the stick. Parsons yelped and ran around in circles about his master's boot tips. O'Mailer's face paled. His mouth hung open and his nostrils flared. He struggled up off the armrest but his weight unsettled the chair and as it fell on its side with a thump, he ended up on his backside, his legs akimbo and his shoulders trembling.

'James O'Mailer. On his arse,' I said. 'What's this turning into? Twilight of the Gods?'

'He's behind you,' said O'Mailer.

'Who? Vernon?'

'Don't be a dolt now. Behind you! Flack, I beg of you. Help.'

473

I turned. Static charged through my hair. I held the starfish tight to me. It was the only thing I could hold onto as standing in the doorway, faceless, hands hidden, feet covered, was the Hooded Figure. And behind the Hooded Figure were more Hooded Figures. The corridor between the library and the lift was jammed with a dozen of them at least. Hooded Figure behind Hooded Figure. An army of the Hooded Figures.

They began to shuffle into the library, parting into three groups, a line each along both of the walls and one coming right at us.

'The Canon have found us,' said O'Mailer, scrambling to his feet and regaining his stick.

'The Arts Council has minions?' I backed away from the brown cowl gliding towards me.

'They were never after you, they were always after me, and this time I have stayed too long and said too much. I have failed to outsmart my destiny.' He stepped up onto a reading table and stiffened his spine so that his girth hardened as he jutted his chin, his monocle glowing like lava as he swung his stick in an arc in front of him.

'Call forth the lofty instruments of war!'

Parsons sprang high in the air from under the table and landed barking and snapping right in the face of the monk about to grab hold of me. Lumps bounced from side to side in the hood and the man, if it was a man, thrashed his hands to his face, then crashed backwards into an armchair, flailing and jerking.

O'Mailer was shouting behind me. Other monks were scouring the bookshelves with their fingertips. I couldn't tell what they were looking for as another monk replaced the one that Parsons had dispatched. Before I could sidestep, the monk pushed my starfish and me roughly over into a chair. Suddenly, arms across my chest pinned me down from behind and hands gripped my ankles and another monk seemed to be trying to undo my belt. I buckled and squirmed, cried out, swore. These were larpers, weren't they? Management monkeys on some sort of debagging jape, some rude practical joke, a nostalgic spree now they were too old for the scrum, the lineout and plucking out each other's pubes in public places. A huge bang came from over my shoulder that I assumed was O'Mailer landing on the floor.

'Varlets, curs, get thee gone!'

The monk at my lap dug his hands into the pockets of my jeans. He found something and pulled it out. He held it up and seemed to study it. The arms around my torso and the hands that held my feet relaxed as the monk ahead tossed my cigarette lighter to one of his cohorts standing by the shelves with a hardback book in his hand. The cohort flapped open the book so the pages dangled. Then he clicked on the flame and wafted it under the paper.

I rushed up off the chair, shoving monks aside as clattering and cursing continued behind me. As I reached the monk who had received my lighter, the pages of the book started to smoulder. The title of the book, I couldn't help noticing, as I always draw an inference from what people are reading or have on their shelves or are setting alight, was *A Farewell to Arms* by Ernest Hemingway.

'Stop it' I said. 'Put that back.'

The monk tilted his head to the far end of the library. His companions were standing back in a rough semi-circle surrounding O'Mailer.

The arms of James O'Mailer were beginning to smoke.

Three of the monks at the shelves pulled out books and spun around as if choreographed. The one nearest to me held up *The Man with Two Left Feet and Other Stories* by PG Wodehouse. The next had *The Severed Head* by Iris Murdoch and the other lofted a copy of *Heart of Darkness*. Other monks were still scanning the shelves, searching, I presumed, for any book with a body part in the title.

'Make them cease, Flack,' shouted O'Mailer. ' New dwarves for a new world. They burn the precious life-blood of Kvasir.'

I stared around the room for a moment, at the phalanx of monks silently watching the coils of smoke rippling from O'Mailer's sleeves; at the others alongside me waiting their turn to set fire to a book; at a chihuahua leaping up at a hood and being battered down again and again. And I felt unable to act, or incapable of thinking of anything that I could do, and then realized that if I did nothing this might all just fade away. The books would return to the shelves and the voices would vanish and I'd either wake up with the starfish on my chest in Erika's too-white room. Or, better still, surface with the mere embarrassment of being found by Gloria, or knowing my luck, Reg, sprawled naked and swastika-shaped on the library floor after a maniacal sleepwalk. It would be eight in the morning and none of what had happened so far today would have really happened. Erika would not have a cock. I wouldn't have seen Cynthia giving Reg a lap dance. My first kiss with Jane, when it came would be experienced as delightful *déja vu*. And I'd never have to hear O'Mailer's over-phrased, cod-Renaissance blather in my head ever again. I would be free. Free of the voices that lured me to the grey ashtray light and the hammerhead silence of the garret. Free of the cast of The

Fumigator. Free of my bad prose, rubbish stories and trickiness to market. I would let O'Mailer frazzle and all this would end. Only a singe on the parquet would remain: the last image from a nightmare that I'd hardly remember.

In the best story ever written for me, I'd wake up and it *was* all a dream.

Outside that beach-front shop in Australia Johanna would not have given me the starfish but, I don't know, a fossilized sponge or a cuddly koala clutching a cuddly boomerang, and later on, that night ten years ago she would not drop my hand in the snow and I'd be call-centre manager man or assistant to Oliver Blox, rubber-stamping past-abroad-celebrities and 3-for-2 table product-shifters, and Johanna and I would be together and as happy as we could be.

It would not be a good story for you, but a great one for me.

My eyes started to sting. I blinked and the monks closed in tighter around O'Mailer. He called my name. The starfish seemed to pulse in my hand and it struck me that whatever was or wasn't real here I didn't want *this* story to end this way, with book burning and the lynching of a wordy ponce. I could do better than that. I spun around to the monk using *A Farewell to Arms* as kindling and ripped it from him. Before my fingers could smart on the burning jacket I swung my arm and hurled the book across the room. It carried in a blur of sparks and crashed into a window with a clang, then bounced into a wastepaper basket.

'James,' I shouted. His head sprang up. All the monks whipped around to face him. I reached out, grabbed the hand of the monk next to me and prized the lighter from his fist. O'Mailer then bounced like a gigantic, smoking ball over the heads of his enemies and Parsons, my starfish and I joined him as we ran out of the library.

In the corridor, we found that the lift door was shut. No way could we wait for it with the footfalls of The Canon rumbling behind us so we pelted on towards the stairs. Parsons leapt up over my head and lodged perfectly in O'Mailer's jacket pocket despite the arms of the suit still blazing. Maybe I should have spat on that Hemingway before I lobbed it. Smoke rushed into my face as I followed O'Mailer onto the walkway above the foyer. At the top of the stairs, I grabbed hold of the rail and had to pause to cough and wipe my eyes.

The Arcana were standing around in the foyer. Their heads turned as O'Mailer thundered headlong down the stairs towards the wedge of light on the mosaic floor the doors let in. Jane and Cynthia and Reg clustered around Frank, big Frank with his big glistening head and spade-beard and his arm around Erika. Or was it Vernon? Or was it possible to say, or correct to even speculate? Vernon? Erika? Verika? Even now they were inside my head, twisting another retcon out of me, changing their names, altering their qualities. And apart from them, a little way back, in the middle of the floor, talking into a mobile phone was Mac, The Paddle, The Fat Drummer Who Beats His Meat With All His Heart, The He, and he was the last to realize, realize that something was bowling down the stairs like a piano ejected from the tail-gate of a cargo plane.

He looked up and took the phone away from his ear just as O'Mailer flew over the bottom step and came to an immaculate halt right in his face. Eyeball-to-eyeball, they stared at each other and from up here I couldn't quite tell them apart, both of them broad and tall and dark suited, black bearded with wild hair, except of course for the telling details that O'Mailer was not wearing a tequila bandolier and Mac was not on fire.

Mac held out his arms and shrugged, perhaps a gesture of disbelief, a disarming gesture; body language learned from years of being bottled off-stage and handling let-down punters demanding refunds; a pacifying shrug, a 'hey, what's up?' A 'how's it going, buddy?' A 'shit happens', a 'yowza, you know you're on fire, man.'

O'Mailer swung out his right arm. Mac took a step back with his hands up as Frank and Jane made a short spurt towards them, but O'Mailer darted his arm into the other side of his jacket, ripped it off, flapped it up into the air and began to stamp on the smoking sleeves.

Then the door to my left crashed against the wall and The Canon burst out onto the landing waving their arms, brandishing their fists, stampeding right at me.

Starfish in hand, I jumped down the stairs, taking them three at a time. The heads below seemed to wobble in circles, shock in the faces, Jane and Reg and Cynthia, Mac and Frank and Erika, but O'Mailer, without even checking back, just ran for the door, out towards the park.

I didn't stop when I hit the floor, just carried on after him. I heard Jane call my name and shouts of surprise and confusion and the vibrating murmur of The Canon's charge down the stairs behind me, and then a drop in pitch as they must have reached the foyer floor and their footfalls changed from tom-tom thuds to a hundred tinny clicks. I heard Cynthia yelp. I caught Mac's eye as I passed, and heard Frank say: 'Them bazzers are chasing our Nathan, c'mon.'

The sunlight almost took my head off as I ran down the Grange's steps and across the gravel, following O'Mailer, following him without

477

thinking, just trailing him as he made it onto the grass and started to heave up the first slopes of the ridge. His graceless body joggled and shook but didn't seem to slow as the gradient increased. My lungs began to compress as the flags and tents of Fort Larper began to come into view. Sweat lashed across my head like a bucket of warm water. The ground started to club at my shins and I could hear shouting, different types of shouting from all around me, raucous, high, screechy, battle-cry, and I realized, as if until now I'd had my eyes closed, that I wasn't alone. The Canon had not caught up with me yet, but alongside me was Mac, Mac with his arms out as if asking for an answer, as if I were blindly leading him over the top in a World War I offensive and he was the only plucky working class soul who saw the futility of this, who saw the truth. And on my other side, head-down like a bull was Frank and with him his new best friend, Erika.

'The He . . . The He . . . The He.'

O'Mailer was still ahead of us; we were getting no nearer to him and along the ridge, as the tents and stalls and caravans of Fort Larper stood up now like a city in the desert, a line of smudged figures began to appear, fall into an orderly line, bristle and widen. I looked back now, and from here I could see the Grange and the carpark as a white and yellow taxi had pulled up and someone was getting out, and Jane and Reg and Cynthia were peering after us with their hands over their brows and between us and them, the last in a line that now ran through Fort Larper to O'Mailer to myself and Mac and Frank and Erika, arranged in a neat geometric square like Roman soldiers and roaring up behind us at an even, indefatigable pace was The Canon.

All this space suddenly closed up. I turned to look up the hill as I stutter-stepped rather than ran now and the gap between O'Mailer and us was merely a few metres. I snatched a backward glance. The Canon were right on our tails and then ahead, on the top of the ridge, the larpers were twitching, drilled, organized, their swords and spears and axes lofted in unison, their pennants and banners flickering in the wind at their backs. They girded themselves. They pushed back their heads and their shoulders and right ahead of me, above O'Mailer's struggling form, bang in the middle of the line, the king's position that must be held, stood Captain Mousy and Ruiner Black, and Ruiner Black raised his sword and screamed.

'Prism of Q'Qth, Attack!'

The larpers pounced off the ridge and for a second all I could see were dozens of pointy things coming right at me just as my legs buckled and a hoard of brown habits engulfed me from behind and in an eddy of bodies I seemed to flow backwards, catching only for a second Frank's white spade beard and Erika with hands pressed together in front of her face as if praying and Mac with his 'shit happens' shrug all marooned in a thrashing sea of helmets and armour, hoods and fists, and just before I went down, just before I lost my footing I caught sight of the downward charge of Captain Mousy and Ruiner Black, sweeping down on James O'Mailer just as the vanguard of The Canon drove into his back. A shockwave of tumbling bodies swept out from around them, like spray erupting from the surface of a lake after a rock has plunged from a stratospheric height. It might have been just my head hitting the grass, but I thought I heard a 'tock' sound.

When I came to I seemed to be a long way back down the ridge, lying on the flatter land closer to the Grange. An orange glow flashed across my face. I could still smell smoke. Something was pressing again on my chest, though this time it wasn't Parsons or The Starfish, which I clutched in my right hand, but Sharon Plum's six-inch high, violently mauve, cheetah-spotted platform sole. Her face glowed with a purpling, bruised flush.

'Where are my happy Miffy bunnies, Nathan?'

I started to laugh, uncontrollably, like I was being tickled. The breeze carried the sound of clashing and shouting down from the ridge and mixed in with this phased the sound of a fire engine's siren. Spluttering for breath, I looked up and noticed that not only were Reg and Jane and Cynthia looking down at me as well but also that the Grange behind them was on fire. From the library windows, orange flame and black smoke swept back over the roof. Glass exploded. Everyone above me flinched. Sharon's shoe pressed down harder on my chest. I'd set the building on fire. My students were fighting with costumed geeks when they should have been inside the still-intact venue filling out forms that expressed what a great course it had been and how the learning outcomes had been achieved and how they would recommend the course to all their lovely, fee-paying friends. It wasn't supposed to end like this. *An Introduction to Prose Fiction* with Nathan Flack was supposed to end with polite 'thank you's and a feeling of marginal enlightenment and renewed aspiration, not a crushing sense of terrible finality. But this was the end, beautiful friends. This is where it all ended up ending. I tightened my grip on my starfish and smiled back at Sharon, realizing that whoever she was pretending to be now must be very jealous. Gender identity confusions. Relentless, commercial and dripping salacity. A Chosen One-Everyman hero with great responsibility forced upon him. An age-old institutional conspiracy underpinning the history of Western Civilization, dollops of toss-awful writing and, crucially, an apocalyptic medieval battle deciding all at the climax. I knew it. She knew it. She'd kill for it, but it was mine, not hers, and she knew that, too. What was happening around us was the end of the best story ever written.

Epilogues

Black Hit Out of Space

I'd never advise ending a novel with a neat and convenient coincidence, but the day I finished *The Girl on the Millennium Bridge* did happen to be the day that I crossed paths with Mac MacMahon again. But when I say 'finished' *Millennium Bridge* I am misleading you. Finishing a novel is a staggered affair. It has no defining moment. Unless you are Mac, of course, and you can write a phenomenal and groundbreaking novel in two weeks, you spend a year or so finding the novel. This means writing a load of old cack. You have a pile of useless paper best kept under the bed, like a pisspot. At least now you have something to change.

You take this pile of paper and chuck half of it away. You change the beginning, the middle and the end and make sure that the story has a coherent sense of accumulation and escalation. You complicate your characters and hone their voices. You cut down on the swearing, the slang and the dates and the overly specific cultural references. You realize that the second person, future tense was a stupid voice to have used and start again, first person, past tense, nice and simple, no grandstanding or showboating, no footnotes or parallel or nested texts, no testing the reader's patience. During the writing of the first draft the wordcount jacking-up every day gives you an immense thrill. Now you get a kick out of seeing it shrink.

You finish the second draft, but this isn't finishing either. Now you need to read the novel over and over again, polishing every sentence, fretting over every comma, paying attention to continuity and tone. You read the dialogue out loud. You wander in circles reading the whole novel out loud. You cut, cut, cut until little of the first draft remains. You check for dangling modifiers and pronoun agreement. You take a scalpel to the adverb, the adjective and the passive voice. You bother about spelling, hyphenation and italics. You make sure that consecutive paragraphs do not start with the same word.

You do this over and over again until stopping becomes a terrifying prospect. This story has been your routine and your ballast. What will happen when it's gone? Will you die? Dry-up and fail? But you have to settle eventually, come to an agreement with yourself that fiddling about with one more semi-colon or changing 'antennae' to 'feelers' and back to 'antennae' again will unsettle the whole anthill. You are now freefalling in the endless whiteness that scrolls beneath that last word on the final page. And these people you have loved like children are never going to talk to you again. They strop off on their own and exclude you from their plans and adventures. Their fate now rests with other more discriminating, indifferent or sharp-tongued people.

When I finished *The Drowners* I was confident that the novel would be met with enthusiasm and a modest advance. But the captains of The Arctic just told me to come back with another one, so I had a little cry in my beer and rolled up my sleeves and started again. At the end of *The Mess* I had similar, vainglorious thoughts. Again, the snowmen only wanted to see what would follow. So I wrote *The Best Man,* and as I waited for Squinty Hugo to get me a deal I paced around the block and could visualize the establishing shots of the film adaptation. Unfortunately, no one else could. With *The Penelope Tree,* though, I knew that I had learned from all my mistakes and was writing at the top of my game. But I was tricky to market now, and had a breakdown, something that I've vowed never to write about.

None of these expectations galvanized me when after four years of the above-described procedure I finally settled on *The Girl on the Millennium Bridge.* Today I'd accepted that there was no more tampering, no more fretting, finessing or brooding. Earlier I had printed off the manuscript, and now, after waiting around all afternoon I was lying on the bed with my hands behind my head. I'd put my headphones down. To prepare myself for the evening ahead I'd repeatedly listened to *Black Hit out of Space* by the Human League, a song about a record so ubiquitous that it sucks in the world as it passes number one in the charts and enters minus figures. I was waiting and thinking about *The Girl on The Millennium Bridge*, seeing it as a dream, a flow of colours. I had not thought of escape and reward. I wasn't even going to bother sending off my fifth novel to Frederick Malone of ZY Haggard. I was just lying here, relaxed and comfortable, waiting for my reader to finish.

I don't know why she knocked. It wasn't as if she could possibly interrupt anything important, and it was her bedroom after all, or our bedroom in her house.

She hesitated in the doorway with the manuscript clutched to her chest. This was bad news, wasn't it? She was not going to say it, but she felt that she'd wasted a whole day-off work ploughing through this turgid tripe, this contrived, clickety-click shambles, this unlovable slab that I'd bricked myself up in the conservatory every day, squandering four years of our time together. She must be imagining all the DIY and gardening I could have done if I hadn't deserted her for the raggedly-aligned bundle she held to the front of her sleek navy blue dress. In her eyes I saw all the doubts I'd had about *Millennium Bridge* rise like the reflections of guttering candle flames.

The mattress dropped as she sat down on the side of the bed. I eased myself up on the pillows as she put the manuscript between us.

'Oh my. It's the best thing you've ever written,' she said.

'You think so?' I said.

'Oh yes, not that I disliked the others, but this, this is amazing.'

'You think so?'

'Oh yes, I mean, the end, those last few pages . . .'

I didn't know what to say and felt embarrassed somehow, so I mumbled a 'thank you.' She reached out for my hands and pulled me towards her and we lay side to side on the bed with *Millennium* between us.

'It's not fair,' she said. 'It makes me so angry.'

'It's for you,' I said.

'It shouldn't be.'

'It can't be helped.'

'And today of all days.'

'I know. Hilarious. Couldn't make it up.'

'We ought to get going, you know. It'll be bedlam out there.'

485

'I think we should stay here, maybe order a take-out, maybe go to the pub, have a few beers . . . '

'It'll look strange if you don't go.'

'You think that bothers me?'

She wasn't having any of it. The tickets were highly prized. He might never come here again. And Reg had gone to a great deal of effort to get us the tickets and expected us there, seven-thirty sharp. Fifteen minutes later, the ex weirdest creative writing tutor in East Anglia slipped the starfish into the side-pocket of his leather jacket and walked out into the October breeze towards the town centre, hand-in-hand with Jane.

Apocalypse Norwich

Every time we passed a pub I pulled her towards it, but she would pull me back and so we kept going. I didn't particularly want a drink. I just didn't want to sit in a hangar-sized corporate bookshop, listening to bollocks for two hours when I could be enjoying myself. I could be cooking Jane a nice beef stroganoff, drinking a nice bottle of Chilean red or something more titillating, like whipping my back to shreds with a rice flail. As we made our way she told me more about what she liked about *Millennium Bridge*. I knew she was trying to distract me, or cheer me up. We'd been together for just under four years now and I realized that about four years ago, on a Tuesday evening like tonight, I was walking in the opposite direction, away from town and up to the campus, ready for my first date with O'Mailer, the Arcana and Jane. Fortunately, in the interim, I'd seen a lot of Jane, little of the Arcana and nothing of O'Mailer. After the Battle of Kollocks Grange – in which it was commonly thought that a rogue band of austerely monastic larpers had set fire to the library by accident, then picked a fight with the Prism of Q'Qth – and after I'd been sacked by Sharon Plum – I haven't taught creative writing at the university since, but neither has she, funnily enough – Jane took me back to her house where I stayed. Writing the new novel proved to be a much warmer experience than composing *The Penelope Tree* in The Garret. It was a My Starfish and I production. We did it on our own. We'd not heard a whisper from O'Mailer. The only voices in my head were characters clamouring and my self-editor begging me to cut this sentence and that sentence and stop using the word 'gob' for 'mouth' and 'whiz' for 'throw'. I'd suffered no spectral catcalls or demigodly interjections. Maybe The Canon had done for him on the lawn in front of the Grange while the library burned. Maybe he never existed at all and I had simply suffered a brief parenthesis of insanity. I could still find no reference anywhere to any James O'Mailer or any Canon, not in any records, nor in the autobiographies of any other writers, or in any works on creativity and imagination. I had no way of tracking down the plate-armoured larper who shook O'Mailer's hand before we made it to the library. But, to stir the broth, the stew of confusion, Jane swears blind that a fat, smouldering man did run down the stairs before me, and then out into the grounds. Jane *saw* him. And Reg and Cynthia saw him. Frank and Erika say they saw him, and although they probably see the most peculiar things at regular intervals, the others, despite their foibles, are not liars. Either we had been the victims of some sort of mass hallucination, or he was real and the Canon had achieved their objective. O'Mailer was dead. But we writers have no need of him now. That much is plain to see.

During this last four years I had watched things unfold from the sidelines. Meanwhile, to make some cash and contribute to the household, I took on proofreading jobs and taught Communication Studies at a local college. I wrote some articles for trade magazines, factual pieces about chickenfeed and tractors, advances in lens technology, pension schemes and cliff erosion. I tried to get some tutoring on *The* MA, but it wasn't running anymore. I tried to get book-reviewing work with several Sunday papers, but there wasn't much of that around. I survived, though, and wrote my novel and lived with Jane and all the while I tracked the developments affecting my most esteemed client. As Jane and I reached the outskirts of the city centre I knew she was going to say something about jealousy and resentment being understandable.

'You behave tonight,' she said. 'Don't ask him any hard questions.'

'Like, "what is more important to you, the tumult or the silence?" Who else is coming?'

'I think everyone who's everyone is coming, but of the people we know, Reg and . . .'

'His Darling Dear, so delightful, so dashing, so daring, so deliciously donkey-faced and cloven-hoofed. Miss *Snobbery Mach Frie.* '

'This is good. Get it out of your system now.'

'You're not wearing a pashmina. You should've. For old time's sake. Reg will have his trousers pulled up to his tits and Cynthia will be donning a fair pair of soggy oatmeals.'

'Cynthia phoned and said she'd come if we were going.'

'And you said that we were going to give it a miss.'

'And then she said that Frank and Erika are coming.'

'We'll, of course. It'll be like The Second Coming for them. Slouching towards Norwich to be bored.'

She shoved me and I almost tripped into the gutter. 'It'll be quite a reunion,' she said.

'It's just like Mac's novel. The bit at the end where it's three thousand years in the future and Ruiner are still going. I hate the bit at the end where everyone gets together and the loose ends are tied together and all the conflicts are wrapped up nice and simply, and everyone loves each other now.'

'How do you know that? You've not read it.'

'I'm the only person in the country, if not the world who's not read it. Well, not properly anyway. If only he'd listened to me, eh?'

We made it to one of the side streets that fed into the market square and found that up ahead heaved a mob of people all shuffling forwards. By the time we joined at the rear another crowd of stragglers had hemmed us in from behind. I'd expected a big turnout for the great man's return but not a mass muster of the buying populace. As weight of numbers slowed the crowd's forward motion I was reminded of the only time I'd ever tried to get into Trafalgar Square on New Years Eve. Johanna and I spent hours stuck in Charing Cross Road, freezing half to death with just a few cans of warm supermarket own-brand lager to keep us alive. Only the glow-sticks, the vomit-splashed kerbs and the sporadic outbreaks of random fistfights were missing from this festive jamboree: The Return of the Mac.

It took about twenty minutes to shuffle into the market square. The centre of town was so rammed that I thought maybe Arnold Bumrape had finally been caught and this was the first instance of a new annual Bonfire Night style celebration. The windows of the pubs and cafes were misty with perspiration and the smudged outlines of coats squashed up against the glass. Another monstrous horde swarmed around a big screen set up by the library steps. A murmur hummed in the air, as if an England World Cup game was about to start and it was the last game that England

489

would ever play because we were being amalgamated into a European super-team with standards too high to include any English cloggers. We inched past gangs of people standing on the street corners with books under their arms. Some held carrier bags of books, a sure sign that the hardcore fan base were out in force, the Macolytes ready to have their whole collections signed by the genius himself. Then I realized that apart from the two of us, everyone clutched at least one book.

'My God,' Jane said. 'It's like *Invasion of the Body Snatchers.*'

'Apocalypse Norwich,' I said.

Eventually we shouldered our way across the square and through a densely packed crowd bunching around the entrance to the arcade. Clearly far, far more people had turned up than had tickets. Teenaged girls cried into each other's shoulders. Old men stood stock-still, wracked with awe and admiration. Press photographers aimed their lenses as we squeezed our way through into the arcade. Underneath the curved arched roof the narrow channel was alive with an overheated mishmash of perfumes and sweat. Earnest young men in raincoats and spectacles tried to jemmy past rapt matronlike women and blokes in puffa jackets with meaty toddlers lifted up on their shoulders. It was like the approaches to Wembley on FA Cup Final Saturday, fifteen minutes before kick-off. No, that's a lazy simile; it was like The Beatles had reformed and were doing a one-off gig in Jumping Jack's Fun Pub next to the Castle Mall. No, it was more like William Shakespeare, Jane Austen and JRR Tolkien had been resurrected and were here on the first engagement of a Three Tenors style gala tour. Maybe even that wasn't accurate. Everyone had forgotten Shakespeare and Tolkien, and even Reg had forgotten Jane Austen.

There was no way Jane and I could ease our way through two abreast. I had to fall in behind her and found my thighs stuck up against the back of her legs and my hands wrapped around her waist as the pressure of about five hundred other people pressed down on us. We jiggled with penguinlike movements until we made it to the bookstore. In front of the entrance, about twenty men in black body armour defended a security cordon. They used night-sticks to turn away most of the people who had made it this far, or brandished pepper sprays to urge them back, leaving only the most steadfast and fanatical of the ticketless shouting and screaming for admission.

'Let's give our tickets to one of those loons,' I whispered. 'It'll be our good deed for the day.'

'Shush, I'm not going through that for nothing,' said Jane. 'We're here now.'

The Death Metal Revelations

There was a time when every major publisher owned a bookshop. Beneath the head office maybe, on a nearby street corner, or elsewhere in some shady precinct would be the little publisher's shop. It would carry only the back-catalogue and the new titles for that month or season, books of a signature design and typography with a distinct and comforting identity on each spine. The publisher thus had an outlet where its books could be sold without surrendering most of the cover price to distributors and retailers.

Of course, the rise of the big chains and then supermarket-selling closed down these little shops long ago; or the publishers themselves were lured into boosting a quarterly accounts sheet by flogging off the premises. Dewsenbury and Madge used to have a shop in Fulham, and one in Covent Garden, but they were sold in the eighties to fast food franchises. But one thing that can be said for the new Dewsenbury, the new trailblazing, far-sighted, dynamic and market-leading Dewsenbury and Madge is that they have revived this august tradition of publishers having their own shops.

What we stood in front of now, as a blood-desperate multitude bayed at our back and Jane rummaged in her handbag for what seemed to have acquired the allure of Willy Wonka's golden tickets in *Charlie and the*

Chocolate Factory, was not the old chain store that I had browsed sulkily one late October afternoon fours years ago, where I invented Arnold Bumrape, and O'Mailer heckled me as Jane and I had our first tête-à-tête in the upstairs café, but a new brash and gleaming Dewsenbury bookshop four times the size of its predecessor.

The security guard verified our tickets with an ultraviolet scanner and ushered us in through the doors. Of course, Dewsenbury's shop was more, so much more than a sideline. For a start, it was not the only Dewsenbury outlet. Nor was it one of a couple or trio. It was not part of a cluster dotted around minor British cities, or even one of a large chain of Dewsenbury bookstores. Dewsenburys had become the *only* high street outlet for the buying of fiction. There were now two or three giant Dewsenburys in every city and one at least in all the small towns. After the Monopoly Commission caved in, and after all the other British publishers were amalgamated, Dewsenbury had bought the retail book trade outright, and with the proceeds absorbed all the mail-order bookclubs and all the Internet vendors, too. If you wanted to buy a novel now, you had to buy it from Dewsenbury and Madge. Except, they were no longer called Dewsenbury and Madge. They were called Dewsenbury and MacMahon. And Dewsenbury and MacMahon, be it found on the high street or the Internet or by way of a mail order catalogue, only stocked one book.

One solitary title.

One title that could be repackaged and reissued ad infinitum and no one tired of it. Between them, Oliver Blox, Frederick Malone and Mac MacMahon had cut the Gordian Knot of fiction publishing, the knot that traditionally kept profits low and the industry the preserve of eccentrics because all books, especially substantive, emotive and adventurous works of fiction are *different*, each one in theory requiring its own marketing strategy, their sales unpredictable in the short and inscrutable in the long term. [95]Blox and Co had gone far beyond the Mills and Boon strategy of selling generic titles in supermarkets to the same sort of buyer at large profit margins. They had gone beyond central buying and discounting and owning shops that were friendly and brash and stuffed with cardboard crap so as not to deter the conformist-impulsive who buys whatever everyone else is buying and wants a passive reading experience akin to flaking out in front of the telly. They had gone beyond thirty-day sale or

---

95 We are not dealing with toothpaste here, Mr Marketing Degree. We're dealing with literary fiction. A novel is *necessarily* tricky to market, you fuckwit.

return, beyond three-for-two product shifting and past-abroad-celebrity. They had surmounted the Everest of marketing fiction, conquered its New World, its South Pole, its Outer Space, discovered its Shangri La, its Brigadoon, its Fountain of Youth.

Inexhaustible market.

One outlet.

One product.

The Death Metal Revelations by Mac MacMahon.

In front of us now, as we stood blinking on the matt black carpet was a curved amphitheatre of shelving and stands crammed with copies of DMR[96]. Thousands and thousands of copies of DMR. DMR everywhere: in hardback, paperback, illustrated versions, graphic novel and pop-up versions; editions with a CD attached, audio-books, CD-ROMs and the DVD of the film adaptation that had taken $900 million net last year; large-print, abridged ("DMR in *Half the Time!!!*), redux with extra bits and missing chapters ("The Author's Cut!!!'); reissued with jackets for young readers, adult readers, senile readers, a toned-down version for prudish readers (very short, I noticed, more like a pamphlet), a sanitized version for religious readers; repackaged into fifty-eight serialised chapter-booklets for easy-reading on the train or tube; translated into ninety-two languages, including Sango, and copy-upon-copy, new edition-upon-new edition with simply a different jacket because the completists couldn't get enough of it and the bookbuying public were now all DMR completists, apart from me. Ahead of us, in front of the stairs that led up to what was usually the café but had been converted into an auditorium to host tonight's event, was a seven-foot high Mac MacMahon dumpbin cut-out figure with its arms out wide as if savouring some heavenly power transmitted from the stars.

'This is the worst thing that's ever happened to me,' I said. 'And I've been haunted by a chihuahua-waving ponce and killed by épée in Ancient Greece.'

'Pardon?' said Jane.

'Nothing.' I glanced around. Everyone else must have gone upstairs already. We were the only people in the templelike expanse of the shop, apart from the kids piling up a mountain of $DMRs$ and related merchandise on what I assumed was a signing-desk. My hesitation here

---

[96] You hardly ever saw the full title nowadays. It was always DMR, always the acronym, as if the novel itself had become fused with Dewsenbury and MacMahon Retail.

stemmed from the desk being an electric guitar-shaped coffin with devil's horns protruding from the fretboard. The coffin's lid sprang back on telescopic rods so that Mac could squeeze into the gap with the guitar behind him and use the lid as a rest. Here he could autograph copies of *DMR* and increase their value by one thousand percent. Now that was market presence, a personalized signing desk, the author's equivalent of the autographed Lear jet.

'I still can't believe this,' said Jane. 'I can't believe that there isn't a little room here for you.'

'Well, Mac is rather chunky,' I said.

I didn't want this sort of thing anyway, to be at the heart of a category five hurricane, a cultural Stalingrad, or become seven-foot tall and made out of laminated cardboard. Two years ago, when this whole bizarre, previously unthinkable *DMR* phenomenon had gone into orbit I realized that no niche would ever exist for me on the shelves. Far greater, more established and beforehand irresistible talents had been ushered into the alleys beyond the wings and the backstage. I could have stopped writing the useless pile of cack draft of *Millennium Bridge* then, but I needed to write it. I did it for me. I did it for Jane. I did it for the girl on the Millennium Bridge. I was sad and resentful, yes. In denial, no. *DMR* was a comforting novel in which ordinary blokes with guitars heroically head off the end of the world by playing big, dumb pub rock riffs. Ruiner: they are us. They are who we want to be. I couldn't compete with Ruiner.

A middle-aged couple in coats and scarves passed us on their way to the stairs. At their side was a jabbering boy in his mid-teens wearing Ruiner-style black leather armour. Their footsteps trailed off. The shop was empty again. I blinked. Whole walls of bookshelves on either side of me housed only copies of a novel by Mac MacMahon, Literature Denial's patient zero. When *DMR* was first published, I didn't think that it would even make the 3-for-2 meat counter. I assumed the pulping machines would devour the stock within a year. It would be satisfying to be able to say that on publication the book received the fatal whirlwind of faultfinding I anticipated. It did not, but neither did it stride onto the scene full of fire and bombast. Like one of Mac's zombie fleshgobblers it manifested itself in increments.

The first copy I saw was in the window of a small independent bookshop close to Jane's house, a little store long since drilled into the soil by Dewsenbury. The proprietor usually pushed novels by local authors. Mac was still a local, not a global writer then, let alone *The Writer*. Propped up behind glass, *DMR* appeared to be a substantial yet garish tome. Embossed, blood red lettering lit up title and name. The jacket image showed four hairy rock god types with guitars, clearly based on the original Ruiner line-up, The Paddle, Strang, Feral and Punter backdropped by a huge white skull with a snake pouring out of its left socket and looming like a low-slung moon. Inside, while no one was looking – the girl behind the till was so engrossed in *DMR* that tears were dripping from her chin – I took it down but couldn't bring myself to actually open it and have a read, so hid it in the poetry section next to Ferdie Paget's *Rich Boy Invents His Blues*. Then I ran away in triumph, like I'd delivered Literature Denial a *coup de grace*.

The next few months were quiet. *DMR* was Editor's Choice in a couple of bookclub magazines but that was down to Dewsenbury's wallet. Jane said that she saw the novel on a billboard alongside the carpark of a motorway service station in Northamptonshire, the skull-and-grebos image staring out over the rain-splattered roofs. But then it started. Word of mouth began; the encouraging babble that even Dewsenbury couldn't buy. I started to see people reading *DMR* on park benches, in pubs at lunchtime, on trains, on buses. I saw it in the hands of students as I passed the laundrette. I noticed it lodged in the bags of young mums outside the school gates at half past three. It began to appear in the front windows of the high street bookshops and the department stores and it started to run up the charts in the Sunday papers and the websites. Reg rang me up and had a bit of a gloat. Cynthia phoned Jane and said she was never going to be the same again. Erika rang us up, but we couldn't make fish nor fowl of what she was ranting about. Then people started to ask me if I'd read it. *You should . . . You'd love it . . . It's amazing. I'm obsessed with it . . . You must.*

There was a minor critical backlash. Columnists wryly commented on the essential crassness of the novel and who on earth was buying this and what it said about us in these apathetic, war-torn and doom-laden days. But the backlash received a major popular press rearguard action directed against middlebrow pomposity and high art boorishness. So the columnists returned to what they do best, their deadlined word-processing about themselves, their mortgages and gardens and children or childlessness. Meanwhile, I sat in the conservatory and tried to put it out of my mind, hoping against hope that The He wouldn't ring when the pulping machines started to rev. My only snidey fantasy here was that Dewsenbury would over-invest in a massive print-run that would eventually bankrupt them. But they changed the rules. They bought the competition. They bought the trade. *DMR* only ratcheted up its stranglehold, sustained by whatever hypnotic suggestion the prose of Mac MacMahon emitted.

'Do you reckon he's already here?' said Jane.

'Oh yes. He'll be pacing around, towel around his neck, throwing shadow punches at the dressing room mirror.'

'He's a little unfit for a boxer.'

'Or, she'll be giving him a massage, kneading his shoulder muscles, whispering words of encouragement.'

When I say that *DMR* was the only title you could buy at Dewsenburys I am exaggerating a tad. Like all publishing phenomena, *DMR* spawned its own sub-genre of related titles. As Jane and I started to climb the stairs to the auditorium I caught sight of a stand of these side-products: *The Death Metal Revelations Bestiary; The DMR Encyclopaedia; The Making of the Death Metal Revelations; Ruiner: From Legends to Gods; The Ruiner Songbook; Mac MacMahon: A Life; The Illustrated Mac* and *Living with Genius: Our Life Together* by Sharon MacMahon. All these books were by The Writer formally Known as Plum-Largo. She'd finally got her wish. She was now in print, now celebrated, now power-coupled. Maybe it was Sharon who kept Mac out of the spotlight, concocted for him a mysterious, reclusive image akin to that of Pynchon or Salinger. There had been no book tours, no interviews and no sequels or other novels. Mac was a figure of mere speculation. We'd not seen them since Kollocks Grange. We were not invited to the wedding. Tonight's event was a one-off. Hence the crowds, the atmosphere, the fever. He could have chosen LA or New York, Paris, London or Berlin, but he'd chosen Norwich as the venue for his first ever-public engagement. Tonight, MacMahon, Britain's Only Living Writer would be reading from the bestest-ever-selling novel, *The Death Metal Revelations*, this object lesson in voice and storytelling being followed by an interview with the renowned and utterly impartial writer and critic Sharon MacMahon and by a Q & A with the audience during which Jane had asked me, politely but firmly, to keep schtum.

I am Legend

We must have been among the last to arrive. At the rear of the auditorium we found ourselves alongside a bar and another long table heaped with ziggurats of *DMR*. Hundreds and hundreds of Macolytes were already seated, as many as could possibly fit into the room that was six or seven times larger than the original café. An aisle led down to a stage encased in a cube-like rig of stainless steel struts and spotlights. Two imposing leather swivel chairs had been set up and a marble-topped coffee table complete with tall glasses and a jug of water. A lectern and a microphone stood centre stage. Behind this arrangement hung a wall-sized image of the original, iconic skull-and-grebos *DMR* jacket. It was flanked by two identical moody black and white images of Mac staring pensively at a middle distance, the artist beset by sensation and visions.

I sighed. He hadn't worked for this, endured the OAP gigs in Chiswick or suffered Moonshot and nights of being unheard in dive bars in Gloucester and Spalding. I felt like a circuit-worn, has-been comedian grumbling when a flash newcomer gets to play Wembley. I touched the starfish in my pocket.

'Stop brooding,' Jane said. 'Where are our seats?'

497

I scanned for free spaces. The Macolytes were hunched, whispering, craning around to fans behind them. Dressed in *DMR* homage outfits, some were propped forwards with the book open, revisiting favourite passages. Others swapped stories, anecdotes, impressions and speculations, creating a warped burble that vibrated in the soles of my feet. I noticed three women sitting four rows down from us, their bouffy, tendrilly hairdos unmistakable. It was the Rom-T Chorus of Lou Lou, Sandra and Buns.

'Jane, can we sit with them, please?'

'There's no room down there, and look who's just in front of them.'

She was chatting to the Chorus, dressed in some sort of quasi-goth costume: kohl, a crucifix, oxblood red lipstick and a slenderizing sleeveless black dress. Frances Mink had gone *DMR* a while back. We hadn't spoken. She blanked me because of Jane and I blanked her because of *DMR*.

The Chorus were at the epicentre of a crew of men dressed in skeleton print T-shirts, piratical pompadours and ripped shirts of blood-smear puce or sickish green. I caught sight of Ruiner Black and Captain Mousy, part of a gang stamping their feet to encourage the great man to appear. Then I noticed on the other side, Stephen King-Human Remains Man from the Department sitting with The Boys of Sewage: Kent Stubble, Kitchen Spray Head and Sam Gamgees on Growth Hormones. The Young Kafka from the bank was about a third of the way down on the left. I noticed UKIP and Myra de Courcy, Bob the Maintenance Man from The Garret House, One Foot in the Dave Cave, Lisa Levankranz and Ferdinand Paget (Hironymous Ponce, the Enemy of All That Breathes). God knows why this last pair was here. *DMR* had put both of them out of work. Olivier Blox, CEO of Dewsenbury and MacMahon didn't need to employ fiction editors now, and nobody read poetry any more. And oh yes, there he was, the main man, the man who sold the world, right at the front, head back, arms folded, one of the richest men in the western hemisphere, Oliver Blox with his Himmler glasses and his sidekick-lackey sat next to him, Tie Man or Smiley-Face, I couldn't remember whatever silly name I'd given him. I would lure them into *Bella Pasta* afterwards, show 'em who's boss. Where was Sebastian when you needed him? Exiled, I knew. Screamed all the way to Siberia two years ago. There would be no Sebastian to intervene here, but I half-expected to find Porno and Hard Drive chanting *Three Lions* at the back or Arnold Bumrape and Sododog jizzing into the *DMR* ziggurat and maybe even

Sylvester Sly Ramos-Pintos serving at the bar, pulling a pint, pulling a barmaid, pulling himself to pieces

The foot stomping spread out from Fleshgobbler Central. The aisle started to quiver.

'Come on.' Jane pulled my arm. Down at the front, the other side of the auditorium to Blox, Reg had stood up. From this far away he looked like a walnut perched on the waistband of a giant pair of tweed trousers, a sight I found profoundly moving. He was guiding us to our seats with rigid arm signals, as if directing traffic during a power cut.

We started to pick our way along the aisle towards him, my guts plummeting as I realized we had front row seats and I'd be noticed. I might be able to handle being sighted by The He, but The Writer Formerly Known as Plum-Largo would stare and point, then hold up her finger to the air-conditioned breeze and mime a sizzle. The foot stamping intensified. Underneath the thump-thump I thought I could hear coherent words: *The He, The He, The He.* As we arrived at the front, the stage with its double Macs and huge jacket image reared up and seemed to topple like a skyscraper against speeding clouds. Reg ushered us to him, past three couples I'd not seen before, a skinny bald guy in a grey suit and pilot glasses next to a plump fiftyish women in a leopard print dress; a chopstick-thin, pineapple-spiked-hair man with ageing rock chick slow-miming some sort of moshpit dance; and a bloke with no chin accompanied by a woman who seemed about three-feet tall. They all thunderously slammed their feet on the floor and I realized that I had seen them before, years ago on a website. Menacingly stupid-looking men in plate armour and a chinless guitarist in a crusader's tunic. Punter, Strang and Feral. *Ruiner!* Ruiner were in the house. That just about topped it. I froze before I could dive down into my seat. Along the line, beyond Reg, I noticed his Darling Dear and Cynthia in her oatmeals and Frank with his sweaty bald head and standing up next to him, arms out, fists raised, shouting was Erika Gretsch.

'The He . . . The He . . . The He.'

'Flack, stop dithering,' said Reg. 'You're holding everything up.'

'Why did you get us front row seats? I don't want to sit here.'

'In my day someone in your position would have been immensely grateful to sit so close to genius.'

'I've missed you, Reginald, I really have.'

We hadn't seen much of the Arcana, this was true. Once or twice I caught sight of Frank and Erika sloping ponderously around the city

centre, but I hid from them if I could. For a while after Kollocks Grange
I'd been haunted by imaginings of their pillow talk and in some ways
think that I threw myself into *Millennium Bridge* to stop dwelling on such
things[97]. I knew that Erika-Vernon-Verika had fled the Garret House
soon after me and nested her love in Frank's Trunch bungalow[98]. We'd
been asked over once, but declined, not just because I was scared of
ending up on the barbecue or having to spend all afternoon under a sky
the colour of wire wool talking to Reg about that shocker Robert
Mugabe. We ducked out because Erika and Frank were the joint
presidents of the Official *DMR* Fan Club. The bungalow was a shrine,
apparently, the walls covered in framed and signed photos of The He. In
the garden was a small pond, the centrepiece of which was a statue of
Mac that poured a stream of water onto the lily pads from a stone lager
can gripped two-handedly at groin height. I'd heard whispers that they
were known to pray to it at full moons, Halloween and Walpurgis Night.
According to Cynthia, Frank and Erika acted out the novel together, had
allotted roles and homemade costumes. They were founder members of
one of the many *DMR* larping societies that overran the countryside at
weekends. Going out for a walk on a Sunday in Norfolk nowadays is like
being an observer at an undead paramilitary coup. I've heard that first
thing each morning Erika and Frank open a copy of *DMR* at random,
underline a sentence and use it as a 'thought for the day', like the I-Ching.

They stood up now, wrapped their arms around each other's shoulders
and stamped their feet and shouted for The He to manifest. Cynthia,
however, was still sat down, legs crossed, oatmeals all wrinkled and saggy,
tapping her white trainer as if she anticipated a nice soft folk combo
called Mystic Whiskers or Just Fiddlin'. I wondered if the Darling Dear
knew about Cynthia's brazen lap dance at Kollocks Grange. I wasn't
going to tell her. *The Last Temptation of Reg Carnaby* had been produced and
directed by Mac. It was an example of what The She Formerly Known as
Plum-Largo, in *Living with Genius: Our Life Together,* called "his sexy, bushy
charisma that burns with a hard, gemlike flame". Remembering this line
from my only ever skim of this particular masterwork (of which the first
three hundred and thirty pages or so was a prologue called *Sharon: My*

---

[97] And oatmeal sweatpants, The Angel of Trunch, Arnold Bumrape and Sododog, The
Justice League of East Anglia, Plumcam, Reg's Winston Churchill boxer shorts and all my
devils and night terrors that were now assembled in this room.

[98] This residence was the inspiration for **The Bungalow of Horrors**, a second PI
Pashminski story, the sequel to **The Black Starfish** that I wrote three summers ago as a
birthday present for Jane.

Struggle) made me feel like I'd shrunk further in stature. All the foot stamping and shouting and this terrible faff in which I couldn't sit down or run away, suspended midway betwixt the Arcana and Ruiner, revealed to me my natural place in the universe.

Reg looked like a fossilized, man-sized trilobite tonight. I did an impression of his hand signalling to encourage him to return him to his seat. Beside me, Jane sat down. I found myself facing the audience, the faithful, the Macolytes. And I remembered then something peculiar, something that I'd not remotely thought about for twenty-five years, something from before I'd read *Crash* by Juicy Gash and realized that I wanted to be a writer. Before I read literary fiction or whatever it is that you want to call it, I only used to read, and obsessively at that, Marvel Comics, bad SF and pre-eighties horror novels. And now I remembered being about fourteen and totally engrossed in a novel called *I am Legend* by Richard Matheson. In *I am Legend*, germ warfare has turned everyone into vampires, apart from a man called Robert Neville (a sort of cross between Reg in his pomp and the thoughtful yet macho person that Mac considers himself to be). Neville lives in a fortified house and goes out during the day to kill vampires (a bit like Frank). He breaks into their tombs and boltholes and gives them a good staking (a bit like Sharon Plum). He's a fumigator *par excellence*. *I am Legend* is high-end schlock, but it's a lot better than *DMR*. There's a twist to this tale. There's no way out, no easy answer, no reversal of misfortune, no semi-pornographic promises of afterlife and agency. Not all the vamps are actually vamps. They can control the disease and to them Neville is a monster. He is to them what they once were to him. Legend. And as I peered at the rapt faces of the Macolytes it seemed to me that I was now Robert Neville, I was legend.

Ahead of me: The Macolytes, The Hoard, Flashgobblers and Larpers.

I am legend.

I was not legend, though. Nor was I myth or fantasy or rumour, suggestion or gossip. I wasn't even a white lie or a bit of a fib.

'I am Legend' was the most twattish, most vainglorious metaphor I'd ever come up with. I was just a hack and a ponce and out of step and out of place and, hey, all these people were oh so happy without me and my carping, correcting and blue pencil slashes. I wasn't a legend. Mac was legend.

'Nathan, sit down,' said Jane. 'It's starting.'

The Biggest Writer in the World

The Three Brides for the Three Blokes out of Ruiner and the Three Blokes out of Ruiner all sprang from their seats hollering and wolf whistling. Alongside me, Reg, his Darling Dear and Cynthia stood up to clap. The end of the row was like a snapshot from a late eighties warehouse rave for Moon-Barkers as Erika and Frank flailed their arms, freaky dancing style. Jane eased herself out of her seat. I stayed down. She wrinkled her nose, held out her hand as behind us the barrage of whooping surged to a crescendo.

'Don't look weird,' she half-shouted.

'Me? I look weird?'

'An hour's time, we'll be in the pub and this will all be over.'

Yes, this was true. Soon this would all be over. Sit through this and be purged of regret and rancour and envy and pretentiousness. This would be aversion therapy. Just daydream through this and have a nice instructive think about what I had learned blah blah blah, as if for the last five years I had been a character in a proper novel, not living a real life. Tonight was not about me. Nobody was actually looking at me. Nobody was going to notice me. This moment belonged to the Paddle and the Plum.

I got to my feet and started to clap. Up on the stage a bulky dark and a slim white figure stepped out from the shadows. For a second I thought that The He must have dumped The She, trading her in for what he no doubt would describe, owing to his tendency to go around all the hairpin bends and convolutions of prose to avoid the cliché or the elegant variation, a younger model. But he hadn't. My eyes strained. My mouth dried up. Try as hard as I could to keep it up for incongruity's sake, I stopped clapping.

A lot of engineering work had been done on our Sharon. At least a third of her bodyweight had been liposuctioned away so she could wear with swagger a white PVC catsuit that outlined restless, newborn, emergency airbag breasts that surpassed in the size the spacehoppers O'Mailer had grafted onto to his Johanna clone when he was trying to convince me to kill Frank the Wank. Sharon's chin had been narrowed, her nose pixified and her lips botoxed so much that she looked like she was sucking on a red plastic lilo. Baby pink blusher smeared her cheeks and her hair was viciously straightened and dyed a startling platinum. At the front of the stage now, she parted her high-heeled white leather, knee-length boots. A white leather devil's tail swung behind her legs as the house lights caught her face. Her cheekbones had been so recklessly machined that I thought I was looking at a Cubist painting, a woman's exploding face that only made sense when viewed from a discreet distance.

'What on earth has he done to her?' said Jane.

'Pity the man,' I said, 'permitted to live out his fantasies.'

Mac emerged into the full-glare of the lights. Wedged under his arm was a church Bible-sized, faux medieval, battered leather edition of *DMR*. The same black beard crawled around his face. He wore a floppy, reddish felt hat with a white feather tucked into the band, a double-breasted retro-zoot suit with wide pinstripes and poncey, pointy French shoes. He was bigger, even bigger than before, as if whatever it was that the surgeons of California and Monaco had siphoned off from The She, The He had devoured and absorbed. Side by side, they complemented each other like a black bowling ball and a white skittle. As he nodded a high-chinned pout across the audience, he looked like James O'Mailer's not-so-much-evil but corruptible twin.

Sharon grabbed his hand and lifted it high in the air.

'Ladies and gentlemen, I give you . . . Mac MacMahon!'

The wave of applause shook my chair. Then the room hushed. After hating the noise for what seemed like months, now I felt as if we were hurtling downwards into a silent abyss.

'He's not wearing his tequila belt thing,' I said much too loudly, but my words were not quite as audible as Jane's giggle. I joined in out of sympathy, amplifying her laugh until it circuited around the room and all the larpers and fleshgobblers craned in towards us. A cackle rose in my throat that I knew I was going to have to stifle. To sober myself I tried to internally picture an air raid shelter packed with cowering townsfolk. But Reg's eyes were homing in on me as if he was a Lancaster bomber pilot and I a ball bearings factory in the Ruhr Valley. I spun my head at the stage, hoping that Mac had already started.

He hadn't. Standing away from Sharon now, his balcony scene strut had deteriorated into a hunched slouch. Stock-still, holding his paving slab-sized book with both hands, he'd let his head droop. Sharon Plum, though, or the casing that housed what used to be Sharon Plum had not moved from the front of the stage. Her eyes seemed to be drawing up my chin to force me into contact. A sideways smirk flinched at the corner of her mouth. Then she winked, lifted her finger to an imaginary breeze and mouthed a sizzly hiss.

A cold wave coursed over me. It filled my chest. I closed my eyes. I wanted to get up and run away however petulant that might later look and then wondered why the petulance of the unsuccessful is always more reprehensible than the petty triumphalism of the acclaimed. I willed a bladder trauma so I could use this as an excuse to get up and hide in the toilet for the duration but instead pictured my head, arms and ribs disintegrating as I pissed myself into the bowl out of shame. I had to open my eyes then, look straight up at where Sharon, now behind the lectern, gripped its sides and took a glance over at Mac.

He still had the posture of a disgraced child made to stand in the classroom corner but had lifted his head to stare towards the back of the room. His face conveyed nothing of the wistfulness of the promo-images that hung either side of him. The fabric of his trousers rippled around the thighs and shook at the shins.

I leant in towards Jane.

'He looks like he's got a rat in his pants.'

'He probably has,' said Jane. 'No, a ferret, he's got a ferret in his pants.'

'A pine martin.'

'An echidna.'

'A koala.'

'Will you be quiet,' said Reg.

'One of those moles with a spiky nose,' said Jane.

'Porcupines, except he calls them porcupenises.'

'He brought us together.'

'We owe him our love.'

'Ahem,' said Sharon Plum. 'I would ask you all to be quiet. Turn off your mobile phones. Ladies and gentlemen, again, the biggest writer in the world, Mac MacMahon.'

To another salvo of clapping and howling, she let go of the lectern and kept her eyes trained on Mac as she walked, tail swishing to the chairs at the back of the stage. Sitting down, she reached out for a glass of water, sipped it, then swivelled around and crossed her legs.

Mac, his face already moist with sweat, seemed to have to think his way out of staring at the back of the room. When he finally moved, his limbs shifted one at a time. The left pointy French shoe slid towards the lectern. The left shoulder spasmed. The right hand readjusted to keep hold of the book, then his right side revolved and instead of taking up the lectern position he shambled over to Sharon. She spun around to face him as he picked the other glass of water from the table and bolted the whole lot at once.

'Nerves,' I said in Jane's ear.

'Understandable,' she said.

On stage, Mac fumbled with the jug, trying to pour himself another glass.

'Get on with it.' A shout came from the back that sounded uncannily like Frances's shout-unreasonably-at-Nathan shouting-voice. Up on the stage Mac leant down to whisper something in Sharon's ear. Her torso bounced up and down slightly, as if she couldn't quite decide whether to get up or not. Mac must be regretting, I reckoned, not having to go through the fortifying Chiswick-Moonshot-Death-in-Spalding phase. For a moment I actually pitied him for having to face this sort of insane adulation. I felt sorry for him as whatever conversation he was having with Sharon grew more fervent and then when he let the book slap against his thigh and almost dropped it. And sorry when he finally turned away from Sharon and then when it seemed that halfway across the stage he wasn't going to go through with the reading and was about to walk off. When he changed course, heading for the lectern, for the first time I felt relieved. Because of Mac MacMahon and *The Death Metal Revelations* I would never have to go through anything like this and the little moment Jane and I shared earlier seemed glaringly precious[99].

Mac lay the great book on the lectern. He rolled his shoulders, then reached out his arms ahead of him, laced his fingers together and cracked his knuckles. He puckered his lips and again started to nod appreciatively at people he recognized in the audience. He even stopped and pointed at someone at the rear, but he didn't seem to notice us. All the pity I'd felt at his fit of nerves evaporated now and I started to stare transfixed at Sharon Plum and what all the King's horses and all the King's men couldn't put back together again. I was trying to work out exactly what Tom Baker-era *Doctor Who* alien she resembled in her white catsuit and platinum hair when I realized she was squinting back at me. I tried to visualize some nice friendly putty balled up and smudged with the fingerprints of a playful child and looked at Mac as he stood up to his full height, leant in to the microphone and, fist raised, declared:

'Oright, Norwich.'

There followed a shockwave of wails, cheers, hoots and foot stamping. Objects whipped over our heads: flowers, knickers, little gift-wrapped boxes, fleshgobbler figures and rubber hands covered with fake blood. I noticed Sharon Plum twist around in her chair and chuckle. Reg was clapping like it was *Last Night of the Proms* and they'd just dragged out Vera Lynn for a duet with Bomber Harris. Frank slapped his gigantic hands together like an emperor penguin plugged into an outboard motor. Mac crossed his arms, chin lofted, Mussolini-style as a rubber hand splatted right on lectern. He picked it up and threw it back to a massive cheer.

'I thought I'd read something from me book,' he announced. 'I think you know what it's known as around these parts.'

He licked his forefinger, then prised open the tome. Pausing, he breathed in so forcefully through his nose that a metallic squeal of feedback jolted the PA.

'Rock 'n' roll eh? Never dies first time round.'

'I can still teach you some things about rock 'n' roll, fella-me-lad,' shouted out one of the Ruiner blokes.

Mac's forehead seemed to ripple, as if he was actively trying to come up with a bit of banter, but then the white bulge of his face flushed

---

[99] Tiptop. I had learned something after all, so story over for me.

shocking-pink as I caught his eye. I smiled. It seemed churlish not to and I didn't want to put him off and delay things any longer. He flinched and broke eye contact with me, tilting his head back and forth, spraying sweat like a grizzly bear cooling off on a hot day.

'Oright Norwich. Where's we at?' said Mac. 'I thought I'd read yous something from me book. I think you know what it's known as around these parts. Rock 'n' roll eh? Never dies first time round' He opened the book. 'This is from the middle bit. I don't want to give away the end.'

Erika Gretsch stood up and contorted her arms almost doubled-jointedly, like some sort of over-stimulated mime artist.

'The End. The He . . . The He . . .'

Mac raised his hand only to lower it. She fell back into her seat.

'Where was I? Zane Champ, right, all this weird stuff has being going on that he thinks is down to the booze playing footsie with his noggin. Anyway, he changes his mind and now is about to bare all to this FBI bird called Fansi Fonda.'

I had, in my report, advised him explicitly to change the name Fansi Fonda to Frankie for reasons I thought obvious to a single-celled organism. But my instincts had proved old-fashioned, wrong-headed, and elitist. I'd wasted a week of my life trying to unpick the novel for him and the only suggestion it seemed he'd taken to heart was to alter the title from *The Grasp of Fear* to *The Death Metal Revelations*. If I'd known that the novel was going to become so successful and ubiquitous I'd have told him to call it something catchier, like *Miss Lobster's Ex's Hijacked Cement Mixer* or *The Handbook of the Institute for Chard Studies*).

'Fansi Fonda,' said Mac, 'was a FBI agent with an interest in paranormality. Zane went to see her. She worked at the top of this big shiny office block in what the Yanks call Downtown LA. Downtown is the city centre and Los Angeles is what the Yanks call The City of Angels. Zane opened the door. Fansi weren't half an angel.'

I elbowed Jane. 'I'm getting a nosebleed already.'

'Shhh.'

'She was sitting sideways at the end of her desk so Zane could see her side on. He thought she might as well have done this on purpose so he could ogle the huge globes her bra hardly were able to keep hold of and the short skirt that rose up her thighs to show off stocking tops and suspenders. She was dressed all in white and had very straight platinum blonde hair . . .'

'There you go,' I whispered. 'Mac's fantasy made flesh . . . ouch.'

507

'. . . Just looking at her made Zane feel horny. He went in and she looked up from her typing. He was delighted to see a big fuck-off gun lying on the table next to some coffee with cream and sugar in it and one of those little *Star Wars* toys of Han Solo. He went over and picked up Han Solo. He pointed Han Solo at Fansi. Then he pointed Han Solo at himself. "Notice the similarity?" he said. "You look like you're Hand Solo to me," she said, "the way you're panting like a dirty doggie on heat. You not seen a living woman before, sugar?" "Funny you should say that, love muffin. I ain't sure glad to see an angel like you."'

Mac paused. When he licked his thumb again and flipped over the page the slight swish was the only sound that carried in the auditorium. When he uplifted his chin to take a breath it was the only movement I could sense in the room, until I sank so low in my chair that I jarred the leg against the floor and again the whole room zeroed in on my blasphemous clumsiness. The sweat on Mac's face now looked blue and translucent, almost like a film of shaving gel as he picked up his thread.

'Fansi got up from her seat and perched on the desk, crossing her legs in a way that pushed up her bouncers even more. Zane couldn't tell but he hoped she weren't wearing a Wondabra . . .'

Frank Denbigh fell forward and let off a giggly laugh.

'. . . "You ain't wearing one of them push-up bras, are you Mizz Fonda?" said Zane lustily. "Call me Fansi. No I ain't, sugar, not that that's any business of yorn. What can I do for you?" she said with sexy mischief written all over her voice. "I got this problem, you see." "What sort of problem, sugar?" "A big problem." "I can see that?" "Can yous help me out with it?" "I'll see what I can do?" "You mean that?" "Let's have a look at it then?" She reached down and started to undo his fly. Out he popped like a unicorn's horn. "The things is, Fansi, you're gonna say I'm nutsack, but every time I, like, have a bit a fun with a groupie, they turn into a zombie." "You mean if I keep doing this, I'm going to go all green?" "You might." "It'll go with my hair." "And your undercrackers by the looks of it." "Oh lookity what I won at the county fair." She lay back on the desk and as he went at it he could see all of downtown LA, all the signs and big adverts for booze and movies and adverts to tell the Yanks that Ruiner were in town.'

'Rah . . . Go Ruiner go!' Another volley of flowers and rubber pelted the stage.

'. . . "Can I tell you more about me problem?" said Zane Champ. They . . . talked.'

Mac hesitated, at first I thought for effect, as if now that he was underway, now that the stuttery start was behind him, that he'd convinced himself of what was glaringly obvious, that he had this audience in his thrall, that he was not merely standing before us but presiding over us, that he was a national hero, a one-man industry, the biggest writer in the world, and he could now afford to entertain us with a little stagecraft. He missed the natural beat, though. The pause dragged out until it became almost Pinteresque. He was staring at me. His eyes had reddened and his beard was beginning to heavy with sweat. A bib of grey moisture had formed across the front of his shirt. His eyebrows seemed to stretch, peaking as he scrutinized me and puffed air into his cheeks as if suppressing a fart during a business meeting. I didn't want to think about this, so turned away. He picked up the story again.

'They talked but she was unconvinced.'

His voice seemed to dip, but inside my head not outside it. Two pinpricks of pain stabbed at my temples, a pain I'd not felt for years, a pain I'd first felt the night I first met Mac MacMahon and the others. All of the others. Not just the Arcana. The Hooded Figure as well and[100] . . . My whole body stiffened until my ears popped.

'Mainly because,' said Mac, 'she didn't start to die as they did it. In fact she felt more alive than she had with any other geezer, Yank, Brit or foreigner. 'Tell me more about your problem, sugar,' said Fansi as he went at it like a jackhammer. "Like I say," said Zane, going at it like a woodpecker. "This town is getting chock-full-o-zombies. I seen em everywhere and they seem to be getting into all the bands." "Don't be stupid, sugar,' she said, as he went at it like a piledriver. "Them folk always look kinda untidy. I think you're pulling on my leg." "That don't seem to be what I'm pulling on," said Zane lustily, going at it like a van driver.'

Mac stopped again, seemed to check that I was still here. He seemed imprisoned by the two Wistful Mac pictures that now really did appear to be depictions of someone else. The pain hit my temples again. I gripped my starfish. Something seemed familiar, over familiar, too familiar. I couldn't work it out. He was looking down at me. He couldn't stop looking at me. Sharon uncrossed her legs. A second after the soles of her

---

[100] **James O'Mailer**: Anon, dear reader, anon. Outside, when the moon is high and the thoroughfares of this outpost deserted and the only sound that of something rustling in the hawthorns.

white leather boots clunked on the stage a frisson shuddered through Mac.

'She was writhing all over the desk,' he said, 'and her hands knocked off the gun, the coffee with cream and sugar in it and the Han Solo. She was writhing and really loving it. She worshipped at his stellar crotch. She realized that all she had known before was boys but Zane Champ was a man, a proper hairy rock god of a man with a massive pipe of a dong and she would never cum like this ever again. He was going at it like The Mole underground digger thing out of Thunderbirds. And then she said, "oh sugar, oh sugar, why ain't I turning into a zombie then?" "I don't know," said Zane, thinking I got a feisty wild one here . . . I got a feisty wild one here . . . I got a feisty wild one here . . . I got a feisty wild one here . . . I got a feisty wild one here . . . I got a feisty wild one here. "Do you believe me?" said Zane. "No,' said Fansi. "Why don't you believe me?" he said, as he gave her a deep, harpooning orgasm. "My pa told me there ain't no such thang as zombies, sugar," she said, standing up. "I think you better stop wasting police time." "Oright," said Zane.'

Mac wiped the sweat from his brow with his cuff, then looked back at Sharon, then out at the audience, his eyes like a black smear across his face. He down-tilted his head and seemed to blink at me and as he blinked the pain seized my temples.

'Zane left,' he said, 'realized that he fancies Fansi, then went back to his hotel for a bit of think.'

It was not just Zane Champ who realized. I realized. I stood up as I realized. And when I stood up, Mac MacMahon realized that I had realized.

He grabbed hold of the mic.

'I'm sorry every one I'm sorry I'm really sorry I'm sorry, Sharon, Olly, mate, I'm sorry. Guys, I'm sorry. Me fans, I'm sorry. I lied. I lied really badly. I didn't do it. I can't go on like this. I can't go on living a lie. It's not mine   . . . I didn't write it. I didn't write it . . . He did it . . . Nathan did it.'

The He

Zane leaves and realizes that he fancies <u>Frankie</u> then goes back to his hotel for a bit of think.

The sentence buzzed in my head as I scrambled along the front row, past a stunned and rigid Jane and over the outstretched legs of the Blokes out of Ruiner. It rippled through me as if it were the most resonant, syntactically ambitious and memorable sentence I had ever constructed. My knees almost buckled as I reached the aisle. The throbbing at my temples quickened its rhythm.

Zane leaves and realizes that he fancies <u>Frankie</u> then goes back to his hotel for a bit of think.

Another shout from the stage. 'I didn't write it. He did it. Nathan did it.'

The pulse at my temples forced me to stop and look up. I half-expected to see the assembled ranks of the brown-cowled Canon lined up ahead of me with a burning book in each of their hands. But I couldn't see anyone dressed in brown, only fleshgobbler replicants and larpers in

511

plastic armour and The Boys of Sewage and Porno and Hard Drive lookalikes and The Rom-T Chorus and hundreds and hundreds of fleshgobblers. The throb seized my temples. My legs started to move and I strode clockworklike up the aisle towards the back of the room. A ziggurat of *DMR* reared up, a tottering pagoda ahead.

'Nathan did it. Nathan did it.'

I reached the pile of books and grabbed one.

'Oi,' said the attendant, a person so indistinct to me that he could have been Arnold Bumrape for all I knew. 'That's a tenner.'

'I'm not paying for it, Arnold.'

Only when I'd scarpered out of the auditorium and was halfway down the stairs did I realize that other footfalls followed mine. At the bottom of the stairs, the shop seemed hazy, as if mist and fog had drifted in from outside. I grabbed hold of the starfish in my jacket pocket as if it were a handbrake and shuddered to a halt within the labyrinth of *DMR* shelves and the mountains of *DMR* and the cardboard cut-outs of Mac the Paddle McMahon, the biggest writer in the world. A hammer blow of throb pounded my brain.

'Show yourself, you ponce,' I said.

'Nathan,' said Jane, her face suddenly in front of me. 'What the Dickens is going on?'

'Quick, run.'

I grabbed her hand and we sped across the sales floor and past the security checkpoint. Outside, the Arcade was deserted. No crowd swarmed around the far entranceway and a yellow twilight seemed to hang above the smudged outlines of the market stalls. I couldn't hear any sound. No voices drifted over from the big screen beyond the market. No Macolytes prowled the shopping streets around The Arcade. The zombie army had melted away. The pilgrimage was over. The book under my arm seemed to be growing heavier and heavier. I somehow knew that if I didn't open it up it would spread into a black hole that would suck me into it, followed by Jane and the rest of the city. I heaved it around the corner, guiding Jane away from the Arcade and along the street until we reached the portico of the Castle Mall. Its doors were blocked by a security grille that clanked as I fell against it and pulled the book up to chest height.

'Nathan, this is mad. What's he going on about?'

'I've got to check this.'

I'd never been curious about *DMR*, not even when it had sneaked into the house under Jane's overcoat before mysteriously ending up in the recycling bin. The first thing I noticed was that Mac failed to mention me on the dedications page, not even for inventing the title. He thanked his mum and someone called Chomping Breda who he'd never forget and his love muffin Shaz and all the Gods of Rock and the Gods of Roll and Ollie 'Ballsonda' Blox. I skipped from the first line in every chapter to the last, flipping forwards, seeing the story build up in a rudimentary sketchlike way, from the first stirrings of the fleshgobbler crisis to Zane's (fiftyish) brushes with sex-zombies, then the emerging occult conspiracy and the introduction of Fansi and the thirty or so close encounters needed to establish her complex role in the novel and into the slow drift towards the climax at Ruinerfest and the saving of the world by blokes with guitars.

I dropped the book. It thunked on the concrete.

'What is it?' said Jane. 'You look like you've seen a ghost.'

'I'm about to.'

'What?'

'Mac's novel,' I said. 'It's the synopsis I wrote for him. It's only my synopsis with the sex scenes . . . put back in.'

'What?'

'It's just a story framework I designed for him bulked out hugely by those long porny bits. If you take them out, the whole of the story is mine.'

'Your writing is much better than that.'

'It was just notes, about fifty pages of rough notes. The rest is about three hundred pages of sex-dross. He only wrote that . . . but if I hadn't . . . none of this would have happened. Shit, I wrote *DMR*. Oh my God, Jane, I wrote *DMR*.'

'You wrote *DMR*.'

'Don't laugh.'

'Oh dear, oh my God, everybody knows.'

'You've got to do something for me. You've got to, please. Go back in there and Pashminski around, find out what's going on. I want to know if they've spannered this.'

'Spannered?'

513

'Sharon and Blox. If I thought like they do, I'd spin this as Mac having a loon episode. The shy genius unable to cope with the adulation. This might go away.'

'You sure?' said Jane. 'Why don't we just go home and find out later? Someone'll call.'

'Just go and have a look, please, Jane, please.'

'OK. But you run away, Nathan, and I'll . . .' She picked her mobile phone from her coat pocket and held it up. '. . . I'll track you with my trusty tracking device.'

I watched her stride back along the street towards the arcade, her pale blue see-through scarf fluttering around her shoulders. I didn't want her to go, or know what was going on back in the shop. The pages of the *DMR* lolled in the breeze. The publishing phenomenon of the twenty-first century was a private joke. Whose joke? Who had played the joke on whom? As soon as Jane disappeared around the corner and into The Arcade, my temples pulsed.

'She's gone now,' I whispered. 'You can come out.'

The yellow twilight dimmed. The store windows darkened. Nothing stirred. I turned around. No one was coming up behind me. A few scraps of paper and an eddy of specks rose and fell. The light seemed to retreat further, as if the moon that now appeared above the rooftops had taken a long, deep breath that it would hold to keep in the light until morning. The streetlamps clicked on, as if by magic not design. The eddy of specks seemed closer, a moving, dipping constellation of glitter. It seemed to solidify into something vaguely man-shaped. A chill raced over my skull and poured down my back.

The throb at my temples.

He's here. He's here.

The chill reversed its flow and geysered into my head as eyes began to form in the dust, the outline of a beard, the wedge of his torso.

A tap on my shoulder.

'Even I am not that theatrical. Behind you, Dame Parlet.'

I spun around. There he was, seemingly as wide as the street, his monocle glinting, dressed in a floppy, reddish felt hat with a white feather tucked into the band and a double-breasted retro-zoot suit with wide pinstripes, his stick crooked in one elbow, the tip between his poncey, pointy French shoes, the chihuahua Parsons under his other arm, peering at me with its golden eyes. I pulled the starfish from my pocket and thrust it in his face.

514

'Put it away, Kiddo, I am not the Vampyre.'

'Oh yes you are. What are you here for? What are you doing?'

'Why, Congratulating you, of course.'

'Bollocks.'

'Come, come . . . you know by now that O'Mailer comes never to gloat. You should be rapt and happy as the lamb at your triumph.'

'Triumph, you call this triumph.' I kicked the *DMR*. It scuffed across the pavement and thudded into the front of a sportswear shop.

'Dear boy, dear sweet Nathan, my last troubadour, my last idiot, hair-tearer and dream-dreamer, as ever you misunderstand O'Mailer. I come to congratulate you on the piece I read just now when I returned under purple skies from the slumber of ages. 'Tis a work of rare sophistication. Urgent. Humane. Moral. Complex. Argumentative. A feast for the senses. A rack for the intellect. At last.'

'Don't patronize me. It's awful. Beyond awful. It's the Sistine Chapel of awful.'

'Kiddo, I mock ye not and do not refer to the Fat Drummer's second-hand slop about the groping of the bosoms that heave and the manual manipulation of the nether parts, but to your newly complete cycle I read back at your billet while the aforementioned drummer met his maker.'

'Oh. Well. It's no thanks to you, is it?'

'"Tis so. I concur, for once. I have been elsewhere occupied since last we met on Kollocks Field.'

'I thought you dead. I saw thee fall. Why I am I talking like you? They killed you.'

'Nay, I vanished into the vaporous wisps. Hid myself from mine enemies under the folds of my defeat. We lost, Nathan. We were sundered. A worse defeat than that of Carthage in the Third Punic War. I know this. I was there. But it could have been different.'

'For Carthage?'

'For us, dolt.'

Parsons pointed his snout at the ground. In the circle of light cast by the streetlamp, O'Mailer threw a wide oblong of shadow. Reflected in the window of the Wax Lyrical candle shop, he was standing in profile: a mane of black hair, an upward-coiling beard and his dog poking its head out at my starfish and I.

'Why are you wearing Mac's clothes?' I said.

'A specious question, Kiddo. Better phrased as, why is the Fat Drummer who Beats His Meat with all his Heart clad in the finest garb of O'Mailer?'

'You're behind this, don't mess me about.'

'Yes, 'tis, true, I have been undoing, you may have realized, what you, the Canon's cats-paw, brought about.'

'Look, I get now why you didn't want me to review Mac's book . . . '

'And why I wanted him dead.'

'You wanted *him* dead . . .'

'Poltroonishly, you thought I wanted the Onanist of the Shed dead.'

'Why didn't you tell me straight?'

'The Canon may have snuffed me. They sensed my first stirrings, you know that, followed you around in case I blabbed. And anyway, one such as I cannot help it. What story would this be if there was no puzzle for you to solve, no twists and turns, no outrageous fortune, no monstrous revelation.'

'That's not fair.'

'Fair? Fair? What role has fairness in any story? Fairness, if it comes at all, comes only after the end and, like patience, seldom in women and never for men.'

'I wouldn't have touched Mac anyway, and nor would Jane.'

'Art breaks everything for the artist, Kiddo. You know that. What I proposed was merely reasonable under the circumstances. Desperate times. Desperate measures. There was a line and you couldn't cross it and the Canon achieved their ends as such. The Fat Drummer showed us all that we can all do it . . . that we all are special. We're all equal in the world without O'Mailer, Kiddo. You've always wanted that world.'

'Not like this. I just wanted you to shut your trap.'

'That's why I've been working on my Plan B. To give you a fighting chance again, not just you but all like you.'

'What? By making me look like an idiot. To the ponces it looks like *that* . . . ' I pointed my starfish at the *DMR*. ' . . . sack of knackers came out of my head . . .'

'It did, did it not?'

'And to the rest it looks like I didn't even have the nous to get paid for it.'

O'Mailer pouted, upturned his hand and shimmied his weight.

516

'Why'd you think The Drummer came here tonight? You think he needed to, wanted to? He lives in a counting house where he can count all his money and dine each night upon four and twenty quinces baked in a pie and never bother himself again with the dust and flesh of your calling. But, he knew. Deep down. You saw tonight that he knew the work was not strictly his. The guilt of it gnawed him, scared him. He worried you might find out, act, complain, employ the services of a Scholar of the Law, tell The Bride Plastique.'

'So you started your little whispering business, I suppose, wound him up.'

'Oh no, be fair. My dear Flack, Kvasir is only party to those with the mead's splash. I tried to flow around in there, inside the mind of the Fat Drummer, but there's nothing in there that conducts my electricity. He doesn't even dream. Do you realize that? Not even of bacon and boobies. Most peculiar. An uncommon void. But I know what you have known this last few years of wind and wilderness. There were only two people still bothering to write. Your good self . . .'

'And Sharon Plum.'

'Yes, The Bride. Was easy to speak to her, to suggest it, how pleasant it would be to have a little jaunt back to the old country, a little ostentatious display, show off her plumage and her medals. She's not like you. She's not reclusive. She doesn't really take herself seriously. It's all mere competition and power play. She needs people to listen without listening. The benign dictatress needs to see the whites of their eyes. She needed you to listen, to be made to listen. This is what I insinuated to her. Once this serpent's seed was planted I suggested a little sartorial reinvention for our man of the moment.'

'That's sly, James. That's nasty.'

He raised his stick and prodded the brim of his hat with the boss. His monocle lens and Parson's saucerish eyes lit up gold for the second. Spreading his shoulders, he lifted his head and swung the stick. For a second I thought he was going to let off some deep, thunderous laugh that would rumble around the city, shudder the windows, unsettle the chimneybreasts and frighten the children awake in their cots. I took a step back, threw my hand over my face, cringing.

He vanished.

Goose pimples marched up my arms like a column of soldier ants. I looked around at the shop windows. O'Mailer had not been here at all. He was just a coping strategy, a brainstorm. He only appeared when I was stressed to my limits. Others saw him at Kollocks, though. Had they? They had not volunteered, though. I had to ask. Mass hallucination. Consensual hallucination. Shit and toss and Bumrape. This was going to be the moment that I realized I needed him so much that I'd invented him. O'Mailer was like a story. He made sense of the incomprehensible, connected the loose wires, exposed the ghosts and the wirepullers. This was going to be the moment that it ends just as I realize how much I needed him, but it was now too late.

A metallic crash at my side. O'Mailer was slumped, panting against the mall's security grille. Then he tocked again and seconds later reappeared star-shaped against the window of Wax Lyrical. Before he could move, he popped out of sight but only to rematerialize in front of me an instant later.

''Sblood,' he said. 'It's started.'

'I want you to meet Jane,' I said. 'She'll be back in a minute. I want you speak to her, and . . . I don't know, come out for capons and sack with us.'

''Tis begun,' he said, cocking his hand to his ear. 'And over there it too has begun.'

'What's begun?'

'The hex of the Canon is dispelled. The Reign of Pewter is ended. Prepare for the Golden Age of Kvasir.' His outline wavered, like an old television screen losing reception. 'Others. Others are drawing off me. The others are back. An hour ago, I sensed only you and the dim glimmer of The Bride. Now I sense a hundred others flare into life. Oh my. Zounds . . . a double hundred now, fancy that? . . . I have not felt like this for nigh on forty years. I've not felt like this since fifteen ninety-eight.' He leaned forwards, dropping both stick and Parsons, and grabbed hold of both my hands. 'My work is done. Our work is done.'

'What do you mean, our work?' I threw off his hands. 'I look like a prick. It looks like I was behind all this.'

'I ought to show you, prepare you. Do you want to know what happens next?'

The stick sprang from the ground into O'Mailer's hand. He flipped it up, studied the shaft then swirled it around in front of me, leaving in the wake of its arc one of his glittery gold portals about the size of a basketball.

'Do that when Jane's here,' I said.

'We can't tarry for Doctor Siren. Come, now, I will return you to this very spot, this very second. I owe you this much. I'll show you all that's in store so you can be guarded and overcome. This is your reward.'

The portal spread out until it was as wide and tall as O'Mailer himself, a crackling, golden hole.

'Come, Nathan, I owe you this much, after everything.'

'Stop bollocking about. Just tell me if you've got something to tell me. I'll listen this time, I will.'

O'Mailer lifted his red felt hat from his head and flipped it into the portal.

'I beseech of you. Come for a ride. Let me show you, not tell you. This is what you spend your whole life insisting. Ride with me. You will be prepared for the lunacy that follows. You will outsmart it, outflank it, use it to your advantage. I know you will.'

The glowing disc rotated. Chevrons of gold spiralled, almost solid at the circumference, then liquidlike as it flowed towards the centre. My eyes glazed and as the image blurred I felt as if my eyelashes and fringe and the stubble on my chin were detaching hair by hair to drift into the shine. An image appeared in my mind's eye. A summer's afternoon. A study where french windows overlook a lake. The bulrushes sway out there and the dragonflies skim the surface tension of the water. Framed jackets of *The Penelope Tree* and *The Girl on the Millennium Bridge* hang on the wall. I write the last line, breathe, feel a warmth inside and tiredness behind my eyes. A printer hums and clicks into life and she walks across the parquet towards me and starts to massage my shoulders and whispers in my ear using my voice, 'be careful, this is a Rom-T fantasy supplied by O'Mailer'.

I edged backwards on my heels and remembered the slopes of Parnassus. If I followed him through that portal I might flap around in there with him windbagging on forever. Jane would come back from the shop and find me gone and think I'd run out on her or died of shame somewhere, alone in a shabby garret by the grey sea. And what would I know if I went? What would he show me? Would I see Mac McMahon slumped on the floor of the washroom of the bookshop that bore his name, rubbery, smashed, exposed now and with Sharon Plastique berating him for screwing it all up? Would I see myself behind a lectern, narrating to an empty room, or a packed room or to only Jane and the Arcana and Arnold Bumrape, Sododog and Sylvester Sly Ramos-Pintos? Would I see *The Girl on the Millennium Bridge* jacketed with an inappropriate nudey image and piled high in Dewsenbury and McMahon, or would I see it in heaps upon a conveyer belt, sludging towards the jaws of the pulping machine? Would I see a thousand more evening classes now that these would surely resume, or thousands of mornings of coffee-overdose, chain smoking and pointless scribble? Would I see Sebastian arriving at Heathrow Airport, giving a press conference? Would I see Reg and Cynthia talking on daytime TV about their role in the rise and fall of Mac McMahon? Or Frank starting a survivalist *DMR* death cult in the Norfolk wilds? Or would I see Vernon-Verika scaling the drainpipe of Chateau McMahon, flintlock wedged between her teeth, intent on taking out the false messiah? Would I see Jane? Jane and I? What happens to Jane and I? She leaving me? Me leaving her? All the things that are always there but you never want to think about, because everything is always there ahead, possible somehow. Or would O'Mailer inflate her breasts to a monster size for his own titillation, like he did Johanna's. Would I see Jane and Nathan Forever and would I want to see Jane and Nathan Forever, or see our wedding with Frank and Erika and Cynthia and Reg and his Darling Dear and maybe even the sorry fool Mac The Paddle McMahon all in attendance and making an exhibition of themselves? Would I see us hand in hand in front of the official just as she asks me 'do you take this Jane Vest?' but O'Mailer materializes looming and spectral behind her and I shout 'Get thee gone, O'Mailer' and the quiet in the assembly room segues from respectful to baffled concern for my emotional wellbeing?

'James,' I said. 'I've never been one to flick forwards to the back of the book to see what happens.'

'Stubborn, Nathan, always so stubborn.'

'That's what you bring out in me. I'll take my chances with the lunacy. I always have.'

'This is it, then, Kiddo. Exeunt O'Mailer and Parsons.'

The portal silently closed, the street darkened and Parsons let off a grizzly growl that was superseded by the sound of hurried footsteps came from behind me.

'Until next time,' said O'Mailer.

'Next time?'

'To be continued.'

'To be continued?'

'It is the best ending. Leave them wanting just a little more.'

'James, you always tell me what I already know.'

'Here's a thought then, a parting shot, the last boulder catapulted over the battlements. Our Vernon, she was not quite as wrong as it once would seem, and, likewise . . . there's only one thing worse than being the

520

next big thing, and that's being the next best thing. These things hold hands. You will find out how . . .' He look a fob watch from inside his jacket, gave it a once-over. ' . . . Just about now.'

The footsteps behind me grew louder. As I turned from O'Mailer to face whatever was coming the loudest ever tock exploded. I couldn't look back, though. Running at me, full pelt, head up, hair flowing, with a fierce urgency to her long strides and her pumping arms, was Jane. She wasn't alone. Someone was behind her, chasing her, a broad, panting outline with its arms outstretched. She swerved, as if to throw him off, her line of approach taking a leftwards tack, but he kept straight, coming at me: Oliver Blox. Ballsonda. And just as I realized this and jumped forwards to meet Jane – of course she could outrun him but I am never one to pass up the role of dragon slayer however cheaply costumed and infant school pantomime the monster – a surge of frenzied and animated people poured around the corner from the arcade, rapt, shouting and unified, fleshgobblers, larpers and Macolytes and heading this second wave, the barefoot Plum, her white boots laced together and slung around her neck to flap out either side like a donkey's ears. The horde that funnelled towards me seemed almost like a gigantic alligator's mouth about to swallow me up, a long-snouted green head with Jane as its pale blue right and Blox as its milky, sightless left eye.

'Run, Nathan, run!' Jane passed me. I turned, staggered sideways and something banged into me, sent me careening into Jane and both of us into the Castle Mall's security grille.

I gripped the mesh as my heels slipped and Jane grabbed onto my arm to keep herself upright. Sweaty pink shirtsleeves wrapped themselves around my thighs and when I looked down Oliver Blox was on his knees and hugging mine, panting like a sick dog trapped in a hatchback on a heatwave afternoon.

'Please, please, please mate. I'll do anything. I'll be your bitch. Write your own figure. Name it. Please, I'm begging you. Can't you see I'm on my knees here.' His arms crushed my shins together. I flapped at him with my hands and tried to kick him off but only succeeded in falling back into the grille next to Jane. He let go and tore something from his shirt pocket as he got to his feet. 'You're right,' he stammered. 'You're right. I am a fat bastard. I am. Look at me. Here's the cheque. Name your figure. Anything you want. You got it. Houses. Birds. Cars. Charlie. Just right me the effing sequel.'

'Ballsonda,' I said. '*This* is the sequel.'

His head jerked. His arms flailed out as if someone had stabbed him in the back, and then he swung sideways from us into the oncoming rush of the others as they now swarmed around the portico. Sharon Plum was suddenly in front of me, panting, her platinum hair slicked wet over her head and her cheeks cherry red and bloated.

'Nathan, Nathan, Nathan, please Nathan, you must understand. It was only ever you that I wanted.'

She slid to her knees in a slobbering mess, as if cast out by Saint Peter at the Pearly Gates when all she'd ever done was pilfer a few lipsticks from Boots when she was thirteen and the others had led her on something rotten.

'Now you're just being silly,' said Jane.

I turned and grabbed hold of Jane's hand, trying to pull both of us forwards through the crowd. It was a dozen deep. They were all around us, Old Reg and Cynthia and Frances there in the mix, forcing us backwards into the grille in their costumes and get-up, dozens of copies of *DMR* pushed out for me to sign.

'What happens? What happens?'

'When's the next one?'

'We can't wait. Help us, please.'

Beside me, Jane centred herself by pushing back against the grille with one shoe and using her weight to try and shove off Sharon Plum who seemed to be trying to swing her white boot at Jane's head and as I tried to edge across to break it up I suddenly feared that Frances was going to steam in and it would all degenerate into a tag team catfight. Why does it always end with a catfight?

'Get off, you cow,' Jane shouted. 'I can't breathe.'

'Thems can't breathe,' someone hollered.

The crowd sliced in two in front of us. Big Frank, a look of transcendence on his face strode through as if ten-storeys high and swept Jane up in his hands. He parked her on his shoulders. He was taking her from me, lumbering away from the portico and into the crowd that now blocked the street, and before I could do anything, shout, berate, follow, big thick arms snapped me up and squashed me flat against the grille. I smelt oily yet lavenderish perfume and something like tweed and there was someone else's hair in my face and something thick and rubbery kissed me square on the lips and held it there until I thought my lungs would explode and there was heat and a scuffling scramble that jittered the world beneath my feet and my soul bottomed out as I realized that it

522

ends not with the revelation of the *Death Metal Revelations* or even an unseemly brawl of a catfight, but with snogging Sharon Plum in front of hundreds of Moon-Barkers. When I came up for air, just as I realized that the lavender-tweed scent was very unlike that of the New Variant Sharon Plum, there she was, Erika Gretsch, Vernon-Verika, The Herald. And Vernon wrapped her arms around my thighs and lofted me up like she was tossing the caber, and for a second I was lost in the dark of the portico and twisted around and then I was being lifted over the heads of the screaming people, Jane ahead of me, swaying on Frank's shoulders and Erika was shouting. Erika was shouting and all the people were shouting in unison with her, the same words, the same mantra booming like jungle drums, but hers was the only voice I could hear. Only her voice was distinct to me. Only her voice was clear.

'The He. The He. The Heeeeeee!'

Ashley Stokes was born in Carshalton, Surrey in 1970 and educated at St Anne's College, Oxford and the University of East Anglia. Touching The Starfish is his first published novel.

Much respect to: Robin Jones, Ian Nettleton, Dan Nyman, Jenny Swindells, Rosemarie Blackthorn, Melinda Moore, James O'Mailer, Gordon I Meacock, Shouty the Eel, Flock Various and Andy and Jo and all at The York Tavern, Norwich.

Ashley Stokes

Lightning Source UK Ltd.
Milton Keynes UK
27 April 2010

153409UK00002B/20/P